AN UNEASY TRUCE

"Mabila, Mabila," the chief said as he stood. The meeting had come to an end. Catlike, he stretched, and Madoc followed his lead, towering over the stubby, little red man.

With a friendly expression on his flat face, the miko made a sign, so elegant in its succinct representation of the rhythm of the girl's hips as she had walked away, that Madoc knew instantly that the old man was asking: "Are you sure you do not want her?"

No, thank you, Madoc replied in his own language and in gesture, praying he was not insulting the offer. The miko shrugged; these were strange people. He seemed to gesture at the trees while saying reassuring words with handsign aimed at Madoc's chest, which Madoc took to mean something close to "You have rented an island."

What the chief actually said before he walked off with stately dignity was, "I take your hard metal, I take your bright grave-goods. This time I will not eat your beating heart."

MADOC

Book I in the
MADOC Saga

Pat Winter

"Come listen to a tale of times of old...
and ye shall hear how Madoc
from the shores of Britain
spread adventurous sail,
explored the ocean paths...
and stood triumphant on another world."

Robert Southey

BANTAM BOOKS
NEW YORK · TORONTO · LONDON · SYDNEY · AUCKLAND

MADOC
A Bantam Book / February 1990

ISBN 0-553-28277-8

Published simultaneously in the United States and Canada

Bantam Books are published by Bantam Books, a division of
Bantam Doubleday Dell Publishing Group, Inc. Its trademark,
consisting of the words "Bantam Books" and the portrayal of a
rooster, is Registered in U.S. Patent and Trademark Office and in
other countries. Marca Registrada. Bantam Books, 666 Fifth
Avenue, New York, New York 10103.

IN MEMORY OF MY BELOVED MOTHER,
EVELYN COOPER, DAUGHTER OF THE
MISSISSIPPI, WHO JUST COULDN'T
WAIT AROUND FOR ME TO FINISH THIS ONE

THE CHARACTERS

The White People

Agnes = wife of Huw
Andrew (Brother)
Bjorn = father and son of Yngvild
Brian (Father)
Caradoc the Mediciner
Cari = daughter of Rhiannon
Cyngar = Gwen's rapist
Dag = Norse sailor
David ab Owen = brother of Madoc & Rhiannon
David Iron = Eagle Ring Man's white name
Dewi = son of Ffiona & Edwin
Edwin = husband of Ffiona
Einion = son of Owen & Teleri
Ely (Brother)
Evan ab Powys = brother of Pawl
Snorrison Fair Beard = husband of Yngvild
Ffagin (Brother)
Ffiona = wife to Edwin
Gurd = Norse sailor
Gwalchmai ab Melir = poet to Owen
Gwen (Gwyneth) = daughter of Madoc
Huw ab Tewdr = husband to Agnes
Wil ab Hennin = husband to Mary
Wyn (Abbot)
Lev = a Norseman
Llywellyn (Llyw) = husband to Tegan
Madoc ab Owen = son of Owen & Brenda
Mary = wife of Wil
Matthew and Mark = Brian's sons w/Hayati
Owen Gwynedd = king of Gwynedd
Pawl ab Powys = brother to Evan
Rhiannon = daughter of Owen & Cristen
Rhys ab Meredydd = husband to Rhiannon
Simon (Father)
Teleri = wife of Madoc
Ulf = Norse sailor
Weather Eyes = Madoc's Yuchi name
Tengan = wife of Llywellyn

John (Father)
Yngvild = wife of Snorrison

The Red People

Aligapas = subchief of the Muskogeans
Black Pearl = Rhiannon's red name
Eagle Ring Man = David Iron's Yuchi name
Clear Seeing Man = Fox's crystal gazer
Fat Tongue = a Cherokee warrior
Fawn-Face = a Cherokee woman
Fox = chief of the Cherokee
Lily = Winnowed Rice's sister-in-law
Little Red Fox = Fox's nickname
Hayati = Brian's Muskogean wife
Komas = chief of the Alabamans
Onwa' Pahta = Gwen's red name
Owl Person = shaman of the Shawnee
Smart-as-a-Beaver = Winnowed Rice's husband
Shell-of-Many Colors = Chief of Mabila
Sitlitiga = an elder Alabaman warrior
Sun Caller = chief of the Yuchi
Tumkis = a Natchez woman
Weather Eyes = Madoc's red name
Winnowed Rice = Rhy's Shawnee wife

This map, drawn from contemporary sources by Wendel Norton, is the way Madoc might have seen the world after his journey over the Western Ocean. It is not a sailing chart—the ocean is twice the width shown here, which is imagined to be the way Brother Wyn hammered it into his golden map. This shows Madoc's river route up the Tombigbee (not named here) and into the Tennessee Valley as well as Fair Beard's route overland across Florida, around the Gulf and up the Great River Road to the homeland of the Natchez. Madoc would have heard Norse accounts of Vinland, which we now know to have been some part of Eastern America, perhaps the St. Lawrence estuary. He would have grown up with legends of St. Brendan and Merlin's crystal sphere, in which King Arthur was alleged to have traveled from the river-port at Caerleon-on-Usk (one of three of the Welsh king's castles and probably the legendary Camelot), to unknown western lands, though this legend may have been borrowed from the account of the great Alexander's crystal bathesphere. But in the little ice age of Madoc's century, when the Norse colonies in Iceland and Greenland were frozen out, icebergs prevented travel along the northern route. Like Columbus, who rode the southern equatorial current 322 years later, Madoc would think he had landed on the eastern coast of China (Cathay) instead of a separate land mass. The names here are contemporary with Madoc's lifetime: The Atlantic was called the Western Ocean or the Flood in Madoc's day and the islands he knew as the Fortunates are now the Canaries. The American rivers are based on tribal names that have survived first contact, including the Mississippi (Great River Road), the Alabama and the Tennessee.

GLOSSARY

ab = son of
amobr = debt
atlatl = weapon
ayas = hunting bird
ayat = from now on
blamen = dark skinned man
bloom = molten iron
bloomery = ancient iron foundry
chunkee = game
coracle = Welsh leather boat
curragh = Irish leather boat
daguna = pimple
ell = unit of measure, @ 45 inches
gambeson = tunic of leather
gihli-gasi = dog pull
hatki ahaka = invisible
hauberk = tunic of mail
kanegmati = blue eyed snake
kanskak = cane
lagana = bread
the Mabinogi = Welsh stories
Magh Mel = legendary land of honey
nipowoc = tobacco
tsalu = corn
tun = container
unapii = a fish
u'yu'gi = disease (Cherokee)
vealh = stranger
yn y cwch = into the boat (Welsh)

Chapter 1

...before Owen himself was vast confusion,
havoc, conflict, honorable death,
bloody battle, horrible consternation....
There was outrageous carnage,
the rage of spears and
hasty signs of violent indignation.
Blood raised the tide of the Menai;
the crimson of human gore stained the brine.
There was glittering armour,
the agony of gashing wounds, and
mangled warriors fallen before Owen
whose wide-wasting sword
shall be celebrated in an hundred languages
to give him his merited praise.

—Song to Owen Gwynedd
by Gwalchmai ab Melir
A.D. 1157

Not far across the dark water winked the campfires of the enemy.

Madoc heard the common sounds of their bivouac behind the suck of a paddle as an unseen boat pulled closer to his ship, the *Horn*, anchored in the tarry shadows of a moonless August night. The attack was set for firstlight. Under Gwynedd's dragon his father's men would descend upon the interlopers, and once again, as in the poet's song, Owen's wide-wasting sword would rout English Henry and send him home cold, hungry, and bleeding from a thousand wounds.

"Hail the ship!" the ferryman called from the darkness.

"Where are you going?" the watch answered with the first part of the password.

"Going to meet trouble," came the answer, an old Cymraeg saying. Only Owen's ferryman would know the spot where the *Horn* was anchored. He would paddle a flimsy coracle into these inky waters for only one reason—to bring a message from Madoc's father, the king.

Madoc held his breath. What wing of premonition lightly brushed him?

The messenger, a landsman from the sound of it, climbed aboard the *Horn* with a sharp curse, the enemy camp pinpoints of light behind him. A shroud of fog was lowering, blotting out the stars, but Madoc's keen eye picked out distant silhouettes of individual enemy soldiers passing by their fires, rattling cookpots and weapons, chopping wood, throwing foreign oaths and stout laughter out into the still damp air.

He expelled his breath, slowly and soundlessly. Ahead he heard tide on beaches either side of Menai Strait, which separated the Isle of Mona from the mainland of Cambria (called Wales by Henry, king of the English, who was determined to claim every acre westward to the waves of this sea and name it all England).

In counterpoint to the breakers, a smith's hammer rhythmically beat an edge on an enemy blade. Though Madoc was not armed, instinct drew his hand to the link that would hold the sword called Durendal. Tomorrow legendary Durendal would be sheathed in the enemy.

Madoc licked his lips. He could almost taste it, the salt-sweet flavor of sweat and blood and his own fear blended with the thrill of the fight.

His anticipation was interrupted by the footballs of two men and the tap of a staff approaching from the pit of darkness that was his own deck. One of his mariners admonished the landsman in a hoarse whisper to keep it quiet, yet stumbled on his own advice.

"Guide me well," the landsman replied in a familiar, husky voice. "If I break a leg, your head is next." It was Rhys ab Meredydd, his father's vassal, blind as a wall, for he had no eyes thanks to Henry Plantagenet, and laughing at the rest of them now, thrown by nature's whim into his own perpetual night. "Greetings, son of Owen Gwynedd, from himself, our lord." Rhys turned to deliver the formal address precisely toward Madoc, whose own eyes found the black-red blur of the hooded messenger only a little less obscure than darkness.

Wondering how the blind man knew where he stood, Madoc said, "You make a dangerous journey, old friend."

"All mortal life is such, my prince," Rhys said, too tired for his years, only a couple more than Madoc, who had just turned thirty-one.

"So my father sends you to sing my battle," Madoc said, reaching out to slap his friend's arm.

"You have no battle, Prince Madoc." Here, then, was the reason for his reticence, not fatigue or premature age brought on by misfortune. He carried bad news for Madoc and could not hide his reluctance to disclose it.

"The battle is delayed?"

"The battle goes as planned."

"What—?"

"The king your father bids you return immediately with me to Aberffraw," Rhys continued over Madoc's exploding protest.

"And my ship, my crew?"

"They play their part in the battle, then sail immediately to Aberffraw Bay to await his further orders."

A long silence seemed to draw the messenger in Madoc's direction. Madoc was too wise to press this unfortunate bard who had been obliged to deliver bad news. Gathering himself, he turned to lean upon the railing, chain mail rustling, hands knotted, enemy fires reflected in his eyes.

There was a noise from below, a rattle of weapons. Sixty-three fighting men crouched down there, each a craftsman-monk who traded tools for swords. Those fighting brothers from St. Brendan's of Mona had long been at odds with Henry's Romish priests, who had exhausted every legal means to seize the Celtic monastery, a fine granary and mill. Their abbot himself would lead his men into battle tomorrow.

The fog smelled of burned seaweed. Thickening wisps began veiling the enemy encampment across the way.

"Tell me all of it, then," Madoc finally said, voice cracking. Only the king's worst circumstance would force this demand. "My father must be dying. . . ."

"When our arglwydd dispatched me, he was in splendid health."

"That is a bald lie," Madoc said flatly, detecting Rhys slumping into a sentimental shrug. The king's men traditionally whitewashed royal woes. It had been years since the king was in splendid health, but Rhys would never admit it. Madoc softened his voice: "For what Plantagenet did to you,

Meredydd's son, I would join this battle even if I had no other reason."

"I am honored," Rhys replied quietly. He knew Madoc had personal motives for hating the English king.

"Then tell me something to help me understand."

"I know nothing more."

"Why are we robbed of our revenge?"

"Your men will take many in your name."

"What in thunder is in his mind?"

"Nobody knows the king's mind."

"Has he gone mad?"

"The arglwydd is not mad, just old and tired. He has worries from the Church—a priest was there when I left—à Becket is still trying to persuade him to set aside Princess Cristen."

"They will hound him to death," Madoc said. Madoc's own mother was an Irish sea captain's daughter. Though Owen was married to another, Princess Cristen, his cousin, he had several children from different women. Nobody questioned that Madoc was illegitimate. Such was kingly prerogative; it did not have the same meaning in Celtic nations that it did in others, and Owen recognized and supported all his progeny, though he expected a son through Cristen to inherit the kingdom, despite Rome's opinion that the marriage was public incest.

"His excommunication still wounds him, and he does not have long, Madoc." It would be dishonorable if any but family heard this. Rhys's voice dropped even lower with strained emotion. "House gossip says he dreamed this battle would cost him a son."

"A dream?" Madoc burned with bitterness to be pulled because of an old man's nightmare. This attack, after all, was Madoc's own design, launched despite the doubts of others. He had quietly submitted many plans to his father, most of which had been ignored. The old man only recently had begun to counsel with this other son who was not in the direct line. "He knows I will protest."

"He knows you will obey." Rhys unerringly placed a strong hand on Madoc's shoulder. "We must go."

"Tell me one thing," Madoc asked while linking his sword. "How did you know I was at the rail?"

"Hear the cry of metal yonder when the hammer strikes? Men are sharpening weapons over there to cut Gwynedd—

where else would you be but at the shield-rack watching the enemy, waiting in serious chain mail, emitting hot waves of battle hunger?"

"So, I burn, eh, storyteller?"

"Bright, my captain."

Another voice from nearby interrupted with a polite, "Sir..." and a gentle nudge.

Madoc took a sheathed dagger from his young armour bearer—several of his crew were sons of neighboring chiefs fostered to the house of Gwynedd.

The bearer held out Madoc's familiar brass helmet. Madoc's fingers knew every dent in the old bucket. He slapped his hands around it and pushed it back.

"Wear it for luck, Pawl." This was a high honor for the lad, a promising swordsman and the baby of the company who would have his first battle tomorrow.

Madoc left brief orders with Snorrison Fair Beard to take the *Horn* up to Aberffraw Bay after giving the crew and the fighting monks below full measure of battle.

"Ten in your name," Fair Beard promised, the white crystal disk he wore at his neck the only thing of him visible to Madoc, who thanked him, remembering a time long ago when that white disk saved their lives together.

"When we meet again, we will head for Ireland to see how goes our little sister." Madoc referred to the new ship he commissioned with the *Horn*'s deep keel and other modifications for deep-sea travel. He and all his crew and their families had been living the past year in Dublin, where he and Snorrison had been working on the near-finished vessel until his father summoned him for this military action.

This soupy weather would probably lift by noon, but he must leave it to Fair Beard to decide when it was safe to navigate the infamous coast between here and his father's headquarters.

Madoc guided Rhys forward with the traditional order to board, *"Yn y cwch,"* into the boat.

By the time he and Rhys climbed down the sidelines to the oval coracle, mist hung just above the water. The enemy camp was hidden. Its sounds faded as they bobbed toward the north shore, the ferryman steering the hide-and-wicker boat by the sound of the rough kiss of breakers against rockwork. To step out onto that slick quay was an act of faith.

"At hand, sir," said another royal retainer disembodied in

the gloom where several horses snorted, nervously pawing gravel. By sense of smell Madoc found the wall of shivering horseflesh, took the lead thrust at him, and mounted. A seaman at heart, he distrusted horses, more this skittish creature on an invisible trail. But the animals were tethered together, and the bondsman guide who led them piped a confident tune astride his mule, which expertly found the way down into a cushion of dunes.

False gray dawn was upon the land by the time they reached the stone barbican that served as a relay station at the edge of the marsh. The round stone tower that dated from the Roman occupation loomed out of the mist. There they rejoined the men-at-arms who had escorted Rhys from Aberffraw, and bade farewell to the guide. His lonesome hornpipe faded behind them as the company of seven horsemen headed north across trickling streams, fens of whispering reeds, bog willow, and tangled briar, where even frogs were hushed by mist that thickened as the horsemen climbed an old road up into the brooding hills.

A blurred pink morning bloomed over their shoulders.

"What is this all about?" Madoc asked. Rhys's horse settled beside his while a large dog drove a flock of sheep across their path.

With a friendly nod to them, the shepherd of the flock ambled along among his stragglers. Madoc's horse led Rhys's behind the dog's shepherd, who had a sling over his back with an orphaned lamb bawling inside and a wicker dovecage dangling from the crook of the staff on his shoulder. When they were a fair distance from the escort and had some privacy, Madoc continued, "Is my brother ranting again?"

"Like yourself, Prince David is preparing for this battle," Rhys replied, treading very close to the lines of his employment.

Madoc's brother was second in line to the Kingdom of Gwynedd, a landsman to the marrow who opposed Madoc's marine command because he saw it eating at what he considered his inheritance. That was why Madoc was building his new ship in Ireland instead of closer to home, where David could interfere.

"That is all I know," Rhys added, face resolutely forward. The hood of his cloak had settled on his shoulders. For the sake of others, he kept a neat sash bound around his empty eye sockets.

Madoc was glad. It was not possible to remember the man

as the handsome youth with whom he spent some years of boyhood, yet he did not like looking at those lidless holes. Rhys's short brown hair was streaked prematurely gray, a trait in many Cymraeg families. Where Henry's hot poker slipped four years ago on the way to his left eye, his clean-shaven cheek was marked by a slick scar. Not even mustaches shadowed his lips, the only feature left to him for gesture. His were subtle, neither too thick nor too thin, but the flawless trumpet of his profession. The beige scarf matched the clean lines of his face, which, to a full-mustached man like Madoc, seemed that of preternatural youth.

"Did the king order David to Aberffraw?"

"These things are not disclosed to me, Prince Madoc," Rhys answered, suddenly formal. His tone was yet another reminder of the rigid court protocol that surrounded the lord of the house of Gwynedd, protocol that never failed to provoke Madoc, who had grown to manhood away from it in the relative democracy of the sea.

As the road sloped downward, the shepherd headed his flock toward higher pastures. Madoc and Rhys cantered in silence for a time, plunged again into shadowed dells.

"However..." Rhys added just before they caught up with the escort, "he told me not to return at all unless I had you in the hall by dawn."

Madoc settled back. Whatever the mad purpose, he felt cold comfort that the old man at least wanted to see him first.

The men had paused on a rise where they were watching a pair of ravens that had been following them for some time. The sergeant of the troop crossed himself while slipping from his mount. He picked up pebbles from the road, withdrew an old-fashioned sling, and began casting at the ill-omened creatures.

"What evil do they portend?" one of the men muttered.

Madoc shrugged. He did not share superstitions and fought such impulses in himself.

"They say," said another, "that ravens predict death."

"Most likely the birds have learned that groups of mounted men lead to fresh battlefields," Madoc replied.

The birds turned lazily on an updraft, sailing toward the south without moving a wing.

"Then why are they not waiting on the beach?" Rhys remarked as the troop took up the road again.

"Maybe they know something," the sergeant muttered.

Madoc noticed that the dark pair had circled and were following still as the troop crested the approach to Aberffraw.

The horses quickened pace when they smelled home ahead. The mist shredded before them as they crossed the bridge upstream of the bondsmen's village that served the king. At the end of the right fork in a gentle vale lay Aberffraw Hall.

Not a castle in the Norman sense, Aberffraw was instead a viking chief's rambling two-story log greathouse huddled close by a nest of thatched outbuildings, encircled by log palisades and a moat channeled off the creek. Pitch-and-tow linklights still smoldered on iron standards around the perimeter as the horsemen approached a gate, their lead man brandishing a shield blazoned with the red dragon that matched a pennant on the roof.

Inside, where sounds of human, animal, and mechanical activity was heard, someone yelled an order. Soon the drawbridge machinery irritated the early hour with its lazy shriek.

The logged ramp dropped, and the gate creaked open to reveal a courtyard full of men and women bustling amid rigged carts piled high with penned fowl, parcels, and household items. A unit of foot soldiers stood at ease near a train of caproned wagons marked with the dragon, while drovers, who would walk beside their teams, harnessed oxen. A monk with sleeves rolled up was working with a hammer on the band of a wagon wheel. Several other brothers were among the throng. Near the stables outriders tested cinches and hauled fieldpacks up behind their saddles.

As he led Rhys's horse to the mounting block, Madoc was paid little heed; he may have been the king's son, but from the other side of the bed, fostered out in his youth to an Irish sailor-lord who educated him. Here in his father's ancestral home, he was an outsider.

The royal household was preparing to move to one of Owen's mountain strongholds. Madoc was impressed by the people hurrying here and there, retrieving children and livestock, stacking wicker baskets outside open doorways. The people seemed of a determination. Even the dogs looked purposeful.

The porter, an angular fellow who recognized Rhys, must have surmised who Madoc was because he did not challenge his entry. Servants here had known every word of the arglwydd's message before Rhys Meredydd had left the king's chamber late last night.

Owen's chief porter had already gone with the chamberlain to the next household to prepare for the king's arrival; this fellow was a substitute who did not take the job as seriously. The substitute porter curtly greeted them as they dismounted and handed the reins over to the sergeant of the troop. Muttering to himself about household problems, he led them down a long hallway into the dim heart of the building.

From far off in an echoing upper chamber the voices of two men were locked in heated argument. The first voice was his father's. Madoc did not recognize the second, which was touched with an unpleasant accent. The contenders were far enough way, or there were enough doors between him and them, so that their exact words were inaudible. Only the muffled echoes of their shouts disturbed the gloomy approach to the great hall.

It was unusual that there was no guard at the far end beside the immense closed doors, beyond which the argument flared. There was nobody to take Madoc's weapons as was the custom, but the porter seemed oblivious of this breach of protocol as the angry words grew audible.

"—archbishop prays daily for your immortal soul, sir!"

"Save your prayers, Frenchman. Go tell à Becket that he has succeeded in driving my wife into a nunnery, but he will never force me to divorce her. God be the judge, and the archbishop will have his own sins to answer for!"

Hardware rattled and a door slammed, leaving the house unnaturally quiet. Madoc was aware of the scuff of his own footsteps. He, Rhys, and the porter came to a door where the sound of a harp suddenly blossomed, as though oil were being poured on waters disturbed by the argument.

The music was lovely, a strange contrast to the argument that had gone before. Relieved, Madoc moved beyond the porter who leaned on one of the two heavy doors and let him pass.

A male voice joined the familiar notes plucked from a crwth, a traditional harp, singing a song of battle, "Before Owen himself was vast confusion, havoc, conflict, honorable death..."

Who would have the leisure this morning to be singing about Owen's glory days? Despite the strength Owen's voice had displayed in the earlier argument, the thought again stole into Madoc's mind that his father must be dying. Bards traditionally sang a lord's victories around his deathbed.

The thought deepened when he saw that the master of the house was not holding court. The great hall appeared empty.

From a side hall suddenly stepped a tall dark-robed priest with a wide balding head—without doubt the man with whom Owen had been arguing. Coming from shadows he seemed to bring with him, he was accompanied by two anonymous priests. Like him their hands were folded in their sleeves, their cinctures swinging with heavy crosses, their cassocks dark in contrast to the lighter robes of the Celtic priesthood. A musty smell wafted up from their rough cassocks as they hurriedly approached the newcomers. Madoc was used to priests wearing light-colored clothing; these dark gowns seemed something other than holy.

Briefly the singer paused, leaving harp notes ringing.

The priest's bald head was down as he strode over the slate floor, but as he passed Madoc and without pausing, he glanced back at the sound of the crystalline music. No emotion traced his face, but his lips drew thinner and his narrow nostrils flared.

Then he and his escort were gone.

Only a small fire burned on the Titan hearth at the end of the hall calculated to dwarf any mortal. Before the fire sat a lone figure who would have been lost in the gloom except for the white garment he wore. It was the singer who raised his voice again in harmony with the music, chanting majestically of "outrageous carnage and the rage of spears. . . ."

At Madoc's elbow Rhys identified the singer: "Gwalchmai," he whispered. Madoc knew his father's chief bard only by reputation, though he had heard this famous song sung by others. Madoc had stopped midstride with Rhys at his elbow; one could be nothing less than arrested by the voice and the splendid harp behind it. Madoc's eyes swept the cavernous room for the saga's hero, but his father was nowhere to be seen.

On a normal morning the women would be weaving up there. The balcony would be lined with children and servants listening to such music. This morning the royal loft appeared to have only one occupant, the musician. Currents of cold air drew smoke accumulated at the ceiling toward open shutters set just beneath the thatch ceiling. Doves fluttered there. A woman sat on a stool on the second landing that housed the royal bed and the hanging loom-threads on their carved warp-boards. Madoc could not see her face but knew by her

posture and golden hair escaping the blue mantle that it was
his half sister, Rhiannon. She played the harp called Llais
Mel, or Honeyvoice, with magic hands and all her heart,
oblivious to all except the singer leading and her fingers
following until a glissando of notes rang it to a close.

Dawn nibbled at the high shadows. The birds flapped
applause, sending a glitter of dust motes and feathers down
across the sudden shaft of light.

The poet at the far end of the hall looked upward at the
harpist. Rhiannon straightened above Llais Mel without silencing the strings. Their pale voices lingered on the dazzling
air, powerful as an echo, as she turned to someone unseen in
the farther corner of the balcony. She stood, a viking goddess
in the new light, the golden brooches that gave shape to her
mantle picking out fine rays of glittering sunlight, looking
downward, smiling at the poet who stood and gave her a
small bow.

Madoc was struck with a swift arrow of jealousy and caught
himself glaring at the graybeard poet. The blue mantle
slipped from Rhiannon's hair and shoulders, revealing more
of their Norse heritage than Madoc's darker Celtic features—
they had different mothers. It was her tall, fair mother
Cristen the priest had been arguing about with Owen.

Rhiannon's gaze shifted downward. Gwalchmai followed
her glance to see that she was looking at Madoc. She turned
suddenly and walked from their view toward the unseen
alcove.

"She keeps us from him," the porter sniffed, then slunk out
when Madoc turned a glare on him.

The chief poet approached as Rhiannon appeared again at
the railing and beckoned Madoc. Gwalchmai watched the
intense soldier in whispering chain mail and worn leather
stride purposefully toward the stair leading up to the royal
apartment.

Before Madoc reached the bodyguard at the stair, a voice of
immense authority stopped him and drew every eye in the
hall toward the balcony. "No, Rhiannon, I am going down."

From Madoc's angle his father's long silhouette seemed to
float on the sunlight. He was pulling a heavy mantle of huge
material around himself, and when he stepped out of the
passageway on the arm of his bodyguard, the cream-colored
bed linen trailed behind him. Closer, he looked immensely
old, a heavy-boned shadow of the huge man he once was.

Even stooped by seventy winters, he was as tall as Madoc. His once-golden hair and long mustaches were white, stark contrast to the black circles around his eyes. Old battle wounds were hurting him. One hip was arthritic and his feet were always cold. But he still had most of his teeth, was still a striking man. The guard helped him to the fire, the train snagging on uneven slate.

"What is this?" Owen demanded as he collapsed into his chair, the highest on the hearth, and drew the bedclothes closer. Voice was all he had left of former strength, still able to shake the war-shields on either side of the hall. "Give us some fuel on that fire."

The porter and two servants who had been listening from the passageway scurried to obey.

The others drew toward the new light and warmth as the king asked politely for some breakfast. Amid the gentle bustle that followed, Madoc watched Rhiannon descend the stair with her harp, followed by a monk who served Owen as scribe. Rhiannon brightened as she approached Madoc, taking his hand in her strong, harp-callused fingers. She might have spoken except that their father beckoned her. She moved away from Madoc to sit below Owen on a step cushioned by his billowing cover-pane.

"Good morrow, my children. No need to look so surprised to see me still alive." He chuckled, gesturing impatiently for the char to bellows the sluggish fire.

The servants moved in briskly with ivory bowls of oat soup sweetened with honey. Madoc made sure he sat close to his father as the monk asked a quick blessing on the meal. Owen was aware that Madoc had set aside the bowl without touching the food, and was watching his father, fairly burning with the question he was honor bound not to ask until the king finished eating.

How this one hates the protocol, Owen thought. "You have missed nothing this day, son," he said softly between bites.

"I have missed an opportunity to slay my father's enemies."

"It is only Flemish colonists from the southern cantrefs on that beach, paid by the English to make soda ash."

The Benedictines had whetted in the English a taste for glass objects, especially bottles and drinking cups. But soda ash was a prime ingredient, so there was always a run on seaweed, which produced the stuff when burned. Military intelligence had reported the foreigners were gathering seaweed, but civilian observers also said Henry's soldiers were guarding the operation.

"It is not a battle for which princes will be remembered. Let David and Rhodri take care of this matter—they will make a morning's work of it, so—" He placed the half-full bowl on the floor so that it almost spilled, but Rhiannon caught it. "—we do not have much time."

"Time for what?"

"Why, for departure, of course."

"Is it the Slate House, then?" Madoc asked, referring to his own birthplace in the mountains on the mainland south of the beach where the battle must be just getting started.

"Travel with me a ways, Madoc, and tell me more about your plan to sail after St. Brendan to Paradise."

"My proposal to explore the western isles was rejected."

"I said I would think about it. Is the new ship complete?"

"The mast has yet to be stepped—What makes your lordship suddenly see the merits of such a journey?"

"It does not matter."

"It does to me."

"You should not ask."

"I must know."

The king regarded him steadily. Everyone in the room hung on what he would say.

"Your brother plans to kill you."

Chapter 2

All those far seas and shores
that must be crossed,
they terrify me; yet
go thou, my son,
swift be thy cleaving prow,
and do not quite forget.

—St. Colman of Cloyne to St. Brendan
Irish
c. A.D. 600

"The deed was to be done during this engagement."

"David?"

Owen shrugged. "The other boys always go along with David." Since childhood Madoc and his stepbrothers had fought, but he could not believe they would stoop to this.

Madoc adamantly shook his head. He knew that not all his brothers hated him. Riryd and Cynan had always been his friends, though now they were off in exile on some pretext of Owen's to keep them out of David's way. Iorwerth, nicknamed Bentnose and heir to Owen's title, had no stomach for internecine war and went off praying in the woods, where his nose was not an embarrassment.

Then there was Rhiannon.

Madoc glanced her way; she stared at the floor, admitting no intrusion into her trancelike study.

"It would have looked like your own men's work," Owen said.

"I am worth more alive to fight the English."

"Curse it, son, I know you want to kill Englishmen because of the raid that took your wife, but they are not the enemy

14

here. Will you not listen to what I say on the most definite
proof?"

"I hear, arglwydd, that the proof is only a dream."

Owen straightened, leveling a withering glare at his son. "I
should have brought you to court sooner to learn manners."

Madoc held that stare but was rattled by its intensity; what
an opponent this man must have been in battle. "I am just a
soldier trying to keep his oath to his lord. The arglwydd
knows better than anyone I have no design on kinghood."

"Kinghood devolves on rightful kings, not necessarily those
who seek it." Owen saw Madoc was not going to break the
stare. "You had best listen to these lessons, son. I do not have
time to play Merlin to your Arthur." The old stories were part
of their tradition—in one tale Merlin himself made a crystal
vessel in which the man who would be king sailed into the
unknown west.

Madoc paced a little, rubbing the back of his neck with a
sweating hand. Buildings made him uncomfortable in the
best of circumstances: His heart was under the sky. About
now the battle would be joined. He tried to imagine the field,
to hear the uncomplicated collision of armament, but his
father's voice was too commanding.

"The people are against Iorwerth because of that nose.
They are afraid of David, who is, after all, only second in
line."

He might have added, and a bastard just like me, Madoc
considered, because the Archbishop of Canterbury had an-
nulled that cousin marriage. But Owen had long ago decided
that David would succeed him no matter who would gainsay
it.

Madoc whirled on him: "I do not seek it—"

"Damnation, Madoc—read the man!" Owen was red in the
face. "You are his only challenge—he will take that sister of
Henry's, mark my word. No, English Henry is not his
enemy, Madoc. You. You are David's enemy, even if you do
not acknowledge it!"

Rhiannon looked apprehensively up at Owen. The poet
stared at her. The porter twisted his hands. Rhys was startled, leaning closer to the fray. Evan the guardsman had seen
his master in all moods but was not used to hearing him
bellow.

The king sensed the distress his outburst had caused and
spoke more softly. "David must destroy you."

"I could kill him first."

"Man to man, of course." Owen found his bowl and continued eating as he talked. "He will never risk personal combat with a superior swordsman." He shrugged again. "Besides," he added ironically, "I want to preserve all my sons."

Shamed by the king's sad glance, Madoc took his hand away from the sword hilt. "What do you want me to do, tad?" using the word for father instead of lord.

"You must go away."

Madoc all but whispered with intensity, "I am bound by oath to protect our homeland."

"This is the home of your people, true. . . ." Owen said thoughtfully. "Claimed by the sons of the sons of Noah and the sons of Aeneas. And like Noah and those sailors from Troy, your destiny sets you on the sea. You wanted to go find St. Brendan's Isle just for curiosity. Well, go. Find this place if it exists, and do as our other ancestors did in Greenland and Vinland." That was a family joke; Madoc's great grandfather was a pirate chief. Only coastal people mixed their blood with Norse pirates a few generations back. It had often been mere rape, so having berserker blood was slightly shameful, a subject politely not brought up since it mostly concerned the ruling families of Cymru's coastal cantrefs. Owen himself was one-fourth Norseman.

"Start a colony in that country you found with Fair Beard—perhaps you did indeed find ancient Vitromannaland," Owen said, referring to a legendary western isle where Celtic people supposedly fled in pre-Christian days. "You have talked about it enough. Take the *Horn* and that other tub you are building." Another joke between them; flat-bottomed ships had served Owen well. He scoffed at the *Horn*'s deep keel. "Provision them from the wagons outside."

"But your household—" Madoc started to protest.

"My household does not need a dozen teams to travel to Yr Wyddfa." That was the mountain the English called Snowdon near the battle now in progress. "We are just moving the flocks to winter pastures," he said casually, licking honey from the spoon. "Those are your wagons out there, Madoc."

"But—"

"This is your legacy," Owen said, wiping his mouth on a cloth handed him by the servant who took his bowl. Celtic fathers felt duty bound to leave no child, even bastards, without inheritance, a scruple outlawed by Henry Plantagenet because it complicated land taxation. "In return I ask only one thing."

Madoc nodded.

"Swear not to harm him, no matter what the provocation."

"Did you ask the same oath of him?" Madoc retorted.

Owen chose not to answer. He himself had spent a decade feuding with one of his own brothers; long ago he had accepted that such was the destiny of princes. The only way to prevent it was to separate them. "Promise what I ask, and I shall send you off a king with a portable kingdom," he said, smiling at his clever words. Behind him, Gwalchmai made a noise of professional approval, the only one to respond to the lord's wordplay.

"Who but myself do you have to sail against the Englishman?"

"Leave the Englishman to David and his marriage plans." To a servant nearby Owen softly ordered, "The small cask." To Madoc he continued, "Besides, Henry has troubles with à Becket these days—even greater troubles than my own." He chuckled. "He will leave us alone for a while, at least."

Owen simmered a wicked chortle at his enemy's ecclesiastical woes as the servant returned with a wooden chest another bondsman had to help lug into the hall. He tripped, spilled out a treasure trove of golden torques, amulets, chains, enameled brooches, rings, antique Roman coins, and other relics and booty.

"Take this and find a new land away from the agonies that are destroying this one." With a canny eye Owen watched the servants return every glittering item to the box rather than to their pockets.

Madoc was speechless. One particularly large ring rolled over the floorstones to his boot. He bent to retrieve it, weighing it in his hand. It was set with a huge red stone relief-carved with Gwynedd's dragon, heavy as a goose egg, a jewel in a setting of such pure gold his fingernail dented it.

"Use it to rig the new ship, whatever. Do not tarry, my son. I can only stall David's plan for you."

"Lord, you stun me." Though he usually did not like personal jewelry, and the setting was only money, Madoc was dazzled by the carbuncle etched with the dragon. "Thank you." He would have stared at it the rest of the morning but reluctantly slipped it into his belt pouch.

"It will probably buy your doom, when you sail over the edge of the world." Owen chuckled, choking himself. After a paroxysm of coughing, which Rhiannon stopped by slapping him stoutly on the back, Owen wiped his eyes on the cover-pane wrapped like a hand-me-down cuff in his fist.

"I have your oath then."

Madoc sighed. "What if he attacks me?"

"Protect yourself in a direct assault, nothing more."

The words would not come. Madoc knew he must say them, however, so he forced himself, feeling as though he were voluntarily shutting himself inside a cage. "I swear."

"The ships are your portion. The jewels are Rhiannon's."

She made a distressed sound beside him.

"Take this my most precious jewel and keep her safe," Owen said, grasping his daughter's wrist.

"Please tad, do not send me away." She knelt beside him, resting her face on his knee. His hand fell to the gold of her hair.

"Daughter," Owen all but whispered, "such displays are why they malign you."

"Have I so displeased you, my lord?"

"I send you away to save you, not to punish you."

Distressed at Rhiannon's misery, Madoc asked, "We are to just pick up and . . . and leave?"

"The steward has been at it all night, packing what you will need. They included her looms, a complete forge, tools, glassmaking apparati. And pepper, Madoc, two pounds of the finest pepper the Florentine merchants sent for my birthday."

This was a remarkable gift, which was probably more than existed in all of Britain except for Henry's own supply, since pepper was a spice that brought its weight in gold on the market supplied out of the eastern overland trade routes.

"Even my beautiful bees," Owen continued. "The hives are loaded. I hope your island has flowers. We remembered oats and flax but forgot flower seeds. Perhaps, Rhiannon . . ." he nodded, mind wandering, hand stroking Rhiannon's hair, "your jewels can buy clover seed in Ireland."

Madoc's mind was racing. He slapped his forehead with a sudden thought of his own daughter at a nearby farm with her mother's people. "I cannot go—Gwen is—"

"Is safe and waiting for her adventure," Owen said. He lifted his hand from Rhiannon and pointed toward the shadows on the far side of the hearth where one of the servants pulled back a hanging. Behind it in a small alcove where the light of day would not reach until noon, Madoc heard a small whimpering sound. It was a batch of puppies in a wicker washbasket where knelt his sweet red-haired Gwen, her blue eyes round and trembling with all that she had heard this morning.

"Tad—"

She stood and ran to him. He swept her up. Holding her, he was startled how much the girl had grown in the past few months, all coltish legs and angles where she had been a plump little girl. She looked so much like her mother with dark Celtic blue eyes and fine copper hair, even at thirteen years, that he hugged her close so she could not see his stinging eyes. Over her shoulder he saw the puppies. The bitch was a good old greyhound who had given Owen many a litter.

"They will not take up much room, see," Gwen was saying, kneeling again. Something bawled behind her, nudging at her back. The lavender nose of a spotted fawn appeared, shagging its chin up and down in the crook of her arm, rattling a bell on a blue ribbon around its neck, making her giggle.

"Pick one puppy, Gwen."

"One—!" She searched Madoc's face bent close to hers, hunting for some sign that he did not mean it. Even as a baby this child loved animals and could charm them and heal them when they were sick. Just like Ann . . . achingly he recognized his wife anew in those eyes, not Owen's icy blue but the warmer, almost purple eyes of the ancient native blood.

One, his lips repeated soundlessly.

Too wise, too penetratingly she reflected his gaze just as her mother used to do. Strong little woman. She had sailed before and knew the space considerations of deep-water travel.

Gwen regarded the dogs, having already rated their points as Owen taught her. Their eyes were open now. They could almost escape from the high basket sides. Gwen touched the head of each pup in quick, nonsentimental good-bye and lifted her favorite into the wide pouch of her suede apron.

Madoc held out his hand to her as he stood but frowned when she dipped to grab the cage behind her.

"It can hang from a beam," she said matter-of-factly, tugging him back toward the company when she saw he was about to forbid it. He held back.

"What if they do not have doves where we are going?" she asked with quiet dignity, as though reminding him of a duty.

"Culhwch and Olwen do not eat much," she said, not blinking, waiting to see what he would say. He smiled; she had named her doves after a story about Arthur Pendragon helping the hero win his heroine from a giant. Feeling like a conquered giant himself, Madoc walked with her toward the hearth.

The fawn nibbled at the basket until the bitch snapped at him. Startled, he tried to trot after Gwen, but Madoc said, "No, daughter." He held his hand up, nodding to the servant who tended the fire. The fellow set down a hod of peat chips he had just brought in and led the creature out.

Owen opened his great arms as she ran to him to be hugged.

"Sweet flower, did you hear?"

"Yes, sir."

The old man searched Gwen's face while addressing Rhiannon, "Give this child a beating, so that she can be witness." It was traditional to use children as witnesses and to fix the lesson with pain so they would be able to document an important event.

"You may hit me," the girl said, offering her hand. "But you do not need to. I will never forget this day."

The king laughed warmly and battered her palm with kisses. "With such women as these"—his gesture included Rhiannon—"you cannot help but begin a favored nation."

Madoc looked downward, embarrassed by this from his father. Brother Ely, the scribe who had followed behind Rhiannon, politely coughed his disapproval of such talk; he was sensitive to Roman criticism that the Welsh church did not oppose incest strongly enough. Had not that French priest admonished Owen because he would not set aside a wife who was also his cousin?

"Brother Ely," Owen said, "have you taken it all down— Princess Rhiannon's dowry, my son's title to the ships, the household stores—all nice and legal, something even a Saxon bishop would appreciate?"

Madoc was dizzy with counting the supplies necessary for what his father was proposing, a long bluewater voyage with nearly a hundred warriors and a train of civilians. How would they organize belowdecks? What about the women, for surely Rhiannon would take her companions, and they must some of them have children. At least two of his veteran mariners would bring their wives, or they would not go. He had planned a small expedition, a sailor's dream in a single ship, but nothing like an entire colony. Details whirled in his mind.

The king helped Gwen off his lap, dislodging the puppy. "You picked the best of the litter."

"Her name is Nona, the first of nine," she replied, settling beside Rhiannon.

Owen signaled to the porter that it was time to leave. His glance wandered upward toward the bed landing, as though he had forgotten something. "And the dream, Brother Quill, did we finish relating the dream?"

Ely nodded.

"I would hear this dream that decides my fate," Madoc said impetuously.

Owen arched an eyebrow at him. "You know about it, then?"

Madoc realized he had already hinted Rhys's indiscretion; messengers should disclose only their commission, and that only to the one designated to receive it.

Rhys, who had sensed this was coming from the conversation, stepped toward the voice of his lord, who said,

"So, you let his impatience forestall your duty?"

"Everyone in this house knows about the arglwydd's dream," Rhys replied, dry-mouthed. His usual aplomb was shaken.

"Hmmm. I suppose."

"I must hear this dream," Madoc insisted.

"You will not like it, Brenda's son." Owen threw him another of those glances carved from the giant's tomb on Yr Wyddfa. "You have her eyes, you know, eyes like stormy weather."

Embarrassed again by such directness, Madoc looked down with his mother's smoky eyes, not blue, not silver, but as changing as the sky over the sea.

Without further preliminary Owen opened those windmill arms again, turned toward the bright ceiling, and started speaking to the shields on the walls:

"I dreamed I was a great tree growing for a thousand years in a wide and beautiful country. I had twenty-seven branches, some on the right side and some on my left, all strong and fruitful in leaves and acorns."

Brother Ely sniffed—the oak was sacred to the Druids long gone from this land, but still around as local superstition.

Since the king had sired twenty-seven children, he was identifying his house with a heathen past.

"But one by one the whims of perverse fate took my limbs—lighting, fire, insects, woodpeckers, disease, rot, hail, wind, and heavy snows took their toll. I, the heart of the oak, lived on in sorrow as I watched life whittle down all but two of my strong and bountiful branches, the right-hand one of which grew a sword and hacked off the left-hand branch. Ivy, meanwhile, had been creeping up from the east and soon climbed around my one and only strong and fruitful limb, strangling it completely, leaving me old and fruitless in the wilderness."

Owen cast his dour glance at the rapt audience of his children and servants. In the blazing firelight Rhiannon was sitting rigidly looking downward, her cheek glistening.

Gwalchmai beside her had an aggressive scowl on his face; his fists were clenched at his sides. The bodyguard in the shadows, a strong, big-shouldered fosterling from the lord of Powys, looked straight ahead with his usual discipline, but he was biting his lip, frowning. All the Powys were gifted with second sight—Evan knew how to read a dream as well as anyone. Off to one side Brother Ely leaned morosely on an elbow, one hand fidgeting on his tonsure, his writing hand idle, the quill slack. He had already taken down Owen's dream.

Owen sighed and found Madoc, the wild dark son who came from Brenda, the tragic love of his youth. Brenda, the old man thought fleetingly. Stormy love, are you so long gone? Her son was a fine-looking man. See how often that hand settles on the sword. Too quick to draw the blade, but that will temper, especially if he has a good adviser, Owen thought, his mind wandering again.

Madoc was the only one who gave him back a resolute eye.

He is seething because I took his battle from him, Owen surmised. But he does not lose his control. By now David, who knew protocol better than Madoc, would be banging doors, abusing servants and generally demanding an explanation.

"Well," Owen finally said, shivering a little and drawing up the coverlet, "it was a dreary dream that woke me with a terrible knowledge as plain as day." His huge hand, once strong enough to wield the wide-wasting sword, settled on the cover-pane. Rhiannon covered the blue-veined claw with her fingers.

The king's glance fell on Rhys, who seemed to be in a trance, chin lifted, listening to something inside his own head. This man was Owen's most trusted messenger, a younger son of a noble house in his own province who had given his oath to Gwynedd. He innocently caused Owen the most anguish because each time he looked at Rhys's ruined face it reminded Owen of his lost twin sons. Four years ago they and Rhys were taken hostage in one of many battles with the English.

Henry Plantegenet, furious after losing miserably to Gwynedd, had taken the eyes of those three and nineteen other hostages. The noses of some were sliced off. Several shortly bled to death. All the others had since died except this one who served with exceptional loyalty.

"Well, Rhys ab Meredydd, you have chosen your master then," Owen said, standing. The cover-pane fell away. He was dressed for travel in green tunic, green plaid trews, and gray boots.

"Your lordship, please—"

"You have served me well, and what I do here is to give you a better life in gratitude." Owen embraced the blind man. "Madoc desperately needs you," the king whispered close to Rhys's ear, "But he does not know it."

"Please—" Rhys began, but Owen stopped him with a soft demand. "Promise me you will make him accept the title— the people must have someone to follow. He must be made to see."

"Sire—"

"Promise me, son."

Rhys dropped his chin and nodded against the old man he had adored for most of his life. "I promise," he said hoarsely. Owen had already turned away, resolute with his main purpose.

Completely in authority, he slapped Ely the scribe on the shoulder, bringing him to his sandaled feet. "You too, Brother Quill." In Owen's mind a plan was forming to save some remnant of the native church from Henry and his alliance with Rome at the same time he saved Madoc and Rhiannon. St. Brendan's had always been a holdout for the old ways, and now it would probably be the only remnant, Owen mused. As a member of St. Brendan's, the scribbler had little choice but to obey Owen, who was his patron. Owen was trying to save a little—a silly old man's dream of some kind of lasting glory after I am gone, he thought. A few of the treasures of

his scriptorium had already been brought here because of
English raids on the monastery.

"But, sire, my abbot—"

"Will be going with you, and the servants packed your
books."

Madoc was disturbed to see there were great tears rolling
down his father's cheeks as he turned to Rhiannon and
embraced her, head against her shoulder, speaking so that
only she could hear. She nodded, containing her emotion,
having abandoned further protests. Somehow Madoc could
tell that of them all, it was Rhiannon Owen would miss the
most.

With gentle suddenness there sounded a flapping of wings
above as a bird arrived through the transom, shattering the
mood below. Gwen sprang to her feet and bounded up the
stair. She reappeared on the landing, tucked her skirts into
her apron band, and began to climb the ladder to the
dovecote under the eaves.

"Immodest child," the monk hissed under his breath.

"There can only be immodesty with a knowledge of sin,
Brother Ely," the king replied, not taking his eye from Gwen
as she removed the message capsule, then scurried down the
ladder.

It must concern the battle, Madoc thought as Gwen delivered
the note, which seemed to ignite Owen.

"We have only a little while, children." He gestured at the
servants whom he had coached for this moment. Gwen
gathered up her menagerie. Rhiannon, with her harp, turned
to ask the porter something. He nodded, and she and Gwen
departed with him.

Owen caught Madoc's elbow, drawing him toward the
courtyard beyond the doors. Brother Ely, the bodyguard, and
the chief bard guiding Rhys were not far behind, deep in a
whispered and animated conversation. Madoc was startled to
see the tracks of tears beneath the sash. The fact that he
could still cry was as diverting as the fact that he was crying.
Gwalchmai had his arm around the younger poet's shoulder.
He tightened his grip in the manner of a man trying to buck
up another. It stung Madoc, who would have approached if
there had been time, but Owen called him.

"Just follow my lead," he instructed Madoc, enlivened with
a new mood of high spirits as though he were a great

woebegone boy playing a trick. "There is not time to explain my plan."

Hand on sword hilt, Madoc asked if there was going to be trouble as Owen pulled him toward the lead wagon.

"David is riding this way fast." He greeted the driver, who appeared to know him personally. The foot soldiers had formed up and were marching out of the gate to clear the road. The horsemen scattered themselves along the caravan, while drovers brought their teams into line, whistling, moving backwards, facing their placid, wide-nosed beasts, their short leather goads snapping, gestures flying between drivers and drovers.

While his driver helped the king climb aboard, Madoc realized the shepherd with the bird cage must have been a lookout. No doubt he was a freeholder, bound to the king only by personal loyalty, as were most of the people.

How entwined the royal threads are woven, Madoc thought, but he could not help but ask, "Did we win?"

Chapter 3

The Emperor gave my Durendal to me:
And if I die, who gets it may agree
That he who bore it,
A right good knight was he.

—The Song of Roland
French
c. A.D. 978

Owen gave him sidelong appraisal and burst out laughing. "We always win." His laughter changed. "We will outfight them down to the last of us; still Englishmen will be coming over the hill."

Madoc did not want to hear what sounded like surrender. Owen saw it in his face. "Many an important battle is won without the sword," his father continued, eyes atwinkle. He had donned a floppy shepherd's hat at a jaunty angle.

Madoc hesitated; he knew Owen meant to disarm him.

"Evan, you neglected to relieve Prince Madoc of weapons."

The bodyguard moved with a serious expression; he knew what it meant for a warrior to proceed unarmed. He also knew the legend behind this blade.

"I will hold Durendal with my life, arglwydd." It was clear he was speaking not to Owen but to Madoc—the first time to be so addressed. His father was the only one who caught the fleeting look of surprise on his face. A man could have only one lord, but here his father's bodyguard was already addressing him as such.

"You are Pawl's brother?" Madoc asked. Evan nodded. Satisfied his sword would be safe, Madoc relinquished it and the dagger. He watched Evan stow the weapons in his gear, close at hand should the need arise.

Madoc started to climb aboard the wagon, but Owen stopped him. "Put this on," he said, pressing rough brown cloth into his son's hands. The driver handed over the reins.

"I like to do this myself," Owen said. He looked ten years younger out here in the morning light. The fog was lifting, leaving every surface glistening. In his green outfit, white hair and mustache shining, Owen seemed a reincarnation of the forest lords from the old stories.

"This is a cassock," Madoc said. This was the second time his father asked him to wear such a disguise. Three years ago he played Brother Madoc of St. Brendan's to deliver a message to the king of France concerning an alliance against Henry.

"Perhaps it will keep you out of trouble a second time."

Feeling foolish, Madoc got into the wool cassock and tied the cincture looped at the waist.

"Get lost back there in the middle of things," Owen commanded gently. "I had hoped to load the ships before David arrived. . . ." He demonstrated how Madoc was to slip his hands beyond his studded leather wristguards into the sleeve cuffs to play the part. "Try not to look so combative." He reached down to pull the cowl over Madoc's scowling face.

The old man had touched him perhaps ten times in his life, and here he was fussing over him like a mother goose. He had always been formidable, chiseled in white rock, but this morning he had mellowed. He was almost benign, except for those arctic eyes that gave him away; he was still an old fighter, would have been down there scrapping away on the beach this morning except for infirmity. Madoc had a swift painful recognition of Rhys's perception—Owen did not have long. This glow about him was the last bloom. Owen turned to speak to the driver, releasing Madoc to his own thoughts.

Rhiannon and Gwen were boarding the second wagon with some of the household women, a frail, pale one Madoc recognized as one of her serving women, a girl named Tegan, and another with brown hair and dark eyes whose name he could not remember. Several children in stair-step ages seemed part of her entourage.

Madoc tried to catch his sister's eye, but she would not look up. The blue scarf covering her hair was tied beneath her chin like a peasant's. She had removed the brooches and gold rings she wore earlier. Her long-sleeved tunic was finely

woven but no different from the other women around her.
Far from seeming a royal entourage, they all looked like the
gypsies he had seen in France, too sturdy and wool-clad
practical to be the court of a king. Gwen saw him and
grinned, then hid the grin behind her hand. He winked at
her and continued moving back. Around him the oxen drovers talked to their animals, wood and metal groaned with
maneuverings, and farther back sheep bawled.

Owen instinctively seized the moment when all were as
ready as they would ever be. He stood to his full patriarchal
height, balanced against the strong shoulder of the driver,
and said in his wonderful voice, "A pilgrimage, my children—"

This startled the oxen who took it as the signal. They
lurched ahead. Owen sat down suddenly, steadied by the
driver, and without further ado they were off.

For Madoc it all had the quality of a dream. Evidence was
everywhere of his father's planning and maneuvering of this
event. Used to being part of command, Madoc found it
graveling to be dependent on this strong, whimsical old man
who had made such a far-reaching plan without him. As far
back as he could remember he desired his father's attention.
He could recall sitting on Owen's knee only once as a child.
Now all this suddenly in motion for him after years of
indifference gave the morning the tingling evanescence of
vision that excited and compelled him. The mood intensified
when he passed the gate.

A sweep of wet green meadow encircled this position. The
air was clean. Smoke from the hall and the village chimneys
rose in thin lines that briefly smeared the overcast, giving
way rapidly to bright blue sky.

Squinting, he looked down the slope to the sparkling water
where he was delighted to see the red-banded sail of his own
ship just clearing the approach to this sheltered harbor.

The *Horn* was uncommonly beautiful riding the swell. He
seldom had this far view of her, a high-necked, red-winged
dragon of a ship—a roar from her direction would not have
surprised him. She moved in very steady, despite a chop,
deep keel slicing the water with only a lick of foam. Fully
laden, she would move even closer to the wind. They were
taking in sail now; the dragon was folding her wings.

Someone, probably Fair Beard, even though he must be
dying for sleep, was at the steering oar. Madoc knew it must
be Snorrison piloting because of the sureness with which the

ship was managed along a line that would bring her parallel to the dock.

Just there the sternman threw out a braking anchor. She curtsied and slid into berth exactly where that sure hand aimed her. Rapid sidelines flashed out, ensnaring the dock and giving the illusion of bringing the stones into the ship's embrace.

Only last year Madoc had talked his father into building this rock jetty out to accommodate the deep-keelers, but it was primitive. No winches, and the only bollards were rough-dressed cubes of stone that ate up hemp. Line, he thought suddenly—they must pack replacement line and cordage for a thousand jobs. And hemp seed for the future. More stowage problems. Where would they put all the people? The two ships could not do it—how to get another, or better yet, a pair?

Behind the *Horn* appeared the sails of two others ships under Madoc's command. Walking so he could keep an eye on the saddlebag where Durendal was stowed, Madoc used the privacy of the monk's hood to continue his calculations. How much food, for how many weeks? What could they buy along the way, and for how much? And sheep, too, for surely the flock behind them was intended for his company. He had little experience hauling livestock. From here the *Horn* looked about the size of a toy as he contemplated how to load her.

The caravan moved slowly down the road to the village. To Madoc, used to the speed of sail, it seemed to take all morning just to reach the fork that led back up the Roman road or down into town. He had drifted back and then around the line to find himself beside a monk to the right of the second wagon where Gwen sat on a huge bound bundle, red hair bouncing like a sunlit cloud around her face, piping a tune on the flute, her legs dangling over the tailgate.

It grew warmer. Their stumbling pace was hypnotic. How long, Madoc wondered, would they need to lay over in Dublin until the *Horn*'s sister ship was completed? It was dangerous—he would not allow himself to think, bad luck—taking the new vessel out so green. These and a hundred other details set a buzz in his brain, but behind it all was the sublime realization that he was being granted his fondest wish—to sail west as far as possible to find again the green, mysterious land he and Fair Beard had found by accident

years ago. They had a bet going about how many days it
would take to find the western isle a second time.

He had grown up hearing Irish and Norse sailing stories.
His first remembrance was someone singing a nursery rhyme
about St. Brendan tossed along the rolling sea. Madoc was
certain he would not fall over some kind of vast edge, as most
landsmen thought. The horizon's winsome curve had assured
generations of mariners that the world was round. And the
movements of the stars made sense only if earth was a
sphere. But nobody, not even those who had been there,
knew exactly what land lay in the west. Fair Beard believed
they had touched Vinland long ago when they first met, a
bastard prince out to prove himself and a veteran sailor on
the run for piracy. Madoc thought what they found was what
St. Brendan had found almost six hundred years before them.

Fair Beard scorned maps, relying on the ones he kept
inside his head. But Madoc, raised in the Irish mapping
tradition, had made a copy of the chart he kept during that
journey. He had grown to maturity believing it was proof he
and Snorrison had rediscovered the legendary island of St.
Brendan because of the many similarities of that voyage to
their own.

Would they find the descendants of St. Brendan in a
thriving Christian community speaking a Celtic language in
legendary Vitromannaland? Or would further sailing bring a
journeyer to the backside of Cathay or the land of Nod,
where Cain went east of Eden?

Madoc was suddenly aware of the monk who walked beside
him and looked up to see it was the blacksmith, his long
sleeves still rolled up.

The monk glanced at his ersatz brother. "I am called Wyn."

"Brother," Madoc replied, thinking it unlikely that a member of St. Brendan's would be fooled by this disguise.

"I know who you are, sir, and I would ask that you speak to
your father the king on my behalf." Brother Wyn was clean-
shaven, stocky, and graceful except for his unnaturally muscu-
lar arms and shoulders. He had light brown hair cut short and
tonsured in the old Celtic manner, ear to ear, rather than
Rome's circle at the crown. That tonsure and the date of
Easter were the major conflicts between the Celtic church
and that of Rome. St. Brendan's had been, along with a
couple of Irish monasteries, the last holdouts for the old way.

Wyn had deep hazel eyes and a shy way of using them,

considering his great strength. He rolled down his sleeves as he continued. "The prince your brother has summoned me to be his armorer, but I have vowed to go on crusade."

Every now and then Madoc heard talk of another venture to Jerusalem since the king of France failed in Christendom's last campaign against the Turks. He had even been approached last year by an Irish bishop who wanted Madoc to donate his ship to an effort. Madoc considered the crusaders mad. However, he suggested he would undertake such a journey for hire, but had not since heard from the churchman.

"My word will not go far in the matter."

"It would if I gave my oath to you, arglwydd." Wyn gestured to another monk who had been pacing them. "My brother Stonecutter the deaf wishes to accompany me."

The other monk, an older man with grizzled beard and wandering eyes, dipped toward Madoc in a bow. He carried, tied at his cincture along with a wooden cross, a mallet and chisel.

"Has he a name?"

"Before he lost all his hearing he asked to be called by his task. None of us surviving is old enough to remember what his Christian name might have been."

Madoc gave them both a long study then finally said, "You will be pledging a mad scheme most likely to kill you both."

"All the sooner to meet Christ on the way to take the Holy Land from the infidel."

Madoc appraised him from a different angle. "So that is what you think lies in the west—the other side of the east."

"According to the holy word of God."

"Not all churchmen believe the world is round."

"I have read a little, here and there," said Brother Wyn. "Our own library had books translated from the east, and of course there is the example of our St. Brendan."

"Why does Prince David want you?"

"I have a trick or two with bog iron."

Madoc shrugged. "You must be good at your work."

"I am better at my profession," Brother Wyn said with great feeling, but his thanks were interrupted by the victory shouts of horsemen cutting down from the Roman road.

Madoc knew instantly who the first rider was by the markings on the lead destrier's tack. Who else would have the arrogance to ride his war-horse into less than battle, when any other warrior would have traded for a palfrey?

Unless Prince David had need of a war-horse still.

Madoc remembered his oath to his father but could not put away the thought as he watched David ab Owen flanked by a dozen of his officers, themselves on saddle horses, whooping and holloing, each blazing with family emblems on shields and helmets. But all ranked significantly below Gwynedd's dragon on a flapping pennant adorning the staff of David's standard-bearer.

The effect on the civilian caravan was near disastrous. Everyone in line turned to see the commotion. Sheep scattered before the riders and the dogs went after them. All the family retainers recognized who it was approaching across the stubble field. Many cheered.

Whistling shrilly, the drovers hastened to bring up their beasts before they were dragged under the yokes. Some had room to bring up, but others were forced to veer off or ram the vehicles ahead.

About halfway to the lead wagon, all but one of the outriders reined up behind David. He continued with the standard-bearer, who slowed to let David ride on alone.

He was a thick-boned man who sat tall in the saddle but was shorter than Madoc on foot. He had a brown mustache, ruddy complexion, and very dark eyes behind the nasal of a steel helmet. Madoc had to admit David looked every inch the king sitting the saddle. He was the handsomest of Owen's sons. He blazed with pride on the back of a huge dapple-gray, himself and the destrier still in bloody gear. So there must have been some sort of fray down there, Madoc thought with conflicting emotions as he watched his half brother approach their father's wagon.

Owen had seen him coming but knew what a knot a halt would throw into his train. He clucked to the oxen and waved a gesture to his drover, who was looking back apprehensively.

Without request David ceremoniously handed over his sword to Evan as he would have done upon entering the chief's hall. A flawless horseman, he matched the wagon's pace, then came alongside so that he could converse with Owen.

The line was cleaning up its own snags. Men were dragging one wagon over to the side for repairs. Amid shouts and whistles the drovers regained control of the teams.

Being on the opposite side of the second wagon, Madoc was unable to hear the royal conversation. He quickened his pace and moved in behind the lead wagon where he could walk with the second drover, eating dust. But he could hear most of what was being said without appearing to be listening.

Owen sat a bit lower than David, who leaned over the saddle on one arm, reciting a tally of enemy casualties.

". . . ten lancers, seven bowmen, a few officers. We took thirty-five horses, sixteen workers, a couple of supply wagons and oxen—and we have fifty barrels of fine soda ash the bastards cooked up for us—"

Owen nodded. "The officers—?"

"—worth a fortune in Dublin," David finished.

"The English officers?" Owen asked again.

"Set upon the road to London, of course."

"Mutilated?"

"Bearing a message."

"You swore not to use Henry's tactics."

David smiled. "Father, you are becoming forgetful."

Owen had in fact ordered several mutilations during his reign. He had had one of his own sons imprisoned for conspiracy.

"I would spare you my regrets."

David made himself more comfortable. "The ash is on its way." He eyed the harbor where a mariner on the *Horn* threw the line to a quayman. "I want the *Horn* to haul it to Dublin."

"How many did we lose?" Owen asked, looking over his shoulder and under his hat brim almost directly into Madoc's startled eye—he had not realized Owen knew he was near.

"Three," David replied matter-of-factly. He rattled off family names among his own troops.

Madoc felt a chill; he knew Owen was asking for his sake, "And the marines?"

"The abbot drowned in the mess of landing."

Owen shook his head. He had tried to convince the fiery churchman to stay behind with his noncombatant staff. What would happen now to the brothers, since the man who owned their oaths was dead? For Owen this news sealed his decision to send the brothers of St. Brendan's with Madoc. "And the sailors?"

"One dead. Took a sword from behind. Slit like a flounder, helmet to haunch." Madoc could get no reading of David from this. He spoke without any emotion, and he did not offer names of men or ship.

"From behind, eh?" Owen remarked.

Letting his destrier lead, the heir apparent twisted in the saddle to give the entire winding line a long eye.

Madoc looked aside to keep his face hidden by the folds of the cowl but was able to glimpse David's lips moving as he counted two dozen house guard, a half hundred outriders, twelve sets of burly drovers and oxen-men, and seventeen, eighteen, nineteen monks. For a moment David looked right at the cowled brother closest to him.

Turning face front, he said to Owen, "I see you have already taken in St. Brendan's orphans."

Owen nodded, thinking. He was trying to remember how many Celtic churches had been taken. "Henry has seized the abbey at St. Brendan's." The five-hundred-year-old monastery was held with the traditional grant from this house. A sister minster to the one founded by the saint in Ireland, Henry's own religious favorites wanted that prosperous mill. "Now, with the abbot dead and a price on the brothers' head if they practice the sacraments, I do not know what will happen to them."

"The smith is mine," David said, gesturing at the line. "I do not see him."

"He is back there."

"He has a way of folding the metal of a sword back on itself—unbelievably thin and strong."

"His oath is to a higher master."

David expelled another mirthless chuckle. "Next they will be calling you father."

"By the covenant they are already my adopted sons."

"You have an excess of sons."

Madoc felt icy strength down his arm urging him to draw metal. But all he had was an empty sword-link rattling beneath this ridiculous garment. David had no end of delight when last he saw his half brother dressed like this. Madoc hoped to make it to the *Horn* before the experience was repeated. He ground his teeth in fury at Owen for his perverse whims.

Owen snapped the reins, not about to bite David's bait.

"I suppose you will still forbid us to burn English churches in retaliation," David continued mildly.

They had been gnawing this bone of contention between them for years. Madoc could see only Owen's left arm in the dark green sleeve, and now and then a trace of white beard as the wagon jerked over ruts. But he could tell that Owen signed heavily before answering, "As long as we do not stoop to their level, He can avenge Himself through us—"

"When does He begin avenging?" David cried, interrupting, an unpardonable offense at court. Around him the king's men drew close on several big horses.

"You will spare all churches and holy places," Owen replied, voice growing more soft and ominous with each word.

"They excommunicated you because you married my mother," David snarled, but careful not to raise his voice, "destroyed half your progeny, ate you from the toes up with unrelenting taxes and war, yet you defend the bastards."

Owen's guardsmen were visibly tense, hands on weapons. David's temper was infamous; he would go along calm for a while, then flare violently.

Owen did not reply—his attention was taken by his drover, who had to lead the team around scattered peat bricks that had fallen off a cart up ahead. The carter had pulled his vehicle with its broken axle aside and waved as the arglwydd passed.

On pretext of helping with the tumbled cargo, Madoc moved closer to his weapon and his stepbrother.

David's officers were also moving in. Madoc was interested to see that they did not surrender their swords, as was the tradition when approaching the king, but did not go so far as to draw them.

They continued on a bit, tension ebbing. The dragon pennant cracked in the fresh breeze that met them along the seawall, scattering the last of the mist. On the southern distance huge lathers of cloud lingered over Yr Wyddfa, veiling the summit and catching rays of sunlight climbing on toward noon.

The interval seemed to cool David. "You are traveling heavy, arglwydd," he remarked in a dry tone of calculation. But his horse was skittish and knocked the carter against the broken cart. David appeared indifferent, but the king leaned over the wagon and called to the yeoman, "You all right, there, friend?"

The carter got to his feet and waved, but he frowned at David, who was distracted by Rhiannon behind them. Madoc watched from his concealment as she held David's gaze momentarily, then with blatant design looked away, leaving Madoc without doubt that she hated their brother.

"Fool," Owen said under his breath without looking at David, obviously not speaking of the carter. He had adored this son above all the others, and despite all that love and devotion, David turned out disappointing. He disregarded priorities, this beautiful, spoiled son who had the audacity to ride a bloody war-horse to the peaceful service of his king. Owen regarded him now in the clear morning light, wondering if it was too late to correct any of his own mistakes.

Looking away from his sister, who was pointedly ignoring the heir apparent, David narrowed his eyes, furious at being scorned by her and admonished by Owen. Evan met his eye, but David outranked and outstared him, bending the guardsman's glance.

This was market day, so as the king's entourage neared the village, they passed more people. Many faces reflected back smiles of genuine affection for their king, oath-holder to most of the villagers.

"See that?" Owen instructed David in a tone of burdened patience. "See that look—that woman's face, there—" He waved to the wrinkled grandmother who blew him a kiss, just as she had done for the past fifty years every time he entered this village.

"You need that," Owen said.

David made a sound like a chuckle but entirely without humor as he removed his helmet, pushed back the mail-coif, and shook out his dark cropped hair.

"You need the goodwill of that carter back there, too."

"I will have all I need when you publicly name me heir."

From here on they were on the high street, a cobbled furlong that wandered through timber-and-thatch buildings to a turnaround at the new quay. The king's drover was heading his team in that direction. Owen had little to do, but he was busy ignoring David, so he jiggled the reins again.

"We could stop and have a little ceremony right here." David gestured with his gloved hand. "Your crones and carters would love it."

Still Owen would not answer him.

"You know you are dying." David leaned farther over his bent arm on the saddle horn, looming over the floppy hat. "Let go, old man." His voice was painfully even, but he made the mistake of putting his hand too close to the arglwydd when he braced himself against the wagon. Seven ringing blades unsheathed around him, including his own in Evan's hand.

David slowly relaxed back onto his saddle.

"Come with us to see Madoc," Owen said amiably, letting the men know they could put away the weapons. "While they load the ships, you can brag about your battle. Maybe Gwalchmai can be persuaded to compose a song for you."

Sucking his teeth, David watched the waterside where men lay down ramps from the *Horn* to the new quay. Others were disembarking down another gangplank. The two other ships had anchored midharbor. A string of oblong coracles was already moving over the water, each carrying a kneeling paddler and cargo or two passengers back-to-back.

"Is this why you pulled your pet bastard from the action?" he snorted. "To be your ferryman?"

"Madoc's people supported you. Why are you so cankered, son?" Owen let his reins follow the oxen handler, who was directing the team to a stop at the turnaround.

Most of these men were freeholding farmers. A few times a year they came together on royal projects. The second wagon's crew was already coming alongside, tailgates pointed toward the quay. "Let us drink to your victory." These projects usually rang with the air of festivity because the arglwydd would feed everyone after the work was done.

The second drover meant to pull up beside the first wagon, likewise the third and fourth and so on, the method these men had devised from long years of working together. Madoc got out of the way, finding himself again on the other side of the line.

He was anxious to get aboard the *Horn*. From where he stood she did not look any the worse for wear. The porters were already unloading the first wagon, while the rest curled into place. A line of village boatyard workers was forming as bearers, their own pledge of service each season.

Madoc hefted a huge bundle of wool from the second wagon, then joined the bearers, moving ahead so that he would be the first to reach the ship. Gwen with her creatures and a small bundle trotted after him.

He sprang up the gangplank, surprising Wil, the quartermaster who barred the way. Wil recognized Gwen behind this strange monk who asked, "Permission to board," as he tossed aside the bale of wool and whipped off the cassock.

Wil swore, slapping his captain on the shoulder in warm

welcome. Madoc told him to expect cargo immediately, and briefly they discussed some logistics of storage.

Despite these mundanities, Madoc knew as soon as his feet touched the deck that this ship was mourning, and he suspected with more than the drowning of the abbot.

"The wandering shepherd is home," Wil shouted. Bruised and bloody, the men gathered around him forward of the open hold. Madoc searched the faces to see who was missing.

Usually under such a circumstance they would all be teasing him about the monk's costume. They were too quiet. Madoc laid his arm across Gwen's shoulder, protectively drawing her to him and wishing she had not followed.

Here and there more serious gashes darkened foreheads and arms. Bearers were arriving with cargo on the gangplank; the younger crewmen began taking it aboard. Many of the fighting monks had already departed with the body of their drowned abbot-captain, but a few who chose to remain had assembled a deck below, near the open hold where they looked up as Madoc scanned them. Bloody bandages here and there, purple noses. Searching for Fair Beard, Madoc went momentarily bone-cold when he considered that maybe his blood friend and irreplaceable pilot was the casualty. But there was Snorrison coming forward, drooping eyelids with pale white lashes—he came off the early watch into battle, then, as Madoc suspected, piloted here.

The Icelander saw Gwen and gave her a wink, but some intuition in her held her back from greeting more enthusiastically the man she grew up loving as "Uncle Snorri," far closer to her than any blood uncle out of Gwynedd's brood.

Usually playful with her, now he too was severe, trudging across the deck toward her father, and what was that stained thing in his hands? Her skin prickled. She knew he had no good news.

Madoc was about to ask who it was who bought the night, when Fair Beard thrust the twisted metal object toward him.

Chapter 4

The name Wales . . . is derived from one of the barbarous words brought in by the Saxons when they seized the kingdom of Britain. In their language the Saxons apply the adjective "vealh" to anything foreign, and, since the Welsh were certainly a people foreign to them, that is what the Saxons called them. To this day our country continues to be called Wales and our people Welsh, but these are barbarous terms.

—Description of Wales
by Gerald of Wales
A.D. 1178

Madoc recoiled.

It was his helmet, the one he loaned to Pawl, split nearly in two from the back forward, still gory. Red pulsed in Madoc's eyes. He took it, bitter bile coming up on his tongue, wishing he could shield Gwen's eyes.

Fair Beard cleared his throat, but his voice cracked anyway when he said, "He never saw it coming."

He made a futile gesture with his big work-scarred hands, which landed as was their habit on the large milk-crystal disk on a chain around his neck. It was his Iceland "eye," a slice of opaque crystal that disclosed the position of the sun in fog.

"I saw it all but was too far away." There was anguish behind Snorrison's words. As baby of the company Pawl had been the butt of merciless hazing from the veterans. But the moment his first battle commenced, everyone had a duty to make sure the youngster survived his baptism of blood. To lose a combat baby in his first fray was egregious bad luck for all.

Their faces showed it, but especially Fair Beard's since he was commander in Madoc's absence. His white-lashed eyes were mere slits in his leathery face, always downcast but now drawn even more deeply and that seemed, with his streaked beard, to be of one weathered piece of old walrus ivory.

Madoc felt their combined misery slide onto his shoulders— the boy died in his place under his helmet and his own horribly ill-timed good-luck gesture.

"This was more than battle luck. . . ." Fair Beard said.

Madoc arched an eyebrow that asked for explanation, Owen's words echoing in his mind: *Your brother plans to kill you*.

Fair Beard gestured at the helmet. "Whoever did this thought he was killing the man who usually wears it." He stared at Madoc. "This was murder."

"The attacker was English?"

The pilot shrugged and looked at the deck, his hand pulling on the stone disk. "Hard to say for sure."

"The killer wore an enemy helmet and hauberk that did not fit," Wil volunteered. He was a short, wiry Cumberlander whose powerful hands cracked together as he demonstrated: "And he smote with Cymreig steel." He displayed the weapon, which was clearly local work—the brass inlay below the hilt would tell the smith who made this sword if one took the time to trace it. "Now who would leave such a fine blade unless he had a purpose?"

Madoc slumped with the implications. He regarded the helmet, wet leather padding inside, broken strap. Such a mute object that said too much. Fury welled in him, and he threw it so hard it bounced off the rail and spun overboard. He turned his back on the men, on the startled bearers, on Gwen whom he once again had failed to protect from horror, gripped the rail, and gathered himself. Across this slice of water the wagons had pulled up neatly and a line of bearers snaked out to the ship.

The sun neared its zenith. Off the Irish Sea a sou'wester asserted itself, strong enough to part hair at the nape of Madoc's neck. The ship creaked with the swell.

Behind him Fair Beard waited for his captain to speak.

Madoc looked around and saw the pilot holding his own sword across chert-hard palms as though it were an offering.

"Let me kill Prince David for you."

Madoc would have laughed, but his throat felt frozen. "No," he muttered. He leaned on the rail and glimpsed the green of his father's tunic like a flag across the water. The old man had more information than a dream. He must have a spy close to David to know for sure he planned murder. The cage of Madoc's promise closed in on him; the vow the arglwydd had extracted was quicklime on his tongue. "No, friend. We eat this one."

Fair Beard would do as Madoc wished. Such was the nature of his loyalty, though meekness did not sit well with the man.

"But listen—the king has granted us a compensation."

Fair Beard straightened, scowling, and replaced his sword.

"The western isles," Madoc said.

"Vinland?"

"Vitromannaland," Madoc rejoined, to keep the bet going over what place exactly they had found years ago.

"He will outfit us?" Fair Beard asked. It was something they had talked of for years. Fair Beard was not a young man. His was a long, rough life sailing out of Iceland. He was sure Madoc and he had found Vinland, the most western of Norse explorations. An outlaw in northern regions now, he figured he would never get to return to Iceland, but he never lost hope of returning to Vinland. They might disagree on the name of the place they found all those years ago, but both Madoc and Fair Beard shared the dream of returning.

"An entire colony." Madoc gestured at the bearers who had loaded a store already. "He knew what David was up to and planned all this to confound him."

Wil and his hands were directing the bearers to the winches to drop the cargo into the hold.

Fair Beard was a man with normally drooping eyelids. He looked like a great sleepy tan hound. Now he absorbed this information with round eyes, but quickly. "Your father always was a master of quick moves. Never lost a battle in his life because he planned out every detail." Fair Beard might also have added that Owen had a bloody reputation even where his own family was concerned. He had imprisoned or exiled several of his sons who had opposed David's ascendancy.

The sheep bawled out on the quay.

"What passage do you propose."

"North by west, island hopping as we did before." By that

he meant Ireland north to the Shetlands, the Faroes, Iceland, Greenland, and finally the far reaches beyond. Some sailors, like the Irish St. Brendan looking for solitude, tried it but never returned to tell the tale. Land in that direction went by legendary names—Vitromannaland or Whitemansland by the Norse, and Paradise, Hy Brazil, or O Florida by Christians who thought it the promised land of Eden where man would be living except for Adam's fall.

"Vitromannaland, or Vinland. Let us get off before the cold winds blow, son of outlaws."

"Vinland's the truth, chief of outlaws' sons, though I still say closer than you think, but so is the ice between us and it." Fair Beard glared at the sea as Norsemen who remembered Vinland would for the next five hundred years, with a slow brooding anger as though they blamed the waters for getting cold, the way they might blame an unfaithful woman. "We were lucky in our youth, Madoc. Have you heard of any captain taking that route since then?" He shivered. "You have been on land too long."

Madoc was sorry to admit this was true. Until this recent military action, he had spent the two years either building the new ship or in his father's service, at best making only short coastal trips of a mercantile or diplomatic nature. Fair Beard, on the other hand, had kept the deep-water end of their partnership, working out of Ireland with Madoc's foster family.

"It is the damned ice, mountains of it floating in the water all year round, not just in winter like the old days." He and his crew had come in not three months ago, June, with tales of icebergs as far south as the Faroes. "Do you really want to find out what it would be like now, with winter coming on?"

"T'would make a good test of the new ship."

"Aggh, you are always ready to leap before you look." It was a jibe at their first meeting, which ended with Madoc, green master of his first command, taking a leap into stormy water from the rail of a Norse ship sometimes known as a merchantman and sometimes known as something else.

They stood there leaning on the larboard rail above the humps of coracles lashed in place of war-shields, watching the vast Western Ocean. It looked at that moment like a flat, glossy animal of immense girth wallowing in the sun. It wiggled and winked under noon-light, and called softly in a different language to each man.

"We could take it from the Fortunate Isles," Madoc said.

The Icelander brightened. "The southern passage?" Mariners from many ports speculated about the legendary route, where a strong current drew ships southwest, where a great floating garden was said to trap ships, where the days were long and the noon sun rode dead center in the sky, and where the pole star—indispensable beacon in the heavens—dropped out of sight below the northern horizon.

Islands that would someday be called the Azores were supposed to lie out there many days west of Portugal but were on no chart Madoc had ever seen. The best maps stopped abruptly just west of the Fortunate Isles—the Canaries. Beyond them maps decorated with sea-monsters labeled everything Terra Incognita—the Unknown. What was really out there depended on how large Vinland was. Fair Beard's Norse grandfathers speculated that Vinland was Africa backside. Most landsmen had never heard of Vinland and thought any land out there was just a story to hide the terrible truth of hell.

"It would be fine to know," Madoc said, gesturing at the western ocean. "To see what kept the old sailors from coming home."

"The southern fields of Vinland the Good," Fair Beard said.

Madoc watched the horizon where Ireland lay due west, and beyond that the wet unknown called the Flood because it supposedly contained all the waters left over from the biblical event. "Paradise..."

"We can sail south by west until the days are as long as the saga says they are in Vinland, then head west by north." Fair Beard could not read, in fact disdained reliance on mere written words; but stored in his mind were songs his father's father's father sang about the sea. Thus his people passed on their knowledge. They jealously guarded their trade secrets, not trusting maps, which could be copied or stolen. Because of his secretiveness, Madoc had mentioned their long-ago trip westward only in general terms, never claiming publicly to have found anything of legend. Only to his father had he told the truth to persuade him to commission the voyage.

The Icelander glanced toward the bright shore where David stood out darkly against shifting colors and shapes. "Still," he sighed, "what a shame to leave this land to such a scoundrel."

"This will be our vengeance—to survive and leave sons in a new land." Madoc thought but did not say, Because this one will be changed into something that is not Cymru. The invaders would subdue this land's wildness with another name. He put his hand on Fair Beard's shoulder. "Bring your family with you."

Snorrison turned his gaze to the holder of his oath. It was said his snow-lashed eyelids drooped because they had been several times frozen in the trackless wastes of his homeland, where he had been chased out by his enemies. But there was only warmth in him now. "It will be forever, then."

Madoc smiled sadly, the best way to say yes. He could not speak of it, but he had been infected by his father's dire vision of the future of Cymru. . . .

Welsh, he thought, that was what the English would call this nation: the strangers over the line. He shuddered when he thought of the Saxon word, Wales, itself the sound of weeping. "A new land . . ." Madoc mumbled when he realized his mind had wandered and the pilot was staring at him.

"A new land except for a few Icelanders," Fair Beard reminded him, recognizing his own exhaustion in his commander.

"And vikings on the run from some killings," Madoc quoted from the song Fair Beard had paid to have sung the last time they were in Dublin. In a little public house near the docks he found an old bard in exile from the Orkneys who knew an abbreviated translation of a long saga that featured numerous explorations of ever-more western lands by viking chiefs always running away from "some killings."

"And Skraelings. Do not forget the Skraelings." They had not encountered any of the strange beastlike men reported by Norsemen. But they had heard wild stories about the red-skinned cannibals of the far western lands.

"We need to hear the Vinland Sagas again. Perhaps in Dublin we can find that old singer to refresh our memories."

Fair Beard regarded his friend and master, not quite ready to believe the dream was going to come true, yet ready to believe anything his commander told him. The hound in him seemed to sniff at strange smells on the wind.

Wil approached with a grimace of more than irritation on his craggy face. The invasion by cargo of this military ship was already causing problems. Now Wil was trying to deal with sheep. He had instructed the bearers to begin stacking cargo quayside until the best way to load was decided.

Later Madoc took Gwen back to the beach to collect passengers. He still did not know his father's exact plan—whether it had been merely a diversion to tell David that the *Horn* would transport the royal household south.

Far up the valley on the Roman road a line of mule carts was making the left-hand turn toward the harbor.

"David has some merchandise he wants you to take to Dublin," Owen said when he saw Madoc approaching.

A pavilion was set up under a tapestry awning at the tailgate of his wagon. There he was holding informal court with members of his armed guard at ease behind him. Everyone held cups of mead or wine imported from France. An air of festival prevailed. David's standard-bearer had left his staff with the pennant upright in a dune where the wind off the sea caught it from time to time, animating the red dragon, casting raging shadows over the brilliant sand.

The village elders, the scribe, the two poets, the royal driver, and several servants, in addition to the household guard, were in attendance while the off-loading of the wagons continued. Among the well-wishers drinking a toast to David's victory were the blacksmith-abbot and the French priest Simon, hanging back behind the others as though he did not want to assert his presence but did not want to miss out on anything either. Brother Wyn saw Madoc's glance and tipped his cup meaningfully toward the *Horn*.

Raising his cup, Madoc said, "I have not yet sorted out how to get all the household aboard," as good-naturedly as he could manage with David casting silent stones at him across the elaborate camp table. Unsaddled, he did not cut the same figure; he seemed more than nervous, watching Madoc like an enemy, his handsome nose more than ferretlike, glancing around to see if men flanked or followed his stepbrother. When he saw there were none, just the red-haired girl, and noticed that Madoc was unarmed, David relaxed somewhat, regaining his seat on their father's right hand, allowing a servant to refill his silver-filigreed drinking horn.

Madoc glanced around for Evan's mount so he could retrieve Durendal, but the guard was gone. By now he must know his younger brother was dead. Likewise, he did not see Rhiannon.

"After you drop us off, you will have plenty of room," Owen said, staring at Madoc as though reinforcing earlier commands.

"How about all three of those ships?" Madoc asked, a subtle request since he was suggesting two more vessels than Owen promised for the expedition.

Owen did not miss it. "Take it all, my son," he said with an expansive gesture while Gwen stationed herself beside him, opposite David. Her nose wrinkled; she did not like the way her uncle smelled of gore.

David scowled. His hackles were up even if he did not quite know why. "I want to get this soda ash to Dublin while the market's good." The breeze shifted slightly, wafting the odor of drying blood from his clothing and gear. "That mess will just about pay for this otherwise unproductive morning."

Owen gave Madoc an I-told-you-so while David quaffed the wine, then held the horn-cup out for the servant to fill again. David styled his manner on those he hated, the Norman English, who despised common mead in favor of French wine. He had already drunk too much, had probably been drinking since the battle. Madoc had to forcibly swallow clawing anger that David would be so blatant. His father caught his attention, however, eyes wide with a reminder of the oath. Madoc was glad Fair Beard was not here; there would have been no holding him back because of David's manner, his English affectations and disdain for native custom and manners.

"I have a better idea," Owen said, turning to regard David. "Madoc will deliver the soda ash in his ship, and the other two can transport my household on south."

David liked this. He nodded, then looked beyond his father where the mule train was arriving as he had ordered.

"I will be glad to take your cargo to Dublin," Madoc said evenly, regarding the carts piled high with hempen sacks. He could not believe what Owen was engineering, yet it appeared that his ulterior design was to send Madoc away with David's spoils of war. "How much will it bring?"

Following every storm that deposited seaweed along this coast, there was a brief soda-ash season. "Nobody else will have ash in this soon after the last storm," David speculated and suggested a price that would outfit another ship.

David caught Owen's grin. "What amuses you, father?"

Owen shrugged. "It is a fine sight to see my two children working together instead of against each other."

Madoc watched the mules amble down the path to the *Horn*. After loading she would then anchor in the harbor while the other ship docked for passengers and the rest of the cargo. It would be a tight, hasty squeeze. They would have to repack in Dublin, where they must take on even more. His eyes were calm, but behind them he was again furiously calculating.

The court watched for a while as the mules moved to the quay. Madoc saw Wil discussing the situation with David's standard-bearer. Even from here Wil was clearly scowling. The bearers began to load sacks onto the ship. As he watched, the *Horn* hunkered deeper and deeper into the water, not unlike a goose full of eggs and riding wider.

His father appeared quite happy, surrounded by adoring townsmen, loyal retainers, and his family. Gwen was handing him his refilled cup. It was all working out just as planned— David's own greed was expediting the operation. Fair Beard and the crew would grudgingly accept reparation in payment instead of blood revenge for Pawl's death. Madoc was beginning to believe that this plan of Owen's just might work.

The standard-bearer, a distant cousin named Cyngar, with the rest of the escort veered away from the mules to return to the chief's makeshift reception hall. They passed to one side, where they dismounted on David's command. Removing gloves and helmets, they ambled over where the servant was already pouring wine for them, when suddenly from Madoc's right Gwen screamed.

She backed away from Cyngar, who had to slouch to stand beneath the awning. A massive block of a man, he had shed his mail-coif to reveal a smallish head and an axe-edge face that seemed all teeth and blue chin.

The girl's cry arrested everyone, including Rhiannon, who appeared at the backdrape of the wagon, her woman behind her startled by the scream.

Gwen fell, trying to get away from Cyngar; her father helped her to stand. Cyngar bent in creaking leather to retrieve the pup, squalling in his hammy hand, as he held it out to the girl; but she averted her face against Madoc, who felt her trembling against him. Rhiannon took the dog and handed it to the serving girl, Tegan, then tried to pry Gwen from her father.

Owen had been startled to his feet. David had an unreadably flat glaze to his eyes.

"What is it, Gwen?" Madoc asked.

She shook her head against him, refusing to look up.

"What is this, girl?" His grasp yanked her toward him. Her face was dirty from new tears on the dust of the caravan, and she refused to open her eyes.

"Look, here, Gwyneth." Owen shook her.

She cracked her lids, but barely, as in a seizure. She was shivering, hysterically cold, her arms limp in Owen's hands.

"Look at me, now."

She threw herself against the green wool of his chest and clung to her grandfather. He looked at Cyngar with glacial eyes.

Cyngar backed away, his glance glued to his lord; David gestured for his vassal to get lost, but Owen's voice froze him: "Halt there, Cousin!"

A wave of cold from within drenched Madoc as he observed Cyngar. He had heard soldiers' stories about this fellow, said to be always at David's side, more than a bodyguard and known for his ability to kill in a thousand ways.

Owen all but dragged the child upright against him. Her hands clawed at his tunic. She was trying to hide her face again. The arglwydd gave in to her and was silent, and thus all around him, for a painfully long moment. He threw an unmistakable warning look at Madoc, then said to Gwen, "Now, lass, I call you to witness."

"My mother . . ."

Only Owen could make out what she said. He separated her from himself so he could see her eyes. "Are you sure?"

She nodded, casting her gaze downward, for all the world appearing guilty with the shame of the raped.

"Gwen?" his voice insisted.

"I saw him this close." Her meaning was unmistakable. "While the others . . . hurt mam, he . . . he . . ." Gwen was not going to say she was raped. The supposed enemy raid happened two years ago. This was as close as she had ever come to speaking of it.

The air in front of Madoc's eyes vibrated in transparent red waves. What happened next was very fast.

Cyngar, who had not relinquished his sword, had his hand on the hilt, but he never drew it. Madoc had taken a guard's weapon and had the blade at the soldier's throat in a smooth slice before anyone else moved. Someone screamed—not one of the women but David, who caught Madoc from behind.

But too late. His half brother had already drawn blood from Cyngar, who had gotten tangled in the poles that supported the awning. His massive arm lashed out, but already blood spurted. He grabbed his throat and staggered backwards, bringing the awning down around the startled court.

David growled in rage when he saw the death throes of his best killer. He reached from behind to grab his brother's sword hand, in effect riding his back, but Madoc was quicker.

He swept back the hand with the sword, bringing a knotted fist full of hilt into David's fine nose, cracking it with a sound like the snap of a deadfall branch. Then he rolled away from the screaming prince and, with a great cry, hauled up the sword with both hands, poising a second at the highest point of the swing above David's head.

It was Owen who yelled this time, throwing himself directly at Madoc. There was a fragment of a second when, to all watching, it looked as though the son were going to behead the father. The old man rolled at Madoc's feet. The blade came down—not even Madoc could have stopped the serve. But there was enough sanity in him to hook it, sending it curving backward, mowing down the hardened pole behind him like a reed. The dragon emblem fell, billowing in the wind, as Madoc slung the sword at the end of the arc out over the sand where it impaled the horse Cyngar had just dismounted. The animal, mortally hit, shrieked and dropped.

Owen gasped on hands and knees in the sand. Madoc had no resistance when the smith and a guard caught him from behind.

"Both of them, both of them," the old man wheezed, gesturing at David while Gwalchmai and the porter attempted to help the king up. With the aid of a guard, they lifted him to the chair.

A guard moved in behind David, who lunged at Madoc, teeth barred, his nose hideously flattened on one cheek. The guard gently grappled with him, bringing him up short of violence.

Rhiannon hurried to the king, who appeared faint, head thrown back, face flushed. "I am all right," he said. "No, no, I am not hurt." He drew himself upright with a huge breath, wiping his mouth with the back of his hand. A flash of blood showed there, which Rhiannon wiped away with her mantel. But he pushed her hand aside, his eyes searching and finding

Madoc. He would have risen if he were able, but he leaned forward instead.

"You—" he said, tight-lipped, shaking in anger and exertion. "Your vow was not a day old."

Madoc was unable to move; the monk and the soldier held him fast. "It is all right, now," Brother Wyn said softly. Madoc's own body seemed without volition. He might have collapsed if they didn't hold him. But he returned his father's stare.

"Damn you!" Owen raged, slamming his fist on the arm of the folding chair, shattering it. He looked over at David, who was standing now, cradling his face. He saw Madoc again and made a feeble attempt to break away from the men who held him.

"And you—" the old man glared at David, unable to find words for his disgust. "You . . . you . . ." Traditionally, wrongs done in secret were more onerous than public murder because they undermined communal trust. He dropped back to the chair, leaning his head against Rhiannon. Gwen crept to him. When he felt her small hand on his knee, he looked up and brought her to him, rocking her back and forth.

The dying horse gave another cry and sputtered, head flailing on the sand. Owen saw it over Gwen's shoulder and nearly crawled over her to get to the miserable creature. He dragged the sword from its withers and plunged it with tremendous force into the animal's neck, silencing it instantly.

The fallen pennant snapped in the breeze. Around the wagon people had gathered at the first sign of trouble. Now they stood gape-mouthed. A few had presence of mind enough to cross themselves as they watched their blood-splattered king turn, staggering to his knees. Ten pairs of hands were immediately there to support him, but he fought them off when he gained his feet. The wind whipped his hair in his face as he gave his family a long study. He glanced over his shoulder, where the last of the sacks was being loaded onto the *Horn*.

In his mind was the pale hope of salvaging some of this great plan he had undertaken, to separate these two sons of his forever. He blinked, clearing his sight, and straightened, letting the porter help him back to the chair. On the way he grabbed the pennant and used it to wipe blood from his tunic and hands. As he did so, he spoke. "Great wrongs have been done here." He dropped the ruined pennant and leveled his gaze at Madoc, then David. "Great wrongs have also been uncovered."

"The child lies, sire—" David started to protest, his voice thick and liquid with pain.

"Be still," Owen commanded quietly, and David obeyed. "This child did not lie. I believe her. I believe you have tried twice now to murder your brother Madoc." He turned to Madoc, who had not moved, and said, "Now perhaps you believe, too."

Madoc accepted this, dropping his glance. When he looked up, he saw Gwen and almost cried out to see the expression on her face as she stared fixedly at the dead man.

"The ancient laws of Hywel the Good are clear." Owen gave Cyngar's twitching corpse a final glance and continued with grave slowness. "The dead avenge the dead." He looked back at the company, his voice changed, assuming the drone he used when he sat in judgment on legal questions brought before his court. "In the case of a virgin raped, her lord, her father, must be paid for the loss of her virginity. The lord of the rapist..." he turned pointedly to David, "must pay her father the value of this loss, considering that this child is royal."

David was sputtering in fury.

"Write this down, Brother Ely," Owen instructed. "I, Owen Gwynedd, et cetera, judge that the price for this girl is equal to the cargo of soda ash just loaded onto the *Horn*."

"No—" David yelled, pulling forward, but was held fast.

"But that is not the only wrong done this day," Owen said, turning to Madoc, "you have broken your oath to your lord, and there is no less punishment than death—"

David's fury descended into an unnatural grin, but Owen continued, "—or banishment. I am a just man. It is the latter. Brother Ely, write this down: You, Madoc ab Owen Gwynedd, are henceforth and forever banished from this realm. So be it."

He walked to David as he spoke. He took his son's ruined face in his hands and examined it with great care, turning the chin this way and that. He palpated the flesh and quickly, expertly, lifted and set the nose back into place. David gave out one hoarse cry, then said, gasping, "This is the moment, father." He moaned again in pain and continued. "Make me your heir, and I will not oppose this play to protect your bastard."

Owen regarded his handiwork, turning David's chin so he could pursue the profile. "You know how the people feel about an ugly nose on their king."

David tossed his head back, replacing the helmet, hiding his face. "Now, father, with these witnesses."

"Very well. I name David ab Owen sole and only heir to the house of Gwynedd." The court gasped. Even David was surprised. This was a sudden, dramatic way to settle a matter of state that would have best been settled at law and in ceremony rather than on a windy beach with the blood of kin staining the sand.

"Let me loose."

Owen deigned not to respond. He turned instead to the smith restraining Madoc. "Take him and tie him to the mast of his ship." The old man chuckled sadly. "To keep him from the siren call of revenge—"

Nobody seemed to get the reference except perhaps Gwalchmai, off to one side, who was stained by horse's blood, too shaken by events to appreciate literary repartee.

"Tell Fair Beard to take the fleet yonder to Dublin. Then and only then can Prince Madoc be untied."

He told all the others that it was time, they must follow Madoc down to the quay, board the ships, and proceed as planned.

The French priest hung back, but Owen saw him. "You too, Frenchman."

"Sire, I am to return to Canterbury."

"I cannot insure your safety, Father Simon. Get your passage back to your master. Go on. You do not have to pay." He chuckled to himself with this and turned his back on the sputtering Frenchman as he gestured to a guard to see that his order was obeyed. Simon saw the guard and stumbled backward against Wyn, who said words of encouragement with some reference to fighting the infidel in the Holy Land.

Owen was brisk in his good-byes to Rhiannon, Gwen, and Rhys. To each one, including Brother Ely, he said, "Go with God," and embraced them all, then clapped his hands as if herding sheep, "Yn y cwch, into the boat."

Only Gwen looked back.

Beyond the wagons Owen saw a raven hanging around the boatyard. The sergeant of his guard was still round-eyed in the aftermath of events. He caught the king's gesture, eyes narrowing with revulsion at the raven and her mate hopping closer to the dead with beaky grins clattering.

The sergeant took out his sling and a pebble from his pouch and started to wind up to dispatch a bird or two, but the arglwydd gently stopped him with a touch on the shoulder. Since before the Druids the ravens of Mona had been protected. All Celtic kings were under strong sanctions to harm no bird, since flying creatures were, by virtue of their wide view, kings of the animal world. Owen retrieved the ruined pennant and offered it to the soldier.

The sergeant relaxed, crossed himself again as he took the shroud and his men to remove the two corpses. The steward whipped his cloak at the ravens, who grumbled in retreat, finally taking wing where they observed all below from lazy, high circles.

Gwalchmai, watching this small episode and unable to resist its poetic symmetry, remarked that what he had seen today inspired him to compose an ode.

"It shall be called 'Madoc's Song,' I think," the poet said as he struck a pose:

> "Beneath the knowing raven's eye
> brother smote brother on the sand
> while Gwynedd's dragon . . . cried."

Behind them David hissed, but the two guards held fast.

"No," Owen said morosely as his other children diminished with distance. It was answer to both his son and the poet.

Eyes following the hero, Gwalchmai quoted from an old song that was part of his profession's oral tradition: "'It would be wrong to leave him unremembered, great were his exploits. . . .'"

Ignoring the poet, Owen continued, "I forbid you to compose a memorial to this day, which will bring my death." With that he sat in the campchair and stared after the dwindling throng.

It gave the poet chills because he had been inspired but had censored himself from saying "while the dragon died."

"Besides," Owen muttered, "the song belongs to Rhys now."

Gwalchmai sniffed with barely concealed disdain. While Meredydd's son was his former student and talented, he was still just a house poet, a rememberer, a courier, cantor of paraphrase and secretary of the ordinary. His seat in the great hall was down near the masters of horse and hounds. Why, he even accompanied himself in public, not usually done. He had never saga'd a king. In truth, thought Gwalchmai, Rhys's poetry was too bare. And the man's voice was too rough for noble redaction, too like a sailor's or a French troubador's.

Gwalchmai, chief of poets, royal storyteller of Gwynedd, stifled his ire, however, when he glimpsed utter indifference, like a hood, settling over his brooding lord.

People came and went from Owen's presence—his own staff, villagers, David's men, nervous and shifty-eyed, the mediciners, trying to ease their miserable commander's discomfort, despite the human chains that bound him.

"I say, brother," whispered Caradoc the physician as he perused Owen's work on David's nose. "We are fortunate that our lord the arglwydd has other duties, because he would take ours from us with his skill."

"Hmmph," Owen was pleased to growl. He loathed Caradoc's obesity and had been the unfortunate recipient of several of his cures for arthritis.

"Aggh—" David cried.

"Sir—!"

"Caradoc, your hands are colder than a witch's teat."

"But, sir—"

"Get away from me."

"He has to release the blood, son," Owen said.

David laid his head back against the men who held him. "Very well, but listen well, you butcher: If you hurt me once more, you will be on that ship yonder."

Caradoc made a small, condescending bow; his portly bulk was sweating from every pore, and his forehead was pink under the bristling sunlight.

"Agh—that is it—" David screamed, slinging blood from his face as he pushed the surgeon away. "Since you killed three of my men with your incompetence, I have been waiting an excuse to get rid of you. Go on."

Wiping his hands on his silk tunic, Caradoc stepped backwards with a silent appeal to Owen, who merely shrugged and looked at David who was holding his face in a once-white cloth handed him by the second mediciner, who had the good sense not to touch the prince.

"But you send me off the edge of the world," Caradoc moaned.

"Kill him," David said to a man, who drew his sword.

They watched the sweating physician tread heavily down the road. Sometime later with the sun slanting down on them, Evan Powys, ashes in his curly brown hair and a hefty bundle on one shoulder, approached and when granted leave spoke intently to Owen, who replied with a couple of soft words to him that sent him off toward the ship.

Around the arglwydd what was left of his household was getting back to business as usual, preparing tonight's feast. The steward, the brewer, the elders, all reported on preparations.

The arglwydd spoke to each in turn, but quietly and with distance in his voice, his attention drawn by activity down near the water as the last passengers boarded.

The ships loosened like thistledown. Feverish with injury, David realized too late that his smith had not returned with the escort from the quay. After a desultory nod from Owen, the guards let the prince slip away. He ran stumbling, screaming imprecations, through the mules taking their oat reward.

"I command you to return—"

But the *Horn* was long into the water and far from reach when he ran to the farthest tip of the rock jetty. The wind caught the sail and filled it, grabbing the *Horn* and making of her a living thing that sprang, despite her off-balance load, toward the greater water.

But those on board could still hear the screamer on the quay.

"You hear me, bastard—" His voice carried over the water, to the man tied to the mast. "I put a viper in your nest!"

And from the hold Madoc called an order, "Man the horn!"

Fair Beard was delighted to comply, sounding the ship's bellowing war horn so that David did not get the last word.

Chapter 5

*Then shall the Britons be
like prisoners
with status of aliens
to the Saxons.*

—Prophecies of Taliesin
Welsh
c. A.D. 500

It took the rest of the afternoon to cross the Irish Sea.

Fair Beard helped Madoc remove the tunic of mail, then stayed a while after fastening him as comfortably as possible with his hands bound back around the mast. It was stepped into a huge oak block on the keel but was braced on the bilge deck by another majestic heart of oak, ingeniously built into the middle ribs and carved like a fish, in fact called the mast-fish by the men who hewed it. The rounded shape made it impossible for Madoc to sit. So Fair Beard had bales of wool brought down to cushion what could have been a difficult berth. They talked about details of the voyage, the crew, the passenger situation.

Throughout their conversation neither mentioned events back on the beach. Cymru was behind them. It would become an unspoken agreement among the exiles that everything in the past was gone. All they had now was the future and the present, which must be used to plan how to crew the ships and apportion the goods.

"But we should always sail together, brother," Fair Beard protested when Madoc gave the Icelander command of the new ship.

"We will sail together—just on different ships."

56

But this did not comfort Fair Beard, who knew it was next to impossible to keep two ships together on the open sea.

"Besides, who else do we have?" Between them they commanded less than sixty men. Among those were fine seamen, strong in the oaths that bound them, but there was not one these two could trust with a green ship out on such a voyage.

Fair Beard could not answer the question, so he went away muttering to himself. But Madoc knew he was secretly delighted to be master of the splendid new vessel, which Madoc named that night the *St. Ann*.

He heard someone approach from the shadows.

"Sir . . ." Caradoc the mediciner stepped into the light from overhead. "Does m'lord need assistance?"

"Oh, no," Madoc said, settling back against the tree.

"That cut over your eye needs tending."

"It is nothing."

"Let me wash it for you—"

"No, it is nothing. I do not even feel it. Thank you."

The plump physician stepped back and turned to leave.

"Mediciner—" he called, bringing the fellow up short before he placed a foot on the bottom rung. Madoc could not see his face in the gloom, but he had turned in this direction.

"Nothing. Never mind."

Madoc watched Caradoc turn back and haul his bulk up the ladder, wondering if David had been telling the truth when he screamed from the quay. Was this the viper?

Rhiannon came to him next, her soft scent a strange presence in the hold. The woman who accompanied her brought pale cheese and lagana, a traditional flatbread, which Rhiannon fed to him with her own hand.

"I am sorry our father forced you against your will to come with me," he said shyly after she dusted crumbs from his mustaches and chest with a cloth that smelled of heather. It clouded him with memory of a long upland meadow full of lavender flowers from a time in his life he thought he had forgotten, when he was a boy in the household where this woman was a small child.

This close she could not avoid looking into his eyes. Hers were gray, the color of steam. It was as though she were completely transparent and he was looking into the piled-high clouds in the sky above. He could look right through her and not get any trace of who or what she was. Yet there was no evasiveness about her. She dismayed him, and even more because as she looked at him, she was so open he suspected it could only mean that she had no secrets to keep from him. Or to share.

It was still afternoon. In light from the square of sky above, he could see Owen's dried blood on the hem of her mantle.

"I do not mind traveling with you, brother," she said simply, helping the woman named Teleri put away the meal. Madoc could not remember her family name. She was a strong-boned, plain woman with small feet and hands that fascinated him in their freckled whiteness as she went about the simple work. He thought she might be mam to one of the children he saw earlier.

"Back there all was blood and death," his sister was saying with a gesture of a lovely shoulder toward the shore they left. "We had planned to go to France when father . . ." She tossed her hand as if brushing away spiderwebs or distressing thoughts.

Madoc had caught a glimpse of the same despair when Owen commanded her to leave. "You were so sad. . . ."

"He will not get the care he needs from anyone but me," she replied with that same disarming simplicity. "Everyone else just uses him." She looked up at Madoc then, melting his heart. He inwardly groaned, for what was he to do with this love for his sister? He was unable to mash it down inside himself; he was only glad that the shadows hid his body's reaction, which he kept further private by raising his knee between them.

She looked down at her hands where a thumb played with a string-callus, almost as if suspicion of his feelings made her shy. Dare he hope she shared them, he wondered, but saw when she looked up again that he must be mistaken; her thoughts were only for Owen. This realization relieved him in a way, but it was a wound, too. He looked away from her and right into Teleri's gaze.

"He will die now, you know," Rhiannon was saying.

Unnerved by Teleri's penetrating observation of his discomfort, he started to reassure Rhiannon, "His servants will—"

"David will find a way through loyal servants. The others he will pay." She shook her golden mane, letting loose the stained scarf as Gwen approached from the stair with a pot of bag-balm. She kissed Madoc's cheek and began without words to rub the ointment into his wrists where the cords were binding.

Rhiannon and Gwen left together. Teleri looked back as she followed, but she did not speak as she mounted the ladder.

"Eh," he stammered, "Lady Teleri—"

She hesitated on the middle rung, bending to see him. "Yes, lord?" A coil of rich brown hair came undone and dropped, unraveling to its full length beside her face.

"Who did Princess Rhiannon mean when she said 'we' would go to France?"

Teleri hesitated, then answered, "Myself I suppose." She turned to mount the stair after her mistress, then paused again, hair swirling like a slow river through rich farm country. "I am not noble, sir. Just a bond woman, with her since childhood."

When she had gone, he could not remember what she looked like or the color of her eyes, if she were old or nubile, fat or thin. Yet he could not forget that loose wave of hair swaying with the movement of the ship against milky skin.

Overhead the sky turned a darker blue. The high clouds changed into red billows with iron-colored bottoms. He tilted his head back on an aching shoulder, trying to lose himself in the dash of colors.

Above the sounds of sea and wind came male voices singing on cooler air; the monks were chanting vespers on deck. The old rituals remained, despite disrupting events. It was an unexpected comfort to the captain tied to his ship. Madoc was not a religious man but loved the music and tonight needed its regularity. The sweet, mournful song drifted like a fragrance, muted by the wind.

They must be halfway to Dublin by now.

The off-duty sailors made their way one by one or in small groups to speak with Madoc. He asked them small things about the running of the ship, which they answered briefly in gesture and jargon. Several of the Norsemen serving under Fair Beard descended the peg-stair to the spot beneath the square hold-opening and approached as a solid wall of sailor-flesh.

The men did not talk much, but they left him with the assurance that he had their loyalty. Madoc wondered how they would feel when they learned where they would be sailing.

As dusk descended, the fire went out of the sky. The clouds

moved on, leaving the hold-opening a purple canopy sewn with stars.

Wyn was there suddenly, quietly, holding a shallow copper basin of water. He set it down and stood formally with his thick-fingered smithy's hands folded over his rough-woven cincture of unbleached flax coming unraveled at one end. Was there anything the arglwydd needed?

"So that is what I am then, of this ratty pack?"

"Your father ordered it so."

"I am not the arglwydd."

"People need a leader." Wyn straightened, and as if to explain this peculiarity of the human species, said, "The brothers have elected me abbot."

Only thirty of the monks stayed aboard, he explained. The others scattered to the four winds with the death of their oath-holder, the fighting abbot. These few were delighted to follow their patron saint Brendan westward, where they believed they would find his descendants living on a visionary Isle of Paradise the Irish saint had seen shining in the west six hundred years ago.

"I am no great churchman, no scholar," Wyn continued, casually untying the sash and draping it across his left shoulder after brushing its fringe against his lips. Now Madoc could see that what appeared to be rough weaving were holy scenes subtly tapestried in the weave. "I think they chose me because I have the strongest body left in our community."

"A father."

The monk nodded, finishing the thought with Madoc.

"It seems to me the brothers made a wise choice." Madoc sighed and leaned back upon his tree. Now his shoulders were killing him. "Surely my father did not mean to cripple my sword arm. Untie me, Brother Wyn."

The monk looked shyly up at him, enough light cast from above to illuminate a wry expression. "I will hear your confession, my son," Wyn said as he unfolded a clean rag. Even though he had so recently been elected abbot of a disinherited community, he was not a priest. But in the Celtic tradition he could hear confession—this was another area of disagreement between Celtic Christians and Rome. Wyn rinsed the cloth in the basin and proceeded to wipe sweat and dried blood from Madoc's brow.

"I have nothing to confess," Madoc said, quietly stubborn. The truth was he had avoided confession for so long he forgot the last time he bowed his head. The rag was cool against his skin. Last Easter, he suddenly remembered, he went to Mass and confession—the least piety possible and still call himself Christian. He closed his eyes, pressing the knotted muscle in his right shoulder against the ghost of a knot in the wood.

The monk moved around the mast-fish. Unseen by his host, he laid a benediction on the wood as he touched it—this ship made him uncomfortable because it had not been named for a saint.

Presently Madoc felt his arms relax forward as the bonds loosened. He was not free, but he could flex his shoulders.

The monk was whispering a prayer. This, too, gave Madoc a fair measure of solace. Evidently accepting Madoc's lack of remorse for a mortal sin, Wyn finished with a simple blessing, his work-scarred hand on his new lord's head. Here Madoc read the monk's true feeling: "Father, watch over this unrepentant sinner and guide him to seek forgiveness through Your light, in the name of the father, son, and holy spirit, amen."

"You bless me anyway?"

"The sins of kings..."

"You will pray me out of hell, then?"

Wyn shrugged. "St. Brendan's has been praying for the souls of Gwynedd for two hundred years." Madoc realized was a start that it was so—the family had endowed the monastery for perpetual prayers on behalf of the line. He thought fleetingly of all the many sins of his family, of David and the warrior brothers Madoc had left behind, of his wild viking grandfather who took the Christian faith only on his deathbed after a career most heinous. Fleetingly, because the thought hurt, he was reminded of Owen, his banishments, his imprisonment of his own brother, and other sins too close in Madoc's own lifetime. It was a violent ancestry to have the task of praying for.

"You really prayed for us, I mean, at the monastery?"

"We still do and will as long as one monk from St. Brendan's is alive." Wyn stood with the basin, a blacksmith again, said goodnight and left as quietly as he had come.

For a while Madoc appeared to be resting, eyes closed.

He heard someone else approach, wood scraping wood. When he opened his eyes it was dark, though someone had a fire going in the rack on deck. Rhys laid aside his staff and crouched down, offering Madoc a water bag. He gulped, happily surprised to taste mead. It dribbled down his chin. He tried to lick it, but it trickled down his throat and into the hairs of his chest, an awful, small itch that he could not relieve. He did not want to tell Rhys, though, because he did not want the blind man fumbling against his person trying to clean it up. Most of the irritation of this position was in not being able to help himself. Again he silently cursed Owen's whims.

He thanked Rhys, indicating that he had had enough. The bard lingered without speaking. Madoc finally said, "I relieve you of my father's commission."

"But, sir—"

"I could not help but notice earlier that you are obeying him with less than enthusiasm."

"I am grieved, lord, that you saw me weep like a coward."

"You do not have to sail with me to prove your courage."

"I will go."

"I want only volunteers, Storyteller."

"I want to go."

"But earlier—?"

"It was just shock. I love Owen Gwynedd. I have served him since I was his page at seven years. He is the only father I remember. For that reason I will go with you."

They talked about their boyhood, how they would never have suspected that life would bring them to such a pass. Madoc said he wanted Rhys to make the western journey on the third ship. He had been doing some furious mental work before he drifted off. He planned to sell the two smaller ships, which would not be seaworthy on open water, and buy a larger one in Ireland.

Madoc considered the possibility that things might not be so welcome in Dublin, and he began thinking of alternate ports. Too bad there was not time to swing by Lundy Isle south of here, where the house of Gwynedd had friends who might be persuaded to join the venture or at least to put up a ship.

He would still have to get to Dublin and claim his new vessel, then sail her and the third ship out the channel as fast as possible. The purchased ship they would rechristen the St. Brendan, which he planned to have commanded by the new Abbot Wyn, with Wil as pilot. Rhys would be Madoc's surrogate with the monks. He must put some of his best mariners with

Wyn to crew the third ship. To spread out his expert seamen, some of the younger monks would accompany Fair Beard. The one commodity he desperately needed but could not buy with all his father's treasure was experienced sailors. There was slim chance of picking up extra crew in Ireland. There might be one or two Norse hands in port with a hankering for a long run, but few would chance the great unknown. The monks had learned soldiering well enough. They would learn still another occupation.

Rhys was surprised Madoc would entrust command to a blind man, but he said he would serve as his lord wished.

"Rhys, please send Fair Beard down."

The poet stood without comment and moved away, staff gently tapping the planks, leaving Madoc with an itch he could not scratch, but feeling even more hopeful.

He felt the tremble of the sea up through the mast at his bare back. His heat had activated rosin in the pine log; the aroma was strong in his nostrils as he opened his eyes.

In the starglow he saw the young strained face of Evan Powys, Madoc's Durendal glinting in his hand. The brass hilt— little man of the sword—had been polished, the edge sharpened.

"Thank you," Madoc whispered, ashamed to look into the boy's eyes. "I am sorry. . . ."

"Pawl adored you, sir. He would seek no finer death."

Madoc swallowed, wishing Rhys had left behind the meadskin.

"I came to pledge my oath."

"But my father—"

"Released me, even before Pawl . . ."

Madoc could only nod, unable to think of aught but that bloody helmet.

"I will serve in my brother's place." Evan laid the sword at Madoc's feet just out of reach, then looked up at his new commander. "It is really Roland's Durendal?"

"The king of France said so."

"You must have done high service for such a gift."

"It was to seal a bargain between himself and my father, who said such a weapon should not be wasted hanging on a wall."

Evan removed Madoc's dagger from his belt and placed it beside the sword.

"We will never return home," Madoc advised the serious young man. Despite his love of sailing, Madoc always loved to come home; this would be his first voyage without such assurance, and he was already missing the isles of Britain.

"My brother was the last of my close kin."

"Then you shall be Gwynedd's kin," Madoc said, thinking that he would station Evan with Rhys. Of all those who would accompany him, Madoc was least sure of the monks, even with Wyn leading them. There were a couple of Saxons in the brotherhood. Evan could act as Rhys's eyes. Madoc wondered if he could indeed trust this man. "Begin your service by releasing me."

Evan bit his lip. "Our lord Owen did get that one promise from me." He grinned lamely. "Do you need anything else?"

"I am thirsty . . . and need a cloth to wash." Madoc relaxed. He would be needing loyalty in the men who followed him. So far he had not let himself dwell on his brother's parting words, but they still echoed in his mind. Had he been able to place a viper—a spy or saboteur—in Madoc's nest? Caradoc was the prime suspect, tagging along at the last minute on David's orders. Was his ire a sham to cover the commission? But Evan also joined the company after Owen's banishment of Madoc.

But Madoc knew David. Unable to inflict injury, he would lumber Madoc with a worried mind. An empty threat, most likely.

Evan brought what he asked and wiped the drip, relieving the itch, then said good night. Fair Beard swung out and dropped the last three rungs to let Evan pass.

He hunkered in front of Madoc, waiting for privacy.

Satisfied that they were alone, Madoc said, "Friend, do you know what will be waiting for us if we are foolish enough to arrive in Dublin?" Hugh de Lacy and Henry II were already cooking up the annexation of Ireland, a viking colony long ago and destined to be an English colony within a year.

"I wondered how long it would take you." Fair Beard leaned closer. "A small wager that the viper is the Frenchman."

"He will leave us in Ireland. Perhaps it is the physician."

Fair Beard considered this, then shrugged.

"Or that young man whose brother fell in my stead."

"Those Powys boys are loyal," Snorrison commented, then with a change of tone, asked, "Dun Laoghaire, then?"

"Too close if we should get hemmed in—they will see us entering Dublin Bay. No, Snorrison, we must get to Wicklow."

South along the rugged coast from Dublin was Wicklow

Head, which boasted a fine boatyard that served the fishermen who followed the cod in those waters.

"That means taking our new ship secretly out of Dublin."

"We have enough friends to help, and money." He laughed; suddenly he had all the money he needed, had needed all these months getting the new ship built and outfitted.

They spoke further on details—trading the two smaller vessels for a third larger one, supplies, the probabilities of getting extra crew, and a couple of tricks that would throw David's dogs off their trail. Madoc had connections in Ireland that his brother did not, which would market the soda ash without delivering it to Dublin.

Fair Beard climbed up the ladder to scramble the crew for a course correction toward the southwest.

Around Madoc the company was settling in. The wind came in at a more belligerent angle, but they would still pull in close to midnight. Even the nervous sheep quieted—he heard Gwen up on deck crooning to them softly, spreading fodder out in the makeshift rope pen where Wil had them hobbled.

The quartermaster brought a bilge-bucket without his captain asking, knowing he must relieve himself.

"Wil, you think your Mary will take a little trip?"

"She tends to seasickness."

"How are your boys?"

"They are six this spring, full of the devil."

"You will never see them again if you take this journey with me, old friend."

Wil stared. "We have sailed too long to part company."

"Then bring your family."

"They are a ways south of Dublin."

During this Madoc felt the internal groanings of the ship as the wind moved against her differently with Snorrison's change in course. Wil felt it, too.

"We put in at Wicklow." Madoc grinned. "To avoid trouble."

Wil nodded, having heard the gossip of this afternoon's confrontation.

"And where is it we are going?" Wil asked, but someone else cleared his throat in the shadows.

"I come to ask the same thing, sir—some say Africa, others say you are thinking about sailing west." It was Huw, one of the senior men sorely missed if lost. He also had a wife living in Ireland who might keep Huw from the venture.

Madoc saw Fair Beard return to stand in the shadows, listening quietly, his arms folded across his chest.

With the shift change the rest of the crew came down with Huw as their spokesman. Each man approached him, some talkative, some merely giving him a wink, a drink of their preciously small store of mead, a look of commiseration and gratitude for avenging Pawl. Monetary compensations were common; they felt he had gotten the best of David. They listened as Madoc discussed their destination. All but a few pledged themselves to the venture.

Fair Beard reported they were making for Wicklow Head with a clear sky full of stars and a good wind.

"Owen said I must not be untied until we reach Dublin."

"You misremember, sir," replied Fair Beard.

"But you were not there."

"By now I have heard the story from everyone who was, and all agree that the arglwydd specifically said you could be untied when we reach Ireland, which by my calculations will be ere the midnight bells." By that he meant the monastery bells on Wicklow crag, which could be heard far out to sea.

As they filed up the ladder, the men grinned when they heard this—everyone knew Owen had said Dublin.

Snorrison left Madoc alone with the groaning mast at his back and the stars above his head. He went over the day's extraordinary events. Instead of the fatigue that should be consuming him, Madoc felt a surge of second-wind energy. There was still a while before they docked. He went over his crew, stowage, and passenger disbursal, and decided what they needed to buy in Ireland. He would also get messages to his brother Riyrd, who held family estates in Ireland, and the Lord of Lundy Isle—both of whom loathed David and his English connections.

Madoc relished planning the entire trip and for the rest of his life would remember that oddly peaceful time bound to the mast shivering in its clever Norse socket, with the strong male voices riding the wind above.

The sea ran high all that afternoon.

Chapter 6

No breeze drives the ship forward,
so dead is the sluggish wind off the
idle sea . . . there is much seaweed
among the waves, and it often holds
the ship back like bushes.

—Ora Maritima
by Auienus
c. A.D. 300

Ten weeks later all that was behind them, and more ocean than could be imagined lay between themselves and Britain.

To Madoc it seemed a miracle they had come so far, a very long way indeed, and still no land in sight. At this moment he could recall very little of the hopeful feelings he had felt during the crossing of the Irish Sea.

Dressed in loose trews and a knitted wool pullover, Madoc gazed at the distant horizon encircling the mast where he was tied again, this time not in the hold on royal orders but secured up on the highest point of the ship as barefoot lookout. The chain mail, hauberk, and leather gambeson were stowed in his sea chest. At his belt hung an astrolabe and a line-knife. He was not even armed. So long had they been out of the sight of land that he feared he would never get to face an enemy again. Ireland was a faded dream. Shortly after he had made port at Wicklow, Madoc completed payments on the new ship and brought her unnamed out of Dublin under cover of night, her skeleton crew of Norsemen nervous because she was not deep-water tested. Wyn had hurriedly christened her the *St. Ann* before a quick afternoon run on the Irish Sea. Their stealth proved their best defense.

Word had come through Madoc's Irish fosterage that David had mounted a warship to chase him down and reclaim the price of the ash, which found easy market. Some of his crew had chosen not to stay aboard; the two most loyal of these he paid to deliver the letters to several men Madoc wished to advise about the true nature of his departure. He hoped he might get answers but dared not linger. Nor did Madoc wait to find out if David would ignore Owen's direct order; he had axed the lines that tied them to the ancient viking dock at Wicklow and took his little fleet out on the next tide heading for the open Atlantic and the passage on south where he found the fabled African current and on which they launched into the great western mystery that yet held them.

After so long at sea they yearned for land, even their captain, who was in his element. Each slow swell lifted and tilted him on his forty-foot perch. Had he not been lashed with a clever seaman's knot to the yardarm, he would have been thrown far below onto the mast partner or into the monotonous swell.

The sea lay five leagues in all directions, a hammered-dull shield interrupted only by shark fins out to the edge of the unknown. Land of any sort was less then a memory. Even Madoc's sea-loving eyes hungered for some blemish on that unchanging circle cast about their small ship adrift in too exact a center.

Directly above, wind hissed in the lanyard that secured a dragon pennant. The red-and-white leather flag cracked in the flat-voiced breeze that for three nights uttered only one sound... becalm... becalm... becalm. Even now his hair was licked by the odd whispering downdraft fierce enough to tease their flag but too weak to swell the sail. Below his bare toes the square sheet rattled like nails in a bucket. He ordered it unfurled last night to catch what he prayed was an upping from the southwest, but the sail would have to be trimmed soon or the mean-dog wind would chew it to shreds. An hour ago he was sure he smelled the tide, a reliable promise of landfall. But now, squinting at the purple western haze, he knew a trick of this strange water had fooled his nose.

What smelled of land was really an immense seaweed growth just below the surface. Its leathery leaves and round berries gave the sea the look of oiled and hammered metal. This was the legendary garden in the sea that becalmed ships until their crews went mad. The old stories were true. If that tale was true, then perhaps the legendary sea monster really did guard hell's gate just over the western horizon.

Madoc scanned the reach.

Perhaps there was no solid land on this side of the world. Perhaps he had led these trusting souls over the edge.

He tried to recapture the elation he felt during that afternoon crossing after Owen banished him. But despair filled him as he regarded the company below, most of whom were flattened with seasickness. The sternman had fallen asleep over his tiller. Floating here in the deadly garden, the rudder was useless for anything except to keep them oriented west, waiting for wind. This was the only time during the voyage when Madoc regretted his decision to sacrifice the oars for cargo space. But, he considered, how long could men weakened as they were row out of this immense desert of water?

None had been spared seasickness. Even his hardiest men suffered from the relentless swell. He himself kept down nausea by not eating at all. Everyone aboard was sick at heart from the unchanging days that wore on the soul too long aboard ship.

Drinking water was scarce. Two weeks since they caught rain in the leather sail spread for that purpose over the hold. They were hungry, down to nothing but fish. Fish they had aplenty.

He heard the doves cooing in the cage lashed to the deck below. The female was fat with eggs—those two of all those aboard the *Horn* were well fed by Gwen, who gave them scraps of fish that Madoc would have said no land-bred bird would eat. But he was wrong; they especially liked the entrails of the catch and had fattened on this diet and under his daughter's care.

He was certain he was not the only man aboard who had imagined the aroma of roasting pigeon.

They ate most of the dried fruit bought in the Fortunate Isles, which were called the Canaries in Latin. His father's gold ring paid for those supplies. He managed to keep the engraved garnet, but the rest of the treasure was nearly gone. He had determined to keep the sack of Roman coins, an urge to preserve something of their former life forever gone. Also, he had managed to hold on to half the precious pepper his father had so generously given him. He figured that the rare spice would eventually prove to be his most valuable trade item. They carefully stowed the monastery's books in chests aboard the *St. Ann*, but Madoc wanted something of more permanent material.

But they could not eat gold, and there was no telling how much longer it would be before they began dying. The wind bore no chill, but Madoc shivered when he thought about today being All Hallows. According to the hash-mark log he kept on the back of his chart, tomorrow was New Year in the old reckoning, the day when the earth of men overlapped the otherworld, when human beings could fall through the crack between to be lost forever. He wished Fair Beard were with him here on the *Horn* rather than on the *St. Ann* somewhere out there in wet eternity. The man's presence could keep Madoc from falling into darkening thoughts. The last time they saw either of the other ships was two weeks ago. It was depressing that they might never be seen again.

Reason seeped in, arguing that the movements of the stars could only be comprehensible given a spherical earth. Land-lubbers could not see it because they never watched the heavens as a sailor must. He continued presenting himself with these comforting thoughts, as Fair Beard would if he were here, and finally consoled himself with an essential truth: Madoc loved this time at sea. It was good to be up here, the eye of the ship, in the dawn watch above the company stirring below.

He saw his sister's red-trimmed cloak on the second deck, where she moved with a water bag among the pallets of the sickest ones. Her head nearly brushed the underside of the top deck, which was slightly wider than a catwalk on the sides of the open center hold. The modified Norse ship was two-storied, much like the chief's house back on Mona. The bottom deck—the bilge boards—was little more than a crawl space used for bulk storage. The sheep were on the *St. Brendan;* likewise fine pregnant sows they bought in Dublin. One of the monks was a stockman back in the monastery, so Madoc was spared their trouble but made up for it by taking on more passengers among the crowded cargo. While the crew and a few passengers slept in the open, the second deck was where about half the company spread their pallets be-tween stacks of cargo and rectangles of unfinished wool cloth hanging on its warp fibers. Before the seasickness the women were at the weaving every day. They had not touched the looms for three days: The stone beads dangling at the warp ends clattered gently together as if calling the weavers back to work.

Presently Rhiannon climbed the ladder to the top deck, where she proceeded to the high, narrow prow to sing a morning prayer. Even without the harp, which she left wrapped away from the salt air, Rhiannon's voice was Madoc's favorite music, strong and clear, "Holy Mother Mary and St. Brigit, thank you for another night of life and another dawn to sing."

The sea in the eastern quarter took on a rich blue cast. The verge seemed to be made of glass. The sun was already up but veiled by milky haze.

"And thanks to you both for a fine wind, from the east, if your holiness does not mind." He was counting—had counted for days now—on the warm rush of air that often preceded sunrise on the open sea to blow them out of these doldrums.

Just as the first rays of sunlight broke through, Rhiannon's face turned toward him with a smile. The contrary wind flung back the dark blue mantle that she had been wearing the day they left. Whispers of her yellow hair escaped the wool material.

He would have sung with her some more, but he glimpsed a blemish of what might be a sail just at the horizon—surely one of the other two ships. Both Fair Beard and Wil had a sunboard and some knowledge of the winds and currents. Chances were good that the *St. Ann* or *St. Brendan* should be brought with the *Horn* to this becalmed spot of sea, considering they were of the same berthen and began from the same point west of the Fortunate Isles. Madoc peered through the tunnel of his curled fingers at the growing shadow on the western horizon. He leaned against the harness to determine which of the ships it might be.

He could plainly see what he thought was the shape of the *St. Ann*'s big dark-banded sail furled into a strange triangle. Maybe the storm had damaged her, he thought. Like rising smoke its foremost edge seemed to tear into rags of separate shapes.

It was not the *St. Ann* or the *St. Brendan*. For a flashing second Madoc thought of what other ship might be at sail on these waters. From the other side, perhaps?

It was no ship at all. Some kind of sudden weather, a waterspout, he surmised. The air felt wrong for such, though who knew what evil winds blew through these heathen quarters?

No. Nor was it a storm. This movement was purposeful, not half a league away, but stretching weirdly back to the horizon. Vague fears laced his heart of some supernatural, myths of old evil let loose upon the world of men. He was not superstitious, but the last few days had worn on him.

Since thy entered this becalmed zone, he found when he took readings that the polestar was closer and closer to the northern horizon each midnight. A slow current, a massive spinning eddy, was dragging them as helplessly as a fishing cork slowly southwestward. It was an unnerving experience to watch his only guiding light sink closer and closer to vanishing below the line.

He was sailing off the map. Sailing blind for the first time in his career. One did not have to be superstitious to know fear. He knew he would be afraid when he looked one of these nights toward the polestar and found it gone below the northern horizon. They would be utterly lost. Lines of an old saga recalled storm gods raging out of the sky.

Then he saw what it was plowing toward them. He hung there straining to see if he should shout a warning. It was coming this way, though the ship was a little west of the flight's southward determination. Fascinated, Madoc watched it grow into a looming fan of laboring wings.

He saw Rhiannon gazing up at him.

"Birds," he called.

Rhiannon nodded, watching the immense flight cast a shadow as vivid as a mirage on the sea. Several mariners climbed into the rigging to get a better view.

That entire quarter of the sky was stained by the flock streaming out in a long veil. The birds were very high, plowing onward on slow-moving wings. None so much as glanced downward as they slipped between the ship and the climbing sun now escaped from the haze. Wings shimmered. Cries of wonder came from the deck, where all but the most seasick dragged themselves to watch the spectacle.

Madoc was dizzy calculating the number of birds that must be traveling the flight. They did not pass directly overhead but stayed on their high course due south. Vaguely he could hear their weirdly human cries.

Through gaps in the living cloud, sun rays shifted here and there as though the birds were sweeping the water with strokes of light, a strange vision. Bright spots on the swell moved in zigs and zags, illuminating the rattled tops of the giant weed. Madoc saw the flash of fins under the sunbeams—sharks swimming in circles, dashing as though attacking the dancing light.

The individual birds, now smaller than the vanguard, dipped lower. They looked like swallows or starlings flapping frantically. A few sought the refuge of the ship—curlews, sparrows, warblers, thrushes. They settled into the lines and on the yard beside Madoc or fluttered to the deck, where most of these stowaways ceased to move. Even those on the lines soon dropped off, taken again to flight or dead in the water.

The sharks slashed the water, war breaking out in a stew of fins and foam tearing at a pair of wings. While the main body of the flight was still some distance away, lone fliers rode far from the throng. Several flew close enough for him to see flashes of blue and white, startled bright black eyes and gaping beak—something very like a nightingale all but panting, battered by the wind. Unable to pump farther, the bird was tossed at the man up on the mast, nothing but bone and feathers, so it did not hurt but was a shock when Madoc saw the bird was dead even as it fell away from him, dead in flight.

What kind of journey had it traveled to break its heart against this bastard's chest? "Stupid bird," he muttered. To challenge all that water . . . the thought furrowed his brow. A brooding empathy scored him as real as the physical ache of hunger through his stomach, chest, and arms when he glimpsed a morbid vision of his own plunge into failure, his child and all below perishing under his misguidance.

The sun blazed against his ear. The other birds flew on, their combined shape dwindling into warmer southern latitudes where the days were longer and sunset came on stronger. This change in the length of days had been obvious for more than a week. Their latitude seemed to be more southern than the saga's description of Vinland. But Vitromannaland was south of Vinland according to Norse lore, and the chart he kept with hash marks each day, done after midnight star sightings, had them moving much farther west than he or Fair Beard gambled. This ocean was much, much larger than anyone had imagined. How much larger the Earth itself must be than the great Ptolemy calculated.

One among the diminishing flock cawed what sounded like a laugh. That seemed a sign of hope so soon on the heels of despair. A good omen is a good omen, no matter how strange.

He heard Nona barking at a clatter below. The long-legged pup scampered between Gwen and Teleri's brown-haired boy Einion, scuttling across the bilge-boards of the lower deck in pursuit of a raucous, aggrieved gull trailing a dislocated wing.

Madoc's heart leapt. Birds of any kind were a good sign, but this was even better. A gull. A shorebird. The others of the migrating flock could have come from far inland, but a shorebird usually did not stray too far from a coast. The gull either had gotten caught up in the vast swarm and flown out of its normal territory, or... or there was a shore nearby.

Madoc shielded his eyes to search the horizon in all directions. The flock brought in its wake a fresh front of cool, dry air from the northwest, which tamed the unpleasant downdraft.

North of east a ship lumbered not half a league away. The great flock had taken his attention, or he would have seen this, undoubtedly a sister ship and probably there all night. It was not moving. At its highest point a black pennant dangled.

Madoc's stomach clutched at the possibilities. Disease, accidents, quarrels? Madness in this becalmed zone? Could it be possible that someone had actually died of seasickness?

He must find out why death was riding the *St. Ann*.

Chapter 7

*The time shall come at length when
Ocean will unloose the bonds he
imposes, when the vast Earth will
lie open, when the sea-goddess will
disclose new worlds, and Thule will
not be the last of lands.*

The Tragedy of Medea
by Seneca
C. A.D. 100

He untied himself and shinnied down the mast, refusing the breakfast of dried fruit Rhiannon offered.

"You will be sick if you do not eat." It was surprising how much she had tanned while at sea; most of the Celts were blistered, but her Norse heritage turned her exposed skin brown.

"Sister," he replied, "I will be sick if I do."

He caught Gwen's gaze as she looked up from her lap of swooning seagull, but she did not speak and went back to setting the wing bone while the boy Einion leaned, watching her labor. He was tall for his age, about six, with Teleri's mild features.

Too impatient to wait for someone to break out a coracle, Madoc did it himself, ordering one man to row the distance between the ships. He asked one of the sailors to fetch him the hen-dove. She and her mate were trained to fly the pennants, that is, home in on the dragon-marked flag whether above a field headquarters or a ship at sea, instead of a stationary coop.

"The men saw sharks out there," Rhiannon called after him. "At least send someone else in your place."

75

Over his shoulder he shouted to the crew to check the rigging for damage and get ready. "There is something coming up from the southwest." Then to his sister he said, "I will take care." It pleased him for her to worry about him.

Around them everyone was watching; he could feel their combined worry, for which Rhiannon was speaker. It was an old tradition—the arglwydd was personally responsible for them all. He did not want to be their king, but here he was, king anyway.

The sailor brought the caged pigeon; then he and Madoc unhitched a coracle from the shield rack. It dropped into the curdled water below, and they helped themselves down the sidelines into the round-bottomed craft and pushed off.

The oarsman was one of his senior mariners, Huw ab Tewdr, who had been with Madoc for years. He was good with the impish oval canoe—he was from the River Severn where his grandfathers were fishermen before Christianity. But the sea was contrary, and for every ten of his strokes, the dipping swell seemed to swallow eight. The downdraft threatened to throw them into a spin, so Madoc picked up a narrow paddle and held the little vessel on course, presently to come alongside the *St. Ann*.

Even as he climbed aboard, he knew something was wrong, some dread appropriate even if the black flag had not warned him. This close he could see the explanation for that: Nobody on board had flown death's color. Madoc could plainly see that the dragon pennant and the entire top of the mast were charred. Likewise the yardarm above the ragged sail, charred black but not burnt clear through. How odd, he thought, wondering what set of circumstances could explain it.

The sail was less of a mystery. It was wind-chewed, its patchwork hides coming undone at a dozen seams, left unfurled far longer than any self-respecting mariner would allow.

How long had the *St. Ann* been a ghost ship?

Behind him Huw drew his sword, uttering a muted curse. He could smell death here. Madoc kept Durendal sheathed, intuiting that the threat on this ship could not be dispelled with metal.

Several of the migrating flock had paused for the last time on this ship, too. Some small bird feebly flapped a wing against the deck until Huw lifted it with the flat of his blade and pitched it overboard. Rigging creaked. Wind teased the sail. A pin cracked against some obstacle forward of his position.

Together they noticed the lidded tun bolted to the forward spar-block, neatly spigoted and gurgling with each pitch and yaw. Other men might pray for water, as other ships have water barrels for crew. But these were Cymry. Neither man had brought a drinking horn, so, of a single mind, both lunged for the nearest low spigot of a barrel and lay down to let the excellent milk of Mona—fermented barley water and honey—flow into their faces. No thirst is so finely quenched than with mead, went the old saying, for it was the best way devised by man for keeping water potable. Sated at last, Huw retrieved his weapon and looked over at his captain with the shyness of shame; they spilled so much.

"I suppose we must save some for the others," Madoc said, twisting the nipple closed and pulling himself to his feet. Already feeling renewed, he slung the ambrosia from his mustaches and turned toward the hold.

He came barefoot to this deck, which groaned up through his bones. It should be rumbling with men about the ship's business, but none greeted them as they stepped onto sun-bleached boards.

Madoc had designed this ship. He knew every splinter of her grave, hollow sculpture, hundreds of interlocking pieces carved to match a partner by masters' hands from knees and elbows and roots of oaks fitted as delicately together as bones in a bird's wing. He had prowled with the master builder through forests to find the perfect tree for each major piece of her puzzle. Not only did he architect the design, he worked here with adz, plane, pumice, and whale oil. He had broken bones on her. His hands bore calluses and scars from the carpentry of strakes and ribs, each a handcrafted thickness that allowed maximum strength with maximum suppleness for great seaworthiness and speed.

He could have traversed this deck blindfolded. But these boards were just her bones. Now he could feel with an ache the emptiness, the absence of her hands and her heart—the crew and Captain Snorrison Fair Beard. All below the scorched mast and ragged sail appeared shipshape, untouched by disaster, evil weather, or hostile hand. For there to be nobody aboard under such peaceful circumstances was incongruous,

even ludicrous. One might expect the men to be hiding and
at any moment to leap out and have a joke on their arglwydd.

Their absence was a grim joke, for Madoc feared only one
thing would force Fair Beard to leave these boards unattended.

He glanced skyward, where rags of sail flapped more
vigorously. He eyed his companion who knew that the slapping from that direction meant the wind was definitely picking up, friendly and strong from the southwest.

On the *Horn*, riding not a furlong away, the sail's belly
billowed now and then in the renewing breeze. Soon they
could leave this deadly garden. Yet the joy Madoc might have
felt was dimmed by this mournfully silent ship creaking
around him as he made his way to the hold and peered down
into the shadows.

An almost overwhelmingly sweet smell assaulted his nostrils.

The cargo looked jumbled as if smashed around some.
Most of the lash-lines held, well knotted and double-tied; his
seamen were the best. But what had broken was smashed.

On the dank air lay a sound Madoc could not identify.

Huw, lanky and sandy-haired with deep-set eyes that had
squinted so long his face was permanently shaped that way,
frowned even deeper at the mystery. Madoc signed that he
was going belowdecks. His heart sank with the thought that
he might have to complete this great undertaking without
Fair Beard.

The stair rungs complained minutely as he descended into
the relative darkness. Going into any dark place always
hoisted his hackles. So by instinct he withdrew Durendal and
leveled the blade, catching a piece of the sky, the only
brightness in the hold piled to the deck above with cargo.
The sword's glint darted here and there, illuminating nothing. Narrow passageways between neatly battened-down cargo led into greenish darkness.

He stepped the last rung. Coiled line swayed. Now he
could see barrels and boxes twisted crazily together beside
the hives. Some were broken, spilling contents out onto the
deck—seed, wool cloth, tools. A cask of apples seemed all
right when he pried the lid and sampled one. He savored the
excellence of its slightly dried pith, still juicy with the taste of
earth and old flowers.

Some of the hives had burst. A great gout of rich brown
honey oozed into a wide puddle on the boards. Around the
puddle were sticky, unmistakably human, footprints.

A flurry of movement startled him; involuntarily he brandished the sword at a soft gray cloud rising from a fragment of blackened honeycomb. He saw immediately that it was a flock of moths, a sure sign of a dead hive.

The bilge was high. He could feel it sloshing beneath the water-logged planks that felt gluey under his feet. The sea-man in him groaned at such abuse of a ship; she must be bailed soon, or caulking would start to pop from between swollen strakes.

The flaxseed was wet, fluorescent with mold where it edged like a miniature forest against the amber lake of honey. That large a mold would take at least a week to grow, Madoc surmised.

Whatever happened here was some time gone.

His attention was caught by the flight of a bee past his face, up and into the forward hold. At least one of the hives was healthy enough to have found new quarters back there.

Just then Huw called from above with an abrupt, "Captain—"

Madoc would have returned to daylight immediately, but for something in the far shadows where the bee had flown. His eyes were adjusting to the gloom. He could just make out two lighter shapes jutting from behind a row of crates. He angled the blade's glint, but it only confirmed that something was indeed out of place there, so he edged closer.

It was a pair of naked feet. Madoc felt himself to be a cage of bones—in this light his own toes seemed skeletal. But these protruding feet were even more emaciated. The toes curled toward the soles. They had to be feet of the dead. Now in the zone of death he could detect the undisturbed smell of it, but heavily veiled by honey, distressingly sweet.

"Captain—?" Huw called, peering into the hold.

"Someone is dead down here," Madoc replied, continuing on because he must know who. There was just enough light to see. He straightened from a crouch and confronted the corpse.

It was the scribe Brother Ely in the cassock of St. Brendan's order, sprawled against an open sea chest set against the extra rolled-up sail. The once-plump scribe was long gone, no fat on him at all, as dried up as a sandal and screaming silently forever. There was no sign of the cause of death except the starved-looking remains with leathery skin stretched over and defining each bone. Had the poor bookman been so over-educated that he did not even know how to rig a fishing line?

But starvation might not be the only explanation for his condition. All the exposed skin was dotted with brownish circles—Madoc would wager they were old bee stings.

He first surmised that the monk had tried to avoid starvation by stuffing himself with honey. A thin dribble cascaded from the corner of his mouth for all the world as though he were a brimming pitcher.

Then, with chilling realization, Madoc saw honey oozing from his eyes and ears as well. He knew that the monk was full of honey, but not because he ate it. He had been hungry, raided the one remaining hive, sustained bee stings until he died down here with his beloved books. The likewise starving bees must have fled the infested hives, found themselves in the middle of an ocean with nowhere to start anew, and took up the only berth available near a food supply. From the monk's startled eyes ran great sticky tears as though he were crying honey. To be host to so much honey could explain the lack of putrefaction, Madoc thought, half remembering something from the scriptures: Samson and a swarm of bees in a lion's carcass. . . .

Used to the hideous variety of form that death could take, Madoc thought he had seen everything until this moment. Involuntarily he shuddered at the image of such a weird demise, which seemed in its own sweet way as horrible as gore or rot.

He sheathed his sword, observing another bee fly directly into the corpse's gaping mouth. Another took off from the ashen lip, zooming past Madoc and back toward daylight.

Ely must have been rummaging the chest he had died against, because several items—books, their cases, and a few scrolls—were disarranged or scattered on the floor. Madoc groaned to see a splendidly drawn frontispiece to the Psalms mildewed, wet and reeking. The hand-printed book and its masterful illumination in gold and scarlet—the product of months or even years of some monk or nun's life—were rimmed with green fungi. Most of the text was already blurred, ruined beyond recall. Humming happily, other bees were working from both sides of the magnificent initial capital enscrolled with an angel's wings in Celtic spirals. Madoc's Irish foster father made sure the boy learned his Latin. He had also picked up working French, Nordic sea slang, and Saxon in his travels and found languages easily retained.

Only one fragment of verse was legible, a verse that

seemed a direct command to the man who could not resist reading it: "Be wise now therefore, O ye princes, be instructed..."

Both of Ely's arms clutched decorated and gilded leather boxes, each the repository of an illuminated manuscript. His stiff right hand was glued to the Gospel of St. Luke, and the left thumb held open a small breviary.

Madoc could not help himself; he breathed out an involuntary sigh of relief that it was not Fair Beard.

"Captain?"

Madoc hurried up the ladder. He was gasping for breath when he scrambled out into the fresh air of the upper deck.

Huw jumped back out of his way; the smell told him all he needed to know, except identity—was it one of his mates?

"One of the monks," Madoc said, knowing the sailor's mind.

Huw nodded and crossed himself, then gestured toward the western horizon, but Madoc had already seen it: a cipher of smoke etched the far lavender haze. As keen as his eyes were, he could not tell what was burning, but it seemed to be a point on the water. He caught no indication of any land whatsoever.

But land it was, they discovered later that afternoon after sending the pigeon back to the *Horn* with orders for seven men to bring their bedrolls to this ship. Giving Huw temporary command, he ordered him to keep the men out of the hold. Together they brought up the apples and some other supplies.

The current had drawn the two ships closer together. The men were arriving from the *Horn*. After consuming an adequate amount of mead, they rigged the spare sail, rafted the two ships together, and tacked against the strengthening wind, which brought them within sight of a low island.

The only vegetation on this frail pate of land was mangrove swamp and a beard of salt grass, which the several very pregnant ewes were seriously barbering. One of the ewes had two healthy-looking ram-babies nuzzling at her flank. The animals lifted their placid faces only briefly when the human commotion began, then went back to nibbling. Just this side of their flock a fire sent oily black smoke into the sky.

Lined up on the facing shore either side of the carcass of the third ship were more than forty crewmen and passengers from the SS. *Brendan* and *Ann,* bloody from butchering the last of the pigs, jumping, waving, screaming, and finally crying with the sheer joy of seeing the *Horn,* and with quite a tale to tell.

Chapter 8

*There are thrice fifty distant isles
in the ocean to the west of us.
Larger than Erin twice is each of them,
or thrice.*

—The Voyage of Bran
Irish
c. A.D. 700

Even Rhys waded into the gentle surf to meet the coracles from the *Horn* and *St. Ann,* which Madoc ordered anchored well away from the island before taking a half-dozen boats to the shipwreck.

The hysteria of rescue was upon the survivors, while those from the ships felt themselves rescued by the islanders, rescued at least from death by thirst because a little spring nearby trickled fine, clear water. This fingernail clipping of an island was less than half a league wide and three long but solid land, no matter how slim, cured seasickness.

Madoc saw only a handful of the monks, who had started singing *Salve Regina,* a hymn of salvation, while others fell to their knees praying loudly in several languages. He wondered where the main community of clergy was hiding—or had they perished?

He tried to speak to each man and woman, to remember faces and names, to take their hands at least, but there were too many screaming for joy. The rays of a lowering sun in his eyes and the din of their voices hit him with a headache despite the race of victory that surged through him. Fair Beard took on more than a dozen more people in addition to his family. Many of these men and women Madoc did not know—who was that young mariner with dark skin, a freak of nature or burn victim?

He recognized the twin boys cavorting naked in the surf as Wil's boys, and there by the fire was Mary, their mother.

And that old man there, muttering foreign incantations to the sky? Bleary-eyed, he suddenly found Madoc and stumbled over, clawing at him, nearly taking them both down into the cold breakers. He cried out something in Western Norse, the language of Iceland. Madoc knew a few nautical terms and the like, but this was more complicated.

As toothlessly pink as a baby, the fellow switched languages: "Who will bury us, master?" he demanded in rawly accented Irish, grabbing Madoc's loose tunic and shaking him so that his astrolabe clanked against his drinking horn. "Who will bury us?"

Madoc would have tried to assure him but saw he was delirious. He stumbled on, grasping another of the mariners who tumbled from the coracles at the water's ruffled edge.

Around Madoc faces were drawn by malnutrition with eyes as deep as wells—a look that reduced all humans to a single countenance. He wondered if he looked as hollow, but they all seemed to recognize him. They crowded around him, reaching to touch him for the king's good luck.

Madoc tried to take a head count—Fair Beard and several of the best seamen were not among those who splashed out to welcome them. He tried to ask several people where they were.

"Off to search for western land," a big blond pregnant woman gasped in Norse-accented Gaelic, salt-sprayed and shivering as she bear-hugged him. "Thank you, thank you for coming," she cried. Madoc was aware of a strong metallic smell about her, then realized when he saw a stain on her lip that it was blood.

She wiped it away. "They have begun killing each other—" Seeing him stare at her bloody hand, she shrugged and smiled a grin marred by bad front teeth, another toll Madoc had noticed that the sea took from human voyagers.

"It is only pig," she said. "The heart they gave to us." She patted her unborn child, but her attention was snagged by the old man angling into deeper surf, so she hurried off to take him in hand. He followed her back toward the fire, where a loose ring of bedrolls and meager possessions marked

their rough camp—men this side of the beached *St. Brendan,*
and the women on the other side.

At least, Madoc thought, they did not waste as much of the
pig as he had thought. He realized that the blond was
Yngvild, Fair Beard's wife, who like the other wives of crew
had moved to Dublin, where Madoc and Fair Beard built the
new ship. She was a different woman now. The old man was
her father, much the worse for wear and not recognizable as
the tough old viking he had met on the dock a day before
they sailed.

He was able to piece together a ragged report in those first
few minutes from their disjointed versions of the sea-toll—
storm, shipwreck, more storm, death, lightning, fire, sickness, panic, fighting, killing, mutiny. . . .

The raven was picking them off by ones and twos, Madoc
thought morosely. Nevertheless, this crazed but not altogether lost remnant survived. He saw Gwen arriving by coracle
with others from the *Horn.* For an eyeblink at this distance,
she might have been Ann— No, he thought, breaking the
cherished illusion, I must not turn the girl into the mother.

Behind her more of the *Horn's* company dragged their
oblong coracles onto the beach.

Einion and Gwen jumped from the boat as though this
were all a romp in a meadow, Nona bounding before them.
From the boat the girl retrieved a wicker cage—he thought at
first it was the dovecote but saw that this one looked quickly
made of an old basket. She pulled out the gull whose wing
she mended. By that time Wil's sons found them and were
laughing at the bird, which reeled drunkenly in the surf.

Standing there with gray water foaming around his feet, he
experienced a moment of keen detachment as he regarded all
of them in the golden light. Were they enough to survive?

Searing doubt scored him.

The gull shook itself and staggered a couple of steps. A
wave came in and flattened it, but Gwen was there, picking it
up out of the racing water. Shocked into flight, the gull
winged up, dripping, not strong, not graceful, and unbal-
anced in favor of the sprained wing. But it flew, placing a
circle over Gwen's head and pulling cheers from her and the
other children. Wobbling, it dipped and beaked something
squirming from the curl.

Madoc felt his doubt heal with a flash of an idea that would
grow in him over the next few months: He would someday

return to his homeland. He knew this with a sureness beyond mere hope; he knew it. So there was reason to be optimistic, even though at the present moment he might not know exactly how he could pull all these strangers together, get them settled, rooted, and viable. He did not even want to contemplate how they could muster fighting men should they find resistance in the western land.

But their weapons had been saved, and everyone would be stronger after a week of rest, water, and food. He thought they might make it if they found a mainland. As surely as he knew some would survive, he knew he would return to Gwynedd. He would settle with David, make his peace with Owen, outfit more ships, and bring more people, because this colony was going to make it. The next few months would be the test.

Then, just as suddenly, his brief moment of awareness passed, leaving him once again cold, wet, and hungry, his hand burning like acid. The salt water was fire on a new blister. Someone crawling with vermin and reeking of pig blood was sobbing against him. He recognized it was one of his own mariners who had filled out the crew of the St. Brendan, Wil ab Hennin, whose wife and twins had been on the St. Ann. Madoc distinctly remembered that, yet the St. Ann had been found abandoned miles from this place. He was dying to hear an explanation of what must have been confusing events on this island.

And confusion still reigned. Madoc looked around; the beach was boiling with people, several smeared with blood, all ragged, dirty, laughing or crying together. Beyond them the few sheep milled nervously.

At least their Celtic love of pork had spared the sheep, far more useful than a mere meal. With wool they could recaulk the St. Ann and continue west. All these people would not fit aboard the Horn. They must abandon half the company to this island or salvage the other ship.

So much was lost. Fair Beard, apparently, and the cream of the mariners, some of the monks, unique craftsmen whose knowledge was lost except for whatever two or three apprentices had learned.

On a shallow rise that marked the sand-buried rocky spine of the island, seven crosses leaned starkly against the sunset. He had not had time yet to find out who laid there.

Doubtful that three piglets would increase to a viable

herd—bad luck two were male. There was a chance, though, that they could save the ship dying out on the dark swell, waterlogged and oozing caulk. But not the fine vessel that fed their fire. They had dragged off most of the *St. Brendan's* goods and rigging: At least some forethought prevailed among them. The fire had not consumed her hull completely, so there would be caulk they could boil down for tar to mend the *St. Ann*. Otherwise, the ship lying across the waterline was a total loss.

He groaned when he had a closer look at the wreck. She was only beached, not breached, and could have been salvaged had they not so foolishly fired her for a signal. Wil looked miserable even with the skin of mead at his lips. His glance told his captain that he tried to save the ship. Madoc bit his anger in the bud and swallowed it; this was not the time to play despot.

But he chewed them out about the sow they had butchered on a stony outcrop where blood still puddled. The last piglet was being born when they slit her throat, wasteful of the blood out of which a nutritious pudding could have been made. Madoc disdainfully remarked they could have killed a ewe for meat.

"I tried to stop them," Wil said, glowering at the butchers from a raw black eye he got trying to stop them.

"But, sir," Evan said, glad that blood hid his bruised knuckles, "it is Martinmas—"

"You are out of your mind," Madoc retorted. "Tomorrow is the old New Year Day, November first."

"No, sir," said another sailor. "It is November eleventh—"

"We have kept scrupulous time," said Brian, newly ordained, and so was Father Brian, though somehow the title seemed inappropriate for his age. He was a round-faced Irish fellow, with sandy brown hair around his old-fashioned tonsure that went from ear to ear rather than a mere circle on the crown.

"Well, you are scrupulously wrong," Madoc said flatly. He had kept his sighting like a religious ritual three times a day and had a chart marked with small crosses and his dates. He could document that this was not Martinmas.

"Our prayers have kept us on date," Brian responded, crossing his arms against his chest.

"And Martinmas demands a kill," Evan said, standing somewhere between Madoc and the clergy.

"Man, I am telling you, your date is off—it is not Martinmas yet—it is only All Hallows," Madoc corrected him. "Tomorrow is November first, the start of winter."

Brian looked chagrined but answered, "Beg to differ, Captain, but Father Simon says it is Martinmas, the eleventh."

Exasperated, Madoc said, "We will settle this later—the point is you could have celebrated with something less than our last pig."

They stood like naughty boys made sinister by the blood.

"One of the sheep, perhaps, which we have more of." Madoc was about to explain the obvious, when Evan spoke abruptly, interrupting the arglwydd.

"It is the fat, sir—the body craves fat." Several sailors behind Evan growled agreement.

"And surely there will be pigs wherever we land," replied Caradoc the mediciner, up to his elbows in blood. His cassock trailed in it. Madoc saw that they would be lucky to get a modest snack for so many people from she who had been hungry. All eight piglets were runts.

"Pigs are everywhere," interjected Father Brian, with a twinkle in his eye. If the lad, probably a monastery orphan, had grown up on Celtic lore instead of bible stories, he would know pigs had been in Britain only a few centuries. Their introduction occasioned one of the most popular old tales about the first pig swindle and swine raid.

Three piglets were stillborn—the butchers trod a fourth in the frenzy of killing. They found another the mam had crushed.

"And if they are not everywhere, then you are three pigs away from your last pork chop," Madoc said, turning away in disgust.

They had all grown to manhood on pork; to do without it was to contemplate starvation, or worse, fish.

While the pup wolfed down the afterbirth, Gwen and the other children took charge of the babies, letting them suck mead from a skin and holding them swaddled in aprons on their hips. If the ewe had enough milk to spare, they just might save them.

"Like this, Einion," Gwen instructed the brown-haired boy, who was more serious than his five or six years.

Despite his fury at the destruction of their swine, he did not stop their spitting the sow over a bed of glowing embers—remains of the fire that Madoc had followed on the horizon. In the frenzy of the slaughter, nobody had seen the two sails approaching. The lookouts were on the western verge.

Soon a heavenly aroma cloaked the island.

The islanders had enough flour to make one biscuit for everyone, so there was stone-baked lagana as good as home. The islanders had fared somewhat better than the *Horn*'s company, but there never was enough. Caradoc had elected himself keeper of the pantry, doling out the food to make it stretch.

Munching the delicious flatbread with Huw and Wil, Madoc discussed how to best use the men to accomplish the deck work. He told them to go take water to the *St. Ann*, and bring mead and apples to the *Horn*'s crew, then the same for the island. But he decided to keep quiet about the dead monk aboard the *St. Ann*, at least for tonight. Madoc had not yet decided what to do with the corpse. They could not bury what was the only surviving hive.

More passengers from the *Horn* came ashore, saying that the meat perfume reached all the way out to her moorings. Huw's wife Agnes was hauling all her earthly possessions— she was seasick and was so glad to be on solid land she was crying. Stumbling ashore behind her was Edwin, an Englishman but many years a loyal crewman, and his young wife and baby. Madoc could not hear their words, but they were obviously at odds with Edwin doing most of the speaking, angrily, while his wife looked dejected beside him.

Among the new arrivals he spotted Teleri crashing ashore with Rhiannon, whose harp case bounced on her back, wet to her thighs and shining so that he must look away for a moment before approaching her.

"My God," Rhiannon gasped, hugging him in a distracted way, searching over his shoulder, "I am going to die with that wonderful smell—" She slipped the leather-cased Llais Mel from her shoulders, letting it drop to the sand, while her eyes found the firepit some ways up-island, and closer, the abattoir.

Her nostrils flared.

Madoc was horrified to see his sister push past him as though he were a gate, running with the muscles of her legs straining under a wet-heavy skirt to fall on her knees where the pup was swallowing the innards whole. Nona growled a territorial warning, but the woman ignored her as she dipped up blood from the puddled rock and poured it from the cup of her hands into her mouth. She drank greedily and grabbed another handful, swooning back in hard ecstasy, her long neck a stained white curve.

Madoc was shocked by the sight of his noble sister snarling like a vixen over the kill. He, who never once was sick in many battles, felt his gorge rise. He staggered and retched.

Rhiannon had turned to see this.

Teleri meanwhile rescued the liver and kidneys from the dog and was pulling as though her life depended on the other end of the intestine. No ratty whelp of a dog was going to keep her from making sausage. Finally she got down on Nona's stubborn level and hanked, the startled animal flying into the air. Still the dog held on until Teleri swift as a thief whipped out a knife. Madoc thought for a helpless moment she was going to kill Gwen's dog, which would have earned his undying emnity. But Teleri neatly snicked the gut instead, tumbling the pup end-over.

"Ah-ha!" Teleri exclaimed in victory, a fierceness in her that he never suspected. He had heard many a warrior cry proudly just like that after a good kill. She grabbed up her prizes and tramped over to the kitchen, tripping on her dragged hem, leaving lesser morsels to the lesser creature.

Rhiannon stood. The western wind was on her back, drying the pale yellow wool tunic that still clung to her fine body. When he looked, she was licking blood from her fingers, making small involuntary gasps of pleasure.

Her face and chest were smeared crimson. Finally, after he had stared for a long time without blinking, she chanced to glance up at him. She straightened, and without breaking the stare, defiantly sucked her last finger clean—really clean.

Madoc knew he would have to turn away from her soon or betray himself, but she beat him to it. She looked down, aware that she made him sick and maybe more. He was close enough to see her skin riddled by gooseflesh, but she was distant. She betrayed no emotion as she touched her ruined tunic. The ends of her hair were bloody, trailing across her perfect skin so white it shone like quartz—the blue white of high anemia. She did not look at him again but strode away high-headed, refusing to be ashamed of dire need satisfied.

Eastward the sky drained color. Soon it would be night.

He watched her walk to the water, where she hunkered down like a common cockle-digger and began rinsing herself and clothing. Her servant, the pale girl Tegan, knelt with her mistress in the surf, where they spoke together quietly.

Finally Madoc breathed. He had forgotten to for too long. Fleeting nausea and other bodily reactions subsided in him, and after a while he felt better. Evaporating sweat cooled him. One of the crew passed with a water skin, which Madoc commandeered but did not drink. Instead he slung it over his shoulder and avoided looking in Rhiannon's direction as he sauntered to the nearest coracle. He deliberately walked with it on his back into the surf. It was cold. Beyond the breakers he expertly rolled into the flouncing little craft and, shivering head to toe, warmed himself with the labor of paddling to the ship.

He had to satisfy a sudden concern that the *Horn* was tight. Only three crewmen remained aboard, pitifully few, and sorely grateful to him for the drinking water. Their loyalty in these circumstances moved him deeply.

He prowled the ship, inspecting every major join. The anchor-line hummed tautly. She was secure, but a current nudged ever westward. He descended into the hold and stared for a long while at the mast partner, prowled into tight, dark crawl spaces to inspect the underwater strakes. His hands were his eyes down here in the gloom; his fingers traced the beveling of each plank overlapping the one below, feeling the telltale dampness in the grain. There were few nails in the entire ship. She was put together with carved interlocking parts held together by their shapes and with clever lashing of iron-tough spruce root—every trick of the shipwright's craft to give this ship and her sister, *St. Ann*, flexibility in rough seas or heavy winds.

Hands out, touching either forward point of the side strakes as they swooped forward and up to be embraced by trennailing into the massive oak knee of the keel, he felt the great ship more as a living body than a mere construction. It was so finely made there was built-in give of more than an inch at any major join; the rail could be twisted five inches out of true and not split.

The loosening of less than a dozen bolts, axing of the spruce cables would leave her within a day of dismantling. Key joins were reinforced by elk-horn plugs, which named her. Drill out those pegs, and she would fall apart like a dry skeleton. And just as remarkably she would go back together again—each piece was unique in the design. His own hands had been hardened at the labor; he and Fair Beard spent six months building this ship. Either of them knew every piece of the puzzle and had the blood blisters, splinters, and unremitting calluses to prove it.

Madoc slapped a strake midway up the keel. Setting this plank, he had broken his right hand, fully healed now, but since then sensitive to changes in the weather.

The wood boomed resoundingly, as if the ship were responding to his slap. It lived and breathed, though resting now under his palms, but with minute groans like a sleeper in deep repose on the goose-feather mattress of the water.

He wandered back amidships to stand below the opening of the hold, the view he had had crossing to Wicklow that afternoon. Now he paused, listening to various familiar squeaks and groans that could tell him many things. Tonight they simply said, all is well. He hefted a couple of leathern buckets of bilge water and climbed back up into the gathering twilight.

He dumped the bilge overboard, noticing that the wind was holding up. It smelled clean and inviting from the southwest. Heavily laden, both his ships could sail even steeper into the wind and make good time.

Content that all was right, he descended to the sea chest secured against the bulkhead aft where he had set up his bedroll. The chest was not locked. Everything he had put there was just as he left it. He removed the leather bag and spilled its contents onto his pallet. Coins—none less than gold, several fine electrum pieces, Roman, French, native Cymreig, English, and a hoard of viking Irish copies in gold of English pennies—winked brightly even in the gloomy hold. The sea was grown—the coins clinked together with the ship's movement. He ran his hand through their slick coolness, probably a goodly portion of his father's royal treasure collected over the centuries the family had ruled. The information stamped into these bits of metal was the history of the line and of the nation itself.

He had an idea there on the beach when it struck him that he did not yet know if he could weld the people together. They were too many to be a family and too few to be a nation. That was the truth of it. Until he could return to Cymru and bring more people, they would have to function as something other than his father's domain. Let them call him what they wished, at best he was a sea captain who owned the mixed devotion of a few experienced crewmen and five times as many noncombatants a few sheep away from eating each other.

But if he could make them see common ground in their

situation, they could rise above their fractional differences and save themselves. Like these coins of several denominations and various mints, they were bears and cats in the same cage.

The coins were all close to pure metal. He fingered a gold piece stamped with an alphabet he did not know, probably part of his grandsire's pirate booty. He delicately eyetoothed it, denting its malleable surface. He rummaged the carpenter's box lashed to another rib forward of his own and found what he wanted, an awl and a fat mallet.

He retrieved Owen's relief-carved garnet from his belt pouch and began restamping the coinage. The work was pleasant, just trying enough to challenge the dregs of concentration, just mindless enough to get into the hammer's rhythm spatting smartly against the carbuncle's flat underside, like the pacing of a smith at a forge. Soon he had a pile of angry little dragons in clear intaglio over the palimpsest of the old stamps left like ghosts on the metal. He counted out enough for everyone with one to spare, then, with a last whack on the awl, pierced each coin.

He used most of the gold. He secured all but three of the new impressions in the pouch and tied it inside his cloak, then put the rest of the money in the chest and went back on deck.

He slipped a coin into the three crewmen's palms, promising he would save their portion of meat and send relief in two hours, in fact planned to stand watch himself tonight.

The last western light was bleeding from the sky when he returned to the island with his charts and a spare hourglass in their cases on his back with his bedroll. The steady wind from the southwest taunted him with smells from the cooking fire.

Back in camp he told some of the men to haul out the cauldron from the *St. Brendan*'s stores. Other of his own and Fair Beard's crew he set to pulling salvageable caulk from the wreck. Then he claimed a spot just below the crest, set up his headquarters, and called Rhys over.

The poet gave him quick report of the situation. His main point was that Fair Beard had to fight some of the monks and men for the coracles he had taken to look for a mainland.

"My boatload of monks has been miserable since the *St. Brendan* went aground and let loose the hive of women, as Simon calls it. They set up a llan on the western shore to maintain maximum distance." They were continuing the old tradition of setting aside a llan, or cultivated plain, for religious purposes.

The sailors had begun hauling old caulk to the cauldron, many of them having boiled down tar in this manner for ship repair. The sheep herded themselves nearby in a fluffy knot. From time to time one of them bleated. The fire roared, and all around the ocean whispered its ancient secrets.

"One of the women is pregnant and heathen, and one old man walks around praying to Terrible Odin, the viking god."

"Bjorn, Fair Beard's father-in-law," Madoc said. He took a brand to light another fire in the pit they had scraped beneath the cauldron a few paces from the ship.

"All the sailors want to turn back," Rhys continued as Madoc blew on the glowing ember nestled among driftwood, coaxing a flame, then stepped back with a couple of his trusted men and Rhys as it briskly grew.

"A couple of individuals have already been measured for the cooking pot, so to speak."

Just then someone rang a hand bell salvaged from the *St. Brendan*—supper was ready. None among the lay brothers was a priest, but one began a quick grace anyway.

Everyone was festive but with an edge of impatience on each face as they gathered around in loose lines, stepping up to cut their own portion when another turned away with a knifeful.

Madoc would have had one person slicing, to make it even. As they filed off, each took an apple from the barrel Wil opened up nearby. They likewise helped themselves from a low basket to the flatbread, which served as a plate as well as the meal itself.

His eye was caught by individual faces—there was Huw's wife, Agnes, a long-boned, handsome woman in her midforties, smiling now, illuminated by the fire and food. They moved away in twos and threes, finding spots to sit, but none were waiting to begin on the meat. He saw Yngvild's toothless father gnawing away on a bone, sucking for all he was worth, then wiping his lip and grizzled chin with the bread like a bishop's napkin.

The monks clustered in their chosen spot. The children and women sat on the opposite side of the fire. Nona poised in tense suspension, watching every move Gwen made eating, snapping scraps from her before they hit the sand.

As Madoc wandered among them, he noticed the dark-skinned fellow standing by himself slowly munching an apple that had been chewed down to the thin core.

Closer, Madoc saw no burn scars. The fellow's skin looked evenly dark brown, his pupils obsidian black in large whites, his hair curly black. When the stranger saw himself observed by the lord of his leige lord, he bobbed an obsequious bow.

"Ari, sir," he said as though explaining himself. Madoc nodded; he would satisfy his curiosity later.

He listened to their sounds as he moved toward the fire, breathing easier with evidence of their benign mood. Nobody seemed to be alarmed at how small the cooked pig was, and none seemed to be taking more than he should. Mouth watering, he was about to draw his own blade when they were all arrested by a screaming male voice,

"You took two—!"

Chapter 9

*...there was another island in that
ocean which had been discovered by man
and was called Vinland, because vines
grow wild there and yield excellent
wine, and moreover, self-sown grain
grows there in abundance; it is not
from any fanciful imaginings that we
have learned this, but from the
reliable reports of the Danes.*

> —History of the Archbishopric
> of Bremen and Hamburg
> *by Adam of Breman*
> A.D. 1176

It was one of Fair Beard's Norsemen who were now staying close to Yngvild in his absence, part of their vow to him.

"By Thor's red hairs, I saw you, you blaman—" The sailor lapsed into Norse as he leaped upon a smaller figure—hard to see in the flickering light.

Madoc moved quickly with a couple of others when he saw the knife. He grabbed the hand that held the blade and pulled. The sailor, a brown-haired Norseman with a scar across his nose, could not be stopped and smashed again with his free fist. The youth cried out, and soon the combatants were separated by the other hands. Madoc handed the knife to Wil for safekeeping.

On the sand lay the dark youth, lip bloody, one eye pinched shut and bruised. He still held an apple with one bite taken out of it. He struggled to his feet with some help as Madoc asked, "You, Dag—what the hell is going on?"

"He took two apples," the sailor spat, still not tame. Madoc let two of his men hold him while turning to the other.

"What say you?"

Wiping at his swollen lip, he thickly answered, "Yes," holding up the apple.

Noticing that there was no grease on his unbearded face, Madoc asked if he had taken his portion.

"I do not eat the meat of the pig, master."

Dag broke free one hand with which he grabbed the lad's free hand and forced the fingers open. The palm was a lighter color than the rest of him, but it bore no sign of pig juice. He forced the hand to wipe on the white tunic, but it left no stain. All who had served themselves were grease smeared and shining.

"Not yet, you mean," the sailor puffed, most of the wind taken from his sails, but he muttered anyway, "Blue bastard."

"What do you mean, no meat?" someone asked.

"Not pork. Pork is unclean."

"He is some kind of a Jew," said Father Brian, the same expert on pigs.

"He is a lying blue bastard, that is what he is," snarled the Norseman.

"Are you a Moor, son?" Madoc asked.

"I am Christian," he proudly answered, wiping blood from his lip and righting his tunic so that a crucifix was revealed on a thong around his neck. "My family does not eat pork."

"Muslim," Madoc said, placing him now. The fellow nodded.

Madoc had met Arab ambassadors at the French court, leather-tan men nothing like this fellow, who was a dusty blue-black as Dag said. Madoc was still puzzled by the man's Gaelic accent, though he spoke Madoc's kindred tongue as well as any seaman from the docks of Ireland might.

"You are Saracen?"

"My people came from farther south, Ethiopia," he replied, adding not without pride, "But I am an Irishman, sir."

Madoc had heard of dark-skinned southerners from the farthest end of the world—the Norse called them blamen—black men. Family and sailor stories told of hot lands down there, strange creatures and people of many colors. He wondered when this man's people came to Dublin.

"His clan forbids him to eat this meat," Madoc said to the

group. "I have no objection if he takes an extra apple to make his share." To underscore his decision, he plucked a third fruit and tossed it to the lad who caught it, grinned, and tucked it into a belt-pouch.

A buzz of approval circled the company.

Snorting his disbelief, Dag shook off his captors as though flexing his muscled arms but apparently accepted the will of the majority. He strode away, grumbling to himself.

People turned away, attention reclaimed by food.

The young man watched Madoc with a wide gaze. When they were alone, he dropped to his knees. "Master," he said, "Ari is your slave."

"I need you on your feet, not groveling in the dirt."

The young man stood as gracefully as a juggler, eyes bright. "My people have always been slaves."

"What did you say your name was?"

"Ari, sir. Al-Ghazal Ari O'Dalaigh."

"It has a ring to it," Madoc said, unable to contain a chuckle.

"The Moor owned us first, then the blondies."

Madoc's stomach growled. "No slaves here," he added in Gaelic and continued toward the fire, knife out to claim a slice of meat.

After they ate the best feast Madoc ever supped, primed with mead and fresh water from the island's southern rock flats, cheered by the presence of friends, warmed by a bonfire and the blessed music they conjured from Rhiannon's harp, Gwen's flute, and the various drums and voices of the company, Madoc sat munching an apple with Rhys beside him, going over events.

The mutiny had begun on the *St. Brendan* not a week out of the Fortunate Isles; it brewed among the younger monks and some of the sailors who came aboard in Dublin. Fair Beard knew he had to find a mainland where they could sustain themselves.

Madoc was thrilled to hear that the lookouts had seen the long blur of land far to the south, but, Rhys added quickly, Snorrison had decided against heading there because he thought the southern landfall was only an island while he swore what he saw to the west was mainland. That was the direction he headed. He did not expect them to wait for his return but promised he would try to get back in a fortnight.

Fair Beard was right: Madoc could not tarry here waiting for their return. The food would not hold out.

"He said he would light a fire at his first beachhead," Rhys said, lips and fingers glistening until he licked away the last of the supper juices like a huge tawny cat. It was too good to waste. "Since he left, we kept a watch on the western beach."

Some of the lay brothers had abandoned piety, forgotten their vow of obedience when they smelled the meat cooking, and stumbled from their womanless llan over the dunes like banshees, teeth barred, drooling. Wyn, however, was not among them.

Madoc noted that Rhys had fared well from his ordeal. He still went to the trouble each day to have his lip and chin shaved by Caradoc, who as surgeon served as barber. Madoc was thinking how good it would feel to have his own whiskers shaved off; he was feeling a bit ratty with the stubby beard he allowed to go ungardened while at sea.

While he kept his face cleanly barbered, Rhys had let his hair grow long, a style often affected by poets. It was tied back neatly at the nape of his neck and braided loosely. His cheeks were sunburned to a healthy glow, which diminished the scar, his brown hair bleached out to blend with its natural gray streaks. The weight loss did not look as mean on him, though he had two weeks of shellfish and pork to fatten him up, Madoc was thinking as Rhys rubbed his hands in the sand to cleanse them, at the same time outlining the situation since they were parted.

"So after we were driven aground where she lies," Rhys continued, "we thought we were doomed. We never expected to find you or the *St. Ann* again. There were arguments about whether land had or had not been seen to the southwest. Thinking one of the pigs would drop her litter soon, the sailors started butchering to supplement fish and oysters." He paused. "They went nearly crazy, Madoc. The meat seemed to help."

He understood their loathing to eat seafood exclusively. He thought he had never tasted anything so delicious as that bite of pork tonight. It was amazing how bright his outlook was now compared to his earlier despair on the mast. Now, glad to have Rhys's company, renewed by fresh water and a little hope, he lounged against a dune watching the stars and smelling the sea, feeling as satisfied as a sated lion.

Over by the fire Rhiannon and her Llais Mel found the

melody of an old song cycle. Everyone knew endless verses, and soon their harmonies covered the surf's murmur. The air was very bright, though there was no moon. The sky, a meadow of stars, was transparent.

Surely the stars could hear this music, Madoc thought. He would take a midnight reading to determine sun time from the guardians of the polestar. They could at least find out how far south they had come. In the few nights they had been becalmed, according to his observations, they moved on some gigantic current many leagues west by south.

If Fair Beard thought he saw land southwestward, Madoc feltt confident in believing him. The man was the best latitude sailor Madoc ever met. He was illiterate but held in his mind a vast store of sea and navigation lore.

The birds were some kind of supporting proof of nearby land. He knew his people could not go much farther, nowhere near as far as they had already come, which was way beyond the reported distance to Vinland. From his assessment of their combined stores, he figured they had enough food for two weeks, plus whatever fish they could catch. Landfall must be soon, or this company would go down as yet another lost westward venture. These thoughts flickered through Madoc's mind as Rhys continued.

"On the third day Wil spotted the *St. Ann*'s sail. Madly they began burning the beached ship despite my pleas. Wil argued with them, but some of the men held him down while the others lit the torch, they were so afraid the *St. Ann* would not spot us. Fair Beard brought his ship close enough to offload coracles, and we had a feast night much like this." Rhys gestured toward the fire's warmth, where the music's tempo had picked up as the company hit the bawdy verses.

"Fair Beard was among the shore party. That night there was an argument about which way to head. Fair Beard was sure he had seen land in the southwest. But some sailors, Caradoc, and half the monks wanted to go east on a current they detected—"

"Ah," Madoc said with interest. An eastern current?

"When Fair Beard refused, they picked up driftwood clubs and went to take the *St. Ann*."

"Which way does Wyn lean?"

"On the back door to the Holy Land, which is all he can see on the western horizon and wants nothing but to go there immediately to fight the infidel. But I do not trust the Frenchman."

"What Frenchman?"

"The fellow in Owen's hall—"

Madoc had to think for a moment. That all seemed to be a thousand years in his past, that day in Aberffraw when he had gotten his father's commission to start this colony. Then Madoc recalled the argument in progress when they arrived at the great hall that day. "Hmmm," was all he said as he picked up a handful of sand to cleanse the grease from his fingers. "Why is he among us?"

"Your unexpected layover at Wicklow changed his plans."

"My father gave him passage to Dublin—I remember he went on one of the two smaller ships."

"Which never got to Dublin, of course."

"So, then, he is ours whether or no." Madoc dusted the sand from his palms. "Do you know the disloyal ones by voice?"

"Some, perhaps. But I cannot be sure of all the men who opposed Fair Beard." Rhys had heard them mostly as an indistinguishable mob.

"Evan?"

"He is one I am not sure of—he was not an instigator," Rhys mentioned names. "But Evan was one of the pig killers."

Madoc could not restrain a cynical chuckle and a heavy sigh.

"So what happened when they tried to take the ship?"

Rhys found a more comfortable position before he continued, "They fought—four men were killed—" He rattled off their names, their fathers' names, and the places of their birth. Such lists were part of each day back in the house of Gwynedd, and old habits were hard to break.

Madoc gently laid his fingers on Rhys's sleeve to curtail the recital of places that no longer mattered. "So," he said, "what kept them from taking off?"

"In the middle of it a squall drove the *St. Ann* too close to the shoals—she rammed so hard we thought she was breeched. The crew poured off, but Fair Beard reboarded with a few men."

He began to add more names and general histories but stopped himself when he realized what he was doing and went on with his story. "They tried to get the sail down, but the squall broke into a full-fledged storm. Brother Ely stayed aboard, determined not to abandon his books."

Madoc reported the reboarding of the *St. Ann*, mentioning the monk preserved in honey. "John can say Mass tomorrow."

Rhys agreed it was a good idea to let them have their celebration tonight. "It is Halloween, after all."

"The mast—?" Madoc said.

"Lightning struck her pinned there. The waves were terrible— we moved everything to the rocks and huddled together, sure the entire island would be drowned. The rain put out the fire on the mast almost immediately, while Fair Beard and his men struggled with the sail. It got dark, and our people could not see what happened. A while later the men dragged Fair Beard and a couple of his sailors from the surf. The *St. Ann* was gone, swept away. We were sure she went down."

"Only Fair Beard saw land?"

"But he was very sure," Rhys answered, nodding. "He said he saw it reflecting on the underside of a sunset cloud the night before, though they tell me fog has kept that portion veiled."

Madoc had heard of such inverted mirages on the open sea; it was something like iceblink. A wide stretch of sandy beach could cast such a light. Likewise snowcapped coastal mountains.

"How many days since he pushed off?"

"Six."

Madoc brooded on that. There simply was not enough food here to sustain them longer than it took to repair their ships.

"He said he would set a bonfire on the first beachhead. Wyn and his hermits have been watching from the western shore continuously. So far, nothing."

Madoc related all that had befallen the *Horn*'s company since the storm, while the music softened again.

Rhys listened with a particular tilt to his head. He was hearing a quality in his captain's voice that disturbed him, something kin to Owen's hopelessness over the past year of illness. Madoc was too young and strong to sound in similar despair. He was hesitating. Rhys hid his true feelings, but he was uneasy with the realization of Madoc's distress.

Rhiannon plucked another tune and called over, "Come sing the song of Culhwch and Olwen, poet!"

"Agh," Rhys moaned, then confided, "I last recited story when I studied the Mabinogi—twenty years at least."

"You are all we have, Storyteller," Madoc said.

Rhys would have said the same thing to Madoc, but someone might hear. "Your father used me as a rememberer and messenger."

"But you know the song—her playing will make it sound fine."

"She knows it better than I and has a better voice."

"You know they need a feast day, and for that a chief poet." The term was masculine; it was not a position held by women.

"But I have never once saga'd a king," Rhys admitted, meaning the heroic verse that was reserved for the chief bard's presentation before a lord. It was the one thing he wanted to do for Owen, but he had resigned himself to be outsung by the renowned Gwalchmai.

Madoc said, "And still you will not."

Rhys turned his face toward him and sighed as though regarding him. "If my duty bids me tell for the arglwydd, then I must have an arglwydd to tell to."

"This is not a kingdom and I am not a king," Madoc said, made shy by the impression that he was under keen observation by a man with no eyes.

"Time to stop doubting." Rhys leaned closer, touching Madoc's arm, speaking in a soft but commanding voice. "Lead us with your whole heart, or we will perish."

Outside the small circle of privacy Rhys's whisper had created, Rhiannon made impatient music.

"Here, here, Master Rhys," called the sailors. A fair harpist himself, he had told a thousand stories and songs that had kept them distracted from grim reality and grinding boredom. Several times since they were shipwrecked, his lampoons had broken with laughter a nasty tension that flickered through the group like sudden flame over banked coals.

"Then your arglwydd bids you play before his court," Madoc said with a sweeping gesture, cuing Rhys to stand.

Rhys grinned in a charming way and extended his hand, which Madoc pulled to help him rise. But their two hands clasped were also the ancient symbol of mutual promise. Madoc took it, realizing as they clasped their palms together that Rhys had maneuvered him around to accepting the title and all the honor—and burden—that went with it.

"It is done," the blind man whispered to his old master, who was on his deathbed thousands of miles to the northeast. In a month Owen Gwynedd would lie in his tomb at Bangor

Cathedral, from which, because he had been excommunicated, the new Canterbury-approved bishop would order his body stealthily removed and flung into the forest.

But Rhys ab Meredydd had kept his promise.

Chapter 10

*Put on more sail and ply your oars
more briskly, that we may get away
from this island.*
   —St. Brendan the Navigator
    Irish
    A.D. *910*

Taking him by the elbow, Madoc led the bard over the sand toward the makeshift court.

Pipes and harp picked up the rhythm of Madoc's walk as he and Rhys approached. Everyone beat upon the nearest solid object or clapped in time. The fire crackled as someone threw on another ship's bone. It flickered shadows off the many faces gathering around; they could have been anywhere on earth, Madoc thought fleetingly, but they were here on an impossible grain of dust in the middle of the Flood, with no knowledge of their position or what lay ahead. Yet here they were more than a hundred souls alive, burnished into a celebratory glow and functioning, at least around this fire, as a community.

Madoc had seen Owen enter the great hall several times. Now he tried to remember every kingly gesture his father had used. People were making room for them where someone spread a sheepskin over a barrel for their lord's seat of honor. He saw that it was Ari, smiling to reveal perfect white teeth.

Madoc nodded thanks and sat down.

Evan and others who had been part of Owen's household remembered the seating positions in the house of Gwynedd as described by Hywel's Law.

Evan drove a staff into the sand for the traditional pillar beside the king. Then he pointed the position for each court

105

officer. It was a rough approximation, out here under the stars, of Owen's impressive hall, but the ritual of it felt good. Even the sailors, less inclined to landlubber rules and sure in their hearts that Madoc belonged first to them—even they participated.

He watched how Evan had placed the officers. Chief bard Rhys sat at his right hand. The mead-maker, Father John, who had been cellarer of the monastery, was placed at the pillar behind him; the musician there, and beside her the place the smith would have sat had Wyn been present. Madoc was thinking about what Rhys said, as Evan acted the crier, striking the pole with the blunt of his sword.

"Be quiet now," he called in imitation of the porter back at Aberffraw. "The lord of this domain is seated." This was the cue for the poet to stand and begin:

"Hear my voice: Madoc ab Owen, a prince of Gwynedd and son of the lord of Mona, stander on the land...eh..."

The people laughed for what estate could their lord command but this slip of an island and those ships yonder under starglow?

"Lord of the brine and stander on the land that knows no other master," Rhys improvised, which brought a cheer from them. It was a strong combined voice that might have contained more than their actual number. Madoc acknowledged it with genuine emotion catching in his throat, but he did not want it to show.

"You should add a line that I command swine-slayers and remorseless murderers of casks of mead," he said good-naturedly, though he was still furious at them for butchering that sow. From the direction of the mistress of hounds, appropriately porcine yips joined with Nona's low growl. At least three piglets were alive, who found mead much to their liking.

Everyone liked the joke; maybe they laughed too hard. Their eyes were as shifty with chagrin as their chins were greasy with porker juices. Behind them the sheep mewed, their backs to the prevailing westerly touched now with fog.

Rhiannon, watching the poet for a signal, strummed Llais Mel in a stair of notes. Rhys turned toward her—she felt for a fleeting moment that he had lanced an impossible secret glance at her from behind his tattered blindfold. He nodded subtly, and she found the preamble to a general introductory melody that could be used for just about anything Rhys wanted to versify, but for which he chose to begin with the legendary genealogy of many Celtic houses, including Gwynedd:

> "Noah's nephews of his father's kin
> forbidden the ark but still good men,
> believing their uncle only half mad,
> sailed north to islands called not half bad
> with fifty-one women and a mighty get the good wind
>   blew.
> Poets call it the last fair deal in Britain. True,
> everyone got enough—!"

"Everyone except the fifty-one women," the harpist said wryly. Everyone applauded Rhiannon's satire. Such interchange was acceptable as long as the interruption did not spoil the music, and without skipping a beat Rhys continued,

> "Next the sons of Aeneas from Troy's ashes sailed
> to the same land of isles, Brutus their leader vowed
> to set a new race upon that place
> his sons called Briton for their father's name.
> Some went north, some east, some west
> to Mona and the sea-bright sunset shore
> where sons in the line of Gwynedd are. . . ."

Now the people joined him, all those who had grown up or worked in the house of Gwynedd, for the long list of names was familiar even to the sailors and ended in Owen's name, politely as one does for a still-living ruler, a crash of music, applause, sword rattling, and another round of mead.

"Has my lord any personal requests?" Rhys called to Madoc.

"Brendan Sails," Madoc said without hesitation.

There were several versions. One took an entire evening to recite. This one was a simple little rhyme that reduced the great saga to bare essentials, something children or rowers sang.

But the song's unflinching hope in the face of circumstances similar to their own served Madoc's purpose. Now he knew he was not the only one confronting the immensity around them. Rhys had given him that. He did not even mind that everyone else, including Rhys and the few monks on this side of the island, was getting drunk.

But Madoc wanted to stay clear-headed. He quietly pushed his drinking horn at someone and asked for water while he let his thoughts wander: What rescue had they achieved to unite two fragments of precarious existence out here in the middle of nowhere, flinging their feeble songs out to indifferent stars? They would need all the hope they could muster.

Remembering the agreement he made with Rhys, he cloaked these intuitions in a mien of fierce kingly optimism. So, he thought, that is why Owen always held himself with such dignity in his court, and why he seldom spoke, but when he did, the walls themselves leaned close to hear what a king said.

Brendan Sails was one of Rhys's favorites because he could get everyone to sing along with him and relieve himself of the burden of entertaining all alone.

His voice fell into cant, as enticing as rich food.

"We are not the first to venture out into these parts. . . ." he almost sang, and Rhiannon followed as he gathered them up again in the net of song. "Long ago in the age of saints, men looking for some quiet place to talk with the creator crossed the Flood to follow lights in the western sky. . . ."

The harpist brought the music up to a place where the voice could take off, and Rhys did on the wings of verse:

"In a leather boat sixty monks
    westward, Brendan sails.
Malo as mate holds the jolly
    rudder and away Brendan sails.
Brendan's sails on the horizon,
    horizon-leaning, Brendan's sails,
    tossed along the rolling sea."

Each time the poet sang "Brendan sails" everyone joined in—it was an old song everyone knew.

"Close to the wind Brendan sails.
Wind-pregnant, full in belly
    forever west Brendan sails.
Giants on one isle, sheep on others.
Fire from demons on the third
    burned the beards off the brothers.
To an isle of ice Brendan sails.
Found another where a holy hermit
    unfed for one hundred forty years but fit and hale
    on his windy rock, away Brendan sails.

Loose the tiller, give her to the wind
for where God blows Brendan sails.
Be thou my pilot, O Lord."

The several monks who had come from the western strand
to break their fast joined in here, enthusiastically repeating
this verse several times. Madoc was fascinated by the way
their eyes glistened unnaturally—was this because of famine?

"Anchored close to another flat isle, much like this one . . ."
Rhys improvised out of meter in a stage whisper, making
them laugh nervously and look around at the darkness, "they
found themselves not on a land of rock but on a monster's
back—" Here he roared and threw his arms wide in a gesture
of menace that made the little boys cry out and the adults
shiver. Beyond the comforting circle of fireglow the waves
mumbled, the darkness seethed. They could feel the sea alive
around them. Rhys, pleased with how he had charged their
mood, continued the song in a dramatic voice of one of the
characters in the story.

"What is this that pits my back?
the whale Jasconius screams.
He flings the men and boat aside.
This is no island Brendan cried,
But a creature full of spleen.
Let us away from here,
himself ordered, raise *Brendan*'s sails.
Fog greeted the final landfall.
Magh Mel, honey-sweet plain,
forever warm and fruitful and
so sweet he designed never again
to unfold *Brendan*'s sails."

They clapped and cheered until they were hoarse.

Rhys leaned toward his accompanist and said, "Thou hast
angel's fingers, m'lady." She was the finest harpist he had
ever sung with, and he would tell her so. "If we but had a
way to make a copy of your Llais Mel, I would beg you to be
my teacher."

But she demurred. "Sing another," she said.

Rhys began the Song to Owen, which Madoc had heard
Gwalchmai sing in Owen's hall far behind them: But he did
not get past the first stanzas before Wyn and his monks

stepped into the firelight with the effect of dampening festivities.

"Praise should be reserved for God," said a balding priest with Wyn, who was thinner and fiercer about the eyes from his ordeal. At first Madoc did not recognize him. But when the priest sternly admonished a couple of younger monks for joining in the song, his hood fell back and Madoc recognized Simon, the sour-faced Frenchman who passed by him after arguing with Owen on that morning that gave birth to this venture.

Madoc remembered Fair Beard's suspicions.

About a dozen of the brothers stood just outside the ring of fireglow, as far from the females as they could stand and still accompany the abbot. They all had those feral shining eyes, Madoc observed. Simon slunk back into the shadows behind Wyn, who stepped forward with his big blacksmith's hands folded over his cincture. Firelight picked out the tapestried pictures woven into the belt, giving them animation in the flickering glow.

Madoc exchanged looks with Wyn and beckoned to him. "We saved portions of meat for you."

"We are fasting," said Simon before Wyn could reply.

"Will you live like the hermit in the middle of the Flood without food for one hundred forty years?" Madoc asked Wyn, ignoring the French Benedictine, who had taken it upon himself to speak for the abbot, and trying to ease the tension their arrival had brought around the campfire. It crackled in the humid air, sending sparks upward to vanish against the night.

Wyn approached Madoc, who stood to greet him. "Come and sit in your rightful place," he said cordially, indicating the spot reserved for him as priest as well as smith to the household. "All of you, come and join us."

Simon hung back, hands folded in his wide cuffs, but the others, gaunt and hollow-cheeked from their austerities, tentatively drew closer.

Rhiannon saw what Madoc was trying to do and found her chord again. But the Benedictine turned on her and said with a low French hiss he was not aware Madoc understood, "Unchaste woman, hide your face in shame." He had no way of knowing that Rhiannon and her brother spoke his language.

Madoc demanded, "What say you—?" as he stood and took a step forward.

"Brother Simon," Wyn warned gently, hand on Simon's sleeve.

"How dare you admonish Princess Rhiannon, you—" Madoc took a step closer to Simon.

"Forgive him his zealousness, arglwydd," Wyn said, placing himself between Madoc and the priest.

Rhiannon looked deliberately away, like a bored cat, from Simon and toward Rhys, without losing her melody.

"Apologize to her," Madoc ordered, stepping around to confront the priest, who watched now with fear in his eyes. He was in his late forties, a long-faced man with the permanent tonsure of baldness and a lipless mouth—tight and colorless from a stern will and hard fasting.

"Do as our arglwydd commands," Wyn suggested gently.

"I call no man lord," Simon said stubbornly, his lips barely moving in their taut line.

"Do as Captain Madoc commands."

The priest complied in word if not in spirit, muttering, "Apologies, apologies," in French, eyes flickering like a liar, then slunk back, arms across his chest. Madoc sat, a stony difference on him now in contrast to his previous good humor, but he said as he poured a cup of mead, "Have some supper. Roast pork and apples."

He handed the horn to Wyn, who took it and drank it down in one swallow, then replied, "I am vowed to fast until morning." He looked haggard by the wind; he spent the last few hours standing cross vigil so that his hair was plastered by salt spray back from his forehead. His eyes were sunk in deep blue pits. His great chest and shoulders were hunched with spasms from the punishing arms-out position of prayer.

Madoc sighed and set aside the skin. "One should practice moderation even in piety."

"So my lord speaks French and argues theology," Wyn observed.

"Philosophy, I believe it was," Madoc replied. "I do not argue theology."

Rhiannon plucked out the first notes of an old hymn, the *Te Deum*, which everyone, even the sleepy children knew. Madoc was aware of the hymn, pleased with his sister's good sense to play something soothing that everyone could sing together.

But not even this gesture pleased the Benedictine, who turned defiantly, then stepped off into the darkness of the western shore, the dark cassock that gave the Benedictines their nickname—Black Monks—like another shadow around him, his pate glistening with sweat and firelight until he was gone. Several others in St. Brendan's lighter garb followed him.

Madoc looked at Wyn. "He is a stubborn man, my lord, and a foreigner to boot, who does not understand our customs."

"Why is he here?" Madoc asked. "He is not of your community."

"When we did not put in at Dublin and left in so few days, Simon was unable to get passage back to England," Wyn said.

"Perhaps he is my brother's viper," Madoc said glumly. Sometimes, usually just before he went to sleep at night, he thought about Prince David's parting words. On a bad night he would run through the possibilities, wondering how an agent of David's could hurt this venture and not doom himself.

Wyn almost chuckled. "The good father would quarrel even more with Prince David the chapel crusher than with yourself."

"Is that what they call him?"

"Among other things."

"Who might it be, I wonder, the viper?"

"I thought Evan, since his brother took the blow for you."

"He has had ample chance to take revenge if that were his motive. No, the lad is loyal. How about the mediciner?"

Another little chuckle, and the abbot spread his hands out in a shrug that said, I doubt it.

"Even as a boy, David was mean. He would say anything."

Wyn was nodding. "That is his viper. Nothing more. To plant doubt in you." He sighed. "As for Simon, it is good to have another priest along," said Wyn, himself only a monk and not ordained, even though he was the abbot. "Unusual times cast unusual people into unusual positions."

"He does not belong," Madoc all but snapped.

"We all belong where God calls, master."

As though he had not heard, Madoc added, "And he is dead wrong about this being Martinmas. It is All Hallows."

"As you say, of course, sir. But we notched a staff—"

"I have a chart full of sightings—three a day for seventy-five now, to mark our course. I will believe that against a stick notched by a priest made dizzy from self-enforced starvation." He threw a quick, piercing look around him. "It is a mess here, Wyn. How could you let the people get so crazed—you should have pulled them together."

"I sincerely believed I would very soon meet the Creator at any moment. I have been here to serve their spiritual needs. Many have prayed with me, have confessed their sins—one of the Norsemen has converted. Begging the arglwydd's pardon, but we have been getting ready to die here."

"You insure it, Domme."

"But God's plan saw you here to save us." His eyes seemed brightened by more than hunger. Madoc decided he would never understand the religious persuasion. Self-delusion, it seemed to him, and giving in without a fight.

"Look, to save this situation, I need your help. This Frenchman, is he going to be trouble?"

"I am not his abbot, but he will obey me."

"And it is not Martinmas."

"If my prince says so."

"I am your commander. The rest of it you can have."

"Then you will listen to me concerning spiritual matters?"

"As long as you get that forge hot the first sight of trees, yes. You can have their souls. But I have their minds and bodies. Think, man, if it is Martinmas, they will want to celebrate all night and do no labor in the morning."

Which was true. It was traditional for the lord to kill a pig to celebrate November 11 and to give to the people generally by letting them sleep all the next day.

"We must get the *St. Ann* aright and get off this island before we begin eating each other here—we have enough food between us to last three days."

"I have one man who is going to stay."

"M'god, you jest!"

"The carver, the deaf priest, my own confessor who wishes to spend the rest of his days praying here." Wyn looked down at his bare toes. "He is old, and his life is nearly over. He wants to reach for God."

"He must be mad."

Again Wyn leveled dreamy blue eyes on his earthly master. "We all expected to die at any moment, sir. None thought to ever leave this place. For one, at least, that is the answer to his prayers, who only wants to devote his life to God. 'Tis the reason Brendan sailed before us."

Madoc shook his head. "Then let him stay, but it is a shame to lose a good carver."

"One of the younger brothers is his apprentice. Ffagan will stay with us."

Madoc saw at the tail of his eye that someone was standing just behind him. It was several of the sailors and Fair Beard's Norsemen in a shadowed, disgruntled knot.

"We do not have enough food to go back," Wil was saying, exasperated with them. "We have to stock up first."

"What is wrong with fish?" Dag asked. "Now is the time to say it, then. Let us take that eastward current back home."

Madoc wanted to find out more about the current they detected. He saw no evidence of such, except for the general westward pull that brought them here. He put it to Dag, who had been lineman of the *St. Brendan*. In this way he not only could learn something but could also open them up and discover his troublemakers.

"And do you think we should take your mysterious current immediately back to Britain, Dag—leave your chief to his fate over there somewhere"—he gestured at the dark southwest—"without even trying to find him?"

Dag slouched into his inarticulateness, looking at the sand at his feet. He was a brown-haired, bony fellow, all ankles and wrists, knees and elbows, and his face in its gauntness was a plain of angles.

"I hate to say it, but my chief is probably dead."

"And?"

Dag shrugged. Still he would not meet Madoc's eye. Instead he stared into the darkness off to the left. "We do need to take on more supplies, of course," he conceded, "but this"—this miserable island, his body language said—"this is no promised land."

"Well," said another voice from beyond their circle, "I say we should take this current as fast as possible back into the Christian world."

Everyone turned to see Simon enter the light.

"This is a heathen place where we have no business."

Madoc had hoped the man had returned to the llan of the western shore. But since he had opened this conversation with encouragement for the men to voice concerns, he let Simon finish.

"We were not meant to come here. It was the height of arrogance to attempt such a journey in the first place. God created the Flood to remind men of the consequences of sin.

There is nothing in scripture about men sailing that damnable ocean this far west."

Madoc groaned at the effect this could have on his sailors, who watched with white eyes as the priest concluded, "We had better repent and go home before it is too late."

None of the sailors went so far as to cross himself against such luck, but one or two frowned or bit a lip curled tight.

"Ah, yes, Father Simon," Madoc said when the man seemed to have finished. "The abbot tells me of your bad fortune to find yourself among us. But I remind you that we will have to cross the same damnable ocean to get back."

Madoc turned on the others who were gripped by silence, fascinated by the ongoing confrontation between the two men. "I am glad to hear about this current, Dag, because someday we will need it. But not this day. I will not lie to you—we have very little food, two, three days at best, and then it is fish and water unless Father Simon can somehow sprout bread from sand."

He threw a low glance at Simon, daring him to work up a miracle, at the same time giving the remarks about the food supply some time to sink in. "Even if all of you here choose to go, you do not have enough men to crew a ship, not to mention that you have no ship." A delicate reference to mutiny since the ships were his own; he wanted them to know he knew their mind even at its worse.

He deliberately turned his back on Simon.

"You men know the arglwydd speaks the truth," Wil said. "It would be best not to give evil the power of naming it."

"No," Madoc replied, "it is good everyone speaks his mind."

"It sounds disloyal," Wil muttered, wanting to remind the captain that some of his own men were grumbling, too. But Madoc knew, even though they had been careful not to disparage their master's course within his hearing. He could read their faces.

"Are you afraid of sailing off the edge of the world like some old nun?" Madoc said to the lad who was biting his lip.

"They are superstitious, you know, Captain," Wil said in disgust. He looked up at Madoc with embarrassment in his squint.

"This is the longest journey I ever made, and I am a seaman most of my forty-three years," said one of the sailors.

Madoc laughed without joy. "I have never been this long at sea, myself, Llew."

"They know that," Wil said disparagingly, catching several glances. "You men should be more loyal."

"I tell you," Madoc replied, "I would have you put it into words, looking me square in the eye, rather than have some man stay silent planning mutiny." That got their attention.

"Wil," Madoc said, suddenly weighed down by fatigue, deciding not to return to the ship tonight. "Take two men and relieve those still aboard."

Wil said good night and went to return to the *Horn*. In his wake the men continued to voice their doubts. But they did not have the chance to continue with this conversation because a voice from out of the western darkness flung hope at everyone, even those who had gone to their bedrolls.

One of the younger monks, falling down he was so breathless, ran calling into the main camp, "On the western horizon! Fireglow—clear and bright—"

A couple of the women stayed behind while the majority grabbed up torches and headed toward the western reach. The sudden news drew them as one single creature, their long shadows stretching out over the dunes, marching like a silent twin companion to each one of them.

On the western beach some of the monks were reciting their prayers, arms outstretched in cross vigils—three of them at all times maintaining the position, working at it in rounds, four-hour shifts not unlike Madoc's crew. The office never ceased, the prayers continued unbroken with one brother replacing another around the turning of the hours of the day like the great shaggy plowhorses back at the monastery.

Oily smoke rose in plumes above the marchers, to be scattered by the sea breeze driving ever eastward as Madoc in the lead climbed the final dune above the low rumbling surf where the sea turned over pebbles in an endless shuffle, sometimes soft, sometimes rough. Tonight the gravel sounded like a boys' choir, brimming with potential, while over there in the unimaginable southwest glowed a beacon on the edge of the world.

The flickering torches cast shadows that seemed to grapple with each other on the sand.

"Light the wreck to signal that we see him," said a Norseman behind Madoc, sounding as though he would dash back immediately to rekindle the *St. Brendan*.

"If Fair Beard is setting that sign for us to follow, why would he come back here, fool?" Madoc remarked, frustrated that all he could see was the glow of fire on the bottom of haze—not the fire itself. It might even be a reflection of the gone sun. At the very least this blaze was far off, beyond the curve of the horizon. It had to be a big fire to illuminate so much cloud. Unless he ignited an entire forest, Snorrison could not set that large a fire. The largest bonfire on the closest beach could be as distant as five leagues—fifteen English miles was the conventional horizon from a mast top—depending on visibility.

There was probably some natural explanation for the fire, other than one started on purpose by a determined Icelander. The truth was there was very little chance they would ever see those men again, given the vast distances they seemed to be lost in.

He did not share these pessimistic thoughts with the hysterically happy people around him, however. They were dancing their joy, the sailors and some of the younger monks, the women and children just arriving from the trudge across the island, their faces bright with hope even in the darkness.

No use to spoil their hope, not at this point. They would just have to follow the glow as soon as possible. There would probably be smoke the next morning if the fire was as large as he suspected. At least it meant land in that direction.

Madoc lifted the small astrolabe at his waist and found the polestar. For his midnight reading he would use the larger instrument, the nocturnal, but for this rough direction the astrolabe would do nicely. Squinting, he held the instrument at eye level and opened it to mark the star's position. He mentally noted where the fireglow lay in relation to the angle of the star. Later he could mark the fire's apparent direction on his chart so they could head that way even if the fire was out by the time they were able to sail.

"Well, master mediciner," he said when he saw Caradoc puffing up from the east, wondering how he had managed to stay so fat when everyone else was at least lean. "Do you still say we should turn around and go back to Britain?"

The stout fellow was breathing hard. He dropped to the sand, panting before he answered, only able to nod.

Dag and a clot of Fair Beard's oath-men stared with the others at the light on the horizon, muttering among themselves.

"What say you, Dag?"

"Well, perhaps. But that may not be his fire."

"It seems too far inland," said another of the Norsemen, Lev, Snorrison's heavy-browed young cousin.

"He said he would set a black fire."

"It would be foolish to turn back now that we are about to find our destination," Evan said behind him. "I am sorry I doubted you, lord."

When Madoc looked, the young man had bowed his head before him. "And I am sorry about the pig."

"Thank you, Evan." Madoc glanced around at the company, catching looks here and there. "I need to hear loyalty."

Wyn was the first. "Willingly I follow you, because I believe you are moving in the will of God."

All the monks followed except Simon, who hung back. Wyn spoke to him while the seamen filed forward. One by one they stepped up to Madoc with their fists across their chests. In Norse, Cymraeg, Irish, and even Saxon they pledged their oaths. Then each woman, including Yngvild, swept his hand up to her lips. Ffiona, wife to Edwin, one of Madoc's sailors, and Mary, wife of Wil, who had returned to duty aboard the *Horn*, curtsied, murmuring their loyalty.

Rhiannon kissed him lightly on the cheek, as she said so all could hear, "My brother, I love thee."

Madoc did not see because he was caught up momentarily in her closeness, but Simon, arms clutched tightly across his chest, turned his eyes from them and snorted disdainfully. Wyn watched him ready to warn him with his eyes, but Simon seemed able to contain himself.

Finally Wil's little boys came forward, led by Gwen, who said, "Pledge to thee, lord," which she had heard Owen's men say.

Madoc felt something tugging at his clothing. It was little Einion looking up at him, his piglet mewing in a pouch.

"I love you, too," the child said, pulling hearty applause from the hands of the company as Madoc ruffled the boy's hair. Beyond he could see Teleri beaming in the glow of torchlight.

Wyn, who had turned away to speak privately to Simon, returned with the Frenchman to face the arglwydd.

"I pledge my loyalty to thee," Simon almost growled. "But only as secular leader."

Madoc nodded acceptance, not believing. But it was good enough for his purposes. Buoyed by the happy tension around him, and the steady glow on the southwestern horizon, he told them, "What we must do now is get our vessels in shape as soon as possible. We still start repairs at dawn. We will need every hand." Madoc turned, satisfied that he had said all there was to say and seen all there was to see. "Day after tomorrow at dawn, we set sail."

Madoc was exhausted and was thinking he must still take the midnight reading. He started walking away, feeling the weight of the money sack clanking against his leg. He turned back where most of them still stood looking west, where some others had begun walking back to the camp.

"Wait!" he called to the broken line of people on the beach above and below his position. "Evan," he said, "call them all here." Behind him someone rekindled his torch from the glowing ember of it jabbed into dry sand.

Almost all the company was here, save for those who stayed at the fire and a few sailors on the two ships and a couple of the monks still at their vigil further south on this beach.

They crowded around Madoc, eyes bright with the torchlight as he whipped off his cloak and spilled the sack of gold coins onto it spread on the sand. Several people gasped. People in back pushed through to see past those in front. A murmur charged through them as one voice, but Madoc silenced them with his own.

"You have given me your oaths—now I have something for you." He began handing out a coin to each person—even the children—amid sounds of approval. He noticed several people tooth-testing the quality of the gold and nodding approval.

"It is the dragon of Mona," said Edwin, holding his coin up to the light. "How did you—"

Madoc pressed a coin into Rhys's hand; the poet thumbed it, a wry grin on his face.

"With this," Madoc said, extracting the garnet. He held it up so each one could see, then continued, "My father's seal-stone handed down for ten generations."

A couple of people, including Ari, had already slipped the amulet onto neck thongs or chains.

"But I am not Venedotian," someone said in a thick Irish accent, meaning he was not a native of Gwynedd; others echoed the same doubt.

"Neither am I, anymore," Madoc replied. "We are something else now, all of us."

"What are we?" Einion asked.

He knelt down on the child's level, lifted his sticky little hand holding his coin, and said, "We are something new, son."

"We need a name," a sailor said.

Everyone buzzed agreement, but no voice stood out with a firm suggestion until Rhys silenced everyone: "Madoc's Hundred."

It was a good suggestion, which was well received by all familiar with the political divisions in the land they'd left. A cantref, meaning enough households to produce a hundred fighting men, was like an English county.

"Madoc's Hundred," Evan echoed.

They all said it at once or twice, a new idea that had to find itself on their various tongues. It sounded right, so they all said it a few times in unison and then clapped.

"So be it," Madoc said, highly pleased. Seeing the weather about to change, he wanted to take advantage of the clearing and get back for his observations in case the fog won over the wind. He slapped Rhys on the back.

"I will stay with the brothers awhile," the poet said.

The women, children, and sailors in several small groups had already begun to walk back to the eastern camp. It had been exciting to see what might be Fair Beard's fire and to be given coin amulets from a king's treasury, but now everyone was tired and wanted to sleep after a long, eventful day.

Liking the feel of the darkness, Madoc struck out over the sand alone, leaving the monks to watch the enigmatic glow through the night. Shreds of wispy haze hugged low spots among the dunes, but thick fog had not materialized as it usually did on the island by this hour.

Overhead a glittering gravel of stars paved the sky-road. He had never seen it so brilliant.

Behind them leeward surf broke and ran, broke and ran, muffled by increasing distance as they headed back to the eastern camp. Ahead breakers from the ocean sounded louder as the company spread out in twos and threes, trudging through fine sand that splattered with each step like dry water against the ankles. The walk, which seemed easy when they were drawn this way earlier by curiosity, was now labor.

"It pulls me down," Rhiannon said, as she reached for him. Her hair seemed to have a light of its own, waving in the wake of her movement that lifted the folds of her mantle beside her like wings. "May I hold onto you, brother?"

Madoc, who last wore shoes in Ireland, gave her his arm, feeling the warmth of her hand as she slid it into the crook of his elbow. "Barefoot is easier."

She stopped without letting go of him and kicked off her French slippers, then tucked them under the cincture at her waist, laughing a little breathlessly because she was shy about her feet, which had always seemed to her to be too big.

To Madoc the silvery strands of hair across her face were like quick clouds in front of the moon.

She was long-legged, almost as tall as he. Footloose like himself, she matched his pace through the sand granular and cool beneath her uncallused soles.

He felt her snug up closer, the angles of her ribs pressing against his arm, telling him something inarticulate. His abdominal muscles clutched as if he were falling. She uttered a throaty chuckle—a delightful sound he hoped she would not repeat—and said, "We are going to make it," as a surety she had just encountered. She was not asking for confirmation of her hope. She was joyfully expressing it.

He made a sound of hearty compliance, not trusting his voice; his throat felt tight, the only part of him that did not feel good. He wished they could go on walking like this together, forever, even into darkness.

When he dared look at her, obliquely, she appeared luminescent, a foam-white woman running over the sand, the water-dark mantle flowing around her with a pleasing sound not unlike a wave against a shore. They were moving up the island's incline, a corrugated sand dune beyond which they would see the fire.

They seemed suddenly to be alone. Behind them bobbed a torch or two, glowing wanly in the vast night. The bright stars blazed overhead, but the usual fog was creeping along the ground; if the shreds built into an overcast, it would be a soupy night. Far off to the left someone was speaking softly in Latin—a prayer perhaps; it was not close enough to hear precisely.

He heard her breathing as they reached the gentle crest. Down through the sand and rock they could feel the pounding water hit the island from all sides. The wind had turned chill.

"Yes," he said, "I think we have a chance."

Pausing, hugging herself and staring out into the night, she sighed. It came from deep within her, made her shiver.

He wondered if this was the right time to ask and was about to when she said, "You will be wondering, I suppose..." she began with a tremor in her voice, "about what the Frenchman said."

Madoc made a light, positive sound.

"You have the right I suppose."

"He is a woman-hating priest," Madoc said to reveal his loyalty. "To shut him up, I will leave this island without him."

"They have been spying on me."

"Spying?"

"Well, spying on our father, actually."

"Brother Ely?"

She nodded, dazzling in the starlight. "He told them I shared Owen's bed."

Madoc turned to face her squarely. Something in him shriveled at what she said. It was an awful possibility he had never thought to consider. He might have wondered for a moment, but the look on her face revealed her innocence.

She waited, tensed. But when she was sure he would not question her, she said, "Thank you," hugging herself tightly.

They stood there a few more moments until she took a step toward the distant campfire. He reached out and stopped her with his touch. Before he touched her, he sensed her warmth beneath the fabric of her clothing, but he dropped his hand quickly when he felt a spark crack between them.

"Rhiannon?"

"Yes?" She was trembling. She knew it was too much to hope that he would not want to know more, but she was unprepared for what he finally managed to say,

"I... I love you."

Chapter 11

*From those who hate us we can often
learn the truth.*

—Metamorphosis
Ovid
c. A.D. *10*

He could hear her breathe but detected no sign of a
response.

Because he might never be able to say these things to her
again, he continued, "I have loved you from the moment I
first saw you. I had to stand on tiptoe to see into your
cradle—you were a few hours old. Princess Cristen permitted
all the others of the king's children to see you because you
were the first girl among all us boys. You were like a glowing
light even then...." He dared step closer and almost dropped
to his knees in gratitude that she did not step back away from
him.

Still she did not speak.

"Your eyes were open and seemed to me to be the same
cloudy-sky color as now. You looked directly at me and
smiled. I adored you, even then."

Her silence threatened to pull him in. He hurtled on,
terrified by what her lack of response might mean.

"I still do ... adore you. ..." He stammered to a stop and
reached out again to close the gap between them. Again she
did not draw back, did not move except to breathe closer to
him now as he enfolded her in his arms. There was no
resistance as he found her mouth, surprised it was open—in
shock, surprise, disgust?—it did not matter, he found it with
his own and closed whatever space had existed between them.

123

He could not break it, could not bear to lose her now that he had found her waiting, because she was surely kissing back. He seemed to be able to breathe through her and she through him.

He was startled that his face was wet, salt was in their mouths, but still they clung together, he not sure which of them was crying. But finally she made a small hurt sound. The sea air was cool on his face after her warmth, but then he knew it was she with tears on her cheek. The starlight was bright enough to see the glistening track on her face as she looked at him, wide-eyed, trembling beneath his hands on her arms. She was trying to speak, swallowing tears and the kiss. He could not hear, and when he did, it burned him as though she spat hot coals in his ear.

"Damn you," she growled in a low whisper, but entirely without rancor, "Damn you, damn you—"

He was faint with apology, though he was sure still that she had complied, kissed back, held him with arms as trembling as his own; but before he could express it, she said evenly, "You are going to make me be the strong one."

He was not sure what she said.

He forced his hands from her; it felt like a loss, and it was all he could to do keep from touching her again.

"You were the first person I remember," she said, barely above a sob. "Ever since I could toddle around, I wanted to be with you. When they sent you to Ireland—I could have been no more than five—I thought I would die, afraid I would never see you again, but glad that I would not because—even then I knew—it cannot be, Madoc—brother and sister—it cannot be." Her voice grew stronger with the words, as though she must say this to herself to make it so.

She was still staring at him.

She loves me, he was thinking, feeling as though he were sliding down a long embankment. It is not just me all by myself with these feelings, she loves me, too—

"Half brother," he corrected her. "Half sister."

But she was shaking her head. "There is sin in it."

"It will put me no closer to hell than I already stand. Besides, you never put much stock in what the priests say."

She did not answer right away; she was still thinking about it, he saw, and just needed time. "What if they are right?"

"Do you feel they are?"

"Please," she begged, "please do not make me be the strong one, not all alone."

"I am sorry."

"Do not sorrow, brother, just help me."

He touched her cheek and she let him, eyes still pleading. "You love me, too."

She nodded. "All my life."

He could not fight it; he hugged her and she clung to him. They rocked each other as the fog rolled in around their ankles, clinging to the ground but leaving the sky starry overhead, until he slowly drew away from her, nodding as though understanding for the first time. "I will do whatever you say, Rhiannon."

"I beg you not to make me be the strong one alone."

He nodded more vigorously. "Of course." He felt giddy because he realized that she would think about it and then, when she had thought about it enough, she would give in to both their desires. He did not have to force anything, would not dare because he wanted her willing, not raped, so he stepped back. Neither could speak as they started slowly toward the camp.

"You . . . you never showed it," he said softly.

"You, either."

"I promise I never will again, if you want it so."

Now she was the one to nod, too vigorously perhaps. "It is not what I want. I never get what I want, but it is what is."

"Yes, if you say it. But I will never stop loving you." He almost touched her again, and as he caught himself, she looked directly into his eyes. "And it is not wrong—not to God, who made us what we are." Lest she have the slightest doubt, he repeated, "I will never stop loving you."

"Me, too." She looked down as she said it, then turned and walked quickly away from him toward the eastern camp that was a small glow ahead. Madoc let her go, full of sweet knowing and willing to wait for her as long as she needed.

He felt bathed in a glow of understanding; he had not been alone all those years. He thought of Ann, sweet Ann whom he had loved, but who was gone, when his reverie was broken by a harsh male voice with a strident accent from somewhere up ahead:

"Run away from your shame, whore of Babylon—" Simon's voice boomed from the blue shadows.

Madoc saw him there, advancing on Rhiannon who had run

several paces. "You do not deserve to live among good Christian people—find the Norseman's savage Skraelings and live amongst them as their queen, woman of Satan, witch, whore—"

As the priest grabbed for her, she started swinging, screaming back, "Leave me alone—"

The priest, who had taken vows against violence even to protect himself, prayed in Latin and backed away from her blows.

He saw Madoc and cried, "I bear formal witness, sire."

Madoc grabbed him. Rhiannon fled.

Simon cowered from blows he expected from Madoc, who tossed him aside and watched the darkness consume Rhiannon. Glancing around, Madoc found nothing to strike, nothing but the cringing priest making begging noises in the sand. Such a display sickened Madoc, who had seen battle break green boys and gray old soldiers—but cowardice from this creature, a man whose hands were callused by no other weapon than a quill pen—well, it was disgusting. He felt sick with fury and must strike his own hand to keep from punching the priest.

Simon peeked up, saw Madoc towering with knotted fists, and ducked again. But blows never came. Muttering a prayer for deliverance mixed with imprecations at Rhiannon, Simon looked around to see if anyone had witnessed his loss of face. He staggered to his feet, heart settling somewhat, his face stinging, then hurriedly and from mindless habit crossed himself.

Madoc had not moved but stood a pace and a half away as far as Simon could make out, glaring in his direction. Simon brushed cool sand from his bare legs, kicked his sandals to empty them, and righted his cassock on an already-lean but now fast-starved Norman frame. He growled in Rhiannon's direction, hissing under his breath a jumble of French and Saxon. "Black-hearted whoring heathen Druid sorcellerie witch Welshwoman—"

Pointing after her with a trembling finger, he was about to voice his accusation in Cymraeg—he felt it was his pastoral duty to enlighten the naive lord about his whore of a sister before she succeeded in seducing him, as she would have done just now in the same manner she had seduced the father had Simon not intervened—but Madoc grabbed a handful of cassock and yanked him almost cross-eyed.

A nose away, even in the darkness, the priest could not

look away from those wide, trembling eyes that had not quite regained the person behind them.

Beyond all caution the priest sputtered as he awkwardly blessed Madoc, or rather blessed the hair's breadth of air between them as he was silently praying to be delivered swiftly, if this be his time, into the arms of Christ Jesus. That was what he was thinking, but he was saying, "My son, as one of your spiritual advisers, do not gainsay my witness against the woman."

"You are certainly not my spiritual adviser, but a Frenchman with a suspicious Saxon accent."

Simon could smell the rich vapors of mead, salt water, and fury from his temporal lord, who did not part his teeth to say, "Speak no more against her."

"Her actions speak—gagghh—she seduced your father, now she would drag you to hell with her, too."

Madoc twisted the rough collar.

"Can you not see her swollen belly?" Simon gasped, determined to do his duty despite the grip that threatened to strangle him. "She is with child, man—why do you think she hungered for the blood?"

Madoc flashed recall of stained Rhiannon washing pig's blood off in the surf. "One more word and you have claimed your sod."

Simon swallowed largely. "But—"

"One more treasonous syllable."

The Frenchman licked his thin lips with a tongue dry enough to remove skin and almost spoke despite the fact that he was well versed in Celtic folklore, which held that a person must find his destined spot of ground before he can die, and having found it, will. He also knew that under Cymreig law and maritime tradition, the arglwydd as war chief and shipmaster owned his life with no appeal if treason were the crime.

Despite his famished condition Simon was a big-boned, lanky man, yet Madoc foot-dangled him so that his hoary-nailed toes just brushed the sand. Madoc clutched the robe tighter under the throbbing Adam's apple, cutting off Simon's air.

Neither of them was aware that the glow of a torch had been moving steadily closer since Simon called out against Rhiannon. Now it flared nearer, a bobbing moon, as someone holding it high trudged downward at a steep angle from the crest of dune.

Wyn's voice rang through the mist, "Brother—"

Slowly Madoc gave Simon back to the beach. Neither man blinked; liberated, Simon collapsed as his abbot appeared behind him, bathing in warm light what seemed the inside of a glassy sphere that contained them on a fogged circle of strand.

"Tell him, Domme, what everyone else knows about her."

Madoc had the look of an owl about him as he swiveled his head and pinned the mouse against the glare. His eyes narrowed.

"So be it," was all he said, and very quietly then turned toward the eastern camp where he thought he saw Rhiannon's diminishing silhouette in front of the larger glow.

"Nay!" Simon screamed, realizing what he had done. "Tell him, Domme, tell him I speak the truth—"

"Brother Simon," Wyn's soothing voice coaxed him to be still, to regain his spirit, and slid into a soft Latin cant from the Psalms. Afterwards, "We will speak with him, we will speak with him, my brother," Wyn promised. "He is amenable; his heart is good. Leave him to me. The woman you must leave to the Lord."

Madoc could hear Wyn comforting again, soothing, Latin again back there, then admonishing Simon to rejoin his brothers on the western lookout.

But beyond Madoc's hearing Wyn whispered to a calmer Simon, "He loves her, brother. Guard your tongue."

"'All wickedness is but little to the wickedness of woman,'" Simon snarled a quote from the Apocrypha. "She bewitched him!"

"She is his half sister, man. Blood kin. If you harm her, even disparage her, he must defend her."

Simon started to speak, but Wyn forced another point. "And all his relatives, too, which accounts for about half the men in this company. They are all related. They raise each other's children. That is how it works—blood ties down through the generations, overlapping and tying everyone together—fealty, fostering and blood, and, my brother, if you are going to survive amongst us, you must not offend that sensibility."

"I suppose you be his third cousin somewhere down the line."

"His father and his father's father's father have supported my community for nearly two hundred years. All of us owe our lives as well as our vocations to him."

"You owe your vocation to God."

"Through the support of Gwynedd for our house."

"If Owen Gwynedd would have put aside that whore of a cousin, you would still be praying in your house, Brother Abbot."

"Brother," Wyn said, a hand on the priest's arm, "if you insist on provoking this man, I cannot save you from him."

Simon smoothed some wrinkle from his garments, brushed more sand from his person. "He will abandon me just because I refuse to call him lord."

"He cares nothing for titles."

"He will exile me for spite because I speak the truth."

"Himself was exiled for much less."

Simon, wide-eyed with bluish orbs under the vast dark sky, turned to Wyn. "I saw them in shameless embrace, I saw them—"

Simon could barely make out Wyn as he gestured with his chin to the immense vault of the heavens splattered with stars to make his point: "'Tis dark this night with no moon...."

"I saw—"

"One can imagine seeing all sorts of—"

"I tell you, I saw them—brother and sister—together in the unspeakable." Simon glanced in the direction she had gone. "She is after his soul. A Welsh witch, like mother, like daughter."

"I believe I can soften his heart this time," Wyn concluded, seeing that argument would not prevail against Simon's stubbornness, and so turned toward the eastern camp. "Let me talk to him. Return to your holy labors and stay away from him. Pray the Lord grants you protection against excessive pride."

Simon blinked and obeyed, walking in the opposite direction.

Madoc knew Wyn would follow and try to change his mind about things. Ahead all was dismal dark around the fog-haloed double point of the campfires.

Now, stumbling in the night, Madoc felt his face under a wet chill. He could not call these tears Rhiannon's; he must claim them. He heard the perfidious priest's words in the waves and wind. Rhiannon and Owen. Owen and Rhiannon. Oil on fire inside him, so that his tears tasted smoky, the darkness turned from black to red with the distant campfires the burning two-eyed heart of his pain.

Thief of my life . . . father, father, father . . .

Depthless perfidious bitch, Rhiannon, Rhiannon . . .

By the time Rhiannon entered the glow, her face was dry. The prevailing breeze from the sea bent the smoke westward, where several men occupied bedrolls. She crouched for a while before the ranked embers of a timber, letting it take away her chill.

Teleri had been the first to return to the campfire. She sat on a short keg near the larger bonfire, her hands dancing away at needlework. She glanced up at her mistress, no word but what passed between them when their their eyes met.

Teleri blended as she often did into the shadows. A few years senior, she had grown up with the moody Rhiannon. Since infancy they were sensitive to each oher's nuance. Through the dancing flames she could tell Rhiannon had been crying. Her eyes were narrow, the skin under them puffy, even as lean as she was. With the same loose-jointed posture she held when washing off the pig blood, she now crouched in bent fatigue as close to the warmth as she could without getting singed, a folded, reedy stem of a woman drawn to the fire, one hand limp and extended across her knee.

Suddenly alert, Rhiannon looked in the direction of men's voices, still far off but approaching—the arglwydd who answered tensely, monosyllabic in response to Wyn's argument.

". . . he has the right to witness, under your father's law."

"I warned him," said Madoc in a voice deepened by resolve.

Rhiannon was up and gone like a moth. The two men did not even see her. Teleri watched her against the surf winking with a faint luminescence, then moving past the wreck toward the sheltered women's camp where another smaller fire burned in the lee of jumbled timbers. There crouched the sheep who presented one pale fleecy back to the upping wind tattering the mist around them.

Madoc and Wyn were speaking softly, rapidly countering each other as they approached the fire opposite Teleri.

". . . but she had a power over the old man that had people talking," Wyn was saying. "She is too old unwed. Your father should have dowried her off long before twenty-two. Many others said this. Father Simon only repeats these accusations—he is not their author."

"He disobeyed me."

Wyn nodded. "Ah, yes, you must have the man's obedience. I promise you he will obey, if you can forgive him."

"Do you believe this slander against her?"

Wyn shook his head. "I never believed these rumors. But what I believe is not important. It is going to affect the men. It is married couples who make a homeland, not a bunch of wild roaming sailors. You have only three mated couples here. If you fail to set a moral standard, well..." Wyn seemed genuinely unwilling to say what the result might be. "Well, terrible chaos could overtake the women...."

Madoc stared into the fire, no indication that he either ignored or listened to Wyn.

The monk glanced at the Norsemen, because his implications were aimed at the unmanageable Dag and his cronies, still on the western side. "And the children."

He meant for this to mean Gwen to Madoc, for if he could not reach him through Rhiannon, then the girl was the only hope of persuading this man.

Madoc and Wyn lingered near the fire only a moment. When the arglwydd spun and stalked off, the stocky abbot followed him, ignoring that Madoc had failed twice to respond.

"... so it is our suggestion that to set an example and forestall trouble, the arglwydd must take an appropriate wife."

Madoc was gone into the darkness, Wyn following with his hands folded inside his sleeves, the heavy cloth around his ankles whipping like a pale shadow after the larger man.

A chill shot through Teleri that had nothing to do with the windy beach.

Wyn continued. "It will not be long before your Gwen—"

"No!"

Teleri could tell Madoc had drawn up short because their voices stayed in one spot before fading.

"Perhaps Evan Powys..."

"She is a baby," Madoc protested as their voices faded.

Teleri gathered up her sewing and brushed the sand from her skirts as she stood to follow her mistress. She walked by the pile of sleeping children, counting silently to make sure each bedroll held a child—three, including her own tousle-haired Einion beside Gwen with the pup between them. The two other women were curled into blankets on either side of the children.

One of the sailors over in the men's camp began to pipe a slow, ancient tune.

Teleri moved among the children and saw they were given to sleep, then made for a carved beam from the defeated ship pulled to one side to serve as a beach before the smaller blaze. There sat her mistress bent toward the fire as before.

"Tell them, my lady, to stop their slander," Teleri whispered behind Rhiannon, who did not respond. The firelight glowed against her skin and hair. Short blue sparks cracked at a knot of rosin or tar on the glowing log as Teleri sat nearby and resumed the needlework.

Rhiannon regarded her without moving anything but weary eyes. "I swore not to expose this child to the abuse of ever knowing its father."

"But they abuse you."

"I will defend myself to no man."

"A word could stop them."

"No—no mere word will ever stop them," Rhiannon said stubbornly as she leaned back on her elbows, stretching her long legs out to catch the fire's warmth. "They slandered my mother and chased her into a nunnery, where she lives like a prisoner away from my father because of the scandal they heap upon her. As her child I was always condemned, no matter what the truth."

"They disparage your child because they think—"

"A nearsighted priest saw me sitting on the edge of my father's bed bathing his face during a fever. They have seen to it that his wife is not there to take care of an old, dying man. My place was beside him in her stead. My brother will accept simple truth before he will believe that priest."

"At least tell him you were raped." That much Teleri knew, that Rhiannon had been raped—she had been with her right after it happened in her father's house at Aberffraw.

"Careful, Teleri—who knows what ears listen?" Her hands fell protectively on her abdomen; she meant those ears, too.

Teleri did not know who was the father of her mistress's baby, but she knew all the possibilities. She glanced at Rhiannon's gently rounded belly, thinking about the pelvis that held the bump of new humanity. Rhiannon was far more athletic than princesses were supposed to be in London or faraway France. She was a Celtic princess, another thing entirely, more kin to Diana of the Hunt than frail Mary of Nazareth. She was spirited, strong, and toughened by this journey, whereas another woman, Edwin's little Ffiona for instance, was laid low.

Teleri judged that Rhiannon would probably have a fairly easy childbirth. It was not too soon to begin these considerations: Teleri had rightly calculated that Rhiannon was four months pregnant. Rhiannon did not volunteer information.

One of the children tossed among the jumble of bedrolls. Off to their left the piper picked up the pace and someone else began humming along.

Rhiannon and Teleri seemed to be alone at the moment, but the fire cast lurking shadows on the fog that swirled close to the ground, shredded in the strengthening breeze.

Scratching one foot with the instep of the other, Rhiannon continued in a softened voice. "I will answer nobody's charges."

"Not even our lord Madoc's?"

Rhiannon abruptly stood and stretched, then took from a covered wicker basket a spindle-whorl and dropped it on its growing cable to begin rotation, enjoying the whispering sound it made, liking the tension it put in her wrists. What she missed most was her weaving. True, she had been able to set up the warp-board of her loom aboard the *Horn* but had not much to show for it of a tapestry she had begun a year ago. She longed to be finally settled so that she could install the loom in a permanent home and so finish the work. Not even music satisfied the desire. Without its exercise daily she felt at loose ends, as though weaving the strands of wool set the pattern of her life. Now, at least until they found Madoc's promised land, she must make do with this, the spindle-whorl.

Her fingers expertly fed the whorl from the sack of wool.

"He will not challenge me." Rhiannon paced a little, hugging the fleece wrapped on a stick, the bobbin swaying and humming its single note. The music coming from the other campfire found time with the whirring instrument, the weight of which now moved more quickly than the eye could see.

Teleri took up another stocking with no heel. The iron needle must be threaded again. There was just enough light from their little fire to see the silhouette of the needle and thread when she held it up against the glow and squinted one eye. She glanced at her mistress busy at mindless labor in the blur of the spindle-whorl.

"He most desires to know, my lady."

Rhiannon eyed Teleri in a new angle, looked around to be sure of their privacy, and leaned close to ask, "How do you know?"

Teleri was practiced a keeping her feelings close to herself alone, but now she almost smiled over the darning; she was fixing Einion's only extra pair of stockings, patched over several times, as was all their clothing by now. Her stitches were perfect, the envy of the women of Gwynedd's household. "I have eyes, my lady. I saw him just now with the abbot."

"He regards me so, he will never ask."

"Yes, mam." A term of endearment, servants often referred to the mistress as mother. But it had the effect here of formal acquiescence, a condescension on Teleri's part because as servant she was not supposed to criticize her mistress.

"He trusts me."

"Yes."

Rhiannon abandoned the spindle-whorl by tossing it back into the basket. She sank to her bedroll, wordlessly slipping into it.

"Good night, my lady," Teleri said, but did not expect an answer. Later she put aside her darning and stretched out the kinks. She needed to relieve herself, so stepped silently away from the fire toward the water's edge.

On her return she saw Wil's wife Mary spreading out her bedroll a few paces on the other side of the fire. Huw's wife was with him on the second ship, but Mary was prone to seasickness, so she and her two children would stay with the other women ashore when her husband was on duty.

"God rest thee," she said as Teleri passed in the gloom.

"And thee," Teleri answered as the older woman dropped to her knees on the thick Cumberland blanket.

"I have some simples here," Mary continued, rummaging a lumpy drawstring bag.

Teleri paused.

"Ah, here," Mary said, coming up with a small tied pouch she offered to Teleri. "Maidenhair for thy mistress."

"She has no distress," Teleri replied, meaning the morning sickness and fatigue suffered in some early pregnancies.

"Ah, but there can be distress in more than the body,"

Mary replied. "It is an old remedy from home." Like the men, the women of this company did not often refer to what they had left behind. None of them had planned to pull up their lives and head into Madoc's unknown. Mary, who suffered terrible seasickness, was not here by her own will. If her husband had not told her they would never see each other again, she would not have come along. But a sea widow would have little prospect for a decent life back on the coast where she came from.

It was a wild, rugged land where the last vestiges of the old pagan ways remained, and where every village had an herbalist. Usually these were older women. But such women were scorned, and Mary had not looked forward to living out her last years in a hovel on the edge of some bleak forest where women would come with small coin to be aborted.

Teleri was counting their blessings that they had such a woman among them. "You have the art of herbs and simples, then?"

"My grandmother taught me some of the old ways," Mary said in the self-deprecating style of her countrymen. In fact, her grandmother had taught her much. But Mary was still unsure if such knowledge might be in her favor or against her in the minds of these people, who were for the most part strangers.

She began to brush out her long, gray-streaked hair. Teleri saw the flash of gold at her neck; she had put Madoc's coin on a braided string for an amulet. Teleri had sewn her own coin to the inside of her apron.

"And midwifery?"

"I helped deliver a few in my time and had my own."

"Myself, only Einion, but I have assisted several."

"We will have the Norsewoman dropping soon."

"Within the month."

"She is as healthy as a sow. No problems there, I wager."

Teleri made a sound of agreement as she hunkered down beside the older woman, who nodded rhythmically, gently tugging against a tangle in her hair as she asked, "And her ladyship?"

"She has four months, thereabouts."

Mary continued nodding. Teleri could tell that she was soundlessly mouthing a prayer. She rocked silently with each stroke of the brush. "She carries a terrible secret."

Teleri stiffened but found a calm voice before she replied in defense of her mistress, "More like a terrible burden, sister."

"Hmmm." Small blue sparks crackled between brush and hair.

"Others have motives to libel her," Teleri said stiffly, ready to walk away if Mary was one of those.

"Not myself, I assure you," Mary said. "But she is bound to cause talk, a high-born unmarried woman like that carrying—"

"Thank you for your concern, mistress," Teleri said, standing abruptly and about to walk away from her. "I will give her the herbs and be glad for your wisdom when her time comes."

"I brought a few things with me—let us pray the Lord plants herbs on the far side, too."

"Surely He must," Teleri said, and would have walked away, but Mary continued:

"And let us pray for the master and his continued wisdom."

Teleri said coolly as a means for good night, "Aye."

"What he needs is a wife."

Neither woman could see the features of the other, and both were quiet for long moments. Then Teleri said softly, "I heard the abbot tell him the same thing."

Mary, engrossed now in her prayers, was not listening; she thought Teleri had moved on.

As she walked back to her bedroll, Mary's muttered devotions faded under the never-silent waves against the shore.

Teleri watched from her blanket as their lord, in the company of several of his men, walked back into camp and to the beached wreck of the St. Brendan. Its stern lay partially in the surf, but the fire-gutted prow was high and dry.

Madoc carried his wrapped sighting instrument and rolled-up charts, while Ari carried his blanket and a tallow light in a clam shell behind the ragged strakes of the ship. Evan held his weapons, sword, and knives and the rest of his gear. She could hear them speaking over there, but softly, not their exact words, but she could imagine. Evan stowed the weapons in a chest someone had dragged from the St. Brendan. Ari began arranging the furnishings of the rude headquarters—he and another of the men spread out pieces of sail to hide the scorched walls of the inner straking. A hatch cover quickly became a trestle table, mounted on casks.

The night deepened. Einion had stopped tossing, and the men of the company were engaged in soft conversation near the big fire as they bedded down for the night; but Teleri stayed awake in her bedroll near Rhiannon, who fell into deep sleep.

One by one the men bid Madoc good night until only he, the dark servant, and one of the sailors were left in the ship's hulk. Presently Madoc and the sailor strolled from Madoc's appropriated headquarters out to the dune that rose on the spine of the island. The dark man stayed behind, arranging crates and other items so the master could live there.

The smaller fire was dying down. Teleri could see their vague silhouettes and hear their quick man-talk as they prepared to take a sighting on the polestar.

Stray wisps of fog hugged the land, but the breeze cleared the sky where stars beyond reckoning spread a dazzling array.

Their present position must be somewhat north of the last star reading Madoc had taken at sea, because Polaris was well above the northern horizon, whereas earlier it had hovered just above the curve of the earth. They discussed this for a while, neither of them voicing the fear of moving farther into southern waters, where they would lose Polaris altogether. That would be a true step into the unknown.

"What think you of the landfall to the south?" Madoc asked the sailor Edwin, who had been with him for seven years. Beyond that tie he was also some distant cousin on Owen's side. In his late thirties, a stout but compact brown-haired fellow of the native stock, Edwin ab Islwyn was from St. David's in south Cambria. His people had been seafarers forever, his father being one of the crew of Madoc's Irish foster father. He belonged to one of the three married couples Wyn mentioned; his wife was the quiet little thing, Ffiona, with a baby of eight months.

"Hmmm," Edwin gave for an answer. "It is a big island. I wager."

"You think it is a better bet than Fair Beard's west?"

Edwin gazed in that direction toward the landmass that would someday be the Bahamas. "I would always gamble on Snorrison, master." Himself, he had never been a blue-water sailor but was an expert at conning coastlines and rivers. This was his first venture into any open sea but the Irish. "And I heard tales that you and he passed as far west as a man might."

Madoc removed the sunboard from its leather bag, which Edwin held for him. "But that was long ago and stumbled onto by accident. This is surely some other place much farther south."

With the sunboard he would be able to determine sun time and thereby mark their approximate position on his running chart, which inked across two widths of parchment by now, indicating a far wider ocean than Madoc had been prepared to navigate. They had now sailed twice as many days as Madoc and Fair Beard had traveled years ago, and these parts looked nothing like the land he had found back then.

"Should we not have made the southern land, sir?"

"That was just another island."

They had altogether missed the Bahamas to the north. Likewise, the islands that would someday go by the names of the West Indies, Puerto Rico, and Hispaniola were fallen below the southern horizon, beyond view.

They were a gnat on the tail of the immense land-beast that would slumber waiting three hundred twenty-two more years to be called the New World. Fate had deposited Madoc's Hundred on one of the thousands of sand bars that formed the San Sebastians, swept into this passage by the great broom of the South Equatorial Current.

Innocent of all such geographies, Madoc with the sunboard stood a darker silhouette against the pale spangled sky, facing north with his arms outstretched as if he were an ancient athlete frozen into a statue of a discus thrower setting up his shot.

Teleri watched from behind as he lined up the hole in the nocturnal with the star Polaris, then moved the arms of the simple mechanism to point to the two stars. He knew the Little Dipper swings around Polaris once every twenty-four hours. The two bright stars of that constellation farthest from the north star were called the guards.

This nocturnal had been a gift from his Irish foster father, dead a dozen years. It was made of rosewood inlaid with walrus ivory, pearls, and gold wire, a piece of artwork from some unknown carver's hand and one of the few material objects he loved.

Behind him in the glow of the shell lamp, Edwin put pins in the worn limp parchment as Madoc instructed. After a muted discussion Madoc carefully wrapped the nocturnal. They lingered on the rise with the infinite sky unrolled over their heads.

"And Ffiona, is she better?"

"Still weak, but holding her own. She never was strong."

"And the sea toll."

"It was a hard journey, yes sir. I am scurvied; half of us are. There was a time or two I doubted even you. But Fair Beard never did—he believes you yet wherever he be."

Madoc smiled and clapped Edwin on the back. "See that Ffiona gets some of the ewe's milk and an extra helping of the pork fat, Eddie. I saw Caradoc hide it away for our breakfast." He thought, but did not disclose, that Caradoc assumed care of the food because he was filching. It was all that could explain his continued weight when everyone else was starving.

"And marrow," Madoc added. "Crack the bones for her. Do it now before the dog gets the best part."

"Thank you, sir."

"We will all be stronger now that we have filled our bellies and have some rest." Madoc was glad to see his gold coin winking on a cord around Edwin's neck.

"It will be good to find our Norseman," the sailor said of Fair Beard.

"You do believe, then? No more doubt?"

"Aye, I believe in St. Brendan the Navigator—and you, sir!"

Madoc could not help but be cheered by Edwin's loyalty, even his simple faith; but himself, he never put much stock in a story about a man who sailed this ocean in a leather boat. Ox-hide coracles in quick dashes across the River Severn were one thing; gluey ox hides stitched together on that great gray immensity he had just crossed, well, that was quite another.

But he kept his cynical thoughts to himself and presently they bade each other good night. Edwin went to break the supper bones for Ffiona, who was asleep with her baby in their bedroll near the big fire, Madoc to the glow of the destroyed ship, where Ari met him with a drinking horn.

They spoke briefly. Teleri could not hear but knew what was being said from the gestures, then was certain when Ari nodded and picked up his own blanket, which he had dropped just outside the wreck. He traipsed back toward the main camp at the big fire where the other men had bedded down.

Teleri sighed relief. Though it looked as though he would be accepting the strange black man as his personal servant, it appeared that Madoc did not want close attendance.

His sheep oil and clam shell light threw gold flickers on the sand outside the wreck as Madoc worked over the chart. The strong mutton incense lingered at ground level inside the ship's carcass, giving a rosy glow to the light and a pungent aroma to the air.

Long after everyone else was asleep, Teleri still watched from the women's side of the ship. The stars made their slow turn overhead. The ocean stroked the island unceasingly. Deep into the night the glow behind the boards was extinguished. Teleri waited, then left her warm bedroll, hugging herself in her linen shift against the chill air to join him.

He was almost asleep and did not protest.

Chapter 12

*Now there are to the south of
Greenland, known since A.D. 985
desert places set amidst ice, then
comes the country of the Skraelings
which in the Cree tongue means raw
flesh eaters, then Markland, then
Vinland the Good; next somewhat
further south lies Whitemansland
where there was formerly constant
sailing from Iceland.*

—by Ari Thorgilsson
Iceland(Codex 770)
A.D. 1120

The morning opened dull and gray. Even the sea was muffled by a persistent overcast that did not prevent Madoc from rising before firstlight to begin work. His mind was racing with plans of how to section out the men as he waked them with his own hand.

It seemed to Rhiannon that every day of her life had begun with Teleri's gentle hand and voice, but today dawned with the flat gray sky overhead, the far-flung shriek of gulls, and Madoc's call under the sea-sound and wind.

"All of you, everyone, this is what we must do," the arglwydd called to them. The primary task was to get the *St. Ann* seaworthy, pumped, and recaulked where the damage was bad. He glanced back over his shoulder at the ships sitting the waves.

The *St. Ann* listed badly amidships and from this point of view seemed about to go down, while the trim *Horn* looked to be backing away from her sister ship in despair of averting the calamity. But he knew they could salvage the neglected ship. To get it done quickly he would need the civilians, even the children, to pump the bilge and haul caulk from the *St. Brendan.*

As the man gazed toward the ships, Rhiannon watched him. She loved seeing him like this and knowing now that his heart was hers as hers had always belonged to him. She listened with the others as he pointed to each group with a task that seemed just right for their strength and skills.

She watched him with new eyes, a wife's eyes, as he instructed the Norsemen to begin hauling everything of value out to the *Horn,* then to coracles over to the *St. Ann* and begin pumping the bilge.

"Tell the women what we need here," he said to Rhiannon, who was braiding her hair as she stood on the sidelines watching him from her secret perspective. "What do you want us to do?"

"The old caulk must be hauled to the ship. Maybe if you work in teams." He had assigned a team of sailors to get a cauldron going onboard to melt down the tar and mix it with new wool, which would replace the water-swollen caulk between strakes.

"I will not!" one of the men had snarled at Evan. "'Tis Martinmas and a day forbidden to work."

Several of the other sailors and three of the religious who had stayed in camp agreed, dividing the work force neatly into two opposing groups before Madoc stepped among them.

"What does it matter what day it is, man?" their commander asked as he separated the sailor from Evan, whose hand was already on his sword hilt. "We must get off this island."

"Bad luck to work on Martinmas," said the sailor, an Irishman.

"What about the dead man on the ship?" It was Brian, the priest who had been reared in the monastery. Madoc privately sighed; he might have known he could not keep that a secret.

There rose a muttering of agreement and surprise from the men, some of whom had not heard the rumor about the corpse.

"We must say Mass," Simon said as he entered the circle.

Madoc's eyes narrowed, but he bit back further comment.

"For Christ's sake," said another sailor, "what dead man?" And that broke them up into gossiping subgroups around Madoc.

"It is ungodly not to say Mass," Simon began a triade, but Madoc stopped him with a voice that was too gentle.

"Very well, say your prayers. Then, back to work."

"It is Martinmas," Simon insisted.

"Bad fortune to work," grumbled two sailors. Several drew the sign of the cross across their hearts.

Ignoring them, Madoc said to Simon, "I will kill a sheep for a feast tonight, but first we get the water out of the *St. Ann.*"

Simon, who had expected otherwise, was taken aback.

"Well, get to it, then," Madoc said mildly.

"We will, eh, ring the bell when we are ready," the Frenchman replied, still surprised at Madoc's concession. Simon and his group of religious backed off while Madoc redirected several of his men to the *St. Brendan.* He told Gwen to gather up the baskets and buckets to haul caulk.

"He cannot expect us to touch that filthy stuff," Mary said.

Rhiannon suggested, "You can prepare the feast."

Caradoc, already sweating, had the intended sheep staked out near the fire he was feeding the last of yesterday's wood. "Go," he told Einion. "More driftwood!"

The boys whooped off, flooding past Mary, who trudged toward the fire with her mantle pulled around her face.

People were catching Madoc's enthusiasm; his decisive commands rallied them with hope. The air vibrated with it, an almost joyous hysteria. They were fueled by it despite the cold, sunless morning that was only a mirror of their bleak situation.

Rhiannon turned to see Teleri shaking out a blanket beside the beached ship. Wind whipped the light gray wool upward, spanking the corners tasseled in royal purple. It was an old but serviceable blanket Rhiannon had packed with her own hand the night before they departed Aberffraw. It had been Owen's—only the king wore purple. Now it could only be Madoc's blanket.

Rhiannon stood watching her servant fold the blanket with a careless caress as she lay it on an arm bent against her heart and turned behind a width of sail Ari had stretched across the open end of the hull. The black man approached, carrying several wrapped objects, speaking with Teleri, who remained beyond view. Rhiannon could not hear what was said, but he set down his burden just inside the hanging curtain and retraced his path.

The breeze flung voices from several directions—children squealing with gulls at the waterline, the men barking to one another on the other side of the *St. Brendan* as they mounted her lines with pickaxes and buckets, the laughter of a woman who must be Yngvild, and the chanting voices of the monks somewhere off to the west as they said their morning office.

Her braid forgotten, Rhiannon shook her own blanket, then stood staring at Madoc's headquarters. Forgotten, the bedroll slipped from her hand.

The air brightened, but the sun was still behind the overcast in the eastern sky beyond the *St. Ann*. Rhiannon squinted at the new glare, watching the hulk, letting the wind rake long, pale hair from her face. Presently Teleri left Madoc's nest and walked toward the main fire without looking back.

Rhiannon turned to the beached ship, where already Gwen had dropped a score of buckets, baskets, crocks, and crates.

Very soon, with the monks' combined voices in the *Te Deum*, Brian clanged the tocsin, calling all to the spine of the island where the monks had set up their makeshift altar using rough-bound sea trunks draped with lengths of sail for the undercloths and an exquisite altar cloth from the monastery's treasure room.

The silver and gold threads vibrated against the wine-colored silk that trailed a long fringe. Jewels sewn into the embroidery winked in the new glow from the overcast that promised sunlight. On the cloth the monks had spread their holy instruments, two hooded silver candlesticks meant for outdoor service, a heavy crucifix, a carved ivory book stand, and the Word encrusted with gold leaf and jeweled bindings.

A gold chalice burned with reflected sunlight under its stiff linen pall; the white of the towel beside it seemed unnatural amid the coarse pink sand. Other gold dishes had been set about under and over pure white linen. The air was very still, considering this was the highest point for many miles around. Only now and again a breeze played with the silk fringes and the hair on the heads of the faithful and curious alike.

The sacred finery glinted with foreign mystery in the rustic setting as Brian the acolyte lit the candles with a flint. The breeze puffed but was still not stiff, and the flames held. The community had salvaged rich vestments and some of the church furniture from Owen's chapel. Now, with the people beginning to gather, Wyn found Simon helping Father John to put on the holy garments behind the crating they rigged to serve as sacristy.

At hand stood Rhys ab Meredydd in an attitude of unreadable emotion, but strong, all but staring at Simon as he went about his task as valet to Father John.

John was praying, eyelids fluttering in a trance. The old man had been fasting. He stood the whole night in cross vigil; his shoulders fell into the posture with arms outstretched, letting the younger man dress him.

The silk and linen made their own sounds together for a second, then Rhys, all but forgotten, cleared his throat politely. He started to speak, but Simon said brusquely, "I have asked the poet to play, Domme—" Then he turned abruptly to Rhys, who might yet speak, "To glorify the Lord."

"Nonsense," Wyn said, and laid a hand on Rhys's shoulder.

"We must have music in the Mass," Simon insisted.

"You were to say Mass," Wyn reminded Simon as he helped to invest John with the last of the holy garments. At St. Brendan's it was traditional for the sermon to be preached by other than the celebrant, who was not to break his trance for the pulpit.

John hummed, nodding in cadence, moving to assist Simon's knowing hands; they had both many times been through these intricate steps, the central pattern of their lives.

Simon made a gesture at Father John as if to say, let the old man have the honor.

"He was to preach," Wyn said evenly, "on Jonah and the whale."

The vestments were predominantly black that day because this was a funeral Mass. Simon slipped the long stole across the bent but still-strong old shoulders; John, son of generations of farmers, was a farmer still with a wiry body that bespoke a lifetime of bending. Back at the monastery he was the chief of cultivation from the kitchen garden and herb-pots to the sweeping acres of oat fields that had been the community's fortune. That a priest would be a farmer and cellarer was not strange, since monastic rule prescribed humble labor.

Wyn, a blacksmith who was a monk and not a priest, was deeply affected by John's sublime attitude, which seemed evidence of divine grace. Smiling like a child now, eyes pressed shut, John hummed a sacred chord, murmuring a prayer as he stepped out into the makeshift sanctuary with the men helping him at the service. They had no altar boys, so Father Brian and a young monk were acting as acolytes as the people joined in the hymn.

Suddenly the sky visibly lightened, the cloud parted to drop a shaft of light that sent a whisper of awe through the people. Several, including some of Madoc's sailors and the women, crossed themselves when more rays from the sun pierced the cloud cover, illuminating a patch of water that glinted like a gilded backdrop of glory behind the altar.

Even the Norsemen who stood aside with Yngvild cast impressed glances at the opening heavens. Odin, too, was a sky god.

Wyn saw that Rhys also experienced the sun's blessing—his face tilted so that his handsome features beneath the band were scored in sharper lines by the good light. He smiled, apparently forgetting his argument with Simon.

It moved Wyn to see this, that even a blind man could see this enlightenment, and he thanked God silently. He knew that this court bard, though nominally a Christian, was not about to lend his music to the Christian service. It would go against tradition of which Simon should be aware.

John, acting as his own lector, began with scripture.

Wyn whispered to Simon, "I believe I have persuaded him to rescind your exile." Wyn crossed himself and gave eyes to the ritual, aggrieved at the necessity of further conversation, but added, "If you guard your tongue, brother, you will be safe."

"Yes, Domme, I understand."

"What is the text of your sermon?" Wyn asked, gesturing at the breviary Simon had taken from a fold in his cassock sleeve.

Simon was watching John read the Psalms at the altar, skipping the Gloria because this was a funeral Mass.

"The Lord be with you," John said to all present, managing in his misty-eyed but magnanimous address to include not only the scowling unbelievers on the sidelines, but the echoing gulls, the cockles they dismembered over the dunes, and even the pink and undulating sand itself.

Christians replied with the formula, "And with thy spirit."

The strengthening breeze lifted the altar cloth to reveal the humble trunk. One of the brothers acting as deacon caught a candelabra about to topple, then smoothed down the linen.

When it appeared Simon would not reply to his whispered

question, Wyn said, "I advise you, brother, to preach on Jonah and the whale. Or Moses and the Israelites."

"Yes, appropriate, yes Domme, thank you," Simon replied humbly, and let Wyn see his eyes.

Without speaking, Wyn mouthed the words, "Moses, then."

Simon nodded, kept his head bowed while John led the people in another prayer and more Gospels, until it was time for the lesson. When the monks began to sing, he stepped forward, his finger marking the book he held, to preach the sermon.

Wyn held his breath. Where Simon should be reading from Exodus, he began to recite from memory and in the vernacular a sermon first preached by St. Patrick four hundred years ago.

"Things hateful to God," the Frenchman intoned in a formal voice of address, his accent a lisp in the language everyone here either spoke as their mother tongue or as a necessary second language of trade and labor.

Wyn groaned as Simon enumerated those things hateful to the Lord according to the saint's own words: "A wise man without good works, an old man without religion, a young man without obedience, a rich man without alms, a master without virtue, a grumbler of a Christian, a poor man who is proud, an evil king, a negligent bishop, a crowd without discipline, a people without law, and," he sucked a breath, "a woman without modesty."

The wind accompanied him as the sun climbed above the layered cloud, widening its light but removing the fiery edges of its glow, turning into an ordinary day. Simon droned on, elaborating on St. Patrick's precepts until he had raked and curried every species of mortal shortcoming. Only once did Wyn glance Madoc's way. His gaze was stony, unreadable as a wall.

Though it was a small blessing that he named no names, Simon saved the "woman without modesty" for the end. Actually he had rearranged the order of Patrick's advice, no doubt to make his point. When Wyn looked back at the arglwydd, he had not moved, nor had Rhiannon nearby.

The abbot silently breathed an ardent prayer as Simon drew tight his noose of words, ending his sermon with a prayer that asked the Almighty to have mercy on whatever sinners might be among the congregation. He loudly asked for divine forgiveness for laboring on this holy day of Martinmas and went on to claim special blessing on labors that must be completed. He finished with a modest reference to the departed monk.

Simon relinquished the service to Father John.

"Let us pray," the old man whispered, facing his congregation with open arms. He led the Christians in the Credo and Prayers of the Faithful, in which he mentioned Brother Ely. The carver had already added another wooden cross to the summit burial ground, but the brother himself had been encasked with the precious hive thrumming inside him. Madoc had the cooper brass-bind the cask lid in place but knock out a bunghole egress for the bees. Brother Ely would have to wait to be buried until the hive found another home.

Wyn only gave Simon a sad, long glance as he returned to the sidelines near the crude sacristy, but the other would not hold it. They stood watching as John began the Offertory and his private prayer.

"Sanctus, sanctus, sanctus..." the old man chanted into the upping breeze. He blessed the wine and bread and took into his huge, work-callused hand the big wafer and broke it.

Brian rang the bell, a peculiar sound on the soft air, and the old priest elevated the host.

Wyn was deep in prayer at this moment symbolizing the transformation of the bread into his Lord's body, but Simon tugged his arm, interrupting the abbot's meditations. He looked up to see that Simon was gesturing at someone in the crowd. He seemed frantic to speak but would not dare during this sacred moment, trying to get Wyn to see what had him so excited.

"The woman," he hissed, and Wyn saw that Rhiannon's head hung despite the elevation of the Host, when all eyes should be upon the hands of the celebrant. The usually dramatic moment was heightened by the glow of the sun streaming down from the sky behind the venerable priest, whose eyes glimmered with the glare and with tears of joy as he turned back to consecrate the wine and elevate the chalice to the breathy chant from the congregation of the great amen, then began the Lord's Prayer.

Wyn was relieved to see that the Welshmen, including Madoc and Rhiannon, though separately, came forward to accept consecrated bread from the priest. Rhys behind him took a step, marking his next with his staff. Wyn saw the poet might trip, so he took his elbow and gently guided him across the scree to the aisle of sand, where Rhys made his own way to the altar.

When Wyn returned to stand beside Simon, he felt the man's pent-up fury like a banked fire and gently laid a restraining hand on the Frenchman's arm, locking eyes with him.

Wyn heard John's words, "Go, the Mass has ended," and his murmured blessing as the monks sang another hymn and the people dispersed. Madoc was already striding away across the sand, with Ari and several of the men around him.

The Norsemen had turned aside with Madoc when he reached their position. Yngvild, her belly huge, lingered to speak to Mary privately in passing.

"You were unwise to ignore my order," Wyn said behind Simon, who watched the women. He searched for Rhiannon, but she slipped away after Communion. "I forbid you to preach again."

Simon was not a member of St. Brendan's and therefore not under the authority of its abbot. But his mission to Gwynedd had placed him where he found himself, an outsider among this community where Wyn as elected abbot outranked him, a mere envoy from the Bishop of Canterbury.

"I could not in good conscience abstain from my duty," Simon said in French. John approached them, with a knowing look at Wyn and a shake of his head, allowing Brian to help him disrobe. They folded away the garments and replaced them in the trunk that had served as altar.

Simon took off his own vestments, withdrawing his gaze from the Norsewoman and speaking directly at Wyn. "I will take whatever penance to make up for my sin of disobedience."

Now he stood before the abbot in the roughspun cassock of a common brother, the trappings of grandeur removed. He bowed his head, but there was no meekness in him.

"Are you determined to murder yourself?" Wyn asked, finally exasperated beyond his usual calm.

"You would be a martyr, eh?" said John, still dreamy from ecstasy as he plucked salt grass from the hem of the chasuble.

The religious as a group moved away from their sandy sanctuary, leaving Brian behind to put away the holy vessels, the weighted silver candelabra, the chalice and crucifix. Lovingly he set the sacred book back into its leather case and shut the trunk, throwing a heavy square of sail material over it that would keep out all but the heaviest rain.

"Did you see her refuse to look at the Host?" Simon demanded through tight lips. "She is some sort of witch, I tell you. She dooms us all."

Just then Yngvild, arm-linked with her craggy father, crossed their path and could not help but hear Simon's voice.

"Even the gods must die," Yngvild said, echoing the grim religion of her people, which saw little hope for mankind in the face of eternal indifference. Her teeth hurt her, but she smiled with her lips pressed shut and shook her head, moving on toward the work she had left to watch the Christian rite. She had never watched a Mass before, had avoided such in fact, and except for the cooperative and timely sunlight, was unimpressed.

"Godless harlot," Simon spat at her back.

"Not godless, priest," she said in her thick accent, taller than he and not about to back down. "A god I have. Mine religion is older and nobler than thine, Christian, and mine god knew the earth a thousand years ere your weakling Christ bled into desert places."

Wyn held Simon's arm, asking Yngvild, "How is it woman, that you have not taken the Christ as have your more sensible kinsmen for two hundred years now?"

She did not have enough of his language to explain that like other wives of Madoc and Fair Beard's crew, she had been living in Dublin only while they finished the new ship. She was from remote northern islands where the new religion had not reached, though some of her family had taken the cross. Among them was not her father, who spat and shoved Simon to the ground when he saw the priest step toward her.

"Do not waste your strength, father," she said in Scandinavian, and the old man let her draw him back from the Frenchman, who was scrambling to his sandaled feet as he growled at her, "Leave this holy place at once, and do not ever come to our Mass again unless you mean to accept the true faith."

"Red-bearded Thor does not go down like a sheep but fights the good fight until there is no more in him to fight, the god of the cold, the god of fierce men and fiercer women."

"You will burn in hell with him, then. What you have seen here today could save your heathen soul if you would but hear."

"Another time, brother, when you are cooler," Wyn advised when he saw the Norsemen stop behind Madoc at the sound of the Frenchman's unmistakable voice. He tried to draw Simon toward the western beach, but Simon pulled back and shook him off.

"And you, brother," he railed at Wyn, "you are a hindrance in God's work here—you with your mindless kindness."

Wyn stopped short, wide-eyed at this as the Norsemen ranged themselves behind Fair Beard's very pregnant woman. She gave them a sign and spoke to them in their own language, saying this was nothing to worry about—we must get away from these crazies. Her father spat out words that seemed to disagree with her, but she only smiled at him.

"This priest is no trouble to me, brothers," she assured the warriors, and turned her back on Simon as she walked away.

Dag, who had let his beard grow out, thrust his chin into Simon's pale face and breathed out a warning in his unintelligible language, then turned with his men following.

When all had gone, leaving only Wyn and Simon standing there, Wyn turned without words to stare at the priest. Simon must have realized he had attacked his only ally. He started to speak, but movement a few paces away caught his eye. Wyn looked into the eastern glare to see what had Simon's intense attention and saw Madoc standing a little way off where he had watched the proceedings, his features implacable stone.

Then, as though the decision were made, he turned and walked back down to the tasks he had set for them that day—to get the *St. Ann* ready to sail on tomorrow morning's tide.

Wyn threw Simon a last wordless look and hurried in Madoc's footprints, leaving Simon smoldering alone on the rise.

There was no arguing, of course. Madoc had decided that Simon would be nothing but trouble. Best to lose him now rather than have him raving later when they would need their attention elsewhere. Wyn argued that they needed the Frenchman as one of only a handful of their company who could read.

Madoc's reply was sardonic: "I can live with verbal poetry and scriptures if I must. Besides, I read. So do you and Rhiannon. Since the man considers himself more holy than we common mortals, let him follow his patron's *Rule* and stay here in humility where nothing can gainsay his holiness."

"Since when does a warrior know of *St. Benedict's Rule?*" Wyn asked, stopping in his tracks.

"I know enough to have it figured out that the Frenchman is a dangerous fool who escaped the enlightenment of his own religion," Madoc said without rancor. He waved a hand to indicate the fleshy dunes that surrounded them. "This will be his cave at Subiaco," he said, referring to the place where the saint achieved enlightenment. He snorted mirthlessly. "Who knows what mysteries will fill such an empty vessel?" His path toward his headquarters crossed that of Caradoc, whom he ordered to tie off two of the sheep: "Let one be a ram."

"But, sir, that leaves us only ..." He turned to count the remaining herd, several ewes and their lambs.

"Do as I say." Madoc did not feel he needed to explain that once, when Owen sent him disguised as a monk to France, he had studied St. Benedict diligently to learn how to appear credible. "I do not want to kill the Frenchman"—he looked back pointedly at Wyn—"just dedicate him to a higher cause."

He returned to work, at the moment the maintenance of his sunboard, which sand had infiltrated so that the movable arm was grinding. He had it on a crate at his headquarters, the parts dismantled. He was rubbing them with oil, about ready to reassemble the contraption.

Wyn knew argument was futile, so he left the arglwydd polishing his devices and made himself useful by helping his monks transport the ecclesiastical cargo to the eastern camp to be loaded aboard the *St. Ann* when repairs were complete.

All that afternoon black smoke rose above the *St. Ann* where the sailors lit their cauldron on a bed of sand, melted the old caulk, and rewooled it to apply in the cracks of the ship.

Madoc crawled around in the ship's underbelly trying to find any burst spruce-root ties, but the seepage had apparently been caught in time. No main members sustained any damage, exceeding Madoc's best hopes. Every task was finished by sunset, and everything salvageable was loaded by dark. Only a few items remained to be hauled aboard.

The feast was well deserved. Everyone had worked to exhaustion and was happy to finally be finished and to rest for an early start at dawn.

Wyn approached the Frenchman back on the western shore to appeal to him to beg for the arglwydd's mercy. Wyn said he was sure Madoc would accept such, but Simon said he would not beg for it, because it was a sin to implore any but God.

"Do you think he will not do it?"

"And risk hellfire?"

Wyn leaned back and sighed, seeing it was useless to importune. He called all the brothers to retrieve their belongings on the western shore and repair to the eastern camp, where they would spend the night and be ready for the early departure. Brian started singing vespers while they walked as a group toward a stain of red light on the southwestern horizon.

Wyn observed the clear bright evening with glittering points of stars, two bright ones very near the horizon, Mercury and Mars, a rare conjunction that augured ill for peaceful solutions. His hands itched. Wyn missed his hammer and anvil and longed in that sunset moment to be settled and firing his forge.

He lingered for one last word with Simon, who sat immobile on one of the two trunks that held sacramental vessels, staring at the west. "We are leaving you and the carver one of the ewes and two lambs."

Simon might not have heard.

"It is all we can spare."

Finally Simon begrudged a nod and remarked sarcastically, "My companions Maurus and Placio?" St. Benedict's solitude had been interrupted by those two, who wished to learn from him.

"It is pride, you know, Simon, that imprisons you here. All you have to do is implore him. I heard Rhys intercede on your behalf. Even the lady asked the arglwydd to rescind his order."

Simon sat immobile.

Wyn heaved another sigh and turned to go. "Watch our sail," he suggested. "If I am able, I will cut a coracle loose for you."

Simon looked up sharply, surprised.

"Perhaps you can catch us later," Wyn added, not sure what would happen in that event, with the arglwydd's intentions.

"You forgive me for accusing you of mindless kindness."

"Of anything you could accuse, that is the least."

Simon regarded his hands when he said, "You are not an obstacle to God's work, Domme, and I am sorry I said you are."

Wyn nodded with the trace of a smile. "You see, you can say the same to the captain, and he will forgive you as I do."

"Only if I relent to his will, and that I will never do." His mouth all but disappeared.

"So be it," Wyn said, and hugged the unresponsive priest. "Farewell and God be with you, brother," he said, and walked away.

Simon watched the burly abbot diminish across the sand, then he relieved himself against a dune, opened the trunk, and proceeded to bury the heavy silver objects in the sand. It was dark when he climbed into the trunk, shut the lid, and pulled the embroidered vestments over himself. With his penknife he began pecking a breathing hole in the wall of his cramped cell and later was sound asleep, his head pillowed by the *Book of Genesis* when the brothers set the altar trunk in a coracle tied behind another Wyn himself paddled to the *St. Ann*.

Madoc and his crew did not sleep that night but worked until departure in the riggings of the *Horn*. They were all overjoyed at dawn that the column of smoke still stained the horizon. Madoc set their course directly for it, though he doubted it was Fair Beard's signal. It had to be some massive grass fire struck by lightning—at least, he thought, it is sure to be some sort of land over there.

The monks had voted to travel on whichever vessel the women did not. Madoc settled it by having all the women, including Huw's wife, aboard the *Horn;* Huw commanded a male contingent, though his Agnes grumbled at being removed from her quarters aboard the *St. Ann*, which was transformed into a sailing llan where Wyn wandered when nobody noticed and lingered just long enough to loosen the ox-hide strap holding one of the oblong coracles tied to the ship. Because their gaze was pinned to the southwestern horizon, none noticed it bobbing back there on the swell. Wyn looked up to see the low smudge that was the island; he could just make out a dark form there on the crest, which must be Simon.

"God be with you, stubborn brother," Wyn whispered, and threw a quick blessing on the little boat already lost in the tossing waves.

Chapter 13

*There would always be fear dogging
them in that place on account
of those who already inhabited it.*

*—Eiriks' Saga
Norse journey to Vinland
c. A.D. 900 (oral tradition)*

With Madoc in command of the first ship and Huw on the second, they followed the smoke all the first day. Soon it became obvious even to the civilians that the western mainland terminated. Madoc kept the conn busy; they were going against a current that bespoke a large body of water beyond that truncated blue horizon. Madoc was betting that it was a large gulf and that the land ahead was a peninsula.

The water very rapidly changed color from the deep blue of the ocean to a translucent aquamarine that reported a sandy bottom. The stuff their scoop brought up contained the debris of beaches and freshwater streams feeding mud and water-tossed pebbles into the larger body of salt water. But the color was apparently as much a factor of the water's clarity as of the draught, because they still had several fathoms below their keel. As they moved southwest, however, the water took on another color—a thick, warm, soupy green.

That night they dropped anchor near a similar island to the one they had left, this one's shore a mangrove stronghold. Madoc ignored it, for they had taken water from the island and he did not want to waste time. But he could not likewise ignore Wyn who, uninvited, took a coracle between the ships to approach Madoc again that evening at sunset.

155

Under a clear moonless sky they carried on low conversation at the forwardmost point of the ship. The cool air was full of smells of oatcakes cooking on deck braziers where hot stones were kept racked for that purpose. Nobody heard their words, but everyone knew what the abbot said angered the arglwydd.

Despite that, several overheard him invite the abbot to stay aboard for the night instead of journeying back over dark waters.

Wyn thanked him but seemed reluctant. Madoc figured he was kneeling to excessive duty—to be with his community—but actually none of the religious wanted to spend much time aboard a ship that had not been christened with a Christian name. Wyn departed finally, Brian paddling him back across the placid water to the *St. Ann*, leaving Madoc standing at the prow, where he stayed until the midnight reading of the stars.

The second day the smoke was gone, but they made for the point where he had seen it relative to his sunboard. They used the wind to cross a strong northerly current that hugged the coastline in these waters. This took them around the peninsula and due north along a swampy coast that offered no landing site, though everyone craved to go ashore. Madoc pushed on, however, tacking against a wind strong enough to overcome the coastal current.

After noon, when Caradoc shaved Madoc on deck, he drew blood. Normally mild about such things, Madoc only winced amid Caradoc's profuse apologies. But when he nicked him a second time, he swore and threw away the wiping towel from his shoulder.

Evan and Ari looked across the desk at the arglwydd wiping blood from his cheek. "Are you trying to kill me, man?"

"Lord, no," Caradoc backed away, but he said, "Though it does cleanse the blood," as Rhiannon deftly relieved him of the razor and proceeded to continue the job.

"My blood is clean enough," Madoc said, closing his eyes against the glare and against the woman who pressed so close.

"I long to be on solid ground," Rhiannon said, her hand sure as it strummed his cheek.

But to Madoc's eye the coast was far from satisfactory, a

larger version of the dismal island behind them, a solid wall of mangrove swamp as far as they could see.

Later, to please her, he took out a coracle to hunt for a landing but found only the gray-green leaves and the fat boles of the trees, rooted like distorted stalking men in the shallows.

Dispirited, he and two men returned to the ship for a supper of fish boiled over low coals in a bed of sand in the braziers. With it they finished off Teleri's cold sausages.

The next day the two ships continued sailing north against the current but with a prevailing sou'westerly that gave them good passage with the soggy mainland to their right, and no sign of the column of smoke they had seen before.

William the Saxon and a couple of the Norsemen were bringing in sea turtles, hanging out over the water and making a sport of it with bow and arrow-line. He had brought in three small ones, but hardly enough to fill the huge company kettle.

Then they caught what at first looked like a big one. When one of the crew spotted the round coracle, ragged and sinking near a headland with a white beach, they did not recognize it at first. Upended, the boat appeared to be one of the creatures, albeit the largest they had spotted since entering the shallow zone.

They caught it with a hooked pole and brought it dripping to the deck, expecting to have a single huge soup that night from this giant alone and much disappointed to find they caught something else entirely. Madoc stood there looking down at the busted craft, undoubtedly a roundish wicker-and-skin canoe, brother to one of several hanging over their own ship's sides.

Silently Brother Wyn peered down at the dilapidated craft, waterlogged and turning, as unprotected leather does in water, to glue. He thought at first report that it might be the coracle he secretly cut loose for Father Simon, but looking at this nearly perfect round shape now, he realized it could not be the one he cast adrift, which was of the oblong two-man variety. He breathed easier and prayed silently for the other's survival.

There was no doubt it was one of several coracles Fair Beard had taken into these waters.

"It could have been caught up from its moorings and lost without their knowing it," someone commented behind him.

Madoc was more cynical. Whatever craft Fair Beard

captained, he never parted from it willingly. The coracle was
beyond repair, so after he stared at it long enough, he walked
away, and the men threw it back into the unnaturally green
sea.

A stronger wind than the current took them up the coast
past bright beaches and still lagoons full of bird calls. Wil on
the rudder watched the prospect slip by as though he expected
a hostile act from the low land itself. He kept three men
sounding at all times.

The crew worked at the lines coiled like great snakes on
the forward deck, while the women set up a sewing circle aft.
There spindle-whorls danced, humming like insects, and
needles flashed in the bright humid air. Gwen fussed with the
dovecote, making sure it was secure in its moorings beneath
the mast. The dove had laid eggs last night, two fat pearls, so
their mistress was concerned that the cage rode easy.

With the whisper of hempen line folding and thumping
behind him, Madoc stood picking his teeth with a broom
straw, leaning against the rail staring at the uninviting mainland, where huge white-and-pink long-legged birds with arched
bills shrieked as they dived to snatch up frogs or fish.
Nothing but swamp, he thought morosely as Rhiannon joined
him.

"At least it is some sort of land," she said.

"Fair Beard would not have stopped here."

She regarded the mangrove jungle where calls of exotic
birds echoed over the water and through the steamy haze
that appeared to rise up from the boggy shore, giving the air
a pearly glow.

"Where do you think we are, brother?"

Madoc held his hands just so, with his fingers spread to
make it seem he held an invisible ball in both hands. He
wiggled his left thumb. "About here, I should think," he
answered.

Then, not without some humor, he tapped his right pointing
finger up on the eastern shoulder of his sphere. "The Isles of
Britain," he explained, and with a wiggle of his thumb, "The
Fortunate Isles are this knuckle. I suspect we are on a part of
Africa that curves around the other side of the world."

Beyond them a slim beach widened and lifted to become a slim
headland, behind which a wide scoop of a bay was revealed—
Madoc took them into deeper water when he saw the peninsula ahead, which defined the outer edge of the lovely double

harbor that men would someday name Tampa Bay. To Madoc's eye it was all too low-lying and swampy looking.

"The Antipodes," Rhiannon laughed a light musical sound. Several heads, including Mary's, raised at this note, censure in a glance or two, but nobody spoke with Simon so recent a memory.

Madoc heard in Rhiannon's laughter a landlubber's stubborn ignorance. He realized his beautiful sister was a flatlander—she had gone on this ridiculous journey believing she was heading for her doom over the edge of the world. To her just being alive at this late date was a miracle, so everything must be tinted with the color of wonder in her eyes.

"Yes, the Antipodes," he said, repeating the word that meant the opposite side of the world—a mere mythology to Rhiannon, who had probably read the word in a bestiary written by a long-dead monk in some crumbled scriptorium . . . that was what this journey meant to her. He had a sudden clear picture of how it must be to her or anyone used to spending their days on dry land.

To him this journey was but another of many to a part of the world he was long accustomed to thinking of as round. It took only ordinary optimism for himself to be here on this deck, his natural home territory in any direction.

But to Rhiannon and the others this was a venture into the true unknown. For a while he could forget Owen's shadow, which Simon's accusation laid between him and this beloved woman.

Realizing her courage made him love her all the more until he felt near to bursting, to do this thing that had brought her to the verge of what was probably her worst nightmare.

It must be especially fearsome to a pregnant woman, he thought, unpleasantly reminding himself of the child. The doubt returned. Perhaps she was guilty, as Simon accused.

"Why not a new land altogether?" she asked, still playful. "Why does it have to be part of some known place? I mean, if we are truly on a world-ball as you say, why not a new part as yet undiscovered?"

"One need not multiply possibilities," he replied, somewhat taken aback by her reasoning. This would be a strange thought for a tough mariner to have, a leap into the true unknown, much more so for a soft-footed woman from a king's court. "Africa I know of." He huffed a dry, humorless laugh. "A new land altogether I must imagine."

She smiled without reply, but her thoughts continued; she did not want to provoke the sound of shortness she heard in his response. This man did not choose to imagine when he could know.

To press his point he continued, "I wager we find black men like Ari somewhere over there—" He gestured vaguely southwest, where no land could presently be seen. "Since this place is most likely some outermost flank of Ethiopia. We are in some southern gulf or bay of immense size. If we had sailed around toward the east side of that peninsula"—he indicated the rising mainland to starboard—"then we might have found the pepper fields of India, which might be our ancestors' Vitromannaland after all."

"Not possibly the fabled Atlantis?"

Madoc shrugged. He would never put much stock in that story as old as the Greeks, because he had seen no evidence. "Then why not Paradise itself?"

She regarded the shore, a low and simmering stew of weird crowded trees that had no proper branches but naked trunks with spiky crowns where garish birds explored here and there in pink shrieks. Closer, a pale line of mottled surf barely stirred the slimy green water, which put forth a miasma of loaded swampy smells and airs buzzing with insect songs.

Wryly she replied, "I daresay it is not Paradise."

They watched together as the steamy land seemed to slither by. "I thought you went this way once with Fair Beard."

He had sincerely kept the secret as Snorrison wished, telling only Owen, and him only recently. "How did you know about that?" Madoc asked, rubbing his right wrist, which had been bothering him. Since he broke it a while ago, it often ached dully before a change of weather.

She regarded him before she spoke. "Our father always talked things over with me."

This clouded his mind further with its implications, but he would never voice them.

"Besides," she said when she saw him withdraw, "Rhys has been singing the song to the men."

"What song?"

"It is a good thing, brother. Some of them doubt you."

"Well, it is true we sailed west a long time ago until we came to some sort of land, but it was not this place." He stared at the swamp. "It was cold, even in summer. Ice was in the sea, and we hopped past many islands to enter the wide mouth of a river. We cut trees and took them back to Dublin. Made a fortune that trip, but it was a place much closer to Britain than this. We have sailed twice as far and still do not know if this is a mainland."

Rhiannon was intrigued by his version of the adventure, though Rhys's song had made it much more exciting.

The sun climbed higher, crashing down on their heads with cymbal clarity, bleaching out colors and stinging the eyes. But Madoc had noticed how quickly clouds were gathering in the southern quarter. That and the aching wrist meant some weather.

After a while she broke his reverie: "As fine and good a man as he is, I do not want to marry Rhys ab Meredydd," she whispered. Then so softly that only he and the wind at their backs, smelling of ozone and rain, could hear, she said,

"I have changed my mind, lord. I would be with thee."

He could not speak, could not even look directly at her so heavy was this confession. A year ago, a week ago, two nights past most certainly he would have taken her without hesitation, no matter whom he had to battle or abandon to accomplish it, but now, now, with Owen's shadow looming between them, all he could do was glance at her abdomen.

Frenchman Simon was right about one thing; she was definitely pregnant. Madoc wondered how he could have missed it. He groaned with the pain this caused him, even though he did not believe it was his father's get—that was a lie from a priest who would turn men into sexless servants of Rome, and who had been preparing to oppose Madoc's taking of this woman to wife.

Madoc did not want to believe. Owen might take a distant cousin, but his daughter—never.

Neither Owen nor Rhiannon could be guilty of that, Madoc's reasoning told him. Yet, she would take him, her half brother. And, who's child was it, and why would she not say?

She was watching him as he gently shook his head. "Do not make me be the strong one all alone," he said, quoting her, putting coals in her ears. When he chanced to look up, she had turned away so that neither he nor anyone aboard could see her expression. She was very still leaning against the rail above the humps of the coracles lashed to the sidestrakes.

"It was a frightened woman who said that to you," she said without looking up, "one who had not sorted out her feelings."

"This enterprise demands firm decision." It sounded lame to him, but he could not speak his mind without wounding her.

"As arglwydd you may do as you will."

"As father did?" He had not meant to hurt her—how could the question wound if the answer was no? But he knew it pierced her that he would question her. It was doubt that did the damage.

She appraised him without emotion, but like the neutral color of her eyes, which contained all colors while appearing to have none, her cool glance held many shades of feelings. Her cloudy eyes darkened—perhaps it was an effect of her lashes lowering or the sky darkening from the south, where the sudden storm brewed—he could not tell. It distracted him because he was thinking they would have to outrun the lowering tempest.

He was immediately sorry for having tried to force a denial from her, but he had to know. It worried at him now like a splinter under a thumbnail.

"Just tell me who the father is. I will keep your secret."

"Will you have me, then?" She met his eye, detecting Owen in him, in the fullness of the lip and the half-dreamy eyelids, in his darker more compact version of the family type.

"Tell me it was Gwalchmai . . . I will understand."

She cast her glance down at the waves licking the waterline, and said, "If you love me, you will not force me to break a vow."

Did she not see that to hold out lent doubt he could not ignore? But apparently this was not as obvious to her, because she said with her face away from him, "I swear to the Virgin it is not Owen's baby."

Well, that was something, he thought, but not enough. "But if you love me as you say, you would give me this small thing I ask, since it will be my child to raise."

"Is my word not good enough?"

He chewed on it, found no answer that tasted right, but because he could not wound her further, he said, "I believe you."

"You have let the priest poison you against me."

"If it were only you and I, there would be no question. I own the duty to all these people. Wyn is right when he says the women and children are in danger."

She seemed to shiver slightly, clutching herself. She saw the way Dag and the other Norse sailors hung around Yngvild. She knew of their oaths to Snorrison, which tied them with Yngvild's protection in his absence, but as a woman was sensitive to the undertone of loose male attention. She had caught a couple of sly glances her own way from more than one of Madoc's sailors when he was not around.

"A storm is coming," Madoc said after a while, turning to shout to Wil who had been eyeing the sky, too. The hands rolled out a huge canvas they lashed over the hold to catch rainwater.

Rhiannon drew the woolen mantle around her shoulders and left the deck.

Below, it was gloomy with the hold covered. Cracks of dull gray light shown around the edges—not enough to see. Someone had a shell lamp aflame that filled belowdecks with a soft light. The civilians had found their spots and settled down. Rhiannon picked up the shell lamp and threaded her way between bedrolls to the place where her loom hung from the ship's rafters. Crates and bales of wool had been shoved back into this portion of the hold to make room for passengers. She dragged a barrel back from the bulkhead, where it had been pressing against the tapestry.

She had not worked on the weaving for a long time, since before the island. About a fourth was begun of the total work, woven from the top, a thin, strong weave too tight to be a blanket. She touched the threads of silk and wool that formed the top of a design. It was a project she had been working on for some time, a red-dragon pennant to fly above Madoc's household when he was off the ship. She and Teleri filled many hours on the voyage with the weaving so far. Now the work had cooled—her fingers were trying to remember it as she touched the weave, longing to return and finish it. The stones at the end of each vertical warp thread clattered with the slight toss the storm gave the ship.

The heddle rod was covered with dust; when she tried to move it, she found it stuck. One of the men had draped a dirty tunic on the end of the rod, which served to change the twill of the cloth. She used the rag to dust off all the apparatus and the top of the weave, then threw it into the shadows aft.

She led a dark woof strand though the weave where she

had abandoned it weeks ago, then was aware that someone stood nearby.

"I could help, if you want me to." It was Gwen stepping from the shadows.

Rhiannon finished the line, beat the weave upwards with the edge of her hand, and looked over her shoulder. She was accustomed to thinking of Madoc's daughter as a child. At Owen's house she was not interested in weaving or other women's pursuits but was always out in the stables with the horses and dogs, or up in the rafters with the doves.

Now Rhiannon could see changes that the press of events had kept her from seeing in her niece. She was dressed in a linen shift with a coarse wool shawl around her shoulders. Her curly red hair was tied back but still blazed around her face, refusing to be held down.

"Will you teach me?" Gwen moved in closer, stepping around to the side so that she would not throw a shadow between the lamp and Rhiannon's hands on the weave.

"From now on I will need three pairs of hands to do it right," Rhiannon answered, indicating the two sides of the dark background and the center red that would be the dragon. "Your offer is timely—of course I will teach you."

Staring at Rhiannon, Gwen sat with her legs tightly together on the short barrel, seeming to draw into her own center. "It will be good to get off this ship and into a regular house," she said, watching as Rhiannon doubled the thread where it touched the red weave, then begin to take it back to the outside border of the pennant. She took the thread back on another course, readjusted the hank of the line, and found a knot in several cables. She brought the coil of wool thread with her and sat near Gwen in the puddle of light.

"I hate being cooped up on the ship," Gwen said, leaning forward, hugging herself.

Rhiannon began separating the knotted skein, listening for what the girl was not saying between her words.

"Everyone is so tense. Nervous."

"It will be good to be settled on land."

"My father is a bear. He has not spoken to me in weeks except to tell me to get something or to get out of his way."

"He has so much responsibility for all of us."

Gwen scowled and picked at a splinter of the roughly made barrel, twisting and pulling at it until it split off the stave.

"I do not think he loves me anymore at all."

Rhiannon let her hands rest on the wool as she looked at the girl's eyes, blue and smoldering in the pale light. She saw none of the father in the daughter, only traces of her mother, whom Rhiannon had not known well. Madoc had married the daughter of a Mona Isle freeholder, a commoner outside Rhiannon's sphere in her father's official household. But this girl stayed with Owen often because she had been his favorite grandchild among many. And because of her favored position, being a motherless child for the past two years, she ran wild.

"I suspect you are the only human being your father does truly love, Gwyneth."

The girl shook her head, catching reflections in her brilliant hair. "No, he does not let me kiss him anymore. I tried to hug him good morning, and he turned away." She looked down at her huddled body, her bare feet and work-rough hands.

Rhiannon reached up and touched her hair. "He sees that you are changing. This happens between fathers and daughters."

"I want it to stay the same."

"You are not staying the same. It is difficult for him because he thinks of you only as his little girl, but look at you." She flung back Gwen's shawl.

Shyly, Gwen said, "The blood is coming again." She pressed the heels of her hands into her abdomen and rocked. "I can feel it starting deep down here, worse than the first time."

The girl's menses had begun in the middle of the ocean. Rhiannon taught her how to use wool to pad between her legs, but Gwen had a miserable week of it.

"Probably not. Everyone has some pain. Walk a lot—that is what I do."

Gwen had seen Rhiannon pacing around the upper deck. She had walked the length and breadth of the island. It seemed that she could not stay in one place too long.

"Gwen," Rhiannon said seriously to catch her glance, "do not blame your father. He is a good man. Everyone watches what he does—you know how the priests harassed your grandfather. . . ." Rhiannon did not say your grandfather and I, but that was her meaning. "Madoc does not want to see you growing up because he would keep you a child forever out of love. It confuses him that the cute little girl with the curly hair is almost a woman who will be taking a husband soon."

Gwen's eyes glistened.

"My grandfather would never act so cold to me."

"He was your grandfather. . . ." The words cut Rhiannon, to put Owen in the past like that, all the more so because she was sure she would never see him again. "But your grandfather reacted to my growing up in the same way. Later we became friends. That will happen with you and your father, too."

Gwen shyly looked down at her hand in her lap. She knew the gossip, but she also knew that it was not true.

"Do not force him, and he will come around after all this worry is off him, after we settle down."

She regarded the knotted skein in her hand, which Gwen took without asking, working at the tangle from the other end.

"Do you mind if I work with you for a while?"

They felt the ship tilt in the wind around them and together leaned over the work for the first time in weeks.

By then half the sky was sulfurous yellow, dark with the squall, high and boiling in a fierce wind on the southern horizon that threw lightning bolts around within the hour. Unable to outrun so sudden a storm, they could but tie down and wait it out. They took in the sail and dropped anchor behind a modest headland—Huw on the second ship had seen it, too. Like every place else here, it was low country, but behind a finger of land that curled north they found some shelter from the western winds.

They were getting battered, though the men had the sail down and tied in plenty of time. Madoc was used to sudden storms at sea, but this one was unusually fierce in a brief time.

An hour into the thundering downpour, he crouched under his cloak in the tent he helped pitch on the watery deck, sharing the watch. Another small tent canopied the rudder on that side of the ship, where a team of two sailors took turns at the tiller. Wil and Evan were taking their sleep shift while he sat talking with Rhys, leaning near the flap where water poured just beyond them, drowning out their voices from their tentmates.

"I hate to give the clergy credit," Madoc was saying, "but he is right. What do you say, Storyteller?"

"I never thought to wed a princess."

"Well, titles hardly matter now."

"What does she say?"

"Nothing of the father. Says it is to protect the child."

"No, I mean about me."

"You will have to ask her," Madoc said with a chuckle, a halfhearted punch on the other's arm. He stared out at the drumming slants of rain. The main body of the storm was spent. The thunder and lightning had died, leaving only the silvery rain that lay down in thundering sheets behind a still-strong wind.

Rhys sat on a rope coil, cloak drawn around him, elbows on knees. His soft leather slippers were soaked and stretched to form exactly over his taut tendons and lean toes. He rubbed his face with his hands, slipping a finger under the sash as though it worried him. Leaning toward the flap, he massaged his temples with one finger of each hand, delineating circles.

"Sometimes I see colors," he said in a softened voice. "Strange, is it not? Colors I have no words for, colors I never saw when I had eyes. I get headaches, sometimes."

"Old friend, I am sorry. Has Caradoc a potion?"

"I would not cure it—the colors are beautiful."

The rain slacked off to a drumming innuendo. Rhys removed the harp from its case slung over his back and began idly to strum the same melody again and again, changing it here and there, as though it were something he was composing and had not finished. He sang only la-de-da, no real words, but his lips moved as though he were trying out a lyric. Madoc laid back against a rope coil and listened to the music and the rain.

He had a satisfying dream about which he remembered nothing when he awoke later in dripping, still darkness. The air was pleasantly damp, but the rain and the music had stopped. The sailor was asleep still, but Rhys's bedroll was empty, though still warm.

Madoc was glad to face the wind beyond the tent flap, where he found Rhys at the rail near the man on the rudder. Had Rhys not worn the sash, Madoc would have said he was watching the dark blur of the land beyond the glistening water that reflected back polished stars from a depthless sky. A few smudges of rain cloud sped off to the northeast. Otherwise the night was newly scrubbed and beginning to fill with the music of night bugs, too.

Madoc succinctly gestured at the pilot. It was an added precaution, though the ship seemed to be lined up fairly parallel to land, having drifted only a slight angle. Two anchors were holding with only some drag from the prevailing current. The sail was trimly fetched; not a single loose line or leather corner dangled. Around them timbers moaned softly in the gentle swell that sent palely luminescent breakers foaming timidly against the dark shore.

"Wake me if I ever fall asleep on watch," Madoc whispered.

"I could not sleep," Rhys commented. "You appeared to need it." The irony of a blind man taking watch was lost on Rhys.

"I must have," Madoc answered, leaning on the rail with him. "What was that you were playing? I have never heard it before, yet it sounded familiar."

"Something I have been working on," Rhys replied. "I will play it for you sometime—listen!"

The jungle was full of small sounds, and between it and them gentle waves washed the shore. The ship creaked around them in a slight chop. It was still a couple of hours before dawn.

"Some of the birds break at night," Rhys continued, inclining his head toward the land that burned a charcoal swath across their field of view, against the star-peppered sky and sloughing watery surface that rocked them gently.

"You hear them?"

Rhys nodded, still inclined to the vista. "They hunt."

Something on the breeze put a chill on Madoc's exposed arms. He sniffed, inhaling the combined smells of a low, fragrant land, birds, rotting things, and swamp gas. And something else.

"You smell it, too?" Rhys asked.

"Fire."

"A dry fire."

"A man's fire." In a swampland it must be either swamp gas or a kindled fire.

"Far away . . ."

"Or," Madoc said, "very small."

"Smells like evergreen."

"Fir, cedar."

"You have an educated nose, sir," Rhys said.

"Rhys," Madoc said in a changed tone that made the hackles rise on the poet's neck. "I see it yonder. A bright yellow flame with a white center—there, there—moving."

"Swamp gas?"

"This appears to burn hot—could be, but no, it flickers."

"Captain—" the sternman called without alarm from the opposite side of the ship. He had seen it, too.

"Yes, I see," Madoc answered. "It moves between the trees."

"A lantern or torch in a boat, Captain?"

"Perhaps."

Chapter 14

Karlsefni and his men raised their shields and they began trading. Above all these people wanted to buy red cloth. This they tied around their heads. They also wanted to buy swords and spears.

—Eirik's Saga
Norse journey to Vinland
c.A.D. 900 (oral tradition)

They sat like that, speaking low, Madoc keeping an eye out for another sign from land. The drip slackened among the lines. Every once in a while something over in the swamp would splash; the surf was down, and all sounds from land were amplified.

Morning dawned with a low cloud cover that had not burned off by noon when they picked their way along the now-westward curve of shoreline. They saw no further evidence of inhabitants, though each man on duty stared himself into a headache watching the shore. They could see that the strand was merely a long, low sandbar that faced the coast continuously along this stretch.

Beyond this narrow margin was more water, then some sort of coast they could see once in a while when the sandbar broke. But like a monotonous refrain, the sandy islands would take up again, affording too small a gate for a ship to pass through; the water looked too shallow. They could hear the surf breaking with a hollow voice a mile from the strand, a sign that the shallow, sandy bottom was a wide trap for their ship's deep keel.

Reluctantly Madoc passed up what looked like good harbors he caught tantalizing glimpses of beyond those bars.

The ship's belly was practically his own, an intuitive sense old sailors had confirmed for him. Sail long enough, and ship became skin. Too near a reef he could feel it in his own breastbone like indigestion and would have him calling out to make for deeper water. Wil had the same sensitivity. Madoc took it slowly, giving the pilot all the conning he needed.

It was on one of these swings out onto the choppy water of the larger body that the sandbar gave way to what was obviously a splendid harbor, the finest so far, with a healthy upland on its far shore. The gap between sandbars here was wide.

About that time the sun came out, highlighting the gateway. Gulls rang from a high breeze that pushed the clouds aside in patches, so that it was alternately a bright afternoon and a gray evening in the time it took to draw a single breath.

Madoc looked at all his officers, then gave the water-road a good appraisal from the mast. He glanced at the *St. Ann;* Huw was tacking now, watching what the commander intended. He, too, had been watching the harbor approaches, analyzing the gamble each one offered in terms of bottom clearance.

"Make for land," Madoc sang out finally when everyone had gotten a crick in their necks from watching him up there brooding.

Back down, and heading due north toward the opening, he confided to Wil, "Looks fine to me. We have a steady wind, and a wide, deep berth. I saw a couple of small islands to the northwest, a green shore behind them."

Through this the craggy-faced Wil gripped the tiller, staring out over the raddled water, where the sun blindingly bounced among the chop. He nodded without enthusiasm, hating that they were sailing without oars, which left them to the mercy of the wind and without much maneuverability—a dangerous situation when sailing coastal shallows. He told two young sailors to do some fishing as the commander had strolled to the prow to watch their progress toward the bay that was called even in those days by the people who lived upon it—Mobile.

The water was calm and very warm for November. Gulls lazily circled, calling to each other. Madoc and Wil and an informal committee of elder mariners discussed each bucket the conn brought up full of coarser sand mixed with mud now, full of the detritus from land—twigs, beach shells, and dead land creatures.

Land appeared to hold the entire northern and eastern quarters. Despite the healthy depth, they took the central channel of the water road, not daring to run closer to shore since they were without oars and would have to depend on the tide to get free. They were seamen who came from treacherous shores and did not trust this benignly smooth one. Their worse fear was to run aground on the sandy bottom, so Madoc kept them in dark green water well away from shore.

Now, behind them breaking against the low gateway isles they had passed, they could hear the heavy surf, long and hollow. Here in the green lagoon the swell was mild.

Madoc climbed the mast again, squinting through his curled hand. He found them entering a harbor about five leagues wide and funneling deeply into the verdant and low-lying land. He could only faintly see the far northern shore beyond the green water and the aching blue of the sky where a platoon of fluffy clouds slouched in from the west.

He would guess that this bay was at least seven leagues long and by the looks of it was the embouchure of several streams that drained higher northern ground.

From above he could see the darker green of the midchannel running up the mouth of this bay, and it was into that maw he ordered his ship. Behind him was the *St. Ann* a half league off.

The mild wind whisked them past several small islands to the west and into calm waters. The funnel was narrowing now—perhaps two leagues shore to teeming shore. He could hear insects or something wheezing from landward, and no surf.

Ahead appeared the first sandy tendrils of a large island with water on either side, which Madoc surmised were the mouths of twin rivers. Their currents poured muddy stains out into the salt water of the bay. The island looked stable between the two streams, heavily forested toward its central height with commodious pink beaches piled with driftwood roots, the rookeries of seabirds, and a silvery strange growth that looked like beards blowing in the warm breeze.

A pelican lifted off a trunk and flew directly over the *Horn* as if curious, then veered off to the southwest and open water.

Madoc had to remind himself this was November. On either shore of the isle itself there was little indication of the season. The wall of a thousand green shades was solid—the evergreen of cypress, weird and otherworldly, with the whiskery long silver moss growing on living and decaying trees alike.

Madoc called orders to put the *Horn* to anchor. Another look at the *St. Ann* reassured him that Huw knew what to do as he saw the first ship begin to swing about, perhaps a furlong from the sandy tip of the river-isle. A gesture to a sailor for assistance, and he hoisted a flag to signal the captain of the *St. Ann* to cross over to the command ship.

Passengers and what crew were not at the anchors and the sail pressed close to the landward rail, remarking with joyous voices the beauty of the island that lay before them. Madoc was about to return to the deck when he was arrested by Einion's cry.

"Oh—look!"

A flock of what appeared to be a million birds, passenger pigeons, was breaking from the forested isle, rising like smoke to darken the sky for more than a minute.

Madoc watched in wonder with the others. He gave Gwen a long smile—so much for her fear that there would be no doves here. As he descended, his higher view afforded a glimpse of a stag's white tail and red haunch bounding into the river to vanish on the far shore. What could be spooking the game?

The sail slid down, hissing and thumping, the men sang their relays as they tied down, and the people cheered Madoc when he dropped barefoot to the deck. He beamed in their goodwill, red-cheeked and suddenly shy, and hurried to watch the maneuvers from several positions before they appeared in place. Then he turned to the civilians, who wanted to land immediately.

"First we take a look around," he said, pointing out individual men to accompany him. They took up light arms and smartly broke out a coracle and prepared a landing party according to their time-honored procedures. "If we find it safe, then tonight we feast in our new home!"

They went wild with cheering and stamping as Evan handed Madoc his sword. Across the span of placid water between the *Horn* and *St. Ann,* the religious raised their voices in a hymn of thanksgiving soon taken up by both companies.

And over all the sawing insect song of the jungle echoed, pulsating, rising, and falling to reveal the single shriek of a bird or water lapping, then the drone would close in again, a squeezed green sound that planted an echo in the ear.

Wil came up briskly behind Madoc with word that a coracle with three aboard had just dropped from the *St. Ann*. Madoc walked to the other rail where Agnes, Mary, and the three boys were watching the oblong coracle approach with Huw's back to the *Horn*, Brother Wyn smiling upward from the opposite thwart in the glare of his pale cassock, and a bent-backed seaman between them paddling on his knees for all he was worth.

Madoc had not invited the abbot, but there was nothing that could be done about it now. He certainly did not need a counselor to plan what they were going to do next.

They simply could not go on. He had personally checked earlier to find their water supply down to one more day. Caradoc's larder was painfully bare, some oats, salted fish, a little more honey. He knew the *St. Ann* was running out of oats for the sheep who would be a day hence the last relief from fish.

This was it. He squinted at the island again, the thrumming of the forest creatures at a shrieking pitch.

He did not wait for the *St. Ann* contingent but took his shore party in three coracles to the curve of graveled beach.

It was a highly situated peninsula, in fact, with only a slim margin of western marshland, in all about five leagues north-south and about three east-west—wide enough to support a fair-sized lake. The local waterline was laced with many inlets where streams of fresh water flowed into either of the two rivers that embraced the isle. The western verge was swampy; the eastern gravelly and littered with sheets of boulders at the waterline of the river that lay about a quarter mile wide.

They found no trace of human habitation.

When they circled back to the headland, they started a bonfire signaling the larger company to disembark.

Amid great cheering, jubilation, hymn singing and all around congratulations, Madoc's Hundred scrambled from the ships and began to set up camp. They could not stop singing and calling to each other, as if this final disembarkation was not to be believed and they must continue confirming that they had indeed reached their destination.

Plenty of daylight remained, so Madoc organized teams to accomplish different tasks. Some went after fresh water, others began unloading the immediately necessary goods— bedrolls, cooking vessels, weapons, and personal gear.

Caradoc, with a fire going and his team of boys collecting driftwood, paddled out to the *St. Ann* to take a ewe. But Madoc despaired of killing one of their fast-dwindling herd, so he sent Dag out with bowmen to see if they could scare up another buck like the one he had seen making for the western mainland.

The hunting party strapped a coracle to the stoutest back and took off to reconnoiter. They ranged far up the peninsula, crossing the eastern river to the mainland that climbed into an upland, more favorable country for game since their arrival apparently had cleared the island of anything larger than a hare.

The isle itself was covered with cypress close to the marshy western verge. Later they would learn the local name for all this greenery—magnolia, pine, and holly marched up the loamy knolls that rolled back from the water, staked here and there with bare hardwoods, hickory, pecan, and an occasional oak or maple still hung with the bright red leaves of a late, lazy autumn. Beneath these the women found the ground littered with ripe nuts and brought back a hoard cascading from their apron skirts. Black grapes clustered lower branches and snarled vines. It was a warm afternoon, amazing for November to these northerners, but as the shadows lengthened, the air cooled to a chill that might mean frost in the morning. The women, their voices singing echoes in the still wood already entwined with woodsmoke, ambled back with their treasures.

Long before the sun angled pink and orange through the tuffed trees, the first of the hunters returned via the river, the boat loaded with a variety of game they dressed in the field—venison, pheasant, and a larger bird unlike anything they had ever seen, a turkey, which they would learn to appreciate.

Gwen, the pup kicking at her ankles, brought back blue-and-white cockles from the eastern gravelly river; Caradoc officiously gestured for her to dump them into the glowing coals to one side of the pit, where they had the largest of the deer carcasses spitted and already crackling over the flames. Frowning, he watched the shells sizzle and pop open, tonged out a morsel of the tender flesh, and flung it to Nona, who gobbled it up, then whined at the heat she had swallowed. But when she did not vomit after a few minutes, Caradoc pronounced the muscles edible.

Dag cheered Gwen and called her little huntress, which made her shy and forced a glare from Madoc. The Norseman paid too much attention to the girl, and his eye was leering when he thought nobody was looking.

Madoc deliberately stepped between them to help cut the meat. Dag caught the gesture but had sense enough to ignore it.

The hunters also brought back reports of what they saw on the mainland, something like a human-trod path through the forest, though no footprints confirmed the suspicion.

Madoc set out a heavily manned perimeter nonetheless and ordered the usual complement on the watches of both ships. The men grumbled but obeyed, taking with them their supper, the next-to-the-last skin of mead, and promises to be relieved after the customary four-hour shift.

He could not find it in himself to relax. It was as though his body had not received the message that the sea journey was over. While everyone worked, he paced, restless and without a specific task since he no longer commanded a sailing vessel. He growled to himself that it was damned early to be suffering port fever. But his worry had a more sinister inspiration. He could not accept that this rich country was not inhabited. Several times he started when a sound broke from the darkening jungle, expecting to see armed men step out into the giddy firelight.

They broke into groups while the poet played beside the fire. Agnes and Huw sat with Wil and Mary, the comfortable old marrieds, their boys slumped exhausted in bedrolls.

Einion was also fast asleep with his head in Teleri's lap while she sang with the others, and Yngvild lounged back, talking with Dag, while her father dozed with his head on her thigh, off in his own world, muttering, smiling idiotically.

Madoc narrowed his eyes at Gwen laughing at something Evan said. The girl glowed in the firelight, bright-eyed, uninhibited, and achingly lovely to her father's eyes. Instinct tightened muscles in his neck and hands when he observed the young man, his attention on the girl. But he sat apart from her, not too close.

Madoc leashed his instinct. It would be out of place if he made something of their innocent conversation with Edwin and Ffiona, who seemed healthier this evening in the light of their founding fire, and from the way she and Edwin leaned toward each other, they must have made up. The journey had put everyone on edge. Now, Madoc thought, they could settle in and return to normal. From here Madoc saw the glint of his golden coin at Ffiona's throat, and it pleased him, though he would not allow anything to lighten his gloom.

Rhiannon had been making music with Rhys earlier, but now she moved between the groups, lingering along the fringe of this one and that but not taking part in any conversation. Firelight gilded her as she ambled with the blue mantle pulled about her shoulders against the chilling air. She paused and looked around, saw Madoc staring at her, brooding in a way that reminded her with an ache of Owen, frowning off by himself. She subtly challenged his mood by placing herself between him and the fire.

He regarded her with an ache that the excitement of landfall had allowed him until this moment to suppress.

She stood above him with her fingers interlaced, thinking as she regarded him that he was beautiful in his own way. Not like a tapestry or a piece of music, but the way a rugged land could be beautiful, or a storm. Some men are plain, even ugly in youth, and only in maturity achieve a masculine beauty that could take a woman's breath away.

Such was Madoc's appearance to her at that moment as he leaned back against a mossy trunk, his dark hair and eyes deepened even further by shadows, his cheeks sunburned, his strong nose and chin made firmer by firelight on the sable lines of his mustaches. She did not remember him as a handsome boy. There was something brutal in his thick eyebrows and sultry lashes, his thicker lower lip that sometimes seemed to pout, his self-deprecating manner, the things that had drawn her to him.

She was close enough to see the double row of his upper lashes—a charming trait that cropped up in the native bloodline—and the feathery shadows these cast on the flesh below. She was so pale, all that was shadowy in the man beguiled her, just as her light bedazzled him.

Madoc set the trenchard aside, his food hardly touched.

He did not want to speak with her because of too much still unsaid. Besides, her presence stirred him; nothing had changed except his will. Again his body was of a different inclination; fleetingly he recalled the priest's remark about possession. Ignorant fool, he thought. Of course it was possession. He wanted to reach out and possess this woman this moment.

His action encouraged her to move closer, eclipsing the fire and placing herself in sharp silhouette. From his position her belly loomed as round as a dark moon, reminding him of too much.

He stood abruptly from the fallen tree Ari had appropriated with a thick rug for the arglwydd, and moved deliberately away from her toward Rhys, where he feigned interest in the song.

Rhiannon alone witnessed his rebuff. She stood there, then turned to get another sliver of meat from a roasted fowl.

The arglwydd's attention enlivened the music making. After a while he turned to Bjorn, who had awakened and was singing, though not the same song or tune Rhys was playing at the moment.

"You are the skald who recited the saga for me in Dublin—"

The old man was nodding, the angles of his face catching pockets of shadow from the flickering fire.

"Sing something about Vinland for us now."

Another nod, and a long, slow sip of mead. He closed his eyes; Madoc thought he was going to sleep, but he blinked and looked upward with his eyes closed, and to the left, his eyeballs moving under the blue, shuddering lids as though reading from their insides. "I know all the old stories."

"About Vinland?"

"Yes. I was never there myself, but—" His eyes snagged back and forth rapidly again, then slowed, and Madoc could trace their path moving as though following a moving object in his field of vision. "I was never there myself but was taught the songs." He was falling deeper into some kind of trance. His voice trailed off and then brightened suddenly with normal speech, though he continued with eyes still closed. "The stories are long in the telling, one for every night of the year."

"This is a good night to begin."

The old Norseman began with a droning keen, launching into a long version of the story of Eirik's journey to the country of the Skraelings—in Scandinavian.

Rhys found some chords that almost accompanied the song, but he was grinning with Madoc, who tried to stop the old man.

"Is no use, Captain," Yngvild said, patting her father's bony back. "Once he starts, he stops only when he falls over." The old man, oblivious to all now that he was singing, howled a long recitation about a series of landfalls from the Faroes, island-hopping across the North Sea. It was with these verbal maps of their sagas that the vikings had picked their way across the ocean, and how they remembered the way back, through long songs.

Yngvild began humming with old Bjorn, and when he was through with the mapping prologue and began the story of their landfall, she began a rough translation with Dag's help.

It was a wild story of landfall to cut mast timbers in a cold country inhabited by the red-skinned natives, who liked the milk given them by the the Norsemen and -women (for there were several women who accompanied those viking crews, one who bore the first European child in those regions). The Skraelings also liked the Norsewomen's red cloth, but only trouble came from them, so the Norsemen went back to Greenland with their stories.

As the night wore on, Madoc's Hundred returned to finish the food, drinking and feasting like demigods, some even to sickness, and sang as the fire simmered down.

Yngvild cried out in pain while eating the last of the oysters—she had found a knotty brown pearl the size of a fingernail, which had dislodged a front tooth already carried.

Caradoc recognized the scream of pain she flung out and remarked dryly that he would be glad to extract the tooth for her. She growled at him, sucking on her pain and pocketing her rustic jewel, which she considered a good luck charm.

The monks retreated to the *St. Ann*, where Wyn decided they would stay berthed until their llan could be established. He was elated to have already found the spot on the north side of the lake. Tomorrow they would start building their sanctuary, but tonight, with all the other religious on their ship, Wyn lingered with the main company. Late that evening, while the dark riverbanks sighed with innumerable small voices around them and the rest of the company bedded down, Madoc sat drinking a last cup of mead with the abbot, Rhys, and several of the men by the fire where they could watch the peaceful bay.

The two ships were silhouetted as one long, double-headed creature. Watch lamps on the vessels gave out blurred spots of orange glow that reflected in the dark, still water, where hung a trace of mist, and a sporadic westerly wind teased the forest tops and the pennants on the two masts gently lifting and dropping on the swell and under the spread of stars.

They had been talking about the different angles the constellations took at this latitude, intermittently discussing the heavens and this new land on which they sat.

"Edwin?" Madoc called, looking around. He wanted to take a reading, and the instruments were in the man's care. Few things had been offloaded. Only Edwin knew where the sunboard was.

Dag snickered. Madoc threw a questioning look around, but it was Rhys who answered, "He will be back in a while."

Evan made an embarrassed laugh, then said softly to Wyn, "Begging your pardon."

"No, no," said the abbot. "Why should they not enjoy the pleasures of the marriage bed?"

"The marriage bush, you mean!" Evan said.

"'Tis their reward," Wyn said, giving Madoc a slow eye.

Madoc ignored him.

"Fun to fight so you can make up," Dag said, elbow punching the man next to him.

With a glance back at the dark and humming forest, where several men were on lookout, he called to Ari, who was always close at hand. "I think you had better keep the sunboard from now on—Edwin will be glad to lose the responsibility."

The fickle breeze changed into a decisive north wind, which moved down through the forest to slap new life into the fire.

Madoc had noticed that Rhys was unusually quiet. The poet sat very still, his face toward the fire but one ear inclined to the tar-black wall of the forest.

When someone caught the arglwydd's glance into the shadows, the group fell into an eerie silence that Madoc felt compelled to break.

"What is it, poet?" he asked.

Dag stifled a sarcastic but nervous chortle. "Fairy folk in the grasses?"

The men grinned nervously, eyeing the woods.

"Did you hear something?" Madoc asked.

"There are seven levels of drone in the insect song," Rhys replied. "At least fifteen local voices, with many others farther out, and the pitch ranges from the highest note I can hear to the lowest. They are singing a complicated round."

He reached for the harp box; exposed, the strings rang with a faint sympathetic vibration to the jungle sound. He hit a single note, blending all the strings that quivered into the other sound like cold honey poured into boiling water. The drone subsided only momentarily as the creatures who made it absorbed the intruder, then picked up their score as though nothing had interfered. Rhys put the harp back into its case.

"Tree frogs," suggested Wil, familiar with swamplands.

"Crickets," another said.

"Cicada," suggested a sailor who had been as far south as Sicily.

"Tree frogs," Wil insisted. "Too late for bugs."

Madoc voiced his concern about prior inhabitants, but Dag reminded him that they had seen no sign of human beings.

"The path we found is most likely a deer trace," he suggested, since they had followed numerous tracks to their kill.

"And where is Snorrison?" Madoc said to keep the conversation going. "I cannot believe he would put in at any of the other bays we passed." He shook his head. "No, he would have stopped at the first good harbor with a decent approach through those narrow sandbars, which is this one." He idly tossed a twig into the fire, then another he stripped from a stout branch, the tip of which he shoved into the glowing coals.

"Safe for a coracle and safe for the *Horn* are two different harbors," Dag replied. "He might not have had a choice."

"Maybe he had to land because of storm," Wil thought out loud, recalling the battered coracle they mistook for a turtle.

"Or sharks," someone suggested.

"And what about the smoke?" Wyn asked.

They played with what they knew and what they speculated, tossing both back and forth like that until Madoc threw a final twig into the coals and made a move.

Ari, behind him, was quick to offer to refill his cup from the meadskin, the last from their now empty larder. All that remained were three sacks of oats and the strange honey from Ely's cask, which nobody cared to eat.

"No, thank you," Madoc said, standing to stretch, and,

when he saw the dark fellow wanted to help him at whatever he meant to do, added, "Some things I must do for myself."

He dropped his hand to Rhys's shoulder, knowing the poet had been quiet because what he had to say would be to Madoc alone.

"Well," Wyn said, standing, "I believe I will join my brothers on the ship," and said good night to all as Madoc stood and stretched.

Evan and Huw glanced up—did he want an escort?

He shook his head. "But keep an eye out," and took up the glowing brand as he walked away with the poet. When they were at the eastern bank, Rhys confirmed Madoc's persistent suspicion:

"Someone is watching us."

Chapter 15

The court of Pengwern is a raging fire.
The hall of Cynddylan is dark tonight,
Without a hearth, without a bed.
I weep a while, then fall silent.

—by Llywarch Hen
Welsh
c. A.D. 700

T hings might have been different if the one who watched had not seen the strangers piss in the river. It was such an ignorant, shocking thing to do, a thing small children of every nation were taught not to do with lessons of pain—and among red nations corporal punishment was generally not used on children.

Rhys had heard more than a bug choir in the woods. He also smelled something, but fleetingly, because when the wind changed the one who watched moved, slipping into the eastern river just below the boulders among watercress and reeds, the surest place to hide his scent. This is where the watcher had crossed to the island earlier, a spot well-known to be too close to the brackish water of the bay for the tastes of the tribe of alligators lodged along softer, sweeter banks upriver.

It would have never occurred to the watcher why the two white men were coming to the water. Below the rocks he had a good view of them crunching over gravel without stealth beneath the glare of the torch the taller of them held high.

If the watcher had not already had some small experience with similar strangers, he would have been lost in their strangeness so that the two might not seem human to him at all. But recent experience reminded him that these whites were

183

human, they breathed as humans, bled and died as humans, with the same reactions to extreme pain as any red man.

They were not spirits; they were human, but very strange.

It seemed to the watcher that the subject between the two had changed. Earlier they exchanged short comments; now the taller man spoke quietly, pausing now and then as though trying to convince the other of something that might be disputed. The blindfolded man did not reply, so the first continued speaking in what could only be a voice of friendly, patient coaxing.

Their language was unintelligible, stranger even than Cherokee to the watcher, who had fluency in two languages and a jumble of dialects spoken in the valleys of these two rivers and their tributaries. But not one word of what these strangers said could he understand. It was coarse gibberish, full of harsh inflections different from the watcher's singsong language, which depended less on the tongue and more on pitch for subtle meaning.

Another strange thing was their color. These people were not red. They tended to be white-skinned, which turned pink in the sun, but with white skin like that on the belly of a fish or a deer. Throughout the day he spied on them he had seen under the clothing of the others where the One Above did not shine. Their blood showed through their pale skin, making them look bluish. In his own mind the watcher called them white-bellies, and except for the young female among them who had caught his eye, he considered them thoroughly ugly.

Then there was their hair, as much animal as human. One of these two had facial hair similar to the others, long, narrow mustaches, though this one's coloring was dark, where those had been yellow. Any warrior known to the watcher plucked chin and lip hairs; red people just did not have much body hair. To the watcher, hairy faces, chests, and limbs looked like bears.

Their eyes were weird, too, ghostly blue or green, something the watcher had never seen or imagined.

The watcher could not detect eye color now, but it was clear that the taller man was guiding the other, whose eyes were bound. The watcher surmised that the first was a warrior who had captured the second and perhaps now meant to ritually execute him, though such an act was usually conducted in a public atmosphere of dramatic intensity.

But it became obvious by their manner that these two were friends, that the first was leading the second to the stream.

It might be some shamanistic ritual, considering the blindfold. Shamans used such techniques to instruct boys in obedience at their coming-of-age.

". . . time for you to approach her," the taller was saying as he propped the torch in a rocky crack.

They stood at the water's edge. The watcher's view afforded him very close perusal of the two men who casually stood at the verge of the sacred water to commit their shocking sacrilege.

By the time he realized what they were doing, it was too late for the watcher to move without being seen.

If a pious Welshman had witnessed a tattooed Muskogean warrior step from a canoe in the Strait of Menai, walk the high road to Bangor Cathedral, and relieve himself on the altar, the effect could not have been more profound. The watcher was outraged, even more because his hiding place lay directly down current from the two barbarians.

The only way for him to avoid ineffable contamination, which would require many moons of complicated, uncomfortable, expensive ceremonial cleansing procedures, was to go immediately underwater and make for midchannel. Being young and agile, he was sure he could make it unseen beyond the torchglow.

At that moment he hated the author of this disgrace, his maternal uncle, who had ordered him here and upon whose head he now uttered a mean, small curse. The uncle, grand miko of the upriver settlement of Mabila, had sent his nephew down into the territory of the low-caste Alabamans, swamp-dwelling cousins to his own nation, after one of their runners had brought evidence of bearded, white-skinned strangers whom the Alabamans reported had set up camp in their territory.

"Bring me back some of these strangers," the miko had said, and Aligapas, as his nephew, heir, and servant, obeyed because he must. Now he saw for himself the Alabaman had made an accurate report; the white invaders had set up camp on the island.

This was the terminal end of the Great Path, which all nations used to get from the saltwater bay up into the highlands known as Head of Waters. It was a time-honored tradition that all nations used the trace; enemies meeting upon its hard-worn dust through cypress, rhododendron, and vast stretches of waving, silvery cane would pretend not to see each other as they passed.

Nobody owned any of this country, but red nations had long ago marked their hunting territories. These were separated by vast, uninhabited buffer areas and traversed by such neutral byways, which included this island.

He sighted his spot on the opposite shore, where he would take the Great Path back to the Alabaman village; gripped the powerbag tied around his neck and the new white-crystal amulet in worked metal, which the Alabaman chief had taken from the first white outlanders; mentally began reciting the formula against the seventh degree of pollution; took a deep breath; and went under.

He pulled as much water as that breath would allow, knowing surface current was stronger than in the deep, opened his eyes to make sure he was beyond illumination, then glided as an alligator would to the surface, slowing down at the last moment so that just his high-crowned head was exposed from the nostrils up.

Suddenly Madoc fell silent and grabbed the torch.

"What . . . ?" Rhys whispered, stepping instinctively back, hand out for balance, reaching for the staff he had set aside.

Madoc flung the flare in a high arc above the water, illuminating a huge circle that shrank as the torch descended. His aim was good; like many of his countrymen, he was skilled with the javelin, which he liked to think was from his ancient Greek ancestor.

The other men were running up, torches in hand, having seen Madoc's flare and been close behind him despite his orders.

They could all hear a swimmer.

"A man—there—" Madoc said, grabbing Dag's fire and slinging it in a circle of blue sparks to let it go at the right moment so that it climbed high and glowing over the swimmer.

"I see him!" Dag cried, staging his spear and letting fly.

Wyn launched another flare before the second was drowned, but Dag's lance fell shy.

As Madoc shucked his bulky pullover, wide tool-laden belt, and heavy sandals, the nearest lookout ran onto the rock face with an arrow already nocked on the crossbow. He took sure aim in the shower of brilliance, but Madoc pushed the device upward, skewing the arrow, and in the same action dived into the water from the rock ledge as others ran up with torches.

The last flare sizzled out beyond the swimmer's advance. Someone followed Madoc into the cold water that threw only a sluggish current against him.

Madoc was an excellent swimmer, the best in his crew. Not even the youngest man could beat him on the longest haul, and cold water was the only kind he had known. This river was a bath compared to the Severn.

The quarry, a younger man, though shorter of arm and torso, made it to the opposite beach, but Madoc had narrowed his lead enough to be able to run him to ground. They went down in a gasping heap with Evan running up, dripping, on Madoc's heels.

They were embroiled in a bloody tangle, but Madoc finally extricated himself and stood catching his breath, watching as Evan nailed the other in a vise grip around the neck.

Sputtering, groaning, they thrashed momentarily before the watcher gave up and ceased struggling. He was mainly strong in the thighs and did not seem to have the upper-body strength of a man used to wrestling or lancework.

Madoc's first impression of their captive was of an abnormally flattened forehead and a slightly lopsided mouth. He had a flat crown, which gave the red man's face the appearance of a trenchard—wide, flat, squarish, and exceedingly ugly. It was strange enough to be called freakish, though later he would learn it was done on purpose by binding the heads of highborn Muskogean male infants because it was believed to enhance male beauty and intelligence.

The only light came from torches far back on the other shore, and from the starglow that afforded only enough light to see outlines and high surfaces as a lighter darkness. For a fraction of a second Madoc saw the other's eyes flash with small points of reflected light. They went black as he attempted to break from Evan's grasp, but was caught in a tighter grip for his trouble.

Madoc called across the river for a coracle. They soon had their muddy captive bound, transported via long coracle, and parading into the glow of the renewed campfire, where everyone, including the growling pup, had been roused and stood watching now with great curiosity to see what it was the arglwydd had caught.

"A Skraeling!" the old Norseman cried. "A raw flesh-eater."

Nona growled and nipped at the captive's heels but scurried away when he tried to kick her with a viciousness that bespoke a man who did not like dogs.

Gwen cried out and tried to restrain the pup.

"A blue demon..." mumbled Mary, crossing herself, and not alone in the act. Some gasped, Agnes and Mary made small sounds of embarrassment behind their hands, the three little boys giggled, the rest just stared with their mouths open at the most naked and tattooed human being they had ever seen.

"Get something to cover him," Madoc said to Ari, and as he ran off, ordered Huw to make the rounds of the lookouts.

"Wager he is not alone, sir," Huw said as they moved off.

Nona trotted a safe circle around the captive. She tried again to take skin, but he growled back at her and kicked her hard enough under the ribs to send the lanky greyhound tumbling end over. Gwen caught her and slipped a braided leash around her neck, then scooped the puppy up and held onto her muzzle.

Madoc cast a glance over his shoulder where the sounds from the woods had died down. It was suddenly very quiet, with a meandering wind that had a cold edge to it.

The captive stared at them as they stared back at his coppery complexion, his long, flat head, his slit ears plugged with disks, his many rings of blue tattoos on his arms, legs, fingers, every surface of him down to his small, stubby toes.

It disturbed Madoc to see Gwen staring dumbly, and Rhiannon, bemused, openly observing the blue and fear-stiffened maleness of the captive who stood in their midst, breathing heavily in the residue of exertion, trailing river-weed, arms bound behind his back, one ankle hobbled with a cord that ran back to Dag's hand.

The Norsemen had found the captive's weapons, a sharp flint dagger and a narrow articulated stick with a wad of clay on one end, tied to a soggy bag of curious short three-pronged arrows. They were inspecting the weighted shaft between themselves, puzzling how it worked.

Dag jerked the line so that the captive stumbled and fell. Iron knives flashed. The half-dozen Norsemen were suddenly all over him, teasing, fired up and ready to do berserker work.

The dog wrenched free and threw herself snarling into the

swarming mess of legs and arms and dust that rolled into the audience, scattering onlookers.

Madoc pulled the sailors off and pushed them back, protesting but finally obeying him. They threw threats and curses upon the red man dripping slime, mud, and blood, but resheathed their blades as Madoc unleashed the hobble and helped him to stand.

The dog was yelping furiously, edging closer with barred fangs, neck muscles straining. The red man shouted, falling back as the dog again attacked his ankles. But Madoc grabbed it from behind. Gwen came forward and took Nona from her father, who did not look at her as he handed the pup over.

He had his other hand stiff against the fellow, who was furious at the dog's attack. The captive fell back and scrambled to his feet, coughing and sputtering because he was throttled with the same cord that bound his hands behind him.

Madoc was aware of a woman approaching and quickly turned to see it was Ffiona with a wooden bowl, which she offered to the red man. He reached to sip the water that slashed down his chest.

Behind them Madoc heard her husband curse, "Woman—" and rebuke her in a coarse whisper when she stepped back into the circle of amazed onlookers.

"Well, he was choking," the girl protested meekly, "and he looks like a human being."

Wyn, to one side, crossed himself.

Edwin, who had grabbed up their sleeping baby in the crook of his left arm, jerked at his wife's sleeve. "You should be shamed to look at all," to which she hung her head.

"He killed my captain," Dag insisted suddenly, and had to be restrained by Edwin and Huw.

Madoc saw as the captive straightened why Dag was so agitated. On the naked chest glowed the white feldspar disk in the silver bezel—the Icelandic eye that Fair Beard never removed from his person. Madoc handled the thin disk, turning it to make sure it was Snorrison's, then jerked it so that the thong snapped.

Ari approached with a dirty gray cloak, which had been used as the dog's bed on straw, but did not dare come near the red man, who stood there bleeding, panting before them until Madoc made a gesture that he be followed to the rug-draped log, thus causing the principal nakedness to be turned away from the women and children.

"Bring more water and a cloth," Madoc said as he ushered the stumbling red man to be seated. "And some food." He regarded the captive.

Ari rushed in behind him with the feeble drape training in the dirt. When the prisoner sat down, the black man threw the cloak across the naked lap.

"Ffiona's right," Madoc said, "he is our first guest."

Ari hurried off again as Ffiona looked shyly down and Edwin bristled beside her. "Here," he said stiffly, and handed her the child who was waking up.

Rhys, Evan, Dag, and a couple of the others sidled over while the main group simmered near the fire, glancing this way amid a low rumble of speculation.

Madoc saw that many hands were on weapons as his escort closed in. He gestured for the bonds to be cut. Evan complied but lingered very near, dagger drawn.

The first thing the red man did with his freed hands was to remove the soiled cloak from his thigh.

Ari, approaching with a basin of water, tried to replace it, but the red man threw the filthy rag off again.

"Never mind," Madoc said, and Ari let it fall, gingerly setting the water before the red man, who stared with even rounder eyes at this black man on his knees offering water.

The captive slowly, not trusting, dipped his hands in the basin, and splashed his face. Ari removed the basin and offered a trenchard with the last of the oatcakes and a venison joint.

Still slightly stunned, the red man looked down and shook his head; then, as though remembering that to refuse food was unfriendly, he took the smallest morsel possible and ate it.

He smiled nervously at Madoc, then chewed minutely and swallowed as though it hurt. Dag made a move to shift weight, and the red man ducked an expected blow.

"What is wrong with his head?" one of the men asked.

Dag laughed low in his throat and informed Rhys what was happening. "A pinhead, is what he is."

"Some kind of idiot," a man agreed.

"Why else would he be wandering out here all by himself?" Dag said, ostensibly to Rhys, who did not answer.

The captive looked at Madoc, who touched his own chest and said his name with a calm voice and a steady gaze. Then, eyes locked on the red man, he touched the tattooed chest of the other, who blinked once and made a sound, "Aligapas..." and touched his own chest, nodding, smiling, then not smiling. "I am Aligapas, I Glitter, I Glitter," he said in what Madoc's Hundred would come to recognize as Muskogean, and gestured at the skyful of stars above. "Aligapas."

Aligapas was shaking in fear, Madoc observed as he scrutinized him. What a weird and incongruous human being, and was he saying that his name meant *Star*?

"A-li-ga-pas," Madoc said, and the other nodded. "Yes, well, Aligapas..." He held out the disk. "Where did you get this?"

The red man looked first at the disk, then at Madoc, staring mutely, though it was clear what was demanded.

"Where?" Madoc repeated, shaking the disk and tapping the man's chest with it.

"Let me ask him," Dag growled, but was held fast.

The captive eyed him and looked again at Madoc, seeing for the first time that this white man had disturbing eyes the color of smoke. The red man said something in about four words, then repeated himself, nodding at the disk. Then he made the handsign for a trade, thinking that surely these people knew handsign; every red nation shared the ancient handsign language.

Now it was Madoc who stared dumbly at the red man.

Aligapas said the Muskogean word for trade, simultaneously repeating the sign. He could see that the white man did not understand, so he bent down and picked up two pieces of gravel, handing one to Madoc and hiding the other in his fist, drawing the fist close to his chest while he said his name. He opened his fist to show the pebble to make sure his meaning was taken, then held it against his chest and said, "This belongs to me."

Madoc nodded.

Aligapas pointed to the pebble in Madoc's open palm, then to Madoc's chest and said slowly, "This belongs to you."

Madoc signified he understood.

Aligapas placed his stone in Madoc's other hand and relieved him of his pebble. He stood back and repeated the word for trade in his language.

Madoc repeated the word. "Yes, I understand, trade. Who traded it to you?" He gestured with Fair Beard's amulet.

"Alabamans," the red man said.

A birdcall split the night, causing everyone except the captive to start. Madoc caught his eyes darting toward the woods. A hunch pricked Madoc, and he said to the captive, "Alabamans?"

The red man lifted his chin as if to defiantly say nothing.

Now Madoc's hunch was a screaming bunch of muscles knotted in his belly, as though the *Horn* were about to scrape bottom.

Quietly, so as not to alarm anyone, Madoc said to Evan who happened to be closest to him at the moment, "Get everyone back on the ship, immediately." Evan saw Wil was listening. With a thumbs-up gesture Wil scooped up his sons, one under each arm. The sleepy children protested and woke, wiggling and mean, but shut up when their father gave them a good shaking. He got their mother's attention and soon the family was in a coracle scooting from the shore while he turned back to help more civilians.

Rhys had suspected a human cry in the shriek, too. He whispered to Rhiannon that she should quietly but quickly get the women and children to the coracles. She looked at him only a moment before they heard another birdcall answer the first, perhaps too precisely, and after an echo the air fell still.

Suddenly shattering the quiet, a scream rang out from the direction of their eastern watch. Then a garbled curse in his own language and Madoc was on his feet, his dagger at the red man's throat, dragging him backward toward the sand of the beach. The women were crowding into the boats, Mary herding her boys, and Einion in a coracle with one of the sailors. Only bedrolls and a few utensils had been offloaded, nothing to linger over.

Madoc's men, who took their cue from their commander, were backing now down the beach. Swimmers had already taken to the water, not wasting time or effort on a boat.

A liquid death-cry burst from the bush. It was the lookout, screaming as he ran pell-mell toward the beach, arms out, staggering into the last of the boarding party. In the tangle that resulted the red man dashed off into the eastern shadows.

Dag would have pursued, but Madoc pushed him into the nearest boat, where Huw restrained him.

Blank-eyed, face frozen in his final scream, the lookout slumped into the last coracle dipping at the shore, with three prongs of a dart lodged in three fatal places in his back.

With tears and sweat in his eyes, Madoc hauled on the sailor, a man he had sailed with and fought with for more than a dozen years, trying to pull him into the two-man coracle.

Evan stopped him. "He is gone, sir."

Madoc stared down at the three delicate wands that pierced the sailors's back with little blood, the angle suggesting penetration of the right kidney, spine, and heart. A wicked, wicked weapon, this, he thought, fingering the central shaft, which appeared to be simple cane.

"It is no use, and he will swamp us," Evan said when it looked as though his commander would not let go.

Madoc saw that Evan spoke the truth and released his grip on his old friend, easing the body into the silky black water. "Farewell," he said, uttering the man's name.

The lookouts dashed splashing into the water. Catching the last of the coracles, they hurriedly pushed off from the shore.

But something was happening out on the water, beyond the *Horn*. As figures scrambled up his ship's sidelines, he saw bright flares on the other ship, which clearly had moved since the last time he had looked.

Incredibly, the sail was hoisting. The north wind caught against the anchors. The ship had already lost steerageway and was out of control; obviously there was no hand at the helm. The ship wrenched into the face of the wind, which struck the sail and with a snap filled it out, rattling and rippling ominously.

Even as he watched unbelieving from the coracle, the sail continued to rise, but crookedly: He knew instantly that only one man was doing the work—it took three sailors at least to hoist that sheet. He could hear the straining of lines as the ship pulled against her anchors. People were yelling at the *Horn*'s starboard, and there was an unusual flare forward where someone was moving about, exhorting others unseen in darkness.

Chaos broke out in the near water with thirty-five bobbing coracles, the yelling crew, crying children, the dog barking, someone calling his name, and the wind, sharp now and cold, and the awful crack, crack, crack of the crippled *St. Ann's* screaming sail as she loomed closer and closer to the *Horn* against the sky just lighter than pure darkness.

He heard sheep bleating.

On the *Horn* he heard Wil's cry of astonishment and the clear information that the *St. Ann* was being badly brought about and was going to ram her sister ship. The screams and prayers from portside chilled him more than the wind as the *St. Ann* sliced within spitting distance of the *Horn,* gouging at her sidelines and ripping several coracles from the shield-rack.

There was a brief, terrible groan of wood scraping wood, and Madoc looked up to see Simon with his arms up shouting something to three monks, who were trying to get the sail down.

Within seconds the *St. Ann* would broadside the *Horn*.

"God, no, not my ship—" Madoc cried, helpless in the bobbing little boat while disaster loomed closer.

The wind changed. It had been coming in from the north, but now, as early winter winds will do, it switched, licking at his hair and the reefed sail from the northwest.

Like a hand clearing a table, it whisked the *St. Ann* at a skewed angle away from the *Horn*.

If someone could only get aboard the *St. Ann* and put down the helm, perform the maneuver of wearing ship against the wind, what little forward motion she had might be put under a man's control. Madoc stood; Evan at the paddle tried to pull him back, but it was no use; the commander was over the side and swimming toward the yawing ship.

Coracles full of frantically shouting silhouettes caused him to lose the stroke and flounder, but he regained his way and made for the ship, which seemed from his low angle to be a crashing sky.

Suddenly he could see. Light was coming from somewhere, far more light than should be available from a single torch. In horror he saw flames dancing along the head of *St. Ann's* sail.

From the far shore lights appeared, glowing against the purple-black wall of undergrowth, as though many torches were held high along the water's edge where limpid, fleeting figures in long, low boats called trilling noises back and forth.

Four of the craft sped out onto the larger water directly in the path of the careening *St. Ann*, where now Madoc could hear crewmen shouting, trying to avoid the impending disaster of rocks ahead. They were trying to get the sail down, but

Father Simon's voice harangued them. "We must go back to Christian places—he dooms us all to hellfire!"

Madoc gasped when he saw the flames leap through the hempen rope of the halyard. Pieces of the glowing landward lights began to soar through the air, and he realized that they were shooting fire-tipped arrows, several of which made their target.

Madoc saw silhouettes on the deck running crazily, shouting and praying. There was a wrenching groan, and the anchor-line pulled taut as the hook found purchase, yanking the *St. Ann* to a struggling halt, throwing people into the water. Then either the line broke or the anchor lost its grip. The ship lazily leaned again toward the land, sail shaking as if the ship had sense enough to be afraid. Seconds later the air was full of an almost soft grinding crunch as she ran aground.

He scrambled up the sidelines in the flickering illumination that was spreading into the bunt of the sail. Many of the lines already glowed as flames sparkled along them. He could hear a familiar voice on the deck, amid others and the bawling of sheep, but it was all going by too quickly to make out who was who in the darkness. Two coracles floundered in the ship's wake, tossing people into the water. He was sure he heard Gwen's voice in the wet darkness, and another woman's. He heard the dog barking out on the water; then, suddenly, it stopped.

He staggered along the tilted deck toward the sheep pen, but fire on a rope coil kept him back. He went around and started hacking at the ropes of the pen where the terrified animals were screaming, some of their woolly back already ignited. They slipped and slid on the angled deck, and Madoc saw that it was hopeless—not only were they penned, they were individually hobbled. Fire rained down between them, arrows and pieces of the sail and lines. He slit the throats of the nearest two, but the heat forced him back as the animals shrieked and crackled.

Knife out, he began to cut at the lines already infected with flame, pulling them out away from the mast. Some came loose, tumbling down around him with sparks flying. He threw them overboard, seeing as he did the flotilla of long boats slithering around the *St. Ann*, full of warriors trilling war cries.

The next few minutes were a hazy blank to him later, full of slashing knives and screams. He connected with several of the wild warriors, but he saw no more of Simon, and when he came up gasping for breath, the swarm of warriors swelled around the Frenchman.

One huge tattooed fellow crouched before him, a long sticker brandished in front of Madoc's nose. They circled each other, and clearly he could see the blue bands around the man's arms. The warrior feinted toward him, playing with him with a malicious grin across his wide, flat face painted bright red, clearly visible in the light of roaring flames that had claimed the entire sail.

Madoc waded into the gigantic opponent, feeling skin part under his long knife, but then fragments of burning sail began to rain down upon their shoulders. Smoke billowed from several points—the flame-tipped arrows had found other flammable targets. A barrel of sheep oil aft suddenly sprang to red life; sides split, pouring the melting fat onto the deck, food for the fire that licked hungrily, turning the planks into a furnace.

Someone caught at Madoc from behind. He tried to bring what felt like another attacker over his shoulder, but both rolled sideways near the spreading puddle of flaming grease. His erstwhile attacker cried out, and Madoc saw a blade coming in the man's hand at his face. But suddenly, also behind so that Madoc could not see, the attacker was thrown aside, screaming, into the flames that caught his feathers and stuck with the grease to his blue-figured skin. Madoc saw him rolling off into the lake of fire and whirled when he felt another pair of hands on his arm.

It was Brian dragging at his tunic, stark naked, screaming something unintelligible to him in the din of fire and human screams, and the roar of the fire as it ate oak.

It seemed the entire ship was engulfed in flames now as Brian pulled him to the rail and tried to push him overboard.

Madoc held onto the priest's sleeve, urging him to jump, too.

Brian said something, Madoc could not hear what as he straddled the rail. His knife was gone, left in the soft belly-flesh of the monster warrior, his tunic was burned from his body—shreds of it smoldered hotly against his blistered skin. He heard a horrible sound and looked up in time to see the boom with the flaming tatters of sail come roaring down toward the remains of the sheep, lines whipping around like snakes on fire. He must jump or be struck by the aft end of the boom. The young priest was gone, Madoc never saw where.

The last thing he saw before he went overboard was a single ewe skittering toward him with the hobble tripping her, sliding on the slick boards, her wool a perfect ball of fire.

The water felt so cool and dark when he plunged in and took the depth. When he came up, people were splashing in the water, and as he breaststroked to avoid debris floating around him, he met others still trying to make it to the *Horn*, bobbing like a duck on the choppy bay. He saw a couple more figures leaping from the *St. Ann*, which was now a ship of screaming fire.

Only one appeared still aboard; Madoc thought with horror it must be Father Brian, but then he heard a strained call from that direction, "Do not let his sin take you into this demon country—this is hell—this is hell!"

Behind Simon's outflung arms the fire completely owned the ship. He stood there, in his final posture of the cross, as the flames snapped at his back.

By now dark figures were swarming from the *St. Ann's* sidelines and back into the sleek canoes that surrounded her. Madoc had reached the ropes of his ship and hauled himself up, watching the horror over his shoulder, hearing the thousand hisses as flying ashes hit the water.

Someone helped pull him in, and when he was able to see was surprised it was Wyn. "Did you see him—did he make it?"

At first Madoc thought the abbot meant Simon.

"Father Brian—did he get off the ship?" Wyn yelled.

"I saw him—" Madoc fell gasping to the deck. When he looked around, Wyn was assisting others to clamber over the rail.

Madoc helped pull people up, trying to see who it was. Rhiannon, Mary, Einion, Teleri clawed their way up his arms and onto the deck, where they fell panting and crying, then dragged themselves to the rail to watch with the others as the *St. Ann* burned. The screaming figure was gone; the last of the long boats melted into the darkness of the far water.

Into the night they heard drums as the fire burned itself down to the *St. Ann's* waterline. The various independent glows of torches melted back into the jungle, where they continued to hear the screams of men and women while they collected themselves together on the decks of the *Horn*.

Madoc, stumbling through the survivors, was trying to piece together what had happened.

"How, how in God's name?"

When none answered, one of the monks said, "Somebody obviously cut loose a boat."

Wyn almost said something then, some lame thing about perhaps Simon held back a coracle and buried it until the *Horn* and *St. Ann* sailed, but Madoc's snort or rejection stopped him. "How could a lone paddle buck that current back there?"

They silently stared at him until Dag said, "I know I did not help the Frenchy son of a bitch."

Several men snickered agreement.

"We tried to stop him," said one of the brothers.

"He tried to talk me into helping him," said another, young Ffagan, apprentice to the exiled carver. "When I refused, he said he would wait for you, Domme."

Wyn's guilt made this an accusation where none had been intended. The abbot stood there, his tongue swollen in his throat, staring at Madoc and expecting the worse. But Madoc seemed not to suspect him, which poured acid on Wyn's conscience and would for the rest of his life, that Madoc so trusted him.

"The next thing we knew, the madman had the sail up."

"We tried to stop him," said a man, joined by others.

"Yes, we tried—"

"He struck me," said one man with a black eye.

"He fought us off—we tried to stop him—"

"But," Madoc said, stepping among them, "how did he get here in the first place?"

"None saw him board," said Ffagan. "He was suddenly there."

All fell silent under Madoc's penetrating gaze. Several shook their heads.

"He was not stowaway on my ship, lord."

"I know that, Huw," Madoc said, sure that he was not responsible, though equally certain that had to be Simon's method. Huw, furious that his vessel had been taken from him and sick with worry about his missing wife, stood with his fists tightened, a little aside from the group around Madoc.

"Who helped him?" Huw demanded, grabbing the nearest monk and shaking him.

Madoc stepped behind Huw and restrained his arms. "It does not matter now."

Huw pulled free, glaring at the monks who cowed back

from him. Madoc put his arm across Huw's shoulder and walked him away from the wide-eyed clergy, who hung back, muttering to each other, reinforcing their innocence.

Wyn, who believed Madoc was wrong about Simon's ability to follow in that freed coracle, shook his head, crossed himself, and wept into his arm later, begging divine forgiveness for what his act of mercy accomplished.

In the glow of the burning ship, they recovered seven bodies from the water. All but one was mutilated with the hearts cut out. The one exception was what appeared by deduction to be Simon, since that corpse was cremated beyond certain recognition. They found none of the enemy dead, though Madoc was sure he had gotten one of them, and Brian had scored another.

Missing from Madoc's Hundred were six monks including Father Brian, three sailors, Al-Ghazal Ari O'Dalaigh, Ffiona and her baby, Agnes, Gwen, and the pup.

Far away, through the trees and over the water, they heard screams echoing all that night.

It started raining again before darkness settled in.

Madoc threw the tightly woven cloak over his head and climbed to the upper deck, a silver river of driving rain. The sounds of its millions of needles piercing the water around him was a thrumming drone, a torture upon the ears. He stood at the rail where only a few coracles remained, listening to the soft din, staring at the shore made vague by the downpour. Everything looked pale around him in the dwindling light. The trees themselves were bearded with their long gray hair, an oddity that gave the feeling of wispy curtains shutting him out. Rain beat down steadily for a while, then slacked off, even more depressing than downpour. It seemed he could distinguish each drip between himself and the soggy land where the veiled trees blocked his view and kept him away from Gwen, lost behind their silver wall.

The sun seemed an old memory, a dream from childhood. All surfaces around him were gray. The only glow in all that subdued wetness was in his eyes, where smoldered determination to find her.

Chapter 16

*All the Britons dye their bodies
with woad which produces a blue
color, and this gives them a more
terrifying appearance in battle.*

—The Gallic Wars
by Julius Caesar
51 B.C.

Dawn sifted down like grave dust. No sun showed through a cloud cover that cast no shadows and colored everything a uniform gray, deepened by smoke coiling up from the smoldering carcass of the *St. Ann,* which ran aground at a sad tilt in shallows off a gravel beach about a quarter mile across the river.

Madoc woke, hurting in a hundred places, slumped against the forward bulkhead, to the sound of a woman weeping below. It was a soft, private sorrow. He sat there listening with closed eyes, trying to identify who it was, until a man's voice comforted her, and the company came awake by ones and twos.

They recovered themselves that long day, taking stock, counting survivors, making repairs, tending those who had been hurt. The sheep all perished in the holocaust, burnt to charcoal in their pen along with many supplies and tools and most of the seeds. About the only things salvageable were a few ax heads and Wyn's anvil, all too hot to handle. The salvagers quenched them in the river before hauling them back to the *Horn.* Madoc was blistered but suffering no serious burns. Others were not as fortunate. Caradoc was busy all morning, the one among them who seemed animated.

Madoc saw Wyn on his knees aft and wandered back to

stop him from praying for so long. "Do we not have enough casualties Brother Wyn?" trying to make a weak joke.

The abbot looked back over his shoulder.

"Your knees will be bleeding if you—" Madoc stopped himself when he saw tears running down Wyn's face. And, closer, Madoc saw he was busy with three illuminated books Brian had managed to get off the doomed ship. Wyn had the soaked volumes out to dry on the rough deck while he and another of the brothers sewed new leather cases.

"These three are all we have left," the monk said, looking down at the books, their parchment pages swollen and tacky, with blue ink bleeding. "I begged Brian not to go back for more." He wiped his rough face with an even rougher hand. "And now he is lost to us, too." Their only surviving ordained priest was John, a man in his sixties.

Madoc realized that when he saw Father Brian last night, it must have been his second trip to the burning ship. Madoc thought what a brave and foolish thing for the priest to have done, just to save some books. But he would not say such a thing to the abbot, and because he would not say his mind, he had no words at all and could give comfort only with his hand on Wyn's shoulder. "It might rain again. . . ."

The monk regarded the leaden heavens, then looked down at his books with their dazzling, unnatural colors. "Yes, thank you," the monk replied, as bereft as Madoc could imagine seeing him, and went back to work.

They had nothing to eat, but the sailors threw lines over the sides and pulled in abundant yellow fish. Wil produced three skins of mead that he had hidden against just such a time.

Late morning Madoc gathered Dag and his men with orders to go out and reconnoiter. "Kill nobody if you can help it," he said, knowing with a soldier's heart how that order would be appreciated. "We must talk with them, show them iron tools, cloth, things like that."

Dag looked at him with growing insolence displayed by a heavy shifting of his weight to the other foot.

"You know the sagas," Madoc argued patiently. "Your people did not have any luck at all fighting the Skraelings, but they made a good profit trading with them."

Arms still locked defiantly across his chest, Dag looked down at his boots. The men behind him shifted their glances between him and Madoc, who found comfort that several wore his coin prominently sewn to their jerkins.

"We have too few men," he said finally. "We could all go down in one heroic battle, and what would that accomplish except to make all our suffering for nothing?"

He turned to the men. "Lev, I know you want to go back."

The red-haired fellow looked chagrined, thinking the commander would consider that a mutinous sentiment.

Madoc scored another point when he continued. "Well, so do I." His candor surprised them and broke through the wall of stubborn will they had set against him. "I have a hunch Fair Beard is alive."

Dag made a doubtful sound, but Madoc turned a steady gaze upon him. "You just want his wife."

"You have women," Dag said, eyeball to eyeball with Madoc. "What do we have?" The men growled agreement, but not enthusiastically, and Dag heard it. They had followed Snorrison not Dag, not even Madoc, who had only their chief's pledge. If he was dead, they were no longer bound to his liege lord.

"We will trade axes for furs, like the heroes in the saga, and go back rich men. You will have all the women you want," Madoc promised. "I swear it to you."

This had some effect on Lev and the others, at least, though Dag's frown deepened.

"I swear on my name that you shall all have an equal share in the cargo we transport back to Dublin." This was the old contract of the sea, the pledge of the argonaut, verbal agreement more binding than iron and more ancient than their grandfather's viking ships resting on the bottom of the North Sea with iceberg holes in their keels.

"For now," Madoc continued in a smooth voice, "at least until we reconnect with Fair Beard, trade with these people."

"Well . . ."

"But," he concluded, turning away from them, "if you choose instead to go to Valhalla together in one splendid bloody battle, the hair ripped off your skulls and the balls from between your legs, your half dozen to the enemy's three hundred, at least do it as far away from this camp as possible."

These boys were not as religious as their viking grandfathers. Valhalla was little more than a romantic story none believed any more than Madoc believed in pink-angel heaven. But the rest of what he said was all too real. They grew up on hair-raising stories about Vinland's cannibal savages. And from where they stood ready to go on patrol, they could see the mutilated corpses from last night laid out for burial.

They took these thoughts with them as they went off to scout the island and eastern mainland.

There was no sign of the enemy during those silvery hours. Nor did anyone hear more of the terrible screams. From time to time they heard rolling thunder, but there was no more rain. And everyone waited, for what they were not quite sure.

Madoc did not leave the rail where he watched the shore all day, turning his back on the bedraggled company. The civilians seemed numb. The three little boys were quiet, contenting themselves with knot-tying and knucklebones. The crewmen went about their tasks slowly, speaking little. The ship was so crowded, people were bumping into each other. Madoc regarded it all morosely, knowing that there was no way he could take this overburdened ship into open water.

Often that day Madoc would catch himself staring at the jungle, thinking of Gwen and those echoing screams.

The men worked on sail repair, sidelines, and coracles that had been damaged. Whatever happened, a ship's crew would go about its traditional duties. From time to time Madoc would call one or the other, and for a while they would discuss the situation, but it was as if they were enmeshed in a dream. They seemed to him to swim in the pale light that threw no shadows.

He missed Ari; he hated to admit it, but he had grown to depend more and more on the black man. He could not find things and growled at Edwin because the sunboard was missing.

"You gave Ari that duty," Edwin insisted.

"Damnation, you should back him up."

Edwin did not reply, and when Madoc looked up, he saw the man was greatly offended at being chastised.

"Edwin," Madoc said when he saw the misery in the fellow's eyes. "You and I share the worse loss."

Edwin brightened somewhat, and they commiserated about Gwen and Ffiona and the child. At this point there was not much Madoc could say except that he would do everything in his power to get them back. "All nations take hostages," he said, offering the only hope he could. "We have valuable

things to trade, things these barbaric people do not know how
to make."

Edwin was silent, his wet eyes gazing upon his commander. Perhaps, Madoc thought, you will appreciate her more if
you get your wife back, but he said no more.

Edwin said he would keep searching for the sunboard and
excused himself to go below.

About noon they heard Huw cry out from starboard; floating facedown in the water was Agnes, caught by the river and
washed back in from the bay on the tide. Huw stared
stony-eyed, his squint deeper than Madoc had ever seen it,
as they put his wife's body into a coracle and rowed her to the
island, where they left it with the others while the grave
diggers finished their work.

The brothers at their appointed hours repeated the Holy
Office in a tight, small group aft. The tone of their incantations was dire, leaving no doubt that none of them thought
they would get out of this alive. They were preparing.

Over on the island, while an armed guard stood nervously
around, the men finished a pit that must do as a single grave.
The religious had to improvise an altar; the great trunk where
they thought were stored all the silver vessels would never
be recovered from the deep mud where the St. Ann's hulk
rested.

"The Mass is more than silver candlesticks," John said
almost peevishly while his brothers fretted around him.
When he had taken a coracle from the St. Ann, he held a
modest supply of the Host he had squirreled away. Madoc
donated a small cache of wine from his sea chest aboard the
Horn. John said Mass on deck with Wyn's anvil doubling as
the altar, spread with a strip of sailcloth. They scrounged the
other necessary instruments but were hard put for the candlesticks, which must be precious metal.

Rhiannon rummaged Owen's treasure chest, coming up
with two dazzling items of pure gold, huge unmatched brooches
that came down through her great grandmother. These served
as holders for the last of their beeswax candles, burned down
about half their length.

The chalice was a common horn drinking cup.

John felt it to be his most inspired funeral Mass. There was
something deeply comforting in the singing. The company
sent hymns ringing across the water while the men covered
the dead.

Madoc stood with Huw during the service.

The sun never did come out; the light slid imperceptibly from gray day to gray evening. Just at slate blue darkness, while Madoc was watching a swarm of bats jerk at insects above the beach, the scouts returned with two turkeys, a small doe, and several hares, along with a wild story about a dragon that hissed at one of the men before it slid into the river.

The teller of this adventure was Lev, youngest of the Norsemen. Madoc thought he had mistaken a big turtle on a floating log, but Lev would not back down from his story—the dragon was the length of three tall men. Its tail whipped. It had bulging eyes. Its mouth was lined with huge sharp teeth.

Madoc expected next he would have it breathing fire, but Lev stubbornly shut up when he saw nobody believed him. The others had not seen the thing and so could say neither yea nor nay.

They saw no sign of the native army, not even a dropped weapon or bent branch. It was as though last night's ethereal attackers had melted into the swamp.

Early evening Wyn prayed down below in a tight circle of the devout. Madoc could hear them from where he stood on deck, grinding his teeth and cursing himself for his folly.

"Blessed Virgin, intercede on our behalf to your holy son Jesus Christ to deliver us from the straits into which we have fallen, and if any among us bear secret guilt that could underlie our misfortune, let him confess now that we all may be saved...."

Public confession was traditional. Madoc bit his lip, thinking, so now I am a bad-luck Jonah. They would blame him for everything.

He heard a woman crying below, the same from this morning, and was still unable to recognize who was behind the tears. Momentarily it sounded like Rhiannon, and the possibility that she was weeping served him a headache. He pressed his thumbs against his closed eyes, stroking them without comfort.

"Father John," Llywellyn cried out, "please marry Tegan and me so that we can die in grace."

"Yes, Llyw, oh yes," Tegan cried with strident joy.

Madoc realized it had been Tegan crying in the early morning fog, and Llywellyn comforting her. He had been right when he supposed they were lovers, and she had been crying not in mourning but in distress at not being wed.

Madoc listened as the abbot called on John. The old man had been faint during the earlier services; he had fallen in last night's scramble. Caradoc had bound his forehead and told him to rest. But John called across the dark hold that he would be happy to perform a wedding. "Affirmation of life, affirmation of love," he mumbled in his dreamy voice, "in the jaws of death. . . ."

"Here, Father, let me help you."

"I can make it," said John, eager to do the Lord's work.

Wyn's voice was clear to Madoc out on the dark prow. "Perhaps there are others who would like to join, so that they will be ready in grace to meet the Lord."

Madoc could imagine Wyn turning to say this in the direction of the hold, aiming his message at the arglwydd on deck.

"A double wedding," Mary said, and others made comments too low to be heard but with another clear message.

Madoc, his glance still on the dark shore where only now and again he caught glimpses of what was most likely swamp gas, said hoarsely to Rhys, "Come with me, poet."

Rhys, moving to comply, should have been warned by the cynical note in Madoc's voice when he said, "Down to final glory," and pushed away from the rail with a curt order to a sailor not to take his eyes off the shore view. Rhys, as familiar with the ship as the corridors of Owen's house so that he seldom needed the staff on board, handed himself along.

A rosy glow poured from the hold where they had oil lamps ablaze, so Madoc could see their upturned faces as he descended with Rhys close behind him. A beaming Wyn said amen, amen, God be praised, and the Christians crossed themselves. They looked like one many-eyed creature to Madoc as he dropped into their midst. Without regarding anyone, he waded among their seated and prone figures, grabbed up Teleri's hand, and dragged her to her feet. Then, causing everyone to draw breath in surprise, he likewise plucked Rhiannon out of the group and walked with the two women in tow at either hand to where Rhys lingered.

Rhiannon was speechless, her lips open in dumb shock. Teleri did not take her gaze from Madoc as he handed Rhiannon over to Rhys, who now understood his lord's cynical remark.

Madoc said to Wyn, "Very well, then. This is what you want?" He glanced around at all the faces, and those of the Norsemen who were not on duty, lined up leaning with one foot against the bulkhead or peering over the edge of the hold above.

Christians grinned approval, and Wyn said softly, "Praise the Lord."

John shuffled forward, pulling a long white shawl around his own shoulders, The brothers fussed over him, whispering together for a drawn-out minute. "I know it by rote, I know it by rote," the old man said when someone tried to shove a breviary into his hand. He was a farmer with a farmer's stubborn, sunburned, wrinkled and squinting face, thick neck and red ears. He had the stockiness of the ancient native line of Mona, where grain had been grown long before the Romans came to Britain, and men like this had been priests and farmers in a single occupation.

"Do it then," Madoc said, tight-lipped. The old man blinked at him sharply, the bandage askew around his leathery brow giving him a jolly aspect, like a holy clown.

"Sir..." Rhys was about to say, but Rhiannon's hand at his tunic sleeve stopped him when she whispered, "Let it be."

With no private word to Teleri, without even looking to see if she was still where he had left her, Madoc drew her forward.

"You two," he said to Llywellyn and Tegan, "come on."

Llywellyn looked back at Tegan, the only person in the hold who was smiling, and she with a teary face glowing in the lamplight. Together they stepped forward, the girl wiping at her eyes, the man with blushing ears and an absurd grin on his face.

Madoc squelched fury at all of them.

Everyone turned to look at Rhiannon and Rhys, who stood speaking together, hands no longer joined, their turned backs their only claim on privacy.

"Poet?" Madoc asked, his voice rough with impatience.

"Sir, such a thing must be voluntary."

"Rhys," Rhiannon whispered, her eyes downcast, "it does not matter." She felt a sensation in her lower abdomen—the child was quickened.

Within himself Madoc felt a wave of anger rise and flood his vision, red again, and boiling. He saw his half sister lingering in the shadows behind Rhys as though she might be forgotten, one hand on her blaring stomach, her head down so that the lengths of her hair fell like golden ropes hiding her face. Stubborn, implacable, holding onto her secrets. He hated her in that moment for saying that it did not matter and wanted to hurt her.

"Since when do highborn ladies get to choose their husbands?" he replied to Rhys.

She looked at him then with steam in her dry eyes. Staring at him with no trace of any feeling, she stepped into the full light beside Rhys and took up his hand in both of hers.

And so, the three couples were married.

It must be brief because they had none of the trappings of a wedding but only the words Father John brought to join them. And when it was over, the people grinned and clapped as though they had something to celebrate.

"And you may kiss the brides," John was saying, but Madoc turned away without a word to anyone, not even Teleri, and climbed heavily back up the peg ladder to take his self-appointed station in the forward darkness.

The night was long. Exhaustion took the company, which fell into slumber where they stood. Curled onto rope coils and wool bales they slept in groups, heads on laps and shoulders, mattresses and pillows to each other while the watch turned in the early morning hours up on deck. Madoc dragged himself belowdecks and stumbled to the spot Teleri had staked out on the other side of his personal trunks.

He could hear Rhiannon and Rhys whispering far aft when everyone else was asleep. Later he heard her soft carnal laughter that ripped into him and rekindled his fury, so he left Teleri's bedroll without any satisfaction to either of them and returned to the rail, where none dared challenge his solitude.

Belowdecks, behind the half-finished tapestry Rhiannon hung to give them privacy, Rhys's hands trembled. She watched him in the light cast by their clam-shell lamp, a strong man in his thirty-sixth year, a man whom maidens once whispered about. There was a trace of that in him still, in the strength of his steady masculine jaw, his stout neck with its muscles firm from the control of oration and song. The tan favored him, made his lips a sensuous plum color. His light brown hair had grown more gray-streaked during the long voyage and was sun bleached from time spent on deck, winding coil and making hempen rope so his thumbs had another kind of callus, that of the common sailor.

Unlike many poets this one had not gone to flesh but kept a youthful leanness. His arms were his most attractive feature, long-boned and fine, the muscles picked out by the labors of making music and rope, run through with outstanding veins and arteries like patterning in rose marble.

All in all not an unpleasant man to bed, a honey-colored man, even with the discreet sash across the bridge of his finely molded nose. Did he remove it at night, she wondered? She saw him once take off the band to wash his face—the memory chilled her. It was disturbing to see that the eye sockets were red, as though they had never healed. What did one see without eyes? Darkness, a field of gray, illuminations from the mind?

She wished she did not have to look into those unmasked zones again, wondering how many times she must witness his mutilation over the march of years ahead.

Sometimes he wept. Several times she saw him wipe away tears with the tasseled hem of the sash. A mystery then, for how can one weep without eyes? She wondered about that and finally decided, after crying over some trifling thing, that the tears must spring from the back of the eye, or beneath it, rather than from inside it, as one without reflection might suppose.

But these things she could have lived with. Prettiness in a man more often than not turned her from him. His face was disfigured, but his body was manly and strong. His mind was agile; he was blessed with a sense of humor and tact.

He was a good, intelligent, honorable man from an old family who would no doubt be an excellent husband and father. Why was it not possible for her just to forget the circumstance that forced them together and love him as he deserved?

And what of me and what I deserve? her heart answered her self-rebuke. Am I never to be regarded in decisions on my fate? And if fate seemed to smile instead of frown, should one question it any less? God had given her a will; when would she ever be able to worship God through its use? The priests indicated that a woman's place was to give over her will. Then why would the Almighty give a women such a useless thing if she was not supposed to exercise it over the most important decision in her life?

He waited, knowing that she was watching him but not quite fathoming the thoughts that kept her silent and separate. He knew when she snuffed out the light; the wick smoldered.

He untied the sash and put it aside. It always felt good to remove the band. He wore it for the sake of others, because he knew they did not like seeing his face without it. Often when alone he would slip the band up and let the sun shine on the scars so he could see the shimmering colors like music dancing just behind the empty eye sockets. He still dreamed in the same vibrant colors but always woke up with a headache if he slept with the sash on.

They lay there not touching in the darkness, but nowhere near sleep.

He might have been thinking along lines similar to her own. He had long admired Rhiannon for her music; he loved to be accompanied by her, to make music with her. Memory was still crisp of the last time he saw her, one of his last pleasant recollections of vision. She had been with other girls leaning on a window casement, her face glowing under the sun, a little over four years ago when he was part of Owen's huge retinue departing for the battle that eventually cost so much for victory and darkened the sun for Rhys ab Meredydd forever.

She had been like a sun herself. No man could deny her beauty on that brightly washed summer morning somewhere back in the dark halls of his recall. The breeze had lifted her hair, catching its color like none other. Not of gold, because gold is glaringly yellow. It had sparkled here and there on a shoulder and at a wrist as she wore pieces of the family fortune, ancient if not vast, beyond counting. The electrum torque she wore at her throat on that lost day was supposed to have been cast in Troy. Her hair was a pristine illumination, not a color at all but finely woven strands of pure light.

She had not looked his way but stared at someone else in the crowd during those few minutes before the mass military departure amid braying animals, shouting men, and creaking metal and wood. One of the soldiers in the caravan—he never knew who.

She had been just a beautiful golden child leaning from a window on a bygone day, but she was one of his most treasured memories. Yet he never entertained thoughts of having her. She was royal and beyond his expectations, but it was more than that. There was something cool about her despite her glow. Like sea luminescence, or lightning that provides light without warmth.

Rhys received his training in her father's households, so he saw her often from afar or in passing. Her beauty always seemed a gulf between them, even more than social station. It still remained, though he could no longer see her. It froze her in his memory and made her a being apart from common existence.

As many times as they made music together, he could never remember her remarking on his performance. She appeared to accept him, for good or ill, and that drew a distilled thread of anger from deep inside him, which he quickly repressed because of his respect for who she was. Such a detachment from the consequences of things had distanced her from him so that now, with her scent in his nostrils and her name his own, he still could not quite believe it.

"I cannot sleep," she said when the silence had grown loud.

"I was remembering..." His usual wry smile lingered behind the words, a kind of irony that lent a subtler meaning than mere nostalgia to what he was saying. For himself Rhys could not shake the feeling that this was an illusion or a playlet they were acting. He still could not believe they were man and wife. In his mind her shape burned a dark red silhouette; he felt the heat of her radiating close to the skin of his arms. If she touches me, he thought, she will know I am afraid, but he said, "... remembering the last time I saw you, beautiful lady."

"That must have been just before the battle of Oswestry," she said with her usual forthrightness.

"You were just a girl." He could feel her getting more comfortable on their rough bed, the cooling of his skin's sensation of her. "Some soldier among us had your attention."

There was a swift breath of air between them when she moved, the spicy aroma of her cool hair rushing in to fill the void.

"Do you know which soldier had my attention that day?"

For a swift second Rhys imagined that she would say it was himself she had watched with hungry eyes. He so wanted to keep the fantasy that he said, "I do not want to know."

"Really?"

He heard genuine emotion in her, that she was glad he did not want to know his rival's name. She remembered very clearly the man she had watched that bright morning in the not so long ago, a dark-haired sailor with double eyelashes in Owen's retinue, who was not going into battle but who left that same morning on a diplomatic mission.

"Lady, I wish to say what is past is past. I mean to treasure you in the here and now."

"Rhys . . ."

"I can imagine how this situation must distress you, married off to a blind man to stall rumors—it cannot be how you imagined your wedding night."

"I have always admired you, Rhys ab Meredydd, for your candor, well-spoken."

"M'lady."

She took a deep sigh. "But it occurs to me that we should make the most of it in what little time we have left." She uttered a throaty laugh that sounded weary.

That was the laugh Madoc heard as carnal and mocking, which provoked him to abandon Teleri and seek refuge on deck so that he would not have to hear what sounded like Rhiannon's happiness in another man's arms.

Rhiannon and Rhys were oblivious to him.

"M'lady?" Rhys said as though he had misunderstood his bride's meaning.

She slid her hand up his arm, feeling the musculature she had long admired as well as the ghost of a chill on his flesh. The long muscles were as firm as she expected; each hair was erect with the pattern of gooseflesh.

She took it for desire. He would have spoken further, but she silenced him with a kiss, exploring the plumpness of his lips—often she had admired them, too, while he sang—and the smooth jewels of his teeth. She found it a small delight that she caught him off guard, had startled him even though he continued to speak while she came up for air. "M'lady, I would tell you that I do not hold you to vows you took under duress."

"True, I did not chose a husband. But I can live with you."

It was clear he did not believe her, though he was unable to frame his doubt in words, so she continued. "We are a man and a woman. Events conspired to throw us together. So be it."

His fingers reached out to her and began to stroke the architecture of her knee.

"Because we are all going to die tomorrow?" he asked wryly.

"There is still tonight."

"I would have had you choose," he said softly.

"I choose to accept."

He laid back on the pillows, arm thrown over his face. It was not completely dark; from the open hold came a diluted less-than-darkness from the overcast that had moved in since sunset. She could see his strong wrist white in the dimness. He was a fascination in that moment to her; what would he do next?

"I would have you love me," he said after a time, his thumb stroking that taut hollow. He knew her well enough to know she would not lie, and she did not fail him, though obliquely:

"My mother, also a wife of political convenience, told me that love does come, eventually. The last time I saw her she said that now, when the archbishop has hounded her away from Owen, she loves him all the more."

Rhys did not for one minute believe that Rhiannon was Owen's bed partner. He had been too involved in that household, where such indiscretion would have been known belowstair as it was happening. But he saw in what Rhiannon said that she would bend to her fate with him.

It struck him sadly. He did not display it, but her frank response cut him. He would have had her lie, though in nothing else. He wanted to fall in love with her, but he knew he would never love this distant woman with or without a fall. This union they submitted to felt suddenly vacant to him, and he recognized that coldness in Rhiannon that had always kept her at arm's length. At the same time he felt a flash of desire for her, just lust of flesh and bone, to hell with further mysteries.

As though she had heard his thoughts, she laid her ear in the valley between his abdomen and thigh. The warmth of her breath and the weight of her hair suddenly along his groin was a shock, a dive into cold water coming up in hot sunlight, for the silken strands of her hair were quite chill to the touch; it was only his own reaction that was heated. He desired to warm the luxuriant tresses, to melt her iciness. His body reacted before he could think, his own fire kindled by hers no longer cool, no longer distant, but flaring inside him between them in the places where they had no words.

Then they slept entwined in peaceful surrender to the gentle rocking motion of the ship.

Irritable the next morning from lack of sleep, ground down by sorrow and loss he could not express, Madoc stared at the island in pale morning light. His wrist told him there would be more rain. There was the true chill of November on the air—bright autumn leaves clinging to oak branches before the rain were now gone, leaving stark limbs.

He decided that a small party would establish an island base from which they would hunt and gather, while the main body of Madoc's Hundred would live on board. No more than a dozen hunters or crewmen would be on the island at any one time. Full watch schedules were in effect on the ship— he had to keep up their morale, not to mention his own, with tradition.

Madoc and six men gathered weapons and tools. His plan was to begin a stockade where Wyn could fire the forge. His hope lay in negotiations with the red men, who did not appear to occupy the island. Therefore, he reasoned, perhaps it could be bought.

Just as Madoc swung over the sidelines to the double coracle lobbing in the water below, he was arrested by the watchman's cry from the yardarm. "Captain—look!"

As one voice a cry of dismay escaped from the company that froze at the sight of a line of many red warriors similar in stature and decoration to Aligapas, stepping out from the green cover and onto the fair sand, each one of them holding unmistakable weapons. They stood just beyond bow shot, but the sight was chilling nonetheless. As though the jungle were weeping the warriors, they continued to emerge from the bush until the sand vanished under their blue-tattooed numbers at the tip of the island.

Madoc felt a thrill course through him, remembering that his own ancestors had once painted blue designs on their bodies. Had they looked like this to the invading Romans?

A sailor swore, a woman gasped, and old Bjorn, sinews strained as he pointed, uttered in a coarsened whisper the word they had all come to know. "Skraelings!"

Chapter 17

...*we must through much tribulation
enter into the kingdom*...

—Acts 14:22

Madoc stepped back onto the deck.

He turned to the people and ordered, "All you women and children—belowdecks—Edwin, help them."

No need to order at arms; the Norsemen had their battleaxes out, the sailors their daggers, and from several positions bowmen were already sighting targets ashore, where a quick perusal confirmed that a defensive force was indeed amassing. They kept coming from the folds of jungle green, red man after red man stepping into place on the sandy promontory.

The women and children fretted as the sailors helped them below. They piled up, waiting to descend, crossing themselves and looking fearfully across the water.

Madoc missed Rhiannon staring at him behind the other women from across the wide hold as sailors rushed around her, jostling her shoulder. She moved to get out of their way, stepping behind a festoon of line and wooden blocks.

When Madoc looked that way again, all he saw of her was an anonymous white hand on a rope.

Satisfied that the noncombatants were getting to relative safety, he leaned staight-arm against the rail, watching the now-unmoving line of red men, appraising as coolly as he was able the enemy's strength. He strained to see what kind of weapons they held, but it was too far to make out details.

He could see shafts of what were probably lances, some large items that looked like clubs, more of the deadly articu-

215

lated sticks, but nothing in any way resembling armor, in fact no evidence, no glint, no clang of metal of any sort. No swords, thank God, but those were bows there in the vanguard slightly forward of the line, which parted even as he watched, allowing a single blue tattooed warrior to step to the lapping waterline.

This fellow, far from being a strong warrior, was rather portly and dignified by three long feathers that bobbed above his head. He held a lance attached to a long, stiff strip of white material—Madoc could not tell what from this distance.

He tried a quick count by tens and came up with three times more armed men on the strand than on the *Horn*.

And silently, like a bad dream from which he could not waken, from both estuaries a fleet of the low, sleek boats slid into view, each manned by a dozen warriors. They backpaddled to hover a furlong from the *Horn*, close enough to see wide, dark eyes in white-painted faces amid splendidly colored feathers, and close enough for the nearest rank to target an arrow.

Except for the breeze in their feathers, not a one of them moved, an eerie sight to see. But it made them easy to count. In all, perhaps three hundred now confronted his pitiful fighting force and dependent civilians.

He was so focused on this hard arithmetic, it was giving him a headache between the eyes.

As he watched, several men began erecting a small pavilion with what appeared to be prefabricated materials carried in bundles. It had no walls, just four long poles and crosspieces over which they threw the flat fan-shaped palm leaves.

Another subordinate was kneeling under the thatch for some reason that became clear when a curl of smoke rose up from the sand. Others spread out furs on either side of the little fire. These workers trotted to stand attention beside the shelter while the entire host behind the chief stood totally still.

Only he moved, taking three paces into the water, pointing his lance with its white pennant directly at the *Horn*. He stepped ceremoniously out of the water and implanted the staff upright in the sand.

"Sir," Evan said at Madoc's side.

The arglwydd saw weapons and miscellaneous gear on his cuirass like food on a tray offered by Evan's hands—Durendal, the broad dagger, the helmet. Dull reflections from the sky touched polished metal as Madoc grasped with an itching palm the pommel of the great French sword and the various daggers. Evan took beautiful care of them. The edges burned blue.

Madoc sheathed his sword and linked it around his waist, then slipped a favorite sticker into his belt and glanced at the beach where the chief sat himself down under the shed: Perhaps from this shaded spot he intended to watch the battle.

Madoc offered his hands to Evan could tie on the wrist guards and held still to allow the ornamental chest armor to be buckled in place. An impressive piece of gear with a red-enameled dragon over the heart, it fit him like a second skin and picked up light on its surfaces.

Evan nodded. "Are we going to fight?"

Madoc did not answer immediately but with a one-eyed squint toward the beach suggested that Evan observe the enemy.

"See the headman," he said, as Evan locked him into the metal skin.

"Yes, sir." Evan was fully armed, already breathing faster with battle readiness.

"And how those with the second-highest feathers array themselves behind him?"

Evan nodded quickly, sweat glossing his lip.

"Outfit ten men in the brightest armor to do the same for me," Madoc requested gently, a memory blowing through his mind of something Owen had said to him not so long ago, and took the helmet, a new one that must have come from Owen's own locker. It was a huge, mean steel affair in the Greek style with a narrow T-shaped slit from eyes to chin, a cooker, Madoc surmised, that would suffocate him and cut off peripheral vision.

Holding it, wishing it was a lighter model with only a noseguard and nape flange, Madoc regarded the beach, where the breeze slapped the stiff pennant against the white pole.

"What do you think that means?"

Evan squinted. "Sir, it looks like a white flag."

"I think you are right." He looked at Evan. "Is it not strange that white means the same to them as to us? And red has got to mean the same to everyone. The man I killed last night was wearing red face paint."

"So were the ones I saw."

"But none of these people are painted red, except— Look at the chief more closely."

Evan peered, leaning, without spilling his tray of armament. "Half his face is white, the other red."

"Yes."

Evan grinned at him. "I was right—he is ready to fight, but he would rather talk."

Setting the helmet aside, Madoc said, "Keep this at hand."

"So we might have to fight them."

"Not all battles are fought with the sword, Evan."

Evan grinned and spun off to follow his orders.

Madoc caught Rhys's arm, succinctly briefed him, and asked for "some grand introduction on my signal."

Rhys was already reaching for the small harp on his back but felt it snag and someone immediately helping him.

"It is I, poet," Rhiannon said at his elbow. "Would you rather take Llais Mel? She is three times louder, at least."

There was a soft note in her voice for her husband that tore through Madoc like a lance. He would rather have her appear miserable in her new situation.

"You would loan her to me?"

Rhys sounded too attuned to her mood for Madoc's comfort. He knew for sure, then, that they had made love last night and loathed them both for obeying him so thoroughly.

Abruptly he said, "Rhiannon, get below."

"What have we in the way of gifts?" Rhys asked. If he heard the edge to Madoc's voice, he did not show it.

Rhiannon did not respond to Madoc either, did not even meet his eye, but wordlessly descended the peg ladder.

"Good idea, Rhys—" Madoc whirled on Evan, instructing him to get below, find a certain trunk among Madoc's gear, and retrieve the jewel-handled knife and a length of cloth.

"But not red," he amended the order. "Make sure it is white." If Bjorn's songs were right, the local people were partial to such goods.

What else might they value? He thought briefly of the precious peppercorns worth a king's ransom, snug in their sealed tin box, but bit off the thought; better to save their most valuable treasure against future negotiations. First he must secure the island as a safe haven. Then he must bargain for the prisoners. Who knew what lay ahead or what price he would have to pay? Anything could happen.

It gave him a fine chill as Evan hurried away, the open-ended possibility that existed on the other side of the brief water. He always felt this way before a battle.

He had been too long without a fight. He understood Evan's heightened senses and wild eyes; battle fever riddled his own blood. But the odds held no chance of success. To fight and die in outnumbered slaughter seemed an untimely end after so much effort to get here. Perhaps a chance with talk; they had not attacked. They were human enough to be able to count. Yet they waited over there as he did, to see what was going to happen.

Evan hesitated at the stair for Rhiannon, who saw him and handed up the great harp she had already uncased. Leaning close, he spoke to her, describing what the arglwydd had requested. She sank back down into the gloom.

Abovedecks the harp strings vibrated slightly under Evan's hands and in the moving air as he delivered it to Rhys, then turned back to wait for Rhiannon at the hold. Madoc was instructing a sailor to guide Rhys to the prow, but the poet shook off any aide, saying, "I know the path well."

"Play something stirring now to take away their attention," Madoc said, thinking out loud, stalling for time as his men finished their preparations. "The *Song of Roland*, perhaps. One of my favorites." It was a popular song among the minstrels who wandered singing in the French style.

"That is a long saga," Rhys remarked, as he tuned the harp.

Rhiannon handed up the folded cream-colored wool and the jeweled knife to the closest sailor, who took them to Madoc.

When he turned back to the rail, Huw and Wyn were waiting for him with Evan, who took the dagger and wool cloth from the sailor and stood there, awaiting Madoc's orders. Madoc adjusted the linkage of his sword to his belt and caught Evan's glance, a questioning look as he peered down at the arglwydd's bare feet.

"There is no time—".

"Wait," Evan said, setting aside the cloth and weapon and kicking off his own soft yellow leather boots. Before Madoc could speak, he knelt to slip them on and tie them midcalf.

Forward Rhys touched fingers to strings, sending a shiver of wet, cool sound undulating across the water, and launched into the many verses of the French ballad that told of the brave knight Roland's exploits with his mighty sword, Durendal.

Aft there was a general bustle as the escort got into the glittering court armor, useless stuff for fighting. They grumbled but worked fast.

"Hoist all but the stern anchor," Madoc instructed Huw. He glanced up at the wind in the pennant, determining its direction. "Make ready to haul the sheet at the first sign of trouble."

Sailors were unfastening coracles and popping them into the water that must have a white sand bottom for all the dazzling light reflecting up through six emerald fathoms.

Behind its heavy veil the sun stretched on toward noon.

Rhys picked up the tempo, sending wave after wave of lucid notes reverberating in the humid air. Madoc could not see what effect this was having on the waiting host, who remained unmoving except for the breeze in their feathers, but for himself it stirred his heart and made him want to take action.

"Do not stop," he urged Rhys as he got a signal from Wil and took to the sidelines with his escort following, clanging and cursing all the way.

Madoc told one of the men to hang the cloth from a spear tip. Just by the way they stood there displaying their weapons but not brandishing them Madoc read that the enemy wanted to talk and not fight. He ordered his coracle and the others behind him to hold a certain distance from shore. If the chieftain on the sand ordered all but an equal number of men back, then they would talk. If not, well, then it would be the end for the white men.

Madoc's gamble paid off.

The blue-tattooed chief gestured to his lieutenants, who in turn gestured to the array of red men. They stepped back to the tree line, a furlong from the water's edge, where Madoc disembarked.

For a long breath the two chieftains stood there looking at each other. Madoc felt he had lost some strategic advantage in that he must now approach the seated man as though he were a potentate. But that was a minor consideration.

He reached back and took the lance with the cloth from the sailor and shoved it into the sand next to the chief's pavilion. The breeze rippled the lovely white cloth, billowing it in a dazzling display across the sand.

The music from the ship swelled at that moment. The civilians had defied the order to stay below. One by one they

climbed to the rail to watch with the crew. It was too good a
show to miss. Someone was perfectly banging a drum—Madoc
would never know it was Rhiannon. Now Rhys's voice was
joined by others who knew the saga, a popular one sung by
beggar minstrals:

"'The Emperor gave my Durendal to me, and if I die, who
gets it may agree, that he who bore it, a right good knight
was he.'"

The wind, the snowy banner, the song all had a grand
effect; they could not have rehearsed it better. The sky even
appeared to be brightening as though to highlight the events
below.

Madoc saw the chief was smiling, an odd effect on his
half-red, half-white face already made strange by flattening.

They shared the same language of gesture that warriors
shared the world over. Madoc unlinked his sword and handed
it to Evan, likewise the dagger.

The chief followed with a similar gesture, divesting himself
of three obsidian or cane knives and an atlatl at his back. The
red escort spread out behind the small shelter. The red
seated chief gestured that Madoc should join him in the
shade.

Madoc looked back at his men, gesturing that they should
position themselves exactly as far from him as the red men
stood from their leader. Then, alert and watching the red
chief steadily, he walked slowly to the pavilion.

It may have been an effect of the new glare, the tension,
the hunger in his belly, and a general disorientation after the
attack, but Madoc's thoughts were strangely calm. His focus
was on the familiar music coming from behind like a friendly
hand on his shoulder. He hummed softly, thinking the words
of the popular song Rhys performed so well.

It was ironic and appropriate, Madoc thought, that the
great French knight Roland did not win final fame with his
sword, but with a battle horn. In fact, Roland personally lost
his final battle. The great sword Durendal—Forever—was
not even drawn when the hero died blasting away on the
horn, warning his comrades of impending attack.

The chief hand-gestured for Madoc to be seated on a
beautiful fur rug on the other side of the small fire. The dark
brown hide was finely dressed, thick, luxurious, and not from
any animal he could immediately identify. It might be bear,
except that it was so woolly. But it was too large to be a

sheep. He had never before seen a buffalo calf and had no comparison.

Madoc was feeling satisfied within that he had guessed right. Negotiation was understood everywhere.

The red man was no longer smiling, but neither did he appear hostile as he seated himself and took a long wrapped object from an aide, who removed a brand from the fire and touched its live end to the bowl of the pipe, for that was what the chief puffed on until the contents of the bowl glowed.

The aide backed off, eyes downcast like a servant anywhere.

The chief drew in a huge breath of smoke and while letting it trickle from his nostrils, offered the pipe to the seven directions—north, south, east, west, up, down, and here, then handed the pipe to Madoc, who had never smoked before, had never even seen anyone indulge in the habit, which would not be common in Europe for centuries. But he imitated his host, sucking in on the straw and lapsing into a coughing fit when the smoke hit his lungs. He understood that it was important to get through this, however, looking backward as he suppressed more hacking. The smoke was vile. His men appeared worried, so he made a motion that he was all right.

The red chief wore an unfathomable look on his slightly plump features, nothing that would be construed as laughing at the white man. But now he knew these people were truly foreigners, not to know about sacred tobacco.

During none of this did the chief speak. Finally he held up both of his palms facing the white man, then launched into Madoc's first lesson in the ancient handsign, amazed at how readily he picked up individual signs.

"I am Komas, miko of the Alabamans," he said with gesture and a language that sang. He did not translate his name, which meant "I Think," but merely pronounced it and pointed to his own chest. The idea of miko came from a gesture to the many warriors, a tight fist and the spoken name, Alabamans, then the other hand fisted and called Komas on top of the first. Clearly this communicated one Alabaman on top of others, chieftanship.

"And I am Madoc, miko of the Hundred." He did not try to translate the number, but pointed to his dramatically outfitted men and the ship out on the bright water, saying the word *cant*.

"Ma-doc," the red man said without gesture.

"Ko-mas," Madoc said.

They both nodded.

"Cant," Komas said, pointing to the ship.

"Alabamans," Madoc replied, gesturing at the red onlookers.

This established with painstaking gestures and simple words, they moved on in the same manner as the sun cruised the afternoon sky. While they spoke, various aides brought water in black pottery vessels and unidentifiable edibles on a woven reed tray.

The water bowl had only one dipper. Komas offered first drink to his guest, but Madoc demurred, insisting in gesture that Komas take the honor. Actually he was fearful of poison and wanted to see the red man swallow first.

He did with no hesitation, obviously used to being deferred to. Madoc gratefully took a long sip from the gourd dipper engraved with an intricate design he could not know had powerful magical significance to protect the chief from his proximity.

Komas nibbled fastidiously small morsels from the tray before he continued:

"I was prepared to bring a mighty offering to the Almighty Warrior. Each of you puny pale hairy persons would give up your hearts to my piety. This I was prepared to do until . . ."

He gestured at an old man who looked more a priest than warrior, who brought forth another object wrapped in soft leather painted with many designs, which he laid at the chief's feet. Deftly, as though handling something dangerous, the aide flipped back the corners of leather to reveal Madoc's own knife last held plunging into the bowels of the big red man on the ship.

As the shaman backed off, Komas eyed Madoc, apparently knowing to whom the blade belonged, and launched into a speech Madoc understood only obliquely, by gesture:

"Last night many of my warriors say you fought with this knife and used it with great courage upon my strongest soldier, who had never been defeated in war or game. You defeated him with this wonderful blade."

Madoc nodded, yes, that is my knife, in answer to the chief's obvious implication.

"You could only have done this amazing thing by magic."

Madoc missed this completely but waited attentively for the chief to say more that might clarify his intentions.

Using a corner of the symbol-laden leather covering so that

he never touched it, Komas lifted the blade and turned it this way and that so that the edge shown blue.

"I am an old man, miko of my people for more than fifty and five summers, but never in my many years have I seen metal such as this, which is as hard as stone, and which pierced the intestines of a man who was invincible."

The chief leaned back, as though to let Madoc chew on this.

Madoc was dying to retrieve his knife but stayed his hand because he suddenly had an intuition that if he did, he would not live to draw another breath. He breathed deeply, forcing himself to be still, and glanced at the chief's escort; sure enough they were watching him, hands on knife hilts. They must have orders to kill him if he looked about to harm their headman.

"Give me knives like this, and I will let your people live."

"We want to stay on this island," Madoc said, carefully choosing gestures that might convey this thought.

Madoc was not sure if he made his desire understood completely, so in the dust between them he sketched the general shape of the island on which they sat with the two rivers opening into the bay. Komas, who earned his name, understood immediately what was pictured, and it seemed he was telling Madoc that nobody owned the island and he did not care if Madoc wanted to use it.

The final deal was that for eight iron knives, one for himself and each of the subchiefs, Madoc's Hundred could stay on the island.

Madoc had his men bring over the white cloth and the jeweled dagger, which greatly pleased the chief. Unlike the Skraelings in Bjorn's saga, however, he did not wrap the cloth around his head. Instead he folded it neatly and handed it to one of his aides, whom Madoc was startled to notice for the first time was a woman. All that tattooed red flesh had become a blur, or perhaps she had only just now approached the pavilion. She was young, nubile, and naked except for her many tattoos and a shy smile she seemed to give only to himself before she turned away with the cloth draped over her arm.

Madoc felt the swift heat of his ears blushing and covered his embarrassment by ordering Dag and the six others to hand over their daggers. "Nothing to worry about," he assured them. "Wyn will be at his anvil tomorrow. We will soon have new knives." The one most valuable thing aboard the *St. Ann* that could not be harmed by the flames was her ballast, iron ingots from the southern heart of home.

Dag scowled: "I do not know if I want a Christian blade," he said, referring to the Mass said on Wyn's anvil, but he grinned when he said it and offered his own Norse knife.

Chief Komas beamed when each white man laid a knife on the pile before him, then nodded to his shaman to take the weapons away and purify them before they could be presented to the subchiefs, who were all smiling to each other behind the miko.

"You like her?" Komas asked, gesturing at the girl who could be no older than Gwen.

For a moment Madoc watched her walking away but then shook his head, no, no thank you.

"She likes you, I think," the chief said, winking, but Madoc tried to change the subject.

Madoc asked about the hostages. Komas made it clear that he did not have them, and he kept repeating a word that sounded like, "Mabila, Mabila," when Madoc pressed him about prisoners.

"The Alabamans take no prisoners," the chief said, and of course Madoc did not understand this military scruple in the strange language, but he got the message, primarily because the chief used the right number of missing people, that the captives were no longer in the area. He could not have explained why, but he got the feeling that the captives— Blessed Mary, let it be true—the captives, despite last night's nerve-rending screams, were still alive.

Chief Komas was not about to give up the captives he had taken to replace fallen warriors. He had no scruple against lying to this stranger. Let him deal with the Mabila.

"Do you know the man Aligapas?" Madoc asked, using his hands in what he hoped conveyed his question and pronouncing the name as he remembered it spoken by its owner in connection with what sounded like Alabaman. In case he was not making himself clear, he took the sun-disk from inside his tunic and held it dangling.

The chief was surprised and obviously familiar with the object. He reached; Madoc pulled it back in a closed fist, shaking his head in the unmistakable negative.

The miko shrugged but eyed the hand that held the

treasure, which had been his own for a short time. Aligapas
had made him give it up along with the hard-metal weapons.

He took a deep breath and launched into a long speech in
which he said that some days past his men had encountered
strange blond, bearded, blue-eyed tangle-tongues on the bay
just before this one—he pointed to the east, then sketched as
Madoc had done in the dust the local, unmistakably westward-
leaning coastline with its long sandbars. He pointed to this
one and then drew another just east of it, the other which
Madoc might have taken had the gateway looked bigger.

"Men like yourself," the miko concluded, and gave their
number, making a handsign at his chin for the idea of beards.
"In this many of your round canoes." He pointed to the
coracle Madoc had taken to this sand.

Madoc felt a chill of hope—Fair Beard might still be alive.

He went on to explain to the blank-faced Madoc that his
men had engaged the strangers in battle, had won, and had
taken them prisoner. But the Alabamans, being a subservient
and small tribe under the control of the more powerful
Mabilans, were required by treaty to report the invasion to
the Mabilans.

"We sent their heads and some of their weapons upriver to
Mabila," said the miko, making a dramatic gesture of cutting
off his own head. Madoc's hopes sank in frustration because
he did not know how to ask if any of those other white men
still lived.

"Aligapas?" Madoc said, connecting the name with the
place.

The chief knew exactly whom he meant, repeating the
name and a long string of other words Madoc could only
guess at.

"Yes, it is true that the lying coward of a Mabilan who
shares the blanket with female alligators, Aligapas, has your
prisoners," the red man said, nodding yes, yes, but he
glanced toward Evan, who stood nearby with Madoc's helmet
and weapons.

Clearly this chief was more interested in iron knives than
in whether Madoc's people occupied the island. He wanted
them here so he could get more of the wonderful metal
things. What Madoc could not know was that nobody owned
the island, that the very concept of land ownership had never
occurred to any red people he had met. And later he would

find out why the chief did not care if the whites set up camp there.

"We would like to trade other metal items for food," Madoc said in a roundabout way with many gestures. He tried to convey not only the knives but more peaceful objects as well—he made a gesture of hoeing in the ground, of hammering, of sewing—hoping this indicated other metal tools.

The chief's eyes brightened as he pointed to parts of Madoc's outfit—the brass fittings on his wrist guards, buckles and rings on his belt from which small tools still dangled.

Madoc nodded, "Yes, we can trade all these things."

Komas was highly pleased by this information. He made the handsign for eating and said words Madoc could not understand: We have much food, many fruits and nuts. The Alabamans did not farm but lived off the swamplands and trade.

Madoc had one more question to ask but was unsure how to go about it. He indicated the black hulk in the bay, then the warriors; he gestured away from the chief's person so the armed men—his own and the chief's—would not misunderstand. "Why," he was asking, "why did you attack us?"

The Alabaman understood and replied with a mirthless chuckle and a long, indecipherable remark in his singsong language. "My men came on a simple raid—that is what Aligapas said it would be. No warfare—a man, after all, cannot fight at night and chance dying to leave a lost spirit wandering about." He gestured at first one then the other ship. "We came because honor binds us to the Mabilans, and to get men to replace the ones your tangle-tongues killed— six widows weep, including that girl yonder whom you refuse to console.

"We came here last night for a little sport, a little blood sport, and what do we see advancing out of the night, spitting fire and calling down curses upon us and our grandchildren? The Uktena—" He more emphatically indicated the *Horn*, and then his men. "My soldiers attacked because they were afraid. Aligapas did not say we would have to fight a spirit being."

He stared straight into Madoc's eyes. "Strange that a spirit-being would burn. . . ."

His people were coastal dwellers and did not have the same regard for the river-spirit as the tribes that fished the rivers. But he still respected the river-spirit. "It was a bad thing that Aligapas had us fight the Uktena. Three of my soldiers died in the darkness—how will their souls find the western path?"

Madoc stared at him, entranced by the dramatic gestures and singing words the red man used to deliver this query. He understood very little of it but the tone:

"Aligapas did not tell all the truth, which is worse than lying." He saw that the white man probably did not understand half of what he was saying, even with his fluent handsign.

"Aligapas," the miko finally said, giving up subtlety and bluntly laying the blame on the man who engineered the raid. "Subchief Aligapas, may his balls turn green—he took your people north to the Mabilan heartland." He pointed upriver. The Mabilan homeland was not on the sea in those days but was seated just above the junction of the Rivers Alabama and Tombigbee, or Coffin-Maker.

"Mabila, Mabila," the chief said as he stood. The meeting had come to an end. Catlike, he stretched out the kinks. Madoc followed his lead, towering over the stubby little red man.

With a friendly expression on his flat face, the miko made a sign so elegant in its succinct representation of two round globes undulating in the rhythm of the girl's hips as she had walked away, Madoc knew instantly what the old man was asking: "Are you sure you do not want her?"

No, really, thank you, Madoc replied in his own language and in gesture, praying he was not insulting the offer. The miko shrugged; these were strange people. He seemed to gesture at the trees behind them while saying reassuring words with handsign aimed at Madoc's chest, which he took to mean something close to, "You have rented an island."

What the Alabaman chief actually said before he walked off with stately dignity toward waiting canoes was, "I take your hard metal, I take your bright grave-goods. This time I will not eat your beating heart."

Chapter 18

I have been a blue salmon.
I have been a dog, a stag,
A roebuck on the mountain.
A stock, a spade, an axe in the hand,
A stallion, a bull, a brick,
A grain which grew on a hill,
I was reaped, and placed in an oven.

—by Taliesin
Welsh
c. A.D. 500

The first night Aligapas slit Nona's throat, ate her living heart, and roasted her over a slow fire in the traditional manner of a dog feast, but was infuriated when Gwen refused the honor of joining him in the meal.

Despite that Aligapas was highly pleased with the outcome of the raid—he had more than fulfilled his uncle's command. There had been only a few red casualties, all of them Alabaman. He even had some extra for himself, and a dog feast was well within his demands as a successful hunter. The Alabamans considered it something of a cause to celebrate that the Uktena they had just fought had not killed them all and left their spirits to roam for a long, long time.

Aligapas had sat on the honored buffalo skins with the Alabaman chief while the preparations continued.

The Alabaman warrior enjoyed his dog feast, but Komas and the men with him were not there from any desire of their own. They had been mustered through kinship duty to help him get the captives back up to the primary village of Mabila.

The captives were fascinating, a variety of the strangers

229

that even included one with the darkest skin Aligapas had ever seen. The Alabaman shaman wanted to see if these were true human beings, so Aligapas had given them two to test. He told them they could test the black man but not kill him because his uncle the grand miko Shell-of-Many-Colors would have to see him to believe him. He said they could test the frailer of the two women, but he wanted to keep her alive for his uncle. The red-haired one Aligapas marked with face paint as his own.

Of the other male captives with the strange scalp-circles, Aligapas gave two for the torture pole. The Alabamans were experts at various techniques that provided a good show.

While the majority of the warriors who participated in the raid drank and ate and danced that night, several sat off by themselves, disdaining food. They had their sandstone grinders at work, sharpening fifty splinters from young pines. While one Alabaman began the drum, and the rest joined in the chant, others tied the two priests down and began piercing their skin with the splinters, using close knowledge of musculature to place the soaked wood between large muscles of the arms and legs.

The white men appeared to be invoking spirits.

But the screams that Madoc's Hundred heard back on the bay came later. After sufficient dancing and smoking, the Alabamans presented the two chosen captives, painted, feathered, and unable to stand without help, to Aligapas as the highest ranking in attendance and proceeded to ignite the pine splinters one by one.

It was a venerable ceremony that produced the widest range of human vocalizations Aligapas had witnessed, and he was something of a connoisseur.

Despite these esteemed festivities that were considered powerful medicine for the individual warriors who had risked their souls to fight the Uktena, the six Alabaman warriors given the duty were glad to be on the trail early the next morning.

It dawned another bright unusually mild day for the season. Komas had bade them farewell and went with the majority of the red men back to his village and his later meeting with Madoc, leaving six to accompany Aligapas north.

These men would have rather been on the burial duty, considered the most onerous because of the lengthy cleansing rituals that must follow. But that would have been preferable to this long, uninteresting march to the foreign upcountry. Their favorite foods were saltwater oysters, sea-turtle eggs, tiny net-caught shrimp, and the great fish unapii, which they hunted with lances. They wanted to go home to their fat, pretty wives. They did not like to be under trees, unable to watch the sky. The Alabamans were littoral—their grandfathers' grandfathers' grandfathers had lived along the beach between the bay and what would someday be Spanish Pensacola. They were saltwater canoemen, feather and butterfly collectors, uncomfortable with upland travel. They told bad legends about upriver country.

At first they totally ignored the remaining captives. On the trail, an ancient pathway from here to there through the swampland, then on up into the pine forests and finally the rolling plateau country forever green in a sea of cane—for that was how the ancient trace meandered like a hard-packed brown stream—the Alabamans spaced themselves back along the slave line.

Aligapas led the line, with the eldest Alabaman behind him and the slaves strung out with the rest of the Alabamans walking beside them. As they moved along the trail, they broke off twigs that grew into the boundary of the path—thus was the trace maintained by its travelers for thousands of seasons.

The Alabamans were on this march only to help Aligapas get these oddities up to his miko, a known collector of oddities. So they ignored them and avoided touching them for fear of contamination. But they sneaked curious perusal whenever possible at the captives without having to look into those pale eyes.

The monks with their bald crowns were especially weird to them, men who looked peacefully scalped, an incongruously upsetting idea to the red men, containing elements of opposites.

So after the raid they had scalped each one, meticulously cutting a ring of hair around the shaved crown, and made special oblong frames, instead of the usual circular ones, for the strange scalps. Each of the Alabamans was working on a scalp in the manner throughout the trip. It was a complicated process—stretching and tanning the lock of skin and hair, sewing it to a reed frame, then painting it and sewing appropriate feathers into the design was a lengthy process that none finished until long after this march was over. These scalp locks would be especially prized for the bald spot within the hair of brown, red, and yellow—a true novelty among black-haired people.

Gwen, behind the red, black, and white paint Aligapas smeared on her forehead and chin, watched the red men pointedly ignoring herself and the others. Aligapas had also pressed his red paint-smeared hand on the back of her tunic, a sign of ownership.

When they stopped—about every three hours—the Alabamans would make a circle and talk in a low, tuneful language, working on their scalp tassels, passing around a little pottery pipe bowl attached to a curving stem that was as long as her father's arm. These swamp dwellers were short, bowlegged, almost plump, with small feet and hands and powerfully muscled but stubby limbs. It was funny to watch them hold the pipe out as far as their hand could stretch, then crick their necks backwards like some kind of owl to accommodate the things.

Aligapas, whom Gwen had nicknamed Shovel-Face for his cranial deformation, did not take part in these relaxations. He stayed off by himself, performing strange rituals over a private smokeless fire. His behavior caused the Alabamans to mutter among themselves, even to make sly, almost-funny faces at him. They knew the song of cleansing and what it was for, if not the specific circumstances that occasioned it.

Disdainfully they stayed upwind of him, suspecting by the degree of his ceremonials the degree of his contamination. It was a satisfying reversal to the Alabamans, who were usually looked down upon as the most ugly, backward, short, unintelligent, and weakest of all the local nations. Here they who were called stinkards among their near relatives of Mabila could look down upon one of the elite.

Gwen watched all this, without understanding specifics, when they stopped and while on the trail as best she could, but perceiving the lines of tension between the two distinct tribes of red men. Studying them in this way, Gwen kept her mind from the bottomless panic she felt when she thought about what was probably going to happen to the captives. She was further discomfited by the warm trickle of menstrual blood that came on suddenly late that morning. At least she was free of the grinding cramps that had hit her before.

By afternoon the guards became bored and began shooting, with miniature bows and arrows and incredibly fine-knapped points, small scurrying rodents that moved too fast for Gwen to see. They strung the furry gray bodies on a stout line and laughed among themselves about how good these were going to taste at tonight's camp.

To Gwen these small, flat-footed men appeared somehow innocent, childlike, not unlike what she imagined the Gaelic little people to be. Their voices, though male, were light and melodic, their movements graceful despite their oddly proportioned bodies. They were extremely brown with a tinge of the metallic, as though they had been burnished. The effect was skin coloration darkened by a lifetime of glare and complete nudity, but they had also plastered themselves with bear grease to keep off the small, terrible flies that deviled the captives with angry red welts that itched like fire.

She had heard that her ancestors the ancient Britons had painted themselves blue and imagined that they must have looked something like these men with their indigo tattoos. She now saw the intricacy of the blue tattoos these people wore, some more than others, guessing that the patterns concerned rank.

Aligapas, who was obviously in charge, had more rings on his limbs and torso than any of the Alabamans. Despite their differences, these people shared a common Muskogean language and tradition—the Alabamans, which meant Thicket-Clearers, somewhat older than the Mabilans. They had the same clan and marriage customs, and the same inherited differences in rank. But the men remaining with Aligapas were commoners, with only a few tattoo rings on each limb and additional designs on chest and faces. They plucked almost all their scalp hair out except for a single long string that fell from the crown and was diligently tended, braided, painted, and fluffed at the end like a vulture's collar.

Aligapas frowned at the Alabamans, his flat, lopsided mouth working as he chewed on some unreadable grudge, but he did not interfere with their rodent-sport. It did not interrupt the progress of the line. They shot from their positions, challenging each other and making a game of it.

They soon had a full catch of these creatures but were still full of spirit. One of them grabbed Ffiona's baby from her arm, which was untied so that she could hold him on her hip. Laughing like small boys, they began tossing the infant back and forth among themselves, the same way they warmed up before ball play.

"Dewi—" his mother cried.

At first the baby rent the air with terrible cries, joined by his mother, who whimpered and cried each time Dewi screamed.

But it soon became apparent that the men were not rough with him and meant no harm. They were good at tossing and catching. Soon the little boy was giggling each time one of them caught him just under his little arms and whirled him around, a sound that seemed strangely out of place under the circumstances.

Aligapas stepped among them and took the baby by his curly, sandy hair and jerked him from the crook of a warrior's arm.

The Mabilan's face suddenly changed. He slyly glanced over to see that enough anguish was being milked from the woman. He held the child up as though inspecting meat. He plucked at one little hand. The baby was wide-eyed in front of him. "Look at this skinny thing." He rolled the arm between thumb and forefinger in an unmistakable gesture of testing.

He shook his head in an exaggerated way, licking his wide lopsided lips. "This baby must be much fatter before I eat him."

Ffiona cried a harsh liquid sound and tried to step out of the line. The cord choked her and she stumbled back, coughing. She was the color of lowland pottery, ash gray.

"I gave him water," Ffiona whimpered to Gwen. "I was kind to him, so why would he hurt my baby?"

Gwen knew from the red man's behavior that he did not remember this woman giving him a drink the night he himself was captive in the white camp.

"That is a perfectly good baby," said the elder warrior. "His heart would be such a small sacrifice, I would not bother to eat him. But he would be a fine son." His own sons were grown now, and his wife had no child to spoil as the swamp people loved to spoil children. "Look at how wise he is—does he cry out? No—" He turned to assay the opinions of his fellows, who all nodded yes, it was true that this baby boy was smart.

That evening when they stopped for the day, his mother continued making her cringing sounds.

The captors did not feed the prisoners but gave them water. But they let the baby nurse whenever he seemed fussy.

Despite the insect bites, which she tried not to scratch, Gwen had been watching the way these men spoke to each other, the way they teased, the way their camaraderie seemed to shut out not only the captives but also Aligapas. When one of them let slip the awl with which he was punching holes to lace the scalp lock onto a small round frame, the elk-horn point scraped an ankle, but she saw he was supposed to pass it off as nothing.

The elder, who had taken out his knapping instruments— an antler, a flint flake, and a leather hand guard with a thumbhole—began working at a blade until a flake stung his face. He looked up with the long, sharp sliver sticking out of his cheek. The others called to him, teasing, "You make a blade that cannot wait to draw blood, Sitlitiga."

The warrior used his tongue to push the shard out from inside his mouth, then plucked out the splinter. "Stand close enough, and if you are lucky, some of my power will rub off onto you." The puncture bled furiously, as though he were weeping scarlet tears. Sitlitiga wiped it off and licked his fingers, fresh wound-blood being considered a healing medicine.

Listening to Ffiona whimper, Gwen saw that they valued a show of courage. It obviously pleased them that the little child thoroughly enjoyed the dangerous sport.

"Ffiona, try to stop crying," she called when all the red men's attention was on the bobbing baby, who gave a healthy squeal when one of the warriors held him for a while, high on his upstretched arm, turning him gently. The child instinctively put out his arms, cooing with delight to be flying.

Ffiona did not hear her. The prisoners' hands were tied in front with clever knots on the underside that teeth could not untie, so they had some use of their fingers. She clawed a nasty bite on her knee and kept repeating, "Dewi, Dewi—"

"They will treat you better if you look strong."

Ffiona did not seem to be listening.

"Are you hurt? Did you hit your head or something?" Gwen tried to move a little closer forward. Ffiona was one captive away from her, with Ari between them. Behind her was the slightly basted Father Brian, then three of the other monks. All of these were suffering shock and loss of blood from their strange scalpings, a war memento usually taken from the dead.

The slave line now was slumped in dumb fatigue, still trussed together only a little less brutally than the rodents.

Ffiona made nonsense sounds, drooling, digging away at her raw knee, crying and pointing toward the baby, whom the warrior brought suddenly downward—the way he trained his own sons when they were small—causing the child to cry out in alarm.

"She is senseless, lady," Ari whispered, himself scabbed in several places where they had tested him with the kanskak knives, as sharp as glass shards. In his case the tests were to determine if he was mortal or spirit. The verdict was split and could not be further tested because of Aligapas's order to keep him alive.

"Try to talk to her, get her to stop it."

Dewi was laughing again as Sitlitiga talked to him. "Yes you are a courageous little warrior, yes indeed you are." And he set the boy down on the pine needles, where he began to explore.

Ffiona still whimpered.

When Gwen had a good look at her, she saw the young mother chewing on a strand of her lank hair. Huge purple circles lined her eyes, though Gwen had not seen anyone hit her. She slumped like a crone instead of a twenty-five-year-old wife. Her movements were uncoordinated; she moaned the baby's name again, her face slick with her juices, her eyes inflamed.

The baby recognized his mother's voice and crawled to her, where he found a breast and happily settled down. Ffiona was so thin, Gwen wondered how she had enough to make milk. Despite Aligapas's earlier tease, Dewi was thriving.

That night, as everyone prepared to sleep, Gwen became aware that Shovel-Face was watching her. She stared back, then curled with her back to him, trying to find warmth in her own embrace.

They were on the trail again before dawn. The elder warrior continued to play with the baby. He went off into the wood and met up with them again at their noon rest, a collection bag full of hickory nuts. He cracked these with his head-knocker and mashed them into a paste, which he fed with his fingers to Dewi while holding him on his knee.

Ffiona cried that they were poisoning her son.

Aligapas complained about the mother's whining, so one of the warriors untied Ffiona. He led her stumbling back to the end of the line behind the three monks.

During that break they gave each of the captives a drink made of hominied cornmeal and a sliver of jerked meat.

Sitlitiga tried to give Ffiona a brew he concocted of herbs carried in his medicine bag and fresh-gathered along the trail. He knew these leaves—wild cherry, thistle, milkroot—worked on what his people generally termed female problems. He also threw in specifics, including dried blueberry flowers, to calm her. But she turned away from the medicine. There was something oddly gentle in the way Sitlitiga shrugged and set the wooden cup at her feet and walked away.

He returned to a hide he had spread out. On it he had put the soft green plantain leaves that he had earlier spread with bear grease from his pack. Gwen watch him as he inspected the leaves, then brought one to her and offered it. She gestured that she did not understand—was she supposed to eat it?

Sitlitiga pointed to the insect bites on her arms and legs, then to the goo on the leaf. He left her and offered a leaf of the darkened grease to Father Brian and the others.

Gwen tried the salve and was relieved to feel an immediate coolness on the stinging welts. She reached over and spread some of it on Ffiona's knee where she had scratched herself raw; the woman did not even notice.

On the trail again the warriors bounced the baby some more.

They were performing fancy passes with him now; Dewi still was happy with the attention, and no accident had happened. Then in the middle of the game one of the lesser Alabamans yelled to the others to look at Sitlitiga's catch. The warrior was holding the little fellow by his curly hair at arm's length while he shat explosively as only a baby can, face pinched and purple.

The other Alabamans teased the warrior with his hand full—he danced sideways to avoid the salvos.

"Now what are you going to do with him?" a warrior asked.

The baby seemed to be finished, then looked up with a happy grin on his little face for Sitlitiga, who gracefully turned and walked back along the narrow corridor between the captives and the wall of jungle, then slapped the child against Ffiona's dangling hand. She grasped, but the baby was slick and starting to squeal because the hunter's grip pulled the hair at his neck. The baby bounced and rolled over the padded ground beneath the pine trees. He did not cry out until he stopped rolling.

The Alabaman casually backhanded Ffiona, curtly addressing her and obviously punishing her for dropping the child. He stepped around her, Ffiona cringing and sobbing and about to fall down, and scooped up the baby, holding him carefully.

Aligapas was furious that the Alabaman had struck a Mabilan prisoner and was advancing on the Alabaman.

"You do not bruise the grand miko's prisoners," he said, gripping him at the shoulder. The shorter but stronger Sitlitiga whirled on him, brushing the other's hand away.

"She is a worthless hole—she will not make it to Mabila, much less pass the test of stones, her spirit's so broken."

Gwen followed their hands, which moved in the sign language as they spoke, the more gestures, the higher the emotion.

But after a while they seemed to tire of abusing the mother. Sitlitiga took the baby to a creek nearby and returned with him slippery pink and giggling. He placed Dewi on the ground, and the baby crawled to his mother, where he curled up to feed.

Gwen glanced away from them to see the slit-eyed Shovel-Face watching her from the shadows. She knew what would be coming and began thinking of what she was going to do. Flashes of memory stabbed her—the night her mother was killed, the smell of their burning house, the heaving bulk of Uncle David's soldier. She repressed a shudder and tried to ignore the red man.

Presently he approached her and untied her hands.

Using gestures, he ordered her to remove her leather tunic tied with a length of silk cord. She stared stonily at him.

He ordered her again with words, but she replied by making the handsign for shovel and face and no, no, no.

He whisked out a flint skinning knife and in an extension of the motion slit her clothing from crotch to neck, like gutting an animal, without touching the skin beneath.

Then he slipped the blade under the drawstring holding up her skirt—this costume was a modification of the long-sleeved, ankle-length, light woolen tunic she was wearing the day they left. A leather tunic of that length was uncomfortable and bulky. But a shorter tunic over a skirt of two leather panels worked quite well and allowed her more freedom of movement at the waist. She had left the sides unsewn in the skirt below the knee to make walking easier. All the women of Madoc's Hundred had come to similar conclusions about all-leather clothing. No material they had was soft enough or thin enough for the comfort of cloth, so they broke the garment in two.

The skirt fell away, revealing her foam-white skin mottled here and there by insect bites. She saw a tick buried in the line of her waist and plucked it off.

Her thighs were all of her that retained some semblance of baby fat. Their inner sides were smeared with dark blood; her period had started during the first hours of the march.

Aligapas dropped his crooked bottom lip, revealing a full face of large, long ivory-colored teeth. A hiss escaped between them, and he backed off. He looked at the knife of particularly opalescent gray flint from far west beyond the great Water Road and traded dearly in songbird feathers. It was his most prized possession, and now he regarded it as though it had turned into a serpent. He let go of it so fast, it might have been hot.

The eyes of the other red men widened at the sight of menstrual blood on the girl. They involuntarily drew back but were not contaminated because they had avoided contact.

Aligapas backed from the camp fire and ran into the jungle.

The Alabamans looked at each other and grinned—this was as close as they came to a dirty joke, since a woman's moon blood was the most profane thing that a man could imagine. In their sport and on their hunting sorties, moon blood figured in their hearty insults to each other.

Father Brian was looking at his bare feet. He too was totally naked, and oddly blistered on the outsides of his arms and legs only. He would not look at Gwen. He seemed to be dazed and would not answer her. She wanted to discuss a plan of escape. She tugged on the line between them. It must be pulling at his neck, but still he had ignored her.

Brian was steadily not looking at her now without any clothes on. Father Simon had given him some advice on how to fight lust in the body. He had given himself a long recital to accomplish—he was nearly through the Book of Proverbs, which he was already planning to commit to parchment as soon as they could settle down and establish some sort of scriptorium.

Passing through an open thicket this afternoon, he saw some startling purple berries that would surely make a usable ink. Without the sheep, parchment might be a problem. But as the day wore on, he caught glimpses, in the thick canopy of the trees overhead, of flying squirrels. His apprenticeship covered the making of parchment from several smaller animals.

Walking through the jungle, tied to the captain's red-haired daughter ahead and the man behind him by a rope around their necks, Father Brian had used the time to think.

A year ago to the day if Father Simon was right—a few days less if it was the captain's date—Father Brian had stood in St. Brendan's scriptorium taking one last look at all those books. The walls from the stone floor up to the ceiling had been lined with more than a thousand volumes, for St. Brendan's was a small monastery; the scriptorium doubled as the library.

The duty had fallen to him, ordained only a few months, to choose what manuscripts the community would take into exile. Its abbot was more interested in fighting King Henry than in preserving any of the brotherhood's treasures, so sure was the fighting abbot that they would win. In the hierarchy of the scriptorium, Brian was an illuminator—he painted initials, letters, and borders of the illuminated books in the style of the great monastery school at Lindisfarne, long gone under the viking ax.

Before his removal to Owen's household, Brother Ely had served as the text writer who filled out the pages Brian adorned.

Only a few monks had remained at St. Brendan's. Many of Brian's seniors had fled to sister minsters in Ireland or died in the fighting that had greatly disrupted the monastery's chain-of-command. That Brian was a priest, albeit a very new one, made him the only candidate for the task of choosing the books.

Brian had found it a terrible decision, knowing as he did that many of the treasured volumes would be destroyed or at least consigned to oblivion in a Vatican subbasement, because as Celtic manuscripts they would be considered heretical.

Scripture was safe—they were Latin, and their illuminations would be valued—that talent the English begrudged the Celts. But the Celtic lore, the secular pieces like Taliesin's poetry in the Welsh vernacular, would probably not survive.

His eyes had misted as he passed by his own work-in-progress, a new gospel, the folio page mounted on his high desk, the fruit of two months' labor, complete but for the foot border, the arch of the initial letter in acanthus leaves adorned with all the birds of Mona Isle. His work lay exactly as he left it the afternoon before. . . .

"Good-bye little book," he said, remembering a poem from the legendary scribe of the woods: *O, little book, a day will come when someone over thy page will say, the hand that wrote it is no more. . . .*

On that day Brian had chosen fifty books—all that would fit into the four trunks. The rest were left as they stood for the English, who were reportedly within a day's march, escorting a community of Benedictines to take over St. Brendan's.

Owen's men had come galloping into the monastery gates with the news that the brothers had only a few minutes to pack everything and be escorted to Owen's estate on the coast.

Then, months later, when Owen told them to make ready for further exile into unspecified territory, the night the arglwydd gathered Madoc's inheritance, Father Brian was once again the man to decide what books would be taken.

That night he had looked over all the fifty volumes again, taking them from the trunks and putting them into three piles in order of priority. He had to choose not only for posterity but also for practical use, because the brotherhood did not know how long its brethren must wait for reinforcement, if any ever joined them in the venture.

But now he had only one trunk—the smallest of the four and more the size of a footlocker—for the precious remnant. He spent the whole night making his selections, which were primarily sacred illuminated masterpieces, most of which were three hundred years old: the *Book of Genesis*, *Song of Solomon*, *Psalms*, the Four Gospels, the *Book of Revelation*, and the *Septuagint Apocrypha*. He packed only a handful of other volumes, none of which were illuminated, including *The Song of Brendan*, *St. Benedict's Rule*, *The Teachings of St. Patrick*, St. Augustine's *Confessions*, and the slim little collection of Taliesin's poetry.

Individual brothers all had their own breviaries, some of which were richly illustrated, and a couple of the nonreligious had small missals, but the fifteen volumes Brian crammed into the trunk made up the primary library.

He had felt even worse about that decision and prayed it was the last of such he would ever have to make.

Then last night the final terrible decision, made in terror and without enough thought. Brian had been aboard the *St.*

Ann when Simon first revealed himself, had been one of those who failed to get the starved and thirst-maddened Simon to relent in his determination to seize the ship. He was one of those who tried to restrain the crazed priest when he hoisted the sail, and he was one of those the priest threw off in his mad strength. Brian was thrown backwards, hit his head, and passed out.

When he roused himself, the ship was in flames. His first thought was of the books. He ran to the trunk in the hold and threw open its lid. In the flickering light from above, for the fire had not reached below yet, with the beginning screams of those caught by the enemy on deck, Brian had tried to concentrate on yet another, more terrible choice.

Each book was lodged in a heavy leather travel case with the title in gold leaf on the cover, decorated with brass fittings and stamped with the dragon of Gwyneth curled around the Celtic cross.

But the screams from above had been horrible, and in familiar voices, so he just grabbed, and what he grabbed was what was on top—the *Gospel of St. John, Psalms,* and *Benedict's Rule*.

He could have carried more, but smoke was starting to fill the hold, and it panicked him.

He threw those three volumes into a burlap sack hanging on a peg and tied it to his waist with his cincture, then hauled himself coughing and choking with his burden up the peg stair. Amid blinding smoke and bright flames, he staggered past bodies of his brothers already bleeding from huge holes in their chests. He had stumbled over the rail into the water.

Someone had helped him minutes later as he heaved himself and his soggy bag up the *Horn*'s sidelines. It was Wyn, who embraced him, crying, "Oh, Lord, what have I accomplished?"

Brian had not thought much about it, figuring the man was delirious. He freed himself and went back to the rail, planning to jump into the water. It was only smoke that scared him, and there would be some time before actual flames burnt through the thick oak planks to the cargo hold.

But Wyn had grabbed him, begging, imploring, and finally ordering him not to return, even though Brian screamed, "The fire has not reached the hold yet—I can save a few more—" wrenched free, and plunged again into the cold dark water.

He had no trouble reboarding the *St. Ann*'s port side, where flames had not yet penetrated. The fire in the sail had everyone's attention on deck, so Brian was able to make it to the hold, where flames had broken out far forward and were burning clean through so that the smoke was now escaping through the bulkhead. Brian sprang down the pegs to the trunk, where he grabbed up more books, this time not caring about the titles. But when he looked around, there was no other sack to carry them, so he shucked his cassock, tied off the arms, and shoved the books into its skirt, then threw it over his shoulder and, pinkly naked in the firelight, hauled himself back to the deck.

At that moment he had seen the tattooed warrior reach out with a knife to grab Madoc from behind.

Brian thought his terrible choices were all made. But in a sliced second he did not know he was making another as he dropped his cassock full of books and plunged after Madoc's attacker.

Brian was young and healthy, but obligatory farm work at the monastery had also made him strong. He caught the warrior in a hammerlock, taking him totally off guard, and spun him into the sizzling pool of flaming oil.

"Father forgive me!" Brian screamed when he saw the fellow burst into flame on every oiled surface of his body, even his open mouth, from which fire like vomit seemed to fly as he ran back into the wall of the blaze.

Brian had to duck as Madoc whirled on him, then he saw who it was who had saved him from a sliced throat.

Brian remembered dragging the captain to the port rail to the only dark spot where there seemed to be no flames, screaming at him to jump. Brian thought he could make it back to the place where he dropped the books, still safe in his tied cassock only a few steps away and not yet burning.

He remembered the captain astraddle the rail, his clothes seared off, pulling at Brian's slick, naked arm.

Brian slipped loose.

Just then the boom and sail had begun to slide down the mast as the lines burned away. It came in stages, so that the two men had time for action—Madoc to leap over into the water, Brian falling back out of the way.

Brian remembered a sheep screaming pitifully, the ceiling of flames crashing down in its final plunge, cutting off that escape. Brian could only depart along a narrow corridor of flame. But far away it seemed he could see the stern in darkness that must lead to the water below. He ran the gauntlet of fire so close it singed the sandy red hair from his arms and legs.

Then he had leapt toward the darkness. Cool water rushing around his blistered body was all he remembered after that when he awoke on the slave line in the Alabamans' temporary camp between Gwen and another monk slumped bloody about his head and shoulders beside Brian who remembered nothing after cool water.

He looked up, halting in line, to see a gray sky overhead far beyond the crowns of the cypress. The man behind him stumbled into Brian, and nearby a red man shouted, coming toward them with a slim kanskak whip in his hand.

"I told you not to bruise the miko's captives," Aligapas said, walking back to the Alabaman with the cane.

"Then you can discipline him yourself," the young warrior said, and turned to his brothers. "I do not know about you, but I am going home." It was his decision. Besides, the large town of Mabila lay just over the next rise.

The warrior turned back down the path and soon was out of sight among the rustling cane of the upland plateau. Four of his fellows immediately followed. Sitlitiga stood with his weight casually on one foot, regarding Aligapas, whose face had gone stony as he watched the escort depart.

The men and women on the slave rope stared from one to the other to see what was going to happen and if it would resound upon themselves. Aligapas glanced their way, calculating his chances of getting over the next rise with these captives.

"Help me get them to the test of stones, and you can take the brat, if you want him."

They did not use gesture, so what passed between them was lost on the whites. Ffiona, cradling the sleeping baby on her soiled hip, seemed to be walking in her sleep.

Sitlitiga beamed agreement, and by clapping his hands together urged the prisoners to move along, move along. Aligapas took his place at the head of the line, and the prisoners strung out behind him while the Alabaman brought up the rear.

Shortly they came upon the forwardmost of Mabila's lookout stations at the river crossing where the Alabama and the Tombigbee met. Mabila was just north and west of the junction.

From here could be seen the tallest of the temple pyramids beyond a shaggy line of low trees that framed the river. Beyond that windbreak stretched the low, rich fields. It was late in the day, so there were no workers about, but from their vantage point on the river's edge they could see upstream several colorful canoes with people dressed in feathers scooting downstream, putting into the landing on the opposite shore, chanting for a celebration.

Aligapas turned to Sitlitiga and nodded curtly.

He walked briskly to Ffiona and relieved her of the baby without waking him. At first she did not notice, but when he turned and without another word began walking purposefully down the path, she weakly called, "Dewi," and started to whimper and tried to follow him. The line around her neck held her back, and she leaned against it, pulling the last monk on the chain.

Aligapas gestured to Brian without touching him, then pointed to one of several dugout canoes pulled up on the gravel beach. Brian saw what he wanted and replied with a tug on the neck rope, which the red man cut on either side of him, but he left on the hobble around his ankles.

Soon they were all in the bobbing boat. Aligapas told Brian to paddle from the middle while he guided the boat with a paddle on the aft thwart. They were met on the opposite shore by the feathered group, who stared with unmasked curiosity at the captives, asking Aligapas a series of rapid-fire questions. He was clearly impatient with them, most of whom were men.

"Help me paint them for the test," he said, and the group cheerfully agreed, glad to witness a grand entertainment.

With gestures and switching of the mean little cane rod, Aligapas had the captives moving along a wide, well-trod path now that wandered down through a bean field where dried vines were heaped, waiting to be burned.

Gwen, despite her discomfort and fear, was taking everything in: the people with their gaily colored feathers and bright face paint, the gardenlike fields on either side of the path, and finally the high angled sides of a brilliant red-clay-covered pyramid that loomed on one side. Smoke drew a lazy smear upwards from its pinnacle where a pavilion had been erected. From here she could see men shrunk by distance along its crown, apparently watching in this direction.

Others along the way joined the chattering, festive group

accompanying the captives. To Gwen and the others on the line it seemed as if a pleasant party lay ahead, but she knew this was mostly hope on her part. She remembered the first night when the Alabamans had been in a similar mood before they torched the monks with pine splinters. They partied all though that long night while the white men died slowly.

Now a cluster of cane-and-thatch buildings lay ahead in the shadow of the great red pyramid.

The almost purple sky was streaked with long orange clouds. A pleasant, sweet-smelling breeze fell about her as she moved behind Ari. Finally, just outside the clay-marked flat area where a large fire burned, Aligapas drew them up. He spoke with the feathered ones, who ran off toward the large pavilion at one end of the square and upon another clay-covered earthern platform. By now many people over there were turning in this direction, and soon a milling, animated, muttering throng of about five hundred men and women were lining up on either side of the plaza, at the same time bending over and picking up something on the ground that Gwen could not see.

Gwen even saw small children grinning on either side of a long corridor that ended directly at the low-burning fire.

Aligapas tried to form them into another line, pointing at that space between the people, some of whom were tossing stones and catching them in their palms.

Ari was still first in line. Aligapas prodded him with the kanskak whip. Ari glanced at Gwen over his shoulder.

"Farewell, Lady Gwen," he said gravely with a smart bow.

Aligapas gave him another prod, and he began trotting down the line. Immediately the crowd on either side began calling imprecations at him, tossing the stones at his legs and feet. A couple of the little red children had switches they whisked at his calves as he tried to run faster.

Aligapas turned to Gwen, who stared him down. His mouth twitched, and he poked her buttocks with the cane. She stepped out of his reach and into the corridor, where women's hands shot out at her, yanking at her hair.

At the far end she could see Ari stumble beyond the last of the switches and leap across the fire. He made it onto the hard-packed field that lay in front of the pavilion on its low, long mound. It appeared that the throng stopped its abuse if a captive could get beyond the fire. In fact, she saw two women offer the black man water.

Gwen took a sight on the fire down the line and broke for it, running as fast her cramped legs could manage. Closer, she was relieved to see that the fire was not too great to leap, and as she came down on the other side of it, she rolled. The crowd cheered her, the same people who had been tormenting her. She had passed the test of stones.

Then she saw one man with more blue tattoos than any she had seen so far. He stood right in the middle of the platform where a series of low steps led to the pavilion. He called to Aligapas, who guided the last of the captives down the line.

It was Ffiona who stumbled and cried. This seemed to make the people angry, and they picked up spent stones to pelt her as she lay in the dust. Gwen tried to see, but the young wife was lost in the press of feathered, painted, tattooed bodies and the din of their derisive laughter.

Aligapas and his uncle were engaged in a conversation that nobody could hear. There were many gestures between them, not all sanguine. Gwen watched, trying to figure out what was going to happen next. The world seemed to have narrowed down to this place and time; she could barely remember the day before yesterday, and then only the worse moments of it.

The crowd was cheering at the other end of the plaza. They were dragging something in the dust, and Gwen knew what because she saw a white limp foot before the colors and sounds closed in. You should have pretended to be strong, she thought at Ffiona as the most-tattooed man looked beyond Aligapas's shoulder directly at her, his mouth moving; she could not see the other, whose back was toward her. But she saw his fists ball up and the muscles in his buttocks tighten as he listened to the older man.

". . . and she is obviously a noble woman, a Sun, Aligapas, and you as a Sun yourself know that she cannot be yours but must marry a commoner. I myself, as you know, am of the common soil, and not noble like my nephew, yourself—but there is a beautiful young stinkard here—" and he gestured to one of the feathered entourage who were righting their costumes and crowding now around the foot of the platform. The woman stepped forward, a pretty enough girl, with the tattoo band of a more northern village across her nose.

Aligapas, barely restraining his fury, gestured at Gwen. "This is no female sun, my honored uncle, miko of Mabila. This is some almost-person the tide washed up on the Alabaman beach."

Shell-of-Many-Colors was a man past middle age, but his eyes twinkled unmistakably as he regarded the red-haired white girl. The copper amulet on his forehead matched her hair perfectly.

"And she has to be of your grandmother's clan," Aligapas continued in the same tone of voice.

"You dare to teach me tradition?" Shell blazed.

Aligapas sullenly dropped his eyes. "Uncle..."

Gwen felt someone's warmth near her elbow. From the corner of her eye she saw Father Brian in profile. He stumbled against her as several women from the crowd continued to pinch and poke at him, albeit more gently than before. They cooed together, making happy faces as they spoke of this strange but fine man.

"See how healthy his member is," one said, reaching out to hand-test it.

"But it is my choice among the prisoners," said the other woman, who slapped away the first woman's fingers.

Brian cringed back, turning his sex away from them and directly confronting Gwen beside him. His face was etched with anguish, and his member was as stiff as a canoe paddle. Gwen saw what the red women had appraised; Brian was hung like a horse.

Close by, several other of the tattooed women were inspecting Ari, who provoked the greatest curiosity among them.

"You women," said the miko, getting their attention. "You will have your chance. Now let's see what we have here...." He stepped down the stair and strolled under his three tall feathers to stand before Gwen.

"A little quail," said Shell-of-Many-Colors, "a little white-breasted bird..." and with great gentleness reached out to touch the flame-colored curls.

Gwen shrank back. This one, too, had a long, abnormally flat face, but his was better proportioned. Still he was as ugly as a mule and as repulsive as Shovel-Face, who stood behind him, his features further twisted by barely controlled rage.

"She is not noble because she is not born among us, honored uncle," he said through clenched teeth.

He purposefully waited until his uncle had actually put a hand onto the girl's person, then he said with exaggerated softness, "She has moon-blood."

The miko drew back his hand after touching only the crown

of her hair. He glared at Aligapas. "My nephew is thanked by his miko for the warning."

"She is not noble, uncle."

The old man regarded Gwen again without blinking. With a succinct gesture to two old women who stood among his people on the platform, he said, "Grandmother and auntie, come and look at what we have here and tell me..."

That one touch would still require a week of cleansing ceremony. He was furious at Aligapas for holding back the warning and was determined to teach him a lesson.

The crones shuffled down the steps, their long old dugs swaying like ropes. Their hair, still mostly black despite their age, was cut in a straight line just above the shoulder and was woven into several slim braids around their faces, tied with small songbird feathers and beads. They were nude from the waist up and wore long skirts that might be woven grasses or the gray moss in the trees and were tattooed modestly in comparison to the men. One walked with a limp, unable to bend her knee, which was swollen with what looked to Gwen like arthritis. They came forward, their cold, dry fingers pinching her here and there while the miko continued his thought, "...so tell me, does she appear healthy?"

"Oh yes, father," the eldest replied, that being one of the miko's honorable titles as father of the village and the nation in these parts. "Hairy, but she has good wide hips."

He would have them more thoroughly examine her in private, making sure she had all her parts. As pleased as he was with her countenance, he still was not entirely sure she was not some kind of demon spirit. He would want to make sure she had no teeth in unexpected private places, which one of the grosser legends described, or a tail, or any other sign that she was inhuman.

The skin of Aligapas's face went rigid, a rectangle of tooled leather.

"Then, honored grandmother," Shell-of-Many-Colors said, using the title on the lame one who was of the same clan as his own grandmother, and who must be at least a hundred years old, "a new daughter would you like to adopt into your noble clan?"

Chapter 19

*It was handed down by the grandfathers
that white people...had crossed the
Great Water and landed first near
the mouth of the Alabama River...and
had been driven up to the heads of
the waters...*

—Cherokee Chief Occonostota in
1782, quoted by Tennessee
governor John Sevier

Even without the mooneyes, war would have come to the blood country north of Mabila. It had been smoldering some time.

Much of the serpentine valley of the Tennessee, in those days called the Yuchi River, was one vast forest inhabited by no tribe. Messengers between chiefs, called ravens and painted nonmilitary yellow, traveled here from time to time. Likewise solitary hunters, because game abounded in the blood country.

But the vast forest heartland was named for its principal human activity, the quick grim dance of war parties. Cherokee sought the scalps of southern Muskogeans, who likewise dreamed of eating still-beating Iroquois hearts. Except for gaming, war was the way young men won their eagle feathers. It was not pleasing to sober men or the One Above that neighbors slaughtered each other over that wide and beautiful territory. But so it had been to the sorrow of all for many generations as remembered by the middlemen, the Tsoyaha Yuchi, who spoke a language all their own, who had lived next to the blood country longer than anybody, and who, from the oldest yesterday to the furthest tomorrow, had only one enemy—the Cherokee.

There had been no all-out battle in more than half a man's lifetime. But old revenges were still rancorous; old feuds pulsed like open sores. Hunting parties would confront, leaving each other bloody and reduced in numbers. Once in a while the Cherokee raided out of their mountains into the lowland Muskogean villages. Muskogeans would sneak upriver and hit the Cherokee in small, silent retaliations, then vanish with the mist back into the fens. On all sides old men brooded over sons lost and women stolen ten, fifteen summers ago.

The smoldering coals awaited the spark.

One sunrise, a little after Madoc's Hundred built their small stockade on Two Rivers Island, about the time Gwen was adopted into the bird clan of the Mabilans, a Yuchi chief called his fastest ravens to spread the word of upcoming athletic games. When there was no war among traditional enemies, they held sporting contests, brothers of war, which greatly pleased this particular raven who had been preparing for the big get-together over on the ancient mountaintop stoneworks north of his village.

At that time the Yuchi prospered under the chieftainship of Sun Caller, who sat beside the council fire in his underground lodge that dawn. The gaming field in the heart of the blood country was Yuchi, so it had been for many generations that their chief told the gaming date among all nations. The young runner was delighted the old man was finally calling the season—he had postponed the contests because he said the omens were bad.

On this particular morning Chief Sun Caller was playing with a lump of clay as he dispatched the ravens to various chieftains of the west, north, and east, including Chief Fox of the Cherokee.

One by one the other runners departed. Sun Caller, well into his dignified and still-keen eighties, saved this last man to speak with alone: "And take this sack of broken days to that disgusting Mabilan pervert in his stinking swamp," he said, carefully modeling the clay between fingers as cracked as an alligator's but strong and unbent, graceful with the deftness of a natural artist. Such well-preserved old age was uncommon, and he was highly regarded for it.

The raven was prepared to leave immediately, complete with personal power sack at his belt, atlatl, arrows, and a small ration of dried food in a sling on his back.

It would have been interesting to see what animal Sun Caller was modeling, since one could often tell their thoughts by this strange habit of Yuchi chiefs to craft seemingly insignificant objects, a habit that commanded the raven's attention because he craved to learn secrets and thereby improve his chances of living another sixty summers to reach this man's status. A chief's thoughts were always a curiosity, but his fingers on the work hid it.

The raven took the last handful of painted and carved willow sticks in their hide pouch. Ten and four days were tied together. Sun Caller had spent the past moon carving the heads of each stick to represent ancient animals of whom common animals today were just puny copies. The Mabilan miko would break one from the bundle each sundown between now and the fourteenth hence. Likewise, all the other headmen would break off their allotted days, for his chief had placed the correct number of sticks in each bundle, accommodating different travel times for the far-flung nations. At the appointed sundown the tribes would come together at the Yuchi's sacred mountain for the contests.

"Take care to notice the behavior of Shell's rancid nephew." Sun Caller spat into the fire. Among other things, it disgusted the Yuchi that the people of Mabila did not elect their leaders but passed chieftanship on for payment. The miko had already bought the position for his nephew, who had named himself the vain title, "I Glitter." He was an opponent the raven looked forward to meeting on the gaming field.

"And hurry back," Sun Caller said, almost as if he did not want his runner to go. "I want to hear about old Shell's new wife." The chief looked down at the thing his fingers had made. "Rumor has it she is some kind of Natchez sun."

These noble women from a nearby tribe were high-handed and more spirited than the usual red female, so they became a euphemism for a red-hot woman. The younger man understood the elder's wink when he looked up, fingers uncurling to reveal the object of smoke-colored clay laid across his palm. It looked like a rope with two lateral knots on one end, perhaps the male sex organs. He gestured with it, then tossed it into the fire.

"A dream," the old man sniffed. The clay sizzled among the coals. He waited, tensed; it was strange for a chief to confide such personal things to a mere raven who was his servant, even if that raven was also his own first-born son. "A dream about the kanegmati."

Ah, thought the raven. That was it, then, which he had carved: the illusive blue-eyed snake that had lived in those hills even longer than the Yuchi.

Sun Caller shrugged, staring at his blackening creation. "Some dreams mean nothing at all," he said finally, nodding, giving the courier permission to depart. But he turned again to stare at the baking toy as if he did not believe his own words.

The raven wrapped his white headband anew, trotting up the slope of the vestibule that led from the chief's underground lodge to the dusty courtyard. He stood for a few moments in the brightening morning of what promised to be a warm day, even though it was deep into Long Night Moon. From his pack he withdrew stoppered horns of the distinctive yellow and white paint of his profession, which he applied with the speed of long practice to his face. As long as he wore the paint, he could not engage in war or sex. And he was bound by blood oath to complete his mission before washing it off.

He wiped his fingers in the dust and began trotting out of the village where round lodges seemed like a great nest of half-buried eggs. The Yuchi palisade was strong; this was a warrior town.

He paused only briefly, to salute the shimmering golden disk of the sun rising above the eastern mountains. His people did not build the huge dirt pyramids of the lowlanders but found naturally high places to confront God every dawn and sunset. Arms outstretched, palms sunward, he stood on a promontory above the village, feeling the strengthening rays touch his skin.

Birds in the oak trees sang with him.

"Great One Who Breathes Above," he chanted as he had done every day of his life since the first day he could stand beside his mother and learn the prayer, "In your light I put my life."

He finished with a long formula that asked the One Above to shine on his clan, to forever remember the Yuchi who called themselves Children of the Sun. Then he took up the trail that led from this sacred place.

Sentries waved him onto the trace called the Great Warrior Path by many nations, which led from the highland meadow beside the Little Duck River south across the Yuchi to the Coosa and her sister streams including the Alabama. Over their bright waters a canoe could descend in a day to the low and croaking swamps of the Alabamans and other Muskogean nations.

The journey was uninterrupted—he had made this run ten times ten and knew every ledge, every branching along the trace and its river-road, an ancient north-south path used by all nations from the Head of Waters to the salt water.

After most of that day on the river, he pulled his canoe in at the landing at Mabila where Aligapas had brought his captives. Beyond the line of trees flanking the banks, high up in the lazy air, a pall of smoke turned the late day a smoky pink—they were burning off the harvested fields to fertilize next year's crop. Sommelier fires of smaller nations farther south had raised the hopes of Madoc's Hundred.

The air was spicy with smoke as he leisurely jogged a raised path amid rice shallows, giving the effect of mounting an island.

He had worked up a pleasant sweat by the time the ground gently inclined, leading the manicured path between fields that were being prepared for planting. On the checkered landscape formed by the dikes here and there sparkled fish-breeding ponds.

The workers—men as well as women worked the fields here—were colorfully feathered so that their patient movement out in the far distant fields was that of large lazy birds. Boatmen on the water seemed to be the plumage of a feathered serpent dozing on water as smooth as the sky. Their soft, rhythmic song floated on the air with the perfume of many ripenings. The sight of them made him think of the Uktena, the great horned serpent of many stories and song, which was supposed to have been one of the ancient animals who called these southern rivers home.

These people were famous as weir makers and farmers, unlike the Yuchi who considered red meat the noblest of foods. They deemed cultivation women's work, except for the sacred smoke, nipowoc. Fishing was beneath Yuchi male contempt except to fertilize the tobacco. That was an old trick the Cherokee brought with them a long time ago from their Iroquois farther north. Even then the Yuchi were old in the foothills, where few things large were man-made, except for the stonework of their ancient playing field. Their name meant the Children of the Sun From Far Away. Other nations considered that an arrogant boast, and called them merely Yuchi, or the From-Far-Aways.

All this wilderness squared off seemed alien to this mountaineer, even though he visited here often since childhood.

He hurried past the bonehouse on an ancient pyramid created over many generations by basketfuls of dirt and clay. These people practiced burial customs that disgusted the Yuchi. Ravens had to ritually purify themselves after passing through these parts; the air around the charnel house alone was considered unclean. That evening the wind was in his favor. A long sunset shadow dogged his heels as he trotted into the village below the scrupulously terraced skirt of the bonehouse mound where labored the long-nailed buzzardmen who gave the Tombigbee—Coffin-Maker—River its grim name.

Suddenly on the path he was face-to-face with one of those hideous old men. When traveling away from their bonehouses, they wore a distinctive garment and mask so that people would not have to look upon them. They would close themselves in a short robe woven of thousands of black vulture feathers, collared with the red neck tuff of that bird. The feather-cloak was more an armor than an article of clothing. To keep it around his shoulders, the bonepicker held onto a strap, with the finger of one hand showing. The bonepickers were proud of the major tool of their profession, a single fingernail grown incredibly long and tough, which they took pleasure in displaying. The mask they wore was a stylized vulture's face, ugly in the extreme.

All that showed this was a man and not a man-sized vulture staring him down through one eyehole on the narrow path through the cane break was that long-clawed hand and the ordinary moccasins below the feathers.

The messenger's yellow face paint demanded respect, but the bonepicker outranked him. He quickly stepped aside, totally revolted when oily black feathers brushed against his chest. The bonepicker imperiously hurried on down the path, used to being made way for. The costume assured instant respect, inspired by terror from the youngest child to the bravest warrior of the community or a knowledgeable outsider.

The bonepicker was gone in a musty cloud of feathers, a few of which his costume shed as he brushed through the cane and on toward the steps that led up the pyramid to the tabernacle on the top, where smoke always curled away from a flame that was allowed to go out only once a year.

The raven took up the path again, headed for the place he knew he could find the miko.

But his arrival in the Mabilan square was untimely. The miko, Shell-of-Many-Colors, was presiding over his council arranged before a fire built in a winding spiral of twigs that slowly burned toward the center. The Yuchi noticed more than a usual number of warriors from neighboring Muskogean nations were present. This being a peace village, the presence of red-village allies meant there had been or was going to be some action. From the visitors' pavilion on the southern side of the square, the raven took all this in while listening briefly to the fast musical speech in progress near the fire.

The creeping flame had a way to go, so the raven decided to find the miko's chief wife, who would feed him without any questions while he waited for the fire to burn to the center, flare briefly, and end the meeting which seemed to concern appointment of a new little miko, or councillor.

This being a peace village, all the poles were painted white. Shells rattled and swamp-bird feathers dangled from the thatched roof in bundles swayed by the breeze. This was muggy weather to the highlander used to cool, dry air. The wind felt fine against his still-hot skin as he perused the scene.

Plumed like the many-colored birds in the jungle around them, the little mikos sat in the north and west pavilions facing the square. But the great chief himself wore three modest white feathers in his headdress. His finery was a shell-decorated robe, his only adornments the copper amulet of his office and the dignity with which he sat his throne covered with fur—a glossy black swamp bear with claws, snarl intact—in the honored western pavilion. The miko's brow wrinkled under the copper insignia of a dancing holy man as he pondered the question argued before him.

The message the raven carried did not concern life-and-death, so it would be inappropriate to catch the miko's eye. But the raven saw him glance this way.

Aligapas was arguing in the candidate's favor, but Miko Shell stared at the Yuchi messenger, ignoring the rhetoric of a nephew whom he disliked but who was a useful subordinate, forehead furrowed with some emotion the raven could not imagine.

Presently the speech recaptured the miko's attention. Here his nephew was trying to get a favorite promoted, but the uncle did not like the candidate. Because of Aligapas's successful raid, however, the miko owed him and must have a good reason not to elevate the nephew's man.

Aligapas struck the ringing pole, thus signifying that his speech was ended. Another man stood, struck the same pole, and began a rebuttal. The raven started to wander away, bored by lowlander squabble, when the debater's words stopped him.

"This man exaggerates his own importance by claiming the great turtle appeared personally to call him." This had evidently been hot gossip, because it provoked argumentative comments from all sides. It piqued the raven's curiosity because he was of the turtle clan.

Aligapas looked abashed at such a possible immodesty in his candidate; the man stood, deeply coloring at the insult against his truthfulness and piety and therefore his honor. Shell-of-Many-Colors pounded his staff on a hollow cavity in his throne, but it was some time before the assembly settled down. The miko deliberately stared at the candidate, giving him permission to speak for himself—almost unheard of in such a hearing.

The candidate was shy in his colorful, trembling feathers. He looked down at his feet and almost forgot to strike the pole. The nephew gestured with his mean, lopsided grin, reminding the candidate of the breech, and after he had remedied it, he began, "A handful of days ago I saw the great turtle on the bank of the Haiwassee. He did not speak to me, nor I to him, considering it sign enough that he let me watch his passing onto dry land." He gulped. "This humble one attached no significance as far as his own person is concerned. Others have assumed . . ." He modestly left the thought unfinished.

Another murmur rippled through the assembly, which Shell-of-Many-Colors did not allow to spill over into debate. He rapped the staff twice, bringing everyone to a hush.

"How close were you to the great turtle?"

"As close as I stand at this moment to my miko."

"Describe what you saw."

"A large turtle under a dark yellow shell."

"What led you to believe this was the great turtle and not some ordinary addition to your wife's cooking pot?"

"The fact that it stood upon its back feet like no ordinary turtle, as well as its size, my miko, whom I have served all the days of my manhood."

"Ah, and what was its size?"

"The shell was as great as my arms open," he replied, demonstrating as he continued, "while the turtle stood as tall as a full-grown man, a man as noble as my miko when he stands to his full height to meet the enemies of his people." The candidate bowed, backing off, lowering his eyes while the assembly murmured.

Aligapas leaned toward his uncle in a heated private exchange. The miko's face reddened until it seemed to glow. He launched into a long harangue on the significance of the great turtle, how it is told by the grandfathers of all nations that the turtle carries the whole world on its back.

While he spoke, his nephew sat immobile, arms tightly crossed on his chest, a rocklike expression of fury held in check behind his strange, flat face while his uncle recited old poetry. The flattening of the head had produced a less fortunate appearance than the uncle, who seemed wise. The nephew, thought the Yuchi raven, looked lopsided. The Yuchi did not practice infant head flattening and thought it a barbaric practice—yet another reason the Yuchi looked down upon the Muskogeans at Mabila.

Shell's was a long story the raven had heard since childhood from many turtle-clan relatives on his mother's family, so despite curiosity about the local appearance of this significant spiritual being, he found the needs of his body more urgent.

Since he was painted for his task, he was hatki ahaka, or legally invisible; everyone ignored a raven with a message, though many watched secretly to catch some hint of news. They knew by the way he was painted face, chest, and knees, that it concerned the games. Even boys looked forward to the games, which only a few chosen by lot would be allowed to attend. Since all the little mikos and their families would go in their finery, the annual competition was the most exciting event of the season.

There was a girl of this village who owned his eye, so he looked around hopefully to see if she was there. But only a few crones, aunts of the candidate he supposed, occupied the woman's shed on the east side of the square.

Disappointed, the Yuchi turned to leave. A raven's duty

involved not speaking with any other than the miko, to whom
his message was directed. All he could do now was wait.

With this in mind he walked from the visitors' pavilion. As
he stepped out under the brilliantly colored sky already
picked with a star or two, he saw that the crones over there
sat in a protective circle around a sixth female. He hesitated,
narrowing his keen glance into tighter reconnaissance.

She was the most stunningly beautiful woman he had ever
seen. It was immediately obvious that this woman was not
Muskogean, whose complexions were burnished dark red.
Once the raven had seen an albino man of a western tribe.
This girl must be one of those human oddities, too. This one's
pale and perfect face was framed by a hood of egret feathers,
hung about with ropes of seed pearls in loops and what
looked like countless fine copper wires brushing her breasts.
This rare metal was found in the mountain streams, but it was
reserved for ritual and chiefly purposes such as the miko's
amulet; never had he seen wire drawn so fine as to make a
wig of it, but that was what she appeared to be wearing under
white feathers.

The raven took several small steps. To anyone watching he
appeared to be stretching the kinks out of his arms and
shoulders as he gazed at the fire-bright sky. Nobody could tell
he was heavily scrutinizing the miko's Natchez sun his father
asked about. Around her waist was tied a baby-alligator skirt
and on her feet were small white fur moccasins. She could
have had no more than fourteen winters, yet she had the
steady, wise gaze of an ancient beloved grandmother. She sat
among the crones, they like withered old fingers holding a
sacred crystal. In her paleness she seemed to glow. The sight
of her arrested the Yuchi—fortunately the miko's voice drew
all other eyes, so the raven stood drinking in her beauty,
thinking he did so unobserved.

But one in the plaza knew he stood transfixed. Like the
moon peeking from behind a cloud, she arrowed a glance at
him. He expected albino pink, but her eyes were plainly
blue, a remarkable oddity. He thought at first it was the angle
of the setting sun or the firelight reflecting like a panther's
eye; the sky was pink now. But he saw quite clearly that her
eyes were truly blue, pinning him to the spot as surely as if
she had used an arrow knapped from a chip of a noontime
sky.

He was often the target of glances from women, who

always liked the runners. He expected a flirtatious wink, tongue on a wet lip, some small secret defiance of hatki ahaka. Women of all the tribes teased the runners when their men were not looking.

The ravens ignored them. Instead of a safe, teasing wink at a man who could not possibly even touch her, the girl's glance revealed a shadow passing over her face, like a weight upon her. She sagged. For one terrible moment she looked grossly ancient, as wrinkled as a chalky moon. She was pleading for help in terror and despair with those extraordinary eyes full of pain far beyond what a maiden's should hold.

Just as suddenly she smote him with a smile so full of portent he knew he must disentangle himself quickly, or she with woman's magic would pull the blood from his eyes and ears.

Though none present had made any move that would suggest it, he recognized this woman. Just the way she was set like a jewel protected on all sides, prouder than an ordinary Yuchi or Muskogean woman, she must be the fabled bride his father bade him spy, only she was not Natchez. Because of her demeanor and the absence of color in her skin, he thought fleetingly that she might be Cherokee. Their women were high-headed, and Cherokee skin was less red and more dusty than other nations. But this pale creature was not a Cherokee. She was not an albino, either.

She was something else, something entirely different.

None of this should have been a raven's concern. Hurriedly he departed, hungers aroused within him.

By the time the miko was ready to receive the courier, the sun was down. Instead of sending for the Yuchi, the miko, still wearing ceremonial feathers, personally sought him out in the men's lodge, where the raven had retired to whip thoughts of the unattainable into anticipation for his Muskogean sweetheart. The headman was slipping the hammered copper amulet with its three attached feathers from his brow as he entered through the flap. He abruptly and ritually asked what message came from Sun Caller.

The raven indicated the bag of sticks, adding that they were meant to be ayat, that is as a Yuchi would say, "from now going on," to prevent a miscount from the next day instead of today. The raven expected him to break today's stick immediately, but he only nodded, slipped the sticks into the pouch where he stowed the amulet, and sat hunched close to the guest without speaking.

At that late moment they were the only two men still in the lodge, but Miko Shell looked around as though making sure they were alone before speaking. Ravens did not question chiefs, so as the young man waited, he started to wipe off the yellow paint since his mission was accomplished. He wanted to quickly become an ordinary visible warrior and go looking for his swamp blossom.

The miko leaned close, several carved shell gorgets rattling, to stay the runner's hand, bidding him not to remove the raven's paint. Without looking the Yuchi in the eye, because what he was about to ask bordered on unforgivable rudeness, Shell said that he hoped the raven would forego the hospitality of the Mabila and retrace his steps immediately to his homeland.

"My women have already provisioned your canoe," he continued. The trip upriver would take considerably longer than descent. What urgent message did he wish to get back to the chief of the Yuchi?

The blue-eyed girl was beyond taboo, unthinkable, being this man's woman, but her forbidden glance had aroused the Yuchi. The miko's request, which must be honored, dashed his hopes of sharing a blanket with a local girl. It was unlikely anyone caught his indiscreet exchange with the miko's bride, but perhaps he had offended the miko or his councilors in some other way.

Before this question could be asked with a gesture or frown, the miko whispered, "There is something I would have you take back to your esteemed chief." He glanced again over his shoulder in a manner no chief need use. Yet it was obvious he feared to be overheard as he pulled at the other's elbow, standing, indicating the Yuchi should follow him out of the mens' lodge. Pungent smells and soft sounds of the evening meal being taken in several hundred lodges joined with tree-frog song from the jungle. These people lived in thatched lodges entirely outside the earth, so the twinkling of their many fires through wall slats glittered the night. Somewhere a woman sang an indiscreet lullaby as the raven followed the miko to the empty council square. The time-counting spiral of twigs had been swept away. In the pit a ceremonial fire burned low at the hot center of four log-points. One ancient man crouched near the fire, its attendant.

The chief and his guest were little more than shadows as they approached the throne under the western pavilion, where a young warrior stood at attention in deep blue gloom.

The miko dismissed the guard but waited until he walked out of sight before removing an awkward package wrapped in heavy skins from the stone coffer beneath the throne where ceremonial regalia was stored. The moon was not yet up, but the fire burnished his face and gleamed off one eye hidden beneath the long slope of that clifflike face as he turned with the parcel.

"Let no other than your chief look upon the contents of this pouch," he admonished unnecessarily, insulting the raven, who knew his duty to protect this thing sealed, until delivered, with his life. Regretting the insult, the miko gently slapped his shoulder in a brotherly way. "I was glad when I saw your chief sent you, son of the Caller, instead of a lesser raven," Shell said. "Tell your honored father that there are at large in Mobilian territory and moving toward the Yuchi more of these—" He gestured with the bundle, forcing it into the raven's hands. "Tell him that I will seek his wise and ancient counsel on this matter at the games."

The raven nodded, surprised at the odd-shaped bundle's weight. He bound the long and lumpy object onto his back, fingers discreetly probing the sewn coverings, but he could get little hint of the contents. Two objects it was, not one. Something long and too heavy for its slender size, something else less heavy and round, nothing more.

The miko's eyes glittered dismissal in the twilight. Without another word, but with many private thoughts and not a little regret for the warm girl he would not hold tonight, the raven moved with Shell-of-Many-Colors through the dark chittering jungle to the riverbank where the canoe was waiting, low in the water with generous gifts, to be paddled homeward.

"I would have Sun Caller know of this before the Cherokee, Natchez, Chicasaw, or any other nation, because we Mabilans honor the Yuchi as the eldest among us. Say that my cousin Komas the Alabaman gave this to me as I pass it on to him. Say these things when you give this to him."

The raven, made uncomfortable by Shell's uncharacteristic behavior, as well as by a moldy whiff of the bonehouse on the breeze, stowed the bundle under a hide aft the paddler's position.

But the miko stopped him. "Lest you be upset by an

alligator, or later by white water in the upper rock canyons, keep it on your back," he ordered.

The raven complied, ignoring this further insult to his canoeing skill. The miko watched as the raven pushed off. Despite the cool night the bundle felt hot. Its shifting, mysterious weight put him off balance and distracted him, wondering what it was that he carried.

The water was dark, flowing so slowly that it appeared on its surface not to be moving at all. Yet it murmured. Had the raven ceased paddling, the current against the canoe nose would drag it inevitably back downstream.

After a while on this gentle stretch he had to put his back into the effort, because the riverbed narrowed between high banks and the water was swift.

Later the almost-full moon rose, vibrating persimmon yellow behind haze. Coming around a bend, he caught its reflection off the water, rippling now as the canyon sides angled steeper.

"I greet you, Moon-Maiden, to tell you that I will be here next time to say the same thing again. . . ." It was an old formula.

Frogs greeted the amber light. Turtles plopped flat-bellied from reedy shores. Night birds cooed from sooty-black banks where cypress gave way to cedar, willow, occasional oak, and finally the sheer rock brow crowned by the silhouette of a hardwood fringe. The current grew even more aggressive here. Paddling became labor. The water talked back.

Even a warrior tires. Soon after midnight the raven pointed his canoe toward a small crescent beach between stone pillars. The moon by now was a spilled white cup glowing behind the haze. From his perspective the river's surface seemed to flow from the lunar rim, a shimmering vision that took his eye while he pulled the canoe into a nook formed by the arms of a waterlogged tree trunk. The night sky was so bright he could make out colors.

He shucked the backpack and its cumbersome burden in the canoe, while his hand found a finely woven basket he knew held food for the first night.

He stood gnawing a shred of venison jerky, stretching, giving the surrounding area reconnaissance, the gravel beneath his moccasins a crisp crunch that silenced the crickets.

Chapter 20

O Mother Mary
O Ladder of Heaven . . .
Let us not for mercy's sake
be carried off in a
foray before our enemies,
nor let our souls be enslaved . . .
O Washer of Souls
O Mother of Orphans . . .

—The Marian Litany
by St. Brogan of Clonnast
c. A.D. 750

T he crickets began strumming again as the raven exercised his arms, relaxing from his labor. He reached among the bundles to find a blanket roll, surely to have been packed.

Those southern women sure knew how to take care of a man. He could safely wager that this little canoe carried enough provender to keep a traveler comfortably alive for a week without hunting, fishing, or gathering. And by the look of the stern heavy in the water, he expected to find a change of clothing, new moccasins, and a heavy robe in case the weather finally turned to winter after this unusually warm Moon of the Long Night.

His idea was to rest for a final push homeward at dawn. His fingers groped around, finding a log shape covered in fur.

He pulled out the bedroll and let it curl out of his hands over a spot of gravel where he could lean against a boulder to keep his back covered while he took a quick nap.

But he saw the current steal the canoe, which he was certain had been secure. He jumped up and waded to his

ankles, catching it before it drifted downstream, then pulled
it back to a driftwood snag, where he made sure it was well
tied. He gave the area thorough perusal. Nobody lived in
these parts. This was blood country, neutral along the river
because it was part of the all-nations pathway. He smelled no
other campfire. There might be occasional hunters from any
one of a dozen nations. It would be unlikely for another raven
to be passing this way in the night. After an assay of all that
came to his senses, he walked far away from the river to a dry
gravel bed and pissed before returning to his spot. Munching
on another shred of jerky, he heard a crisp snap of a dead
branch, looked up, and saw the canoe swing into the channel,
where the current immediately snatched it.

He crashed into the swirl and grabbed again for the canoe,
but the river was stubborn. With the jerky still in his mouth,
he plunged into deeper water. He had his flint knife, all the
equipment he required. The boat was no great loss except for
Chief Shell's secret bundle, but he would be sorry to have to
walk the rest of the long journey home.

A few powerful strokes, with the aid of the current, and he
had it in hand again. He worked his way around to the
leather cable still knotted on the broken branch and towed it
back to shore, the rough gravel almost alive beneath his tread.

This time he tied the line to a stouter branch and tested it.
He stood there in the shallows, dripping, remembering to
chew the rest of the jerky still clenched between his teeth,
looking down at the canoe sitting low in moonlight and water.
The current enticed it only so far; the branch held.

He was turning back to dry land when he saw movement
under the hide covering the bundles like a gopher channeling
loose soil—subtle, small, but directed.

Fascinated now, the raven crouched to watch where the
towline joined its loop with his knot. His eye had no trouble
tracing the forward movement of whatever was beneath the
hide.

He grabbed at it before he knew what it was, his hand a
vise—it closed and he pulled in one motion, bringing up and
out from under the hide the hand, wrist, and arm of the
white girl whose piercing blue eyes had snared him in the
plaza at Mabila.

Somehow he was not surprised.

But it was a shock. Letting go as though she were hot, he
stepped back. The canoe rocked; she grabbed both sides and

expertly stilled it by finding its center beneath her own. From that center, with the moon over her shoulder, she regarded him.

It was the shimmering blue-whiteness of her skin that held him entranced. Under moonlight it shown like rock crystal. Her hair likewise had taken on an incandescent glow from the arching light in the sky no longer squash yellow but paling as it rose. Behind the halo of her hair the moon shone ice blue, the color of a lightning strike or afterglow when one looks suddenly away from fire into darkness. What he wanted most was to touch her to see if she would melt like smoke or a vision.

In addition to all this illusion, the girl was unnaturally still. She was nothing like his giggling Muskogean sweetie, or the quietly overworked Yuchi mothers and aunts of his father's fireside, or a wise Cherokee grandmother. Yet there was something of all women in this one and more. No other woman had prepared him for this one who seemed, despite her obvious youth, to be old to him as she appeared in the chief's court.

Gwen was quiet because she was trembling with cold and fear. Her legs were stiff because she had remained still for so long folded into an unnatural position in the canoe, daring not to move behind her unknowing host. Water splashed by his paddle over the sides of the canoe had run down under the hide and soaked what little clothing she wore for a warm afternoon rather than a chilly midnight in Long Night Moon.

Long Night Moon—that is what the chief's wife told her they called this month of December. Gwen kept a notched stick, though the grandmother had knocked it from her hand, telling her such things were for sachem, not for women, and would make her barren. Thereafter Gwen hid her calendar stick.

It was December 27. Tomorrow was Holy Innocents' Day, ill-omened. Perhaps Christian luck—good or bad—did not exist in this strange place, but to be on the safe side it would be best to complete work before midnight, to be finished here before the twenty-eighth day of the Moon of the Long Night.

The crone had patiently made the handsigns Gwen found infinitely reasonable—thumb and forefinger crescent-shaped, then the sign for night, a quick covering of one hand over the other. Then she made pointing fingers of both hands one in front of the other, bringing the right finger forward, quicker done than told.

Why had people back home not figured out this way of speaking? In her several weeks among the Mobilians, she found increasing sense in the words they pronounced while signing. But she was making faster progress learning handsign. She was amazed when they told her all the many nations here used these handsigns, even though they spoke different languages. The red people were amazed to hear of a nation that did not use handsign.

Under the messenger's wide gaze, Gwen's shiver became a shake. She hugged herself, seeing the moon from the corner of her eye, as if for the first time.

Long Night Moon, she signed rapidly, teeth chattering. It scared her that this pillar of startled red man had not moved. He might kill her. She thought, he might be as cruel as Aligapas.

But somehow she did not think so.

He stood tensely crouched, eyes wide, sensuous lips parted. In contrast to the flat-faced Muskogean males, she found this red man to be quite beautiful. His face was very regular with a fine long nose dividing it neatly into two symmetrical halves like nut meat. His eyes were vibrant pit black in the moonlight. Some rippling movement happened in his shoulders, but he did not relax, though something in his eye softened as he touched her cheek.

His touch was as warm as supper, as pleasing as Nona's nose when she used to snuggle against Gwen's neck.

"Who are you?" he asked in the ancient Yuchi tongue and in fluid hand-talk—a quick finger pointing to her, and a quizzical frown between the eyes.

"Gwyneth of Madoc of Owen Gwynedd," she answered. The handsign she used for herself was back-of-hand-mixing for color, plus white (her teeth, her boots) and stiff fingers down along her face that signified woman, the literal meaning of her name in her native tongue minus her pedigree, which was untranslatable.

Then she used her hands to ask, "Who are you?"

He answered, lip and hand, "Eagle Ring Man, Tsoyaha Yuchi of Yellow Pheasant Village, Turtle Clan," pointing as the crow flies toward the northeast. She missed the part about the pheasant, but she repeated the sounds and sign, understanding his name to be something like Bird-of-Prey (?)

Ring Man (!) from the Yuchi place over there. She tried to say the Muskogean word as she had heard the people of Mabila use to name his tribe.

He smiled at her pronunciation—definitely Muskogean.

"Yuchi," he said patiently, but was suddenly self-conscious because she was looking at him without the slightest hint of female modesty. To hide his sudden sense of vulnerability, he translated quickly into the Mabilan she obviously knew:

"The From-Far-Aways," he said, shyly. Among Tsoyaha Yuchi, the nickname was derogatory. But the philosophical Yuchi accepted what others called them behind their backs because other nations disdained their claim to be children of the Sun.

Yes, she nodded. She heard this word in the plaza when she asked—the grandmother told her the young stranger standing in the visitor's pavilion was not to be approached—was invisible?—because he was a messenger from a barbaric northern tribe of hunters called Yuchi—the From-Far-Aways.

But this man could not be ignored. She noticed him because of his height. Among the lowlanders this mountaineer stood out, all the more so because of the mulberry-bark turban around his head and the almost complete absence of tattooing on his body. A discreet stylized turtle swam up the rippling wave of his right thigh. His was still a low degree in the brotherhood lodge, so he had only one ear slit. Otherwise his body was unmarked.

As she watched him, he watched her. Her name in her language made about as much sense to the raven as his did to the girl. In his mind in that moment with the moon burning behind her, he named the woman, and it must be spoken.

"Onwa' pahta," he said, pointing to the moon and making the sign for fire.

"Moon Fire?" she translated.

"Onwa' pahta."

But of course he would not presume to name her, a very intimate thing, and so made the sign for joking.

"I like it," she said. "Moon Fire." She cocked her head, looking him up and down, then signed, now it is my turn to name you. She walked around him, sagaciously nodding her head as she had seen Grandfather Owen do, stroking her chin the way he stroked his white beard. Then she paused, deep in thought, or pretending to be, for she had already nicknamed him. Then she grinned and carefully signed Flying Turtle.

Think about it, she signed, gesturing at her temple and his tattoo.

He grinned with her, yes, the turtle is flying.

In the glow of the girl's presence, he had forgotten to be wary. Remembering, he froze, listening to the sounds of river and forest around them. The wind was up a little from the south. What was that he smelled on it, a breath of the familiar Mabilan stench that seemed to have followed him from the confines of that village? Eagle Ring Man always took the sweatlodge before entering Sun Caller's presence after a journey to Muskogean country, because his father said their odor clung to him.

Her aroma was baked nuts and oysters to the raven. She might look like spirit, but that scent told him she was woman.

But the smell that disturbed him now was Muskogean male above hers and the flavors of pine, leaf mold, and watercress growing in a thick blanket in an eddy below this beach.

"What . . . ?" she handsigned.

His quick glance said be silent. She obeyed, looking around as he listened further to the night. He touched his finger to his lip and led her with a touch back toward the canoe, where he held up the hide so she could reclaim her secluded place.

Just before he tied it down, she held up two fingers like two small persons, one short, one tall, close together and asked near his face in husky Cymraeg, "Friend?"

He held up two long slender fingers in imitation of her gesture and gave her a trace of a smile, then secured the flap. No sooner did he stand but there burst into the river canyon an echoed war shout from downwater. A Muskogean tongue uttered it, joined soon by a hoot of male voices spilling from log canoes suddenly aiming from downstream toward this beach.

But his canoe was tethered so that the nudging current that had vexed him before would sweep it around the shelf of the beach and beyond them before they could remount their canoes. He freed the canoe with a firm shove of his moccasin just as Shell-of-Many-Colors and Aligapas stepped from the last boat.

The river cooperated, grabbing up the sleek little craft and arrowing it out onto the silvery rippling water.

Chief Shell called a curse, but his several warriors were too closely ranked around him to move efficiently. Several were red-village warriors the raven noticed in the square, armed to the teeth and painted for battle. They stumbled in the shallows and on the coarse sucking gravel around Chief Shell, himself still yelling, the nephew clutching the canoe but fumbling the paddle so that the boat skewed and threw him into the water.

"Can you do nothing right?" the uncle railed.

Still designated noncombatant, the raven knew that his yellow paint would not stop them from dismembering him. He took advantage of their momentary confusion and dived into the water.

He was a beaver, slick and waveless as he swam underwater to the canoes tethered together. He quickly hauled them along until he could no longer touch bottom. But his trick was not perfect, and the canoes got away before he could board one, not an easy task in white water under any circumstance. The jagged rocks littering the opposite bank seemed to reach out for the canoes.

Only by powerful swimming was he able to escape their grinding collision. Finally rocks snared them, soon far behind as he felt the jealous current pull him out into the channel.

Coming up for air, he was on his back. He opened his eyes under the water so that the moon was a shivering pale face glowing about him as he surfaced and, accelerated by the river, swam rapidly down the way he had come.

Around the first bend and then another he failed to see the canoe with the girl, but when he broached the left side of a small island, he saw that the canoe was far ahead and about to vanish into the blue shadows of another steep-sided run before rounding a meander of the river, when it widened at a gentle meadowland. The canoe would slow down there in thick reeds and cress that swamped the north shore along that stretch. He could increase his pace and overtake it here or lose it for another long racing stretch, which ended above the landing at Mabila. At that natural bight the canoe would likely drift in to be claimed by warriors on the shore, surely stationed specifically by the chief to stand watch.

The moonlight would be his enemy there, but if the runaway canoe escaped notice, it might smash on the rapids that lay below Shell's village where the Alabama and Tombigbee Rivers merged.

The river here was shallow enough for the raven to stand and take a look around. He saw the canoe too late, unbound by cattails or hyacinth tangle, and sailing on the current's rush around the fat headland and on into the approach to the rapids. If it shot the cataract, there waited endless marshlands where it would vanish altogether in a labyrinth of waterways. There were old stories of people going into the swamps hereabout and never being seen again except as undead and never-buried wraiths during certain seasons when the eclipse monster nibbled the moon's shoulder.

Some people around these parts had the strange belief that the sun was female and the moon male, but the Yuchi knew that to be a gross error that could be corrected only by looking up there at the lovely face of the woman half-hidden by her hair. And anyone who thought the sun was female—well, some people would persist in error in the face of the obvious.

He thanked sister moon for friendly illumination of the canoe several paces ahead. Now he was close enough to see the girl shining in the light, struggling to sit up and gain balance, but where was the paddle? He remembered putting it in its usual snug place, but she would probably not know how to use it.

Suddenly a whirlpool snared the canoe and spun it end by end around a stony outcrop that had caught debris not washed away since the last high water. He saw her clutch a branch and would have cautioned her, but what happened next was too quick: Gwen was good with round canoes—this long one had a different handling on the current. Of course it spun around too fast and smacked against the rocks but was slowed down enough for him to gain on it. A final push brought its rim under his hand.

The war cry of a Muskogean atlatl thrower filled the echoing canyon. The lookouts had managed to capture at least two of their craft now rounding the bend and swinging toward this eddy.

The warrior crouched in the prow, patiently taking aim with the slim spear thrower that could put its missile through a three-year-old oak. The raven ducked beneath the water, thereby losing the canoe, which sped on down the stream.

The arrow sliced the water above him as he dropped down below the foamy surface and let the current take him.

In the canoe Gwen suspected what was coming because of the bucking motion beneath her. She gave up trying to get to the paddle secured just under the edge of the canoe amidship. She stayed low, unthinking at that point, hanging onto her father's golden amulet on a thong around her neck, and repeating an old prayer. "O Mother Mary, O ladder of heaven..."

The roar of the rapids drowned out her chant, "...nor let our souls be enslaved..."

A wall of water lifted a huge hand and smacked the canoe, batting it even faster into the shoot.

"O Washer of Souls—"

Boulders flew by, starkly white under the moon.

"Mother of Orphans—"

The water seethed tar black and blue-white, screaming, echoing, roaring as it cast the tiny vessel along.

"O Mary, O greatest of Marys, Queen of Angels..." The prayer had many pleas.

Free-floating Gwen lost time. To her left the moon lit the way. The current was gentle now; watchmen at the landing saw only a log sliding down the far side of the channel. A little way farther, the Alabama was joined by the sluggish Tombigbee River from the west. As the river widened, its banks now indefinable in a maze of islands and sloughs, the current almost died. Eventually the canoe nosed into a still backwater.

Gwen had no way of knowing that she was within a league of Two Rivers Island, where her father's men had finished the stockade and where, for the past month of her captivity, Wyn had been busily making ax heads, crowbars, and chain links. She sniffed the air tinged with oak smoke, which might have given her a clue—her captors did not use firewood for heat, only for ceremony and cooking. What was left of a chill breeze idled her canoe in a slow spin on the black glass of the marsh.

Silently the canoe found a niche among lily pads that covered a vast surface rimmed with a forest of cattail, their heads blown. What sluggish current was left under her urged the canoe toward the swooning branches of a willow.

In the moonlight Gwen had a clear view of her situation out on the polished surface of the lake. Night birds echoed calls across the water. It was too late in the season for the tree frogs Madoc's Hundred had heard their first night on these shores, but a bullfrog somewhere off to the right had discovered his voice, a booming thurdle like no other sound.

Just as she was about to sit up and find the paddle, she

froze. Another canoe had entered this estuary, and a single shadowy figure paddled it silently in this direction.

The canoeman had not seen her; her craft was blocked by the reeds where the bullfrog sang in the willow's shadow. Nearer now, the moonlight opened the shadows of his face to reveal that it was not one of the shovel-faced Muskogeans but Eagle Ring Man.

He must have caught one of their canoes.

She melted back down into her own blue-and-purple shadows, trying to think like a log. She gave it plenty of time.

She counted to one hundred, then allowed one eye to lift just enough to watch the other canoe move farther up the estuary from her position. Now the moonlight was behind him as he gracefully paddled toward the eastern reach of water, where land must begin somewhere in the murk. The boat beneath him was so low in the water it seemed to disappear. The man looked as though he were merely floating uncannily on his knees just below the surface, raising barely a duck's wake and no sound at all. He backpaddled expertly, bringing himself to a standstill, shipped his oar, and sat there listening to the night.

The air was humid and vibrating, but above spread a rash of stars midheaven. She heard something clicking on the far shore, where his canoe was pointed. Something small fell into the water. An egret broke from the jungle, lifting a silhouette against the moon, which took on sharper edges and lost its blush as it climbed out of the low mist.

For what seemed to Gwen a long time, he sat there, still as moonlight, watching and listening.

She could almost hear the moon squeak along the sky.

Finally, after a patient time of it, he made for shore, his pull making crystalline echos over the still water. He beached his canoe, sliding it through watercress and up into a clay bank until none of it remained in the water, then turned to look out over the sleeping lake. A faint breeze came up, rattling the reeds. A fish jumped nearby.

She knew he was calculating the situation. This man was a hunter. By instinct she knew what he hunted. What she could not know was the potential of the enemy. The men from Mabila would not attempt to shoot the rapids—he knew they always portaged there except for young men proving their mettle. The Mabilans were not known for bravery generally. They were farmers.

He also knew that in the morning Shell would send out hunters who knew every branching of the fickle water and would have help from their froggy allies, the Alabamans who knew every cypress tree in their territory.

His own old man would be expecting him home soon. If he began walking immediately back north, stole a canoe at the landing, and headed for Yellow Pheasant Village as fast as possible, he might be able to make it before word got through to Sun Caller about this night's events. But the system of runners was efficient. Soon his chief would be hearing from Shell, who would lodge protest and perhaps even declare war on the Yuchi village because of the raven's apparent theft of the new bride.

In Muskogean culture this was one of the highest insults, since they put great store in their great suns, members of old families who claimed nobility through descent from the first people to colonize these swamps.

It would be best if he reached home before formal protests were made. Above all he must free himself of charges that he kidnaped Shell's bride—by appearing at home without fleeing and without the female, he might plead innocence. After all, she hid herself in his canoe. He would tell them the truth, that he had nothing to do with her running away.

Eagle Ring Man went about settling the canoe where he could sleep in it. The men from whom he stole it had left behind various items—a reed mat, some travel rations, and a fishing pole with a bone hook on a stout line.

He canted the craft slightly so he could sit upon one edge while he went over these items, listening now and then to the stillness marked by animal sounds.

Gwen held onto a willow branch to maintain her hiding place. She was thinking, too: She was unsure where she was and had no clue that this was the same river where her father watched the jungle, his eyes stranger, his manner more withdrawn with each passing day that she was lost, despite the settlement they built on the island. She knew this river would take her to the sea but was not sure if she needed help to reach it.

He said he was her friend, and now, watching him in the moonlight, she felt compelled to trust this beautiful young man who stretched, yawned, and began unwrapping the elaborately tied turban he wore. His hair fell loose on his shoulders.

She brought the canoe expertly around, aimed directly at his camp, still not quite sure if she was making the right decision.

He looked up to see her illuminated in the warm light of the setting moon. This girl knew something about boats. She would have rather brought the canoe's nose entirely out of the water so she would not have to put her foot in the dark suspicious river where anything could be lurking. But she wanted to appear brave to him. Boldly, though her heart was pounding in an odd mixture of fear and excitement, she exited the canoe, tied it up without any trace of hesitation, and turned to walk the few paces up the bank to stand before him. She brought up her right hand with the first two fingers side by side. "We are friends, remember?" She startled him—no woman he knew could handle a boat like that, or looked like her, or had such directness.

In handsign she asked, "Will you help me beach the canoe?"

He smiled and walked with her to do as she asked.

But the men from Mabila were coming; he could hear the splash of their coordinated paddles. He gestured to her to jump in. Without hesitation she complied, excited and suddenly warmed by him despite the gathering chill. She heard the approaching canoes, too.

He quickly dragged his craft back into the water, then boarded her canoe. Using a long leg, he pushed the empty one out onto the water beyond the reeds. Momentum carried it into the reflection of the moon as the three canoes entered the backwater from the main stream where their fellows prodded other estuaries.

Meanwhile, Eagle Ring Man pulled them under the sheltering willow. The moon was nearly gone, but the eastern sky paled with the approach of dawn.

The canoes advanced, sliding by like snakes as Eagle Ring Man and Gwen watched, hidden a canoe length from the hunters, who moved on into the other end of the pond. Several birds screamed and dragged themselves flapping into the sky.

Eagle Ring Man watched the mouth of the backwater to make sure no others were following, then, satisfied, he pushed them off from the tree, parting the veil of branches with their prow. Gwen felt the slight current of the main channel tug at the canoe. The Yuchi gave several more powerful digs into the green water, sacrificing silence for speed.

About half a league above Two Rivers Island the current speeded up as the channel narrowed. Now Gwen suspected where they were from the shape of the isle and the general lay of the eastern shore, which she had a good look at the day of landing.

Almost home, she signed back to Eagle Ring Man, in deep partnership with the river, pulling, pulling, not yet daring to believe that they had shaken the warriors who were experts at such hide-and-seek games. He tried to keep lookout for the others in the war party, who surely must be using the river in the same way as he as they searched for the girl with bright red hair, who was turning to him now with triumph in her eyes.

Now they could see the larger bay. Swift as gulls there broke from a stand of reeds on the eastern bank two more of the painted war canoes. They made no sound until about a dozen canoe lengths from the prey, then the warriors began an ominous humming chant that had the Yuchi's immediate attention. Gwen cried out when she saw the attackers gaining.

Suddenly Eagle Ring Man jerked and slumped forward, the long pins of a blow-dart impaling his right shoulder. He twisted in agony, dropping the paddle.

Instinctively Gwen snatched it up. She bit back terror and pulled with all her strength as the river opened into the wide bay. The revealed vista in the almost-dawn light smote Gwen like a blow, for there was the *St. Ann* a burned wreck in the eastern shallows. It brought new tears to her eyes. She was especially fond of the ship because it was christened for her mother.

But there was no time for sentiment, for no sooner had she sped beyond the wreck but the enemy broke from around the curve at the head of the island, their echoing war cries stilling birds and chilling the blood, as they were meant to do.

The most immediately startling thing about the island was that it was almost totally denuded of trees. A forest of stumps riddled it from this shore clear across its midlands, a triumph of the ax and saw, she knew. She recognized woodsmoke from new-cut logs she had been smelling the past few days. The red people used deadfall for their cooking fires. She should have known her father would have the forge going. All those trees had gone into the fire or into the construction of the two stockades she saw widely separated on the island.

Gwen saw white people running from either enclosure. Down the gravelly beach a monk was carrying a coracle on his back. He turned to run with the abbot, who was stripped to the waist and wearing his smithy apron.

Gwen allowed herself to look back just once; the enemy were close behind and closing. There were more of the sleek boats now, at least a dozen. The leader was fully loaded with what looked like thirty warriors. They were chanting, singing a low, almost seductive paddling chant that in itself seemed to draw them closer and closer. Just before she turned away from the awful sight, she saw Eagle Ring Man slumped in the stern.

His chest was bloody. One of the short brightly feathered darts delivered with a blowgun was embedded in his neck, another high on his shoulder. Several more nicked the wooden canoe. She could look no more and pulled with all her might, buoyed by the current and the fact that she had only a few boat lengths to go.

If the cremated hulk of the *St. Ann* was a blow to her, the sight of Two Rivers Island was a haven, even with its deforestation.

She could see more of Madoc's Hundred running toward the shore but was still too far away to see their faces. She called, "It is I, Gwen, do not shoot!" when she saw two bowmen prepare arrows in longbows.

Men in the familiar buff-colored cassocks trotted along the beach now, pacing her descent. But the main channel had her, though she had driven an angle across it that would eventually beach her about the rocks where Madoc had first encountered Aligapas. She had about a furlong to go. Without looking she knew the enemy was gaining because their chant was louder. She knew enough Muskogean to understand they were using magic against her, urging the river spirit, the Uktena, to give her to them.

She saw on the waiting shore one of the monks stop an archer about to let go an arrow. They were pointing back upriver now, where they, too, could see the enemy break around the bend and come into full view. They were well out of arrow shot, though Gwen knew from experience that these rivermen could launch a lance from an atlatl twice as far as a bow-driven arrow. She had no doubt they could do so from a moving canoe.

Lances sliced the water, each closer than the last. The marksmen were bracketing their quarry, a sitting duck.

She saw she must maneuver out of their range, so she deliberately used her paddle like a rudder to aim downcurrent, nearly doubling her speed but moving parallel to her goal. She did not dare look back for fear she would see the enemy too close. They would not want to get close to shore, where the white archers were lining up their targets behind her. Rhiannon and Yngvild appeared on the shore, and three children running along before them.

Gwen's arms and shoulders ached; it felt like prickling fire between her shoulder blades. She felt sweat course down the channel of her spine.

Only a little way to go. Her lungs were on fire. Downstream a furlong, then the quieter waters of the bay would swing her in a gentle arc. Neck muscles were cramping; she ignored the pain and kept paddling.

The enemy song was close now. She knew they would not harm her, just board her craft and enslave her. She had that advantage, that they would not hurt her because of Shell's fondness for her. She shuddered in revulsion when she remembered his fishy breath and his bony forehead.

Ahead she was surprised to see the sturdy round wall of upright logs that made up the stockade at the tip of the island just back from what used to be the tree line.

She heard Eagle Ring Man moaning behind her, trying to sit up, staring out at the island. He had never seen so complete a deforestation. There was not one living tree on that side of the river. The sight of hundreds of stumps shocked him beyond pain as he tried imagine what could amputate every tree on the island. But amazement piled onto amazement as he saw the monk running along the beach, close now, with the coracle strapped to his back. The Yuchi stared through his pain with amazed eyes; here he was looking nearly into the face of the spirit head of his clan, for it was surely the Great Turtle himself.

Eagle Ring Man, who was having a religious experience with this vision of his totem animal, called out a prayer-formula and then must have fallen back, because Gwen heard him no more. But when she glanced back, she saw that there was barely a canoe length between hers and the lead war-boat full of chanting, grinning warriors pulling with many coordinated muscles. It chilled her bones to see the front man in the lead canoe was Shovel-Face, his teeth barred and gleaming like a naked skull's.

She heard her people on the beach urging her on. "You can make it," Wyn called between cupped hands, then appealed to heaven to help her.

"Only a little more, girl," cried a strong familiar voice among the many, and she saw that it was her father clapping in time to her paddling, but she knew as he must that there was no way she could outreach the powerful oarsmen whose canoe was now bumping into the stern where Eagle Ring Man slumped in delirium. It hurt to see Madoc standing as helpless as any other man, so close but so far. She wanted to scream, "Tad!" the way she did as a child when he had come home from a long sea voyage, flinging herself into his arms: He would lift her up, up and whirl her around, and everything would be wonderful, she would be safe and mama would be smiling. Nothing bad ever happened with him home; when he was away, something bad always did.

She felt another ominous thump aft and heard the slaps of strong hands on the canoe rim.

Using the paddle-edge as a weapon, she hammered the red fingers clawing at her, feeling the satisfying sound of bone crunching under her blows. There flashed before her eyes the memory of what he had done to Nona as she brought the paddle back as far as she could swing. She turned it so that as it came down again, it was the edge-on that caught him a stout crack on the side of his face, peeling back his left ear. Aligapas screamed and fell back—a quick look, and she saw the enemy canoe falling slightly away.

Now the shoreward archers had range; several of the white men's arrows pierced the canoe and its riders.

Even so, they were pulling toward her again, closing the gap of only a hand span between the canoes, while one of the rowers crawled over Aligapas to take his place at the prow. His hands were already making claws with which to snag her canoe—they would connect near the spot where Eagle Ring Man's head was thrown back against the canoe rim, which was carved a little wider than the body of the craft.

She kept paddling, determined to keep on as long as possible, but she was sure that sweating, plump hands would grab her at any moment. She realized she had been repeating the Litany to Mary unceasingly. Muscles in her neck were cramping, too, from her strained recitation. Just a little more, O Mother

Mary, ladder of heaven, let us not for mercy's sake be carried off by our enemies, O washer of souls, mother of orphans. . . ."

Aligapas would be horned with anger; she was sure she broke his hand, as well as slicing off an ear. She could not know that Aligapas and two others in the canoe were over the side, pierced by arrows and pulled by the current into deeper water.

The canoe slid alongside her own. She tensed, still paddling for all she was worth but sure each stroke would be interrupted with the inevitable.

Instead she heard cheers from landward, and calls of astonishment from the war canoe. She looked back; Eagle Ring Man between Gwen and the enemy boat had pulled himself on one elbow and was staring at the island, as were the warriors behind him, paused midstroke only inches from her, eyes round and staring at something that made them forget their attack.

She did not stop paddling, just plowed on, head down, not caring if her arms fell off. She was jarred as the canoe nosed into the rocks. It rattled her, made her dizzy. She tried to keep paddling but finally realized she was not going farther as she nosed into reeds in the shallows.

It was then that she looked up to see what it was in the air that had everyone's attention, because everyone—red and white—was looking up, and up, and still farther up, following something climbing, craning their heads back, shading their eyes against sun, pointing, making sounds of wonder.

It was the bees in a brilliant, scintillating, pear-shaped swarm, rising up, climbing the sky like a single organism, undulating, marking the air with their one-note song. It was a massive hive, hundreds of individuals nurtured on the rich contents of the barrel, blackening the air like a knowing cloud, groping and spiraling as though sniffing the breeze and finding it to its liking. The swarm moved without speed above Gwen and directly east toward the frozen red warriors, who had never seen a domesticated swarm of honeybees before this moment and thought they were being attacked by a spirit-directed cloud of dire intent thrown out by the white people's magic.

The swarm's trembling tail cleared the barrel the monks had set up inside the stockade, the gates of which were thrown open. Father John was trotting this way, nearly stumbling as he kept his eyes on the bees. People were pouring out around him, calling and running toward her. From somewhere a bell was ringing.

Gwen could look no farther upwards into the dawn-bright sky. Dizzily she brought her head upright, seeing that her father was running this way, arms waving, her name on his lips. His plunge threw fans of spray out from his ankles, but he could not throw the knife he had drawn because Gwen was in his line, upstream across a small bight between the rocks and her position.

"Look out behind you—" he screamed as he lunged toward the canoe to strike the huge, bloody red man looming behind her.

Chapter 21

Women's hearts are shaped on a turning wheel.

—Ancient Norse proverb

Madoc's knife flashed in sunlight. The long boat rolled, throwing Gwen into the shallow water, where she floundered but held onto his arm.

"He saved me, tad—" she yelled, dripping mud from her breasts and outlandish feather costume.

Eagle Ring Man was thrown to his knees in pain and amazement and about to lose consciousness.

By the water's edge William the Saxon and two sailors were sending arrows at the red men within range. The boat that carried Shovel-Face turned back. Aligapas's body and the others in the water had been pulled out into the main current.

Few of the attackers were aware of the whites, because their attention was drawn to the bees now moving like a dream over the water and what must have seemed directly at the Muskogeans. Several of the red men already slumped back under the stings of the white men's arrows.

And now another combatant entered the fray as Huw aboard the *Horn* ordered the anchor raised when he first saw the enemy canoes enter the harbor. For several days the sailors had been working to shape oars to replace the ones left behind for cargo space. Now they set the long paddles the way the original Norse designers of the ship intended, poling because the harbor floor was shallow. The great high-prowed ship eased around the tip of the island and into full view. The red men not diverted by the bees now confronted the ship looming toward them, bowmen studding the sides with the prickling spines of nocked arrows. A volley let loose, and a moment later several canoemen screamed.

The red men were in full rout from the bees in one direction and the ship that fulfilled their worse legends from another.

Wyn came running up behind Madoc with others—Dag and Lev with weapons drawn, several of the brothers, as well as most of the civilians of Madoc's Hundred, including the three boys. They stood gaping at the girl they knew as Gwen in the strange mix of wild clothing and nudity.

Most of the canoes were maneuvering back the way they came, not a turnaround but merely a switching of direction. It was a maneuver accomplished many times by the expert paddling teams, but with the demon cloud of hot bees coming at them like a curse and the dragon ship cutting off downriver retreat, they lost their discipline and crossed each other's bow.

The sun broke from the trees on the eastern shore, bathing the ship in a glorious light and adding to its mystery by puddling gold ripples around her high prow. The anchors splashed.

Those canoemen unfortunate enough to have chosen downriver retreat were picked off by the bowmen, who were yelling challenges to each other as they tallied score. With the enemy in retreat, it was Gwen who provoked shocked stares among the Hundred.

Madoc seemed the most shocked. He stood staring at her, whom he thought never to see again. He had been mourning her for weeks, but here she was, pink goose bumps on her skin as she clung to the canoe between him and the swooning red man.

Wyn, who ran from his forge so suddenly the hammer was still in his right hand, threw the towel from his own bare shoulders over the girl's chest.

It seemed to wake Madoc from the trance. "Oh, Gwyneth," he all but moaned, embracing her, his knife still in his hand.

Wyn asked, "My brothers, how do they fare?"

Gwen shook her head. "They tortured some to death."

It was not that much of a surprise because of the screams they had heard the night of the raid. Wyn crossed himself and said a silent prayer. "And the others? Who survives?"

"Brian and a couple of others, I never knew their names."

She described them as best she could remember but admitted she had not had much contact with the brothers.

Wyn nodded, accepting, his lips moving in prayer.

"Ari is alive," she said. "Three women claim him."

"Lady Gwen?" Edwin said, his eyes wide with anxiety.

With Madoc's arm still across her shoulder, Gwen reached out and touched the man's hand. "I am sorry. . . ."

"Both of them?" he cried, unbelieving. He shook his head in stubborn disbelief, trying not to cry. "My boy, too?"

Gwen was not sure if it was worse that little Dewi had been taken alive. In either case that baby was dead to this man. To spare him bitter hope she said, "They are both gone."

Edwin's face crumpled. One of the sailors tried to comfort him, but Edwin shrugged him off, face twisted.

Over Gwen's shoulder Madoc saw the canoe fleet making for the opposite shore. The stain of bees against the sky had moved slowly only a few feet off the water. The red warriors—maybe thirty-five in all—were trying to get out from under it, scattering as they hit the beach, abandoning canoes to the current. They shouted to each other as they ran, their shamans rattling gourds and chanting at the swarm, but too terrified to stand their ground for proper magic to be made.

Madoc, arm around Gwen, signaled to Dag to go after them.

A sudden grin on his face, Dag drew the sword he never removed and used a foot to shove the red man forward, skewing the canoe. He placed the sword's tip parallel to the ribs, "I will begin with the blood-eagle on this one."

Gwen made a move, but Madoc stepped between her and the canoe, placing his hand on Dag's thick wrist. He gestured with his chin at the far shore. "Over there," he said, eye to eye with the scruffy Norseman. Dag relented, nodding to Lev, and they were off with the other Norsemen to grab three beached coracles.

"I will go with them," Edwin offered through clenched teeth.

Madoc slapped Edwin's shoulder to send him with the others.

Gwen pulled away from her father, Wyn's sweat-wipe falling as she stooped to drag the canoe to the beach before the current took it downstream. Reflexively Madoc helped her beach it, speaking softly to her, "What trouble do you bring, daughter?"

She devoted her attention to the man slumped in the canoe. "Please, tad," she begged, trying to pull Eagle Ring Man from the craft. She looked up, seeking Caradoc in the crowd that pressed around them. "Someone is hurt here!"

The plump fellow stepped forward, his right arm in a leather sling, while Wyn and Madoc pulled the patient onto the beach.

Madoc stood back, scowling.

Caradoc bent over the red man, examining the two wounds. The one in the neck had missed the carotid and only barbed the skin. Caradoc probed for the tip of the cane implement and skillfully twisted and removed it.

"Let me see that," Madoc said, examining the whittled cane sliver, amazed that such a fragile thing could be used so effectively as a weapon. It was little more than a toothpick.

The one in the shoulder was deeper.

"We must cut that one out," Caradoc said to Ffagan, who had been drafted to be mediciner's apprentice. Madoc, alarmed at how vulnerable the community was when only one person knew a craft, had ordered that everyone, including the women, must apprentice to two craftsmen so that they could preserve their skills. Because of Caradoc's injury the apprentice's first surgery would be to remove that dart from the red man.

"But," Caradoc continued lecturing the young monk, "neither puncture is bad enough to explain this fellow's condition." He thumbed back the patient's eyelids to reveal white, rolled eyes.

Ffagan was a dark-haired youth from Bangor, with warm brown eyes under thick brows and a quirk of musculature that made him look as though he were smiling on the right side of his mouth and scowling with the left. He was only a humble monk, an apprentice stone carver, and not prepared for what had been thrust upon him. Scared of his first real test with the scalpal, he was thinking that it was a good thing his debut surgery would not be performed on a member of their own community. He doubted this red man would make it. There was not much blood, but he looked about to die.

It was obvious he was convulsing, tongue lolling from his mouth. He seemed very pale for the savages they had seen so far, the color of ashes. His limbs were beginning to shake; his back arched. The white turban had come undone, unrolling down the riverbank, revealing glossy black hair let loose like a woman's.

Caradoc leaned back on his heels, shaking his head.

Gwen said, "I am sure the darts were poisoned." She had seen the Muskogean warriors preparing their blowguns, dipping the cane projectiles in a muddy boiling mixture before storing them carefully, without touching the points, in thick leather wrappings.

She cradled the red man, holding his ear close to her breast, using the end of his turban to wipe away blood.

It infuriated Madoc that she would succor the enemy. He wanted to drag her away, rip the filthy barbarian costume off her, and cover her nakedness to make her what she used to be.

Caradoc stroked his arm, broken the night of the raid. "Well, that explains it, then." He regarded his patient, then spoke to Ffagan. "We can doctor the wounds, but..."

Mary pushed through the crowd, her hand in a shoulder bag. "Mandrake root will draw the poison," she said with authority that surprised everyone except her husband.

"Mary—" Wil warned gently. The couple had discussed her avocation, deciding not to talk about it until they knew the feelings of the others on the subject, especially the clergy. She had only hinted to Teleri that she had specialized knowledge.

Mary opened her hand to reveal a small drawstring bag, which she fingered open before handing to Caradoc. "A poultice of this mixed with queen-bee jelly."

"Yes, yes," Caradoc interrupted, nodding some impatience as he took it from her, sniffing the powder. "Mandrake works on gangrene." He had not heard of the jelly medium, however—on the battlefield they used axle grease of heavy sheep lanolin.

Mary stepped back beside Wil, her hands folded across her apron. He said something only she could hear, and she responded by saying, "No, husband, I can keep silent no longer."

Caradoc eyed her suspiciously.

"I was afraid you might think ill of me," she said.

"She is a master," Wil said proudly.

She looked shyly down at her medicine bag.

"No Druid magic, now," Father John said, teasing.

Mary smiled nervously. Not everyone regarded herbs and

simples a Christian woman's work. In fact, some considered it
the first step to witchcraft. She had been terrified of provoking Father Simon, whom she overheard disparaging witches.

Shyly now she glanced at old John, who replied, "My own
mother was an herb woman, Lord bless her soul."

Yngvild, now in advanced pregnancy, stepped forward. She
usually said little in public because she was shy about her
thick accent. "You—midwife?"

When Mary nodded, the Norsewoman said, "Thank Freyja,"
clutching her blossomed abdomen and grinning toothlessly.
Caradoc must have finally removed those front teeth.

Meanwhile, Rhiannon pushed gently through the onlookers and draped her old blue mantle across Gwen's shoulders.
Gwen pulled the shawl around herself, exchanged a glance
with Rhiannon, then laid her hand on her aunt's belly, a
question in her eyes.

Rhiannon nodded, yes, we are both doing just fine.

Yngvild nodded. "Praise Freyja, we have a midwife."

"So I hear," Rhiannon replied.

"Praise the Queen of Heaven," Wyn said firmly, "for
answering our prayers."

Yngvild smiled. She had no need to argue.

With a glance at the arglwydd, who made the decision
about who would study what craft, Caradoc said, "Looks as
though I have a new apprentice."

"Or," Madoc said dryly, "perhaps Mary has."

"The red people have good remedies," Gwen volunteered,
remembering the salve that relieved the itching insect bites
among several instances of healing she witnessed.

"Get him inside," Caradoc said as he stood. "That is, if the
arglwydd agrees we should tend the wounds of our enemy."

The arglwydd was staring at his daughter, who looked up at
him with supplication in her eyes.

At that moment across the river, Dag and his men had
taken advantage of the surprise caused by the bees and were
engaging the last of the red men. While the cane knives were
wicked projectiles, in close combat they were no match for
iron blades. Someone over there shouted a battle cry; someone else screamed.

"This one is not an enemy," Gwen said to her father. "He
is not like the others—see—no tattoos."

Madoc looked down at the red man. He did have that long
womanish hair, but she was right. He was a distinctly differ-

ent type in physique and costume. Unlike the shorter, naked, blue-stained, and skull-deformed Muskogeans, this one was a tall specimen of young manhood in a decent pair of leather trews, bound boots, and a jerkin similar in cut to Madoc's own.

Madoc sheathed the knife before he gave Caradoc permission to treat the red man, while Gwen hugged him in silent thanks.

Caradoc gestured at the nearest men to help Ffagan lift the patient, who had lapsed into a muttering half-consciousness.

"Carry him," cried the doctor. "Walking speeds the poison!"

Huw, Wil, and a couple of others hefted his dead weight toward the log shelter, Gwen and Caradoc close behind.

Another scream echoed from the other side of the river as red men fled from the iron weapons. Dag chased one into the forest, where presently he reemerged cleaning his blade against a palm leaf. His men meanwhile were hacking away at three of the enemy unfortunate enough to have been stopped on the beach.

Madoc regarded the group making toward the Hundred's main camp inside the stockade. Because of good trading relations with Chief Komas, they had relaxed security. Now all but a skeleton crew stayed aboard the *Horn*. They had their strange beehive here, and the two fledgling pigeons that had hatched while Gwen was gone. Madoc had personally taken care of the birds in her absence, and they were sleek now and learning to fly to their homing signal, the dragon pennant on the ship's mast. The women, children, and other men had set up housekeeping in the stockaded little fort, where they plied the looms, leathercraft, and other labors aimed at restocking their stores of food and materials. All the civilians slept ashore.

"Wait!" Madoc yelled.

The group around the red man halted clumsily.

"Take him to the llan instead."

Wyn at his elbow started to protest. The brothers had built their own small stockade farther up the island, where they set up the forge and their makeshift chapel under a cane pavilion. Madoc had protested, but the brothers insisted on isolation, ostensibly to conduct their daily offices and austerities without disturbing the rest of the community. But everyone knew it was because Wyn wanted to maintain his brotherhood away from women.

Wyn saw the determined look on Madoc's face and thought better of arguing.

"He can be better guarded there, Domme," Madoc said. "Caradoc cannot tend that giant with a broken arm. Ffagan can take care of him."

Wyn did not comment that it appeared to be too late to protect Gwen from the influence of the handsome young red man.

They turned toward the llan.

"Gwen," Madoc called.

Reluctantly she watched the others carry Eagle Ring Man away, then turned back as her father approached her.

"Get her some clothes," Madoc brusquely ordered Teleri. Gwen noticed the tone because he had never ordered the lowest seaman on his ship that way.

Gwen felt sorry for her new stepmother, who turned to obey without making eye contact, while Madoc put his arm around Gwen.

"Lord, Gwyneth, but it is good to see you." It was as though this moment was the first he allowed himself to believe she was alive.

"I was so scared." Gwen, too, seemed to give in to emotions that she had been holding back. "They have horrible tortures they use to test people."

"Did they hurt you?" he growled, tensing with fury.

She shook her head morosely. "My test was even worse." She leaned against her father, comforted by his strength. "Aligapas killed Nona and . . . they cooked her, tad."

He held her close, patting her as though she were a child again who had come to him with some child's pain that he could soothe away. "It is all right now, you are home."

"I would not be here but for Eagle Ring Man."

He held her away from him at arm's length so he could look into her eyes. "I believe you are a true witness, daughter."

Her answer was a hug that he let her break.

"I have many questions," Madoc said, guiding her with him toward the stockade.

It looked like a more complicated situation than he had imagined. When he asked Owen for permission to come to these unknown western lands, he thought he would be arriving on uninhabited shores. But now it appeared he was dealing with not one but several red communities. He had not bargained on invading someone's country, but here he was and must make the best of it. The Hundred were so few they could hardly be a threat, and had such attractive trade goods that he hoped to get by without any more fighting. In that direction lay quick doom. But Gwen would have observations that could help him understand his military position if they were forced to do more battle.

But she was not his alone. Others approached with a welcome and questions. Was she hungry, thirsty? Had they abused her? Those were genuine pearls, were they not? Was that gold wire they were strung on?

"They beat gold and copper," she said, "but I did not see iron." She saw how her captors prized the captured iron weapons.

Teleri came with a robe from linen that she, Rhiannon, and Yngvild had been weaving to replace their cloth goods; their supply of flax and wool was abundant, and now everyone had cloth as well as leather clothing again since they set up the looms.

"M'God, girl, they marked you," Teleri cried when she saw the blue tattoo on Gwen's thigh.

Madoc groaned at what he considered a mutilation.

Gwen regarded the clan mark the red women had pricked into her thigh, then stained with ashes. She rather liked it, though the procedure had been painful. Healed now, it was a clear outline of a stylized deer.

Father John was speaking urgently to Wyn, pointing at the bees hesitating in their humming swarm above the jungle. His bee veil was thrown back over his straw hat, the only personal items he brought from the monastery, where his responsibilities as Brother Farmer included beekeeping and mead making.

"They do not usually swarm far," John said, more agitated than any had ever seen him. He had expected the swarm because Brother Ely's barrel was overflowing with honey with no more room for the queen to lay eggs, a condition of overcrowding that often caused swarm, although it was late in the season.

The barrel had long been buried because of its primary occupant, the lid being all that remained above ground. The bees had for days been restless and noisy, so John built several bell-shaped willow hives. So far he had not succeeded in coaxing them to depart from their human hive and into the fine new quarters. Early this morning he blew smoke into the barrel hole to calm the creatures, reciting scripture, "Be not afraid ye beasts of the field, for the pastures of the wilderness do spring," while skimming off excess honey—when suddenly, with its group mind, the hive decided the time was ripe for flight.

With all his expertise and spiritual assistance, the swarm rejected traditional hives. It had risen like a ghost, its queen at the throbbing heart, off in search of bee promised land.

"If we do not find them, we may never have honey again."

As a farmer John knew it was more serious than not having mead. There must be bees to fertilize his crops. The thought of losing them was a catastrophe he did not want to imagine.

"Yes," said Wyn, Welshman to the core, who did not want to think of the rest of his life without mead. "Those red heathens acted as though they never saw bees before."

He regarded John, his personal confessor and authority on all things agricultural. "Father, is it possible we have found a land without bees?" In the back of his mind was the thought that poor Simon may have been right in his madness—this truly might be Satan's country if it did not contain biblical types.

John shrugged. "I have seen deer, but I don't think there are cows or horses here, either. The people who come to trade do not seem to have any knowledge of them, or sheep or even pigs."

"So," said Evan who was listening, "Father Brian was wrong. Pigs are not everywhere."

Madoc shot his aide an I-told-you-so.

In that look Gwen recognized Owen. Mourning her and sustaining so many losses had worked on her father. The subtle changes from a month ago gave him a sharper countenance that reminded her so much of the grandfather she sorely missed, it brought tears to her eyes.

"God protect Brian in his ordeal," Wyn whispered, overcome by the combined loss of his men and the threat of losing his way of life. "God protect them all." He had expected tribulations on this journey, had even desired them the better to serve God. He welcomed the chance to go to the Holy Land and battle the Turk with his bare teeth if necessary, but to contemplate a world without pork roast, clear mead, and wool to make the brothers' traditional cassocks was to contemplate a place too much like purgatory. He regarded the hammer in his hand as though he had forgotten what it was, then beckoned to the brother who had been carrying the coracle, asking him to follow the bees to see where they finally landed.

John, his eye on the swarm, was ready to plunge after him, but Wyn held him back. "Take help," he called after the old man, who waved affirmatively as he trotted after his bees.

"I will go with him," Evan offered.

"Good idea," Madoc said, and Evan hurried off to join the monk, who was helping the brother launch his coracle.

"Take a couple of other men," Madoc called, thinking of security. He trusted the Alabamans because they wanted more of his trade, but now he must double the watch against this new threat from the Mabilans. He would not assume they would let Gwen go without a fight, since he had already learned that among these red people loss of face and wife-stealing were the most provocative offenses. He could ill afford to lose any more of his specialists. If manpower had been a problem before, it was a crisis now as every few days took another life from the community. Never voiced, but always lurking in his darkest thoughts, was the fact that already they were too few to make an enduring colony, a problem he must confront sooner or later. Immediate survival seemed the first priority.

Across the river it looked as though the Norsemen had concluded their grim play. Even from here Madoc could see what looked like a blanket of blood over there. The Norsemen knew terrible torture rituals passed down from their Odin-worshiping ancestors that would compete with the Muskogeans in brutality. Madoc accepted the necessary carnage of war, but it was his style to kill quickly. He was glad he was not close enough to see what they did to the red men they caught. It was probably the hideous blood-eagle, which Madoc was thankful he had never seen.

However, the commander in him was glad the Norsemen had this diversion to drain building aggression. They had been picking fights among themselves. They sounded mellow now, singing some old victory song as they cleaned weapons, took ear-trophies, and prepared to recross the river.

Madoc's hand on Gwen's back urged her forward to the little fort at the tip of the island.

Wyn was left alone beside the canoe as people returned to their various occupations. He stared a moment at the long foreign boat marked with what looked like evil signs, then called a brother to help unload it and see what cargo it held.

The first item was the long bundle with a bulge in the middle. He lifted the thing, wondering what it was. While the brother exclaimed over a set of exquisitely carved horn eating utensils in a polished turtle-shell bowl, Wyn hurriedly unlaced the odd package, suddenly plied by curiosity that was all too soon shockingly satisfied.

He threw the bundle away from himself with a startled gasp and crossed himself twice.

The brother cried out when he saw what the abbot had uncovered, crossing himself and backing away with a cry that caused heads to turn and people to stop in their tracks.

Madoc was the first to return to the canoe, with Gwen hard on his heels. One by one people hurried back to the spot and stood staring at what they saw on the ground, while newcomers pushed to see; then they, too, froze at the sight.

On the gravel in the leather wrapping was a beautiful Norse short-sword and a mummified human head.

Madoc stared at the grim memento, trying to remember the faces of the men who accompanied Fair Beard. He knew only a couple of the six. He seemed to remember that at least three, including the commander, were blond. This shriveled parody of a human face might be any of them, or—yes, he had to admit, though God in heaven let there be some justice in the world—it might be his partner and blood brother Fair Beard Snorrison.

"Who?" Gwen asked. She had not known about the bundle Eagle Ring Man was delivering to the Yuchi from the Muskogean miko. But she knew the grisly remnant had belonged to a blond man.

"Lord, I do not know," Madoc said, beyond horror. He could not help staring at the thing, but as hard as he looked, he could not see Snorrison in this pitiful object. It was some kind of Norseman, but he could not swear that it was not the Norseman.

The head was well preserved, somewhat shrunken, but the blond mustache and hair were the living man's, though it had been scalped. A circle on the crown was hairless, and the remaining hair, including the mustaches, were braided into several coils.

Madoc gripped the sun disk hung around his own neck. He knew Fair Beard would not have willingly parted with this artifact. Someone would have to take it from him by force, if not kill him.

The pouting, desiccated face told him nothing. The eyes had been removed and the lids sewn shut. Likewise the lips, so the features looked only human enough not to be something else.

Which individual human could not be discerned.

The skin had darkened with whatever mummification process the Muskogean bonepicker priests had used to preserve it to the consistency of old leather. It had been sent to them in salt from the Alabamans and preserved immediately, so there was no sign of putrefaction. They had used a rendering of oak galls after removing the brain and other soft parts, performing a mummification that would last for a long time if it was kept dry.

Dag and the other warriors were crowding in to see what had everyone's attention. They stood staring at what could well be the head of their chief and an answer to their several questions, not the least of which was one Dag persistently tendered to Fair Beard's wife. Yngvild had been able to forestall him like some latter-day Penelope with the argument that she waited for her husband. As long as she could reasonably anticipate Fair Beard's return, she could keep Dag off her.

Dag handled the broadsword, turning the blade and nodding. "It is his." He caught Yngvild's eye and held up the weapon so that she and Madoc both recognized it as Snorrison's.

"Come see your widowhood, woman," he said to her, never having used that tone before because she was his chief's wife, and he was bound to protect and defer to her.

Yngvild came forward, her hands across her abdomen as though protecting the child within. Nervelessly, not a muscle twitching to give away her feelings, she looked down.

Dag and everyone, even Madoc, were bound up in the spell of Yngvild's stillness as she stared at the severed head. She bent as well as she could at seven and a half months of pregnancy and took up a stick, with which she rolled the hideous thing over.

She stood, still staring.

Dag gave out a hoot of triumph, but Madoc's hand shot out to hold him back. The Norseman's shout soured to a growl at the man who owned his liege lord's allegiance. "My oath is broken on Fair Beard's death," he sneered. "This is between me and her."

"She decides," Madoc said evenly, holding Dag's glare.

Several around them, including Lev and other Norse sailors, agreed. They did not want to believe their Snorrison dead.

"It is the woman's decision," Lev said.

"Let her choose," agreed another.

"Is it Fair Beard or not?"

"Take your time, daughter," said Bjorn, crouching to study what might or might not be all that was left of his son-in-law.

The chorus faded, and still Yngvild had not taken her eyes from the thing on the ground.

"You know it is him," Dag hissed.

"No," she said, breaking one tension and drawing another. "You know it!"

She turned an unblinking gaze upon her husband's first mate. "He has a mole on his left ear." She used the stick to spin the head around. "See with your own eyes."

Everyone pressed close. Someone reported back to Rhys and those at the rear, "No mole."

"How can you tell with the skin so dark?" Dag fumed.

Yngvild stood defiantly before him as he was about to speak further, when Lev whispered to him in Scandinavian, "Her choice, brother. Think—"

Dag pulled away when the blond lad held his arm.

"Think of the consequences if she is right," Bjorn said coolly, standing stiffly. He turned to Dag and confronted him directly. "Think about what Fair Beard will do to you."

Dag bared his teeth with a response, clenched his fists, and stalked off with several, but not all, the Norsemen following.

Rhiannon behind Yngvild gave her a little sisterly handshake. Mary spoke softly to Yngvild, asking how many weeks before the baby came.

Again they scattered. Madoc took up Fair Beard's sword and said as he walked away with Gwen, "Wyn, will you bury that."

"Snorrison was no Christian."

"I will take care of it," said Lev, who swooped down on the ugly relic and wrapped it in its leather covering.

Wyn hefted his hammer and returned to his bloomery. The ax head he had been forging was dead—too cool to work. Andrew, who was apprenticed to him, kept looking toward the dormitory section of their little monastery, where they brought the red man.

The apprentice had not stayed at the forge but followed the commotion down to the riverside like everyone else.

"The bloom is gone," Wyn remarked of the unworkable lump, but Andrew was not paying attention, so curious was he about the barbarian moaning under Caradoc's ministrations across the way.

Wyn tonged the metal back into the crucible in the oven, humming to himself and calling silently on the Queen of Heaven to intercede on their behalf now that Madoc's Hundred had crossed over into this ungodly place. While waiting for the metal to renew its bloom, he let the hammer ring rhythmically against the anvil-altar, chanting the prayer, frightened for the first time about what might lie ahead.

He had promised himself that he would complete ten ax heads this day, and he determined that he would not let the interruption prevent him from his goal.

He peered into the furnace to see if the metal had returned to that consistency that would yield under his hammer. He was thinking that there were fifteen members of St. Brendan's left, including himself and Father Brian and the monks still in captivity, God preserve them.

Wyn decided that he would make fifteen ax heads instead of ten, and he would pray continuously during the forging. He turned with the evanescent bloom of buttery metal between the scorched tongs and laid it on coals aside from the main furnace. He moved the forging around on the carbon-rich charcoal, which pass he must complete several times to harden the blade.

He removed it glowing white hot, laying it on the anvil that seemed to him to have increased power since it served as the table of the Lord. He observed the bloom, seeing an ax head within its coruscating white-hot core, the first of the last fifteen, and symbolizing in his mind. *I will forge myself in thy service O Lord and dedicate these fifteen blades to thee*.

He lifted the hammer and began reciting the *Book of Psalms*, prepared to work all night to make his sacrifice.

There were no trees left anywhere on the eastern side of the island, so there was no place for the mockingbird to be singing, yet a mockingbird sang that dusk and late into the evening when the sun burned the sky the color of the ripening persimmons in the mainland forests.

The mockingbird, perched on the corner eave of the llan, was what Eagle Ring Man heard when he wakened next morning, thinking that he was well on his way to the west and the land of the dead. Other sounds filtered through his consciousness—the roar of a fire muted but close, and the rhythmic clangs of Wyn's hammer on the fifteenth ax head.

Slowly the Yuchi opened his eyes, turned, and found himself awash in the glow from the throat of the furnace.

While he watched, Wyn removed a dollop of metal from the crucible. It was a small sun of bright orange light, a spongy incandescent globe of pulsing fire that seemed to the red man to be captured by the huge wooden tongs of the white man, who bent over the anvil now, chanting while he brought the hammer down rattle, down rattle, and down again, beating out the impurities.

These people have found a way to capture the sun! Eagle Ring Man felt awash with enlightenment. All his mythology, the stories handed down by his people, said that their ancestors had come from the sun, whom the Yuchi worshiped as a supreme masculine deity unlike other red people, such as the Cherokee, who prayed to the sun as Our Mother.

The Yuchi brave staggered from his cot, the sleeping brothers snoring around him. He followed the glow as he made his way from the dormitory pavilion to the forge.

Several times Wyn plunged the sizzling bloom into a barrel of water, sending clouds of steam up to vanish into the cool night air. Then he placed it on the charcoal, letting the carbon adhere to the iron edge. Then, the hammer.

Wyn was chanting his rhythm on the last ax head. Throughout the compound Madoc's Hundred wondered why their smith had to work so late, keeping everyone awake with his clanging hammer. None had been able to dissuade him from completing his vowed fifteen ax heads. Everyone but the lookouts had finally found sleep, though punctuated by those hammer blows.

Eagle Ring Man knew he was witnessing a holy thing as the glowing object fell from white to yellow to orange to a fleshy scarlet, bruise purple, and now, as the monk quenched the thing one more time, a powdery black still hot enough to send a halo of heat waves above it.

He tonged it onto the wooden block, looking for minute cracks or blisters he might have missed. He saw a blister, lay it on the coals momentarily, then returned to the anvil.

Continuing to hammer, he called his apprentice, but Andrew did not hear him. More metal must be cooked. The fire must not be allowed to die but must be fed more oak and hickory and ore and sand piled over it so that after he had rested, Wyn could return and bend again over the bloom. He called for help again, and Andrew stumbled from the dormitory.

"You should stop, Domme," he said sleepily, then came instantly awake as he saw the red man entranced in the shadows.

Eagle Ring Man watched, feeling his world change. This was a thing of greatest wonder; his eyes had never witnessed this glowing of the captured sun. He knew in that instant that he could never go back to being his father's runner. He must learn to speak with the piece of the sun, to mold it and shape it as he watched Wyn do with the fifteenth ax head.

The abbot went about his holy hammering, unaware that he had an audience. He had gone through the Psalms by the thirteenth ax head and started over again. Each stroke was accompanied by a phrase as he worked his way through the Psalms a second time.

Eagle Ring Man watched through a fever veil as the white man bent over the labor, sweat glistening on his arms and running in small rivers through his hairy chest.

"O clap your hands all ye people—"

Clang!

"Shout unto God with the voice of triumph—"

Clang!

"—He shall subdue the people under us and the nations under our feet—"

"Eh, Domme . . ." Andrew said, and Wyn looked up.

Beyond his anvil Wyn saw the wide-eyed red man approach, his stare riveted on the glowing ax head.

Wyn recognized the look of the awestruck. It was holy work on a dedicated anvil—it seemed a sign from heaven that this heathen youth recognized what he was witnessing. The look on his face transcended any language; he knew he was hearing sacred words because of the way Wyn delivered his recitation.

The abbot quenched the work a last time and tossed it onto the sandhill banked around the half-buried forge. "Come, come, lad, help me feed the fire," he said as he tossed several hickory logs into the firebox and worked the bellows of the oven so that the apparatus began to hum. Heat waves shimmered around him.

Andrew obeyed but kept a wary eye on the looming red man.

Eagle Ring Man drew close enough to feel the heat and stood there mouthing his own prayers of thanksgiving at being given this wonderful vision.

On inspiration Wyn reached with his tongs into the crucible for a small petal of bloom that remained.

He whisked the blob of metal onto the anvil and began hammering something that was not an ax head. From time to time he looked up at his one-man audience, continuing with the Psalm as he flattened the metal, then with a chisel whittled off excess, and with a swift whack of mallet against awl, punched a hole in one arm of what gradually appeared to be a cross.

"God reigneth over the heathen," he sang, laying the cross on the coals for its measure of strengthening carbon, then bringing it back to the anvil. With a chisel edge he grooved it and quenched it several more times, each time bringing it to the wet block of wood for the final smoothing of its edges.

He held up the darkening cross with the wooden tongs.

"You see it . . ." he said in awed tones to Eagle Ring Man.

The lad was still in a trance, but now his gaze was fixed on the monk and not the metal.

Wyn pointed upward. "Not me, son, but the Lord!"

Eagle Ring Man looked upward, so still he might be listening to the dawn approach.

"Praise the Lord," Wyn sang. "He worships the Creator and not the created."

Andrew fell to his knees, his whole face smiling, whispering, "A miracle, a miracle . . ."

Wyn, himself moved to tears at the ways of his Lord, set the cross on the sand around the forge, put aside the long paddle tongs, and wiped his face and hands with a rag.

He put his hand on the red man's shoulder and said, "Come, you must rest," trying to lead him back to the cot.

Finally Eagle Ring Man took his eyes from the reddish cross and looked at Wyn.

"Teach me how to shape the sun," he said in his own language. His handsign indicated to Wyn that he wanted the cross, the forge, the hammer, the anvil—he wanted all of this for himself, which he communicated by hitting his own chest.

Wyn, with missionary zeal over his first red convert, nodded, speaking in a soft and comforting voice, "Yes, my son, yes, I will teach you. First, you must heal." He could see that much of the glistening in the man's dark eyes was wild and unfocused—no telling what poison Mary's simples had left in him.

To Andrew he said, "Feed the fire, feed the fire!"

The kneeling apprentice crossed himself and rose to obey his abbot who could bring the heathen to the altar of the Lord.

Wyn tried to pull the red man back to bed, but he resisted, indicating that he wanted the cross over there on the sand. He moved to pick it up but drew back when he felt the heat. Still he would not leave it, because he knew Wyn had made it for him.

Wyn nodded, picked up the tongs, and dragged the cross through the cooler sand, hoping that it was not cracked from cooling too fast. He said a silent prayer that the work would not be spoiled and dropped it into the water trough, sending up a cloud of steam above the water that sizzled and foamed. He tonged it out, pleased to see that the Lord had spared it. He plunged it into a barrel of water until he could handle it.

It was a crude thing, but without blemish, a Celtic cross thin as a coin. When he was satisfied, he gave it to the Yuchi.

Eagle Ring Man let himself be led back to the pallet, where he laid back clutching the warm cross over his heart, closing his eyes, visions of the sun burning there and coloring his dreams.

Chapter 22

The red dragon leads the way!

—*Welsh proverb*

"What in God's sweet name are you doing?" Madoc demanded, the first time he raised a blasphemous voice directly toward the abbot, who interrupted his stroke to answer mildly, "Putting the finish on our only plowshare, since Father John tells me all we had are under a fathom of mud with the *St. Ann.*" Their several attempts to claim salvage had yielded one tin cup and an anchor, only because it had been hawsered.

Madoc stood at the edge of the monks' pavilion, rubbing his wrist and scowling. The moody sky behind him had been threatening to turn nasty for two days. Wyn stood with his hammer resting on the anvil beside the glowing plowshare. He lifted and bounced the hammer, letting momentum rattle it as though the tool itself were impatient. He glanced skyward; he had only a short time before it opened up.

Madoc glared at him and shifted his gaze to the Yuchi warrior who stood to one side watching the abbot work. It had been several days since Gwen came home with her stray red man. Standing beside the bellows, obviously already schooled in its use, was the fellow, bare-chested like Wyn and wearing a chain and cross around his neck and an old singed leather apron. He looked hale, hearty, and wide-eyed, the new iron cross within a circle on his thoroughly-muscled hairless chest.

"A miracle," said Andrew nearby.

"He has found the Lord Jesus," Wyn said, resuming his

301

rhythmic hammering before the metal lost its bloom. "Besides, you said each of us should take on another apprentice."

"You are teaching the enemy how to make weapons." Madoc was furious at having to explain so obvious a thing to a grown man. He hated to give Simon any credit, but the arglwydd might this moment agree that Brother Wyn suffered mindless kindness.

"I tell you he is converted." Wyn turned the share with the tongs, inspecting edges. "And a plowshare is hardly weaponry."

"What is the difference to the hammer?" Madoc felt himself shaking with astounded fury at the monk.

Wyn continued minutely scrutinizing the plowshare until he found a blister in the metal, which he showed to the red man.

"How can he convert?" Madoc asked, forcing himself not to become shrill. "He is not able speak our language!"

"That is the miracle," said young Andrew, beaming joy.

Wyn smiled at his man's enthusiasm. "I tell you David Iron has seen the Lord in the metal. He is Christian now."

"See," said Andrew at Madoc's elbow, "he wears the cross." The red man must have understood a few words, because he clutched the cross Wyn made for him.

"Accept that the ways of the Lord are indeed profound, Captain," said Wyn, laying the plowshare back on the coals to carbonize. Then, standing back from the heat, he took up a cloth with which he swabbed sweat from his eyes. "Some see," he said pointedly to Madoc, "and some are blind and cannot see."

It was a cold day and getting colder as rain approached, but Wyn moved in the warmth of his own sun, the humming forge.

With a look of devotion the new apprentice offered him a gourd of water, which the abbot took gratefully.

"If you had come to Mass yesterday, you would have seen him baptized. His name is David Iron—his own choice, by the way."

Madoc smiled bitterly. "I might have chosen another name."

"The patron saint of our homeland seemed appropriate enough," Wyn replied between hammer blows.

"Too many Davids in this world, Domme."

It surprised Wyn that Madoc would be so sensitive, with an entire ocean between himself and his stepbrother. "It was the iron that showed him the light," he said with a benevolent glance at the red man, who ardently watched as the abbot removed the work and began to pound out the blister of impurity.

"I forbid you to teach him to make weapons that he might turn against us."

"Who will be my other apprentice, then?"

Madoc swore vehemently, "Myself, if there is nobody else," then felt a threat standing too near his side. He whirled and found himself face-to-face with the object of discussion.

The red man did not speak or move. He just stood there with an intense look in his dark eyes, Wyn's measured hammer strokes ringing behind them. Slowly, without breaking the deliberate stare at Madoc, the Yuchi brave offered his palms outward as though presenting his own hands to the man before him. "I am David Iron," he said slowly in Cymraeg as the white shaman had taught him. "I know that you are arguing with this shaman about me, honored chief," he continued in the measured tones of his native tongue while simultaneously translating into handsign. The intensity of his stare was a palpable thing that struck Madoc with physical force. "But I am your friend."

A tight fist drawn across a man's heart while uttering such words, whatever the language, must be a basic human signal of loyalty.

The Yuchi said, "I pledge my fighting arm to you as my chieftain." It was a variation of the formula uttered by pledges to the all-male lodge of his father and grandfathers.

Madoc had seen the gesture many times in his fighting career, had performed it himself upon his knee to Owen's service.

"I explained to him that you would be stubborn," said another unexpected and incongruous voice in the circumstances of male domain. Gwen stepped up behind her father as he turned. He might have thought she was crying because there were drops on her face, but her smile was too merry.

Beyond the pavilion it had begun to rain, a slow, loud pattering on palm leaves. Wyn scowled at the heavens, gave the plowshare a couple more whacks, and made to shut down his forge. The sky was leaden, and from the way the weather had crept in, growing more and more cloudly with the smell of moisture and rolling thunder from the distant greater water beyond the bay, it looked as though it were going to be a steady downpour that would not blow over like a sudden thundershower.

As the rain began to leak through the palm-frond roof, Gwen stepped between Madoc and the red man. She had a basket over one arm, which she handed to Andrew, who could not resist peeking inside, letting a puff of delicious steam escape from hot corncakes. He quickly covered the food and set the basket aside to await his master's pleasure and began gathering everything made of iron out of the rain.

Her back to her father, and in subtle handsign, she said to the Yuchi brave, hello, my beloved.

David Iron responded with a shy smile.

"Tad," Gwen said without preliminary, "David Iron says we must get off this island." She spoke before Madoc expressed whatever it was he was about to say, which she anticipated would be some sort of protest.

To Gwen her father seemed too much like her grandfather when he said, "Tell him that Miko Komas traded us the use of it."

"Komas!" the red man exclaimed in his own language and sign. "That slippery old lowlander has played a trick on you."

Gwen continued, "He says that if it rains much, this island will be flooded."

Madoc scowled, watching the red man make a sign for high water, entirely eloquent as his palm moved up in jerks until it represented waves lapping under his nose.

Beyond the feeble roof rain hit the rock, banking the exposed metal of the forge, and sizzled, sending up singing little wisps of steam. They had not built a permanent roof over the anvil and no sort of roof at all over the forge.

Madoc swore to himself, naming the Alabaman chief an obscenity. In hindsight he realized that the Alabamans, who had been trading with Madoc's Hundred, had not been seen for two days—since the first sign of threatening clouds.

Wyn tossed his tools under the flimsy shelter, where his two apprentices were collecting them for dry storage in the dormitory. Beyond the little shelter the air was already a wall of silver needles. Puddles rapidly filled up sinkholes, and all beyond the pavilion looked dismally gray.

"He says it happens every rainy season. All the rivers swell, and these lowlands become swamps."

"Only lying, web-footed, half-alligator Alabamans can live in these places," David Iron added.

Madoc sat back on a barrel, catching several references to Komas's tribe. Well, he thought, so much for diplomacy. "Where shall we go?" he asked nobody in particular. Even David Iron understood what the chief's posture expressed.

Madoc was unable to keep his glance from straying to the *Horn*, leaning away from the slant of rain out on the leaden water. If only they were not too many for her, he would climb aboard and sail away to that alluringly blue southern shore they had seen on the island in the Flood, instead of this disastrous northern place. He should have given up on Fair Beard in the interest of the survivors and let the polestar be damned. Old sailors had told him a legend about a group of guiding stars in the southern skies, not a solitary stationary point like Polaris, but a cross of stars one could depend on.

He wished now Lev had not cremated the head. The lad was convinced it had been his chief and gave the relic a flaming funeral, which sobered all the Norsemen into chanting grim old songs. He had packed it in pine shavings, oozing natural turpentine, and set it on a gravel bed in an expendable coracle, which he launched out onto a shallow arm of the bay where it flamed for an hour, its glimmering doubled, itself and its mirror image on the still water until the gravel got hot enough to set the grease-soaked boat afire in a sudden flare-up that sent pine sparks cracking off like shooting stars over the water.

Everyone watched the heathen viking funeral, even the Christians on land and among the ship's crew, though they pretended to be doing something else.

Yngvild refused to attend the ceremony, because she said it was not her husband, though they named the names of all the men it might have been. She, Gwen, and the three children went looking for nuts as far away from the ceremony as they could wander. Evan, who disdained anything Norse, took his sword to protect them.

Madoc wished he had taken a better look at the head before Lev destroyed it. It haunted him that it was probably Snorrison. He knew he should give the man up, be content that he would never know for sure. It was naive to hope in light of the evidence.

The rain had intensified to a single sound, a boring drone that went right to the center of the brain.

Gwen picked up the basket and began passing it around to the men, saving David Iron for last. They exchanged a shy,

lingering glance when their fingers touched, which Madoc
caught as she gave him a morsel of food. It was a blow to him
that his daughter had given herself to this stranger. He
breathed a long sigh, the cooling corncake in his hand
uneaten. "Oh, Gwyneth . . ."

She turned and looked him directly in the eye.

Wyn chose that moment to rasp a quick benediction. When
he was finished, Gwen continued as though there had been
no interruption. "We need him far more than he needs us."

Beyond her, too close at her shoulder, the red man had
quickly crossed himself, which he did every time he saw Wyn
or one of the other brothers do the same. He had the move
down so that he looked as though he had done it all his life.
He said to Madoc, "I believe if you take the blue metal to
him, my father would welcome you and your people."

"What is he telling me?" Madoc grudgingly asked.

"He knows where we can all find sanctuary."

David Iron crammed the whole corncake into his mouth
and dropped on one knee to the dust under the pavilion. For
an awkward moment Madoc thought Wyn was teaching the
convert to truckle but quickly was relieved to see that was
not the case.

Chewing as thoroughly as an elk, he traced with his finger
the general outline of this island very clearly situated between two arms of a river that broke into two rivers farther
upstream. His sketch was similar to Madoc's own done on
leather, making the lakes as Madoc had placed them relative
to the general shape of the long, pointed island.

He continued drawing several northerly paces from the
map-island, looked up, and made the hasty sign for a long
way—the side of his hand moving in increments even farther
northward to what appeared to be another river, which he
named as he traced its course east to west.

"Uktena Yuchi," he said, swallowing the last of the food
and looking up for Gwen to translate.

"Uktena is their word for river," she said.

"That is what they called the *Horn*," Madoc replied.

"Uktena is the name of the great serpent who gives his
name to all big streams. The Yuchi is a big river that flows
from east to west named after his people," she said, having
worked this out earlier with the red man. They had talked
much during the past three days. "Their homeland is north of
that river on a smaller stream, the Little Duck."

David Iron indicated with his finger moving above the north-south river that opened around this island, that its headwaters sprang very near a bend of the Yuchi. He made a dotted line of fingerprints in the dust that bisected both rivers and followed the Alabama to the higher country of the Yuchi homeland.

"The Warrior Path," he said, demonstrating a man walking.

"Portage," Madoc said, munching the corncake as he observed what the red man had drawn.

David Iron saw understanding on his new chief's face, and he smiled a thoroughly human smile, pointing his finger at a spot above the northern bank of the river. "Tsoyaha Yuchi," he said, hitting his own chest. "That is the homeland of the Children of the Sun from Far Away."

"His father is a powerful chief, and they have a huge territory that David Iron is sure his father will share with us in return for some things made of iron."

"I do not doubt that," said Madoc cynically.

"What choice do we have?" Wyn asked.

"He wants to go home and help his father," Gwen said in a tone of witness. "He knows he is in trouble over me. He must go back, because the Muskogeans will blame his father. Tad, we must help him."

"You are moving too fast, girl," Madoc said, backing off.

"You can trust him," she said more evenly.

Madoc regarded the red man, who had not taken his eyes off him, then pointed to the crude but clear map. "How many days?"

Gwen translated in pure handsign, but David Iron had anticipated the question that any warrior would have asked.

"Many sunrises—you have pregnant women and much to carry. Nearly a moon of days, longer in this rain." His dark stare was intense as he paused for Gwen, though his handsign was eloquent without her.

Gwen realized it and stopped translation. She was warmed when she recognized mutual understanding between these two men. She knew in that moment that they would someday be friends, perhaps not right away, because her father would have to test him. As she watched them, she thought how alike they were.

"But . . ." David Iron turned slowly and pointed to the *Horn*, "in the snake canoe on the high water of the river, two days to a portage, then another ten to get to my father's village."

He pointed to a spot.

"Up the Alabama River—past hostile Mabila?" Madoc pointed a stick at the junction of the Alabama and Tombigbee rivers, where David had indicated the enemy village lay.

"Not the Alabama," David replied. "The Uktena is too wild in that river past that village. An upriver canoe must portage where that river races through the canyons." Most of this he illustrated in handsign—one hand the fragile canoe shooting an imaginary canyon and the other pretending to be rocks. This was the way he had descended to Mabila.

"But the Tombigbee is a swamp river, a female Uktena who spreads her thighs like a full-bellied mama about to drop a litter. She runs only so deep and flows past her banks. An easy river, much water, little current, a mother Uktena."

Madoc did not like the way the red man used Gwen to demonstrate these ideas, handling her hip when she translated the word, female.

"And in this high water, no Muskogean scouts will be on the banks of the Tombigbee because there are no banks. They do not like the swamps, either."

"How deep?" Madoc asked.

She handsigned to David Iron that the *Horn* had a draught of twice her father's height—two fathoms or about twelve feet.

"Well, then," David Iron replied in like sign, "that snake canoe can take the Tombigbee all the way to its headwater, which is a deep lake in the rainy season."

Madoc chewed on this information. He did not like to take his deep-breasted ship up a stream that might evaporate.

As he stared at the map, the downpour drumming, another idea came to him. He placed the tip of the wand at the junction of the two rivers, which David Iron said was Mabila, and drew a line from that place westward to the river David was suggesting that they take. "How far overland from here to there?"

"Not far. From now to midday."

That would be about two hours, Madoc calculated, and before he could ask further questions, a commotion erupted nearby.

Several brothers began to move trunks and other items from the leaking roof.

Madoc regarded the stretch of ground between this shaking pavilion and the little stockade farther down the treeless island. Now the stumps looked like tombstones in the gray wash. Madoc's Hundred must get out of here. They would be uncomfortably crowded on the ship. His mind circled itself, trying to think of an alternative. They could put out to sea and likely go down in the storm. They could stay here and drown.

"Look!" Andrew cried, pointing to the courtyard, already a muddy stream that washed away some of their kindling.

The monk started to run after it, but Madoc stopped him, "Let it be, brother."

Gwen, recognizing her father's decision-making process, smiled at David Iron.

Madoc was aware that the others, including the intense red man, were waiting for him. Finally he said to Wyn, "Tell your people to get that cargo aboard the *Horn*. Gwen, get the women together." He gave the stump-dotted, rain-pocked sward morose regard. He had never seen such a sudden downpour. "If this keeps up, we will not be able to stay the night."

"We push off immediately," Madoc said.

Each turned to obey him, the red man following Gwen out into the throbbing downpour, walking so that they touched. Madoc ground his teeth.

Then Wyn turned back, almost whispering to the arglwydd, "'Twould be best to drown here on sanctified ground than to board a demon ship."

"What?" Madoc thought he had misheard.

"That ship, you did not give her a Christian name. What sort of name is 'the *Horn*,' but some heathen Norse reference?" Decent ships were named after Christian saints.

"Domme," Madoc said in a softened voice, "she is held together with staghorn pegs, a trick of the Norse that makes her as flexible as a fish."

"Nevertheless..." Wyn said, holding back, not looking directly at Madoc. Andrew behind him had paused to watch his abbot instruct the arglwydd, who stood poised. Brother Andrew thought he was going to invite the abbot to stay, so the novice's heart was pounding when the arglwydd replied, instead, "Of course, her full name is *Gideon's Horn*, Domme. A pun, you see."

Andrew, who was Saxon and knew it worked in both his own and Madoc's language, almost laughed out of nervousness.

Wyn looked up sharply at Madoc.

"I thought you knew," the arglwydd said smoothly, his eyes betraying a twinkle of mirth.

"Well," Wyn was flustered, and it looked unnatural on him as he found another tool to rescue from the rain and handed it to his apprentice. "In that case, of course..."

"Perhaps Ffagan should carve her full name on the header."

Wyn smiled up at him, but any reply he might have made was drowned out by a clap of thunder and intensified downpour, which had the effect of spurring human activity.

There was sudden group movement throughout the llan. One corner of the roof was sagging; a waterfall cascaded from that point to the flooded, trampled grass of the yard. As he watched, the small lake forming on the roof burst through. The forge was sizzling, sending up a cloud of steam now.

Madoc stared at the map David Iron had drawn in the dirt, memorizing it even as the tendrils of water filled the lines, making miniature rivers that eroded their banks, dissolving the map. Later he would copy it from memory onto leather to add to his growing chart library.

The river was just as the red man said it would be, a swollen but gentle swell that lifted the vessel as their sail caught a breeze from the southwest.

The rain pounded relentlessly, sheets of it appearing solid before the wind.

As the river narrowed, they reefed the sail because it moved the ship too fast—the obstacle here was not rocks, but shifting sand. There were also drowned trees drifting below the bow that scraped their new oars, which the sailors had busied themselves carving for what they imagined would be more coastal sailing, never dreaming their captain would dare take such a stream.

Soon they must use the oars as poles, gondola-style. The trees overhanging the channel threatened to snare the mast, so Madoc ordered it struck—an easy task given the way it was constructed in the socket of the mast-fish. But it took up more of the deck, displacing people who were already back to back. The hold was crammed with people and materials. One could not walk around the deck without stepping over a dozen figures huddled under tarps against the rain.

A sailor rigged their dragon flag on the tall prow, and Gwen removed the dovecote from the mast to the deck forward so Culhwch and Olwen's nestlings could see their homing signal.

Below, Rhiannon worked at the hanging loom-threads on the pennant that matched the dragon flag on the prow.

With her wing clipped the *Horn* cut a more somber figure, moving silently up the glassy river. They were a sorry lot, but the ship rode high. The rain was cold but not freezing, and the sailors were used to much worse. As they conned their way northward, the rain slacked off, though the southern sky continued gray behind them.

As the south wind died, they rode into a land of mist.

Late one dark afternoon Madoc saw something in the water below his position that looked first like a lumpy log, then it moved, blinked open a pair of eyes as the log split at one end, yawned, and made a frothy, sibilant sound in the ship's direction.

"What is that?" he asked David Iron at the prow.

It was difficult to tell how long the creature was, because so much of it was underwater, but it was at least a man-length. While he looked, it made a sound like a hiss and a snort and opened huge jaws lined with small sharp teeth.

"Ha, a grandfather alligator," David Iron said, repeating a formula against the hideous creature: "We have no babies to feed you." Muskogean mothers never bathed their children in these waters; horror stories abounded, and at least a couple of the lowland clans sometimes worshiped a particularly big man-eater wounded but not killed by a careless hunter.

David Iron assured him, "They do not bother people unless you get too close to their nests."

Madoc felt his flesh crawl; he had leaped unthinking into the lower waters of this same river to chase the red man. The thought of swimming beside this monster ruined his lunch.

Here, then, was Lev's dragon. They used their oars to good purpose, poling her like a ferry scow, and with David Iron riding in the prow, avoided backwater bays and dead-end meander lakes around every other bend. He had canoed this river many times. Sometimes it was an easily defined channel between the overhanging trees—except for the river bed, the canopy of the jungle was flung unbroken on either side of this slim lane where the iron gray sky hung so close it seemed to rest against the treetops.

During a drab chill sunset, they dropped anchors at bow and stern. They ate whatever they could find of what they managed to get off the island. They might have hunted, but not even the most daring of the Norsemen wished to step onto the soggy islands, where David Iron assured them nested more alligators.

Rhys sang a while—stories from the Mabinogi, and the Hundred seemed cheerful and glad to be out of the rain as its people bedded down. Madoc paced the ship, stepping over people, peering over the rail, watching the water as a breeze from the west lifted the higher clouds and polished the sky so that by midnight stars glittered behind the shadow-cypress as though snagged in the lacy crowns.

"So it would rain for days," Madoc said to David Iron. Gwen helped with handsign, but the red man had a quick answer:

"It probably is still raining on the bay," he said, indicating with a licked, uplifted finger that the wind was from due west, pushing the southern rain away from the uplands they were entering. "After rain, fog. After fog, clearing."

After they ate, Madoc became even more restless. He moved from one post to the other, talking softly to the men on watch, and finally leaning against the long prow, trying to identify the squeakings he heard below while half listening to the forest.

He brooded as he regarded the eastern darkness. Somewhere over there were his men held captive by the same savages who kidnaped Gwen. He had been thinking of Brian and Ari. The others were probably outside his reach, having been taken by other tribes, according to his daughter's report.

But Brian and Ari were but two hours overland in the village of Mabila.

Madoc had been feeling lately that he was in the grip of events. He needed action of his own to sweep away the dull ennui that threatened his peace of mind. Restless still, he walked the deck as it grew mistier again, stepping over the sleeping forms of people under blankets. Suddenly he stopped, for what he had stepped over were two persons deep in slumber, holding each other tightly. Even in the cold, misty night he recognized his daughter lying there under a single coverlet with the red man.

He stood regarding the sleeping faces tilted together. He almost cried out, because he did not want to see that she was no longer a girl. With all that had happened, it was not fair to expect that she would be. But this, why this?

Now even he would admit that Evan was an appropriate husband for her, but she had to bring home this creature, as she had taken in strays since she could toddle. Dogs, cats, frogs, birds—once she brought home a baby wolf. Madoc could still remember the cold terror he felt when he saw his little girl with an armload of wolf-pup. No bitch ever showed up, however, and she kept the wild thing until it started after the geese, and Madoc turned it loose on the slopes of Yr Wyddfa.

Here she was again with another dangerous stray.

Madoc turned away in sick disgust. A night bird called from the darker trees of the eastern bank, echoing on the still water that lay around them like a spill of Wyn's molten glass. What light the mist created was reflected back by the lake surface.

The ship creaked.

He felt anger pooling inside him. Suddenly he wanted to rouse the entire company, shake them out of their dreams and force them to share his woes. He wanted to do something that would pry his Gwyneth from the red arms around her. He heard her stirring minutely, reaching in sleep toward her lover. Watching them, he thought of ways the red man might die. Madoc's hand was on the knife hilt. It would be easy. He could even blame the Norsemen—Dag hated all the red people and had complained about their keeping this one.

Another bird shrieked; he saw it against the sky, heading east toward Mabila.

Before he realized what he was doing, he was shaking David Iron, who came instantly awake, a warrior at the ready, unblinking and taut under his hand. Madoc was pleased to see discipline in the fellow but showed no sign as he gestured that he was to come forward, where the chief headed without speaking.

The red man stood and stretched behind him. Madoc glanced back as he tenderly replaced the blanket over Gwen, then soundlessly followed Madoc to the prow.

Madoc took a deep breath and said, "Mabila?" while pointing eastward, where no light yet showed the dawn that was hours off.

David Iron was completely awake. Madoc could see the whites of his eyes glistening as he nodded curtly. "Yes, Mabila," his gesture said.

"Gwen says two of my men are there. Will you go with me to get them back?"

"Go? Now?"

"Can we be back before the sun rises?"

David Iron knew the word for sun. He glanced at the sky. "If we run."

Madoc was already moving to get his sword, some rope, an extra knife. It was his fervent hope they could stealthily accomplish what he had in mind, but they might have to fight. He woke two of his men who were good with their knives and veteran enough not to use them unless absolutely necessary.

The men had two coracles loose from the rail and dropped almost soundlessly by the time David Iron caught up with him. Together they went over the sidelines and into the oblong boat.

"Where are you boys going?" someone said above them, silhouetted at the rail.

"Gwen—"

"Onwa' Pahta!" the red man exclaimed.

So, Madoc thought sourly, that is what he calls her.

She was coming down the sidelines and had dropped into the coracle before either man could react further.

"Go back to sleep, woman."

"He is right, daughter. This is none of your business."

"How can you rescue Brian and Ari without me?"

"Why do you assume we are going to rescue them?" Madoc demanding, holding her wrist.

"Mabila is a big village. Only I know their lodges."

David Iron looked at Madoc for direction.

"Come on, then," she said, taking up a paddle, which David Iron removed from her hand. She sat the third thwart between them, facing forward, facing her lover's back as he began pulling them toward the murky shore.

"How did you know?" Madoc said behind her, marveling that she could know what he had only just now decided.

"You asked how far it was when David Iron drew the map. Why else but to go there?"

"Perhaps I was concerned about how easily our enemies could be upon us."

For an answer she uttered a throaty, cynical chuckle as they moved on in silence, paddles cutting the still water as easily as knives. Through a winding lane of dark cypress and

swaying moss like old men's beards, David Iron piloted their
little boat.

Finally they nosed onto a shallow beach. Madoc helped the
two men beach the coracles, which they flung up onto the
broad branches of a cypress, securing the lines, shaking them
to make sure they would stay put until needed upon return.

Off the water darkness was complete. Gwen between them
held onto David Iron's shirt, and Madoc onto her tunic
behind her, while the two men held behind. In this way they
crossed low, flat ground through the densest forest, then up a
long slope to one of the endless canebrakes of the uplands. At
each possible junction David Iron paused to make a mark—a
cut on a tree or a cane tied just so, pointing subtly toward the
lake where the *Horn* waited.

Cane leaves rustled dryly with their passage, which continued for half an hour. David Iron was right—the ground was
dry. It had not rained here for days. Madoc felt no trace of
the telltale twinge in his wrist that signaled wet weather.

A pale crescent moon lingered behind the foliage ahead,
illuminating nothing with its alabaster smile. For a while it
seemed they were walking directly into its mindless grin that
was pretending to hide behind the trees. But it finally broke
loose and rode the sky free of branches.

On the air was the smell of woodsmoke.

Then suddenly ahead they saw a wide sward of stubble
field that had not yet been burned for fallow. Now risen above
the night shade of the trees, the moon cast feeble illumination, reflected by the mist and smoke that lingered near the
ground in these low places. They edged around the field.
David Iron knew the lookout posts were along the river,
where the Muskogeans figured an enemy might approach.
The backsides were relatively unprotected, the swamp being
their best ally.

Gwen saw immediately which neighborhood they were
near in comparison to the miko's centrally located lodge
where she had resided. "Ari is in the far hut along that path,
and Brian is..." she looked around—all the huts looked so
much alike, but there was one where the big pottery kiln lay
half-buried near the clay-pit. "Brian is there—that one beside
the low mound—that's where the women come to do the
blessing-work on their pots." Blessing-work was what the red
people called decoration.

With a gesture Madoc indicated David Iron should find the

black man on the far side of the plaza, where it appeared a meeting was going on.

Gwen, huddled under her woolen cloak, had already explained to him how he would recognize Ari.

Suddenly a dog barked not far off. The five at the forest edge froze, trying not to breath in the slight breeze that might give them away. But there was a lot of smoke on the air. Gwen had brought pieces of dried meat for them to nibble, but she did not take them from her shoulder bag immediately. Presently another cur answered the first, and both barked together farther off toward the other side of the village.

Each of the five relaxed in the darkness.

"Now," Madoc whispered to the men he had brought for defense he dearly hoped would not be necessary—his blood tingled as it always did at the promise of action. "We will be thieves in the night. . . ."

Chapter 23

*Let there be fóg
And let there be phantoms,
Weird marvels to baffle
the enemy . . .*

—Njal's Saga
Iceland
A.D. *1011*

Leaving the two armed men to hold the rendezvous point, the three raiders crossed the stubble field, where the corn-stalks leaned like miniature versions of the great clay-covered pyramid glowing with a rufus light under the climbing moon, which cleared the treetops and floated free on the lighter darkness of the sky.

A path bordered the huge field skirting the pyramid, where the glow of the eternal flame smoldered on the pinnacle. From their position they could see human figures moving about up there, but down here on the shadowed ground they seemed alone.

David Iron was right—the elders of this village were complacent with the great swamp protecting their backs. The watches were stationed along the river, leaving the rear alleys of Mabila deserted.

They stopped where the path forked. David Iron was rubbing paint onto his face as Gwen peered through the gloom, pointing for her father's benefit to the kiln keeper's hut; that was where she remembered Father Brian living when she left this place. They agreed by sign to meet back here with their prizes, then return to the rendezvous together.

She pulled the hood around her against the cold and against

317

recognition, while Madoc watched David Iron applying the weird yellow paint in a striped pattern on his forehead, cheeks, and chin. "It makes him an invisible messenger," she explained.

Madoc scowled thinking that Gwen would support such nonsense, but he understood when she added, "People will look away from him."

She gave him a small wink, was gladdened to see him wink back, then he was gone.

Just as she and David Iron started out, they heard a dog growl to the right. They froze. The dog investigated, rumbling hoarsely in its throat. She quickly pulled out a piece of jerky and tossed it in that direction. A low shadow snatched up the offering; they could hear hungry munchings behind them as they made their way along the path he had often trod as Eagle Ring Man, she holding onto his tunic, he going by memory.

There was some foot traffic on the wider lanes, but most of the villagers were in for the night. The smells of food were enticing on the air for those who dined only on jerky and water.

They passed through blue shadows behind the main pavilion, where David Iron had first seen Gwen as the miko's Natchez sun. A ceremonial fire still burned, and David Iron wondered what important guest could be keeping Miko Shell in council so late.

Gwen spied the hut where she remembered Ari living. She led the way between lodges, where vegetables and gourds grew in patches, careful to step between the plants that might trip her.

She found one of many cracks at her height and peered through. Inside she could see several persons, none of them Ari. Beside her David Iron found a peephole; Gwen had earlier described the man they were searching for. He had to see this man with black skin to believe it, he thought, but did not see him inside this lodge.

Confused by darkness Gwen realized she was at the wrong house. Across the way she saw it, the shabbiest, smallest lodge. She remembered its owner, a widow with two daughters, and as she peered through the cracks of the second hut, she saw she was right this time.

Meanwhile Madoc had taken his fork toward a long, low-raised platform where Gwen explained the potters decorated their ware. Beyond it were the rounded roofs of the half-buried pottery kilns and their accompanying high, neat stacks of firewood cut the right size by women's labor to fit the ovens, none of which seemed to be in operation at this time. That precinct of the village was dark except for the banked fires in each wicker hut, which could be seen glowing from cracks here and there.

When he tried to see inside the hut Gwen indicated, he saw nothing. He cursed the darkness and began whistling the tune of an old hymn. After a few phrases he stopped, poised and listening, hand on knife hilt.

He thought he heard someone stir inside the hut, and began whistling again the tune that any Christian would know.

Presently a tall white-skinned man wrapped in a tanned deerhide stepped from the hut's doorway and, whistling the same tune, proceeded to relieve himself in the bushy shadows.

Still not able to see each other in the darkness, the two men greeted each other, Brian unbelieving his rescue, Madoc weak with relief that he had found the man.

"Wait—!" Brian whispered when Madoc started for the path.

"No time for baggage—come on—"

But Brian pulled away and darted back into the hut. Madoc could see that there were several persons asleep inside the lodge, one of whom seemed to be a large man curled up in a bedroll nearest the low fire.

Madoc growled when he saw the priest rousing one of the sleepers on the far side of the slumbering giant, then groaned when he saw the man had been successful. A woman with long unbraided black hair and naked to the waist sat up on a bedroll, rubbing her eyes as Brian tried to hustle her from the hut.

He must have prepared her for something like this, because she glanced calmly at the doorway where Madoc stood outside and pulled her blanket around her.

It was an agony watching the two of them pick their way delicately between the several sleepers, including not only the large snoring male but a couple of children.

Madoc was drawing a breath to protest when Brian whispered, "I will not leave without Hayati."

Madoc looked at the yawning woman.

"She is a wonderful potter," Brian said lamely, as though

this might tilt Madoc's decision, though it was clear he meant it when he said he would not leave without her.

This was no time for discussion. Madoc swallowed any comment and turned to go, leaving Brian to follow or not, but he froze when he heard the unintelligible but loud woman's voice back at the hut. He whirled to see now there were two women beside Brian, one pulling his left hand, the other his right.

About this time on the other side of the village, Gwen realized she had the wrong hut. She tugged at David Iron's shirt to get him to go to the one that looked more likely, and he gestured for her to stay put while he walked around to the wicker arch that served as a doorway in the second hut. She repositioned her eye at the crack and heard David Iron's voice from the other side as he scratched on the doorpost and called in Muskogean for the husband of the house.

With a sinking heart she felt something furry at her ankle. The wet nose brushed her leg; the beggar was back. She broke another fragment of jerky, let the mutt sniff it, and then tossed it away from her. She heard the dog go after it, and returned her gaze to the crack.

She saw the woman inside approach David Iron, whom she could now see in the doorway through the slats.

"Yes," the woman answered, "the husband of this fireside is here." The woman stepped back to invite the guest inside, but he declined, saying, "I come from the miko to speak with this man."

Gwen could now see Ari stand inside the hut, obviously out of curiosity for the stranger at his door who would not come inside. He had affected completely the winter costume of a brave, with a beaten mulberry-bark jacket, tall leggings, and fringed moccasins beaded on the toes. His fuzzy hair was braided into several coils, decorated with small shells and feathers, and he had let his beard grow out. What a cause for curiosity he must be among these people, Gwen thought. The only thing on him that bespoke his other life was Madoc's gold coin still on the thong with the cross, but even among the darkly complexioned Mabilans, he would still stand out in any crowd.

She remembered that the miko had to choose between three women who claimed a replacement for their dead husbands. There had been quite a debate around the council fire as to who would get him, and the miko finally chose this

woman, because he deemed her need the greatest with two daughters to raise.

Ari spoke to the elder woman, and David Iron, upon hearing his voice, called out in the only Latin phrase he knew: "In the name of the father, son, and holy spirit."

"Who goes there?" Ari replied, himself with little more than church Latin.

Having used up his store of rote Latin, David Iron did not understand more than that it was a question, but Gwen suddenly at his elbow replied in Gaelic, "Friends, Al-Ghazal Ari O'Dalaigh."

"Lady Gwen!"

She gestured for him to follow.

But Ari hesitated, his glance darting not to the older woman to whom he had been given as husband, but to a sloe-eyed beauty of about sixteen. Instantly Gwen knew there had been some rearrangement of the original situation. One wife was bad enough to have to explain; two would be impossible.

The young woman clung to him as Ari implored Gwen with a pleading glance. Meanwhile the girl had reached back and caught her mother's hand. The older woman immediately swung into action, picking this and that from the pegs or baskets scattered around the shabby lodge. Everything in here had a secondhand look to it—even their clothing, which appeared stained and old, though their hair was glassy black and shining in the firelight.

The woman spoke to the third female in the lodge, a duplicate of the sister in beauty, a girl of about ten years. The three female faces turned with wide eyes, three variations on a tattooed theme, from a single rayed cross beside the child's right nostril, to the same, plus wrist bracelets, on the younger woman, and the many tattoos of the mother.

Ari's protective stance with the younger woman clearly said, I cannot go without my wife, while she said something that clearly meant, "I cannot go without my mama," and the elder woman pulled the sleepy little girl to her, muttering words that clearly said, "I cannot go without my baby."

"They will starve without a hunter to bring them meat," Ari tried to explain to Gwen. The Muskogeans were farmers but still depended on the men of each fireside to hunt for meat and leather.

"Everyone else treats them as charity," Ari continued. "I

was supposed to replace their hunter, but..." He shrugged, certainly no species of hunter and clearly delighted with rescue.

David Iron wore a look that was also easy to read, which said he was not sure about this situation. "How will your father feel about having three more women to take care of?" his gesture said.

"He will have to tell them himself," Gwen replied, not about to reject those pleading faces. She turned to the door, setting everyone in motion. The women smiled to each other at the chance of a new life with these exciting strangers. They hefted a few pitiful bundles and were ready to go.

The women recognized Gwen even under her heavy cloak. The miko's Natchez sun had been the subject of gossip since she ran off with the famous Yuchi raven, here with her in his yellow paint of invisibility, which confused the red woman because she was not supposed to acknowledge him. She was shyly deferential to Gwen because of the white woman's notoriety and strangeness.

As Gwen left the hut, she almost tripped over the shaggy mutt waiting for her just outside the door. She had one shred of jerky left. She let the dog smell her fingers, then took out the jerky and lured him back into the lodge, where he all but knocked her over to get the treat.

The dog, now revealed in the low firelight, was of a motley reddish yellow coat, with a lean muzzle above bright, intelligent eyes, which he focused on Gwen with a look of expectancy.

The woman saw the problem and reached up into her sooty rafters among undistinguished materials drying there. She flung down a lump that looked to Gwen far too much like a dried rat and hurried out of the hut, followed by Gwen, who pulled the hide hung for a door over the opening. Inside they heard the dog going at what sounded like the first square meal of his life.

They hurried away from the lodge without a look back.

"Who is the miko's guest?" David Iron asked in Muskogean.

The woman shrugged shyly to him she was not even supposed to see—who was she that the miko discussed his guests with her?

As they hurried behind the council pavilion, David Iron longed to linger at the wicker wall, which screened but did not obstruct the voices of the two chiefs beyond in intense conversation. He had to find out who was meeting with

Shell-of-Many-Colors that would keep the council fire going long past sunset, the traditional hour to break up such meetings.

He bade the women pause momentarily while he veered into the shadow of the pavilion's wicker wall. He peered through, seeing Shell listening to the other man, whose back was to David Iron's position. But he could tell by the shaved head of the stranger, the scalp lock, and other details that this was a Cherokee.

David Iron moved to better see the stranger's face and was not surprised to see Fox, war-chief of the largest band of Cherokee in the eastern mountains.

He hurried back to the women, urging them on, keeping to the trail that would lead back to the intersection where they had parted with Madoc, who should have been there first, having a shorter distance to return from the potter's. But there was no trace of him.

David Iron herded Ari and his household into the darkest pit of shadow, where he pressed them to crouch and wait silently.

That is what they did for far too long. David Iron was nervous against Gwen, who was imagining all sorts of trouble that might have detained her father, when suddenly there loomed an ominous shape coming toward them along the path.

It was not the mongrel dog.

There was just enough moonlight to illuminate the vaguely spherical object moving rapidly down on them. Gwen almost screamed when she got a better view of it—a grotesque face with a long beak and bloated body that smelled like a nasty dovecote.

"Step aside, woman," a man's voice demanded in Muskogean from inside the muffled shape approaching Gwen. "What business have you out of your lodge so late at night?"

David Iron was quick and not as intimidated by the monster as Gwen, because he knew what it was. He muttered a formula to dispel evil that must be touched, caught it by the neck, and had it down on the dirt, where she heard the muffled curses of the man inside the odd feather clothing.

Then she realized what David Iron had seen all along—this was one of the Muskogean bonepicker priests moving about the village in his official costume.

David Iron applied a twist to the neck, and the man inside

lay silent, the Muskogean women whimpering at this sacrilege of a shaman. He hurriedly had the costume off the scrawny old man inside and rolled his body from the contraption.

Now they had done it, for surely this would bring attention. And where was Madoc? David Iron's face held all this, which Gwen realized as they divested the priest. The odor of mold wafted up from him. He was entirely motionless, and Gwen knew David Iron had broken his neck.

Gwen bit her lip to stifle any comment she might make or question she was dying to ask.

David Iron rolled the body into a shallow ditch.

Now what? her gesture importuned as David Iron stood from the disagreeable task, the odor of decay lingering around him.

Ari behind them was trying to console his women, but they moaned so loudly that David Iron quickly looked around to make sure nobody heard them. Get them out of here, David Iron's gesture ordered.

"My father—" Gwen started to protest.

"Take them to the tree I blazed at the forest edge."

She nodded. That was where the two armed men waited.

"Do not wait for us—get back to the Uktena." David Iron persisted in calling the *Horn* by the local name.

She held him back.

"Go, Moon Fire—I must find your father!"

"I love you," she said, and kissed him fiercely before turning to grab the nearest woman's plump arm.

"Come with me," she said to Ari, who was able to move the women along without silencing their terror or their murmuring incantations against evil.

David Iron watched them vanish, then bent to slip the stinking suit over his shoulders. He found the strap by which he held the thing on, feeling polluted beyond the seventh degree.

The dead man had dragged the mask into the ditch with him, so David Iron retrieved it, lingering only long enough to snap off the grotesque fingernail that was as long as a dagger on the end of his pointing finger.

David Iron poked at the corpse to make sure there was no life left and shifted the entire bulky wicker-frame and feather costume more comfortably onto his broad shoulders. He managed to get the mask into a position where he could see through one of the two eyeholes, almost retching with the smell.

He grabbed the strap, conspicuously holding the broken fingernail outside the edge of the suit, and went off at a trot toward the hut where he found Madoc with two women and a tall red-haired man.

The second woman was standing in the doorway trying to pull Brian back into the lodge. From what Madoc could see of her, she looked identical to the first woman, who was pulling Brian in the other direction.

Madoc felt the situation slipping out of control. His first instinct was to let Brian be damned, but instead he remembered this man saving his life on that burning deck; he whispered hoarsely, grinning what he hoped was an ironic smile, "I know you are new at this, Father, but the rules are, you only get one."

Brian blinked at him; Madoc figured his timing was wrong to joke because the man seemed dazed.

"You are going to have to choose," Madoc said, trying to imagine Brian's first conversation with the abbot.

"Eh..." the priest said, and Madoc might have thought even he was having trouble telling the twins apart. "That one."

Hayati seemed to be the strongest of the two, or perhaps Brian was pulling with her against the second woman, for they had moved away from the lodge.

Madoc reached swiftly behind the other woman, who now was yelling at the top of her voice, cupped his hand over her mouth, and grabbed her by the waist.

A dog barked somewhere nearby in response to the woman's voice, which broke off immediately.

"Do not hurt her—" Brian whispered with real concern. He bent close to her, apparently trying to apologize. Madoc cast a knowing glance that Brian did not refuse. His chin went up a bit. Ah, Madoc thought, the sin of pride.

Madoc was a little jealous, remembering how it was. These twins were beautiful women; he would find it difficult to choose between them himself. He smiled back, but the woman squirmed, and he gave Brian a look that asked for help; they soon had her trussed and silenced with a long strap of leather.

"Thank you, sir," Brian said with a twinkle in his eye. "The last person I want to take is my mother-in-law!"

Madoc could not respond; conversation would wake the man he had seen slumbering inside the flimsy wall. He left the youthful mother-in-law silenced for a while at least and stood to lead Brian and his bride out into the tarry shadows beneath an evergreen tree that stained the air with a clean, tingling aroma.

But luck was not with them. They were barely twenty paces from the hut when the tied-up woman slipped her gag and screamed in fury, which brought the hefty fellow—in fact her son—lumbering out of the lodge, trailing his blanket.

Madoc expected an army of Muskogeans to appear suddenly at the sound, but something else entirely different happened that he was unable to see clearly in the darkness. From the path there hurtled a roundish dark shape fully as large as a man. It flew at the Muskogean, who had been roused by the screams of the woman still trussed in Madoc's bonds on her own doorstep.

It was amazing to see the huge red man stagger back as the thing bore down on him making an awful racket like a crazed bird squawking. The fellow cringed back, muttering incantations against the apparition, stumbling over the woman, who also cowered from the bird-thing that was pointing a long pale stick or dagger at them as they tried to crawl back into the house.

The monster croaked a Muskogean formula for asking forgiveness and ordered the man to help the woman. He fumbled with the ropes that tied her but finally was able to get her ankles loose and drag her into the lodge.

It stood there swaying back and forth, rumbling incoherent words and phrases, pointing the long sticker or whatever it was at the two terrified Mabilans, who were not even allowed to look upon the person of a bonepicker.

"Begin the prayer," commanded the voice of a man inside the thing, and Madoc suspected who it was.

The man and woman abased themselves on the packed-dirt floor. By now several others in the lodge were awake and staring wide-eyed with fear at the bonepicker priest hovering in their doorway, a sign of egregious bad luck in any circumstance and a positive death knell in the middle of the night.

Even the children fell to their knees and brought their foreheads to the ground.

David Iron inside the costume turned and snagged Madoc by an arm on his hurried way toward the path. Madoc let himself be pulled along for several paces before he tried to pry David Iron from the odorous contraption.

At the fork in the path they scurried across the stubble field, the light up on top of the pyramid seeming to float in the misty darkness. Madoc gave out a low whistle familiar to his men, and one answered him back.

As he shucked the grotesque apparatus, David Iron was speaking rapidly to Gwen.

Madoc saw there were more persons with them than expected, but there was no time to discuss it. And he saw what was clearly a large dog at Gwen's feet. But he had more on his mind than his daughter's strays. He kept looking back over his shoulder to see if the big fellow had sounded an alarm, but Mabila remained quiet under the misty moonlight.

"He says they will be busy with the prayers he ordered," Gwen whispered, getting the gist of what happened back there.

"We must get out of here," Madoc said, finding the trail, but David Iron held him back, speaking rapidly under his breath as Gwen translated.

"He says there is a guest back there who is still talking into three spiral fires."

"Who?"

"Fox of the Cherokee."

Madoc had heard of this Fox from the red people, including Komas, who told him he was a lucky war-chief who had been elected to lead raids across the blood country into Muskogean territory.

"Why are they talking?"

David Iron shrugged. "We need to find out." He already had an idea, if he could just communicate it to Madoc.

As he continued speaking, he opened the two halves of the bonepicker costume and motioned for Madoc to put it on. He demonstrated with the strap how to hold it.

He sat back and removed the small hollowed deer horn at his waist that held his paint. He brought out a fingerful of the thick yellow pigment and freshened the marks on his face. "It is just over there," he gestured with a toss of his head.

"You," Madoc said with a hand against Gwen's arm. "Go with these people back to the *Horn*." He pulled the feathered suit up over his shoulders, and David Iron set the mask in place.

Through the eyehole Gwen could barely hear her father speaking, "We will be along in a while."

She threw a telling glance at the red man, then turned without another word, the dog at her side. The men were anxious to get on, one taking up the point, the other moving behind the women as rear guard.

Shortly Madoc and David Iron were left alone on the edge of the misty field.

David Iron was trying to right the costume's shoulders for him, but Madoc accomplished the balance with a jog in place.

"I have it," he said, feeling as though a disguise as a priest was some kind of minor curse he must encounter over and over again all his life.

He gave David Iron a mean stare through the peephole, and the red man did an odd thing. He stared Madoc down behind his sulfurous face paint, lifting his hand in a gesture that meant he was masking himself. "Hatki ahaka," the red man said, drawing the veil of his hand over his eyes.

"Invisible," Madoc said, urging the other on.

They walked across the field, where they encountered a villager hurrying in the opposite direction with a bundle of kindling. He did not acknowledge the painted raven, casting his eyes downward when he caught a glimpse of the shadowy bonepicker.

The invisible guided the grotesque along the path to the rear of the council pavilion. Beyond the wicker the two chiefs had not even changed positions. They had been served a light meal, which lay on trays before them. From time to time one or the other would place a morsel of fish or corncake in his mouth and slowly munch while the other man talked.

Their conversation was formal and slow, much of it polite address or repetition of each other's titles and honors. They circled their main subject several times and were targeting on it again. David Iron sensed from having sat through many such meetings that this round would end with some sort of decision.

Madoc got a good look at Fox, feeling a chill run up his sword arm at the sight of the bare-chested Cherokee, who had many battle scars despite his obvious youth. He was a big, well-porportioned man with an erect bearing that told of pride and prowess. He was taller than the average red man Madoc had seen, taller than David Iron or himself, for that matter, and not bronze red like the lowlanders, but a dusty tan. Madoc could see no tattoos, but Fox's earlobes were slit and plugged with what looked like copper coins. From a lifetime habit Madoc could not resist sizing the man up as to what sort of opponent he might make, should he and Madoc ever have to face each other.

But the tone of the discussion was dull, no matter what might be the subject. Madoc felt himself nodding more than once. At least this stinking suit of feather armor was warm.

They stood there in the growing cold, eavesdropping on the Muskogean and the Cherokee for a long time. The fire finally smoldered in the firepit when the two mikos stood, stretched, and ambled off toward the steamlodge.

The last exchange between the chiefs that David Iron was able to hear began as an inquiry from Shell-of-Many-Colors about Fox's health. The Yuchi strained to hear their exact words, but they were fading as the two men left the pavilion, where the attendant was already cleaning up behind them.

It was very still in Mabila, a good two hours after midnight as the bedraggled bonepicker and the smudged invisible messenger slunk across the stubble field. Up on the pyramid over their shoulder the eternal flame sent a wavering column of smoke up into the bleaching sky.

David Iron was concentrating on how to explain what he had heard to Madoc, who was shucking the awful suit as quickly as he could without stopping. But he held on to the mask as though it were a war trophy. It felt like that to him, anyway. The sense of being cornered was gone. His action was accomplishment in the midst of staggering losses and setbacks. This felt as close to victory as he had felt on this trip so far, so he claimed the soldier's pleasure of it and went on his way.

David Iron stared at the unlucky bonepicker's mask his new chief insisted upon keeping. A scalp lock would have been a safer memento. He would try to explain that complication later with Moon Fire's help. For the moment he struggled to explain the significance of what they had seen.

Fox invited the Muskogeans to join him in a war against the Shawnee, an invitation Shell-of-Many-Colors would be unwise to refuse. Fox had a team of crack raiders with him who had several times tangled with the lightweight southerners.

"Why does Fox fight the Shawnee?"

How could the Yuchi explain generations of emnity to this stranger? He would have to understand that the Shawnee and the Cherokee shared ancient rivalries. The Shawnee stubbornly refused a limited territory imposed by Cherokee expansion and often sided with the Chickasaw against Cherokee.

Now, for some reason the conversation did not disclose, the Shawnee provoked the Cherokee further. Fox was using an excuse to go after a weaker enemy and rid himself of bothersome nomads.

All this was too complicated for David Iron's modest Cymraeg and too abstract for handsign, so all he said was, "An old hatred between brothers," and Madoc nodded with bitter understanding.

"My father needs to know this," David Iron said. "The Yuchi," he said, trying to bridge the gap between his and Madoc's understanding. "My people are between—" He hit the two edges of his hands together, forcefully implying conflict. "Fox is a terrible enemy," he added, something Madoc had intuited.

David Iron thought about Shell's inquiry into Fox's health, an odd question for as young and strong a man as the Cherokee chief. David Iron thought the miko said something about the old-bone, but David Iron could not imagine that he heard right—a warrior as powerful as Fox with the old-bone? He dismissed the Muskogean's comment as too insignificant to repeat to Madoc. Most likely he had misheard, and Miko Shell was asking about Fox's grandfather, reputed to be the eldest still alive in all the head of waters.

Ahead they saw the ghostly shape of the ship in the mist hanging above the lake. Fish jumped after bugs. Echoing from across the water were the clear sounds of breakfast being prepared, and Madoc wondered how they had cooked the fish this morning. He could make out distinct voices on the moist air.

They had left a coracle in the tree.

He went to the water to relieve himself, but David Iron drew him back, trying to explain that he must never, ever put any body fluid into any stream of running water. Madoc felt mildly chastised by a subordinate who was right. He slunk behind a cypress and filled a deep depression in one of the tall knees of the odd trees that sprang up around the main trunk.

First to see them pulling through the swirling fog was Rhiannon, who gave a revealing shout of joy that brought the company to the rails of the ship, a scattering of dark faces among the white and pink ones, all smiling, cheering them on far too loudly if the two men had been followed.

The weight of Madoc's Hundred tilted the *Horn* slightly in a little bow as her master reboarded.

Chapter 24

*I was young once and walked by
myself, and lost my way. I knew
myself rich when I found a friend*

—Sayings of the High One
Norse oral poem

They poled the ship out of the lagoon and up the Tombigbee, David Iron's mother river, living off the water and land. The red women cheerfully offered advice about this leaf and that root, thereby increasing the Hundred's store of many things from amaranth seed for a not-unpleasant gray gritty bread to sassafras root tea.

They were too crowded, but for the most part everyone was tolerant in circumstances that felt extraordinary. Even the children seemed to appreciate the treasure of each moment they remained unmolested by the Chickasaw on the west, Mabila from the south, or Fox from the east.

It was not a king's royal cruise. But there was a renewed spirit on board with Father Brian and Ari's return, though they could not help listening for the sound of the Muskogean war call, and Madoc and David Iron had to tell their story many times.

Finally Rhys made up a satire about "the raiders three, who did the deed so quietly. . . ."

All ears were attuned for some response from Wyn and John about Brian and the complication he brought from Mabila. Hayati, whose name meant Dawn, was a sweet-natured young woman with permanently stained and dry fingers from her work with the clay. Like the other red women, she was shy among these tall, pale strangers. Brian obviously adored her. The naive young priest, who lived his

332

life behind the monastery walls, had fallen in love with the first woman he met outside those walls. Now the question was, what would happen to his vows if he lived with her.

Wyn had to have some thoughts about this, but he made no sign. It was the object of gossip, though Brian was discreet. He traded the deer hide for the buff-colored cassock of his order, and the permanent tonsure given him by the Muskogeans gave him the younger monks' awe and respect. But so far only John celebrated the Mass; Brian seemed satisfied to be a parishioner, as though he did not want to test the delicate issue of celibacy.

But his and Hayati's glow could not be suppressed; still there was no response from the clergy. Madoc figured it was because there was no way to have privacy aboard the crowded ship. But everyone watched the principals for some sign of what must eventually be a confrontation. The clerics held their morning Mass with no sermon, just a prayer for God's protection.

The sailors continued to pole the ship almost due north along a river that remained high and muddy, indicating upriver rain. Mist continually hugged the water. At one point the high water obscured David Iron's reference points. They had come to a place where the river was so spread out she had no course. There were seven channels, six of which could lose them forever in the twisting lanes between high watergrass. Birdcalls echoed from those labyrinths, and things moved beneath the water. They heard a growl, which their guide assured them was a swamp bear. He went out with hunters and bagged a huge specimen. The red women fell upon the carcass and swiftly butchered it. That night they feasted on the rich meat. Teleri meanwhile prepared the intestines and taught the red women how to make sausage, for which she stole a cup of Madoc's trade pepper without remorse.

Because David Iron wanted to study the signs, they stopped poling. There was so little current or breeze, the *Horn* lay as becalmed as she had adrift in the Sargasso Sea.

David Iron cast a dour gaze at the cloud cover; without his signs and the sun, he could not tell due north, the direction of the primary channel.

Madoc saw his distress, took out Fair Beard's translucent disk from under his tunic, and walked forward, where his pilot frowned at the dismal sky, holding the thing between his eyes and that part of the sky where the sun was hidden.

David Iron grabbed the stone. Madoc took it from around his neck and gave it to the red man. The crystalline substance of the white stone polarized the light and clearly showed the sun's disk. Knowing that could tell him which way was north. Madoc told the sailors to take up the poles, and once again they were on course, moving along the northern channel. Only reluctantly did David Iron return the sun disk, which Madoc put back around his neck, where he would wear it as a sign that he considered Fair Beard still alive.

Dag watched nearby. He glared at David Iron and spat into the water to provoke the red man, knowing how he felt about polluting the river. David Iron chewed back comment and returned to the prow, where he stayed all day, watching the water with the men handling the conning lines.

They had plenty of bottom left in this swollen channel, which was too deep for poling. They rearranged the cargo once again, further crowding the passengers below, set the oars in their sockets, and sang rowing chants. They made good time, but their pace was not killing, though the weather turned colder. The sailors traded off rowing shifts, singing their songs in time as the ship slipped through the compliant river.

After a while, the river began to narrow. Shortly their oars would be scraping each bank, so they shipped them and returned to two men poling her ever so slowly along, their footsteps thumping on the deck.

They could feel drowned branches scraping the ship, an eerie, hollow sound and vibration that sounded like the ship screaming. Madoc's and Wil's guts had been hurting all day with the grab of snags below her waterline. Madoc ordered all cargo shifted aft of the mast to bring the deeper keel up, thus giving a little more draught to the ship's bottom.

David Iron assured them that the deep lake that supplied the Tombigbee was around the next bend, and sure enough, before a sunless noon, they slid into this almost mythological waterway, solid and green like glass slag with bubbles rising from the oak-stained murk below—at least four fathoms, so that finally Madoc's stomach relaxed.

Around the lake empty limbs of a drowned forest forlornly clawed the low sky. It was a dreary place where Madoc hated to leave the ship. But his handpicked crew looked forward to getting her ship shape after close quarters with civilians.

They would spend their days adding several more oars, refurbishing the rigging, and mending the sail.

They had a small fire going in the deck sandbox, where Caradoc fried the last of Teleri's bear-sausage in his skillet, and Ari's Muskogean bride made small thin corncakes by spreading dough on a hot rock she brought for the purpose. A rock so perfect for baking was a prize she would not leave behind.

Wyn insisted that day was a Sunday, and Madoc lodged no protest. He was interested to see the abbot and Brian speaking to one side while John and Andrew set up a hasty altar. This was the first Madoc or anyone had seen of what the abbot might think of his betrothed priest, and Madoc half expected conflict. The only sign of it, however, was a long, slow shake of the head by Wyn, who turned to assist the Mass.

Brian obediently turned without any sign of his emotions and rejoined Hayati, who was making sassafras tea in her boiling basket, scorched black along its bottom and sagging at its rim. But everyone enjoyed the spicy tea she concocted in the thing by tossing red hot stones into it full of water.

The Mass proceeded without incident, Brian remaining one of the congregation, standing back with Ari and his woman, whom he was teaching the rudiments of the Mass. Brian showed Hayati how to hold her hands, how to kneel, and was beginning to instruct her in the congregation's responses.

Madoc had already worked out with Wil that the main body of the colony would be walking east to the Yuchi. They restepped the mast and flew the dragon flag. Shortly after Mass the company said good-bye to the sailors, sent their cargo across the emerald water to shore, where everyone balanced bundles, and set off before noon eastward into the jungle.

The forest fell behind them as they mounted the slope away from the swamp. Dead into January of the year 1171 if Wyn was right, and slightly short of that if the arglwydd's calendar won out, the bundled and furred contingent overburdened and cold in single file through the rattling cane fields and murmuring freshets of the leafless Alabama woodlands.

All the adults weighed more than their normal stone because their outer clothing had been sewn with the long, narrow loaves of iron ingots to spread out the burden. Wyn was the heaviest with their gold and silver stitched into his cassock hem. The burly abbot left deep footprints behind him and would not leave the *Horn* without his anvil, though no one person could handle it.

The red women had a simple solution. Among their people women always accompanied warriors away from camp. They were good at burdened travel, because they carried back the butchered buffalo carcasses from the far hunting fields to the villages.

They improvised from materials at hand, throwing together a sled made from a single huge buffalo hide folded over lightweight hickory poles. Onto this they lashed the anvil, sewn into a harness of their strongest gut straps. The red women made several of these to carry bulky items.

These contraptions were the source of much hilarity among the Hundred until they saw how efficient the things were. David Iron said that in all but a couple of narrow defiles on their proposed route, the fully loaded dog-pulls would easily pass. They were not breaking any virgin trails. This journey used an arm of the Natchez trace, over which ravens of many nations ran for untold generations, so it was a beaten track.

Everyone took turns pulling the half-dozen gasi over the packed dirt of the trace. Madoc was amazed to see Gwen's stray Mabilan dog allow himself to be strapped into a harness the women rigged for him, taking to this task like a veteran. "Gihli-gasi," said David Iron, which meant dog-pull. It was an old idea among all the red nations, who had legends of a time long ago, called the dog days, when everyone was a nomad.

The red women showed no surprise—that was what dogs were for, as well as feasting upon at appropriate times, which is why they never named their pups.

The company walked parallel to Bear Creek, then turned east, where it met the Yuchi River below two leagues of shoals. They stood on a high bluff looking north across the river, which at that point was a wide, peaceful expanse of water, having thrown itself against the shoals that marked the river farther eastward. Walking along the southern cliff, they could see beyond a long slender island against the far shore, where another large red-clay-covered pyramid stood out on the riverbank against the green of foliage, its eternal flame sooting the sky in a shallow layer along that stretch. They were too far away to see people except as minute specks, but David Iron explained that this was the oldest pyramid hereabouts, and one of the most northern of the structures the Mabilan ancestors built to mark the farthest boundary of their territory. Beyond was blood country.

They walked the cliffside that bound the river along that stretch, then down a slope of stairstep ridges to a wooded plateau that was still high above the river. Here they forded the first of many small streams that communicated with the mighty Yuchi, which ran raging over leagues of tumbled rocks called Muscle Shoals for the freshwater clams abundant there, far below their left hands—often the precipice was immediate, where a misstep would plunge the hiker down into the boiling water of the ravine. But most of the path was well away from the river's edge, though they could hear its roar and feel the spray of its troubled journey most of the time on the trace, which paralleled the river until the fork below Lookout Mountain.

Several men carried coracles lashed to their backs, which they had to use more than once to cross swollen creeks. All the men carried additional burdens hung over their shoulders in nets, so that they looked like winter-coated bitches with clinging pups—these were the meadskins and honey bladders that they expected to sustain them until they arrived at the promised land.

John was slung all about his person with bags of seeds, a sampling of every variety they had with them, including clover for the bees. In a special satchel he carried the dormant hive cluster with the ever-humming queen at its heart, wrapped in finest wool. She would be dormant as long as it was cold, so John was sure he could get the hive to its new home before a swarm.

Gwen had the dovecote strapped to her back in addition to her share of ingots in her cloak hem and around her waist.

All the men carried their own weapons in addition to their allotment of cargo and iron. Caradoc was bent under his load of surgical tools and his skillet, which he would not leave behind.

David Iron grew more nervous about their lighting a fire the closer they drew to the blood-country border with the traditional Cherokee line. Once across the Yuchi River, they would be safe in Yuchi territory, but the crossing was another two days away if the weather held out.

The red people called this Snow Moon, but so far the month had not lived up to its name.

They had not seen the sun, now, except for patches in more than a week. The Norsemen eyed the sky with wry disdain. Bjorn spat and placed a curse up there.

To Madoc it smelled like snow. Likewise to those of his men who would say, because such predictions were of a pass between them for small bets. Wil kept a crabbed record of points amassed by each crew member. This sport was kept strictly among the sailors of the Hundred, who would not let on to the civilians such a thing was in progress.

Rhys made up a satire about it, spoken in puns and veiled innuendo that had everyone laughing around the fire, which David Iron did not like. Cherokee patrols could be out, though it was unlikely because of the season. But Madoc felt that comfort and the wonderful tea were important to keep up everyone's spirit, so they continued to build a small fire whenever they stopped. The red women were good at stacking fuel so that their fires threw off very little smoke.

"If they are going to see us," Madoc said to counter David Iron, "they are going to see us, and there is nothing we can do to hide such a troop as this. Just keep a tight watch." Which he did. Discipline had never been better among his crew, now ironically without a ship.

Everyone expected snow at any moment. The trees around them had become very quiet. They had seen no flying squirrels for days. The forest floor was still; shrews, rabbits, and rats had gone underground. The only birds around were the bright redbirds, who fought with a few frail sparrows over the Hundred's meager garbage. The hunters ranged far from the trail and found their quarry of turkey, quail, and deer out on adjacent meadowlands, where there was forage under the lowering sky.

But one in the Hundred did not see snow in the signs.

"I cannot smell snow," Yngvild said, arching her back for comfort. So far she showed no sign of going into labor, but Mary and Caradoc agreed that it was past her time. "All great Norsemen are born in snow," she said, insisting that it was not time as long as it did not snow. She thought she had days left, and they should go on.

Madoc watched her carefully. By the third afternoon something in the way she walked told him she should not push her luck further. He did not want to make the whole party vulnerable, having to stop for possibly several days while the Norsewoman gave birth and recovered. They camped that evening under the looming slopes of Lookout Mountain, called "rock that comes to a point," or Chado-na-ugsa. While others gathered wood, the red women got a fire going, and soon the wonderful smell of sassafras wafted through the quiet, cold wood.

David Iron and Madoc hiked to the brow of the mountain. It was a wide, bountiful view that spread below Madoc's handsomely moccasined feet. The forest was gray and green, leafless hardwoods and evergreens. Massive rock formations were covered with lichen; mistletoe knotted in oak crowns. This could have been Yr Wyddfa, where Madoc was born. He had often looked out on a similar view from his father's stone house on the pinnacle, the highest point in all Britain, contemplating the plain.

The Cambria that he had left was a small country, bounded by the sea on three sides, not a hundred miles at its widest. His father's kingdom would fit into one bend of the river below.

From the vantage point he now commanded, he could see a hundred such kingdoms in the expanse of twisting river valley to the north, east, and west. In the oak forest at his back, he envisioned hundreds of ships like the *Horn;* all possibility seemed to lie around him, more land and resources than his father or any British prince ever imagined, all here just waiting for a man with the spirit to grab it.

He was full of these visionary thoughts, wishing he could return to Gwynedd immediately, provision a dozen more ships, come back to this wide-open country with the necessary materials and hands, and begin the realization of this dream. But he kept all this to himself, sucking on the possibility like a starving man on a piece of jerky, and kept his comments to the here and now, limiting his public concerns to the well-being of those under his immediate protection.

"How many can live in these caves?" he asked in handsign.

David Iron thought for a moment. He and his new chief were only now becoming comfortable about conversing without help of their translator.

"Ten or twelve," he replied. He had earlier explained that since this was disputed territory, nobody lived nearby. There was plenty of game hereabouts, and the caves had access to water. They were up a steep cliffside, which could be defended by one man sitting in the correct position.

David Iron knew Madoc was proposing to leave behind the

women and children with armed men to defend and feed them. He, too, was feeling held back by the slower members of the party. A few men could make it in a short morning to his father's village north of the Yuchi on the Little Duck River. Madoc was calculating who would stay and who would go on with the main party.

They sat there looking out over the promising territory. The north wind with an edge to it hit them unobstructed above the course of the river, which looked like a foot, called Moccasin Bend by those who traveled these parts.

"So much land," Madoc said to himself, bracing his back against the wind that flattened the hairs of the hooded fur tunic the elder Mabilan woman had given him in gratitude for letting her family join the Hundred. Her earnestness was touching; Ari had carefully coached her, for she said the halting phrase in Cymraeg.

The coat was of winterkill wolf, and he loved it like a friend. Soft and as supple as a baby's bottom, it even smelled warm, with cuffs he could roll down to make quick mittens. The red women would let no scrap of the game they caught go to waste. Every shrew pelt was tanned and put to some use; they had a way of twisting rabbit strips of fur to make a lightweight, warm comforter. They spent hours around the fire at night lacing furs, working teeth and quills for bead-work, pounding leather, scraping slivers of bone for needles, and stretching gut for line—which they ingeniously cut in a spiral to make an exceptionally strong, fine cord.

David Iron may not have understood the exact words, but the way his new chief was gazing at the wide view, his meaning was not hard to imagine.

"Cherokee," he said, dropping a sour note into Madoc's reverie, pointing to the hazy eastern horizon, where a mountain shoulder lifted its moody purple mantle above interven-ing layers of peaks, misty valleys, and forest ridges. "From there the Cherokee will be pushing this way," David Iron continued in a halting mix of his own and Madoc's language. "Sooner or later we will have to fight them." The handsign was much more clear. "Will you teach me to use the great sword?"

"I suppose I must if we are to fight this enemy together."

David nodded his thanks; this was a new acceptance.

The wind was blistering now, so they climbed down the promontory. The last of sunset was fading as they returned to

camp with the aromas of sassafras and roasting fowl. It would
be good to warm the insides, Madoc thought. He went to the
fire, where Hayati shyly offered to fill his drinking horn. The
red women were extremely differential to him, even more so
than to the priests. Hayati had worked up a pair of supple
laced boots to replace the worn-out pair Evan had given him.

As Madoc thanked her for the tea, and as he gratefully took
in the warming drink, he saw standing off to one side John
and Ari, speaking in hushed voices. Several pairs of eyes
glistened with movement, watching expectantly.

Everyone had eaten the fine prairie hens the hunters
brought to the fire. They skewered the fowl on hickory spits
and served them with broiled landfish—morrel mushrooms—
wild onions, and tubers the women found nearby. Ari and his
Muskogean sweetheart caught perch from a nearby pond with
her nets. Her mother baked the catch on hot rocks at the
edge of the coals.

Now, drinking sassafras around the fire, all cheered as Ari
announced that Father John had agreed to marry him to his
Muskogean lady. The red women were laughing and singing
little songs to help the bride get ready. Their customs were
different in ways that might have disturbed Wyn and John if
they had known the truth. Marriage was not a sacred ritual
among any of the red nations. It was a ceremony of elegant
simplicity, which they performed just before the Mass without the whites ever being aware of it, although Ari knew
when he sliced a morsel off a fish he caught and pressed it to
his lady's lips. That was the custom—he offered her meat and
she fed him a bite of corn bread. All the red women and Ari
grinned with their secret ceremony as he and she stood up to
John's beckoning hand for the Christian ceremony. In the
other hand was his little missal. He was glowing in the pale
mantle taken from Andrew's backpack, along with the makeshift sacred vessels set out on a table of rock and spread with
a piece of linen not long from Rhiannon's loom.

Everyone gathered around with smiles and a sense of
well-being. A wedding back home would have been more
complicated and more thoroughly planned, but it could not
have generated any more radiating good feeling than did this
one under the darkening sky. The fire crackled as Evan threw
on more wood.

Rhys tuned up Llais Mel, and the old man began, "We are
gathered here together..."

His voice was melodious and tender toward the young people before him as he recited appropriate scripture, recalled ancient admonitions, and promised a future of bliss and fertility to them.

Father John was an old man who had performed many a marriage. He knew the ceremony by heart, but each of his services was unique and unrehearsed. His little sermon wandered, his dreamy eyes making contact with others in the congregation. He was inviting others to join in matrimony. Madoc realized that he was forcing Brian's hand, because he was gently admonishing anyone among them for living in sin.

It was unheard of for anyone to carry on a dialogue at this point, but Brian evidently felt moved, because he said from one side, standing beside Hayati, "In the old days, Father, the Celtic clergy had wives as did the apostles of the early church."

"This is true," John said in his sleepy way, "but over time we agreed with our Roman brothers that a life dedicated to the Lord does not leave room to take care of a family. There are two paths. For the priest God is the spouse of the soul."

"It must be one or the other, then?" Brian said, not in a tone of argument, but in explication.

"The householder's is not an unbeloved path," said John. "Priesthood is only for a few, while God said man should mate and multiply as a general rule."

Madoc could see David Iron and Gwen speaking quietly between themselves, she evidently responding to a question of his.

"There is glory in both paths," John said, and Wyn cast his gaze to his feet, hands crossed in front of his belted cassock. No doubt he was mourning the loss of their last priest. Madoc wanted to comfort him but was too far from him even to catch his eye. If he could have spoken, he would have said to the abbot that Brian must take on a student, for he could pass his priestly knowledge on to another, who with John's help, could carry on the colony's priesthood. He wanted to assure Wyn that he would be bringing back other priests to carry on the work.

Brian seemed lost in Hayati's dark, lovely eyes. He took both her hands and kissed her in full view of all, the first open gesture of affection for her. It drew a small gasp from several among the onlookers, able to be shocked by a priest kissing a woman. He murmured something, and she nodded shyly.

It did not yet show, but Brian knew his seed had found hers and new life grew inside her. He loved his vocation but having grown up in it, had thought of little other possibility. "I accept your invitation, Father John," he said. "God will still be the spouse of my soul, but this woman is the spouse of my body." He turned to the little altar, drawing Hayati along after him to stand with the other couple before the priest.

A sign of approval rippled through the Hundred. John was nodding, slowly, as if saying something to himself.

"Brian had to choose," Gwen was saying to David Iron.

"Is this true?" the red man asked Wyn, who nodded yes.

"To be Christ's sachem I must reject Onwa' Pahta?"

"Yes."

This was the strangest of all the white strangeness to David Iron. He was used to the idea of a sacred priesthood, but even the stinking bonepickers would take a wife if they found a woman who would have them.

"But you have shown me so much wisdom in all other matters," David Iron said bluntly to Wyn, though some of the handsign was too subtle, and Gwen was glad.

David Iron confronted her with an intense stare. Behind them the ceremony was suspended. John had not moved above the pages of his open book. Ari and his woman, Brian and Hayati, all seemed frozen in their steps, because everyone could hear what was being said between the arglwydd's daughter and the Yuchi warrior who had saved them all.

Then David Iron's glance sought out Madoc.

The silence was tingling when, as a group, all turned eyes to the arglwydd standing off by himself in the shadows. His thoughts had been drifting, returning to his wide vision on the mountain, when he realized everyone was watching him for his decision. No words had to be expressed. He saw Gwen and David Iron holding hands, the frozen tableau at the altar with John's thumb holding the page, and Teleri's expressive face across the way, which seemed to be urging him. He wished she were close enough for him to touch.

"Tad?" Gwen asked, not sure if he was going to break the spell, and unable in her youthful impatience to remain suspended.

Teleri almost cried out to him. He could see her urgency

from where he stood; a toss of her hand gave her away. She brought it to her lips as if to curb herself.

Let go, he imagined he could hear Ann whispering from long ago and far away. It is the same advice Teleri was offering. Only she saw his shoulders slump as if he had taken a blow.

He could not trust his voice to say the words, so he nodded, breaking the fine, invisible wires, freeing everyone to resume. Now, with all attention on Gwen and David as they joined the other couples before the altar, Madoc slunk back into his private shadow. But he realized he was not alone. Teleri had moved to his side. It was good to have her there to lean on while the priest said the words, and later when the meadskins were opened and everyone sang with Rhys into the moonless night.

They had planned to cross the Yuchi River before dawn, but Madoc saved his decision until after everyone had a good night's sleep. Yngvild, Mary, Tegan, the children, Caradoc, old Bjorn, and several other men would go with David Iron to the caves and wait there until the main party was settled among the Yuchi. Very soon Madoc promised to send his son-in-law back to fetch them to their new home. Amid tearful good-byes, the two groups began dividing supplies.

Rhiannon flatly refused to stay, even though Rhys pleaded and Madoc threatened her. But in the end she would not let anyone prevail against her will. But Mary did not argue, and neither did Tegan, both of whom were weary to the marrow and gladly moved toward the promise of a warm cave with a safe fire and plenty of venison.

There was never any question that Gwen would accompany her red man, and Teleri would stay with Madoc, though her little boy went with Mary and her sons.

David Iron returned shortly after noon to the larger group, which was growing restless in the shadow of the mountain. They spent the rest of the afternoon rigging line at a wide, slow spot of the river, which had for generations been the only ford along this stretch of the Yuchi.

It was cold but not freezing, and miraculously the snow everyone smelled still had not fallen. The coracles hauled on the backs of the monks became the only transport for the precious iron ingots. None dared try to swim that current with iron sewn in their clothing, even with the line.

They made it to the other side without casualty. The only

way to dry their clothes was to walk until body heat took care
of them. Everyone agreed not to pause to eat but to continue
on for the short time David Iron assured them would finally
settle them at their destination.

Madoc rubbed his wrist all that afternoon.

Then, suddenly, in the last blue light of evening when the
snowflakes drifted down between the bare trees, they came
to a ridge, beyond which they could see the meadow where
the Yellow Pheasant Village was situated like a nest of giant
eggs behind its strong stockade.

Snow dusted the round clay roofs of the half-buried lodges.
David Iron approached the first sentry above the village,
hidden in his cane-covered blind on the trace as it broke from
the woods. He spoke softly to the man, who was trussed up
in heavy bound fur so that only his eyes showed.

Presently the lookout whistled a high note, and several
other bundled warriors, their weapons ready, strolled into
view.

David Iron turned to the whites crowded behind him.
"There is no lodge big enough to hold everyone."

Gwen translated, so everyone in Madoc's Hundred—
considerably fewer in numbers than their name—was watching
her rather than the principal speaker. "So you will go in small
groups with these men. They know you are friends. They will
take you to warm lodges and feed you."

They could smell the aromas of supper cooking on the crisp
cold air, where the snowflakes drifted thicker than before.
But they waited for Madoc to speak before anyone moved.

This is it, Madoc thought. If he is going to betray us, it will
be now. He looked at Gwen, who was of course gazing at her
husband. He looked at Rhiannon and Wil, Teleri, and the
Norsemen who seemed to blend into one furred, many-eyed
beast, so close were they standing together. He tried to catch
each man and woman's eye, because if he had misplaced their
trust in this red man, they would all soon die.

"Let us get in out of the cold," he said briskly, slapping his
hands together and blowing into them.

Rapidly they reformed, their packs all the more heavy now
that the end of the trail was in sight. Wonderful smells drew
them on, and soon they were no longer one group but many,
and gone from each other's sight into the half-buried houses.

David Iron turned to the center lodge.

He entered without ceremony, which was traditional among

his people. His father was lounging back on his buffalo robe, smoking from a large platform pipe, while his aunts prepared the sleeping platforms along the back wall of the spacious household which served as Caller's private home and as the council house.

His son entered and dropped to his knees. It was in no way a gesture of supplication but merely the etiquette of a man entering a house with only cane rugs for furniture.

Sun Caller stared for a long time at him who had been given up for lost. As Madoc looked upon Gwen, this father regarded his son as he had never expected to see again. The young man would stay in that position of waiting all night if necessary, until the old man decided to recognize him.

By now the aunts were stiff with curiosity, for they knew the man who had left here a boy only a few sunrises ago. They and Caller immediately recognized changes in his son. Except for the iron cross hanging around his neck, he was dressed much as he had been the day he left this lodge. But he was different, and anyone looking could plainly see that the differences went below the surface.

"So," Sun Caller finally said. "You have come home."

"Many things have happened since I last saw you."

Caller nodded, yes, he could see that.

"The games, how did we do in the games?" He was sorry he had missed his last chance at his boyhood challengers.

"Many things have happened here, too."

The son would not press. There would be plenty of time to catch up on everything.

"You have been long on the trail," Sun Caller observed, and gave a gesture to the chief of his women who was in charge of food. "Have something to eat, ease off your muddy moccasins, and rest closer to the fire to warm your bones."

"I have much to say, father. I will wait until I have said it all before I take any rest." This was the traditional way for him to bring up the subject of his extraordinary companions.

Caller nodded. His heart was filled with great joy at seeing his son alive, but he was not about to lose his dignity over it. Later they would speak in private and he could express his feelings. For now he held himself slightly aloof as he said, "Miko Shell has made serious charges against you."

The son nodded, insisting on discussing his own subject.

Finally Caller relented when he perceived the boy was hinting at some real news.

"I do not come alone, father," and he launched into a brief version of his adventures since he left this lodge.

The father listened, and the women behind him, without a word and hardly breathing.

"So, father, I come to you now to ask sanctuary for these people who are small in number, but who bring wonderful gifts to make the Yuchi strong, stronger than the Cherokee."

And when it appeared the son was finished with his remarkable story, the father said, "Call a council."

The women moved immediately—some to prepare food, some to bring out the council robes, which were laid out behind the chief in the traditional ranking. Another woman went out to find the assistants who helped convene the council of seven elders, most of whom were in their lodges on this night of first snowfall and the beginning of a slow-coming winter.

"And," the chief said to his son, "you may bring me the chief of these people and his counselors."

Madoc led them, Rhys, Wyn, Wil, Dag, and Gwen, to translate. The others stayed behind in the lodges where they would be boarded for the night.

The counselors whispered and muttered about these people, who were exactly as the complaining Muskogeans had said—white-skinned, pale-eyed, and light-haired.

Sun Caller could hear them speculating as the strangers filed in and took seats on the hides behind the white leader, who placed himself opposite Sun Caller and beside David Iron.

The extraordinary red-haired female, mother of so much Muskogean distress, sat behind them, already translating when Sun Caller called for his formal pipe.

The lad who took care of it for the chief hurried up. He brought a coal from the newly fed fire with a long tong of hardened hickory. As Caller puffed to ignite the mixture in the bowl, the boy touched the coal to the stuff. Soon aromatic smoke twined around the poles draped with all manner of carcasses, dried vegetable materials, and coils of rope and cable.

Madoc took it all in with a slow gaze that did not pause. It was a huge room, capable of seating more than thirty persons. He noted the intense stares of the women over by the cooking fire, amid the festoons of various-colored buds—yellow, green, and red—which he suspected were some sort of fruit.

Other things hanging from the rafters were unhusked corn, rabbit, and other small creatures' hides stretched over wicker frames, bundles of yellow or white flowers, and strings of leathery mushrooms.

And in the center of it all, like a dark jewel on his slightly raised platform covered by the luxuriant buffalo wool, was the calm, steely-eyed chief staring back at Madoc.

The counselors were speculating about whether or not these were human or spirits.

But Sun Caller knew in those first few moments that these were indeed human persons, as Eagle Ring Man had reported, and not spirits, as had others. A deeply devout man, Caller nonetheless had never seen any sort of spirit in the flesh.

These people were weird, but this was surely another flesh-and-blood human man looking at him with silver eyes. Caller, who felt aligned with gold as his own personal metal, representative of the sun, gave the stranger back as glittering a stare as he was getting, eye for eye.

David Iron introduced Madoc, then, and introduced Sun Caller to the white man, then named all those with him, men, women, here in the Caller's lodge or housed throughout the camp, several hands of them, he explained, plus another dozen who stayed in the Chado-na-ugsa caves, where one of their women was having a baby.

"We welcome peaceful strangers here," Sun Caller said formally, and Gwen translated but had to have help from her husband. He gave Madoc the sign that he could speak.

Madoc spoke slowly, because now Gwen and David Iron were translating by committee, giving their results in a strange mixture of Cymraeg, Yuchi, and handsign and much discussion between themselves alone about specifics.

"Chief Sun Caller, I come to you with gifts, asking in return for the use of a small portion of your vast country. . . ."

This was a difficult concept, which had the two young people in near argument. There was no notion of a country to the Yuchi or to any red man. And the notion of the vague clan community that transcended geographical locations may have been a part of the Welsh tribal experience back in the hazy past of ancient Celtic clandom, but was almost mythological to landowners like Madoc, who had for generations been gentry.

The concept of a red nation was intangible, while the white idea of nationhood was tied to a particular piece of real estate.

Each phrase took some time to work out to everyone's satisfaction. The red counselors had no scruple against interrupting whenever they needed clarification. Wyn and Rhys behind Madoc whispered between themselves.

Meanwhile the women of Sun Caller's household had begun to cast gestures at each other as they recognized the signs in their chief that he was about ready to have something to eat. Among the red people this was rarely set at a specific time. People ate when they were hungry, and in a meeting like this the host chief would call for the prepared dishes to be brought out at any time. A couple of the women slipped out to go to other kitchen lodges where they had the food wrapped and keeping warm, now that Sun Caller was rocking forward, as was his habit just before he called for food.

The old man gave the high sign, and the women began to move.

Sun Caller's elder sister was the hostess for this meeting, and it was she throwing subtle gestures to the various assistants in her charge. The girls returned with soft mulberry-bark swatches and shallow pottery basins of water so that the strangers could wash their hands and faces.

David gave Madoc a sign that now was the time to bring out the gifts. Madoc beckoned Wyn to unwrap the iron implements he had brought specifically for this meeting—a cooking pot, some needles, a spade head, an ax head, an adz, and a single short knife suitable for gutting fish or skinning a small animal.

Sun Caller inspected each item, making comments and passing them back for his counselors to puzzle over and comment upon.

Gwen produced a wire of blue beads, which caused more comment than the knife.

And when Rhiannon unrolled a length of her finest soft woolen cloth, every red person in the lodge wanted to touch this wonderful woven thing. Yuchi women had small hand-looms on which they wove headbands and belts, but they had never seen anything like this wide, strong, supple cloth made up of interwoven fibers like small basketry. Just like the Skraelings in the Vinland sagas, they each wanted it, and even started pulling it from each other until Sun Caller clapped his hands for order.

Madoc unsheathed his knife and began hacking the cloth into pieces, passing these out to all the woman and the counselors, an awful thing to have to do; but it satisfied them.

Since the meeting had begun, the audience had swelled until there was no standing room left inside the lodge and people were even crowding into the long passageway to see who it was the chief's son had brought among them.

"And," Madoc said, "I have brought other gifts of even greater value."

As David and Gwen translated, Sun Caller was wondering what could possibly have more value than the incredible blue-metal knives on the hide between him and the white chieftain.

The blue beads, likewise, he thought the most beautiful mystery—their color, their hardness, their shiny surfaces.

Madoc gestured for someone to hand him a specific bag. He had brought only a miniscule drawstring purse that held a small amount of the treasured peppercorns ground into a powder. He remembered there being more in this bag and knew instantly that someone had pilfered it. Probably Caradoc, he thought, but now was not the time to be distracted.

Carefully, because to him he was handling black gold dust, Madoc laid a pinch of pepper in the red chief's hand.

"A spice," Madoc said, and Gwen and David were at it again. The red people used fireplace ash as a seasoning, salt when they could get it and various herbs. Bunches of those items were hanging from the curved poles of the domed lodge.

Madoc made a hand gesture for eating that was almost exactly right; chief Sun Caller understood without translation.

Since Madoc had not mentioned pepper to his son-in-law, David Iron leaned with his father to see what the treasure was.

Madoc put his own little finger in his mouth and dipped it delicately in the precious dust and tasted it. He loved the rare treat of pepper, the way it vitalized the tongue like a kiss.

Sun Caller eyed his son. David Iron nodded, go ahead. He had no idea what this stuff was, but he trusted Madoc without reservation and wanted to try it for himself. Madoc saw that expression on his face and offered his hand. The young man took some of the granules to his tongue.

What could the chieftain mean, he wondered, calling this mild-tasting stuff a treasure?

Sun Caller was coming to the same conclusion, but he was not polite about it. He threw back his head and laughed.

Madoc stared at him, not sure what joke he had missed.

David Iron was embarrassed for his new chieftain. The way Madoc treated the pepper, in the little silken bags inside the metal box, he could tell he really thought it valuable. But he could see why his father was having a good chuckle over this one.

"Here," Sun Caller said to his two nearest counselors. "Taste it." They obeyed, and broke into laughter.

Gwen was figuring out what was happening, with David's help.

This might be the official lodge of the clan, but it was also Sun Caller's home, where his aunts and daughters boiled his corncakes and kept his pipe cleaned. The tools and storage baskets were hung and stacked around the sides of the lodge. Bundles of herbs swayed overhead. Hanging near the firepit was a long beard of flaming red chilies, and on another pole were their green and yellow cousins.

Sun Caller saw the look of perplexity on the face of the man he had nicknamed Weather Eyes and stood gracefully, for an old man, reaching up to pluck a chili from the nearest bunch.

With a thin, unreadable grin that might be simple host-pleasure, he handed it to Madoc.

Someone made an exclamation behind the chief. "Not the little shooting stars!" said his eldest counselor.

David hurriedly told Gwen what the reference to a star meant, and Madoc overheard. He was smiling, but it was a smile of resignation. He regarded the small red cone-shaped fruit and saw David Iron warning him in gesture not to eat it.

Will it kill me? Madoc asked with an arched eyebrow.

"No, no, but—" David Iron tried to explain.

"It does not hurt my feelings that they have pepper, too," Madoc said as he took half of the chili in one bite with his usual enthusiasm for new adventure.

None of the red people breathed as they watched the white man munch the pepper. Suddenly, eyes wide, he stopped chewing and regarded the watchers all around him, intuiting that it was a point of honor—he must swallow what he had bitten off.

David Iron was proud to see his new chief act with the honor of a warrior by continuing to chew the mouthful even though tears ran down his reddening face. Finally he stopped, swallowed a final time, and stared at Sun Caller.

"Well done, well done!" Caller exclaimed as he pounded the nearest pole with his open hand, joined by every other red man in the lodge, and David told Gwen that her father was a good sport and had won approval, though it was fairly obvious from the faces of the chief and his counselors.

"May I have a drink of water?" Madoc was barely able to speak. Now he felt the thing slide down his innards.

David Iron said a word to one of his aunts, who was suddenly beside Madoc with a dripping gourd dipper, which she offered shyly and backed away. He drained it, and she brought another, the counselors and the chief all the while commenting, nodding about the warrior spirit of the white man, though he was a crazy fool to have swallowed it. He would pay in the end, a couple of the old men said with nasty chuckles Madoc could not miss.

"What are they saying?" he asked Gwen, still gasping.

"I am not sure, tad." She was, but did not want to say it here and embarrass her father. "That you are a 'great shouting warrior,' whatever that means."

"High rank for bravery," David Iron interjected, himself unable to suppress a grin.

"Tell him I like his joking spirit," said Sun Caller. "Your new friends bring wonderful gifts. Tell them they can stay all winter if they want."

"Sun Caller," Madoc said after he had gotten some of the sting out of his mouth, "we appreciate your great generosity, but we do not wish to become permanent guests who quickly wear out their welcome. We wish to have a place to stay apart from your own people, but near, so that we may be allies and help each other, trade and learn from each other."

He paused, letting his chorus of translators sing on.

"We do not want anyone's charity, however."

Sun Caller liked what Madoc said about learning from each other. His eye strayed to the metal weapons held by the other white men—the battle-axes and swords—and the sword at this man's belt, which was itself made of fascinating links of yellow metal, his sheathed knife, and his clothing, which was a strange, beautiful cloth unlike anything made by red people.

Yes, Sun Caller thought, looking at all that loot, yes, Weather Eyes, there is much I would learn from you.

Chapter 25

I shall not sing, I shall not laugh,
I shall not jest tonight.

—Juvencus Englynion
Welsh
c. A.D. 850

The snow stuck the next day, then melted off when the wan sun came out. The first cold snap of an unusual winter had overnight turned the persimmons orange-pink with a purplish glow. Bitter as bile only a day ago on the trail when Dag tried to eat one, now they were lusciously sweet.

The Yuchi women were collecting them this morning where they fell out beyond the chief's snow-patched tobacco field. Sun Caller saw the tall, light-haired men with the women of his village, holding their baskets. He saw no hostility there, only young men attending young women. The white men were armed with nothing more than their knives. They appeared amiable and obeying what was, no doubt, Weather Eyes' orders.

But Sun Caller could already see influences. The girls looked shyly at what he had to admit were handsome strangers.

He saw the one called Dag eating from the hand of Sun Caller's own niece, who was betrothed to a warrior of a nearby Yuchi band. Sun Caller himself had arranged the match.

In the innocent tableau of young white men and red women gathering fruit, Sun Caller saw his problem grow thorns: how to benefit from these potentially dangerous strangers.

He turned away so he would not have to see, but he could still hear the girls' piping voices as they moved under the persimmon trees with their overflowing baskets. It was a joyful sound, which recalled Sun Caller's childhood. But nostalgia made him feel suddenly old with the weight of changes happening too quickly. He was glad when they moved away and he could no longer hear their youthful sounds.

Caller's heart was heavy as he walked his field, desiccated now and nothing but empty stalks. He had harvested the tobacco leaves one by one, an old tradition, and hung them in the little log lodge his father used before him to cure the sacred nipowoc in the traditional manner of the grandfathers.

He made his way toward the shed, poking at the stubble with a moccasined toe. The stalks were ready to be burned and turned back into the ground for next season's crop. This was the only agricultural effort practiced by Yuchi males. The women harvested corn crops mixed with squash and beans near a creek on a sloping meadowland used for generations by the grandmothers.

This field was male territory, and only the chief and his men attended it, the chief's field where the ceremonial nipowoc was grown. Even the young girls and their fecund influence over there with their new admirers stayed out of the tobacco.

Caller entered the aromatic shed, which had a heavy roof like other Yuchi lodges, but with latticed openings under the eaves through which diamond-shaped holes provided the only illumination except for the golden leaves suspended from the ceiling, aglow with their own vegetative light, curing in the essential empty space between the upper and middle worlds.

Curing always reached perfection after the frost. He wandered through the veils of leaves sniffing, tasting, taking samples of the crop. Finally he found a favorite sitting spot against the south wall of the tobacco lodge, where the lattice let in the day's strongest sunlight, pale shafts dancing with motes angled in to drop splashes upon Sun Caller's leather-clad thigh and foot. He leaned against a peeled cedar post, where a buffalo robe had been hung for that purpose, and laid out several tobacco-leaf bundles and the knife Madoc had given him. At hand were personal items, covered baskets, a long bark tray, and a flat, scorched rock. Sun Caller removed a thumb-sized shard of clear crystal from the basket and began to inspect his specimens, peering through the natural lens at veins and mottles, finding rainbows in the golden grainy surfaces, then cutting leaves into diagonal strips with the blue-edged knife and laying them out on a split-cane mat spread over the dust in that corner.

Presently someone stood in the doorway.

Sun Caller was not surprised to see the familiar silhouette. He and his son often talked in this place where the tobacco enhanced in power as it dried.

This was the first day they had been able to talk privately since the son's return. At first the father did not speak, and the young man would not out of respect.

Sun Caller had seen that Eagle Ring Man was changed. This change Sun Caller sensed in his son was more than physical, however. It disturbed the chief who had been beyond joy to see the son whom he had never hoped to see alive again. He gestured for the youngster to be seated on the mat.

"They are teaching you how to make the blue metal?" Sun Caller finally asked his son, as his thumb moved on a leaf.

"That and much more, father." He was making progress learning swordplay under Madoc's tutoring.

"Because of the Natchez sun?"

"She is not a Natchez sun!"

"She was the Natchez sun of Miko Shell-of-Many-Colors." He had in fact paid a large bridge-price in flint and buffalo hides to his old enemy to avert revenge for the girl's kidnapping.

"Against her will."

"Someday I want to hear the story of how you took her from him," he said, delighted that his son had accomplished such a feat that would cuckold his enemy. But there was a sadness in him, too. He saw that the whites had put their mark on his son.

"You have been adopted without first becoming an orphan," Caller observed.

"I have seen the One Above in the melting iron, father. See, the white sachem made this from the metal I saw changed."

Sun Caller regarded the amazing amulet his son wore with such pride. This one was so earnest, had striven so hard among all the young men to know the secrets of the sun. He had pushed hard at the grandfather's lodge to admit him into higher degrees, had endured the austerities of the isolation rituals. Ever since he was a child, this one had sought the higher. Now the father could see with sadness that something other than the Yuchi way of life had given Eagle Ring Man what his heart desired.

"So they know of the circle within the cross, too," replied Sun Caller as he let go of the Celtic cross while thinking all those sorrowful thoughts. Himself, he had always followed the traditional forms but never felt the call of the higher. Sun Caller's own personal call had been from what was in the middle world, not the upper of the One Who Breathes Above. Sun Caller was rooted in solid, stubborn earth. Every day of his life he had meditated on the rising sun. He knew all the phenomena, all the body's reactions to its unimaginable power, but he, personally, did not wonder any further about what that power might be. The circle within the cross was familiar to him. It was the opening and closing of each day, nothing more or less than the shape of the light made by the One Above at dawn and sunset when one in the correct meditative posture squinted at His Face.

Sun Caller picked up one of the fleshy tobacco leaves, rolled and crushed its tip, then bit through the roll with his front teeth. He sat back tasting the juice, smoothing out the leaf as transparent as a baby's ear so that the fire's glow showed through. Curing the delicate, fickle leaves was a lifetime art, a skill passed from grandfather to grandson. Who would be his grandson to pass along the secret of the sacred smoke? If his son went away with the kanegmati, he would have to find some boy to adopt, now, as a formal apprentice.

"In each generation," he said, still analyzing the flavor, "there is the perfect leaf. This season I know it is one of these two. I must wait a little longer to see which one holds the purest spirit of the nipowoc."

He offered the leaf he had just tasted to his son, who timidly nibbled at the stem.

"So it is with every generation," Sun Caller continued, "one deer, one wolf, one turtle, one tobacco plant, who perfectly represents the nation of deer, wolf, turtle, nipowoc, or whatever, because each animal and plant—even grasshopper—has this one who is the highest blossom. That one represents the best the nation can be, given the weather and the hunt and all the other things that can go wrong."

He regarded the other, who was, as always, hanging on the chief's every word. "My son, in this Yuchi generation that one is yourself. Let me finish—it is not because you are my son that I say this. When you live a long time, you begin to see generations of things. It is because I have observed it over the seasons in the nipowoc that I observed it in the people around me."

He took up the second leafy candidate for this season's honors, rolled its edge, and bit into it gently, then sat back and sucked on the juices around the rest of his words. "You will take this Yuchi blossom away from the soil in which it grew, and you will break the heart of your father."

"My father has always told me that the duty of the son is to leave and the duty of the father is to let go."

"Do you not love your homeland?"

"Father, it is an affair of the heart . . . a call from the One Above."

Sun Caller nodded, humming to himself. Respectfully his son sat back on his heels and stopped speaking, for it seemed the chief was meditating on the taste of that particular leaf, but finally after a long silence, he said, "Fox of the Cherokee says the Yuchi no longer have the right to call the games."

He looked up to see his son staring with his mouth open. The lad had grown up with the annual games; they were as much a part of life as the round of seasons, the hunt, and the male lodge ceremonials. To have them suddenly ended was shocking.

"The Cherokee say that from now on they will call the games, which will be held in their territory."

David Iron had grown up with the threat of the huge tribe of Cherokee living to the east, and the more distant, but no less hostile Muskogeans on the south and west. All the stories of his boyhood revolved around warfare that broke along those lines, as did competition in the games.

"But surely the other nations defied him."

Wearily Sun Caller answered, "Fox has made an alliance with the Muskogeans except the Natchez and the Alabamans. Even they will not go against him."

"So nobody showed up for the games?"

"We were there," Caller said laconically. "And the Shawnee." He began meticulously to shred a leaf.

"But the sacred mountain—"

"—Fox says it is not sacred to the Cherokee, not since the earth shook," Caller said as he continued working on the nipowoc.

Last spring an earthquake tumbled some of the ancient dry stone walls atop the mountain. Earthquakes were unspeakable terror to all the red people, but more so to the Cherokee, who were burdened with a belief about the nature of the middle world of earth, which made them even more superstitious. Their tradition said that earth was the Great One's trophy hide, stretched out and hanging by ropes from the roof of heaven. Any movement meant the ropes were getting old, their knots fraying or slipping loose from the great lodge pole in the sky.

To the Yuchi this was nothing more than a story with which one might scare bad little boys; they held a more mystical view of the status of the earth, thinking of this middle world as an idea in the mind of the One Above, rather than His triumph robe. Their earth was held up by the eternal breath of God. There were no cosmic ropes to rot in the midnight of a Yuchi soul.

But others were more gullible. Fox was using the quake to denigrate the mountain as an excuse to achieve his own ends.

Both Yuchi and Shawnee were small in numbers compared to the lowlanders and the highlanders; united, the others would swallow the Yuchi, who had only their respect as elders to protect them.

"Fox has declared war on the Shawnee," David Iron said, now knowing the answer to the question that he could not answer for Madoc back in Mabila.

He briefed his father about what he had overheard in the Muskogean village. "And what about the Yuchi?"

"So far," Sun Caller wearily replied, "he says he honors us as the oldest brothers in the Land of Head of Waters. He has no objection to our holding our own games, alone." He removed his pipe from a pouch. "The Shawnee, by their traveling, claim more territory than any settled tribe. We are too small to matter to him, you see. But it is only a matter of time now." He gestured with his pipe at the blue-metal knife. "That is why your white friends interest me."

"I feared you might take Shell's side in the discussion of the Natchez sun," Eagle Ring Man confessed.

Sun Caller chuckled as he tamped shredded tobacco in the pipe bowl. "It was worth the revenge-price to know you deprived him of that beautiful creature. How is she?"

David Iron shrugged. "Better than a Natchez sun!"

The old man removed his flints and proceeded to ignite a small flame on the stone blackened by that function many times in the past. A covered basket of pine shavings supplied his fuel. He fed the little flame, which was all but invisible in a shaft of sunlight. When it was hot enough, he took a long splinter out and lit his pipe, drawing in a strong breath that made the tobacco flare in the carved stone.

He handed the pipe to his son, who took it and slowly inhaled, held the smoke, and silently prayed to the Christ, whom he was sure was the same as the One Above, that this fire, too, would enlighten him.

He gave the pipe back and released the smoke, saying, "Father I believe it is my destiny to fight Fox. Tomorrow I go into retreat to take eagle feathers."

"There is an aerie on the south ridge, on the rocky point."

"I will bring you one from the tail."

"Do you think I am crazy enough to fight him, too?"

"Perhaps he will leave the Yuchi in peace."

"And the kanegmati. What will Fox do about them?"

David Iron shrugged that he had no idea. "What will *you* do about the kanegmati?"

The old man took a long draw on the pipe and picked up the knife, testing its keen blue edge against his thumb. But he did not answer, and his son was too polite to ask again.

The next morning the sun was warm enough to melt off all the snow, and Sun Caller personally took Weather Eyes for a stroll over to the sacred mountain.

The white people were scattered throughout the village with individual firesides, and because it was a bright day after snow, many people were outside at various tasks and pastimes. Red and white watched the two chiefs walk out of the village stockade, past the sentries, and onto the broad trace that led to the plateau several leagues away.

Behind them a few respectful steps trailed their children, at hand to translate if either Sun Caller or Madoc needed it and shouldering backpacks of food and water for the day-long sojourn.

It was not to a towering peak that they traveled, for they were already on the high ground of the wide upland plateau that the several Yuchi bands making up the nation claimed as their homeland. They were walking a well-worn path almost due west, crossing several minor creeks as they paralleled the Little Duck to its junction with the Duck River. Where these two tumbled streams converged lay the steep-cliffed tip of this plateau. Madoc had been hearing about this sacred mountain now for some time, but nothing prepared him for what he saw when, just before noon, he walked out onto a rampway beside steep ditches, obviously a natural feature enhanced by the work of many men.

Across this causeway loomed the most ancient walls Madoc's eyes had ever seen, as old or older than Roman ruins back home, massive, venerable worked stone so long in place the lines between each stone were indistinguishable and covered by moss. There was a great doorway that led in to stony darkness, on either side of which towered what he could only think of as barbicans, round stone towers that dotted his native land from Caesar's occupation. These vaguely conical towers stood well over Madoc's head and appeared to be flat on top.

A hush seemed to fall about the four as they approached the high doorway. Inside was a gloomy, long enclosure with another opening at the far end, communicating with the south side of the building, if that was what this roofless room was. It felt to Madoc more like a maze. He saw no evidence that it had ever been roofed, yet the walls were high enough for it to have been a room people could live in.

All four were silent as they passed through this entranceway and out the other doorway into a courtyard bordered by other walled, roofless structures.

The sun felt good on his arms after the shadowed enclosure.

They walked out across a meadow that must have been twenty-five acres, completely bare of any sign of grass or other vegetation. The ground of this plain was a smooth beaten clay that could only be a mudflat—impossible up here on this mountaintop—or it had been purposefully leveled by men.

Around the perimeter of the plateau grew oaks and other varieties he had seen on the journey to this place.

Their shadows were directly below their feet as they walked across the gaming field to the far verge, which ended in an absolute drop of a hundred feet to the rock-strewn bed of the Duck River below on its inevitable plunge toward its meeting with the Little Duck a short distance downstream. It was a dizzying drop with only enough angle to the slope for Madoc to see that it was a natural cliff enhanced by more of the monumental stonework he saw at the entranceway. It looked as though many human hands had been at work on this mountain for many generations.

So far nobody had spoken. The chief was watching him, however, analyzing the white man's response to this place.

They walked along the south verge. At one point Caller pointed, for his son's elucidation, to a bony ridge, where even now a lone eagle rode an updraft.

Below, the two streams joined in a noisy green and foamy crash of waters. At that point more than two thousand horizontal feet of wall had been constructed from one stream to the other. Having supervised the building of several stone projects, including his father's quay, Madoc tried to calculate how many men and how many days of labor it took to raise the capping of the island's tip.

On the far sides of the Y-shaped chasm loomed cliffs of equal steepness, topped by a thick fringe of hardwood. Around this side of the plateau was that natural gray cliff, enhanced at various points with obvious handwork.

Now that he could see the riverbed, Madoc knew the source of this perfectly squared stone. The channel was layer upon descending layer as perfectly finished as giant stairsteps. Where broken, it cleaved along parallel lines, fracturing into rectangular or square stones that would have only to be slightly dressed to fit into a wall.

On the northeastern side of the enclosure were ancient stepped embankments under a small oak grove that shared the rocky banks with willows. The sunlight was dazzling on the bright cascading water that formed a pool on one level of a rocky basin that spilled out a wide shallow horseshoe falls.

Here the four found a mossy clearing with monoliths for sitting. Gwen broke out the luncheon while the water played before them, filling the canyon with its wash.

"What is this place?" Madoc asked.

"The oldest man-made thing we know," Caller answered. Madoc had some Yuchi now, simple words, but no real grammar. But Sun Caller used handsign while David Iron muttered behind him.

"Is it for defense?"

"Only the games. I can name ten generations of grandfathers who have played chunkee and ball on this meadow. But there are not going to be any more games here."

David Iron with Gwen's help had explained the situation with Fox. Now that he declared the mountain profane, Sun Caller had decided to take Fox at his word: "Do you think your people would be happy here?"

Madoc looked around and with significant understatement nodded, squinting, yes, this would do very well. It was one of the most perfectly defensible spots Madoc could imagine and reminded him of the hundreds of hilltop forts in his homeland.

Sun Caller betrayed no emotion as he continued. He was proposing that the white people could live there for the cycle of two seasons—one year. "In return for this you will give each of my warriors a blue-metal knife."

This site was the best, after their own village, on the whole plateau. Yet it was far enough away from the Yuchi enclave so that the whites would not be a daily influence on his young people. He knew Madoc would like the security of this place.

Madoc wanted to know if he would be able to build a roof over the entranceway and use it as a headquarters.

Sun Caller said as long as the original works were not permanently disturbed, the whites could use the whole plateau.

Madoc said to David Iron, "I do not understand. If this is sacred ground why would your father let strangers have it?"

David Iron and Gwen discussed this, with much head shaking, gestures at Sun Caller, the land around them, shrugging of shoulders. "This is a hard thing to explain," said David Iron finally, with a frown that matched Weather Eyes' own. "This thing Fox has done is a great..."

"Disgrace," said Gwen.

"Disgrace," David Iron agreed, but clearly this was not a strong enough word for what he wanted to express. His hands moved against each other as he continued. "My father is far too outnumbered to send men to fight Fox and too old for personal combat on behalf of his honor. So, he says, very well, if you say this place is no longer sacred, then it is worthless, and we will allow outsiders to take it off our hands. He is insulting by being so agreeable, do you see? Insulting and threatening at the same time, because with you and your iron, he might have a chance against the Cherokee."

"Will Fox use our being here as an excuse to attack?"

"How can he?" Sun Caller said, laughing. "He says this place is worthless."

"Fox will not want to go against what he himself has said to so many chiefs," David Iron explained. "It would cost him face."

"Disgrace," Madoc said.

"Disgrace, yes."

Gwen said, "It is as though Sun Caller is following Fox exactly and thereby opposing him in the only way he can."

"Yes, opposing," David Iron said, hitting one fist against the other hand.

"We may plow the meadow?"

There was no way to explain what a plow was, but the concept of hoeing a field prior to planting was easy enough.

"I would advise your women not to plant on the gaming field," Sun Caller said sagaciously. "This field has never been planted, and to hoe it would take a hundred women a hundred seasons." David Iron did his best to translate, then explain to Sun Caller that the whites had a big hoe that worked fast.

As yet David Iron had not seen this plow work, but he trusted Wyn, who said that it would, though he was as shocked as his father that men did the planting.

"And will their women take up weapons when the enemy approaches?"

David Iron briefly explained that these people were more like the Muskogeans in that regard: The men did most of the field work because they planted more than the Yuchi and needed the men's greater strength.

Caller removed his pipe while absorbing this information. David Iron scurried to assist him by taking his flints from a bag at his waist. Soon, with pine-shaving tinder from another pouch, he had a flame.

Madoc did not like inhaling the foul smoke but he took the pipe when Sun Caller offered it because his new son-in-law had earlier explained the significance of the tobacco ritual to bind agreements between chiefs.

What Sun Caller was proposing was adoption of the kanegmati. That meant they were allies. Did Weather Eyes realize how much a threat Fox was with his push west?

David Iron told his father what he had explained to Madoc.

Sun Caller was imagining what iron battle-axes and swords could do in close combat against cane and flint knives. It had been a long time since the Yuchi defeated a Cherokee force, and he would like to live long enough to see it happen again. "Will he fight with us if the Cherokee attack?"

"Yes," Madoc answered emphatically. "We will come to your aid if you need soldiers. Will you trade food to us until we can get in a crop?"

"The Yuchi are not farmers," he answered, "but we will

trade from our abundant stores of meat and hides." They had traded profitably with neighbors for corn and had enough to share with the whites. And, he added, the Yuchi would share their vast hunting territory with the kanegmati bowmen.

They wandered through their terms in this way, finding common ground and little to obstruct alliance. Sun Caller had planned to return to Yellow Pheasant Village, so they concluded their discussion and prepared to leave.

But David Iron had not eaten. Gwen commented upon it because his appetite was usually strong.

"I hunt the eagle today," he answered, and protested when she said she would stay behind with him.

"This is not a thing a woman can do."

Madoc urged her to return with him, but she refused.

"I cannot . . . be with you," David Iron said, a final attempt to get her to go with her father back to the Yuchi village.

"I will not abuse you, husband," she said wryly. "And I can be of help, keeping your camp for you while you do this thing." She figured he was going to snare a bird and snatch a couple of tail feathers, then let it go.

They bade farewell to their fathers, who took up the trail walking together. Gwen and David Iron watched them until they were gone, then she quietly, as promised, began to gather kindling. He must practice austerities, but she would be warm.

The next morning he was gone when she woke up alone in their blanket. The mist had returned so that there was no sun. She found banked coals from the night before and built up her fire, waiting for his return. But noon came somewhere behind the low clouds, and he stayed gone. She killed the fire and gathered their meager gear in the blanket, then walked to the verge.

She had seen Sun Caller point out the promontory yesterday on the south canyon wall, making the quick sign for eagle.

Now she found a comfortable sitting spot and sat to watch that point directly across the hundred-foot-wide chasm. The eagle was nowhere in sight, but after a while she spotted it far up in the sky. It was very similar to the golden eagles of her homeland, with a good five-foot wingspread. At the same time she also caught sight of David Iron's movement on the far ridge. She had to watch patiently for some time before she was sure, because he was moving slowly from cover to cover.

As the bird swooped on some other flying creature still far away, her husband paused. Now she could clearly see him watching the far speck of the bird against the sky as it killed with its talons and ripped with its beak, then fed in the air.

With a bloody tatter in its beak, it descended to the nest, which Gwen had not seen until the eagle located it, a rough pile of sticks in a cranny just below the cliff reach.

The bird took off after feeding its young the liver. Only when it was completely gone from the sky did David Iron resume his careful movement. But he did not approach the nest from the ridge. Instead he crawled along a sloping table of the same dark stone that littered the river canyon below, coming up under the nest from below, where the bird could not possibly see him.

He wedged himself into a breathtakingly small cleft under the aerie ledge and the sheer rock wall that plunged eighty feet to the foaming water below. There he waited.

Midafternoon, at least three hours later, the bird returned with another morsel in its beak.

She watched in admiration the parent bird clutch the nest's rim and bend to drop dinner into an unseen eaglet's mouth, then her husband reach up deliberately and grab the nearest unfeathered talon of the great bird.

The creature was taken completely by surprise, flapping with sorrowful majesty because there was no way he could free himself of the line the man had twisted around his foot, then looped around the other; then, with a final twist, the man caught its ruffled neck before that slashing beak could aim at his eye.

David Iron jerked the line, flipping the eagle down in a wide arch, yanking it on the downswing so that the eagle's neck was instantly broken.

Gwen stood in shocked dismay at the efficient violence of her husband's act. She could not hold back tears that burned her eyes as she watched him drag the bird back to his position and begin working his way to the plateau.

She screamed across the canyon, startling David Iron who up to that moment concentrated on his task unaware that he had an audience. She had promised not to speak to him, but that was before she knew how he was going to collect the feathers.

When he killed the bonepicker priest back in Mabila, it seemed like an act of war and not murder. But the unnecessary destruction of a beautiful creature looked to her like a senseless act that negated her promise to him. Why, she wondered without any understanding of the solemnity of the eagle-hunting tradition, could he not have just plucked a couple of feathers from the bird and let it go free?

"What about the babies?" she called with a haunting echo across the verge.

David Iron recovered, nearly dropping his prize in astonishment and anger. "What are you doing, woman?"

"Go back and get the babies—you cannot just let them die."

"There is another parent bird." Actually David Iron had been surprised there was a chick in the nest at all this early. Usually the eagles didn't breed until spring. He figured the warm winter had fooled them.

She scanned the wide gray sky. "Where?"

In fact he had seen only the single bird, a large male feeding the single nestling.

Perched precariously en route back to the plateau, he did not answer her and started to backtrack along the sloping path.

"I will not leave the babies."

"There is only one!"

"Go back and get it."

He hesitated, struck by the sound of pain and fury in her voice, something he had never heard in this woman he loved. His eyesight was excellent. He could clearly see her face across the way. Without speaking, he tied the line that still held the dead eagle dangling above the long drop to his belt, then eased himself back to the cleft below the nest.

Now she could hear the faint cries of the baby bird, which David Iron reached for above his head and without being able to see it. His hand found it, but it struck at him, quite a large baby with the beginning of adult feathers on its fuzzy body.

David Iron endured the hacking of its sharp beak and brought the creature down, fighting him all the way. He checked his line to make sure his prize was secure, then, with the eaglet cupped in one hand, its little talons tearing bloodily all the way, he edged back up to the trees along the verge.

She met him by crossing over the ditched path to the gaming ground. He did not speak to her but handed her the shoulder bag where he put the chick. Still not speaking, he turned, wiping his own blood from his fingers, and began walking back to the Yellow Pheasant Village, leaving Gwen to follow or not.

Though she was sure she could have found her way back alone, she trotted after her silently furious husband as she peeked into the bag to see the little fellow who squeaked inside.

She had a little of the jerky left that they had brought. She slipped these morsels to the bird, letting her hand stroke the prickly little head as the beak ripped into the food, then opened for more immediately, forever hungry.

They returned to the village before sunset. David Iron took his dead eagle to a private spot in the woods where he would stake the carcass out over an anthill. During that time he would not eat or have sex and would meditate in the men's lodge until the flesh was gone from the bird. Then he would remove the feathers, distributing them to various brothers in war.

He gave one to Madoc, who put it away somewhat embarrassed. It felt too much like a superstition for his comfort.

His mission complete, David Iron found Gwen in the lodge that was hosting her. Everyone in the village was gossiping about the kanegmati woman who had named a wild creature. The Yuchi did not even name their dogs. The old men of Sun Caller's counsel thought the whole affair tainted. None were feeling good about an eagle born in winter, and because of the anomaly thought the creature unclean.

"His name is Arrow-Eye," she said, stubbornly refusing to look David Iron in the eye, hovering over the eaglet like its mother. It snuggled to her breast, looked up with its ugly pin-feathered head thrown back, beak open, begging for food. She dropped a bit of jerky from their store into the mouth.

To name a wild creature—this was surpassing strangeness, which he reacted to as Eagle Ring Man instead of as David Iron. Gwen kept it in her shoulder bag close against her so it could feel her warmth while she fashioned a hood and braided leather jesses, as well as a kind of heavy glove for her hand.

Owen had fancied himself a falconer in his younger days and from time to time had kept hunting birds, so Gwen was familiar with the practice. This baby had been taken too early from the nest, so for the first few weeks of his life, Arrow-Eye almost didn't make it. But she was diligent, and the creature was spirited, and soon the ayas was thriving on jerky and hominy. Madoc was doubtful that a male bird would take to the hand, since it was traditional to put only females to falconry. But he helped her with the equipment, axing the weathering block and whittling the perch. Well away from her dovecote, because the sound of even an infant eagle terrified the pigeons, John helped her build a hawk house of withes, for by that time Madoc's Hundred was settled on the mountaintop with the rivers nearby.

The day they moved into the Big House she let loose old Culhwch, the male of the original breeding pair, with a message attached to his foot. There were bets placed among the men about the bird's chances of making it back to the swamp where the *Horn* was anchored with its dragon displayed— the only sign for the bird of its home. The message was not crucial, just word that the Hundred had found what looked like a permanent home, and the arglwydd would soon be coming south to the ship.

They built a roof over the entranceway of the stoneworks building and set up housekeeping before the second snow buried that whole region.

The hunters went out every day and brought back plenty of meat, leaving the butchering to the red women, who with their usual frugality had a use for every tendon, bone, and hair.

Once they dragged in a mother bear found outside her den. She and her twins, which they rooted out, were full of fat—something everyone found their bodies to be craving.

Despite Madoc's help with the eaglet, it took a dislike to him, hissing and rousing feathers when he stood near Gwen.

Several weeks after she had adopted him, Arrow-Eye had lost all his baby down and was growing real feathers. He was a huge bird, already ruffling his young, untried wings as though anticipating flight.

Even before beginning to fly, the creature would seek out Madoc and steal food from his hand or scream at him, picking him out of a group to upset his drinking horn or to flap wings in his direction. It was a grand joke, for which Rhys could not resist composing a satire.

But the arglwydd had more than a testy eagle on his mind. He was already making plans to return to the *Horn* and bring the rest of the men and supplies to their mountaintop.

When that snow melted, he commissioned David Iron to return to the caves across the Yuchi and fetch the rest of Madoc's Hundred. Gwen stayed behind on this trip; she and her husband were still touchy about the bird, though he was wearing the new eagle feathers in his turban now.

Every day the men went out and cut down trees, dragging them in teams to the forge Wyn constructed of clay and the flat boulders of the cliffside. Soon he had his fire roaring, fed by a constant supply of firewood ten men spent all their waking hours taking down.

The first products he turned out were knives, one for every Yuchi household in Yellow Pheasant Village, to fulfill Madoc's contract with Sun Caller.

St. Brendan's remnant refused to live in the Big House but built its own small log lodge over on the far side of the plateau across the meadow.

Brother John began building more wicker beehives, and the women mounted the broadloom on the ceiling on the new top floor of the Big House, which is what the Hundred began calling the entrance building they enlarged, repaired, and topped with heavy rafters and a log second story.

Rhiannon threw herself into work on the pennant she wanted to have completed before her baby was born, which would be sometime in late March.

The red women were skittish about going inside the ancient sacred stonework, and refused to live inside it even though they surrounded it many times with formulas in and around the walls.

They built their own hide-covered lodges along the river, where they did not have to walk so far with water.

Two weeks after he left, David Iron returned with the cave contingent, including Yngvild, carrying a hefty, red-faced boy she named Bjorn, after his grandfather who did not survive him. Sadly Madoc's Hundred was reunited without everyone who had stayed behind in the caves. Young Tegan and old Bjorn had died during the first few days when it had gotten very cold. They left them entombed there in the deepest rooms of the caverns, where many years later their mummified corpses would be a great mystery.

Llywellyn cried bitterly that he had lost his young wife and blamed himself that he had not stayed with her. Yngvild missed her father but was content that he had lived a full life doing what he wished, living on the sea most of his eighty-plus years.

Despite this further loss there was a celebration that night, with mead and a feast for all, their last until warm weather coaxed the bees from their hibernation.

And the winter wore on with more snow, as though the sky were making up for time lost. The Yuchi kept their promise to help supply the Hundred, but there was hardly any need because the hunt was so bountiful.

Arrow-Eye took to the sky without any trouble, Gwen watching him just as his own mother would have on his maiden flight. From then on she worked with him every day, and despite Madoc's fears, he proved to be amenable to the human hand. It was traditional in her family to let the bird get used to human beings immediately, then hack it, that is, let it fly free while feeding it by hand until the bird mastered flying and striking.

She spent hours watching the ayas learn its wings.

The weaving Rhiannon had begun grew with each day, as did her belly. Then, on schedule, the last week of March her water broke. Mary, Yngvild, and Ari's Muskogean mother-in-law attended the birth, which proceeded without incident.

Rhiannon's cries woke Madoc, who was sleeping in the alcove Teleri claimed for them downstairs.

He went upstairs, where he watched from the shadows beside Rhys until the pale light of dawn, when it was over.

Rhys joined Rhiannon on the pallet when he heard the baby's husky cry. Madoc moved forward to see her. His heart was heavy as he trudged across the rough planks of the loft room where Rhiannon lay with her head in Rhys's lap, against a pile of hides and pillows stuffed with cattail fluff.

Madoc looked at the infant in the crook of her arm and almost cried out to see that she was not fair, but a raven-haired little beauty who must have had a brunette father.

He dropped to his knees beside his sister, who lay pale in morning light coming from the window, opened despite the chill in the air that smelled like rain.

He stared at the baby, who could not possibly be Owen's, after all that sorrow, all that doubt and suspicion, and laid his head on his stepsister's hand and wanted to cry, though his eyes were dry. "Please, please forgive me for doubting you."

Her hand rested on his hair.

"Please, Rhiannon, say you forgive me."

He looked up at her. Rhys was stroking her cheek with his thumb. It was so tender a gesture, Madoc wanted to reach out to him, to share this moment of love for her between them.

"I forgive you," she said, no trace of feeling in the words.

"We are going to have a celebration," he said. "We will bring the feast up to you."

She shook her head and closed her eyes. Rhys placed a kiss on her ear, and she drew close to him in a way that Madoc did not want to see.

Later, when he returned to the fireside downstairs, he said miserably to Teleri, "She was telling the truth."

"I told you so," Teleri said for the first time to him.

"It is not Owen's child."

Behind them Einion ran through the kitchen, grabbing a leftover breakfast corncake from the skillet on the hearth.

"Wipe your feet, son," Teleri called to the boy as he ran back outside, slamming the heavy oak door and ignoring her completely. It occurred to Madoc that Einion was lanking out, suddenly growing. He was going to be a big man someday.

Madoc caught Teleri's glance, and something behind it they had never discussed before.

"What?" she asked.

Thinking out loud his sudden realization that here he had yet another brother, Madoc answered, "Owen is Einion's father."

Teleri regarded her hands folded on the tabletop.

Madoc sighed. It was so far away, it might as well be long ago. "It does not matter to me, Teleri," he said, patting her hand.

He gnawed his lip, wondering about Rhiannon's black-haired baby.

Chapter 26

...they sought to give me a husband against my will

Rhiannon in The Mabinogi
Ancient Welsh tales

"Rhys," Rhiannon said one morning during the week the little girl was born, "I want you to name her."

Back home it was very good fortune for a bard to name a child, who was then supposed to carry a song through life.

"That is for the mother," he said, one arm thrown over the bridge of his nose. With the other he found her hand.

He knew the tradition. Still, he hesitated.

"It would mean so much to me if you would name her."

"I will think about it." He lifted and lowered her hand in a measured rhythm. The sash had slipped upward under his arm. Now his still-handsome head and its leonine cap of brown hair streaked with silver was nested among the cattail-stuffed pillows she had woven. His high, manly cheekbone caught some morning light. He would have been beautiful but for the red, empty pit illuminated by the same neutral sunbeam that enlightened his beauty and his scars at the same sweep. She had tried to remember him the way he was before. But there it was, the glaring red concave flesh above the slick scar where the Englishman's poker had caught him. She would never get used to it, never be able to see beyond his mutilation.

She almost made a sound and had to look away. His hand was warm on hers. She made sure nothing of her moved but her head, conscious of it because more than anything she did not want to hurt this man.

"What troubles you, dear one?"

Master of subtlety, she thought, leaving silence her answer.

"I am learning you, wife," he said, turning as if to watch her, a strange habit, she thought, to be lingering in him. He, of course, turned to follow sound. "Something just now, something you saw, made you turn away."

His hand climbed her wrist. "What was it?" he asked again.

"A passing thought . . ."

"About myself?"

She did not answer, so he knew. He sat up in a swift rolling motion, stretched, and stood above her on their bedroll, righting the sash across his face. His movement disturbed the baby, hidden among blankets in the wicker basket beside their pallet high up in the loft rafters of the Big House.

The baby gurgled without distress; it was Rhys who found the basket and lifted her out.

"Good morning, baby-one," he said mildly, his cheek close to hers, but not touching lest his night-beard sting her. She cooed back at him as he strolled a bit with her, then sat back down on the pallet with Rhiannon.

She watched him with a great and secret pleasure she felt each time she saw how much he loved the baby.

Except for Teleri and Mary down below baking venison, corn, and tuber pies Yuchi-style in clay, they were the only ones in the house.

Later Rhiannon planned to come up here and finish weaving the pennant. She could see it over there in the gloom. The scarlet dragon burned from the shadows, hanging on the long warp threads from the cross beam that was part of the roof. A couple of afternoons and it would be finished. If Teleri helped her, they might be able to complete it tonight.

If not Teleri then Gwen was sure to volunteer, though she was not as fast as the more experienced women.

Someone was chopping wood with powerful strokes somewhere in the compound.

The voices of the three boys at competitive play echoed up from the open door in the kitchen area. They were playing under the last of the oaks beyond Rhiannon's view. She heard Teleri speak to Einion and Wil's sons—what were their names? She never knew. She had distanced herself from the group in these last few weeks, even from the other women, who considered her eccentric, spending all her time walking back and forth under the threads of her masterpiece.

Outside, birds warbled a salutation to the sun.

Rhiannon crawled on her knees to the shutters and threw them open, careful not to get splinters from the new wood. A torrent of buttery sunlight washed into the loft, smelling lightly of woodsmoke and warm earth from the field where the men had been taking turns playing oxen since false dawn. She leaned against the rough boards, letting the breeze take her hair up like wings.

It was a strange but peaceful scene she would never forget.

There he was, down there setting his example among the men, Madoc, pulling the plow. They had argued about it last night. The monks were docile and used to obeying, but his sailors scorned the task, and the proud Norsemen balked at being draft animals.

But how could one of them refuse to do it now that their arglwydd played the ox? His gesture was infallible.

She leaned against the sill, squinting to improve her vision, watching him with an ache deep in her womb. It was probably an aftercramp from the birth, but its timing struck her hard enough to bring a mist to her eyes. It lingered like an intense menstrual cramp, then suddenly was gone, like lightning, leaving an afterimage of receding sensation. But the mist remained, rimmed her eye, and stung like salt. She quickly wiped it away with the back of her hand lest Rhys detect it.

"Tell me," he said behind her and close to her ear, his breath on her neck as he spoke, "what is it that you see?"

He seldom had done this, asked her to witness for him, though she remembered him asking others, the sailors often. During the birth she remembered someone in a far corner of the loft whispering a detailed description of everything that happened. Who was his reporter? She had been so lost in the birth process she could not remember the voice, or if it was a man or woman.

Ironic that Rhys chose this moment to ask her to see for him, when it would be impossible to lie with her heart in her throat. He leaned against her in a relaxed way, indicating that he really meant for her to be his eyes on this splendid morning in March, which the red people called Crow Moon.

The rhythmic strokes of the woodchoppers continued ringing as she spoke. "Well..." she cleared her throat of its tremble, easily caused by just waking up, "the day is bright. There is a haze to the south, the direction of this window."

She took his hand and laid it palm up on the rough wood in a puddle of sun. His fingers uncurled like a flower. "Hmmmmnnn," he said, a burst of reddish gold the shape of his hand pulsing in the nerve endings where his eyes used to be.

"I do not see a single tree." She made a disgusted sound. "They left three old oaks on the other side of this stone fort or whatever it is, but all other trees were cleared for planting."

Off in the distance on the far ridge on the other side of the chasm beyond the field, two men continued chopping rhythmically. Soon would be heard another tree crashing to the ground.

Wyn's was a hungry forge.

"Do you not find it comforting that oaks grow here, too?" Rhys asked, stretching out across their pallet, chin on his wrist on the sill.

Rhiannon made a small sound of agreement, a kind of loud smile, and continued, "The field is big—I was never good at estimating distances."

The baby wiggled between them, grabbed Rhys's thumb, and started to suck.

Rhiannon continued, "Some of the sailors and monks are working on the far verge of the plateau. Brother Wyn's forge is throwing up heat-shimmers—I wonder if he started the glass."

For the past three months, Wyn had kept the forge roaring while he hammered out short knives, axes, shovel and hoe heads, cooking pots and needles—iron trade merchandise for their allies, the Yuchi. That trade had kept them well fed on the red people's corn and dried beans all through the winter.

But Madoc did not like trading anything that could be used as a weapon, even to allies. The Yuchi expressed interest in glass beads, which were cheaper to make—the ignots they carried up here sewn in their clothes were almost gone, and Madoc had not found another source of iron, though he and Wyn made several explorations with Madoc's new son-in-law.

"Father John has staked out the field—it looks to be more than forty acres to me. The dirt is rich and brown—smell it?" Rhys smiled.

"Some of the men are taking turns hitching themselves to the plow, one man playing farmer, the other playing ox."

"Well?"

"Well what?"

"Who is the farmer and who is the ox?"

"I, eh, cannot see from here." She felt the baby's feet pressing at her back.

"Someone is hungry," Rhys said, pulling his finger from the baby's mouth. She started to cry, but he quickly slipped her beneath Rhiannon's arm. The baby latched on so tightly it hurt.

Rhiannon helped her get a better hold. "I am not making enough milk, Rhys," she said softly after gasping with the pain.

"Maybe Yngvild can help."

"How do you know?" Rhiannon teased.

"The men talk," he said, laughing a little. "They say she has enough for a litter."

They were silent for a time, the only sounds in the room the baby sucking. Outside the men called too far away to hear their words, but their voices sounded strong and almost playful. Downstairs Teleri threw another log into the fireplace. She spoke to someone while the soft sounds of food preparation continued under the good-natured shouts from the men out in the field, which at this rate would take days to plow. They had been at it since dawn with only two furrows cut.

"That is Madoc's voice," Rhys said.

"Yes," she said. The bright light dazzled her so that when she looked away from the window, for a moment she could see only silhouettes. "He is the ox."

Rhys cocked his head, listening. "He would do that. . . ."

"They love him for it." She looked down, willing her eyes to stay dry, focusing on the men at the far end of what used to be the red men's playing field.

While Madoc and his crew worked, another group plowed from the other side of the field, leaving what would be a gradually shrinking balk unturned between the two darker swatches of disturbed earth. Their ox was one of the white-cassocked brothers, nearing the end of a row at the forge and swinging around to begin another.

Rhiannon saw it all through wet eyes despite her strong will. Madoc seemed to shimmer in her vision, focused in the center of her view and larger than the others. He leaned into the labor, the wide straps drawing his bare shoulders back in a way that looked painful.

"John thinks the growing season starts earlier here," Rhys said in a tone that bespoke thinking out loud. "The Yuchi told him their garden plots have been in a month, and our spies say the river-bottom corn of the Muskogeans is up to their knees. I wonder how they know when it is safe to plant?" Rhys mused.

Madoc had put off plowing because he wanted to use the men to cut wood for the forge and to build this house over the ancient foundations. Besides, even a sailor knew planting must be late enough to avoid frost, common back home in these first days of April.

Manpower was Madoc's problem. There were not enough hands to spare with that labor, so vital to make trade merchandise, as well as the diversion of the river below the southwest cliffs. Flowing as it did directly out of Cherokee territory, the Little Duck River would bring an enemy speedily to their southern flank, where the flat island would give footing for a good climber to scale the cliffs.

Madoc was working everyone at double tasks and shifts. Rhys did not say these things, but they lay under his words.

Rhiannon saw the forge flare, a small bright white-orange sun on the edge of the plateau.

She closed her eyes and remembered the ancient recipe for making glass: In a clay pot, in a furnace built into the side of a windy hill, melt one part flint sand, cleaned of earth and stone, with two parts ash, then mix, melt for two days and two nights, skim off the foam, and you will have pure white glass. . . .

She felt as the sand might, melting into pure white glass. She closed her eyes long enough to feel the sunlight glare when she opened them again. Madoc was there at the end of an imaginary line that stretched between her eyes and the field. She could almost see the invisible halyard tying her to him. Since he had spoken to her after the baby's birth, she could think of little else, his head on her hand. Watching him now was a crystal moment, frozen on her eyelids when she blinked again.

I cannot live without him. The thought seemed a thing apart from her, an arrow from an unseen bow that sliced directly through all her defenses straight to the heart of the matter.

"You have not been playing Llais Mel," Rhys remarked from the other side of her clear vision.

"I have been busy keeping up with my brother's orders." A

shallow laugh. She meant she was spending all her time weaving. Just before the birth she began memorizing glass-making techniques from Wyn. Rhys, too, was memorizing procedures from Wyn, including the smelting of iron, the casting of silver, and the making of brass and other alloys. Her words carried double meanings, which she did not realize until she spoke them. She regarded Rhys, but he did not show any reaction to what could also refer disparagingly to their marriage.

"I miss your playing."

"But you are are mastering the strings." As a poet in Owen's house, Rhys had neglected the harp. Poets were most often accompanied by others. And his particular tasks did not require formal recitation like those Gwalchmai performed. Rhys was delighted to be finally improving his skill, especially with Rhiannon's fine old instrument, which he used to set rhythm and aid memorization.

"I will never play as you do," he admitted, and they both knew it was true.

"But you make the harp happy," she said, and he knew that was true, too. He loved playing it.

While the baby suckled, her little hand still closed tightly around Rhys's finger.

"So you will name her?"

He brushed the baby's fingers across his lips, nodding yes with the same movement of his head.

On impulse Rhiannon began changing the baby—the cat-tail fluff was working just as Hayati said it would. Rhiannon had never regarded it, because at home there was wool and flax cloth for these kinds of tasks. The red people had uses for every stick and stone around them; she had learned much from observing the newest members of the Hundred.

She pulled a bunch of fluff from a basket and lined a new leather diaper with the fiber they harvested along the river-banks. She tossed the soiled fluff out of the window, where a sprightly wind picked it up and broadcast it beyond her view toward the unseen river.

She pulled an apron over her shift, quickly braided her hair in a long quoit that felt heavily between her shoulder blades, then hefted the baby in the fold of the blue mantle, which she wrapped carefully around her shoulders.

"Where are you off to so suddenly?" he asked, disappointment in his voice. The company had purposefully left the new parents alone, and this morning they were the only people in the Hundred who were not laboring at some task.

"I want to see Wyn make glass." It was not a lie. She was curious about the color. She remembered Wyn's brief lessons. Traces of tin would make milk glass. Manganese would make it purple or brown. Silver nitrate produced yellow glass, and red, the most precious of all, could only be made with gold. Iron from ordinary rust made it green.

But satisfaction of her curiosity was not all the truth, either. Would Rhys detect a possible other motive? *Build the furnace on a windy hill . . . she wanted to see that verge.*

Madoc said it was a vertical plunge of nearly thirteen fathoms below, where lay tossed boulders washed down by the narrow, strong river, which had cut a channel through the ancient rocks, and which must boil with turbulence when the water was high.

One must be careful along such an edge. A fall would surely be fatal.

"Well . . ." he said.

She heard the sound of disappointment in his voice. It had been three days since the birth. A little stiffness was still in her loins, but she had fully recovered. Her flesh had not torn, because this baby, though vital and perfect, was small.

Rhiannon looked down at Rhys, brown and sweet smelling and previously so attractive.

But now, stomach flattened and flesh loosened by water loss so that Rhiannon felt abandoned inside her own skin, her mood shifted with sea changes, she did not think she could ever make love with this man again. While she was pregnant, he had been a wonderful diversion. She had heard it was not a good thing to do, but their lovemaking had brought on labor, and the baby looked none the worse for it, a fine, delicate little girl with a lusty cry and long bones. And big feet, Rhiannon thought, like her mother.

She let her hand touch Rhys's silky hair as she stood. "I will be back soon."

He caught her hand, but gently, as if to read its palm with a restless thumb.

She tugged back. Movement beyond the window caught her eye. Madoc reached the end of his row nearest this position. He was stripped to the waist, glistening with sweat and sunburn and pulsing with power that seemed to shimmer from him under the hard sunlight. *I must live this close to* him and never touch him, she thought, feeling the pang again in her lower abdomen. Piercing. Would she always feel this ache for what she could not have?

"To work on that damned rug?" Rhys asked without true rancor. That was what he called the pennant over which she labored every waking moment now, driving herself to finish it.

"I want to have it done before Madoc leaves for the south."

"He does not care about such things."

"Still," she said, tugging against his grasp, "a pennant should fly over his house. It is tradition."

"He hates that sort of thing, the protocol, the title, the way people treat him differently. Of all your brothers he is the one who does not care about having power. Yet of all Owen's sons, he has it most."

It chilled her that Rhys saw, though from a different perspective, what she saw in Madoc.

Below, still harnessed in the tack, he took a break and a long drink of water from a skin. The men laughed among themselves—Wyn had promised them another plowshare but had been diverted to make glass for the Yuchi.

Rhiannon watched Madoc as he wiped his face and made a small wager with Dag that he could finish the next lap before Dag finished the brother's. Dag roared and ran over the huge unplowed expanse of packed, weed-picked game field to relieve the monk of the harness. They got in place, facing each other with the field between them while the other men lined up on the sidelines to cheer each man on and to make bets.

She saw Madoc's back now, powerful among the men, pulling the plow to set an example and making an entertainment of it, and likewise powerfully drawing her along behind, forever tied to him and unable to love him as her body wanted.

It would be a torment to live so near and so far, to have to watch him growing to love Teleri, for Rhiannon knew that would happen. Teleri would make it so; for all her gentleness, she would forge chains stronger than iron with her devotion to him. Rhiannon keenly knew that devotion by its absence. Teleri was polite, but clearly and without a word being said of it, she was no longer Rhiannon's servant.

Is my impurity rust? Rhiannon wondered, because I am

surely rusting away here. Is my soul's glass the green of
jealousy?

She could feel Madoc's power drawing her now on the
invisible rope. Her pelvis angled toward him. Her soft parts
were leading her, her juices flowing in his direction.

All this was too close to her surface, which suddenly felt as
brittle and as transparent as common green glass. She must
leave now, or Rhys would know.

He felt her hand suddenly gone from his hair. He sat there
alone for a while, his face turned in the unbreakable habit of
observation listening to Madoc's voice from the field.

Rhiannon went downstairs where Teleri and Yngvild were
cooking. The lower floor was humid with steam and thick
delicious smells.

This part of the Big House was the ancient fortification of
the red men. The huge squared stone of the walls was dark.
There were no windows down here and only one doorway,
because the back passageway served as a chimney. Ffagan
had built up a false wall behind the opening, using the same
river stone that made the original building. There had been
much discussion among the whites about the purpose of the
ancient walls they found here. Dag thought it was a fort, but
Madoc doubted it, since this side of the plateau was ap-
proachable from across the north fork of the Duck River.

When he first saw this plateau, he thought it the remains of
some ancient military object. On three sides it was all but
impregnable except by single rappelling climbers. But on one
side it could not be secured without a large force, yet all this
stone had been massed unlike anything he had seen by any of
the red people he had met so far, who appeared to be little
more than farmers or hunters who left no permanent
construction.

Now he agreed with the Yuchi that this had always been a
game field.

"Skraelings did not build this," Dag had said, insisting on
the name his grandfathers had given the red people of the
western lands. He believed this was undoubtedly the southern parts of Vinland his people had called Whitemansland, or
Vitromannaland.

"You believe your ancestors came this far south and inland?" Madoc asked, knowing that pride made Dag want to
believe it.

"There is no place on this world that Norsemen have not traveled," Dag boasted, and the other Norsemen agreed.

Rhiannon did not know who had built them, but she could feel the age of the rock walls around her as she moved from the loft's blazing sunlight down the new oak stairway into the first-floor gloom, past hastily crafted barrels and crates full of the red people's trade, piles of leather and furry hides, hanging strands of drying onions and herbs, and into the kitchen proper, where the other women turned to greet her.

What the carpenters of the Hundred had done to the ancient building was to put a second story of oak logs on it and build the huge hearth and fireplace on the south side of the original walls, which had no roof at all when they found it.

"I want to finish the tapestry," she said, walking around the long trestle table hewn from the soft, sweet-smelling cedar. Rosin still leaked from several knots. Already its surface was polished with many meals celebrated upon it.

Yngvild and Teleri looked at each other.

"If I had help," Rhiannon continued as she sat on a bench and brought the baby onto her lap, "I could complete it tonight."

"The arglwydd wants everybody on the field this afternoon to prepare the ground for seed," Teleri said as she bent to stir the stew of venison and quail, wild onions, tubers, pine nuts, shelled corn, and various herbs. The iron pot was her pride and joy, which took seventeen of their precious ingots to fashion.

It irritated Rhiannon that Teleri called Madoc by his formal title when she knew that he preferred they use his name, at least among his family. The men called him Captain now; it had been a while since anyone had used his father's title.

"I will help with the hoeing, of course," Rhiannon bargained. "Will you help me weave the last courses after supper?"

Teleri hesitated, but Yngvild jumped in with an enthusiastic response. "I will be glad to help you finish."

"Of course," Teleri replied, not looking at Rhiannon, but banking the coals in the fireplace.

"Unless you have something else to do, of course," Rhiannon said coolly, because she felt Teleri's unspoken hesitation.

"I want to help you finish it," said her former servant, tapping the wooden spoon against the pot rim. "The master should have a flag flying over the royal household."

Rhiannon narrowed her eyes. Yngvild saw it, but Teleri chose to ignore her former mistress's displeasure.

Because she did not want to engage Teleri in an argument about the manner in which her brother wanted to run his household—that is, informally—Rhiannon stood and bade the two women good morning.

The sunlight was a welcome comfort after the dank gloom of the Big House. Rhiannon did not like the place and was always glad to leave it, even the more comfortable, lighter loft, which held the looms and sleeping quarters for the married couples. Madoc slept elsewhere, either downstairs with Teleri in an alcove off the kitchen, or out on the watch, which he shared with the men. Nobody would dare ask why they did not share the warmer, more comfortable loft, but he refused to sleep near Rhiannon and Rhys.

It was a fine blue-domed day with small flocks of fluffy clouds skimming overhead in a brisk, fragrant wind. Even from here under the oaks where she could not see the field, Rhiannon could smell the rich brown perfume of the plowed earth.

The three little boys were under the trees down by the river catching small creatures in their nets, squealing and pushing each other in play.

Dag won the ox-pull. Having nothing else to wager, he and Madoc had bet time. So, as Rhiannon crossed behind the field, he and a couple of his men were preparing to go hunting, while Madoc and the sailors stayed with the labor of the plow.

Over there, halfway up his row, the monk leaned into the labor, while still another of the brothers guided the plow behind. The going was excruciatingly slow, even for big, strong, work-toughened men like the sailors and the monks, who had worked this hard at the monastery. Two other brothers walked along guiding the oxen—they would trade places at the end of this next row, back and forth, until the great space was turned. Rhiannon wondered how long it would take . . . a week?

Father John wanted the women and children to go along behind the plows, breaking clods and refining the soil, removing roots and rocks. It had consistently rained every other day or two, so the ground was soft and loamy, not at all unpleasant to walk barefoot. She did not want to show her big feet but caught herself. What did it matter, now that she had made her decision?

She walked into the shade of Wyn's pavilion, but under the thatch it was furiously hot with the forge roaring over on the blunt edge of the cliff. The thatch roof did not extend that far because of the danger of fire, but the dormitory and kettle-kitchen of the brotherhood, as well as the huge dull-gray anvil, were shielded from the sun and rain.

Wyn crouched on his ankles inspecting a small oven adjacent to his huge, roaring, smelting furnace, which had just been stoked and stocked with the last of their ingots. By tomorrow evening the iron bloom would be hot enough to begin working.

The smaller furnace of stone lined with clay was mostly underground on the west face of the cliff, a trapdoor of iron set with clay into the living stone. The firebox that fed both ovens was down a few steps where the apprentices had stacked hickory and pine, sawed and chopped the right length for the firepit. It took five men working every hour of daylight to keep the forge supplied. Soon they would have to move the forge deeper into the forest or cut down every tree within a league of this position. But before that happened, they would run out of Welsh iron. They had found traces of copper and other minerals, but no iron. Because of this Madoc planned to return soon to the *Horn* and remove the last of the iron ballast from her hold. That gone, they must find another source of the ore.

Several steps west on the narrow path, and there was the deadly edge. A slapping wind continually blew up the stone face, which was more than the thirteen fathoms Madoc guessed from this spot to the rock-strewn chasm below.

She saw Andrew return from feeding the fire; he saw her and momentarily was shy in her presence, then went about his duties assisting the abbot without looking at her.

Wyn was just opening the smaller oven door, his face shimmering with sweat.

She knew the monks hated having women here and tolerated her only because of Madoc's insistence that all the crafts be remembered by more than one mind. He saw she had the baby with her, that she looked strong and fit after her labor. He wondered if this would still her restless heart, for he had seen it in her long ago and forgave her for it as he would a wild creature. Still, she was so beautiful, so dangerous.

She regarded him before she drew nearer. The baby fussed, and she spoke gently to it, rocking it in the makeshift cradle of the long blue mantle. Wyn could see the shape of the baby's head and spine in the pulled cloth.

"I have come to continue my lesson, Domme," she said demurely, lowering her lashes.

He nodded and caught up the steel rod, or punty, with which he removed a glob of glass from the white-glowing crucible.

Andrew stepped back, anticipating his master's movement.

Wyn swung the punty around in a tight circle with his wrist as the center, keeping the parison or bubble of hot glass from sagging. With each turn of the rod, the glowing morsel of liquid glass became denser, darker, and longer as gravity drew it out into a smooth, thick rope of malleable glass. It made a small, intense humming noise, a one-noted song, with each pass.

When it was just the way he wanted, Wyn stopped spinning the punty and let the parison hang, its weight drawing out the glass rope even finer. Then, quicker than the eye could trace, his hands swung the punty, and brought the heavy, cooling blob of still-soft glass onto the wooden block, where Andrew was ready to hand him a flat-bladed tool of hardened hickory he used to roll the glass.

The damp wood sizzled under the hot glass.

His other hand flipped a few drops of water from a barrel onto the darkening thread, then, with a single tap on the glass string, he neatly severed the hotter blob from the shaft of glass, which he continued to roll on the wooden block that had been soaking as long as the glass cooked.

Even as they watched, the string cooled from red to dark orange, as though life were ebbing from a living thing. Whack, whack, whack, Wyn used the knife to chop the string into disks, which his expert motion separated from their other brothers in the line.

He flicked his wrist, positioning a loop of wire he had put there like a bracelet, and began quickly pricking each shimmering blue disk. By that time they were the consistency of hard butter, but as he neared the end of the line of about thirty beads, the last two or three had hardened beyond piercing.

With the wooden blade Wyn whisked these and the severed parison onto a corner of his apron and threw them back into the crucible resting on its bed of sand in the glowing oven, the door of which Andrew opened precisely, then closed.

Back at the wooden block Wyn rolled the soft beads on the wire under the paddle to mold them to uniformity, then raised them. So they would not cool too rapidly and crack, he hooked the ends of the wire and lay the coil on the oven roof.

Rhiannon watched from one side, sweat drawn onto her face as Andrew cracked the oven door and Wyn started the process again, taking out another dollop of glowing glass. Despite the inferno of the forge, the glass of the beads was cooling to its final color.

"Sky blue!" she said, amazed. She had forgotten what substance made the brilliant color.

"There must be copper in the sand," Wyn said, looking up at her with his face glistening. "The holy color of heaven!"

He laid the circle of beads on the hot sand.

Rhiannon refused to be gladdened that they were not dark green.

"You never know until you put it through the fire," he said in a tone of instruction, but watching her sideways as if something in her stance had alerted him.

She stared at the flaming throat of the forge, thinking what he said about how the metal needed potassium. Bones, he said, were a good source. She felt all bones at that moment, with no flesh on her, lean after bloating for nine months.

But the fire blistered her, pushing her from it. She knew she could not climb into a furnace to do what she must do. She had not the courage or craziness to burn alive. It must be something quick, she was thinking, something I only have to begin, not even as complicated as a knife, which I must continue pressing into my body, but something I do not have to think about once the step is taken. . . .

Wyn put aside the tools, wiped his face, and took a gourd ladle full of water from one of several water barrels set around the pavilion. He wiped his lips with the back of his hand and said, "Daughter?"

Then he turned to her, casually laying the sweat-wipe across his shoulders as he might a clerical stole.

Andrew, ever the sensitive assistant, withdrew to tend to the fire, for it needed feeding all the time.

Wyn drew closer. "Is everything well with thee, daughter?" he asked in Latin, his scarred hands folded on the sweat-wipe.

She nodded without speaking.

As abbot he was offering to hear her confession.

As dutiful and obedient as a nun, she knelt so that the weight of the little girl dragged in the dust, and folded her hands. Wyn knelt behind a water barrel while she whispered softly to him.

But her sins were minor; he gave her penance, a certain number of prayers to the Holy Virgin, and she said the right formulas and thanked him. She turned to leave but hesitated, mentioning that it would soon be time to christen the baby.

She felt as though she were afloat in a dream; she was more calm than she had been in years.

They spoke briefly about godparents—Madoc and Teleri agreed to stand for the child.

"Day after tomorrow, then," Wyn said, glad to see in Rhiannon a concern for the babe, which meant she was probably going to be all right. "It is a Sunday, according to the arglwydd's calculations."

Rhiannon said good day and left without further discussion of glass or sin.

Wyn went back to the glass, wondering where were the others whom Madoc had ordered to learn this craft. He began another batch of beads alone, chanting from the Psalms.

He saw Andrew staring after Rhiannon, who walked along the western verge close to the edge.

She could hear the river grinding away and the sounds of workmen's sledgehammers and picks unseen farther around the point. Pebbles rolled under her toes and took forever to faintly ring on the stones below. Through the tumbled boulders the river ran gray green and foaming, but far enough away from the stone foot of the cliff to be unable to cushion a fall.

The drop fascinated her as she stood above it, the baby making small noises in the folds of the blue mantle.

Chapter 27

We hanged our harps upon the willows ...

—*Psalms* 137

She backed away. It was not yet time. No need to take the child with her. Rhys would make her his by naming this baby.

Rhiannon would finish the tapestry, and then she would leave.

Just then she heard a bell, which was supposed to call everyone to the Big House. She supposed it meant Madoc was ready for his peasants to begin breaking up clods. She was glad, though, because she meant to ask Yngvild if she would nurse the little girl.

They worked all that hot afternoon, refining what the human oxen had turned in the morning, and later when they ate Teleri's soup, the hunters returned with a good bag of turkeys. They also dragged behind them an enraged creature that brought out every soul of the Hundred to stare and wonder what it was. It was sort of a cow, but with thick brown curly fur all over its huge humped shoulders.

Dag explained that this was a young one of a small herd they found munching prairie grass on a northern meadow.

While everyone looked on, the Norsemen attempted to harness the animal to the plow, but it dragged them through the dirt, their harness stripped and trailing after them. The creature snorted, making feints at the men with immature little horns.

As the Norsemen grew tired of the sport, they were astonished to see what must be the creature's mother stamping onto the field, followed by a dozen huge creatures hoofing dust and making hostile wet noises through their nostrils.

388

Dag quickly cut loose the buffalo calf, which the red women informed him was what he had caught. Dashing this way and that, the creature answered its mother's howl, pink tongue lolling as it trotted after the cow and the big-shouldered males flanking her.

Apparently the woolly creatures only wanted the calf back, for as soon as he was nipping at his mam's dugs, they were off. The Hundred had run for cover as a single creature at the first sight of the dark herd. Now they peeked from the doorway of the Big House to see if it was safe to come out.

But William got off one arrow—a direct hit that brought down a bull—when Hayati urged him to shoot it, and the red women butchered the carcass faster than buzzards.

Yngvild saw that the woolly animals had left hunks of their pelts on the bushes growing beyond the Big House. She called to the children to come help her gather up armloads of the stuff, a soft, strong fiber she was already sure would weave into a serviceable blanket if they could get enough of it.

They took that and the wool from the slaughtered animal into the Big House, where she and Teleri combed it, discussing its properties and testing cables of it with the spindles to see what kind of yarn it made.

Gwen was amazed that it was soft, because it looked rough. "I wondered what animal it came from when I saw this stuff at Mabila." She had not seen any buffaloes there, but she saw other red people coming to trade bales of the wool for food.

"Well, lady," Yngvild said, standing and arching her back with her hands on her hips, stretching her abdomen as far back as she could, "did you say we could finish the pennant tonight?"

Teleri set aside the spindle-whorl and stood without speaking. She called Einion, but the child yelled from the outside that they were catching fireflies. Madoc called that he was watching the lad—the men were talking, watching the stars, tossing plans around. Tonight they had much to discuss, with Madoc soon headed south to bring supplies from the *Horn*.

The three women climbed the stair and began to work, Gwen following with a skin of John's newest brew. Soon their weaving song flowed with the mead. Mary followed soon after and joined with her rich alto. Wil growled when Mary met him at the top of the stair, turning him back.

Rhys came inside, where he found Llais Mel and began to

play along with the weavers. He leaned back, feeling warm and full and hopeful with the harp, elaborating on the melody.

Into the night they sang, treading on the squeaking floorboards overhead as they moved under each other's hands, back and forth, completing the wine-colored dragon by midnight and aiming to finish by morning the tip of the tapestry that would measure a fathom in length and three ells wide at its widest before it sloped to a point.

Rhys could tell after a while which woman was making which step: Yngvild's was heavy, flat-footed, and firm. Teleri, used to moving silently to serve a master, walked soundlessly on the balls of her feet, while Rhiannon dragged her heel at the end of each turn. They were moving in and out of the warp threads, which hung vertically against the weight of stones. Each woman guided a thread while one of them, probably Rhiannon, beat the weave upwards with a broken coracle paddle. One of the treasures she left behind was an elaborate iron weaving sword. The wooden one made a less satisfying sound, something like the whack of a paddle against a child's padded bottom.

The muffled clacking of the heddle rod, which arranged the twill of the weave, from time to time added a syncopation that Rhys traced with the harp. Once in a while he could hear the clack of the stones as the women's ankles brushed against them. He could see with his mind's eye the dragon they were weaving, the attacking dragon with three claws on each hand.

He had touched the fabric as she wove it, feeling the dragon grow. Here and there she slipped in by hand strands of gold his fingers could detect against the softer wool. She told him it was a dark red beast outlined and scaled in gold upon a dark background. Now he envisioned it completed in their song, which lasted deep into the night.

Rhys awoke with the harp in his hands in the cold night. Madoc had taken the bench beside him, though he did not speak at first but threw another log onto the fire, which had died to coals, and the two of them sat there for another hour, drinking some of the wonderful mead Father John made from Ely's honey. None would eat the raw stuff, but it produced a remarkable beverage, clear and not at all sweet, but flavorful and glowing in alcohol content. There would be only one batch, but the bees were making new honey, ensconced in more traditional housing, John's bell-shaped hive fairly humming with their endeavor. He was sure the hive now contained two queens and would soon divide. He had another wicker hive waiting their pleasure.

Madoc's back and arms were aching with the day's labor, but he felt satisfied they would get the field plowed in two days. The other men who had been talking with him outside wandered in one by one and sat at the table, taking the meadskin when it was passed to them.

"I leave in the morning," Madoc said unceremoniously.

"I thought you wanted to see the planting in."

"Dag can handle it." Madoc took a long drink of the mead. "The truth is, we are short of iron. The ingots I will bring back will be the last." Glass would continue to be a trade item, but they needed iron to replenish their own tools and weapons.

He had arranged with Sun Caller for several Yuchi warriors to accompany him south to help with transport. When he returned from the south, he planned another expedition north, where David Iron said there were mountains of red rock. That, Madoc hoped, would be their iron.

"Well, then," Rhys said, holding out the skin, "to a pleasant journey."

They drank a while in silence, Madoc staring at the fire.

Overhead the women's tread creaked the boards.

"What is going on up there?"

"A surprise for you," Rhys said, wiping his mouth with the back of his hand. "You must pretend to be pleased."

Madoc looked around; they were alone but for Wil dozing at the other end of the table. "What?"

"A pennant. Rhiannon has been working like a madwoman."

"A pennant?"

"The dragon of Mona. To fly above your household."

"No," Madoc said, leaning back, not rejecting but only not believing. The Hundred had demanded so much practical cloth from the looms, he did not see how she had time for anything else. He looked up where the tread increased—they were nearing the narrow tip of the tapestry. All that would remain to do was to roll-stitch a border—two more hours at best in daylight.

Suddenly the tread ceased, and they heard the three women clap and cheer.

"Beautiful!" Madoc heard Teleri exclaim.

"We must take it downstairs and look at it in firelight," said

Yngvild, followed by a series of scuffling steps as Rhiannon cut the warp threads and rolled the tapestry.

Shortly they appeared trooping down the stair, Teleri leading with a candle that suddenly illuminated her husband staring at her out of the darkness.

"Lord, sir, you startled me!"

Rhiannon glanced up over her armload of rolled material.

"Show him, show him," Teleri said, as she stoked the fireplace, throwing on another pine chip that instantly blazed up with a rosy light as Rhiannon walked to the table and unfurled the splendid tapestry.

Madoc was speechless as he fingered the rich weave. The men crowded around, highly appreciative of the work, touching it and exclaiming the colors and the resplendent blood red dragon.

"It must be edged yet," said Teleri, "but is it not wonderful? Fit for a king."

The men agreed, the women exclaimed, but Madoc bit his lip as he caught Rhiannon's glance. This was a gift of love from her. It was so beautiful it hurt, her masterwork. The wine-colored silk had come all the way from Cathay overland on the backs of camels, and in long ships across the Mediterranean to Florence, where his father's agent had bought it for an ingot of pure silver. The golden threads of dragon's scales were from an ell of cloth-o-gold from his father's treasury. The royal creature that symbolized the House of Gwynedd looked so real it seemed to breath in the flickering firelight.

She had put her essence into this work for him, and it showed in her eyes this moment. She was smoldering in there, he realized, as he was over here. How were they ever going to live together? he wondered miserably, hiding his feelings behind continued inspection of the tapestry. He looked back at it lest Teleri catch what passed between himself and his sister.

But he was not quick enough. Teleri saw and looked away. Rhys could only wonder at the sudden silence in the room as his hands stroked the tapestry. The outline of the dragon was easy to follow by touching the golden thread. He felt Rhiannon in the piece like a cool light at his fingertips.

Madoc saw the bard absorbed in the texture and, without being asked, began a detailed description of the pennant for Rhys's benefit. They all listened politely—his report was a form of abundant praise that made Rhiannon shy, and she suddenly realized who it was that had given Rhys a verbal description of her labor. The realization flooded her with a blush that went from the soles of her feet to her scalp.

"Well," Madoc said when he finished, moving to the alcove he and Teleri shared, "I want to make an early start."

"You are going so soon?" Teleri protested.

He watched Rhiannon. "It is beautiful," was all he could say, and that was a strain. "Thank you, sister."

Rhiannon hurried upstairs so she would not have to look at him anymore.

"Goodnight, then," said Yngvild, who followed Rhiannon upstairs where she had a bedroll on the other side of the looms.

Everyone drifted off to bed, leaving Madoc and Rhys alone beside the renewed fire, where they talked as it died back to red coals.

"I can never sleep before a morning departure," Madoc confessed, though he saw Rhys stifle a yawn. Madoc felt like talking and described the route David Iron would take to get them back to the *Horn*. It would be little better than a forced march down the Warrior Trace, a faster but more difficult route than that they followed along the Yuchi River to get here. He planned to be back by the next full moon—less than three weeks.

"You and Wyn are in charge," he continued, adding that he also wanted a few men to continue working on the canal they had finally opened between the south and north forks of the river. Madoc felt that deep moat of water was the best protection they could have against an attacker crazy enough to approach the cliffs from the south and west. They talked of this and other practical matters, drinking from a common cup, until their voices slurred.

A night bird called somewhere outside.

"She does not love me," Rhys said softly.

"Since when do we get love in marriage?" Madoc almost snarled as he got drunker. Most nights now he pretended he was holding Rhiannon rather than Teleri, who took on a grossness that repelled him in comparison to the other. But the pretense dampened what pleasure he found between the short, stout thighs that fate and his religion had given him.

"I do not please her," Rhys muttered, too far gone into his own misery to help Madoc with his.

Madoc listened with mixed emotions as Rhys talked of his attempt to please Rhiannon.

And finally they said good night, banked the fire, and went to their separate beds. Rhys was asleep before his head hit the pillow, but his hand found Rhiannon's.

A couple of hours later Madoc left with David Iron, their Yuchi allies, and Lev and another of the Norsemen to relieve the crew on the *Horn*. By dawn they were out on the Trace south the way David Iron had gone as Eagle Ring Man.

They were gone when Rhys awoke with a slight headache and the feeling of Rhiannon's presence nearby. He felt for her, but their bed was cool.

"Good morning," she said from the far side of the pallet where she sat in sunlight, hemming the pennant.

Outside someone was chopping firewood into quarters: Woodcutting was the drum rhythm of all their daylight hours.

He crawled over to touch her leg, felt the distinctive texture of the pennant completely covering her as she sewed. He heard the baby in her wicker basket cooing at dust motes dancing in a ray of sunlight coming through the open window, which he appreciated when he leaned forward, burrowing beneath the material to kiss Rhiannon's naked leg.

Below, the men were dutifully plowing, each of two teams taking turns as oxen. Every spare hand, including Teleri and Yngvild with little Bjorn in a sling on her back, was working with hoe or rake on the swath of brown earth.

"You are going to work on that damned rug all day."

This time he really sounded disgusted with her, and remorselessly jealous of her project. She did not answer.

"Well," he said, standing abruptly, "I shall make myself useful elsewhere," then grabbed his staff and went downstairs.

For a while Rhiannon stared outside, listening to the evenly spaced powerful strokes of the unseen woodchopper.

Presently she saw Rhys striding out toward the workers, where he spoke with Teleri, who gave him her hoe and turned to get another, a wide floppy hat that covered her face. She and the other pure Celts were beginning to burn under a sun unbelievably fierce for April, which the red people called Grass Moon.

Rhiannon kept stitching. Today, she thought, I will complete the tapestry. Midmorning she made the final stitch and sat looking at her handiwork spread out on the rumpled bed. She stood, still looking at the tapestry, feasting on its completion. It was her masterpiece; she knew it though she never would have voiced such a thing. Rejecting further sentiment, she rolled up the tapestry, took up the sleeping baby, and went downstairs, where she found Gwen alone in the gloomy kitchen. She one-handedly unrolled the tapestry on the big table, delighted again at her work that glowed in the light from the open doorway, where just outside bees buzzed in puddles of lacy light filtering down through the oak leaves.

Gwen admired it anew and began rolling it up to hand it over to Ffagan.

Rhiannon saw someone approaching with a wave from the glare of the field but could not see who it was until he was upon her.

Wyn came closer, in his full cassock and evidently not yet at his forge or perhaps not blacksmithing that day. He spoke to Gwen, who was hurrying off with the tapestry under her arm, responding to whatever he said by gesturing at the Big House.

The abbot wanted to talk to Rhiannon about the baby's godfather. Teleri had agreed to be godmother, but with Madoc's sudden decision to go south, Wyn asked Llywellyn to stand for the child. The man was despondent over losing his wife, and Wyn thought this would do something to help fill the void.

In the kitchen he found Rhiannon and asked her about Llyw. Rhiannon said that was fine with her.

"And what will you be naming the little angel?" Wyn asked, plucking back the mantle to see her flowerlike face framed by curly black hair.

"Her father is going to name her, Domme."

Wyn straightened, nodding. He was aware of the traditional naming by the song-maker.

"I have something for you, Lady Rhiannon."

From his cassock Wyn produced the string of blue beads he had made the day before. "They are for you, daughter," he said, gesturing that he would place them around her neck. She rarely wore any jewelry except gold, but she let him so as not to hurt his feelings.

"Thank you," she said, touched at his gesture.

"Do not forget," he said, "heaven is with us even if we are unaware." He patted her hand on the child and hurried off.

Looking down, each bead seemed to Rhiannon to be a miniature globe of pure sky, so shiny she could see her reflection in each round surface about the size of the baby's thumbnail.

Rhiannon went to find Yngvild and work on the field with the others to while away the time. All she had left to do now, she mused, would have to wait until the cover of darkness.

Behind her someone called. She turned, and so did the others out in the field to see who it was trying to get their attention. Up on the roof of the Big House Ffagan rigged a staff and a line with a wooden pulley for the flag.

Gwen was standing on the ground looking upward, as Ffagan raised the pennant, flapping in a strong wind that stretched it out to its full glorious length. The red dragon by this movement seemed alive and ready to attack. Everyone cheered the ensign of their lord's house, which now was the flag of Madoc's Hundred.

Everyone was exhausted that night from the field work. Few stayed awake past sunset. But Rhys played Llais Mel by the fire. It was late when he climbed the stair, his tread barefoot as he made his way to their bed.

He nuzzled his wife's neck, but she feigned sleep well enough to get him to turn away, a great sigh escaping from him.

She waited until his breathing deepened and his arm beside hers relaxed. She peered into the blue shadows of the wicker basket where the baby peacefully slept. She could barely make out her lips sucking a dream teat.

Rhiannon soundlessly removed Madoc's gold coin from around her neck and laid it at the child's feet beneath the blanket.

Silently, on strong toes, she stood and walked across the loft, making only an occasional squeak. There was a faint glow from the kitchen fireplace, where coals were banked, but it was enough to make out her harp sitting on the table—he always neglected to box it. She took it in passing, holding it close to her so as not to vibrate the strings.

The night was cold. There was no trace of breeze, but it was very dark. The stars seemed far away behind a faint but darkening mist.

The three great oaks were stark against the sky, their young leaves hardly moving in the still air. The boys had made a swing with a hempen rope hanging from a stout truncated branch low on the trunk. She felt with her hands along the rough bark until she found the branch, then looped the strap around it with a knot. Let loose from her touch, the harp vibrated slightly, bringing up the faintest trace of music.

Then, stilled by her hand, it was silent.

She felt the chill damp earth of the plowed field beneath her bare feet. But it was so dark she could not see where she was going. The forge lay over there, but she was nearsighted and the distance escaped her.

She realized she was still wearing Wyn's beads. She closed her eyes, fingers on the slick glass, imagining clear sky.

She seemed to have walked farther than when she scouted the verge. It must be there somewhere. Not to worry, she thought as she walked past the plowed furrow and toward the precipice. She could hear the river now; she would just keep walking, and that would be that.

It was a mortal sin, but she could not see any other way out. God and the church seemed very far away, and she had never been sure about having an immortal soul, anyway. She did not feel immortal.

An owl hooted. She felt scree roll under her heel and with the next step felt on the sole of her foot the cool breeze blowing perpetually up the side of the cliff.

Forgive me, Mother Mary, for being too cowardly to go on living.

The next step was easy.

Chapter 28

Her hair was yellower than straw flowers. Her flesh was whiter than sea-foam. Her palms and fingers were whiter than the clover among small pebbles of a gushing spring. No eye was fairer than hers, not even the eye of the mewed hawk. Whiter than the breast of a swan were her breasts; redder than foxglove were her cheeks. All who saw her became filled with love for her. Four white clover flowers would grow up in her footprints wherever she walked, hence she was called Olwen, meaning White Footprint.

—Culhwch and Olwen
The Mabinogi

The darkness of eternity dawned into an ordinary morning the color of the beads around her neck.

There was not a cloud in sight. The sky was scraped as clean as her own mind, for in those first few moments, her head pillowed on a mossy stone where the river had flung her, she had blissfully forgotten everything.

She made the mistake of moving and was blinded by a gush of pain at the back of her skull, flooding in with memory of who she was and how she came to be here.

The Duck River might as well have been named the crazy snake river because of its many turns and switchbacks as it rushed down through hard, ancient rocks to join the Tennessee. Though it was swift, there were no more shoals after its bed passed below the Yuchi sacred mountain. It could be canoed in the dry season with a minimum of white water. Here and there along its course, however, were stalwart outcroppings that blocked the stream, forcing it into abrupt kinks. Behind the outcrops were widened spots where cattail and cress fringed the shallows.

The first of these stony sentinels caught Rhiannon about three leagues downstream, where the Natchez Trace, another of the red people's well-traveled paths, crossed the river.

In the dry season it was possible to wade the clear pool trapped this side of the rock. Even now it was only a leisurely swim. Near this pool were camping spots used by everyone who used the Trace, usually solitary hunters or messengers.

This warm spring season the southern bank was the temporary camp of another group of red people who shared ancestors with the Cherokee but were allied to the Mabilans and, because of their way of life, disdained by both. Their camp hummed with the activity that morning of perhaps forty-five persons, mostly women and children whose ancestors for a thousand generations camped this spot in their annual migration between hunting fields.

The Shawnee of the Whippoorwill Band did not plant. They hunted and gathered and so were the sole nation in those parts to keep the ancient ways of the ancestors before the arrival of corn from the south. They were the last nomadic holdouts, claiming hunting rights throughout the vast territory, which was currently disputed as blood country among the more settled nations.

The Shawnee trod lightly here, having scouts out at all times as they moved in their endless circle through eastern forest and western prairies all the way to the banks of the Great River Road, hunting first the deer and beaver in snow, then heading into buffalo country in the time of heat. Everyone was their enemy, the corn-growing Muskogeans and the hunting Cherokee originally of the eastern cavelands but now depending like the lowlanders on corn they grew in permanent camps. They still hunted, but by individual warriors and not as a clan.

The Shawnee had no permanent camps. They were still dog-people; their means of transportation was by dog-pull, the gihli-gasi, which had surprised the Hundred when Gwen's stray hauled Brother Wyn's anvil.

The Shawnee were a people unto themselves, and the Whippoorwill Band was more conservative than their cousins in the Shawnee homeland of the Kantuck, who had already begun planting corn in the Illinois river bottoms. The Whippoorwills were relentless hunters, and because of it their numbers stayed small.

Corn fed more people, but the purists among the Shawnee believed any plant not found as it grew was not fit to be eaten. They allowed collection of all plants and herbs and had a vast medicinal knowledge. They did not use much pottery, because it was too heavy. But they made the finest baskets of any people in the valley of the Great River Road.

They excelled in all things portable, and most in the most portable—storytelling, magic, and the divination of portents.

It was into the eyes of a woman thus nurtured that Rhiannon stared the morning after she died.

The face was upside down, utterly neutral as the eyes there stared back at her own. It was a cedar red face of a woman in robust early middle age, high-cheeked and dark-eyed. Her lips were puckered in what looked like the act of sucking something. Braids of coal blue hair hung down the front of a fringed tan dress scattered with small colorful quill beads sewn to the leather in geometrical designs.

Rhiannon felt herself awash in the water, the hard stone beneath her head. She blinked and the face was gone, then suddenly reappeared right side up as its owner walked around to stand above her in the shallows. The woman spat a pit into her hand, took from a beautifully beaded shoulder bag another of whatever she was eating, and popped it into her mouth. She sucked at it, obviously removing the meat from a pit.

Rhiannon got to her elbows, scraping her skin. She shaded her eyes and looked up at the woman, who was scrutinizing her with the intensity of a hawk while she casually munched.

Made uncomfortable by such unblinking appraisal, Rhiannon struggled to stand. She was immediately dizzy and fell back into the water on her knees and crawled onto the warm sand of a small beach. She sat and pulled her matted hair from her face.

The woman had followed her out of the water but was circling around her like a curious but cautious animal. She was humming a tune—a chant to ward off evil. Rhiannon heard a low growl and saw a yellow shaggy dog heel at the woman's feet.

She spat out another pit and with the hand that held it instantly stilled the dog, who dropped like a stone in a menacing crouch, muzzle pointing directly at Rhiannon.

The woman likewise sat her ankles, having not so much as blinked, keeping her focus on Rhiannon.

"Stop it!" Rhiannon flared.

. The woman sat back, relaxing somewhat at hearing the white woman speak.

The dog gave a stout bark; the woman silenced it again with a subtle twitch of a finger and muttered something in the same low tone as the dog.

The dog rumbled back, exactly as though they were exchanging speculations about this intruder.

Rhiannon had sunk miserably on all fours. She rubbed her neck, which was hurting so badly she thought she might vomit. Hanging her head between her knees, she saw darkness reaching up again, but it passed, and she saw only the wide bead blue sky when she fell back against the sand. Eyes closed, she thought, let the woman sic the dog on me. What did it matter to a dead woman? When she opened her eyes again, it was later. The sun had moved toward the west. Now instead of one red woman there were several of various ages sitting in a circle, all dressed like the first one, who was still there.

Her reawakening provoked comment among them. Rhiannon struggled upright and saw they completely encircled her, each sitting cross-legged about three paces from her at their center.

"It is most certainly a spirit," said a younger woman.

"I thought so, too," said the first. "But she speaks."

"No color in her," said a third. "No earth. Only air."

Now Rhiannon saw that in each woman's lap was a shallow basket full of what looked like dried leaves and stalks. Each woman was slowly grinding this material in her hands while continuing to watch Rhiannon.

She dragged herself to her knees, and the women began throwing the odorous stuff at her. She plucked it from her hair, filthy with mud and slime, and threw the mess back at them.

This provoked more startled comments from the circle.

"I have never heard of a spirit refusing the nipowoc," said the elder among them, ceasing to crumble the leaves in her basket. Quickly she set it aside and edged closer to Rhiannon, peering at her in that hawklike manner that made Rhiannon feel like a bug under a child's inquiring fingers.

"But the white skin, auntie, what about the white skin?"

"It must be chalk, for some ceremony," the elder mused. "In the water."

"Chalk mixed with bear-grease and stuck on with magic. Such does not wash off easily."

"Then, the hair, what about the hair?"

Clearly the first woman and the elder were debating.

The old woman reached out and handled the matted coils of honey-colored hair. Rhiannon drew back, but the woman held on, rolling it under her fingers. This close Rhiannon saw that while old, the woman was very lean and dry, her skin wrinkled only at the eyes and around the mouth. She had the look of youth because there was not a gray hair in her luxurious black mane, which had been braided into a dozen coils hung about with beads.

Because she felt no menace, but only curiosity from the crone, Rhiannon let her continue touching. The red fingers lingered over the strange woven material of the white woman's clothing—these people did not have the broadloom. Rhiannon was still wearing the light wool shift and a heavier black-and-yellow plaid tunic she had on when she jumped.

The old woman's nimble fingers found the blue beads under Rhiannon's shift collar.

"What is this?" Her eyes widened and she leaned closer, smelling of pine and whatever it was she had been handling in the basket. "Look at this."

"Yes," said the first woman, and they crouched closer, forming a leather wall around Rhiannon. "Sky blue beads."

"What are they made of, these amazing blue beads?" The old woman squinted closer, drawing the strand into her mouth, where she bit at the glass and pulled back even more surprised when her teeth could not make a dent.

"How did she pierce the blue rock, and where did the blue rock come from?" The crone looked at the first woman. "I have never seen anything like these, Winnowed Rice."

The first woman shrugged. "What should we do with her?"

"Let us wash the white clay from her skin," suggested the youngest, and others thought that was a good suggestion.

"Here now, what are you doing?" Rhiannon protested when they clasped her ankles and wrists and dragged her back into the water, where they grabbed up handfuls of sand, with which they began vigorously scrubbing her skin.

"Stop it—" she screamed when they drew blood from her knee. She tried to twist away, but there were too many of them. She kicked, bringing them down with her into the water.

"It does not come off," said the first woman, leaning back, letting the river wash her hands of any contamination.

The others drew away, leaving Rhiannon sobbing in the shallows. She washed off the blood and turned her back on them.

They backed away from her while they continued talking.

She washed the salt from her face and stood to confront them, hitting her chest the way she had seen the Yuchi begin conversations in handsign. She wished now she had learned more from Gwen, but then, she had expected to be dead. She indicated her arm scoured raw by their curiosity. "My skin is this color. Look, you have made me red like you—" She gestured at the burnished red arm of the nearest woman, the younger, who drew back and made a sign against evil.

"You hurt me!" She shook her head. "No more."

"What are we going to do with her?"

"She is crazy."

"Let us leave her and see what she does."

"Too dangerous," said the elder. "What if she is some kind of Cherokee witch they sent to do magic against our men?"

"She does not look Cherokee to me," said the girl.

"She is certainly not Mabilan or Chickasaw."

"Perhaps . . ." said the youngest shyly, suddenly hiding her lips behind her fingers, "perhaps she is a Natchez sun!" She made a sound very much like a giggle.

The others made small laughter without opening their mouths.

The first woman had not joined this debate but reached into her shoulder bag for a morsel of what she had been chewing earlier—it looked like a dried plum, which in fact it was.

She offered it to the white woman, who watched intently as she took it. She looked it over to make sure it was not something horrible—David Iron had told her his people considered delicacies things like locusts and grubs. The morsel smelled fruity. While she sniffed it, the woman took another and put it in her own mouth, sucking the pit as she did before. Then, seeing Rhiannon's unspoken question, the one they called Winnowed Rice did a strange and wonderful thing.

She reached up and plucked with perfect pantomime a piece of fruit from a tree, twisting the stem and yanking.

Rhiannon could feel the tree letting go. The red woman then smelled her imaginary plum, rubbed off the bloom, and bit into it slowly and luxuriantly, wiping away a dribble of imaginary juice, which Rhiannon could fairly taste so good was the woman's mummery.

The eloquent handsign complete, the woman and she shared a smile. Rhiannon was suddenly starving. She ate all the fruit and sucked the seed, imploring with her eyes for more.

"Let us go back to camp now," said the woman to the others, giving Rhiannon another bite as she would to lure a puppy. She took several steps backwards, then offered another plum. "Just walk back as though there is nothing to worry about," Winnowed Rice said to the others.

"Owl Person will know what she is," said the old woman, who was the sorcerer's wife.

The others agreed, as it was polite and politic to do to the wife of the most powerful sachem in these parts. Why, even the Cherokee were afraid of Owl Person. Even the Cherokee had to admit that Shawnee sorcerers were the most powerful. Their great lodges that exalted members to the hundredth degree and took a lifetime to attain were predecessor to the Cherokee and even the Yuchi. But it was to the Shawnee that the Cherokee went for advice about the rules and traditions of the secret organizations. By secret sign and subtly informative decoration that might vary as much as a single stained feather, their officers outranked those of all other nations, and they were arrogant about it.

Rhiannon followed Winnowed Rice and the others to the knoll above the riverbank, a pleasant spot in a ring of poplar trees that rattled in the wind like tambourines. As they entered the village of cone-shaped skin lodges, the people's attention was caught by the white woman following Winnowed Rice into the compound. They turned from tasks or play and stared openly at the stranger, whose likes they had never seen before.

She spit out the seeds, but they hardly touched the ground before the old woman grabbed them up. To the Shawnee nothing was garbage. Every plum pit was planted—that was why there were so many plum trees marking the wide route of the Whippoorwills' migration. Likewise wild patches of nipowoc, which the Shawnee did not smoke like others, but which they shredded on live coals or upon mysteries or water as an augury.

Rhiannon's appetite had been kindled, and she could not stop eating. But something warned her that she would lose it all, so she did not take the next plum offered. She made up a handsign she hoped conveyed that she needed something more substantial—one hand a bowl the other a spoon she pretended to gobble with, then rubbed her stomach and made a smacking noise with her lips as she pretended to lick her fingers.

Winnowed Rice brightened and nodded. "Come with me," her gesture said, and she led Rhiannon toward one of the lodges marked with the painted history of the band. Peeking from the far side of the lodge were several more of the yarrow-colored dogs. The one with Winnowed Rice trotted back to what was obviously her family, an almost full-grown litter of five. None barked, though their ears flared. Mam grumbled they should be quiet, and they obeyed, nipping at her flank.

The white woman felt many eyes on her. Winnowed Rice turned, smiling, urging her to come inside as she held back the tent flap, exactly as she might sweet-talk a reluctant puppy. The old woman went inside, huddled on a fluffy robe of buffalo wool near a younger girl in her late teens.

"Sister, is your moon-blood finished so soon?" the girl asked as Rhiannon entered after Winnowed Rice, who answered, "No, but something unusual has happened. Will you come warm this meal for my stray here?"

Winnowed Rice gestured at the fire, and the girl, who was wide-eyed now at the blond stranger, scurried to poke at a small smokeless fire in the center of the lodge.

Under her hand a thin stream of smoke curled up toward a single hole showing blue sky where the poles met at the apex of the cone. From a small pile of dry sticks, the girl fed the fire, tonging with a springy piece of cane hot stones, which she flung expertly under the lid of a tightly woven basket that was sitting on its wide bottom near the firepit. Soon the soft roll of a thickened liquid boiling could be heard as the girl kept the basket in motion, no doubt to prevent the bottom from burning out under the stones: The Mabilan woman cooked the same way.

The cook unhooked a long ladle from a peg on a pole and filled one of several wooden bowls stacked on a short shelf near the wall of the tent. From inside, the pale leather tent skin was thin enough to see the designs painted on the outside. Rhiannon took the bowl and began eating with her fingers because no utensil was given her. The girl leaned back, a look of unblinking curiosity on her face.

While she licked and slurped, Winnowed Rice watched her with that same bright-eyed gaze. Rhiannon could not know that she was expected to have her own buffalo-horn spoon.

Once the girl reached out to one of many dried bunches of leaves and twigs hanging from many pegs on every pole.

It must be cedar, to judge from the aromatic smoke that puffed above the little fire when she tossed a twig onto the coals. Not taking her eye from Rhiannon, she passed her open palms through the smoke, rubbing them as though they were being scrubbed in water.

The broth was unidentifiable but delicious. Rhiannon could feel strength and clarity coming back to her with each sip. Over the rim of the bowl she watched the watcher, aware now that the crone in the shadows was also keenly observing her, and that the strange humming sound Rhiannon had been hearing the past few moments was coming from her wattled throat.

But the chant seemed to upset the girl, who whimpered until Winnowed Rice whispered, "No fear, Lily. She is a woman like you or me, but not from around here."

Whatever she said, it quieted the girl, but the grandmother still hummed, her obsidian eyes nailing the white woman.

"Yes, mother," Winnowed Rice said softly as she settled in a more comfortable position from which to continue watching the stranger, "you are right to sing against evil, because one never knows when it will enter the lodge." She tossed a pinch of nipowoc onto the flames, which shot up in a sudden blue flare that startled Rhiannon.

"She is a witch!" exclaimed the old woman, interrupting her song, eyes white with excitement. "A Cherokee witch!"

"A witch!" cried the girl, backing away.

"You saw the nipowoc flare toward her," croaked the crone.

"I thought so, too, at first," Winnowed Rice soothed. "But now that I have seen her shadow, heard her speak, and watched her eat, I have my doubts." As she spoke, she watched the beads around the stranger's throat. It was as though she had somehow coaxed small pieces of sky to arrange themselves around her neck. The Shawnee had wonderful skills at coloring quill beads and piercing river pearls, but they had no way to produce anything like this material or its dazzling color.

"She relieves herself just as you and I," Winnowed Rice observed coolly.

The old woman stubbornly intensified her chant, drawing her buffalo robe more tightly around her shoulders, giving a cold shoulder to the stranger.

Rhiannon did not like the sound of that last exchange and decided to do something to soften the old woman's reaction to her. She set the scraped bowl down and said thank you in her own language and what handsign she hoped would convey the same idea.

Winnowed Rice made to give her more, and Rhiannon was glad, because she still felt a bottomless pit. But before she began eating, she set the bowl between herself and her benefactress.

"Thank you for the good food," she said, taking a tin cylinder from her cincture—a little sewing kit with a dozen needles and a thimble.

Winnowed Rice drew back in wonder as Rhiannon offered it.

Winnowed Rice reached out and took the box before the white woman could change her mind. The metal was cool to the touch, like the flints from which the men made their hunting points. But so shiny. So slick, almost wet. Crystal-like, Winnowed Rice thought, seeing her face in the surface. "Who are you?" she asked, using handsign.

Rhiannon touched her own chest. "I am dead. I jumped into the river to die." She made handsign, acted out being dragged in the current, hitting her head. "I have no name."

"This one is crazy," said the older woman, tossing a small pinch of nipowoc onto the tiny flame. It flared blue again, but this time the white woman did not flinch.

Winnowed Rice watched her.

"Let me stay here," Rhiannon said. "I will work for you." She made a motion to feed the fire, to offer water to the crone, to carry burdens.

"You better get your moon-blood out of here," said the old woman, as surly as a thistle to her daughter-in-law.

"I must stay to explain this woman to Smart-as-a-Beaver."

"He will kill her, anyway."

"You are an old woman too mean to die," Winnowed Rice said evenly. "You could offer to sponsor her for me."

The crone curled tightly into her blanket, offering her entire back to her daughter-in-law and the spirit-woman.

The girl, Lily, watched one and the other during this exchange as though observing a ball game.

"Why do you want to keep her, anyway?" asked the old woman without looking from behind her huff.

"You had another daughter once."

"Yes," said the crone.

"The Cherokee took her from you when she was just a baby."

"I will never forget her. She was my baby."

"I give you Black Pearl as a replacement."

"She is a little older than my baby would be," said the crone as she looked back at the newcomer, who saw that there were tears on the old woman's cheeks.

"Only a little," said Lily, who was about sixteen years old, and who never knew the sister taken before she was born.

"She does not look like my family," said the old woman.

Winnowed Rice regarded the white woman crouched by the fire. The mother-in-law was right; this stranger was definitely weird looking. The Beaver was a conservative man who would be suspicious of such strangeness.

The red woman's eyes spotted items hanging on the poles. When she moved, it was very fast as she grabbed a bladder of bear-grease. In a wooden pestle she tossed a couple of nuggets of charcoal, which she began grinding with a stone mortar. She scooped out a mortarful of grease and mixed it in the pot.

On a finger she held out the thick black goo at the white woman, but the mother-in-law said, "It will not fix."

"What do you know or care?" asked Winnowed Rice.

"I am telling you it needs something to fix it." Her hands moved quickly into a basket near her in the shadows, then tossed what looked like a light-weighted wooden ball at her son's wife.

Winnowed Rice caught it in midair. "Ha!" she exclaimed. "The next time they say you are a bear-woman who eats her cubs, I will take your side, old woman."

"You should have more respect."

Winnowed Rice crumbled the oak gall into a puff of dusty-brown spoor, then dropped it into her paint pot and ground it for a while, while regarding the white woman who had been

following her actions like a hungry pup. She gestured with
the mortar, then with a finger gestured at it and at her hair.
She nodded encouragingly at the stranger, who looked down
at the matted coils of her pale hair. When she looked up
again, she was grinning.

"Yes, of course, that is a wonderful idea," she said, holding
the long ribbon of hair out. These people wore their hair full
of oil anyway, which they were constantly grooming. The
custom would hide a dye.

Winnowed Rice brought the mix to her, the grandmother
found a square of leather, and together she and her daughter-
in-law changed the stranger's hair to more normal-looking
black. Lily joined them in the grooming, handing her mother
a wipe, scraping off the goo from the burrs, and handing
them cleaned back to her. They talked and giggled together
like girls, with no trace of acrimony in their voices.

"So you intend to name her Black Pearl?"

"The river brought her, and she is one of a kind."

"Very rare," agreed the mother-in-law, pulling a spiny
halved seed pod through the tangles. The white woman cried
out just like every little girl whose mother pulls her hair, but
she knew that they were going to let her stay.

"As rare as the black pearl."

"Good."

"Black Pearl," Winnowed Rice said, taking a small basket
from among several stacked against the tent wall. She unlaced
the lid and poured out a dozen pearls of various sizes and
colors—none of which was black.

"Black Pearl," Lily said approvingly.

Winnowed Rice held up her prize specimen, a radiant pink
beauty as big as her thumbnail. It had been passed from
mother to daughter for more than seven generations.

"Pearl," she said to the white woman, who nodded, waiting
to see what she was trying to say. Winnowed Rice dipped the
pearl in the mixture, which the grandmother was rubbing
thoroughly in her hair, wiping away the excess grease. The
hair beneath it was not black, but it was much darker than it
had been, a light sable. As the white woman watched Winnowed
Rice, the grandmother began braiding the changed hair,
running thin ribbons of red and yellow plant fibers into the
coil.

"You are now the Black Pearl," said Winnowed Rice,
holding up the pearl with the carbon coating.

"Black Pearl?"

Winnowed Rice pointed at the woman. "You. Black Pearl."

Black Pearl nodded, tugging against the grandmother's tension on her hair as she deftly braided it, weaving feathers into it here and there. She instructed Lily to find a clam shell sealed with pitch in a basket. She lifted the cover with a thumbnail and took a fingerful of red ocher, which had been set in a bear-grease medium. She massaged this into her hand, then wiped her palms on Black Pearl's fair cheeks and forehead. She rubbed it into her hairline and on her ears. The rest she rubbed into the backs of her hands.

Black Pearl saw her admiring the cloth of her sleeve, which this old woman had never seen before. She unpinned the shoulder brooches and slipped out of the shift, kicking it onto the grandmother's lap, saying, "take it, take it."

The old woman's hands were shaking as she said thank you, taking the amazing material and the metal fasteners. She fondled the material with its tight weave, sniffed it, and peered close to see how it was made. She knew basketry, even hand-loom weaving of river-weed fibers, but nothing so fine as this. After a thorough inspection she carefully folded it and stowed it in a basket along with other treasures of a long life.

"Look at her—she is as hairy as a bear!" said the girl, hiding another grin behind her fingers.

Rhiannon felt keen embarrassment, though she did not know what it was about her person they found so amazing.

Winnowed Rice and the grandmother saw that this woman had more hair than they had ever seen before between the legs, under the arms.

"Here," said Winnowed Rice as she rolled a bundle from the storage baskets. It was her own dance tunic with mink-trimmed cuffs, made from pounded mulberry inner bark, softer and more supple to Rhiannon's touch than suede. She handled the edge, wondering what this material was—not woven, but too fine to be leather. It had long sleeves and came to Black Pearl's ankles. She and Winnowed Rice were both tall—these people were taller than the other red people she had seen.

"Well, that is some improvement."

"Where are you going to say she is from?"

"Some western tribe across the Great River Road."

"Smart-as-a-Beaver will never believe that."

Winnowed Rice shrugged. "The Cherokee took her hostage, but she escaped."

"I do not know. . . ." said the crone doubtfully.

"My brother is never going to believe that," said Lily.

"Lord, but I do wish I knew what you are saying," said Black Pearl, wondering if she looked like some mummer. She was sure that she did not look like one of these women.

Just then they heard a masculine shout outside, then another, and then several. The woman all jumped to their feet, even the grandmother, who hurriedly replaced the baskets and clam shell and all other evidence of their work.

Winnowed Rice backed off across the tent away from the fire. She and the old woman exchanged a look that said they were ready, then the crone stood and went outside, leaning on Lily's arm.

Winnowed Rice and Black Pearl were left alone. The red woman motioned for the other to sit down, over here, beside me.

Black Pearl obeyed. "Thank you," she said softly, hearing the voices outside. "Thank you for letting me stay here."

Winnowed Rice touched her lips with a finger, saying be still now.

Outside they heard a terrible sound. It might have been some animal being butchered with a dull knife. But it became obvious as the keen continued that it was human. She did not move from her spot, however, but watched the tent flap, where soon there entered a big red man with evidence of combat all over him, followed immediately by Lily and the grandmother, who brought her moaning song in with her. He threw himself onto the buffalo robe of honor on the other side of the fire. That place was slightly raised above the other robes spread around the firepit, and several of his weapons were speared into the packed ground or hanging from the nearest pole.

Contrary to the behavior of every red woman Rhiannon had seen with a man, Winnowed Rice did not rush to serve the warrior.

Lily began to bring him things—a damp wipe, a cup of sassafras, his pipe—speaking to him softly, but he ignored her.

He saw Winnowed Rice in the shadows with the strange woman.

"Husband," she said.

"Wife," he answered, letting Lily help him shed his muddy moccasins.

"Before I return to the woman's hut, I want to introduce your new sister."

Winnowed Rice came forward on her knees, taking up Black Pearl's hand.

The red man regarded her as he took a gourd of water from his younger sister.

"May I ask why your mother is crying?" Winnowed Rice inquired.

"The Cherokee took Owl Person," he answered, letting Lily touch a wet swatch to one of the many superficial wounds that scored his body.

The old woman keened anew at the name of her husband, rocking back and forth. Outside they heard others making the same sound of mourning.

"Fox is forcing him to dance against us."

"Owl Person will never dance against his people!"

"No," the warrior said grimly, a catch in his throat. "My father will die first."

Lily moaned, throwing herself down on Smart-as-a-Beaver's knee. Very gently he stroked her hair.

Winnowed Rice looked down at her fingers, where some of the black grease had gotten under her nails.

Black Pearl watched them, wondering what was going on.

The red man caught her glance, gesturing that she should move closer to him.

Winnowed Rice drew her forward by tugging her hand. "The Cherokee took her prisoner, but she ran away from them."

"What nation are you from?" he asked.

"Her name is Black Pearl," his wife said.

"Black Pearl, where are you from?"

"Far away," she answered softly, making a gesture she hoped conveyed a distance. But it sounded like the word for Yuchi. Beaver scowled; this woman did not appear to be Yuchi.

"She was very young when she was stolen and does not remember her true people," Winnowed Rice said hurriedly.

"Then let her speak to me in Cherokee."

Winnowed Rice was about to say that the Cherokee had cut out her tongue, but her husband reached up and wiped off the red paint his mother had put on the white face.

He looked closer. "What is this in her hair."

"She is an albino. We thought to make her more normal, so we painted her hair. Since she is from the Cherokee, it seems right that she replace your infant sister taken by them so long ago—"

"This is no red woman!"

Black Pearl cringed under his close inspection of her hair. The grandmother had not ceased her low keening throughout this, and now she intensified the noise.

"We thought she might be some kind of spirit. . . ." said Lily.

"This woman is no spirit," said Smart-as-a-Beaver as he threw himself back on the buffalo robe, apparently without curiosity. "Her people fought the Mabilans. They are all pale like that." He took a drink of water. "Weird looking."

Winnowed Rice stood and shared a glance with the man, which he ended with a curt nod. He looked away from her as he took food from a tray the girl offered.

"I do not care if she stays," he said. "What does it matter? The Cherokee will be here at the next moon."

"But we always camp here for the summer moons."

"Fox says the Whippoorwill must never come back to these places again."

"But our grandmothers' grandmother's grandmothers—"

Smart-as-a-Beaver stopped her with a gently raised palm. "Fox says we may join his people if we wish, or we may leave, or he will kill us down to the newest baby born."

"Then there will be no more dog-people."

"So you see why I do not care if this weird woman stays."

Winnowed Rice saw that her husband was suffering despair. He could count. "They were ten times ten more than my men," he said morosely. "There is no way we can fight and win."

"I have no desire to live as a Cherokee," Winnowed Rice remarked.

"I fear the Cherokee," cried Lily, leaning on her mother. "What do the men say?"

Smart-as-a-Beaver shrugged. "We will not be here next moon."

It broke tradition, to leave this camp before midsummer, but there were many camps on the prairies north of here, deep in the country that was so uninhabited the buffalo had no fear of hunters.

Winnowed Rice leaned back. "So we outrun them."

The man said softly, "Beautiful wife, I long to hold you. Go and finish your moon-blood and come back to me clean, so that I may wipe away my tears with your hair."

Black Pearl was surprised to see the huge red man crawl over to his ancient mother and lay his head in her lap, where he moaned in time with her mourning song. She did not miss a beat but kept keening, rocking as she dropped a hand to her son's forehead.

After a while he sat up and took food from the tray.

"So," Winnowed Rice said. "I return to the woman's hut."

He shrugged as if to say, I should hope so. He proceeded to eat, ignoring her as she slipped out of the tent.

Black Pearl made a noise, thinking that the woman had been turned away because she brought a stranger into his lodge.

Lily threw her a warning—stay where you are. But Black Pearl repeated the sound she connected with the departed woman.

"Moon-blood, moon-blood," the girl whispered, leaning close to the white woman. "Do you not understand?"

Black Pearl stared blankly back at her, then cast a worried look toward the flap still moving with the woman's passage.

The girl gestured vaguely at her own crotch, with her back turned from the man so that he could not see. She made a whispered sound, mouthing a phrase, "Moon-blood."

The man spoke behind her. She scooted back to him on her knees, taking the empty bowl and starting to refill, while giving Rhiannon a stern, warning look.

The grandmother droned away while the man spooned the stew into his mouth, watching Black Pearl over the bowl.

She broke and darted toward the flap, but his forceful voice stopped her, even though she did not know what he was saying. She turned and looked at him, repeating the word, "Moon-blood."

The man's nostrils flared, and he leaned involuntarily back.

He made a handsign that clearly said to Black Pearl, "Get out," and she hurried to comply.

The sunlight assaulted her as she searched for Winnowed Rice. Several persons were among the trees and low bushes of the knoll. She could hear the mourners across the way, who were tearing their hair and keening like the Beaver's mother; and she could see others of the bloody veterans being cared for on the hard-packed ground of the central camp. The sachems were rattling their gourds, shaking feather staffs and chanting away in competition with each other.

Nobody paid her the slightest notice. Suddenly she saw the woman's back just vanishing, with the yellow bitch trotting at her heels down the other side of a sloping path that led back to the riverside where she had found Rhiannon. Walking quickly, but not drawing attention by running, she followed Winnowed Rice away from the lodges and down among the willows and cattails. Winnowed Rice was moving with a purpose but not with any speed as she broke from the trees and into the open ground of the riverbank. About ten paces behind her, Black Pearl saw her turn slightly; surely she must know she was being followed. The dog knew, growling over her shoulder.

Black Pearl called, and Winnowed Rice stopped, then turned abruptly, the hawk returned to her eyes. For a moment they stared at each other like that, then the woman indicated with a succinct sign that Rhiannon was not to follow.

"But I have my period, too," Black Pearl said, closing the distance between them.

The woman cocked her head and said the words, "Moonblood?"

"Me, too," Black Pearl nodded, folding her hands over herself in a significant gesture.

Suddenly from the west a wind tossed leaves between them.

"Ah," Winnowed Rice nodded, perhaps speaking to her new sister, perhaps to the wind. "Then, come."

So began Black Pearl's training under the Shawnee Beloved Woman, who considered the wind coming up a good sign since it was an old Shawnee tradition that wind was woman's friend.

Chapter 29

*A roaring flame
has consumed my heart:
I will not live without him.*

—Liadan Laments
Irish
c. A.D. 800

The Whippoorwills followed the ancient trace in a wide northeastern loop, keeping several camps ahead of the Cherokee, who were in strange country that was old familiar hunting territory to the Shawnee. They lived on the buffalo out on the grassy meadows, staying in one place long enough to kill one or two of the great shaggy beasts, eat for a couple of days, and then move on, leaving little more than a grease spot where the creatures fell.

The band roamed into the spring moons, its scouts keeping a rearguard watch on the lurking enemy, its old men making their travel plan only moments before the entire group of warriors, wives, children, and the elderly would pull up the tent stakes, harness dogs to the gihli-gasi with all their household belongings, and set off over the next rise.

It was a game at which the Shawnee were very good players.

Most days through Rose Moon the weather was mild and sunny, with some hot afternoons, some rain, much wind across the rocky barrens, and the bowls of meadows tossed with flowers and nodding grasses. Often they stirred up dust and were forced to stop beneath a grove so they would not give away their position.

It grew hot with late afternoons that bleached the colors out of Black Pearl's eyes. Her face and arms tanned almost like the red people. She kept her hair dark, for although it fooled nobody, the yellow hair would make her feel too different.

Sometimes there were swarms of flies buzzing in the eyes. She took up the Shawnee practice of smearing her skin with bear-grease to keep the flies away. One dark night in Heat Moon she felt something crawling in her blanket-roll and cried out to feel many scratching legs slither across her foot. She fairly flew out of the sack, which she kicked aside so that it fell on the Beaver's bed. He casually picked up her blanket with thumb and forefinger, shaking out from the folds a scorpion as long as his thumb. He laid the hem of the buffalo hide across the scorpion's path and flipped it with a magician's finesse into the fire, where it writhed until it burst into flame.

Black Pearl shivered with revulsion, and her host said slowly so the outlander could understand, "Many small creatures like warm, dark places."

Even little children knew to shake out their blankets. He was too polite to say it, but she looked as though she got the message as an old man tonged the crisp scorpion out of the coals, snapped off the tip of the tail, and ate the creature, sharing with a child at his knees to protect him from future stings.

As the days wore on, she understood more, such as why August was called Thunder Moon. Along the creeks or into the depthless green forest-sea or climbing the highlands, rolling thunder seemed to follow—distanced on the meadows and as near as a shadow up in the hills.

Black Pearl stayed close to the household of Smart-as-a-Beaver, but found the pace killing. She never before minded travel, but when she was pushed at it constantly without enough time to get used to one vista before setting out into another, adventure grew stale. Despite the fact that the women accepted her without question, initiating her into Winnowed Rice's own bird clan, she did not feel her soul content among these rovers.

But she ate well among them and, strong after the softening effects of confinement, danced their droning patterns around the fires, and learned many things like snare making from Winnowed Rice, who was so fast at butchering a rabbit, the old men made up a song about her prowess. The droll Shawnee were entertaining storytellers, who carried as mixed a bag of grave, cynical wisdom and fantastic beliefs as any people she had encountered.

They wasted nothing, using every part of a kill. Longing for something permanent of her own, Black Pearl had dreams of making a harp. She filched rabbit gut for strings but found nothing to make the body until, when they were pulling up stakes yet again, she saw a young mother abandon a cradleboard because her nursling was starting to walk. She waited until the clan moved, then darted into the underbrush where the mother had buried the cradleboard after removing its decoration. Now it was just a long, flat piece of willow wood with a handhold along the top. It had the general shape of a crwth, though it was not hollow. But the wood itself resounded—it had been an old cradleboard from a single unknotted piece of wood, scooped out in a sort of sounding box where the baby had lain.

She shoved it into her travel pack and hurried after the people, and over the next moon began to assemble her instrument, creating much curiosity. She rubbed it with sand to smooth out the grain. Antler tips provided the pegs. She spent many an hour by the fire, listening to the old men's stories, shaping a bridge of bone, but she snapped it in two and had to start all over again on that final, vital part.

One afternoon, as they approached a campsite up a high ravine gained only by single file, the sky darkened with sudden, thick, and low-bellied clouds threatening a downpour before they reached their goal. She saw the men glancing dourly at the sky and heard the women muttering among themselves as the clouds moved in and squat directly as the Whippoorwills approached the pass.

Black Pearl saw that in a storm the narrow defile would turn into a sluice for run-off water where the Whippoorwill Clan must mount the slope.

They milled around as the sky lowered, becoming more agitated, but not unhitching their dogs, who moaned at the tension among the people.

Scouts had seen evidence of the Cherokee too near the last camp—that is why they had jerked the tepees and moved so suddenly before dawn this morning. Now everyone was exhausted, even for Shawnee; they wanted to get to the safe campground before dark.

Winnowed Rice's mother-in-law began a low chant, picked up by the other women, that vibrated the air, stirring the

blood and the feet to dance. Black Pearl was baffled. She had
seen that they loved to dance, but that they would take this
inopportune moment to dance distressed her so that she
pulled at Winnowed Rice's sleeve, trying to make her see
reason.

But Winnowed Rice only grabbed the fretful white woman's hands, calling to the other women, who clasped hands
and formed a slow circle, babies laid aside in cradleboards.
Black Pearl pulled back, not sure what was happening, but
Smart-as-a-Beaver nudged her forward. "Go on—they need
all the women to do it," he said, as he shooed away a
bothersome fly from his face. They had been plagued with
the nasty things since they began climbing the rise.

"Do what?"

Now the women had their arms about each other's waists,
stamping down the high, dry grass in one spot, while the
men, some holding babies or the hands of little children,
formed an audience around the dancing ring. Before long the
rhythm of the chant had caught Black Pearl up in its movement. She found the timing and was even muttering the
chant that hummed like the heart of the mountain around
them.

The circle moved widdershins, then changed direction,
getting rougher as the women intensified the sound, and the
circle drew in tighter on itself. They had raised a small storm
of dust whipped up by the wind, but she could see that the
men and children had turned their backs on the women's
dance ring, while the women speeded up the line, taking a
step every fourth beat toward the center of their circle.

In the western sky a cloud with a black underbelly moved
before the wind along a line that would bring it to this pass.

With each syncopated step the women uttered a single
sound like, "Huunh!" then jerked their circle around another
few steps, then, without warning, Winnowed Rice's mother-
in-law growled a single sharp syllable that brought the winding line to a halt.

Fascinated, Black Pearl watched the solid wall of red flesh
that was men's backs, and the women standing amid dust
devils as they threw their heads back to look at the sky. Then,
without further sign among them, they suddenly turned as a
group, bent over, and flipped up the tails of their fringed and
beaded skirts to expose their round red bottoms.

Black Pearl staggered back, almost falling out of the line as she regarded the collection of full, withered, sagging, plump, and bony rear ends like fleshy fruit under the gathering sky.

From their bent positions the women began a staccato trilling that undulated through every human vocalization, then faded off as the women flapped their skirt tails rapidly against their skin, causing a sound like birds' wings.

They continued this for several minutes, behind the stalwart line of their husbands' averted backs, then they stood as though nothing out of the ordinary had happened while everyone scanned the sky. A few hot drops of rain puckered the dust. The women shook their heads, and all looked uncomfortably at the gaping newcomer, the strange one with the weird hair and colorless eyes, the one Winnowed Rice adopted.

"You did not talk to the wind," Winnowed Rice accused.

Black Pearl was still speechless at what the women had done. The men had not moved, though one little child, a small boy, peeked back only to be pulled by his father and held firmly so that he, too, had his back to the women.

"Do your women not talk to the wind?" Winnowed Rice asked when she saw her friend's confusion.

Black Pearl shook her head as Lily caught up her hand and drew her into the re-forming circle where the humming began again.

"I do not understand," Black Pearl said to Winnowed Rice as they started the one, two, three, step again.

As though speaking to a small child, Winnowed Rice said, "We are telling the wind to blow that cloud away."

A few more drops plopped into the dust at her feet, but the women ignored them and brought their circle around, pulling the white woman along, catching her up in the chant. Flip, and the skirts went over again, and the trilling, flapping sounds rattled around her as she felt her skin exposed.

What a funny thing to do, she thought, biting back her humor so that it would not show and hurt anyone's feelings, and expecting to feel the raindrops at any moment on her bare skin.

But the rain did not come.

After this round the mother-in-law observed the sky and pronounced their effort successful.

Black Pearl straightened her leather dress and looked up; it did seem more windy than when they had started. The pregnant cloud veered off, already spilling its burden on another slope. The men cheered, the children ran around in circles and clapped, the dogs barked from their harnesses, and the women looked at one another with shy pride, accepting their men's accolades.

"We must hurry," said Winnowed Rice, eyeing the sky, which looked as though the women had won the Whippoorwill Clan only a brief respite from flood.

With speed unimaginable for so large a group of mixed individuals, the Shawnee hurried up the narrow pass one at a time, barely squeezing the overloaded gihli-gasi through the most narrow points, soon arriving in the hidden meadow in a cleft of the mountains where a huge overhang marked by smoke of many past campfires offered shelter to the whole band, every man, woman, and child, plus dogs, cargo, and all.

"It always works," Winnowed Rice said later to Black Pearl, who asked about the dance. The mother-in-law was happy to tell the story of winds and women around their snug campfire protected from the all-night downpour.

Everyone had eaten, the little children were bedded down, and now was the time for storytelling. Winnowed Rice sprinkled a small pinch of nipowoc on the coals and leaned against the Beaver. Black Pearl sat beguiled by the old woman who began in words and handsign: "Long ago when the moon and the sun were still innocent and the middle earth as we know it now was only a dream, everything was peaceful. The moon had his part of the sky and his sister, whom we now call Old Red, because she is no longer the girl she was in those days—she had her part of the sky. They were young, merely children playing in the starry meadows.

"But the moon looked upon his sister as a man looks upon a woman, and he began to chase her around and around even though she told him to stop. He would not, and soon he caught her and threw her down to spread out her legs and find her pearls. Ancient Red had pearls all right, and the moon her brother was a happy man for a short, sweet time until she kicked him away and in fury ran to the other side of the sky.

"Ancient Red brooded over the rape as her belly grew. She swore she would never forgive her brother, not because she did not like to play with him, but because he had taken her pearls without permission. Now she was fat with a child and the moon was ashamed, so he hid from her. But soon Ancient

Red gave birth to a daughter, earth, which we live on to this day with Ancient Red's benevolent light shining down on us, her children.

"The moon moved closer to play some more now that his sister was slim again. But she spat on him and ran away, him hot on her heels around and around the sky-meadow. But giving birth had made Ancient Red smarter and stronger and hotter and more angry with her brother for tricking her, so she flared at him and singed his face to ashes, burning his eyebrows and scalp lock off and making blisters that left ugly scars.

"Ancient Red gave all her attention to her child, the earth, and so it is to this day, that the sun loves the earth and hates the moon, even though he still keeps chasing her around.

"As much as she loves the earth, Ancient Red cannot be here with us because of her heat but must shine equally on all, even her wicked brother, so she sent the wind to be nursemaid to the earth to help when help was needed, and she said, 'Go and listen only to women when they call you, because men cannot be trusted, but the women will never ask in vain.'

"But," the old woman concluded as the fire died down and sent sparks up to the cave roof, "because of the male trickery of the moon, the wind, who is also a male, was forbidden ever to look upon a naked woman. The wind heard Ancient Red and obeyed, and to this day he still befriends women, but..."

All the eyes of the Whippoorwill Clan were wide with the old woman's melodious words, which all except one among them had heard many times before. Black Pearl leaned with the others to hear the end of the story.

"But, if he sees a naked woman, wind must move along because he would never disobey the command of Ancient Red."

The men politely beat upon the cave walls with sticks, and the women trilled softly in approval of the telling.

The mother-in-law told many stories over the next moon of nights, and Black Pearl increased her understanding of the people's language. They kept ahead of the Cherokee through Heat Moon. The Shawnee knew many more secret places, the band having traveled these parts for a thousand seasons. They often found remains of old campgrounds with blazed trees, which the eldest among them could remember mark-

ing as children. They passed high, sacred, stony places where
the Shawnee put their dead on scaffolds adorned with narrow
woven strips of cloth made from fibrous plants they showed
Black Pearl how to soak and pound, and which were as strong
and pliant as flax or silk. She learned to use their small
hand-looms and wished they would settle down so she could
teach them how to make the broadloom.

But they stayed in no camp more than three days. Once on
a far purple ridge they saw smoke their scouts assured them
was Cherokee. The clan's three magicians ceased their chanting
only to sleep, one of them always at it, even on the trail,
making magic, erasing signs, doubling back to spy on the
enemy and throw prayer-formulas in his direction.

They returned in their feathers and black paint to tell of
the damage their magic inflicted upon the enemy, who still
held Owl Person alive and tied up. Each night, the Shawnee
spies said, Fox would have Owl Person brought before him as
he sat smoking with his counselors and his Mabilan allies.

The mother-in-law groaned and rocked herself as the report continued concerning her hostage husband. Lily laid
her head in her mother's lap, both whimpering softly as the
spy continued.

"Each night Fox speaks to Owl Person. They discuss the
various degrees of the male lodge."

Cherokee and Shawnee shared many customs. The Whippoorwill knew that even though Fox was the stronger warrior,
none of his sachems were as powerful as Owl Person, who
had the highest lodge degree of any red man known to be
living south of Iroquois territory. Most of all Fox wanted to
have the secrets of those advanced degrees, but so far Owl
Person held out, not giving away any of what Fox wanted to
know.

"Owl Person gave Fox a nickname, which infuriates him—
Little Red Fox." As a more advanced lodge-brother, Owl
Person could give nicknames to other lodge members. He
could play tricks on him, the idea being to humiliate the
junior brother. The reporter added that Fox was not well but
sat huddled under a blanket like an old haggard man.

"What is ailing him?" someone asked.

"He moves slowly, sometimes with a look of pain on his
face, and sometimes his men must help him. The mediciners
and conjurers are fussing around him all the time."

"Ahhh," said Smart-as-a-Beaver and others around the fire, because they recognized the sign of magic.

"Hee-hee," cackled Owl Person's wife, "my husband is sucking his soul. He gave that young fighting man the one thing a warrior does not want—the old-bone!"

This pleased the Whippoorwills, because they prided themselves on being the finest of magicians. In the end Fox would loose his battle against them even if he killed every Whippoorwill. He would lose because the Whippoorwill sachem had given him a curse in his bones. There was no hope for him.

"Now Fox has ordered Owl Person to take away the curse, because tonight our shaman admitted that he is the cause of Fox's pain." The reporter looked up, catching individual glances among the Shawnee, and cried triumphantly, "Tonight I saw Fox's knees and elbows swollen like an old man!"

"He did this because he is bargaining," said the Beaver, and his counselors nodded around him on their buffalo hides.

"His counselors say they can find more powerful magic to counter Owl Person. It is a matter of face, now, of who can make the most powerful magic."

"What a fool!" someone exclaimed.

"He does not realize what he is dealing with," a woman said.

But one night when the band was still in the sheltered valley under the rock overhang, a spy returned—one of Winnowed Rice and the Beaver's grown sons—with a report nobody wanted to hear, but which none could ignore.

"They have begun to use the fire to get Owl Person to change the curse," the spy said, still shaking from what he saw.

The mother-in-law keened in earnest now and tore at her hair, knowing what would follow.

"Fox's men forced him to hold coals in his hand."

The young warrior said the Cherokee knew where the Whippoorwill were camped. Sure enough, the next morning, when the Whippoorwill scouts looked out over their watchtowers of tall boulders guarding the narrow pass, they saw down on the grassy place where the women danced the wind the many-fired encampment, complete with camp followers, yellow dogs, and portable bent-willow lodges thrown up overnight.

Owl Person was tied to a stake, nearly dead, suffering

burns and cuts all over his naked body. But he was singing, far beyond pain. Mixed with his death song were little verses he composed against the Cherokee chief, who stayed by the main fire surrounded by his sachems and his doctors.

"Little Red Fox caught a bird on a mountain," Owl Person called the derisive nickname so loudly his people could hear.

"He is never going to dance against his people," Fox's eldest counselor said. "Kill him to shut him up."

"You lose face before him," another whispered.

"Kill him, kill him."

Fox did not respond but sat stiffly in his robe, in full war-paint, frowning at the old man dying on the torture pole.

Up on the ridge the Shawnee women extinguished the fire.

The Shawnee men prepared to fight, their women helping them to dress and paint their faces for their last battle, beaded-sole moccasins on their feet to guide them into the western land of the sun, where they would go in death.

The little boys smeared mud on each other's faces and ranged themselves along the ridge at the command of the clan's oldest man, an ivory remnant of leather and bone who might have gone to sleep in the last snow if the tribe had been hungry. It had been a bountiful year, however, and now this male crone assumed the tutoring of the baby males.

To Black Pearl it was a dream. Having no warrior to assist, she wandered the camp, watching the strangely silent Shawnee. Not even the smallest baby cried. All the dogs laid their muzzles in the dust and sighed heavily. Their ears would prick and their heads jerk up when a Cherokee dog barked below. Then the men stood one by one and walked out into the sunshine and down the narrow path, disappearing into the laurel that clung to the rocks. The women painted their faces with soot. Now babies and dogs fussed and were hushed or fed a strip of jerky to chew on.

Below, they heard the first shouts, the war cries, then screams, more screams in Cherokee than Shawnee.

The white woman followed the defile between the scrub and rocks to a point that looked out on the grassy slope below.

Winnowed Rice found her on the ledge, watching the Beaver fall trying to free Owl Person from the stake where he had been tied, each portion of the killing field writhing with human movement in feathers and paint, weapons flying and hauled back, men floundering, catching each other in deadly embrace, red paint, so much red paint flying but it was not paint, she knew.

Black Pearl was glad she was nearsighted and did not see details, because hearing the death cries was enough.

Winnowed Rice had excellent eyesight and could see at that moment Smart-as-a-Beaver get back to his knees and attack two screaming Cherokee.

"They are killing him now," she said softly, face tear-streaked but smiling because she saw he died honorably. "He is taking both with him," she said, because she knew Black Pearl did not have good far sight.

"Which one is Fox?"

Winnowed Rice pointed to one figure standing aside from the general blur, a huge buffalo skin around his shoulders, thigh-high white fringed moccasins, and a breechclout made of a full wolf skin, his scalp lock tasseled with a multitude of feathers and his face and chest marked with a distinctive red design even Black Pearl could see.

The Cherokee and Mabilans still boiled up from the lower slope, while the Shawnee had chosen their ground where the women danced and went no farther, taking on all comers. Many Cherokee and Mabilans laid around the Shawnee, who seemed to have no concept of strategy but simply took their ground and held it. Soon there were only a few Shawnee still standing. No grass could be seen from Black Pearl's position above the battle. Bodies piled up two and three deep, and still a few Shawnee men continued to enjoin the enemy. Now so many Mabilans and Cherokee had entered the meadow there was nobody for them to fight, and they helped their brothers, a tide of red flesh washing over the last Shawnee.

Black Pearl watched the Cherokee drag themselves from the stew of bloodied bodies, limping back to the tree line, where fully half of the force fell to the ground nursing wounds. Shawnee were still screaming down there.

The Shawnee women moved out of the camp and stood near the edge of the highest ridge among the low trees, keening to the wind. Cherokee no longer engaged in the fight had already glanced up at them.

"The river saved you for another death, Black Pearl," Winnowed Rice said behind her, adding that it would not be a pretty one. "Of course they might take you for your oddity, your sun-hair, if you wash out the dye." Of if she was quick about it, she might be able to escape from this pinnacle by climbing down the precarious backside. "You can go back to your people."

Black Pearl laughed ironically; for the first time she told Winnowed Rice why she had been in the river. "According to my tradition," she said, using handsign and speaking Shawnee words when she knew one, but mostly speaking her own language, "I committed a mortal sin by trying to kill myself."

How much of this Winnowed Rice understood, Rhiannon did not know. "It seems only proper now that my desire to die will be fulfilled," Black Pearl concluded, "but it is a tragedy that all these beautiful children and fine women have to go, too."

"It is the way," Beloved Woman replied as she stared down at the Cherokee, one of whom was pointing this way. Arrayed among the trees and stone, the women were keening their mourning song; some were tearing at their hair and clothing. One young bride had gashed her arms as the death song mounted.

"Now the Cherokee are taking scalps," Winnowed Rice said. She removed her knife and started to slash the back of her hand.

"Wait—"

Winnowed Rice looked trancelike with the screams of the dying behind them.

"Even I can see the Cherokee have gotten what they gave. . . ."

Winnowed Rice regarded the battlefield. "Our men are the best. They lose only if outnumbered."

"See how many Cherokee fell beside the Shawnee?" Black Pearl ventured. "Perhaps a few more Shawnee warriors could make a difference." She looked around—how many of those women back there rending their clothes were as skillful with a knife as she knew Beloved Woman to be?

Winnowed Rice understood what Black Pearl was saying. "Yes," she said, "that is the way! We are doomed anyway—even if they do not kill us, without our hunters, we cannot last the winter." She called all the women who would listen and began admonishing them as she ran back up the sloping path. "Take up your husband's reserve weapons. Paint your faces and put on the men's honor shirts—we must die anyway this day, we may as well share the honor with our husbands."

Some of the women were too far into mourning to listen—their faces were dripping blood, their hair hacked off, their children abandoned and crying at their ankles. But others heard their Beloved Woman: "See how the Cherokee sink to their knees—they are worn out killing our men. They think there is nobody else to oppose them," Winnowed Rice said, moving among the wives and mothers, their children clinging to their legs.

"But there is us!" she said quietly but triumphantly, and could see the spark move among the younger women. "After they rest, they will be coming up here. . . ."

"We must not let them rest," said the young wife who had begun the mourning song. She was the first to run back to the camp, where she tossed through bundles to find her husband's extra weapons and honor shirt, and wiggled into it.

Hysterical with grief and expecting Cherokee wrath, the women shouted their approval as one voice and fell without instruction to their preparations.

Meanwhile, down the slope, the Cherokee had suffered for their victory. At the edge of the verge, Winnowed Rice counted the enemy. The ones who were not wounded were busy helping the others or setting up camp.

Like all the red nations, the Cherokee welcomed sunset at the end of a day's battle, because nobody in his right mind would fight at night when the medicine was wrong for the spirit's passage to the land of the dead.

The women regrouped with their men's knives and bows. Some caught up their own smaller bows, used on rabbits and birds. Even the children were filled with the spirit of what they were going to do. They were filled with the excitement of it, like a great dance for which they had been preparing all their lives. Each one called to another for help with this shirt, with the red paint, with the youngest babies, whom they kissed good-bye and handed to the oldest grandmother, watching from an honored spot where she had spread a buffalo robe. Five babies wiggled on the fur beside her twisted old bones, and she grinned and called at what the young women were doing.

"Yes, yes," she muttered, clapping her hands, tweaking one baby here and pinching another there, "see what your brave mamas are doing little one—these are Shawnee women you see going to war. These are Shawnee!"

The little boys with small mud-painted faces watched their mothers become warriors. Their old mentor wagged his head back and forth but was smiling to the gums.

The Cherokee victors seemed to be biding their time about coming up here. They knew there was no place for the Shawnee women to run.

Sunset stained the sky the color of late persimmons, and the enemy's woodsmoke wafted up as one by one the Shawnee women spoke to a friend, a sister, a mother. Black Pearl was swept up with them, helping with face paint and the war-turbans. She felt the hysteria of fear and excitement coursing through her veins. Time to die, time to die, her pounding blood seemed to say. She would close the circle begun on the cliff. She smeared red paint on her arms and face and grabbed her knife, ready to take a few Cherokee with her. She chose Fox to kill. He would be hers.

"Come along, now," the crone croaked to the older children, who sat tear-streaked or who still clung to their mothers. They ranged in ages from toddlers to a twelve-year-old girl who would not let go of her mother's leg.

"Go along and sing songs about this day," the mother said, trying to shake off the child.

"I want to fight, too, let me fight, too," she begged, but the mother leaned, said something to her, then disentangled her fingers and pointed toward the old woman.

The boy-children tagged along behind the women, lingering on the ridge, pushing at each other and whispering.

Finally more than thirty women stood in the slanting shadows, flint knives in their hands, their faces covered, their eyes bright, their cheeks bloody from the mourning gashes they had slashed with their cooking knives.

"We will fight them," Winnowed Rice began a chant.

"We will kill them," someone counterpointed, and Black Pearl joined the chant. She fumbled in her small bundle of personal things and found the slim iron weaving knife she had carried in a dainty sheath at her waist the day she jumped from the cliff.

"We will fight them and kill them, the enemy is a bird and we are the hawk," Winnowed Rice continued the war chant the men danced before a battle. Behind her even now the old man was shuffling the dance, chanting the ancient words that sounded red.

"I will have songs to sing to you," the crone told the babies, "I will have this great story to tell you, and you will tell it to your children's children's children, how your mothers took up the war-paint against the Cherokee. You will sing how your mothers and your fathers died, and you will be proud!"

The women formed two concentric circles with the old man at the center and began working themselves into a battle frenzy as did their men, winding around and around until their combined voices were strong enough for the enemy down on the meadow to look up from cleaning their weapons and dressing their wounds, one by one, wondering where the war chant was coming from.

One of the babies started screaming, and his mother scooped him up, still dancing in the war-circle, without breaking her stride, and gave him her breast.

"Oh, it is a lucky warrior whose mother feeds him the milk of battle!" cried the crone, clapping her hands and giving the babies little dabs of prepared hickory nut meat mashed with blood. The babies kicked on their pallet. The young girl who wanted to fight grabbed the suckling babe, or his mother in her trance would have taken him to the battlefield with the other women who began to file down the slope around the sentinel boulders of their camp and onto the killing ground where their husbands, sons, and brothers lay bleeding, scalpless, in the dirt.

Others who were good with their own bows ringed the upslope behind the boulders, nocking arrows their husbands had sung over while hardening the hickory shafts in winter fires.

They were Shawnee arrows full of magic and power; they would find their targets no matter whose hand sent them.

The Cherokee were counting their scalps and casualties and patching their many wounds when they looked up in amazement to see what appeared to be a reserve Shawnee force boiling down from the plateau in full battle array—weapons and war-paint and echoing shouts that rang off the stone face of the mountains.

At first the Cherokee were threatened to see a fresh force coming at them. They grabbed weapons, some struggling to rise, suffering wounds inflicted by the Shawnee men.

Then the arrows started raining down on the unprepared Cherokee braves. Several fell dead or mortally wounded, but it was not until one fierce old woman threw herself screaming on a warrior and drew blood that the Cherokee started fighting back.

"That is for Owl Person whom you unfairly murdered," the

sachem's wife raged at the warrior, striking again. Fox came to his man's aid by grabbing the woman and slitting her throat.

Black Pearl stabbed with the iron knife—just walked up to one of the startled warriors and started slashing. It was Fox she confronted with the gory knife in her slick hand, and she lunged without aim. They rolled together, his robe flapping, wrestling for the blade, which she was about to grasp when he stepped on her wrist and sat on her, kicking her knife away from them both. She fought with her hair wildly flying, but he caught it up in his hand and yanked back, looking at the crazed warrior who attacked him. His surprise loosened his grip so that she struggled free and bit him, then tried to crawl away. He grabbed her ankles and dragged her back, flipping her over and falling with a grunt to pin her shoulders to the dust.

For a brief moment they were eye to eye. His were dark as night, close enough for her to see her reflection there.

Hers, steamy silver, watched him lean closer.

Later, when she recalled that moment when she first knew Fox of the Cherokee, she would think of the shock that coursed through her. It was like the small spark of touching someone wearing wool. She knew he had been surprised by it, too. In his bewilderment, and as she would find out later, his pain, the man searched her eyes as she searched his. They breathed together, frozen in that glance. He pulled her hair from her face, brushing the flesh of her temple with his wrist. He blinked because he felt her coolness against his inflamed wrist joint. He stood quickly above her, looking at the hand that touched her as though she had left a stain only he could see. She made a sudden move. He grabbed her weaving knife, inspected it, then walked around her, their eyes locked as she sat up, threw her hair back, and felt for broken bones.

Fox uttered a formal shout that ordered his warriors to cease fighting. "Hold that woman there—" he called to a warrior who was about to kill Winnowed Rice.

"Look! These are women," he cried, his painted buffalo robe sliding from his shoulders as he dragged another brave from a bloody woman. "There is no honor for us in killing them!"

Gradually the warriors shook off their battle trance and observed that their individual opponents were indeed females in Shawnee war shirts and paint. One Cherokee ripped the baggy, borrowed honor shirt from the woman who had drawn his blood. He stepped back, spitting off to the side, and threw his knife polluted by woman's blood to the dust.

"Are you women crazy?" Fox demanded. One woman lunged at him, but he did not hurt her, only caught her around the neck to hold her struggling while his men laughed nervously around him.

Black Pearl saw it was Lily under the war-paint, and she held her breath thinking he would kill the girl.

But he did not. He pushed her against a young brave, who held another woman Fox recognized.

"You—you are wife to Smart-as-a-Beaver."

Winnowed Rice nodded, escaping from the warrior who had both hands full with the young wife, standing up to Fox with defiance in her eye.

"Why are you bringing dishonor to good fighting men?"

"You killed all our men. We defend their honor."

The brave got a good hold on the young wife, twisting her arm up at her back so that she cried out. He moved behind Winnowed Rice and caught her arm to pin her in the same way, because she looked as though she might attack the chief.

Fox placed his arms across his chest, staring at her as though he had no response. He reached out and wiped his thumb across the paint below her eye. "Such women cannot be killed, but what am I to do with you?"

Winnowed Rice lifted her chin and narrowed her eyes at her husband's old enemy. "Give me a knife, and I will show you."

"Hear that?" he asked the man who pinned Winnowed Rice. As he talked, Fox strolled among his warriors and the women they held, rubbing his elbow. He walked slowly, even through he was a beautifully muscled man without apparent wounds, favoring one leg.

"I will tell you what will happen," Fox said with a glance up at the ridge, where the rest of the Whippoorwill Band stood watching—the ancient grandmother and all the children.

"You fought more bravely than your men and you are well rid of them. Come and become Cherokee, for you have made yourselves honorable enough to become one with the Principal People."

His braves agreed that this was a most generous offer,

which surely these headstrong Shawnee would do well to consider.

"Well, what do you say?" he asked Winnowed Rice, who was waiting for him to return to striking range.

He lifted his hands and called out, "All you Shawnee up there—grandmother, bring the babies. Come, you will not be hurt. Your daughters' daughters have done you proud—come now and join the Cherokee!"

"We came out here to die, Little Red Fox, not to crawl into the den of the serpent."

She caught him in the right eye with a well-directed stream of spittle. The man holding her twisted her arm back so that she felt the bones grind. Spittle, second only to blood in power, carried huge scorn when delivered in this manner, especially from the mouth of a woman.

"And I am in my moon-blood!" she cried at him, which was a lie, but she said it to pile further insult upon him.

He was a brave man; none saw him shrink back under the barrage of pollution. His magic men at the sidelines muttered chants for his continued bravery, while the chief of the Cherokee attempted to stare this immodest Shawnee female down.

Fox lifted one of Winnowed Rice's braids and carefully wiped her spit from his face, then threw it back at her. "Let her go."

The warrior stepped back and wiped his hands in the dust.

Fox retrieved his knife and turned to leave. "Do any of you wish to come with me?" he called to the women and the children up on the ridge. He ended the sweep of his gaze by staring directly at Black Pearl, who felt her heart leap and her stomach fall.

His men joined him, straggling and limping forward, receding like a tide from the unyielding Shawnee slabs of them, getting out of the way of women who must surely be possessed with bad spirits.

But the Shawnee only bunched up, glaring, still bloody and fierce in the smeared paint. Several threw curses; all spit on the footprints made by the Cherokee.

The Cherokee said formulas to ward off the evil eye, which everyone knew the Shawnee had, saying to each other that it was a good thing these wild, dangerous women had not taken Fox's offer. Imagine trying to live with such a female, one said to another as he staunched blood on his bicep.

This was such bad luck, the Cherokee and Muskogeans had decided without conferring, that they did not even want to camp in this place where women fought like men.

"With so many children you will not make it through the coming winter," Fox called over his shoulder. "Break their weapons—" he remembered to shout, and his men complied.

"Who will hunt for you foolish women?" Fox taunted as he limped eastward over the meadow. His laugh echoed off the stone. His men took courage from him and yelled imprecations back upon the silent Shawnee women.

Finally Black Pearl relaxed her body, which still seemed to be vibrating from the encounter. "What will you do now?" she asked Winnowed Rice.

The Beloved Woman of the Shawnee was shaking.

"Who will hunt for all your people?" Black Pearl insisted.

Behind them were more than sixty individuals, among them two old men who had somehow survived the battle, a gaggle of children, and the disheveled, trembling army of women, who were gradually waking up to their situation. Some turned to throw themselves on the bodies that littered the trampled yellow flowers of the meadow. Some were beginning to cry, the children first when they saw their fathers with bloody heads all stuck with dirt and twigs.

The women threw stones to chase off the dogs licking at the corpses. The Shawnee practiced exposure of their dead, sewing them into robes, placing them on scaffolds in sacred groves along their migration routes with the old and desiccated dead—as they swung by, they would gather the bones and inter them every thirty moons.

Black Pearl helped bring down the buffalo robes and paints for the grim task and brought her own travel pack with the unfinished harp and her few possessions along with the full buffalo robe the Beaver had given her from the last kill. She sought out Winnowed Rice, who was stitching the Beaver's torn body into his shroud.

"You will never make it alone," Black Pearl said.

Winnowed Rice, her face streaked with blood and dust made muddy by tears, looked up, alarmed by the sound she heard in Black Pearl's voice. She saw that her friend had her belongings at her feet.

"A little way up the Duck River where you dragged me out of the water is the camp of the white tribe," Black Pearl said, trying to make herself clear. "They have many men, few women. I think they will welcome you."

Winnowed Rice stared at her. "So Smart-as-a-Beaver was right about you. You are not a spirit-woman after all."

Black Pearl shrugged.

"I was hoping you were a spirit-woman," Winnowed Rice said with a wry smile. "I have never met a spirit before."

"Sorry, just a human woman like you."

"The white strangers who fought the Mabilans?"

"They will take you in."

"That mountain is only a little way from here."

Black Pearl saw that she did not have to convince the Beloved Woman of anything. "There is a man among them...."

Winnowed Rice cocked her head, listening to anything at this point as her people mourned around her. The little children were all crying for their fathers. From many throats the mourning drone had begun.

"His name is Rhys, a good man whose wife left him."

"Ahh..." Winnowed Rice said, beginning to understand. Black Pearl had never mentioned anything about her former life.

"He deserves a better woman," she continued as she righted her clothing and smoothed back her mysterious hair. "Perhaps you are she." Black Pearl stepped back lightly on her feet as though getting ready to run somewhere.

"Surely you will come with us."

Black Pearl hefted the travel pack. "I am dead there." She took a step toward the path where the Cherokee had gone.

"You are not going with the Cherokee!"

Black Pearl turned but continued walking backwards, skipping now and then to keep from stumbling. "That warrior I almost killed—I must follow him. I do not know why."

She waved and trotted toward the eastern forest, staying cautiously behind them, thinking about what she had seen in the warrior's eyes.

The Cherokee were arrogant. They were not taking any precautions to hide their trail. Blood splattered some of the moccasin prints. Bushes were broken, twigs bent aside through a cedar grove where hands had reached out to take incense twigs. Farther along the way she found a broken atlatl with the carved and polished weight still attached, a greenish piece of soapstone about a hand long and a knuckle wide, expertly notched with a dozen grooves for bindings that held it to the shaft. The weight had been hollowed on its reverse side to lay along the cane—a beautiful piece of workmanship she could not believe anyone willingly threw away. She had seen the other red people working this soft stone, which reminded her of weaving weights. If she was settled in one place, she could make a loom with weight stones carved from this material.

The grass carpet of a meadow bent by unceasing western winds was marked with the slash of the Cherokee passage, many men in a staggered line, darkening blood smeared here and there on the young green stems. More than one of the war party was tearing off bunches of the grass, then down the path tossing the dressing aside, crushed and bloodied.

Shawnee gihli-gasi did not cut as wide and untidy a swath as these tired warriors carrying their dead.

From her light pack she took Shawnee insect repellent and smeared its piney essence into her skin as the flies came out with little whispers and silent stings.

Now she could hear singing up ahead, more chanted dirge than tune, and soon afterwards she smelled woodsmoke on a breeze coming out of the northeast. Behind her almost all the sanguine light had drained from the western sky—ahead the heavens were deepening blue to purple.

Bats swooped overhead.

A thin layer of sky near the western horizon was the color of blood. Ahead was darkness except for the wink of several stars above, and below, yellow campfires between the black pillars of tree trunks.

It was getting cold. She drew the supple buffalo hide around her shoulders, thinking about the man and how to approach him. She did not doubt that some of his companions would kill her outright if she walked suddenly upon them. That would lose them face they were capable of making her pay for. From intimacy with the Shawnee, she knew she must dazzle them so that she could go directly into Fox's presence, rather than through subordinates.

Black Pearl found her spot on a flat lichen-coated boulder in a clearing among young cedar trees, drew the unfinished harp from her pack, and in the last light fitted the atlatl weight under the strings. She tightened the deer-horn pegs, and the tension held the notched stone against the old wood that had served as a cradleboard. When she had first seen the carved green stone she knew it would work as a bridge. She plucked the gut-strings experimentally.

Throughout this twilight time she heard the Cherokee over the next rise. Their masculine voices rose on the upping breeze. They were cooking meat now. A scout must have returned with fresh kill because it smelled like venison. Black Pearl's mouth watered. When was the last time she ate? It seemed as though a thousand years had passed since the battle.

When she had the strings tuned, she began to play.

Chapter 30

. . .and those that had not fled,
were braver than were wise.

—by Taliesin
Welsh
c. A.D. 500

"The woman knows her scripture," said Wyn the morning Rhiannon left, for it was he who found the harp dangling from the oak branch, making its own soft song on the breeze.

Rhys had just come downstairs with a whimpering baby to ask if anyone had seen his wife, when Wyn called to tell everyone in the Big House to come outside. They pushed out, bowls of corn porridge in their hands, to gawk at it.

"'We hanged our harps upon the willows in the midst thereof,'" Wyn quoted his beloved Psalms from memory. "'They that wasted us required of us mirth, saying, Sing us one of the songs of Zion. But how shall we sing the Lord's song in a strange land?'" He unhitched the harp and put it into Rhys's hands. "I think she was trying to tell us something."

He looked around at the huge spread of oak just coming into new leaf, small red velvet curls on gray branches. "This was as close as she could come to a willow." They had cut down all the willow for caning and a hundred other uses. "I blame myself," Wyn added morosely. "I should have known something was wrong."

Rhys clutched the harp and stumbled back to the house, leaving Cari at Yngvild's right breast while her own child nursed the other. She looked like a ruddy-cheeked earth goddess with her arms full of plump babies.

438

Back in the kitchen Gwen said, "She always was moody, likes to be alone."

"Somehow I do not think she will be back," Mary said, ladling a bowl of corn porridge for the abbot, who took it gratefully.

"We planned to christen the babe today," Wyn said around a mouthful of the honey-sweetened broth almost as good as oats.

"Then we still must," Teleri replied.

Wyn continued eating until he scraped the bowl. He lived at the llan, but more often than not he ate here, complaining of the brothers' cooking. Others around him ate in silence, each with an opinion about the Lady Rhiannon.

"Maybe she was captured," Wil said.

Wyn scowled. "Did she take anything?"

"The clothes on her back," Teleri said, gathering the bowls.

There was no trace of her. The only evidence she might have left were footprints across the edge of the plowed field, but the ground was so disturbed by so many prints, none would notice. When a couple of the men went down to fish for trout in their moat, they found her blue mantle snagged in the deep green water below the cliff. They searched the rocky riverbank but found no bloodied remains, and finally, giving up and postponing their fishing, they took the mantle back. Teleri confirmed that it had been Rhiannon's. It was she who told Rhys, who clutched the damp silk in one hand as though to convince himself that it was hers.

By evening most were thinking Rhiannon had jumped, a heinous sin none wanted to pin on her. So they said she might have been sleepwalking, but nobody remembered her up at night. Gwen insisted that her aunt was a restless pacer. When not at the loom pacing with the weaving, she would in her long stride roam the perimeters of the plateau. "Remember how she used to pace the ship, walking around and around the deck?"

But the cynics said she purposefully jumped, expecting to die on the rocks. She did not realize that while she had a baby and recovered, the moat had been opened as Madoc ordered, connecting the two forks of the river below the spot where she stepped off. No other trace of her was found, so they assumed she was dragged downstream.

Rhys stayed in the loft all that day. The women left him alone and worked in the field, which everyone hoped to finish that afternoon, ready for John's seeds that day. Everyone would help with the planting—it would be another long day.

Hunters returned before sunset laden with game, which they roasted over a pit fire outside, and as the evening progressed, their mood became festive, celebrating the completion of the field. John prayed for a prosperous planting. The brothers joined the festivities, and by moonrise they were devouring the spoils of the hunt.

Rhys came down and without a word about Rhiannon began to pluck the harp strings. Teleri offered him food, but he would not eat, and he would not stop playing sad old songs even when the fire died to sputtering coals and people began to drift away.

Late into the night he played the harp but did not sing.

It rained the next day, a slow shower that caused John and Wyn to sing songs of thanksgiving because they could not but think that their prayer was answered with this blessing upon their newly planted field. It was warm and did not pound the earth, but soaked in slowly, then cleared to a brilliantly sunny afternoon with pink clouds piled up on the western sky and even a rainbow that blazed suddenly before the sun finally set fire to the edges of a long bank of western cloud.

They started building the chapel the next day, halfway between the Big House and the monk's pavilion.

Gwen appointed herself keeper of the dragon flag, ringing it up of a morning, hauling it in at night and when it rained. When it was not flying, she kept it draped on the wall behind the dovecotes at the other end of the loft, where Culhwch and Olwen's nestlings grew fat on worms she hand-fed them, making sure they saw the great red dragon that would be their homing sign, as it was for their mother, who cooed and flapped nearby over a new batch of eggs. Gwen was training the fledglings daily; already they flew between the monk's pavilion and the Big House.

She watched for old Culhwch's return. If the bird made it south to the *Horn*, the plan was to send him back with the message of the arglwydd's arrival. With the dragon flying over the house, Gwen figured that Culhwch would have no trouble winging his way back here, and she watched for him daily.

Others had been more skeptical, what with all the wild pigeons who might lure the old flyer away from human beings, but John believed the bird's instinct to mate for life would win out over local temptations. But Culhwch also had to run the gauntlet of hunting birds, not the least of which was Arrow-Eye.

Gwen continued to train the eagle. She hoped to bond him with the sight of the dragon pennant, though hunting birds were usually imprinted on the trainer rather than on an object.

For the first few days after Rhiannon disappeared, Gwen expected to see her aunt striding in her long-legged slouch up the approach to the Big House, breathless with the story of adventure. Gwen would be at work at one of several tasks—especially weaving—and would suddenly look up expectantly.

Rhiannon's baby was the most content of infants. Yngvild kept her fat and happy, but she slept on her tad's pallet and woke to play with him every morning. She was starting to sing with him, it seemed, though Gwen knew the baby was too young for that. But Rhys made it sound as though they were singing together.

After a while Gwen ceased expecting Rhiannon. Nobody mentioned her out of respect for Rhys's feelings. He never expressed anything except quiet, playful delight with the baby. But there was a change in him noticed by those who knew him best. It could best be heard in his music, especially when he played the great harp. He withdrew even further into himself, speaking now only to sing. Away from her husband's hearing, people might softly speak of her, seldom mentioning her name. Bets were made, but the odds were long, and there was no real doubt that she was gone for good. Some even breathed easier and began watching for the return of the arglwydd from the south.

Several mornings later Father John joyously entered into the Big House, calling for everyone to come out and look. The sailors, who bunked down in one corner of the kitchen, were playing a gambling game with stones. They did not look up as the monk entered, excitedly telling all that the field had sprouted. He let Mary serve him breakfast of boiled corn and honey.

Mary had made a crock of the red-root tea. A recent trade with the Yuchis was a bushel basket of the dried root for a shovel scoop, but Mary was learning to gather it and other herbs so they would not have to rely on trade.

"Oat sprouts as tall as my thumb," John exclaimed, gesturing with big flat fingers permanently stained with the brown of earth, the cuffs of his cassock rolled back to expose his sunburned arms. "And weeds," John added when he had had a gulp of tea. "Time to start hoeing."

Teleri groaned as she entered the kitchen from upstairs. "I still have blisters from planting." Since Rhiannon was gone, she had moved her and Madoc's bed and belongings upstairs in the weaving area between two rough blankets of the buffalo wool.

Now that there was less field work, she and Yngvild spent several hours a day up there. They set themselves the task of making a new blanket for everyone in the Hundred. The hangings were those works in progress.

They divided their time between crafts that increased their trade stores, and field work as the oat crop raised fine, strong stalks into the sunshine. John continued joyous over the crop, which seemed to be thriving in this foreign soil, its stems straight and full of healthy growth.

One bright early morning that felt more like summer than spring, when Gwen was working with the eaglet outside, she saw him mark something in the air on the far side of the field. She was teaching the ayas to respond to a whistle and so called him in, because she wanted him not to eat his catch but remain dependent on the baited lure. He swooped but turned back without another attack; Gwen was delighted to see that he was learning to respond even with prey nearby.

Shielding her eyes against the sun's glare, she saw a smaller bird coming in from the south, heading for the loft window under the dragon pennant rippling in the breeze. She scrambled upstairs to find Culhwch flapping after a noisy arrival on the perch of the dovecote. The old bird did not have to be coaxed to take her familiar hand, and she pulled him in, exclaiming over him. He seemed none the worse for wear after a journey of more than a hundred miles. He ruffled his feathers, rubbing his beak against her, and cooing a response to his mate, who called nearby.

In the message capsule on his ankle, Gwen found a note so short as to be code that said Madoc had arrived at the *Horn* and would head back this way with supplies as planned. No real news, but this meant the birds could adapt to this new countryside and would respond to the dragon pennant as a homing device.

April, which the red women called Grass Moon, turned on its bright warm days, delivering rain that brought John's oat crop up to their knees in a dazzling blanket of green. The bees came and went above the heads of the women in their floppy hats, hoeing at the weeds, which were as healthy as the crop.

Through Flower Moon everything thrived on the mountain; it was a garden that the visiting Yuchi found a marvel. Sun Caller's oldest counselors predicted that nothing would grow on the plateau, used since time began for male sporting, considered an enemy to fertility.

But May was May, no matter what side of the world it was on or what other name it was given. Seeds grew where nothing had been allowed to grow before. The earth flourished below the sun that climbed steeper each day.

The monks finished the chapel, using another one of the ancient rockworks near the Big House for its walls.

Dag and his men went out every day and returned with bountiful game. The red women taught the whites more about gathering local edibles, and as Rose Moon arrived with its warm scented nights and blistering hot afternoons, Madoc's Hundred began to amass a good store of food and leather.

Any day the red women would be working on hides out in the open near their lodges. Ari lived with his wife there, and Brian roamed between the red compound and the llan, where he had begun a school for the children and the red women.

My mid-June, Hayati's belly was round and solid, while now Yngvild fed the babies one at a time because they were getting so big, too much to handle together.

One day in the last week of Rose Moon, Arrow-Eye screamed and swooped out of his usual pattern when Gwen released him. He flew straight up, then made his dive, an unusual behavior. But he was not stooping on a prey—the pigeons were safely inside the dovecote and there was not another bird in sight, which was usual these afternoons when Gwen had the eagle out and weathering. Before he plunged to the ground in a jelly of feathers, he curved upwards and made for the wood on the other side of the Big House, the approach between the ancient ditches to the plateau.

Gwen watched to see what had the bird so agitated. Shortly he came sailing around the other side of the Big House, rattling the pigeons she could hear fussing, and winging his way back to circle her. She whistled, but he ignored her.

He completed another circle far above her head, then made another drop toward the path, where she saw a group of men with bundles pouring from the forest.

"Tad—!" she cried, running toward her father, who looked up as she approached, his beard full, looking even leaner, more sunburned and trail-weary than before.

The eagle swooped with fierce intensity at Madoc, who threw his arms up to shield his eyes, but the angry, hissing bird veered off at the last second, climbing higher and setting up another stoop. Gwen was surprised at the bird's disobedient ferocity and whistled, holding out her gloved hand for his perch. She whistled again, moving away from her father, who stood back as she coaxed the bird down, screeching and fussing all the way, flapping his wings and puffing out his neck feathers. She slipped the hood over his stiff and hacking head, speaking softly to calm him as she slipped the jesses over his talons.

She saw her husband at the rear of the line of Yuchi warriors burdened with all manner of cargo they carried on their backs, balanced by trump lines across their foreheads. Now the bird was docile on her arm as she caught at David Iron, who bent her back in a long kiss that had his Yuchi brothers grinning and jabbing each other in the ribs.

Madoc stood back scowling but was there when David Iron let Gwen loose so that she turned to greet her father, the arm with the hooded bird held stiffly out from her body.

"Forgive him, tad—" she started to apologize, but he would not let her finish as he embraced her while she balanced the bird, who gave another muffled squawk when it heard Madoc's voice.

"I do not know what he has against you."

"He knows I will eat him, feathers, beak, and all," Madoc joked, his eye straying to the shimmering green field that pulled a smile from him. He had warned her against a male sporting bird—his tradition held with female hunters only.

The rest of the Hundred had heard the commotion and were running, cassocks and aprons flying, singly and in twos and threes to gather around, everyone greeting the travelers.

The bearers stood back, a little embarrassed and not a part of the white people's greeting, until Madoc gestured for them to continue on to the Big House, where they set the cargo

outside under the oak trees where they stayed, stretching
shoulders and arms and drinking from the river.

Wyn paid the Yuchi in blue beads—all arranged before—
and the Hundred planned to celebrate the arglwydd's safe
return.

Rhys and Madoc walked beyond the waving field of oats,
speaking alone for a long time. Gwen watched from the loft,
imagining that she knew the moment when the poet told
Madoc Rhiannon had vanished.

They had stopped, facing each other. She could see Rhys
was speaking and her father listening. Gwen wished she
could see Madoc's face, but he was angled away from her, so
she saw nothing to indicate how he was taking the news.

She was amazed at how the Hundred seemed to heal so
quickly over such wounds. It had been the same when the
group returned from the caves; the ones were gone whom
they had to leave behind in the dark still cavern, to be
mourned briefly and then forgotten. She could not see how
her father could treat Rhiannon with the same indifference,
but he never mentioned his sister again, not by name or
reference.

If anything, he seemed more amiable, treating Teleri with
greater respect after he came back from the south. It was a
puzzle that had Gwen wondering, but she had nobody to talk
to about such a murky, sad circumstance.

A few days after his homecoming, Madoc was off with
David Iron to scout for iron deposits, but they returned
grimly silenced by failure. They planned another trip with
Wyn into more northern regions where David Iron said the
red people found copper nuggets in a certain stream.

Meanwhile the red women had begun a flurry of house-
cleaning that was remarkable even for their industry. Brother
Andrew asked them what they were doing when he saw them
stacking bundles of twigs in the stony yard between their
lodges and the Big House, where the Hundred often had a
communal fire.

Ari's wife handsigned that they were preparing to light the
new fire on midsummer day, the most important festival in
their year. This was too heathen for Andrew, who went
immediately to Wyn, who took up the matter with John. The
flying wedge of religious flew against the obsidian-eyed con-
verts, but they could not shake the red women loose from

their traditional customs no matter how well the Mabilans had learned their catechism.

"There must be a fire renewal, or bad luck will follow our footsteps," Hayati patiently explained to the clergymen who came over to talk to her. The women's plans were to hold a ceremony to kill all their fires and start new ones.

"We cannot put out the forge fire, Hayati," Wyn explained. "It takes days to get it hot enough to melt the blue metal."

"Then we"—and she indicated Ari's mother- and sister-in-law and wife under the oak tree—"we will go to the Yuchis," and she made as if to gather the other red women and leave for Yellow Pheasant Village, much to Brian's distress.

"You are not able to hike half a day across that mountain in your condition," he said to her, blocking her path. She went around him, stubborn for the first time in their marriage.

"Wait—" David Iron called after her, and spoke to Wyn in favor of their ceremony, himself trying to explain how important it was to keep the fire healthy. "Our lives depend on it," he said, unable to understand how this wish to renew the fires offended his friend and teacher.

Brother Andrew was stubborn—no heathen practices. He implored Madoc to back him, lest their faith be eroded.

Madoc did not want to judge this and said so plainly.

"It is stupid not to make new fires," Hayati was saying in her own language. "In this way the One Above leans down and hears and gives life to our children and our crops." Her belly was big with Brian's get and her glance suddenly shy when she found her husband's eyes watching her as he avoided the theological discussion.

"No, daughter," Wyn said to Hayati, straining to be patient with her. "These things are not pleasing to the Lord."

She pouted and hung back, refusing to argue but not wanting to gainsay this respected sachem.

David Iron threw a pleading look at Madoc.

"What about St. John's day?" Madoc asked, rubbing down the chill in his sensitive wrist, looking first at John then at Wyn.

"Midsummer's eve," said Brian, who had grown up in St. Brendan's parent minster in Ireland. "Back home it was a big day, Domme."

"Yes," Madoc said, "midsummer bonfires and all. Call it heathen, but it seems to me both celebrate midsummer with fire."

"St. John's day has come and gone," the abbot insisted. "It is closer to the eve of saints Peter and Paul." In other words, it is still a week later than you think.

Madoc regarded him from under low brows. Their calendrical differences had been smoldering since their time on the island. There had been so much work so far, there were no days off, but which day was Sunday was a weekly argument that the abbot won by scheduling Masses for everyone on his designated sabbaths.

Now Madoc nodded, his features in a wry twist. "Very well, Domme. This argument is over. I accept your reckoning of dates."

"You admit you were wrong?"

Madoc grinned. "I said I will accept your dates."

Wyn could not suppress a grin of triumph in this the only confrontation he had maintained. "If it is the eve of saints Peter and Paul," he said to John, "we should have a bonfire."

"It still seems heathen," Andrew grumbled.

"It is an old celebration," Wyn said to the younger brother.

So the red women got their fire renewal and the men and boys their fire, a climbing, towering, massive pillar of flame, which everyone fed with bundles of deadfall and leaves from their lumbering, and debris and garbage from the household and from the butchering and leatherworks. Yngvild cleaned out her hairbrush, Teleri scraped the supper pot, Gwen swept the kitchen of house moss, and the red women quenched their individual fires.

Gwen even changed the straw in the dovecote and in Arrow-Eye's mews, throwing the old stuff into the flames.

And Father John had no difficulty intoning the old prayer to St. John, too, even though the exact day was missed. To St. John's belated fire he donated an impossibly stained scapular no amount of stone scrubbing could get clean.

They sat around singing to harp music as the fire settled into embers and sparks, then small blue flames that danced on the heads of rosy coals. Brian remembered that the men of Ireland leapt through the fire, and so they rekindled the blaze and began a competition, at which Madoc and Dag jumped the highest.

Einion, who had memories of Owen's household on such a night as this, picked out a brand from the inferno and tossed it into the air. The torch blazed and sputtered midpoint in its arch, where a breeze hit it, flinging out a shower of sparks.

Soon all three children were sending sputtering brands into the night.

The watch changed, and lookouts came in from their posts along the cliffside, where fireflies picked out low yellow constellations against the dark chasm.

They let the bonfire die again with another round of song. Madoc missed having mead and had been disappointed when it appeared no trade for such was possible among the red people: His son-in-law did not seem to understand fermented drinks at all. He and John agreed that their first crop would go into a new batch of the honey-beer.

As the night deepened under a starry sky, each member of the Hundred scooped up warm ashes and threw them between the rows of rustling, night-cool grain. This was an old custom that surely must date back to Druid times, which Andrew did not tire of reminding them. The red women saw nothing strange; in fact, this was precisely their own custom after all the village fires were quenched and relit from the sacred fire made by newly knapped flints.

Tonight they settled for coals from this bonfire lit by the arglwydd's own flints.

Madoc engaged Wyn in a friendly discussion about the remarkable coincidence of custom between the red people and the Celts. Long after everyone else went to bed, they talked about this and other mysteries they had so far encountered.

As though the fire ceremony had been some kind of signal to the sky, the next day burned down with fury, even though it was still a couple of days until the beginning of Heat Moon.

Gwen missed Rhiannon. As the summer wore on into July, she spent more time than any of the other women at the looms up in the loft. She grew to understand Rhiannon's fascination with the weaving process, the comforting rhythm of walking the weave, the delight of watching the pattern emerge, though for the blankets they contented themselves with stripes of buffalo wool, which ranged from a dark brown bordering on black to a light russet.

She would stare out the second-story window over what used to be Rhiannon's bed, looking at the far ridge of trees, wondering where her aunt was and how she was getting along. Gwen could not accept that Rhiannon was dead, for she had no understanding of Rhiannon's despair. She had not confided her feelings to anyone; only Madoc knew why

Rhiannon was gone, and he knew it as a certainty and with some secret relief he hated to admit to himself. He did not even share his understanding with Rhys, who never did quite understand what had passed between his wife and her brother.

So it was another mystery with no solution. Like Fair Beard and the monks taken by the Alabamans and Ffiona's baby . . .

Gwen had dreams about Ffiona's baby, innocent of his terrible danger, tossed from stranger's hands. It woke her up in a cold sweat more than once those hot nights.

Nobody ever mentioned Rhiannon, and only Gwen seemed to think she might return.

The babies grew fat, the bees buzzed in tune with the harp music, and the summer blazed through Heat Moon and into Thunder Moon with a deepening intensity of sunlight more fierce than any Briton could imagine. Madoc's Hundred settled in, made profitable trade with their Yuchi allies, wove blankets, pounded iron, rolled their glass beads, felled trees, and cast their Latin to the brassy heavens.

But there were signs that everything was not as they might have hoped in the promised land. In mid-August David Iron and Madoc failed on two more expeditions to find iron. They brought back high-grade copper picked from the surface of a northern plateau under a rocky ledge, but not the slightest trace of iron ore or even reports of formations that might have given them what they needed to keep Wyn's forge busy.

Then there was the crop. It was a subtle thing that John first saw in the oats coming to fruit in late August. Despite the alert, healthy stems, the grain panicles were very short and fat—a couple of inches instead of the twelve that John expected—and the awns, the small hairs at the end of each flower cluster, were short and twisted, or nonexistent. Their beautiful emerald and waving field was making underdeveloped, even deformed, grain. They would get something out of the crop, but not half what John expected, and it would serve as animal food better than human so tough were the kernels. He would get a batch of mead from the field, but there would not be enough for a big store of winter grain as they had hoped. John figured that they did not get the crop in early enough, or that their seed was not adapted to the hotter weather of this southern latitude.

The truth was that the field turned over poor soil. The whole plateau, which would someday be called the Barrens, lacked nutrients for a maximum crop, as latter-day farmers would come to realize. But at the time John was left with stumpy, distorted grain he was unable to crack with an eyetooth.

David Iron's dreams started about that time.

He later imagined that the mountain itself was aware of the changes on the plateau and was displeased. The nightmares started in Thunder Moon, right after Hayati was delivered of twins, two lusty little boys with the cries of panthers, whom their father promptly named Matthew and Mark.

David Iron did not tell even Onwa' Pahta about the dreams that invoked troublesome images of earthquakes and male invective against the domestic and female uses to which the sporting old man of the mountain had been put.

But these troublesome ideas had not yet come together in the last days of Thunder Moon, when the women put on straw sunhats and the men stripped to the waist to bring in the crop. The red women had spent the last moon making cane baskets to hold the grain, but the crop did not fill up all the containers.

The sun was low in the west, the view of the mountain made ruddy by all the dust their work had stirred.

They were working in teams, just finishing with the reaping. Now everyone, including the reapers, was stacking the bunches on spread-out buffalo hides. They were exhausted and filthy, already telling each other how fine it would be to jump into the river. Some were dropping their sickles and wandering with bone-weary steps toward the water, when they stopped in their tracks.

Dag among them stepped forward in amazement, clearing his vision of gritty sweat with the back of his arm. His mouth dropped open, and he swore a small curse of unbelief.

Someone called, "What is it?" from the field, and the laborers turned to see, trudging the path between the ditches overgrown with short grass, the Shawnee women, children, and old men with everything they owned piled on their backs and on a convoy of gihli-gasi pulled by sweaty little boys and panting dogs.

Chapter 31

Long ago there was a mighty snake....
This mighty snake hated those
Whom he hated....
They both did harm.
They both injured each other.
Both were not at peace.
Driven from their home
They fought with this manslayer.
The water ran off, the earth dried,
The lakes were at rest.
All was silent
And the mighty snake departed.

> —*from the* Walam Olum
>   *Leni Lenape (Delaware)*
>   *(pre-Columbian oral tradition)*

Rhys stayed close to Yngvild that season.

Handing the baby back and forth, he was put into her company already. She spent many of her daylight hours weaving, because cloth turned out to be the one thing their Yuchi allies prized above all other trade goods. She and Gwen taught the Shawnee the innovation of the broadloom. From the branches of the biggest oak they rigged looms, using river-stones as weights and living limbs as warp beams.

They dyed buffalo fleece and with the natural reddish color made distinctive striped blankets. Yngvild concentrated on more finely woven widths, all of which they traded to the Yuchi for corn and squash so that a wider path was beaten between the two nations. Not a day passed that someone from Yellow Pheasant Village did not bring a pipe to be smoked and goods to be traded.

Rhys sat with the red women learning to make yarn with spindle-whorls, himself sometimes making thread and sometimes making music. He picked up Shawnee chants and the old Norse songs from Yngvild, for weavers almost always make music with the work. She taught him lullabies more beautiful than love songs in French or a hymn in Cymraeg, surely the most sublime human sounds on all the earth.

She was a good guide, never patronizing, being a woman who expected everyone around her, even her suckling infants, to be strong. And she did not talk too much. Rhys needed only a few visual cues to place himself in any situation. Talkativeness was not her nature, and Fair Beard's woman did not have that many words in Cymraeg, anyway, though she was glad for the practice over those sultry months of summer.

He wanted to know everything about the Shawnee, what symbols they beaded on their babies' cradleboards, what their moccasins looked like, and how they folded the hide of the gilhi-gasi to be able to carry twice as big a load as the Muskogeans. They pitched their quick tepees out by the other red women, with whom they already had agreeable connections, and quickly fell into the ways of the Hundred as though they had always been there.

About a dozen of the women quickly paired off with the sailors, who were happy to move from the crowded lower room of the Big House and into the cozy lodges out on the grass. There was some shuffling around, but they settled down. Some sailors and a few of the older women still mourning husbands did not make couples. One or two of them, notably Winnowed Rice, did not keep their lodge flaps loose. Lily found Evan's attentions agreeable, but they were slow courting, so the girl continued to live with her sister-in-law.

There were a few fights, a scratch or two, a broken nose and loosened tooth because the Norsemen and Madoc's crew never saw eye to eye. Most of the time everyone was working too hard to do aught but eat and fall into exhausted slumber at sundown. One or two of the sailors asked to be married. John dispatched hasty blessings, while the monks taught the Shawnee the basics of the faith. They were indifferent students, just humoring their men.

The Norsemen balked at submitting to Father John's nuptials, however. Madoc, who had privately vowed never again to involve himself in anyone else's love life, refused to take sides. The red women laughed at the bickering white men and went about their business weaving baskets, finishing off an abundant supply of buffalo hides from the last kill and reluctantly helping with the field work. The Whippoorwills did not plant. Gathering was their specialty. Winnowed Rice's own name came from the wonderful foodstuff found in wetlands, which they harvested in boats, beating the wild grain from the stems and letting the harvest fall into their skirts until they had to have help carrying it, the load was so heavy.

But taking an entire field of grain planted for that purpose was something new. It went against their customs but was a curiosity and something that pleased the men. The grain stalks had been cut and stacked in the field. When Wyn decided it was dry enough, every available hand went out to thresh the grain from the chaff so the air was full of floating fragments of husks.

In private the Whippoorwills mocked the settled life-style of their new friends; they made comments about the white men and their roots, a double meaning in their language that made them giggle when the men were not around. Talk circled among them about the old days on the trail.

One hot afternoon after threshing, Lily remarked, "The dogs are getting fat," to Winnowed Rice, who was working on a width of trade wool under the big oak.

Most of the adults in the compound were off gathering, hunting, or woodcutting, so it was quiet outside the Big House. Lily sat on one of the flat stones that stepped down the north bank of the Duck River. Beyond them the wide but shallow crescent falls glittered with ripples and sun-dogs, whipping up a rosy-tinted foam in the weedy pond, draining toward yet another level of cascades where the two branches of the Duck commingled in ragged shoals beneath looming cliffs, then rolled on down the grade across the old Whippoorwill range and eventually to the Yuchi River.

Winnowed Rice glanced at her big yellow bitch snoozing in a cool nook of oak roots. "So are the babies." Winnowed Rice had often sorrowed over hungry children. "And so are you and I."

Lily started to answer, but saw Yngvild and the storyteller, himself carrying a rolled-up buffalo hide. Winnowed Rice peered around the tree trunk to see them in the sunlight. She had said nothing about Black Pearl to these people. But she knew from the first day who Rhys was. Casual gossip with the Muskogeans relieved her worry that the man had since taken on another wife; he was in Yngvild's company so often and seemed to share children. Though they were obviously friends, they did not speak like lovers, and they rarely touched except when Rhys lightly grasped the big blond woman's elbow for occasional guidance.

Yngvild, the two babies wiggling under each arm, called good day in Shawnee. Winnowed Rice and Lily answered, trying for the same in the white people's language, but that exhausted conversational possibilities.

Close to this tree Yngvild stopped, and Rhys flung out the hide where she set the children. She had fed Bjorn and now unlatched the broach holding up the left side of her bodice for Cari, while Rhys stretched out in the shade.

Stillness took them all while the river and the weaving put small sounds on the air.

When the baby was finished, Yngvild put her down and went to the third loom hanging from a branch on the other side of the tree, where she paused to look at Winnowed Rice's work, pleased the red women took so quickly and expertly to weaving—then she set about finishing the work on the other loom.

The babies were settling into a nap, though Bjorn could crawl by now and could not be trusted in Rhys's care not to ramble. Today he sat playing with a toy boat David Iron had carved for him, beside Cari sleeping in the warm buzzing afternoon while the women chatted back and forth, weaving halting foreign words among the strands of cloth.

"What was that?" Rhys cried suddenly, apparently brought out of a doze beside the snoozing babies. "Something tried to fly into my mouth."

"Too many bugs in this country," Yngvild said, patting her last course up with the edge of her hand.

"There it is again—" He ducked, protecting his face.

"Agh—a bat—" Yngvild cried, knocking over the stool she had been sitting to get away from the creature that moved too fast to see, churning up a soft vibrating sound.

Rhys's hand dropped to the nearest baby's back as he moved around on the pallet dodging the high-speed murmur of what seemed to be the attacker.

"It will not hurt you," Winnowed Rice said, then tried it in his language: "No hurt, no hurt you!"

Lily was laughing behind her hand. One of the babies was beginning to fuss.

"It stung Cari," Rhys said, reaching for her, patting the buffalo hide here and there as he sought her.

Winnowed Rice dropped to her knees at the edge of the pallet and spoke close to his bound face, "No danger, Storyteller," she said in his language, but used the Shawnee word for his title.

The old white shaman had made a strange, sweet drink from some of the grain they harvested, mixing it with river water and the honey captured from their bees. This was all a wonder to the Shawnee, who timidly tried the drink but found it too sweet, with an effect that left them light-headed. Winnowed Rice was so close to the Storyteller now she could smell the not-unpleasant aroma of the sweet drink on his breath.

"Perhaps the hummingbird was tasting your lips," she said in a mixture of both languages. She put her hand over his searching for the baby, who by now had gone back to sleep, guiding it to assure him by touch that the child was unhurt.

"Who are you?" he asked, exploring her hand, touching soft new calluses.

"Winnowed Rice," she answered, because she knew that was what he had asked, without knowing the words.

She tapped handsign on his palm and asked in Shawnee, "Who are you?"

He amended his long family name to simply, "Rhys."

Across the way Yngvild and Lily exchanged a glance that confirmed what they were witnessing. Yngvild smiled, keeping her lips shut, and returned her attention to her busy hands, which would finish this piece before nightfall. Lily did not smile but watched her sister-in-law as she and the blind man continued speaking to each other about unimportant things.

"What did you call it, the buzzing creature?" Rhys asked.

She imitated the creature's characteristic humming sound, then said, "Bird," in his language, having learned that one from Gwen with her tame eagle, which had come limping home with a sprained wing. It was strange for a woman to keep animals; all the red women gossiped about it. The closest things to pets they knew were dogs, never named and often eaten in hard times.

A Shawnee word for hummingbird meant "small one whispering secrets," but it was too difficult to translate.

"There it is again," Yngvild cried, delighted now with the

iridescent green color flashing by. "Oh, Rhys, the color, the deepest green it is—and, oh, wonderful! In the air it hangs!"

Rhys's fingers were still speaking with Winnowed Rice's hand.

"Wings move so fast I am not seeing—"

Winnowed Rice pulled away and stood, returning to the loom, but the man did not go back to sleep. He moved over to sit near her, listening to the soft weaving sounds and talking with her about hummingbirds, which were as unknown to the white people as social bees were to the red, until the shadows drew long, the woodcutters dragged in a log, the hunters returned, and woodsmoke laced with dripping venison juices turned the air blue.

Over in the llan the monks sang vespers.

Yngvild took the babies inside. Lily wandered off with Evan when he and the other woodcutters returned.

"There is no more light left," Winnowed Rice finally said, and tied up her threads. She rolled the various small tools in a worn deerskin and found herself standing beside the man as tree frogs strummed and the last smoky color faded from the sky.

"Come inside and eat with me," Rhys said, touching her arm.

Winnowed Rice saw the communal fire of the red enclave not far off. The aromas of flame, corn, and meat pulled her in two directions, but she walked back with him to the house.

"Another time," she said at the open doorway, where the fire threw a glow. She had never been inside the Big House and was not prepared to enter a place that had negative connotations to her. Her men always came here to do mock battle. Over the years some of them had not returned from this gaming place, which could kill warriors as well as bring them honor.

That night she thought about all the things Black Pearl had said. The next day she sat with Rhys again under the oak, talking while she worked at the loom.

Madoc and David Iron came and went on still another fruitless exploration to find iron. Gossip spread when people saw Madoc and his ironmonger-abbot deep in conversation.

They wandered back to stand outside the Big House, where several men joined them, including Wyn, Andrew, and some of the sailors. They continued talking about the poor crop and iron, then veered off into other topics, namely the clergy's concern about casual alliances between the men and women. "There are strong influences," Wyn said. "Already your poet is taking Shawnee ways."

"Look there," young Andrew suggested, pointing to the oaks where Rhys sat among the weavers. "Already he looks like a red juggler," Andrew said, indicating Rhys, who had let Winnowed Rice braid his hair.

Madoc glanced where Rhys sat beneath the oak with the red and white children catching frogs in the stream behind him, sunlight turning the riddled surface to a spray of diamonds. The poet sat still on his knees while Winnowed Rice delicately applied yellow, red, black, and white paint to his face. Madoc was fascinated by the design his keen eye could discern from where he stood. The woman's steady hand had outlined Rhys's eye sockets with white and yellow pigment, bringing rays over his eyebrows and forehead.

It was stunning and strange to see Rhys this way after that silent scarf for so long.

"It is heathen," Brother Andrew said, "and pitiful—look at him like a painted savage—" but Madoc silenced him with a look.

Across the sunlit yard the woman turned Rhys's face toward them to put the finishing touches on the mask. Madoc was struck with the impression that Rhys had eyes—dramatic dark centers outlined with the sunbursts rayed with crimson.

David Iron had joined them, so he overheard Andrew's comments. "It is for the harvest ceremony," he said.

"It is unholy," Andrew insisted.

David Iron threw a pleading look at Madoc, who drew his attention away from the scene under the tree. Rhys's painted face was an arresting vision, not at all repulsive. But it put a chill on Madoc's arm, and he did not want to comment upon it.

He threw his arm around Wyn's shoulders and began walking toward the Big House. "Domme," he said in a different voice, "I hear the new mead is made—let us give it a taste."

That night Winnowed Rice slept in the Big House and Evan slept with Lily in the tepee, and in the early morning, even before the monks stirred, Winnowed Rice's normally quiet dog started an aggrieved barking at the door downstairs. Farther out, the other Shawnee dogs answered in a clamor that could only mean trouble.

Madoc, furious, dragged out of bed trailing bedclothes, stumbled downstairs, and flung open the door to stare wide-eyed over the dog, who dashed inside and hid beneath the trestle table.

Winnowed Rice beside Rhys upstairs flung open the shutter and saw in the sun's glare not a bow shot across the ditch the encampment of Cherokee war-lodges sprung up overnight as silent and quick as mushrooms at the edge of the lumbered meadow.

Chapter 32

Listen! Ha! Cover her in loneliness.
Her eyes have faded. Her eyes have
come to fasten themselves on one man
alone. Where can her soul escape?
Let her be sorrowing as she goes
along, and not for one night alone.
Let her become an aimless wanderer,
whose trail may never be followed. O
Black Spider, may you hold her soul
in your web so that it shall never
get through the meshes. What is the
name of her soul? It is mine!

—Cherokee love formula

Fox had not taken another woman since the death of his young wife a year ago, and the only stipulation on his taking another was that she be of any clan but his own. Shawnee and Cherokee shared many ancient traditions, not the least of which was the seven clans, so it had been a lucky one-in-seven chance when Winnowed Rice gave her new sister her own family name and totem, tattooed now on Black Pearl's thigh.

The ideal pairing for a Cherokee who maintained traditional standards would be to "marry his grandmother," that is, a woman of his mother's mother's clan, and here she was in the strangely white flesh beneath the Shawnee jerkin and leggings. Fox had kissed the little mark Winnowed Rice had cut and rubbed with ashes and Black Pearl's own blood on her initiation night. Long healed, the tattoo was now a fine blue abstraction of flight.

His being with this woman in the privacy of his own lodge was of no importance to the men he led into battle, now that the fighting was over and they were on the trail home. No red man took sex before a battle, but afterwards it was traditional if available with an appropriate woman. But some of his counselors did not like this particular woman as a matter of principal, appropriate bird-clan tattoo or no, because of her connections with the Shawnee, who had caused them loss of face.

Black Pearl had been careful to stay with the few women of Fox's war party, sisters or childless wives who accompanied the warriors to cook and keep their war regalia in order. She stayed within their behavior patterns, working with them at communal labor, being quiet while she learned their language and ways, so she would not offend.

Fox had accomplished the rest by taking her immediately into his womanless traveling household, displacing two old war cronies who could not complain because it had been they who counseled their Beloved Man to take another wife to cure the old-bone.

Black Pearl leaned back on their blanket while Fox kissed the tattoo again, murmuring the musical chants he was forever muttering. The vibration of his lips against her skin gave her gooseflesh, which made him laugh, a rare, wonderful sound. They were exhausted from love-labor, but if he kept that up, they would be at it again until they both passed out.

"Tell me about the homeland," she said, and he rolled over to use her for a pillow. She was thrilled by his descriptions of a settled country in Cherokee possession so long that there were standing council trees planted by the grandfathers in huge circles used for ten generations as sacred meeting places; where families occupied permanent lodges of peeled cedar logs with firepits so ancient the puddled clay floor was baked as hard as pottery. Black Pearl longed to be settled in such a home.

She understood much of what he said; sometimes he used Shawnee words for her, and sometimes sign with his strong, stout hands. He was teaching her his language and was delighted to give her some tribal history.

The Ani Yunwiya were originally a cave-dwelling mountain tribe from the uplands that bordered the Leni Lenape nation. The name the Muskogeans called them—Cherokee—meant cavemen. They had many villages over in the eastern mountains beyond the treacherous lower Tennessee upriver from

Muscle Shoals. They were the most prosperous and numerous people in that country, which Fox described in great detail in a form of rhymeless poetry she came to recognize from its repeated patterns and phrases.

She said she could hardly wait to go home with him and meet his mother and sisters. This pleased Fox immensely, because it was exactly the right reference that a prospective bride should make to the grandmother's clan of a man as important as himself.

"But we are going to take a shortcut back to those peaceful valleys." Fox had already sent men back there carrying the corpses of their fallen brothers, while his main war party recuperated from the fight with the Shawnee. He sent word that more men should come because he anticipated another battle. Fox rolled over onto his stomach so he could look into the woman's depthless eyes. Softly he repeated a fragment of the love song to ensnare a woman's soul, uttering the words in a low, melodious murmur that vibrated down through her wrist bones and into her deepest parts. "O Black Spider, may you hold her soul in your web so that it shall never get through the meshes. . . ."

She giggled with the tickle his vibrato put in her. It was an effective formula that worked even better when mouthed against the living flesh of its object.

"This shortcut will take us close to the Yuchi mountain," he said softly after repeating the formula three times.

Black Pearl became very quiet as Fox pulled himself off her, leaned on one elbow, and continued, "I hear there are some strangers in the land of the Yuchi. My allies tell me these strangers look different from ordinary red people." He stroked the white skin closest to his hand. "They have pale eyes and hair and skin and hard metal knives, which will cut anything. I want to know more about them, so I must go see for myself."

She had become even quieter.

He continued, "I think you can help me."

Black Pearl took a long sigh and replied, "I will tell you what I know, which is considerable, but you must make a promise."

"What is it you want?"

"You will not do any harm to any of these strangers, and I will tell you some interesting things."

Fox took out the small knife she had given him, which he

kept in the medicine bag at his waist. "Can you tell me how to make one of these?"

She shook her head as she removed from her travel bag the blue beads, which she had not shown to him, and laid them on the clipped buffalo fleece. "But I know how to make these."

He picked them up with the same reaction as the Shawnee and any of the red people who had never seen glass before. He had seen the color of the sky repeated only in the rare stones from the far southwest that had to be traded through many hands to get this far north and east.

He looked up from the amazing beads and into her cloudy eyes, wordless in the presence of his own wonder. "But these do not come from the east," he said, letting her know that he knew her origins, rumored by the several tribes who had encountered Madoc's Hundred, to lie in the opposite direction, the home of the new sun over the Great Salt Water.

She looked down at another circlet of beads that slid from her kit, playing with them idly, not answering him.

"Beads this color come from the land where the sun dies, across the Great River Road in a place next to the underworld, where the sun is so hot it cooks men crisp as corncakes if they are foolish enough to go out at midday." He jiggled the beads on their wire, itself a strange and wonderful product found in his nation only among shamans who hammered it out of copper nuggets found in the streams. "I have heard this from the Muskogean traders."

He cocked his head at her and gently lifted her stubborn chin with a thick red finger. He stared deeply into her eyes the color of rolling-thunder sky, to see if she betrayed any deception, and held the stare as he continued in a measured voice, slowly enough for her to catch his every meaning: "They say the armies of roasted men were long ago baked in their tracks and there they stand to be seen by any traveler to this day, their arms raised upwards in supplication to the cruel sun—like this"—he demonstrated—"the fringes on their shirts as stiff as fish-gutting knives."

He fumbled in his medicine bag and produced a thin, spiny object about the length of a bonepicker's sacred fingernail; it looked like nothing more than a fire-hardened stick, sharp enough to needle medium-grade deerskin. He ran his finger over the point, rasping against his coarsened fingerprint, then, quick as a magic trick, flipped his hand open, palm up, where a single bead a little larger and darker than her glass ones glowed a blue as blue as a sky that could hold such a cooking sun.

She took it in her hand, weighing it and peering close at the striations of dark veins that laced the turquoise, a type of stone she knew from Owen's treasure, and named for Infidels from whose country it came.

"The traders say the sun is so hot over there it cracks the sky and pieces like this fall down to the middle world to be gathered only in cold moonlight and taken to the underground caves, where the nation in those parts puts holes in the pieces while they are still warm with stickers"—he gestured with the cactus spine—"like these."

She returned his stare defiantly, not quite sure what had rattled him but not about to let him bend her glance. "Sounds like a story to me, a desert place, maybe the land of the Infidels." She used the Cymraeg word Twrc; he did not seem to recognize it. "They are darker than Muskogean bonepickers."

She shook the blue glass nodules made for her by Brother Wyn not so long ago in what now seemed like another world, perhaps a world she had imagined, wrapped her hand around his hot arm with the cool beads between their flesh, and said softly, "Let us go home instead of to Yuchi territory." Very subtly she began stroking the elbow that had caused him so much pain.

"Afterwards," he replied, taking the beads from her, but letting her keep the turquoise.

"Will you make the promise?" she asked.

"They cannot stay where they are."

"Perhaps they can be persuaded to leave. But," she added, "you are too great a warrior to waste the blood of harmless strangers." She did not have to tell him all her secrets; her flesh and her pale hair she kept well oiled and painted like any modest red woman; her rainy eyes, and now her intervention on their behalf, told him much.

"Perhaps Black Pearl will sit in on councils with these strangers, since she knows so much about them and cares that they be spared, though they are intruding where they do not belong."

"They would think you were holding me captive." She was threading the big bead on a thong already tied with a few pierced shells and porcupine spines.

He thought about this, now feeling distant from her as she settled the necklace back inside her collar and stared into space over his shoulder. "Well," he concluded, "perhaps they can be persuaded to leave without a fight."

"There are women and children among them."

"More now that your Shawnee sisters found refuge."

Black Pearl was warmed that the Whippoorwills had made it to the mountain.

When he saw she was not going to speak, Fox said, "I have no wish to tangle with those Shawnee women again," and ran one finger sinuously up her thigh to stop on the bird tattoo. He said it to play with her, to have a friendly joke between them, but she did not laugh. It chilled him, so he tried again, and this time he succeeded in warming her—she laughed with him when he said, "One of those women is all any man can handle."

Rumor had sped through his contingent that the strangers possessed great powers, so by the time Fox and his hundred warriors approached the mountain, they expected to see some spectacle. The reality was something less as the war party came in late one night and set up Fox's lodges.

Not a tree still stood on the stumpy meadow where Fox camped, effectively putting the gaming field under siege. Red people burned deadfall in their cooking fires; they lumbered very sparingly, mostly saplings for lodgepoles, bows, and other shafts. When they needed a large log, which was rarely, they would gird a particular tree so that the next season it died. This was a patient lumbering process and never involved the flattening of an entire grove like the one where Fox camped. Even beavers left a few trees. Nothing short of a wildfire left a forest so leveled. Fox looked around at the sight of it, unable to imagine a reason to cut so much wood.

Fox sent ravens out, one to Sun Caller of the Yuchi, informing him that the Cherokee and Muskogeans were protecting Yuchi interests with the encampment and requesting his presence at the council between Fox and the strangers. The other messengers sped to allies—Mabila, the Chickasaw, even the Alabamans—calling for more big chiefs who were Fox's friends and lodge brothers to gather (he held the highest degree in the secret society now that Owl Person of the Shawnee was dead), ready to fight at the gaming field.

Fox was disdainful to see that the white people were complacent and had no watch out that night; it was the

Shawnee dogs who set up the alarm and brought out the
white people, wrapped in their bedrolls, their pink skin
strange in the dawn light, a curiosity to the red men, who
quietly backed Fox and his several counselors sitting dressed
in their most splendid regalia in a crescent just on the other
side of the wide ditch that separated the gaming field from its
approach through what had once been a grove of hardwoods.

After the initial shock, when the whites saw that they were
not under attack, they returned to their lodge. Presently the
white chief came out, dressed in something other than his
sleeping blanket—a bright metal skin that impressed Fox,
with a red snake emblazoned on the chest.

Fox's attention was also taken by the blue-metal weapons
the white man and his men were wearing, knives, swords as
long as a man's arm and glittering helmets, sharp lances and
other metal fittings that caught the sun.

The Cherokee stood to meet the white man, struck by the
similarity between his eyes and Black Pearl's. He noted that
Madoc had even more retainers than himself, including a
young Yuchi warrior dressed like a white man, a red-haired
white girl who stayed close to him, and a man with sunbursts
painted on his face, a powerful symbol that unnerved Fox,
though he did not let it show. Also with him were what Fox
interpreted as personal guards and a couple of sachems
dressed in long, loose robes that did not look like the hides of
any animal Fox ever skinned.

The first meeting was a brief conversation in which Fox
introduced himself and offered to smoke tobacco in "celebration
of your departure from this place."

The young couple translated what Fox and the white
chieftain said to each other after the Yuchi introduced himself
as Eagle Ring Man and the white chief as Weather Eyes,
since Madoc's own name was meaningless in translation,
explaining that this was the name Sun Caller had given him,
and it pleased him to retain it "for his other red friends, with
whom Weather Eyes wishes only to live peacefully."

Weather Eyes continued speaking.

"We have many interesting things to trade for the goodwill
of the Ani Yunwiya," the Yuchi interpreted for the white
man, who motioned for several of his young men standing to
one side to bring out the gifts—luxuriant widths of buffalo
cloth in two weights, three thick loops of blue glass beads
exactly like Black Pearl's, and a splendid ornamental brass

dagger inlaid with opals, from who knew what place far across the salt water.

Fox stiffly accepted the gifts and went through a polite tobacco ceremony in which Weather Eyes joined him with precise attention to tradition and some coaching from Eagle Ring Man. When all Fox's counselors had finished the pipe, Fox presented the long beautiful red soapstone object to the white chief, who handed it to the Yuchi for safekeeping.

Then Fox said that they should come back to this place again when Sun Caller arrived, since it was unseemly to continue speaking of Yuchi territorial claims without their speaker present for negotiations.

Visibly nervous the whites filed out of the red encampment, where Fox and his allies and counselors retired to his lodge to discuss the situation.

The younger braves began a chunkee game and had time to play many rounds while the council dragged on, each of the Muskogeans having his say. They wanted the white people killed immediately just for what they had done to the mountain.

Fox sat back against the buffalo furs, only half listening to the august chiefs of his own and ally nations, withholding his opinion and allowing each chief to have his say after all of them handled the strange gifts and marveled over their manufacture.

Around the central lodge the huge camp settled into afternoon activities. He could smell food on the breeze and welcomed it. The voices of the earnest councilors droned in his ear. They all looked around when he stood—a breech of tradition, which held that they be allowed to argue until the eldest turned and formally petitioned his opinion.

He stood still among their dwindling conversation, but soon they took the hint: The Most Beloved needed to take a piss. The eldest acknowledged him.

"Let us continue at a later council," he said politely but coolly. Several of the elders of more than his own tribe were stirring on their buffalo robes. It had been an extraordinary day. Stomachs were growling; older bladders were even more impatient than Fox's.

Fox left the lodge only to be met by Clear Seeing Man with some formula that must be said as he extended his hand with a leaf smeared with medicine. He was pleased to take credit for curing his chief's bout with the old-bone by doing greater magic against the curse-magic of the departed Shawnee sachem. Now all that remained was for Fox to continue rubbing his parts with this salve Clear Seeing Man prepared for him daily.

"Old friend," Fox said, pushing the sachem's hand aside, "I am cured of the old-bone, see?" As he walked toward the chunkee players, he manipulated his own firm wrist in an agile circle. In fact, Fox had felt only a twinge now and again of the crippling pain since he let Black Pearl share his blanket the first night she had followed them.

The sachem frowned behind his speckled white-and-black paint. "Beware the gift of a woman," Clear Seeing Man intoned. It was an old lodge password.

The sachem and Fox stood talking to one side of the game, a dusty, noisy affair that drowned out their conversation for any who might have overheard.

"But who dares refuse the mother's gift?" Fox retaliated with still another piece of Cherokee wisdom, a reference to the sun, Ancient Red, the female parent of everything on earth.

Clear Seeing Man coiled his lips around distaste. "I will continue to repeat the formulas for as many of the blue beads given to us by the Beloved Man." They were not about to lose that treasure, Fox noted. The sachem wanted to be sole holder of all of Black Pearl's beads.

"I wager this—" Fox said, holding up one of the beads, "that Fat Tongue's nephew there wins this round."

Clear Seeing Man raised his eyebrows when he saw the little treasure. "But it is not much of a bet, since the lad is by far the best player."

"True."

"I wager he wins the next three rounds."

It was a sure thing, but Fox wanted to lose to the sachem and be rid of him, so he accepted the bet, and when Fat Tongue's boy took that set and went on to win the next two, Fox handed over the bead and took his leave.

He was tired of being near so many men all day and wanted to breathe open air. He saw Fat Tongue and another warrior working on their scalp tassels and removed his own from the powerbag slung at his waist. It would be good to do blessing work on his war memento for a while until the light was gone. Together they strolled away from the game.

Black Pearl walked by the dusty spot where the men played chunkee, a wild game that involved throwing lances at rolling stones. She thought maybe Fox would be here watching the play, but he was not, so she circled the camp, looking for him among the warriors. A little way into the uncut woods, where they were working on their war trophies, she saw him bent over his work as intently as a child with a toy. As he meticulously shaped the dried Shawnee scalp on a small hoop of cane, he murmured a chant she did not understand, with words she had heard him mutter before. He had been at this work since she caught up with him and his soldiers that day after the battle.

Now he had tanned the small circle of skin and hair and was sewing it to the cane circle about the size of a copper penny. She did not speak but crouched a few paces from him, bringing tension to the air. He felt her watching and glanced up but did not interrupt the low song of power he sang as his fingers went about the work.

Each time they locked eyes, Black Pearl felt the surge she had felt when they first met. He felt it, too, she could tell. There were no doubts between them, had never been, and now even away from the bedroll she knew she could approach him like this.

Fat Tongue gave her a dirty look and walked off to express distaste. He had vowed never to accept his chief's new woman.

Fox did not smile exactly, but the black centers of his eyes softened as he repeated once again for the magic seventh time the prayer formula to ensnare a woman's soul.

To Black Pearl the chant had only scattered meaning. She knew the word for spider and web and figured this was a song to ensure successful hand work on the scalp tassel, which was like the work of the spider.

When the other men had moved far enough away, and it appeared he was finished singing, she approached.

"Do not fear, woman. I did not kill anyone." He tightened a stitch.

"Did you tell them you would let them go?"

Fox chuckled. "First he will tell me the secret of the blue metal."

"The white chief will never do that," she said emphatically.

He held up the almost complete scalp tassel, regarding it and hoping she would see his fine workmanship. He looked from his work to her colorless eyes. This woman, he thought, has bewitched me, and I let her. He stretched out his arms, feeling the strength along his muscles, no pain, but the twinge at the elbow, all that was left of the old agony.

He touched her, feeling the tingle of spark that always passed between them.

"Is your elbow hurting a little?" she asked, rubbing against him, beginning to massage the elbow.

"You are great magic," he said, leaning back to let her work against his muscles.

He knew some of his advisers such as Fat Tongue did not like the idea of his taking this strange woman, but how could he explain to them that when she touched him that first day on the Shawnee killing ground, the pain ceased. How to explain it even to himself, except that it was a gift from Old Red? Her hands touched, and he could feel strength coming from her.

She had broken Owl Person's curse.

This sachem had told him all he needed was to fast, sit naked in the sun, and ask Her to send him a sign. He had followed Clear Seeing Man's advice, and here was his sign, this amazing woman who walked into his life so full of mysteries he was afraid of her. But she stopped the pain.

Black Pearl did not know how she accomplished this for him but had been aware from the first it was happening. Some men could practice sexual abstinence only so long. Among the Cherokee masturbation was considered unclean. Black Pearl had heard old women's gossip—back home his condition was called monk's gout; the touch of a virgin child was supposed to cure it. She had no knowledge if that worked or not, but she suspected what burned Fox's elbows and knees could be cured, and she had no doubt she could administer the medicine.

Sun Caller arrived with a large contingent, and later Shell-of-Many-Colors and his war-band. The Mabilan was ready to slit every white throat because of the losses they had inflicted upon him, but Caller reminded him that a bride-price had been paid for the red-haired woman. Shell also wanted revenge for his nephew's death, but Fox warned him to await the outcome of council. That morning they joined another meeting with the whites, where Fox demanded the secret of the blue metal and Weather Eyes refused. It was now a raw negotiation, and even the polite discourse of Cherokee tradition could not hide it. They ended the meeting in late afternoon with plans to meet again the next day. Fox concluded by telling Weather Eyes he could cut no more trees.

The white chief did not answer but turned and went back to the lodge his people had axed three hundred trees to build.

Fox went off looking for Black Pearl. It was against his nature to spend all daylight sitting down and talking. He felt a stiffness in his elbow all afternoon, not a pain surely, but something he wanted Black Pearl to rub away with her cool magic.

A long sunset still lingered. It had gotten cooler.

The aromas on the air were enticing. He found several of the women near the big fire, which had been set a long way from the riverbank and well out of visual range from the mountain compound. Black Pearl was not among them, and when he approached the eldest woman, asking for her whereabouts, he was told that she was not cooking tonight but was among the water carriers down at the river. She gestured toward a raw trail that angled toward a part of the forest the white men had not cut because it was on a steep grade leading to the south fork of the Duck River.

Fox took the trail at a fast jog, which he relished after inactivity. Nearer the river he came up behind the women, who all were shyly deferential toward him, a great hero in their nation. He caught Black Pearl's glance, and she walked away from the others toward him. Without a word she followed his lead back up the way he had come and down a short draw to a dry arm of the river where a forest of brown cattails rattled.

Finally he stopped on a rise of ground. For a while he stood listening with her to the sounds of the wood around them. The camp's murmur, the growl of the river not far away—all faded in the cricket-strummed blueness of evening. They stood together watching the campfires through the trees.

"Do not fear, woman," he said, holding up his hand in mock rejection. "Your precious white man is safe behind his women and his blind sachem."

She smiled and let his fingers touch her arms. "Why did you seek me out?"

"I . . . I missed you."

"But you know sometimes I must leave for a while," she said, using an old formula that made him draw suddenly away from her. "No, not yet, but I was going to walk to the isolation hut with Fawn-Face since I must go there in a few days, anyway." She was not sure she had said it all right—there were so many polite formulas the Cherokee used so that a woman did not have to come out plainly and say to a man that she was menstruating. Even the word for moon-blood was considered a pollution to a warrior.

He nodded, needing no further explanation, while he rubbed his elbow. She was not yet unclean.

"Is it hurting?"

When he looked at her, she knew that was why he had sought her. His face looked suddenly drawn—it would be at least six sunrises before she would be back. He had grown to need her touch every day.

She gently began massaging his wrist and arm.

Her thumb kneaded the base of his thumb, which had been bruised blue in an earlier accident on the trail. He all but moaned with the relief of her touch, which was an agony at first, fading into sweet release of tension wherever her fingers moved.

He sighed and leaned away from her, tugging a little against her pull as she worked her way up to the sore elbow, driving the first hint of pain from him like the wind against high clouds.

"I will be back in a few days. Do you still keep your promise to me even though I am not here to rub your pain away each night after you confront the white man?"

He stared back at her, enthralled by her eyes glistening in the pale darkness. Overhead stars cluttered the sky.

She cupped his face in her hands and spoke very softly. "I have been coming toward you all my life. What does it matter to us if some strangers are allowed to flee? Much honor will stick to you as the man who sent them away."

Her fingers felt so cool and soothing on his temples where she rubbed small circles, but he said anyway, "What will happen if I kill this arrogant white chief as I should?" he asked.

She removed her touch from his face.

"A little more, a little more," he said, grabbing her hand again, but she pulled away from him, her silence answering his question. She would cease her healing touch.

Among the Shawnee she had felt no desire, as though her body were healing from the birthing and the fall, as well as the months of sadness that had gone before. But since she first touched Fox, she had been on fire, so he healed her as much as she healed him. She denied those feelings now as she stood abruptly and walked away from him back toward the other woman, with whom she would retire to the menstrual hut.

He watched her depart as he repeated the formula. He felt a twinge in his wrist. It must be because he had been working so hard the past few days on the scalp tassel, he thought, and massaged it with his other hand.

Chapter 33

At least I can say this—
Spears will be shattered where
I shall be;
I do not say I shall not flee.

—Saga Llywarch, the Old Cycle
Welsh
c. A.D. 500

Madoc rolled up the sliver of squirrel parchment and slipped it into the message capsule on Culhwch's pink leg, then handed the bird to Gwen, who blew it a feather-ruffling kiss and released it into the sunshine.

She watched her father watching the pigeon course out over the dead oat field and catch the cliffside's constant updraft, thinking she was seeing resignation in him, but when he glanced back, she saw his eyes were silvery instead of gray.

"I do not want to give up everything we have worked for here in this good place," she said.

"There are many good places."

"A sailor never wants to settle down," she replied, echoing her long-dead mother.

"I am quite a rover, I grant you," he said cheerfully and held her hand. "But I understand some other people are not."

"This is a good home," she said. "If we and the Yuchi stand up to Fox with iron weapons, we could win."

"Is that what the men are saying? Dag and the others?"

A muscle twitched in her lip.

He squinted against the glare as he gazed at the river

473

chasm and surrounding forest. "It is not as good as I first thought."

She cocked her head. She knew about the crop failure but believed John when he said they would have better luck next season if they planted in early March instead of April.

"There is no way to hold off a siege," Madoc continued. "When the ancient builders raised these walls, they were not thinking about defense. Maybe they were marking a sacred place in their religion."

"They have no word for religion."

"Well, their gods or something," he shrugged, thrown off his track by the threat of a religious discussion. Since her experiences among the red people, she had taken a philosophical turn that put him off. "And there is no iron anywhere around here. Odd, is it not—we have several pounds of gold left of our treasure but are desperate because we have no common iron."

"Golden swords would not work?" she asked playfully.

"On a pudding, maybe." He shook his head, reminding her as he more often did these days of her grandfather, which put a pang of loss through her because she had a dream that Owen was dead.

"What about the Yuchi?" she asked. Her husband was tormented by the position into which this alliance placed his father and his small tribe.

"They are our allies, after all, and not our partners," Madoc replied, but he knew what lay behind her words. Each day of negotiations David Iron watched his old father grow more hollow-eyed as the Cherokee chief assumed more and more power.

Gwen could not forget her father's words as they went to more meetings with the Cherokee, who had been joined by chiefs from other nations. She saw that Madoc was not even trying to keep this place but was stalling while he waited to get word to the crew in the south. He had been able to keep Fox talking for almost a month, when Fox declared that Weather Eyes must take his people completely away from these parts.

"You must also agree not to violate any Muskogean territory," Fox said, eyeing his ally, Shell-of-Many-Colors, who had given Gwen a hard stare until she changed positions with her husband and could no longer see the miko of Mabila who once had her as his bride.

"You must take the Duck River west to the Tennessee," Fox continued, and Madoc recalled what he knew of the rivers from his son-in-law's drawings. "You must take the Tennessee downriver away from this place and never return." Fox eyed Rhys. It gave him chills when he looked at the painted face of the kanegmati sachem. No matter where he was in the lodge, the blind man seemed to be staring at Fox.

Later Madoc asked David Iron where they could go, given Fox's option.

"The Yuchi leads to the Shawnee homeland," said David Iron, stubbornly refusing to use the river's Cherokee name.

"Your father tells me the Yuchi runs into the longest river in the world."

David Iron nodded. "I have been to the banks of the Great River Road, but Winnowed Rice has been farther up its course."

"My people would welcome you," Winnowed Rice said when asked, "especially if you bring beads and knives."

Through these discussions around the council fire and with his advisers, Madoc tried to imagine using the Great River Road to return to the bay and eventually the sea to recross the ocean back to Britain. He did not share these thoughts with anyone, but he could not shake them, despite the fact that he knew to descend the river would take them directly into Chickasaw territory. Recently Wyn had passed by while he was dust-sketching the way he thought the rivers ran down to the sea. Wyn had taken the stick and added the western coast of Europe with Britain better defined than the rest, which the abbot knew only from maps in the monastery library. Together they had tried to piece together the world as they knew it but could not finish because it rained before they had positioned Cathay in relation to this new country—was this the eastern edge of the Orient or Africa? Even now, listening to David Iron beside the communal fire burning in the compound between the Big House and the llan, Madoc could not stop thinking about the possibilities.

"Winnowed Rice knows many trails, river branches, and salt licks where animals gather," David Iron was saying.

There were vast wildernesses, she explained, where no tribe lived. "Beyond those in the land between two rivers, my people will welcome us and you, too, as our adopted family."

Madoc sat in the next session listening to Fox give a long

speech about the size of his war-band and the extent of territory now claimed by the Cherokee. Madoc listened to the translation with only half his mind. Privately he was thinking about building a ship as soon as they arrived at this land of Kantuck, where Winnowed Rice said great oaks grew, to accomplish his larger plan—the idea haunted his thoughts and his dreams.

Fox launched into a long poem about the moons of fall, which were considered excellent for traveling since the weather was no longer too hot and not yet too cold. They smoked a round of tobacco, amiable as old women now that the line had been drawn. Madoc's people had been working on the coracles for a week, but he was not sure they could be ready within Fox's deadline.

He was glad to leave the red encampment that day—in fact, was beginning to anticipate leaving this place entirely without any remorse. As he walked back to the Big House, he heard someone with a hammer at an anvil over in the llan; the furnace was cold for lack of metal, but as he approached, he saw Wyn bent over his work, all alone and happily singing some old Latin hymn.

He was working on a small piece, a shaft of light striking him from a hole in the thatch overhead. When he straightened to give it another thwack, sunlight smashed against the metal, igniting the fire of gold so that it momentarily blinded Madoc. "What is this?"

Wyn beamed at him and wordlessly turned the tray-sized object his way. Madoc saw when the glare angled away from his eyes that the monk had been using a mallet and chisel to stamp marks into the plate. He bent closer and understood Wyn's earlier interest in the dirt map, surprised with admiration to see what the holy man had created.

"I am more used to parchment," Madoc said in wonder. Wyn brushed his scarred fingertips across the lustrous surface Madoc likewise could not keep from touching.

"It is so beautiful," Madoc said, but he was thinking what an impractical object this was, useless to a sailor. "But why?"

Shyly, betraying a touch of pride, Wyn answered, "Because what we have accomplished should never be forgotten." Then, looking at Madoc, "Do you think it is accurate, arglwydd?"

Wyn had etched the familiar European coast at the right margin of his golden map. Between those coastlines and the imagined western boundaries were the pockmarks of the

Fortunate Isles and the vast expanse of the ocean they had crossed not so long ago. The western coast Wyn had drawn according to ecclesiastical charts of Cathay with its many islands. His theology was clear in his drafting because not far left of Cathay the deserts of the Infidel stretched to the Holy Land, and beyond, the Mediterranean Sea and the bulk of Africa taking up any unknown territory. He had encompassed the world as it was known by the most knowledgeable minds of his time, but what drew Madoc's attention was a broken line from Ireland southward and westward and into the hollow of the gulf that brought them to this place by way of Mobile Bay.

"The route is as true as we can ever know, but you forgot Vinland," Madoc observed, tapping the North Atlantic.

"Do you think it is the northernmost point of this place?"

Madoc shrugged characteristically. "Make it a large island. . . ." This interpretation sorely reminded him of his lost pilot, and he wondered as he often did where Fair Beard might be. Madoc traced a remembered coastline with his finger. "At least three times larger than Britain, with Vitromannaland below it, across a wide river."

Madoc left him to his task, still dazzled by the chart of gold and the implications of that broken line that belonged to him, being his mark upon the world however invisible, and to his great ship abandoned in the swamp. We have done something, he thought for the first time, something marvelous, which other men should know about. Wyn's useless map had done that for him, recalling the larger view.

Precisely because of that, Wyn's map irritated Madoc because of its insistent vision—to see the world in one wide glance and remind him of potential, which seemed at this moment tantalizingly outside his grasp. He stood at the cliff for a while, watching Rhys and the Shawnee women working on the coracles below at the river edge, then, thoughts still dazed by golden lines and great possibilities, he walked home with Rhys in the late afternoon.

"It has been too long since we sent the pigeon," Madoc growled to Gwen as he entered the gloomy kitchen, sweating and tired and distracted by his thoughts. "I think your bird is not going to make it, daughter," he said, seating himself at the end of the bench after the others made room for him. Ari handed him a bowl full of steaming soup and a cake of amaranth bread, which Madoc hated. He took it anyway so he would not hurt anyone's feelings. Teleri was especially proud of how she had learned to use the native plants as the red women were teaching her. But this bread made of crushed seeds was as gritty as river bottom.

"Fox says we must leave before the new moon," he said to about twenty members of the Hundred at the big table. "I cannot get us any more time." He frowned, the steam off the soup tickling his mustaches.

David Iron nodded, smiling at the joke. Fox was not being subtle. "Traveling Moon," he said, which was what the red people called October.

"There are more watchers over there today," said Evan who had just come in from the watch. As he spoke, two others entered, went to the kettle, and helped themselves with wooden bowls. There was no more room at the table, so they crouched on bales and crates, wasting no time, drinking the soup.

"Mabilans?" Madoc asked around a spoonful. Onion and turtle, he thought, trying to place the undertaste.

"Some other kind of pinhead," answered one of those who had just entered. "Pig-naked with many tattoo rings."

"Chickasaw," said David Iron, and at that word everyone stopped eating. Both the Muskogean and Shawnee women had filled everyone with tales of the terrible Chickasaw.

"How close are we to launching the coracles?" Madoc asked Rhys, who was the expert on their construction. For several days he had been working with Wil and the Shawnee women down on the riverbank, where the women were learning how to handle the oblong craft they fashioned from willow, cane, and buffalo hides.

"We sealed most of them today."

"Indeed," Madoc said wryly, because the stench of bear fat was still strong from Rhys's direction, even though he bathed in the river to get the mess off his hands and arms.

"They need a week to cure."

"We can load in a morning," Madoc said, thinking out loud.

"What about the crew?" asked one of the men in the shadows.

"We must get word to them, assuming the pigeon did not get past the buzzards."

"Arrow-Eye has not brought down a pigeon in weeks," Gwen remarked.

"No offense, mistress of the mews," her father said, looking squarely at David Iron, who was the logical choice. "Someone must go and get them. We quit this mountain day after tomorrow."

It shocked them all full of protest.

"This hill has been bad luck to the Hundred," he added.

They stared at him for saying things they had all been muttering about.

"We all know this is true. The sooner we leave, the better. So, son, you must hightail it to the *Horn* and bring our men up to meet us. We will be at the junction of the Duck and the Yuchi rivers two sundowns from tonight. We cannot stay there long." He did not have to remind anyone about the Chickasaw.

Gwen behind her husband was surprised by her father's decision, but not David Iron, who had suspected the chief would want someone to reconnoiter the river ahead and to rendezvous with the *Horn*—the pigeon obviously had not made it.

David Iron was frowning. "You mean to abandon the great Uktena?"

"How else?" Nobody could know what this meant to Madoc, to leave the *Horn* to rot in the swamp. He still could not let himself see her tilting in the mud, going down with each high water, coming apart, and finally, how many years in the future, disintegrating back into the murk of the earth. He knew he should order her burned—at least give her a warrior's funeral. But he could not. However impossible it was for him to go now, someday he might be able to reclaim her.

"I will do what my father asks," David Iron said sorrowfully.

And the next misty morning half the Hundred went down to the river to see him off below the cliff where the women, the monks, and Rhys were already at the last stitching of the buffalo hides to the wicker frames.

"I am going, too," Gwen said.

"No," her husband said flatly.

Madoc grinned at his son-in-law, who replied without looking at his wife, "It is not proper for her to go."

"She is a good traveler, a sailor's daughter," Madoc said mildly, making her smile. There was a new glow to her; Lord, but she was a beauty.

"A new mother must not travel," David Iron said adamantly.

Madoc turned to her. "Is this true?"

She still had fight in her but was so happy to see her father beaming his joy.

Everyone was full of congratulations to the two young people, shaking hands and clapping shoulders. Teleri put her arms around Gwen, who smiled shyly.

David Iron took possession of her with a long arm. "Your father is wise. He will agree with me now."

Madoc cocked his head and looked at her to see what she was thinking. He did not want to see Ann in her, but how could he not with that red hair and those blue eyes?

He stepped closer to her. "I think this woman can make up her own mind, David Iron." He put his hands on her arms and drew her toward himself, rocking her and making a happy humming deep down in his chest only she could hear. He held her until she broke it, a long time to make up a little for the distance he had been unable to keep from forming between them.

"Thank you, sir," she said, standing back a little.

Madoc said, "Admit it, you want her with you."

David Iron shrugged, feeling maneuvered without an ally.

"Now," Madoc said, "before you go, tell me about this river we must ride."

David Iron broke off a twig of laurel, hunkered down, and began drawing in the wet sand. "A pleasant journey." His voice drew others near. Little boys pushed in close—Madoc was aware that among them were Wil's boys and Einion. He hardly recognized him now. The little Celt, his own baby brother, was as red as a sassafras root, mud painted and be-bangled with the trinkets the several little Shawnee boys put in their hair as they remembered their fathers and elder brothers. The astonishing change in the boy's appearance drew Madoc's attention so that he had to force himself to concentrate on what David Iron was saying.

"The Duck is a young male river running through gullies in high water, but during this dry Hunting Moon he is lazy." He indicated with a sketch where the river would buck and turn on its fickle western course to the wide, placid Lower Tennessee, which he called the Yuchi. "In high water this place"—he pointed—"is portage," continuing in a combination of sign, improving Cymraeg, and his sketch map on the ground. "But now—easy—white water for sport. The Duck—friendly, flowing through blood country where no tribe lives."

Camp on the northeastern shore of the Duck, and whatever you do, do not set foot to the western shore of the Yuchi."

Madoc knew that was Chickasaw territory and nodded. "And should I have to navigate the Yuchi without you, tell me a little about that river, please."

"Winnowed Rice knows more about the Yuchi downstream."

"What about upstream?"

David Iron gave him an odd look; why would the chief want to know about the river upstream of the stretch he would take?

David Iron bent again over his map. "Some say the river my people named was cut by the great Uktena, making a burrow where it supposedly laid a crystal egg."

As he spoke, he drew a jagged U-shaped line that began at the far right of his area—about a yard of powdery red sand just damp enough to hold the impression. "It is not a natural river that flows in one direction." From its beginning he brought the line southwest, where he angled it west for a few hand spans.

"This was the stretch we walked along when we left the great canoe last winter."

David Iron drew marks to indicate Muscle Shoals, then abruptly he curved the line back due north. "Here it swallows the Duck River." He indicated with the stick the river gurgling from two forks behind them.

"The Duck flows the way it should, directly east to west. If you leave by dawn, the Duck will take you to the Yuchi before nightfall. But the Yuchi it joins gets even stranger." He curved the line of the major river westward again. He stopped it there, keeping the twig at the termination.

"Downstream from the Duck it joins another river that flows from the east—the River of the Shawnee."

Someday, long in the future, Englishmen would rename the Shawnee the Cumberland and would use it to enter country that would be known as Tennessee, as would the Yuchi River itself be called by its Cherokee name.

Madoc's homeland had some mighty and strange rivers, a couple of which flowed northward, and some which wandered in several directions before spilling into one of several seas. But never had Madoc seen a river quite like this one David Iron described. What massive upheavals had destined its progress to give it so many kinks and bucks over so large a country?

"Our strange river and the Shawnee continue flowing westward, where they meet a third river that is more natural, falling from the northeast to the southwest—the Ohio. Now our river made bigger by these and many smaller streams continues on west until it meets one larger than itself—the Great River Road."

In the language of the Sioux, who alone knew its source, that would be the Mississippi.

He drew a long north-south slash all the way down his map, then terminated it with the curved line of the Gulf of Mexico. "The Great River empties into the sea." He watched Madoc carefully to deduce his reaction to the drawing. "This is the picture my teacher drew for me."

Madoc knew this was the sea they had first entered.

"Very large salt water. The grandfathers say that long ago a mighty people who loved the sun came from the south across this sea, and up the Great River and Duck River to became the Yuchi."

"So where are we now?"

David Iron placed his pointer at the confluence of the Yuchi River with the Duck, then followed the latter eastward to a fork. There he placed a large cross for this mountain.

Madoc absorbed the map, feeling the press of people all around him so that the light dimmed. They were mostly children, but several Shawnee women and the monks were busy at the wicker frames a few paces away. They had managed to draw nearer so they could listen, while continuing to work on the new coracles.

"How many days from the Duck to the Great River Road?"

Leaning back on his knees, David Iron thought about it. "As I said, I have never been that way, but my teacher went there often in the old days. He never said exactly how many sunrises." He looked over at Winnowed Rice. "From here on ask her."

"I know," Winnowed Rice spoke up from her place beside Rhys. They were working on the coracles. Rhys had a skill at weaving round frames, while Winnowed Rice, the baby asleep on her back, tied off the joins. So far he and the other men had woven thirty-five frames; the women stretched a buffalo hide over more than half and were busy at stitching them now. Others rubbed the shaved leather with bear grease, which had proven to be as good a lubricant as sheep lanolin.

Madoc nodded that she should speak, and she did so in

Shawnee, continuing to bind the joints of the completed frame with rawhide thongs, her stained fingers quick and sure. "We make this journey many times." David Iron translated what she said for Madoc so that the murmur of his voice was a few seconds delayed and overlapping her Shawnee, sounding like poetry sung in a round. "Three days."

"So two days if we push it," Madoc said, musing about the possible size of this country. Downriver travel was fast. Even at two days this country was far bigger than he had imagined.

"And," Winnowed Rice continued, "we can all camp where our grandmothers still follow the buffalo."

"Rumor says the Leni Lenape have invaded the Kantuck," David Iron reminded her between themselves and without translating.

"You have the blue metal. They will be only few in number while the Shawnee are many in those parts." She set down the work and used sign—hands together at the palms thrown outward implying absolutely no limit—to add, "It is a big land."

Madoc looked expectantly at his son-in-law, who interpreted what the Shawnee said in sign but left out references to the Leni Lenape. Madoc caught the word, however, and wondered why the translator used only a few words to represent her long speech without mentioning the northern tribe known for fierceness.

Her remark seemed to answer his unspoken questions about the territory. He came here thinking this was an island called Vinland by the Norsemen who stumbled upon it accidentally, the way he and Snorrison had hit upon some large unknown island farther north some years ago. It gave him a chill to think that perhaps it was one huge island they had found, or the other side of Africa, after all, or . . . or another Europe. He tried to imagine such a landmass, a hundred, a thousand times the size of the little country his father was fighting to hold onto. If he could just get back, Owen would believe him about this place, would see it as the salvation of the house of Gwynedd—why, a hundred Britains could fit into the uninhabited lands he could see in all directions from the top of the mountain above them, and now Winnowed Rice was saying in eloquent handsign that still more unimaginably immense lands lay north and west.

He knew if he could return to witness, Owen would believe.

Yes, Madoc thought with a surge of hope that pulled a rare smile from him as he asked, "What would you say is your most difficult problem on this trip?"

"Finding the mouth of Bear Creek," David Iron replied, wondering at the odd question. "It is easy to miss, but it changes the river to a dark green along the southern bank."

Madoc pointed to the Yuchi and the Tombigbee, joining the two streams with a broken line, less than the width of a little finger on David's map. What he was seeing was something that would strike later observers as obvious. At its Great Bend the Yuchi River should have flowed southward. As David Iron said, it is a strange river that does not flow naturally. Maybe humans will never know why, but it has to do with the hard ancient rock of its channel, and the rising of the land over thousands of generations. It should have flowed south.

Instead it heads west. Only a few miles away lies the source of the Coffin-Maker, where they poled the *Horn*, a stream that cuts a tame course due south to empty into the southern gulf. With a simple portage across the finger width, one could make the journey directly from the place where they stood to the sea where Madoc's Hundred first landed on these shores.

"From Bear Creek to the Coffin-Maker, less than an afternoon over the well-worn path," David Iron said. "I travel faster alone."

"You need a tender giving you water and food."

"I will do as my father asks," David said formally in the language he was quickly learning, but in the voice of a Yuchi male bound in reluctant duty.

Madoc was distracted by Rhys's hands bending the wickerwork, when suddenly, in one of those uncanny moments when it seemed the blind man was observing him, Rhys turned his face in Madoc's direction. He was wearing the sash instead of the dramatic face paint. The breeze lifted the fringe beside his ear. His hair was braided in several neat Shawnee ropes, while the back hung in a single luxuriant quoit. Rhys smiled.

"You had better get started," Madoc said, gesturing at the new sun on the ridge over David's shoulder. "Yn y cwch."

David nodded and stood, dropping the pointer. There was no time for a moment between himself and his father-in-law, but, David Iron thought, finally he is beginning to trust me.

David Iron, with great feelings of love for his new people, watched as Madoc held out his arms to embrace Gwen, who was holding many parcels and, now he saw as the fragrant breeze lifted the red cloth covering it, a wicker cage on one finger.

When he saw the eagle inside, David Iron's face darkened: He wanted her to release the bird, considering it bad luck.

Arrow-Eye gave a harsh scream and flew against the bars of his cage when Madoc moved too close in his attempt to relieve Gwen of some of her burden and help load the coracle. The bird startled him with its vehemence as it raked talons in his direction and gave a hissing attack shriek.

But he laughed at it and there were hugs all around. Teleri pressed a small wooden cross into Gwen's hand before she took the canoe. "It is made of splinters of the true cross," she said softly. "I do not know if that is true, but my father believed it when he carved this."

Gwen took the amulet and thanked Teleri, warming even more to her stepmother.

Yngvild was there with her son clutching his toy canoe. The boy had taken a shine to David Iron and now wiggled to be allowed down to cast his own little ship upon the waters with the red man's.

"No, Little Bear," the Yuchi said to the child, who solemnly listened with a reticence beyond his age and temperament, "another time we will canoe together."

"We will pray for you," Wyn said, and launched into it, "Oh, heavenly father, hear the prayers of these your children. . . ." He kept it brief, though, and on his amen David Iron launched the coracle onto the rippling silvery water. Their coracle was an oblong craft with one wide thwart forwards and a wide bilge deck of woven wicker, where David had arranged their gear. Wil was handing them a water skin and food. Gwen's friends among the Shawnee women shyly stepped up and gave her little things, as though she and David Iron were going away for a long time.

Teleri watched these small rituals, chilled by her feelings that she would never see her new daughter again. She slipped her arm around Madoc's waist and stood close to him, letting the warmth where they touched dispel the premonition.

Throughout all this the young couple were engaged in an argument they were trying to keep private, impossible under the circumstances, as David held the coracle and Gwen leaned to stow the re-draped cage under the wide thwart.

". . . and I want you to release it," David Iron whispered through tightened lips as he stood, his hand on her arm.

She stood up to him with the wicker dovecote dangling from a finger. Inside it Arrow-Eye protested his confinement by slapping against the bars.

"With that wing he would be dead before noon."

"It is not fitting to keep such a creature prisoner." Her husband could not begin to explain all the bad luck and evil that attended those who were not careful with eagles.

They would have said more but saw Madoc watching and bit off further argument. Gwen boarded the canoe, stowing the cage under the thwart. "Your threatening words frighten him," she whispered to her husband.

"It is not me that bird hates." David Iron looked up shyly at Madoc, who shrugged.

He had no idea what the creature had against him. He took a few steps away from that end of the coracle, as David Iron held up two small bundles of sticks, one of which he gave to Madoc.

"Break one each sunrise. When you break the last one, we will see you where the Duck meets the Yuchi."

Madoc saw that each stick was meticulously carved with a miniature animal head. "And we will keep the pennant flying," he said, wondering at the tradition of counting by sticks—so much labor to put into something that would in any case be broken. He was hoping that the crew was holding the pigeon; if so it would need the pennant to home in.

Gwen looked back across the rippled water as her father bent forward to free a trailing line.

David Iron called some encouraging word to Gwen. She nodded, repositioning Arrow-Eye's wicker cage more securely.

Everyone waved and called after them—Godspeed, good luck, and successful journey in a stew of languages—as their craft dipped into the course.

Gwen watched her father and Teleri diminish across the water. She raised her chin, hoping that he would see her. But he looked at Teleri instead. Shreds of mist fell between them.

One moment he was there, the next he was gone.

Chapter 34

. . . a wood your curragh sails;
a forest, heavy with mast,
sleeps under your keel.

—The Double Vision of Manannan
Irish
c. A.D. 700

She could not see anyone now and felt alone, moving backwards in a world gone fuzzy with all-enveloping fog. It gave her a strange, suddenly cut-off feeling, as though she had just been born. Then she felt the muscles moving in David Iron's strong back against hers and heard a muffled grumpy croak from Arrow-Eye. She asked her husband if he wanted water; he said no and kept steering.

The eagle rattled the cage. Gwen whistled. It seemed to please the bird because he settled down, cooing under the wrap.

Effortless passage down the singing river was soothing. Gwen's strange detachment faded, replaced by contentment as she leaned against her husband's back.

The mist did not burn off, so though the day brightened, they flew downstream into continual clouds. This was common along these rivers in the dry season. Midafternoon they pulled over where the Duck met the Yuchi for a short break—they wanted to get as much upriver travel in as possible before dark.

They left a stack of river-polished rocks with a feather from Arrow-Eye under the top stone as a sign for those who would follow, and very soon, cloaked in the mist that afternoon only thickened, they were on the water again, this time not driven by the current but paddling against it. Now David's back muscles strained against his woven shirt, Rhiannon's wedding present, soaked with sweat between them.

The sky glowed like alabaster with the sun behind it. They could hear birds lifting from the marsh that was the east verge of the Yuchi, and once a bear's rumble in the shrouded distance.

Without stopping they ate from pouch stores—jerky, a couple of the uncooked crunchy white tubers, hard corncake. She fed David over his shoulder so he did not miss a stroke, even though the current was stronger against them as they drew nearer the shoals. The mist was so thick it would shorten their daylight. Sure he could make Deer Creek before darkness, David was pushing it, dreading the water at night.

They heard what sounded like a hawk. The covered golden eagle hissed, ancient rivalries stirred in its breast. This was a bird that hunted other hunting birds.

The far bank was lost in swabbing; passing on their left was a ghost land of leafless, dead-looking trees in shallow water.

"Hmmh?" she wondered.

"Mmmmh," he answered, his voice vibrating her back with an ominous rumble.

"Hawk?"

Stroke, pull, stroke, pull.

As sharp as a blade, the shriek echoed again off the enshrouded trees. Arrow-Eye hissed a response and flapped inside the wicker bars. David increased his pace, breathing heavily.

The shriek ripped the air a third time, but instead of ending like a hawk's, it rose in pitch to become an unmistakable human cry. Arrow-Eye battered himself against his confinement, shrieking, rattling the cage at Gwen's feet.

Suddenly from the foggy curtain on their right, a low boat appeared, pacing their own. On it were three bald, brightly feathered warriors. Coming suddenly from the west upon the man and woman, apparently materializing out of nothing, the attackers were a trio of naked Chickasaw with bright blue tattoos ringing their arms, legs, and red-rimmed eyes.

David Iron groaned with a glance over his shoulder when he saw that two were rowing, while the man in the prow held in his snarl-bared teeth a short blowgun aimed directly at Gwen and waiting only for better range. The gap of black rippled water narrowed as the Chickasaw canoe swung in closer behind them. There was enough light from the dull red west to see the grinning headman at the front of the canoe. His teeth had been filed to sharp points. His rowers were chirping a repeated sound like, lee, lee, lee, as they plowed the water with almost lazy strokes in time with the chanted trill, entreating the river spirit to give them the enemy canoe.

David Iron tried to swing the canoe around so he and not Gwen faced the onslaught, but it was a tricky maneuver even his strength could not accomplish while still keeping their forward motion against the current.

One of the pursuers could not resist giving another hawk call. It was all the challenge Arrow-Eye could take; the eagle whipped again at the cage door, talons clawing as he shrieked.

David Iron was ready to leap out onto the attackers when they were close enough. "Swing around, swing around," he called to his wife in both their languages. She grabbed a paddle and tried to help.

The grinning headman leaned his faceful of garish blue tattoos so close, Gwen could smell him as she reached for the latch of the cage door. He obviously did not want to shoot her with the blowgun as he reached out to grab her. In that moment Arrow-Eye exploded from the cage directly below him in a wrath of feather and shriek.

The startled Chickasaw covered his eyes and fell back. The two others behind him shouted as the eagle gained its wing and ascended, screaming all the while. It cocked a menacing head, found its target with one obsidian eye, and plummeted down on the naked scalp of the Chickasaw headman.

He fought off the talons that had already drawn blood as his rowers backpaddled, pulling the long canoe out of its cross-current as David Iron threw a leg up, then powerfully down to kick the enemy prow, tilting it farther against the current. The feathered chieftain had made the mistake of standing as he defended himself against the eagle's claws. The canoe tipped, sending him and the others sprawling backwards with a splash.

Just in time Arrow-Eye let go of a shred of his face and lazily dipped a wing in Gwen's direction as he circled clumsily; the left wing was still not strong. When he landed awkwardly on the wicker cage, he was making small crying noises and nodding his bloodstained head. Gwen, whistling to comfort him, saw that none of the blood was his own. She scooped up water and cleaned him, then guided him back behind the gate, which she firmly latched. He began cleaning his beak against the wicker as she covered it with the flannel.

She pressed her spine close to David Iron's in unspoken need of his closeness. His muscles rippled back a silent reply.

There was no trace of the attacking canoe or its riders as David Iron pulled them upriver, his breathing labored now, sweat and liquified mist running down his hair, face, and neck.

"Better . . . leave . . . a sign. . . ." he whispered. Gwen took the red cloth off the cage; it was the last scrap of woven goods she had left from home. David detoured them slightly around a stand of willow where driftwood had piled up in the shallows. Gwen used the cloth to wipe sweat from his face, then tied it with a strong double knot to a stout snag a little above eye level.

Last light, a sickly purple, faded around them. David Iron looked around, assaying the lay of the land along this stretch. Something about the way the bank curved at this point, about what he recognized as the muffled steady vibration that signaled the shoals, told him that Bear Creek emptied nearby, so he swung them out across the current of the river toward what gradually became the southwest shore.

The worse luck of all was to be on the river at night, especially when fighting might have to be done. No matter how much he believed Jesus would look out for his red children, David Iron could not let go of his old beliefs. No red man wanted to die at night and have his spirit lost forever, trying to find the sun and follow it to the land of the dead in the west.

He worried that not even the Christ could help such an unfortunate man, though Wyn assured him it made no difference to Jesus. Their conversation had been recent, and Gwen knew her husband was thinking about these things as he paddled with maximum strength across the current, which urged them further back downriver than he might have wished, so they lost some distance covered but soon were skimming parallel to the other stony bank.

With just enough light to see, he followed a stream of clearer shallow water now pointing to the confluence he sought. Bear Creek did not rush into the larger stream but more gently opened into it, lying low and giving little evidence of its shy entry. A long clear stream of water along the now-southern bank marked the approach from downriver. Once into the Bear, there was little current.

By now he was going by sense of touch, using his paddle to conn the shallow bottom near the bank, poling them slowly along. He took them onto the gravelly beach and rolled out of the coracle, Gwen right behind him. The sky above the leafless trees glowed faintly enough for them to see each other's silhouette. They held each other for a long time, hearts pounding.

All the while David Iron was listening as he held her, hearing small scratchings to the left—a mouse or weasel. A snake or newt scraped sinuously along an upright snag at the edge of the forest, where the trees dripped condensed moisture.

Nothing sounded threatening. Soon they stood and stretched sore muscles in the quiet pine wood. To the right, up a clay embankment, a blue jay launched itself behind a ringing call. Not far away now the final mighty stretch of shoals teased the river into a snarling beast. They could faintly hear it, muffled by the forest around them.

They relieved themselves, careful not to let their water return to the creek, then moved inland, where he determined it was safe to start a small fire.

He took out his flints. Soon he had the dry kindling he always carried sparking with healthy flames. He set it behind a stand of boulders between themselves and the creek and began feeding it splinters of deadwood, while Gwen tied the coracle in the lower branches of a huge cedar tree.

The fire caught, and she tossed pebbles into it to get hot enough to boil water.

While she prepared sassafras tea from their supplies, they nibbled jerky. David Iron pointed with a piece of it to indicate the tumbled wicker cage rattling at an angle on the ground where Gwen dropped it. She retrieved her fowling glove then unlatched the cage to let Arrow-Eye clutch his careful way up her leather-sleeved arm. He rubbed his beak on either side of her lips as she whistled to him while giving her husband a glance.

David Iron held up his hands as if to say, very well, you win, as she stood and walked with the bird back over to him sitting on a log. "Soon now," she said as she rejoined her husband, setting the cage on the gravel where the eagle found a perch. "To live an eagle's life is best. Animals are smart about these things. He will leave when he is ready."

"Wife," he said seriously, spitting out a shred of jerky, which he offered carefully to Arrow-Eye. "That bird can stay as long as he likes."

In the morning they took Bear Creek south through a piny wood full of the tangled coils of briars, sharp green thorns on long, tough, wiry strands. It was as thick as a wall in places, overhanging the creek where recent high water had undercut the banks. Eroded slopes bled red slick clay. Emerald green patches of moss covered whole trunks of downed trees, while here and there long white beards of silver moss swayed eerily in the vapors that rose from the ground. The ripple of a snake marked the water briefly, but the surface settled quickly back to glassy smoothness. As the coracle slipped along, small, furtive, furry creatures raced back under ferns or rocks. Smaller branches fed into this one, some stained with green or bright red organisms or oily rainbow scum. The water grew more still, like polished metal, the farther away from the Yuchi they paddled.

They had not been long on the water when a scrap of something floated by slowly enough for her to catch.

"Woven cloth," she said, puzzling over it, showing him the dripping rag that was definitely a piece of what might be wool.

He made no comment about it. She continued to handle it until it dried with her body heat. She knew some of the tribes used small hand-looms. The swatch was stained with some sticky substance that smelled like turpentine and was so ragged she could not be certain what it was, though why it would be cast downstream on a creek that drained no inhabited banks was a mystery. She finally put it aside and forgot about it.

It was easy now on the placid water. All David Iron had to do was keep them sliding effortlessly upstream between the crowded evergreen banks, where here and there the foliage of a maple or sumac oak flared briefly red or gold. He had time to watch this stretch he had traveled in the past but saw no sign of any hidden observers in places they would have been if any of the Muskogeans were patrolling. This approach to the Tombigbee was a branch of an ancient path and water-road open to any nation, but it crossed their territory on the eastern and southern banks of the twisting Yuchi, as it did Chickasaw territory on the west above the Great Bend of the Yuchi.

They could see sky through swampy overhang only in the center channel of the stream so that they continuously slipped in and out of shadow.

He had two choices of route back to the *Horn:* Ahead, the first landing would lead them over a rougher shortcut to the source of the Tombigbee. Farther south, near the source of the Bear, was a wider trace that would take longer to cross.

"Soon," David Iron said, choosing the first and surest option, bringing Gwen up out of the floating trance into which she had fallen. Some insect was buzzing nearby. They went from gloom to shadow to gloom again. He gave one last long pull that brought them skipping up onto a mudflat directly beneath a low stand of cedar. The red roots of the ancient trees were exposed along the stretch nearest the creek, where swift water had plowed much higher than its present level.

They squished through wet red clay, dragged their coracle up onto dry ground, and listened for a moment to the whispering wood around them. The path was a natural grade around the generally rising forest floor that sloped under cedar cover before cutting across a level meadow of waist-high drying grass, which was colorless under the overcast sky. Many generations of moccasins had widened and leveled the grade; many campfires had burned on this traditional stop-over on the trace used by all nations. By nightfall across this last stretch they would find the wide swampy headsprings of the Tombigbee where anchored the *Horn.*

Ever-watchful, David Iron scouted a wide perimeter. Gwen could not hear him when he approached from the opposite direction. He stood watching her as she set the cage to one side and fed grains of corn to the golden eagle.

He dropped to his knees, silently removing his travel pack, continuing his alert reconnaissance while watching her feed an animal who should be free. Whenever he saw how these people interfered with things it made him fearful and excited at the same time. He removed the quiver full of arrows.

No red woman would keep an eagle. She would be too afraid of disastrous events that would certainly befall her lodge.

He had these same feelings when he first saw the blue metal being made—the red glowing bloom of the soft iron, a thistledown of fire, malleable under Brother Wyn's hammer as he struck it again and again, singing his hymn that spoke of beating the devil out of the world—all this was wonderful and awesome to Eagle Ring Man of the Yuchi. The thing they did that was so different, he mused as he watched his red-haired wife speak to the wild, intractable creature, the different thing about them was the way they interfered and apparently escaped the consequences.

It gave David Iron a shudder every time he saw them at this contrary work. They changed things from the natural course, and yet it did not bring them misfortune. He longed for their secret, thinking as the fire settled into the thicker deadfall branches, this must be due to the intervention of Jesus Christ, which is why he had taken their strange beliefs along with their clothes. His memory of the bloom of iron glowing out of the fire was renewed again, as it was with each recurrence of their sure, almost childlike, eagerness to re-make things the way they wanted.

She smiled when she saw he was observing her.

Without a word he stood, listening to the pines. Satisfied of their complete solitude, but made uneasy by the lack of animal sounds, he walked to her. His long hair was braided without the decorations he wore at their first meeting. He liked the loose suede trews affected by her father and his men, and their woven tunic and buckled belts with all the tack that went along with iron tools and the fine sheathed knife he finished under Wyn's tutelage. He kept the huge traveling moccasins—no boot invented by her people could match the moccasin for the foot of man. But like the white man, he cut off the fringe, which was so prized by red fashion.

She stood to hang the cage from a tree limb and turned to meet him. "You could be traveling faster alone," she reminded him as their hands touched.

"Not much." Again his glance darted around their center.

She followed his scan of the perimeter. "Perhaps we should move away from the path."

"I wish to stop for only a short rest," he said softly, pulling her a little closer.

After an intimate silence she said, "We have time."

David Iron uttered a husky little laugh as he slipped his arms around her.

Arrow-Eye battered himself against the wicker bars, causing the cage to swing on its branch. She untied the apron and tossed it across the cage, then turned back to David Iron, who kicked off his muddy boots beside their buffalo hide he had unrolled on the sweet-smelling nest of moss and pine needles.

They undressed each other down to the leather thongs about their necks, hers with Madoc's golden coin and his with Wyn's rustic cross. These, too, they set aside.

Arrow-Eye subsided. David Iron rolled himself and his wife into the buffalo fleece, so that later when the three Norsemen came strolling along the trace, they walked into the clearing without realizing it was occupied.

Lev had thrown himself down on a fallen log some few paces behind Gurd and Ulf, searching inside his boot for a pebble that had been worrying his progress through this dismal wood. They had hunted into the bush, where too much recent activity had spooked the game, but homeward bound now, they trudged the easy trace. They bagged only three small partridgelike fowl and had a long walk to get back to their base camp.

Ahead, Ulf and Gurd stepped into the worn clearing, where the eagle set up another racket, tossing Gwen's apron onto the ground. The startled sailors were further surprised by the lumpy buffalo robe quivering on the pine needles. They had their weapons drawn as one of them kicked back the hide to expose the glossy couple entwined and heaving beneath it.

David Iron rolled away from Gwen toward his knife, but the nearest white man intercepted with a sword tip and a kick at the red man's travel pack, where the knife was tucked. He lunged with the blade at the red man on his hands and knees while his partner barked out, "The captain's daughter—"

The other struck with the blade, but the quick red man rolled out of the way, bringing himself too near the screaming sailor, who hooked a kick that caught the man on the ground in the belly and rolled him into the low bushes near his backpack.

Gwen screamed and held back the arm of the nearest Norseman, the one named Gurd, whom she vaguely recognized as a member of Fair Beard's old crew. The third fellow, Ulf, who scuttled now to retrieve his blade, she did not know because he had joined Snorrison's ship in Ireland.

"What have you?" Lev asked, hurrying up behind the others at the sound of the commotion and limping a little because he had not found the pebble.

"This savage was raping the captain's girl," Ulf yelled across the clearing as he caught the struggling red man and began to kick him, pricking him here and there with the sword tip to divert David Iron from his pack.

Gwen abandoned Gurd and grabbed at the sword arm of David's attacker, screaming "No rape" to him several times, but he only flicked her off and turned back to finish the work.

"See, Ulf," Gurd said with regard to her as though continuing an old conversation, "I told you they like it."

But David Iron had taken that moment to reach for his tormentor's ankle, which he yanked, bringing him down, and at the same time pitching himself sideways so that he was able to strike with a heel at Ulf's sword hand and grab for the dropped weapon.

Lev called loudly enough to stop the Yuchi, but the white man kept coming so that Lev had to grab him. "She is his wife."

The sailor halted abruptly and stared at her, glancing from the red man at his feet to the copper-haired Welshwoman simmering before his eyes, naked, her shadows pink and forbidden. He scowled while righting himself and sheathed his weapon.

Gurd turned and spat into the bushes, then leveled disdain upon the white girl.

Suddenly covered with chill, Gwen grabbed the robe up around herself while David Iron stood, all his surfaces glistening with their juices and here and there stuck with dirt and leafy debris.

She handed him his tunic, and for a few uncomfortably silent seconds the three men watched David Iron slide into his clothes.

"The priest married them," Lev was saying, turning away from Gwen, who took her shift and moccasins behind the trees to dress. She could hear them commenting disparagingly on Lev's disclosure.

David Iron put the cross around his neck.

"Sounds as though some things have been happening," Gurd said, unable to keep from glancing Gwen's way.

Fists knotted, David Iron stepped menacingly between Gurd and the trees that screened Gwen, but Lev raised his voice to call to her, "Things have been happening here, too, lady."

She straightened the folds of her garments and ran her

fingers through her hair to remove a twig, then took a deep breath and walked back into the clearing, speaking briskly to dispel the tension. "My father says to abandon the ship in the swamp and join him where the rivers meet." Without pausing she walked purposefully to her pack and began rummaging it. "We had to leave the mountain and—"

Lev interrupted, "The ship is not in the swamp."

He heard Gurd and Ulf chuckle and laughed softly with them.

"We took her apart," Gurd said matter-of-factly.

Lev grinned at Gwen's astonishment. "Now," he continued, "we are putting her back together again."

Gwen looked at the three men, first in disbelief, then in realization as her gaze settled on Ulf: She did not know this white man. "You are . . . you are one of Snorrison's crew."

He grinned. "That I am, lady, boy and man these twenty years bound to Fair Beard Snorrison in a blood oath." He was a lean-faced fellow with bad teeth and dull, sun-bleached hair, not over thirty, whose speech reverberated with the accent of the northern islands.

"You went with him at first landfall."

"Aye."

"We thought you were all dead."

He chuckled, stuffed with delight at her ignorance.

"The head," she stammered, "it had to be one of you."

The fellow sobered only slightly. "My brother," he said, sniffing and snorting. "We lost him on the first beach." He blew his nose between his fingers off to one side, utterly disgusting to her, but a common thing to see the sailors do.

"Come along," Lev said, retrieving the pack he had dropped during the commotion. "You have some other surprises."

He stubbornly refused to say more as he hurried them to gather their things and continue along the trace to the camp, where he said the hunters were expected with the game.

"But you are going in the wrong direction," David Iron informed Lev with handsign.

"We are not going to the lake," he answered, kicking his foot as he tramped along, trying still to shake loose the irritation. "We are headed farther south."

David Iron was frustrated that he did not have enough of their common tongue to express what he was thinking, namely that if what they said about the great canoe was true, the Bear was too shallow any farther south. He muttered enough of this for Gwen to translate his concern.

Lev ahead of her on the trail shook his head and fell silent as he managed to kick off his moccasin without stopping, lumbering along with one foot bare while he shook his boot. He hopped to one side, replacing it with a quick twist of the laces then, picking up the pace, he led them back to the junction of this trace and the more southern one that led east from the lake that was the Tombigbee's source.

David Iron continued to grumble, certain that these foolish white men were lost and leading him in circles.

Arrow-Eye cawed a forlorn plea. Gwen fed him jerky and clucked back to both the eagle and to David Iron, smoothing their feathers and urging them to be patient and see what came, but she was the most surprised, stunned speechless in fact, when they approached what surely must be a unique spectacle in the heart of that ancient brooding forest.

Bear Creek was a gathering of springs at the foot of a cleft in a timeless limestone bed. It ran all year long, even in the worse drought, but as David Iron recalled, was usually too shallow during this dry season to navigate this close to its headwaters. It meandered through loamy forest over the limestone underpan, spreading out over polished stones, and not finding a stable depth until it neared the Yuchi River in what was traditionally Chickasaw territory but was observed as the neutral trace used by everyone.

But there had indeed been changes at the head of the Bear.

David Iron and Gwen stared in innocent surprise as they stood on the edge of a wide clearing of what used to be poplar trees, now a graveyard of telltale pointed stumps around the engorged pond David Iron had not seen for many seasons.

But these stumps had not been made by Norse or any man's axes. Each poplar had been gnawed to a conical point, leaving the gold-leafed hardwoods and dull evergreens untouched. David Iron immediately recognized the dam as the work of industrious beavers. Instead of the shallows sparkling over polished stones, the water here was now a small lake behind a thick beaver dam, which they stood below at this point so that behind the embankment there seemed to rise up close to the very sky itself the lean, graceful lines of the *Horn,* vast bulk on the watercourse, which was several acres in area, completely out of place and riding like a great swan dozing on the placid water, a thin stream of which spilled

over the dam in a melodious silver trickle to wash on down
the deep rocky draw lined with rank upon rank of logs, the
obvious product of human labor.

The sight pulled a gasp from Madoc's daughter, who could
not take in all the scene at once. She stared at the incongruous ship riding above the beaver dam like a dream, huge and
towering, men moving about on deck, jabbering, hammering,
yelling, pulling at lines and bringing aboard the delivery
point of a long line of red men, many with flattened foreheads, who handed off items plucked from a pile on the
shore. It was a swift, efficient relay, full of the shouts of men
working at their best pace. In addition to a few white men
were perhaps fifty red men of a nation unknown to Gwen,
though David Iron quickly surmised an alliance with the
Natchez, a little out of their usual territory.

The ship shimmered like a vision on the bosom of the
raised lake. Gwen and David Iron stumbled forward, led now
by Lev and the others as though addled, up and around the
inclining bank as men on the deck saw the hunters returning
with supper.

Lev, followed by Gwen, David Iron, and the two sailors
bringing up the rear, stepped through a wide treeless bank,
where there were scattered in obvious patterns many wooden
parts of the great ship with peg-holes empty, notably the
intricate rudder assembly, deck housings plus the massive
mast, yardarm, and a hundred other ship's bones.

Beyond these a squadron of red men hacked away at stark,
long pine oars, the full complement which Madoc had sacri-
ficed in Ireland for cargo space. Now that the *Horn* was a
river ship again, she needed human power.

To one side and occupying a large area of trampled grass
were what looked like bales of dark smallish pelts and rolls
and rolls of sail set amid a dozen red women, who sat or
knelt, their speedy hands stitching with long iron needles—
the sheet looked to be about three-quarters complete.

"Not much of a bag there, Lev," one tall white-bearded
giant called, relaxing against an adz. "That skinny red-haired
vixen would not be more than a couple of bites," he said as
he stood and walked toward Gwen.

"Uncle Snorri!" she cried, setting down the cage and
running to him to be swept up around him, around and
around the ducking red people and the stacks of barrels,
crates, bound parcels, and other cargo.

He set her down and looked up to see David Iron looming near, a scowl on his face and his fist already knotted.

Gwen stepped between him and Fair Beard, grabbed up the Icelander's hammy hand, and dragged him to face her husband.

"I would have known from the glow on your face alone, lady-girl," he said, eyeing David Iron but not really worried.

From behind Snorrison someone stood closer. Gwen saw it was a woman, a lovely dark-haired girl with skin like burnished bronze, not much older than herself and farther along in pregnancy. Fair Beard's eye caught the movement; he reached out for the girl, whose eyes flashed an unmistakable shaft of love for him, almost twice her height and more than twice her age.

Fair Beard chortled self-consciously, pulled at the mole on his left earlobe, and put his vast arm around the little girl, pulling her to him, where the top of her glossy black hair barely reached his sword link. "This is Tumkis," Fair Beard said, fairly blushing above his full beard and mustaches as he looked down upon the diminutive red woman.

Gwen and the girl shyly exchanged glances.

"Her name means dancing water," the Icelander said, obviously dashed by this lovely little blackbird. Gwen sensed something special about her and would come to understand what her husband already knew—this woman was a Natchez sun.

Snorrison seemed to pulsate for a second amid all his marvels. Then he caught Gwen's eye and looked self-consciously down at the adz.

"I still cannot believe you are alive," she said.

"I had some close calls. We landed on a big peninsula— Skraelings took us captive, but the iron is a miracle to them, so we were traded along with our axes to another tribe farther west on the saltwater gulf. During the trade negotiation we took our axes back, and from then on we were doing the trading as we heard stories by then about the *Horn* taking the Tombigbee—" He saw her watching him wide-eyed. "There's a trading network, and rumors of a grand city farther up the Great River Road. There is much more here than you would first suspect, lady-girl."

She thought of the Yuchi and their sacred mountain, the confrontation with Fox, and now the further migration of the Hundred northward to the land of the Shawnee—it was too much to tell him, and she guessed it, too, would sound like too much adventure.

"How did you accomplish all this?" Gwen's gesture indicated the incredible ship almost reassembled on the water behind them. "And who are all these people?" She recognized vaguely that they were more like Muskogeans than Cherokee or Shawnee, but their particular tattooing and dress suggested a strange red nation.

"They are Natchez, and how they and the beavers helped us get this ship across ten leagues of dry land and to this place is another long story," Fair Beard said, slapping the adz handle in a small, impatient gesture against his palm, glancing at his company stopped in the labor and staring in curiosity at the strangers.

"Get back to work," he shouted in what was evidently the Natchez language, not like Muskogean at all, but, she would learn later, still another tongue in this land of many languages. Behind him Tumkis authoritatively gestured at several people, indicating they should resume work, which they did immediately.

Still, they could not resist peeking at these two newcomers, an oddly dressed Yuchi and this startling flame-haired white girl.

"How did you find the ship?" Gwen asked, David Iron moving closer to her, avidly following Fair Beard's every word.

"News of the *Horn* on the Tombigbee traveled with the ravens," Snorrison laughed, looking down at the adz in his work-scarred hands—the right knuckles were barked, and the left thumbnail was carpenter blue. "We followed the story westward to the Natchez's territory on the banks of the Great River Road. The crew had received your father's message when we found the *Horn*. We have been at this more than a moon, as the red people say."

"You disobeyed his orders," she said wryly.

"I could not leave your father's beautiful ship to sink into the swamp. No, I could not believe his pigeon message when Lev read it to me, abandon the ship, no, I could not do it, and neither could your father if he were here."

"Then old Culhwch made it."

"I guess he did not make it back to you, else you would have known about all this. . . ."

"Poor old thing."

"Lev let him loose, oh, must have been a fortnight past, with our old code. Sorry."

"Tad wants you to meet him at the junction of the Duck and Yuchi," she blurted.

"Yes, and we will if we can only get this rig together," he said, gesturing with the adz.

"Chapa . . ." David Iron said, referring to beavers in amazement as he regarded the pond, fully twice as deep as the last time he saw it.

"Clever little beasts," Fair Beard said when he recognized the old trade word used by many nations for beaver, whose pelts were always an item of barter. The Yuchi could not help but notice a fortune in the pelts baled behind the sail-tenders, and not a single beaver on the water or near their dam, which was two-men-thick and spanning the creek in a wide bow that might be a full arrow shot in width—a good furlong by Gwen's measurements.

"You killed them all?" Gwen asked, staring at the pelts beyond counting. Behind her on the ground Arrow-Eye announced his ire by flapping wildly and giving a short, impatient screech. Fair Beard shrugged. "I see you are still looking after the wild beasts," he said without inflection, meaning not the departed chapa or the eagle but the broad-shouldered young red man in the woolen shirt behind her.

"And you, too, friend of my father, have taken in a wild thing," she replied coolly.

He squinted down at her and sideways, shrugged, and bent closer. "How is she?"

"Yngvild and little Bjorn are both in good health." Gwen thought about telling him how his wife had resisted a rival's insistent attentions—something Fair Beard had not managed. But she bit her tongue, figuring he would find out soon enough.

"A son? Well, well," he said, unable to conceal his self-satisfaction when he glanced at Tumkis, whom Gwen could tell knew very little of the language he was speaking.

"But your father-in-law did not make it through the winter."

Fair Beard listened, nodding. "He was a good man, a lusty warrior in his day and a fine storyteller."

He looked at the adz and back at the ship, beckoning Gwen and David Iron to follow him. "We will have her together by tomorrow afternoon," he said looking around, meeting various glances and silently giving the order to resume work, which was obeyed by everyone his eye encountered. The sounds of labor resumed.

"But what did you use for caulk?" Gwen asked, all too familiar with that necessary ingredient to shipwrighting.

Even as she asked the question, she got her answer. She saw a red man using a scrap of rough wool to swab pine rosin against a crack his partner was stuffing with sticky buffalo fleece. She remembered the rag she found floating downstream.

"We reboiled some of the wool and tar, but pine rosin and buffalo wool work as well," Fair Beard said. He paused amidships to stare down into the hold, where two of his men were working on the mast-fish. "We also had a bit of worm damage."

She glanced out over the lake that brilliantly mirrored the sky. Below the keel of the ship through the crystal water she clearly saw the hundreds of logs laid along the direction of flow, a vast, long mound of stripped saplings packed with mud that rose up past the waterline in a neat dike of stubby, nibbled twigs that so efficiently plugged the stream.

"Before nightfall we can step the mast," Fair Beard was saying as he calculated the light left, then swept his gaze to the sail stitchers. "The sail by noon." He looked directly at Gwen. "You, m'lady, can stitch. Your husband can help the bearers."

Gwen glanced at David Iron, who nodded that he heard. "But you must promise to teach me the Iceland hook," David Iron said.

"Where did you hear about the Iceland hook?"

"My swordmaster and chief, Madoc Weather Eyes, who told me that you are his master in that and several other tricks."

Snorrison clapped him across the shoulders. "When we finish the ship, I will give you some pointers."

Tumkis was smiling, guiding Gwen gently back down the gangplank and toward the women, where she found Gwen a place between two matrons, one of whom had a baby cradleboarded on her back, its forehead bound with a flattening board. The child cooed at Gwen, who took up her position feeding the supple rawhide thongs along the line to the woman with the needle, who was very deferential to Tumkis, nodding what was unmistakably a little bow when the girl came near.

Tumkis herself did not join the labor but trotted back to

Fair Beard's side, where she stayed until dark, handing him tools, scurrying here and there on his errands as he went about several tasks, giving enthusiastic orders until darkness when he ordered torches lit, blazing up the night while the women continued their harmonies over supper preparations. The Icelander joined the Natchez men in a long smoke from their dainty covered-stemmed pipes carved in the shape of water frogs; then it was back to work for everyone.

They lit bonfires around the lake, which reflected brightness long past sunset.

Gwen glanced up to see David Iron engaged at several duties that night, while the men shouted and the ship grew. By midnight, when Fair Beard finally let everyone rest, the mast was a dark, tall needle pointing arrogantly up into the starry night. She and David Iron spread their buffalo hide out on the open deck, looking up at the stars, while he softly informed her about the Natchez, how they had rulers who were treated with great honor and served by common people. He loathed the Natchez on general principles but had all kinds of interesting stories about them.

Long after everyone else but the watch slept, Fair Beard stayed awake at the lines, working with the night birds, making knots he would trust no other hand to tie.

Gwen crept from her pallet, where David Iron snored. "Need some help?" she asked the Icelander, who worked by the light of a candle, perhaps the last among their stores, for she had seen no other in many moons.

"Hold this," he said brusquely, knowing that she understood, because it was he who taught her knots. She took a seat on Old One-Eye, the rough-polished stone drag anchor, and held his knotting for him.

"How is he?" Fair Beard said.

Gwen did not answer right away as she thought about her father. "He is happy, I think, with Teleri."

"So that is who finally netted him."

"Rhiannon ran off. Some say the Cherokee got her. Wil said she killed herself, but I know different."

"Why would they think that?"

"Tad made her marry Rhys."

Snorrison nodded but said no words that gave away his thoughts. "Lev told me some of these things," he said.

Gwen ran through more recent news of the Hundred while Fair Beard worked on the intricate slipknots that would be used in the sail rig. When she had passed on the best of the gossip, she asked him about his Natchez adventures. "How did you get these red people to be so helpful?"

He shrugged, dismissing whatever must have happened to bring him here. "Like everyone else, they want our knives and axes and even our iron cooking pots, and they will do just about anything to get them. The people of the peninsula are cannibals, but we were too much of a wonder to eat, so they traded us overland to the Alabamans, along with our ax heads and knives. They killed Ulf's brother before we were able to reclaim our weapons and run westward along the gulf coast until we came to a delta country of the Great River Road, where we found the Natchez living a little way upstream. We traded some, fought some, eventually persuaded them the wisdom of alliance. Tumkis helped. She is the niece of their big chief." He winked at Gwen, whom he considered his own niece, saying, "Better than a daughter among these people." He shrugged. "It was easy, as these things go. Promise iron knives, and we are princes among them."

He heaved a sigh, looking his work over for flaws. "And they have a legend about a giant river snake," he concluded. "Can you believe our good fortune that these ignorant Skraelings actually worship this load of glorified firewood?" The quiet ship, all shadow except for the guttering candle glow, received the sweep of his loving glance, which belied his disparaging words. Among themselves, but never within an outsider's hearing, the crew belittled the vessel with such reverse affection; it warmed her that he considered her one of them.

Gwen eyed the huge Norseman. How mighty he must look to the short, dark Natchez, who already revered inherited status. They might even think such a gigantic white man, armed with an iron sword and riding the back of the river snake, was some kind of god. She had seen the looks of adoration and fear in the Natchez eyes. She did not express these thoughts but only nodded, relating how they had found a coracle in the water that must have been one of Fair Beard's lost in the storm that beached his landing party, and added that she knew of the Great River Road.

Now he was weary. The candle burned low. She bade him go to sleep because of his plan to get an early start.

He moved to comply, about to fall over. She held the wavering light while they walked together to the stern where he and Tumkis made their bed.

"Among her people she is a princess, too," he said, looking down at her sleeping form.

"She is very beautiful. Some of the men have taken red wives."

"And your jealous priests let them?"

"The red women took the faith."

Snorrison let a cynical chuckle escape his throat; he knew these red people better than that. "And one red man?"

"He is very special. Thank you for promising to teach him."

"We may all yet have to fight," Snorrison said, adding that he thought that he must say good night.

"Uncle Snorri, why did you choose this spot for shipbuilding when you could have had deep water farther down the Bear?"

"Downstream would have put us too close to the Chickasaw, who are enemies of the Natchez and bound to do mischief to us."

"We barely escaped them near the mouth of the Bear."

He nodded, letting her own report stand as proof.

She was still frowning. "What will you do when the ship is finished? How will you get her out of this place?"

"Break the beaver dam and let it fill up the lower channel to the place where we threw up another log dike. That way we can ride the swell to deeper water not half a league downstream."

Gwen could not suppress a shudder. "What if the ship does not get far enough, if the water runs out?"

"We will proceed in stages you see, the way they do back in the Low Countries. We will make our depth as we go." He gestured expansively at the dark wood around them. "Plenty of logs to make the dams. Plenty of hands to do the work."

"But the *Horn* will be unstable—if she is beached, how will we ever get her to right?"

"Not all in one big splash—it may take us a while, but eventually we will reach deeper water and enter the larger river, where your father waits for us."

He looked over at his sleeping woman, then back up at Gwen across the sputtering little flame. "The channel is deep and narrow—just wide enough to let her pass at one point. We shored up the draw. I think it will work. We just have to have faith, I suppose, that we will make it." He sighed. "That is what you Christians always say."

Chapter 35

I was a listener in the woods,
I was a gazer at stars,
I was blind where secrets were concerned,
I was silent in the wilderness.

—The Instructions of King Cormac
Irish
c. a.d. 600

"And we have faith, O Lord," Wyn was praying loudly
so that all could hear, even the ones far back who did not
believe. "We have faith that thou wilst lead us your humble
children to sanctuary, in the name of..."

It was firstlight. After prayer they started loading coracles.
It was already hot. It would be a sweltering day, but not so
bad on the water.

Using a gihli-gasi, they hauled Wyn's anvil down to the
river beach with the idea of loading it onto the strongest of
the round boats. But the thing sank two coracles, and now
Rhys was working to strengthen a third.

His strong, nimble fingers worked faster than even the
eldest of the Shawnee basket makers. He had picked up their
habit of singing to the work in a low humming voice. Sweat
beaded his forehead, and the only thing that flawed his effort
was the frayed end of the sash getting in his way. Finally he
tied it back, and he and Wil quickly reinforced the bottom of
the craft with a solid weave of withies, rather than a simple
frame.

Now they had the double hide stitched and ready for
launch.

Wyn and Andrew maneuvered the anvil to the center of

the curve, where they lashed and sewed it in under strong rawhide.

They had to drag this coracle because it was so heavy. A couple of the brothers helped them get it into the water, where it rode like a dream. Wyn proceeded to lash his cargo vessel to the single-man coracle he would pilot downstream.

Everyone cheered their success, then broke into separate twos and threes to make ready individual coracles. Madoc was determined to leave at dawn to make it to the Yuchi before dark.

The Shawnee women had taken to the round boats immediately—as nomads they had more boating experience than the settled Mabilan ladies, and the coracles were about the same size, if not shape, as the skin canoes the Shawnee were famous for building back in the Kantuck homeland.

Everyone had his personal gear to load, plus whatever community stores the boats could handle. The plan was to lash cargo between people, plus string riderless cargo vessels between manned coracles. The men all carried full meadskins—John got a good batch with their first honey and had some to spare, which was stowed among the cargo. Even now Madoc could see that twice as much cargo was stacked on the bank than could possibly be accommodated in the vessels at hand.

Madoc observed the people going about their preparations, wondering what they would have done without the Shawnee buffalo hides. Walk, heavily burdened in this searing August heat, is what they would have done.

He helped Rhys and Winnowed Rice set up their train of four canoes and worked out plans with Wil, who with one of the brothers would ride point and scout a place to pull up at noon.

Wyn had secured his anvil-float and was now lashing down the altar supplies, which were sewn into another of the buffalo hides.

Brian had the books wrapped and secured in a small one-man coracle to be tied between his and Hayati's canoes—each parent's back was adorned with a cradleboard full of fat-cheeked baby, he playing horse to Matthew while their mother carried Mark.

The men had fitted themselves into the thwarts of coracles stacked so high with cargo the paddler could not be seen behind piles of goods on the little boats, which, like obedient little mules, took a great deal.

The dogs were yapping, nipping at the children's ankles. They would have to follow as best they could, either swimming behind the convoy or running along the banks.

Madoc walked back up to the plateau for a last look around the Big House. He felt as though he were forgetting something.

It was quiet and cool in the kitchen that still smelled of the remains of this morning's duck eggs burned on the hearth. They had mounted the big kettle still warm from breakfast onto one of the cargo boats and packed it with the last of their salt, which Madoc hoped would keep dry. But many of the smaller, replaceable utensils had been left where they hung— wooden spoons, bright red pottery, Shawnee baskets and bunches of herbs swaying from the ceiling in the breeze let in by the open door.

His eye scanned the dark room with ceiling beams so low he often hit his head upon them, this place that had been a comfortable home. He could see nothing they had forgotten. The things they left behind could be duplicated by clever hands.

He gave brief notice to the alcove he had claimed for his own, where he had kept his charts and other personal items, all of which Ari double wrapped in leather and stowed on the cargo boats. A hastily built and slightly leaning table, which had served as his desk, looked shabby now. Nothing here he wanted—then he remembered the bonepicker's mask, the one they had captured in Mabila. He turned to remove it from the wall where he had hung it, but it was gone. The peg was still there with a shred of a leather thong hanging from it as though the weight of the mask ripped it loose. He searched behind the table to see if the mask had fallen, but there was nothing but a mouse scurrying along the rough halved logs thrown down for floors.

Disappointed, he looked around, then walked out of the Big House forever. Under a lighter sky he found the field dry with stubble that crunched underfoot as he walked to the verge and looked down upon the Hundred involved in final preparations.

Each of his people stood out, yet from this vantage point they moved together as one. Among the children was Teleri under a wide straw hat shading her fair skin.

He watched for a while, counting heads and coracles, and when he saw they were short at least two positions, he counted again, and again it added up to two adults without a ride.

He was about to return to work out a solution—double riders, toss some cargo or something—when below he heard someone shout in alarm.

It was Andrew, who was trying to haul the coracle with the anvil back to shore. The craft yawed badly; even from here Madoc could tell it was shipping water. Only with the help of several others was Andrew able to get the overloaded vessel to the sand—it sank completely, and they dragged it out of the water. He groaned, hating to see that they were probably not going to be able to haul the anvil. It was just too heavy for the perturbable little boats.

Wyn seemed truly distressed down there, gesturing, trying to remove the bound anvil from the coracle full of water. People were standing back from him, shaking their heads, coming to Madoc's conclusion about the anvil.

Wyn could forge usable weapons and tools without it. A particularly hard rock would serve, or even a wooden block, but the metal needed metal to strike against to make the keenest edge. Wyn's anvil also had sentimental value to all the Christians, not the least of whom was Wyn, who looked as though he were trying to change Wil's mind about the anvil's chances.

Madoc could see Wyn wanted to pour the water from the coracle, remove the anvil, and reload it for better balance.

Wil was one of those shaking his head, but he helped the abbot unlace and reposition the anvil, anyway.

Now everyone who had a coracle either as a paddler or as a rider had stationed themselves near their craft. Madoc could see two of the Shawnee women standing to one side talking intently together, one with a toddler snug in a cradleboard on her back.

They were the odd women out.

Wil experimentally relaunched the anvil in its boat without tying it down. Andrew and Evan waded into the water to stand beside the coracle, which was a good thing because some slight disturbance in the water caused by people climbing aboard nearby threatened to swamp it again.

Wil was again shaking his head as the men pulled the coracle with the anvil back up onto the beach, a rush of water pouring out of the craft as they dragged it up the gentle slope.

From here it was easy for Madoc to see that they were going to have to leave the anvil behind in any case, thus freeing up the last coracle for the extra women. Already one of the Shawnee was speaking to Winnowed Rice, who in turn spoke to Rhys—from here it was a wide view for the arglwydd who rather enjoyed this brief moment of solitude.

Rhys was speaking to Wyn who stood, unmoving, staring at the dripping leather-covered anvil. His big smithy shoulders dropped. Finally he nodded. It was the only solution. Madoc was touched to see Wyn bend and lay his hand on the thing, after the others turned away to help the women load their parcels.

When Teleri caught a glimpse of Madoc standing upon the brow of the mountain, she shielded her eyes against the first glare of the sun just breaking through a thick haze and waved.

He cupped his hands and shouted, "Are you ready?" and they called back an affirmative, noisy cheer punctuated with whistles and applause that echoed off the canyon walls.

As he walked back across the field and around the Big House, he saw across the sward of dry grass the Cherokee camp. It was far enough away to be unable to see individual faces, but he knew many were turned in this direction, watching as the mountain was finally vacated. He looked at the sky, recalling his promise to Fox that the Hundred would be off by dawn.

By the time Madoc returned to the beach, everyone was already aboard except for Teleri, who stood up to her ankles in the river, holding onto the long coracle she and Madoc would take.

"Did we get everything?" she asked.

"I could not find the mask," he answered, hurriedly shucking his boots, which she put away in a bundle aboard their coracle.

There was trouble with the heavy coracle that last sank the anvil. Water had gotten between the two layers of hides. With the women and all their goods aboard, it rode so low in the water, ripples splashed over the rim. The women were trying to get it back to shore, but already it was underwater.

They grabbed bundles before the current took it all.

One of the Norsemen ran to help, but the river pulled the waterlogged craft out of the women's hands and whisked it in a spin out into the channel, where it sluggishly sank.

The two women huddled, the young mother frowning with the thought that she and her baby might be left behind.

Madoc told her not to worry as he looked around to see who could be doubled up. They all watched him with that wide-eyed stare of the herd that he hated—they would gladly leave the responsibility to him. There was simply no more room on any of the occupied boats. Some cargo would have to go. Madoc was handling bundles on unmanned craft bobbing at the waterline.

"No, not the cooking pans!" Teleri said. She hoped that in all the excitement, Madoc would forget about that awful bonepicker's mask, which Gwen had warned her was considered very unlucky by all the red people.

David Iron had told his wife that it was generally believed that even a priest touching it without the right prayer-formulas would die or suffer terrible loss. Gwen translated this as bad luck without going into detail to Teleri.

Teleri was glad to make sure the mask disappeared and did not want to be asked any questions about it, because she could not lie to Madoc.

"My bedroll—" a Shawnee woman said as he felt a big parcel tied on top of other bundles.

He scanned the possibilities. Nearest at hand was Brian and his train of boats. When Madoc waded out to look at the middle coracle, Brian cried, "Not the books!"

Madoc gave him an apologetic look as he began unlashing the bound volumes. This coracle could hold the woman with the child. As he hurriedly freed the bundle, Brian making noises beside him, Madoc glanced around to see how to accommodate the other woman.

"Not that!" Teleri said when she saw his glance light on a particular boat. "Not your sunboard."

"Did you pack the mask with it?" He let go of that coracle and waded to another.

"Carded wool," she said with a worried look on her face.

Madoc shook his head and loosened the bale, motioning to the woman who hurried over to help him cut the bale loose.

"But that is the last of our wool, husband."

"Please, Teleri," he said, pulling the lashes loose. "This is an emergency here."

As the Shawnee woman bent to help, she chanced to see the ridge out of the corner of her eye. She made a startled cry and pointed.

On the ridge above the Cherokee had taken possession of the mountain. A line of unmoving warriors stood ringing the head of the naked cliff, where Madoc's Hundred had reinforced the stonework, and fanned out on either ridge towering over the gorge where the company was preparing to take to the river. From here the red men looked like so many oddly shaped trees, about the same colors as the autumn leaves around them. All had long-range weapons handy—lances, atlatls, a few longbows, and the flying axes some nations called the tomahawk.

The rising sun cast bright rays behind them. Idle breezes blew their scalp-lock tassels and ornaments, but none in the red rank so much as shifted position.

The Hundred muttered in its several languages.

Madoc caught Wyn's eye across the crowd and nodded. It would not hurt to say another prayer.

The abbot raised his arms and called out loudly enough to make an echo that silenced all other voices except the river's. All the Christians, old, new, and recalcitrant, joined the amen and crossed themselves, while the Shawnee tossed shreds of tobacco into the water and mumbled even older prayers. The Norsemen watched cynically, their faces smug, a word or two between themselves. Their gods did not listen to such supplication.

"Very well, then," Madoc said, "yn y cwch!"

"Into the boat, into the boat," the sailors urged the Shawnee women, who picked up the refrain and made a chant of it.

The heavily burdened monks took oblong coracles two by two, they and the boats looking like the same material, as though the coracles were animate creatures and the monks were merely the slightly lighter-colored heads of them. It was an odd notion Madoc caught himself thinking as the clergy floated away downstream.

He had grown up around the distinctive wicker-and-hide craft. One of his earliest memories was of maneuvering one of the things in a pond—it must have been at one of Owen's farms, because ducks played and pecked at the little craft as the child Madoc tried to make it do something besides slide around in a circle, while the even younger David screamed that the drake behind him was a sea monster.

Madoc watched the convoy assemble and one by one drift out onto the water and then westward in the pearly morning light. These single-hide boats rode higher in the water than the ones made back home, which were usually pieced together with clever overlapping seams that required great skill to accomplish and large amounts of sheep grease to keep watertight.

These coracles did not have that problem. The Shawnee buffalo skins were perfect for an intermediate size of round vessel, which allowed one or two passengers or a rower and a centrally balanced load of cargo. Almost none of the original coracles from Britain had survived this far.

He wondered only briefly if he would ever be able to take word back about the excellent materials here for building the traditional boats. Such was the least of what he wanted to accomplish on that dreamed-of journey, when he would go home, rally a larger colony, and finally do the work he had not completed upon his stepbrother back on their father's beachhead. He would revenge Ann. He let himself think these thoughts only briefly, because they were sweet; but without carrying them through, they were bitter bile on his tongue.

The thought of return made him glance southward as he recalled David Iron's map. He could not forget that short portage that would take him to the sea.

No, Madoc thought, not this time. The return to Britain was not yet provident; he would now have to wait until he had this company settled somewhere in the allegedly fertile northern lands of the Kantuck. Then he could go down the Big River Road to the sea. How many years would that be, he wondered, as the Shawnee women jostled around him with their neatly wrapped parcels and their neatly wrapped babies.

"These are fine little moon-boats," Winnowed Rice called, paddle in hand and already master of the current.

Behind her in their coracle, Rhys with the harp case on his back held onto the withy rim; his lips were moving, but whatever he was saying to Winnowed Rice or to the baby lashed in her cradleboard to his chest was lost to any but themselves and the river. Madoc saw Rhys whip off the sash and throw his head back with a whooping sound, letting the sun shine on his uncovered face. An eddy took them, swirled them around, but with the paddle Winnowed Rice found forward motion and let the river propel her downstream, laughing with her braids flung out as they whizzed through the narrow channel and out into a wider lick.

Her Shawnee sisters in round and oblong coracles bobbed

after her, dark dandelion fluff riding the rattling water. Their laughter echoed off the rock faces on either side. Once in the pool they pulled at the paddles, calling to each other. Children lashed behind their mamas giggled and shrieked as the boats spilled down the rough course and splatted onto the quieter water.

On the riverbank Madoc saw Brian trying to find a way to balance the huge book boxes and the little boy. Taking a cue from Rhys, Brian had moved the cradleboard around to his chest and was strapping one of the books to his back.

But there were still two books on the wet sand. It was impossible to tell which they were, because they were still bound in protective leather sealed in beeswax. This time Brian had not even been able to choose but had grabbed the first of the volumes that came to hand.

The singing Shawnee voices called to them, and more boats peeled off. Brian sat there for a second, looking at the two books that must be left behind.

Madoc saw that his anguish was immobilizing the man, so he went over to push Brian's canoe into the water, the others on his string following. Close, he saw tears rimming Brian's eyes. He tried to wipe them away when he saw Madoc watching him.

The arglwydd gave him a stout slap on the shoulder that seemed to snap Brian out of his daze. Without another look back the ex-priest picked up his paddle and let the river take him.

Coracles leaped into the swell—little Matthew squealed in delight. Their mama with Mark on another cradleboard right behind them sat her own small round boat. She sang some untranslatable Muskogean song from her homeland as she held her paddle ready to use against any obstacle.

The other baby was not as happy about the river as his brother and started to cry, both voices fading downstream.

The Norsemen and sailors finished checking the cargo. They peeled off from the rock slope in a loose squadron, yodeling, trilling dirty old songs.

"Shawnee women, here come we!" Dag's voice echoed in twisted Shawnee down the echoing channel. His men around him called out modified battle yells with a roll of the tongue that was used by cattlemen in Norse settlements.

"Promises, promises, Tangletongue, always promises—" some laughing female called from downstream.

Under all, the river sang against rocks, muttering to itself.

Madoc waited until all the coracles but one were launched on the silver water. He regarded the staunch line of red men up on the ridge. Teleri followed his glance. His company was already far downstream. He could hear layers of male teasing and women's laughter and squalling baby off wet rocks far from his view.

Brian's canoe dashed around the bend, the sun glaring off his permanent bald spot.

Madoc and Teleri were left, the last of the Hundred to stand below the mountain.

"The wool—maybe I can sit on it or—"

He was shaking his head.

"So, husband, we travel together," she said, giving up on the wool, her bare toes clutching at the rim of their coracle. She had pulled her hem between her legs and tucked it under her belt but was soaked to her waist, very fresh looking and rosy. Even under the broad straw hat she was squinting. Her legs bared to the thigh pulled against the current's tug, her eyes following Madoc above new freckles sprinkled on her sunburnt face.

"Appears that way, m'lady," he replied.

She squinted up at him.

He took the weight of the coracle, not much at that, but bulky, and swung it about, expertly catching it by the rope that played out as the river pulled it. With his other arm he swept her up against him and bent her with a rough kiss.

"And what was that for, m'lord?"

He rubbed at a freckle that would not come off. Her cheek felt warm. The wayward coil of sable brown hair had come loose, so silky that it would never stay braided. It was the first thing that he had noticed about this plain, simple, sweet woman he had married under duress. Yet here in the fresh light of a sparkling new day she was beautiful.

There was so much to say to her, but surely she must know already. "You . . . you are very dear to me," he stammered.

She brushed his cheek with her fingertips and tugged at his mustache. "And thou to me."

"I . . . I have not said it, before."

Her cool curled knuckles stroked his face. "You said it—"

"No," he said, hushing her with his hand against hers at his ear. "No, do not take up my slack for me. I was too stubborn to say it. But I thought it many times during the last months.

You put up with me, you let me take it out on you, you forgave me for not loving you as I should. I never appreciated you enough."

She let him hold her, feeling his strength. His great heart throbbed against her ear. His dear rough hands were hot on her back. He smelled of mead and salt, perpetually salt as though his bones were made of it; the sea was always with him. Teleri thought she had never been as happy as at this moment, as simple as it was. She never thought he would admit these things and had been prepared never to hear him speak them, saying what she most desired to hear.

She was so gladdened she almost told him her news but decided to wait another month to be sure.

Arm in arm they stepped to the water. He climbed first into the rocky boat, then held her hand as she joined him and sat so that they were back-to-back. She had never learned to use the paddle—she was upcountry-born, so she settled back against him as familiar as being in bed against the bones of his spine and happy to be his passenger.

He drew in the line and stowed it at his bare feet tucked beneath the thwart, which gave him somewhat the appearance of praying on his knees, then sped into the current that sipped at them. Madoc kept a firm paddle so they did not spin at the base of the gentle rapids, but when they skipped out of the foamy white water and onto the sparkling green pool at the wider spot, he let them pivot lazily, a leaf in the flow.

He laid his head back on her shoulder and saw her smiling face, the only stable thing in a world racing dizzily around, as she turned toward him in the light from the spinning blue sky.

"I do love thee," he said.

"And I thee." For a second time she thought of telling him she was pregnant. She knew it was true, but still she hesitated. She would tell him that night when the world had slowed down.

The spin was delicious. Though it meant letting go of almost everything they owned, this leave-taking did not feel like defeat. To kiss her again, he let them drift along in a general downstream direction, then took up the narrow paddle nearly as long as he was tall to set them with the current.

Around the bend they found the tail of their flotilla, several Norsemen and Shawnee women lingering in the gentled current midstream. From their boats the women were gathering watercress that grew in a great carpet along the north bank.

Together they rode the water on down, through rhododendron that grew all the way to the lapping edge, and laurel, willow, and fern in the sheltered places where boulders had washed down aeons ago. Here and there dogwood and maple flamed in autumn colors, but the predominant tree standing back from the river was a species of oak letting go of golden leaves.

Occasionally they passed startled deer, poised, ready to leap away but for the curiosity of seeing the strange humans bobbing by. Then the Shawnee dogs following the shore would scare game away, bounding with white tails into the low bush.

At a rough beach a bear with twin cubs growled above the wriggling bodies of fish they had snatched. What looked like trout leapt at the margins of the stream, where cattails waved blunt brown spears, sending clouds of fluff into the sunshine. One large fish with long flesh mustaches flopped into Dag's coracle, almost capsizing him, but nobody else was the witness, so his men laughed at his fish story across the echoing water as he thwacked it unconscious with his paddle.

And over all, the great blue bowl of the sky brightened, pulsing and expanding as the sun climbed toward noon. Gradually the land flattened. The oaks thinned out so that beyond the river banks only the jade leaves of rhododendron grew interspersed with tall waving grasses. When Madoc looked back, he could see the last of their mountain home as a diminishing bald knot on the misty horizon. It was too far to see if the red men still stood watching, but he was certain they did.

With a hunter's eye he reconnoitered the banks sliding beside them. He saw no watchers but felt watched, nonetheless. A buzz of unseen insects filled the air. Jays flung slicing notes from plum trees, and blackbirds shrieked from the canebrakes. Several times quail exploded upslope. In the quieter stretches where the river fattened and seemed to snooze, frogs gargled gravel as they plopped among cattails and cress.

Another glance over his shoulder and Madoc saw the mountain for the last time. He would never regret leaving. It was almost as though he had known all along that it was not theirs but was only a temporary camp they would someday have to leave.

He was thinking that the wilderness was vast and his people very small—a memory of his thoughts on the mast in the middle of the Sargasso Sea. Once again they were fleeing westward. There they had crossed an unknown sea; here they faced an unknown wilderness. He wondered if they were doomed to search for a home they would never find but toward which they must march forever westward.

The river, which long after these days would be called the Duck, meandered like a broken snake through the land. Its long passage across hard rock had polished its channel. In high water it was fearsome, but as David Iron said, in the dry season it rolled on gently, rounding its bends without a ruffle as it zigged and zagged but never overran its banks. It knew its channel and stayed to it like a tame duck, though, as could be seen by the high-water marks in debris and tumbled boulders, it could be a roaring thunderbird.

Sometimes the sun rode on their left shoulders. Then the river would switch, and they would bob directly into midmorning glare. As suddenly, they would coast through a long, shadowed gorge where the canyon walls loomed like ancient fortifications laid down in layers of squarish somber gray stone. It was a dazzling journey unmarred by any event.

By noon the women were calling over the water.

Wil and Madoc had worked it out in advance that the point would call the noon rest. Way down the channel Wil saw the sun as high as it would climb and called a yodel, which was relayed back up the line, for everyone to pull into the sandy beach in a protected bay beneath a steep cliffside. Even before beaching the monks were singing the noon office, their mellow voices echoing off the high rocks and the water.

Dag was showing off the catfish that leapt into his canoe—it had no marks of a hook on it, so they must accept his story. Finally he gave it up to one of the women to cook at tonight's camp, but it took two men to carry the carcass to the fire.

Madoc was fumbling at the bundle Teleri said was his sunboard when she came up behind him asking if she could help.

"What are you looking for?" she asked, knowing.

"I want to see if my mask is packed with the sunboard. Did you pack my things, or did Ari?"

"Uh, the mask..."

Warned by the tone of her voice, he ceased pulling at the lines and looked up at her. "Yes?"

"I had forgotten." The glare off the river's surface had turned her nose pink.

He straightened.

"I did not want it to get broken." This was as close as she had ever come to lying to him. The thing was so nasty, so full of bad luck. She told herself she burned it to protect him.

He cocked his head as if to say, yes, where?

"In the wool." Ah, the lie. She was surprised it was so easy.

"The wool," he repeated, slumping. "The bale I tossed?"

"Sorry."

Madoc scowled. He could only blame himself. "Well, you tried to stop me."

As he glanced around, he saw Rhys and Winnowed Rice sitting face-to-face, he poised very still, she painting his eye sockets with charcoal while one of the Muskogean women looked on, giving small advice here and there.

A school of children swirled past Madoc as though his legs were trees, hollering, waving small bows they had made from sticks. Each of them was also painted—he knew Einion only by the light brown of his hair. All the red people used paint in some way, paint or tattooing. Even the sedate Shawnee, who disdained the blue-tattooed Muskogeans, tattooed clan signs on their own thighs and on the soles of their feet to help the soul find its path out of this world when it was time to go.

That was what David Iron had told Gwen, who had told Teleri, who told Madoc, because she told Madoc everything. David Iron still wore face paint for specific tasks and would not even argue with Wyn about it. A couple of the Norsemen who had talked a specific Shawnee woman into taking care of them had let the women paint symbols on their cheeks for special occasions. What worried Madoc was that it was beginning to look ordinary for any number of the white people at any one time to look more and more like red people. Everyone had been darkened by the blistering sun, although some like Teleri tried to keep their faces under wide straw hats the Shawnee women wove from marsh grass and tied on with a ribbon of leather under the chin. The men of the Hundred were in various stages of sunburn and peeling; Teleri was not the only one with freckles.

Even as he looked around now, the people were blended together—for a moment he thought that was Teleri there, but it was really one of the Shawnee women in her own straw hat. They loved the plaid shifts made on the broadloom and the sharp little paring knives from Wyn's forge. But Teleri was not the only white woman who had begun braiding her hair in the red fashion. Yngvild had always worn braids.

His mind was full of these thoughts as they made a quick meal of dried meat and travel corncake the Shawnee women had prepared in advance, drank their fill of water, sassafras tea, mead—soon Brother Ely's brew would be only a memory— and climbed back onto the coracles to journey the short distance that David Iron had assured him would bring them to the Yuchi's north-flowing arm long before sunset.

After about a hundred switchbacks, the Duck took a long swing north. Then, whiplike, it broke abruptly south among a gathering of water-polished stones, and gradually, opening its jaws, the river began to widen. Madoc heard the monks singing a hymn before he saw the encampment Wil had established on the north bank of the Duck, where it finally flung itself into the open, lazy current of the north-flowing River of the Yuchis.

Everyone on shore cheered when Madoc's coracle hove into view under the brassy light of afternoon.

The flotilla had not made as good time as David Iron's single boat, but they still had an hour or more of light left. Madoc was easily convinced that this was a good place to camp overnight. The monks had established a secluded enclave near the larger river's bank, where they would not be disturbed by the sight of women, who, ignoring the clergy, had started a huge cooking fire on the first beach, where they found Gwen's eagle feather in the stacked stones. It was cheering to Madoc and everyone else that their scouts were moving according to plan.

The fruits of autumn lay all about them—roots for sassafras tea, grainy black amaranth seed by the skinful, pine nuts from a neighboring bottomland, plus several edible fungi the Shawnee prized. White tubers were boiling in several baskets the women kept turning with a humming song to keep the hot rocks they tossed in from scorching the weave. Someone had already found a clutch of oysters on rocks a little pace upriver.

People were repairing boats or retying cargo, working and talking together in small groups in their several languages. Even the monks were not too far away to contribute to the satisfied buzz prevailing over the camp that pleased Madoc greatly, as though they caught his own buoyant expectations for the continued journey.

The woman who had cleaned Dag's fish was dropping chunks of it into the soup with wild onion and herbs from community stores. With these pungent smells and pleasant sounds on the air, Madoc, still barefooted, wandered with Rhys over to the larger river's bank, hoping the crew might soon arrive from the south.

"Do you really expect them this early?" Rhys asked mildly, leaning on his staff.

"If they followed my orders, they would be here by now," Madoc said, gazing upriver into the gathering mist.

"They will surely follow your orders."

Madoc regarded the poet staring upriver with painted eyes, about to discuss his plan to stay here until the others joined them rather than go on and take the chance of being separated forever. What he really wanted to say was, we need all the white men we have to offset these red influences upon us.

Rhys shifted his weight in his sturdy Shawnee moccasins, turning his face toward the westering sun. Madoc could not fail to see it was an obvious pleasure to him, as though he were drinking in the persimmon-colored light.

Words clutched in Madoc's throat. How to confide to this man that he was afraid they would lose themselves among the red people, lose the very thing they fled Britain to preserve. How could he voice such concerns with Rhys's face painted like that?

He was about to confront the poet despite his hesitation when Rhys suddenly asked, "Gwen has you worried, yes?"

Rhys was so often right in his intuitions that it startled Madoc for him to be wrong. It did not help at all that the arglwydd was having trouble speaking his mind.

This was not some tenured servant, some sycophantic oath-holder, but his old friend speaking from genuine concern.

Quite without warning Rhys embraced Madoc. "You must not worry about her—she is living a wonderful adventure with someone she loves, which is what young people wish to do."

He stood Madoc at arm's length, treating him more as an equal than ever before, creating in Madoc's chest the tight constriction of painfully grateful love, and added, "Only when we get old do we want everything to be safe."

"You are actually enjoying this," Madoc growled, just to have something to say, to cover his keen feelings as he pulled away. "Since that first afternoon crossing the Irish Sea, you have seen it as some grand adventure—" Madoc stopped himself in embarrassment when he realized what he had said.

"Yes, I see it as a grand adventure, a fine and splendid song, a saga if you please, and so does your daughter. After all I have been through, I am quite amazed to find myself still alive, still able to feel the sun and quench thirst and sing and eat that wonderfully smelling food—Lord, but I am hungry."

"You are happy, then?"

"You mean without her?"

Madoc could not help himself; he looked down at his toes as though the blind man could detect reaction on his face.

"Will it offend you for me to be honest and say yes?" Rhys took a deep breath, looking upriver again with his magic face to speak of things he had never said to Madoc before, things he had never shared with anyone about the time five years ago when he was among Owen Gwynedd's men held hostage by the English king.

"When Henry took my eyes, Madoc, I prayed to die. While I watched him blind the others, I begged God, Jesus, and Mary to let me die. The guards held us kneeling around the smithy's fire; then he came down the line, renewing the poker for each man. I have never seen anyone as angry as the English king that night after your father defeated him. He quite enjoyed his revenge. I was last in line. I prayed for quick death as he worked his way closer. The last thing I saw was his freckled face in that ugly French beard behind the hot poker."

Rhys straightened away from the staff that was worn silken by his hands upon its grain and stamped it against the ground in an impatient gesture that gave away his discomfort in speaking of these things. "Afterwards they dumped us on the road to Bangor. Half the hostages were already dead. I will never forget the mud, my whole world had turned to mud, gray endless mud. Seven more of us died on the road."

Two of Madoc's half brothers had perished among that contingent. Madoc himself did not take part in the battle of Oswestry. Owen sent him instead to entreat the lord of Lundy Isle to throw resources into the fight against the

English. Rhys was giving Madoc the first personal details he had heard of events on the mainland after that battle.

"Again I prayed to die, but I was not given that charity. Somehow, I do not know how, I lived through that night and woke the next morning. After that night I find life a delicious banquet at which I continuously feast." Sniffing the cooking aromas, Rhys inclined his head toward Winnowed Rice singing beside the fire with the other women.

Madoc felt shamed by the poet's ability to rise above loss and entertain joy. He looked anew at the painted suns on Rhys ab Meredydd's face in the slanting afternoon light out here in the middle of nowhere and would have said more, perhaps asked Rhys what he saw when he looked at the sun, but Madoc was moved almost to tears by Rhys's words and by his own inability to articulate his feelings about the painted eyes.

The people called for their music maker, so they returned to the fireside, relinquishing a chance for further discussion.

William the Saxon and the other hunters returned shortly afterwards with enough game to feed twice their number. Everyone feasted far into the night.

Fox promised safe passage, but Madoc kept five men on watch, holding to the ship's schedule, which meant he would be part of their relief before dawn.

When nearly everyone else had retired, Madoc and a few men sat around the fire as it disintegrated into bleeding coals, discussing the trip so far and going over what David Iron had said about the river they would be entering. Madoc had not yet told them he planned to wait here for the rest of their company to come up from the *Horn*. Something kept him from announcing his plans just yet, so his advisers were assuming they would be on the water again in the morning, heading downriver on the Yuchi.

They agreed they had covered about forty-five leagues in today's pleasant downriver sojourn.

They took one last round of mead, leaving only a few full skins, and began to wander away to blankets, until only Madoc, Wil, Wyn, and Rhys remained in conversation.

Wyn bid them all good night after saying a short prayer.

Rhys and Wil continued speaking in softened voices about the Chickasaw nation whose territory began at the western bank.

It had been some time since Madoc had spoken. He was staring into the sizzling coals, hoarding his thoughts, David

Iron's rough map still in his mind. All day on the river, which had kept his attention, he could not shake the recurring thought of that short portage that could take him back to the sea, and the eastern current that could take him home.

Idly, while his men continued speaking, Madoc sketched the map in the dust at his feet.

From the far northeast, as faint as mist, it seemed that he could hear Gwynedd calling him. If a land could make a sound, hers would be a cry, like a wound on the hip of Britain. How many could be saved? How many would believe him and follow him to this new land, where the earth was supposed to have an edge? Perhaps his brother Riryd, if David had not killed him, or young Cynan, if he could be found, would like a chance at another life. How many ship-masters could he convince of this truth thousands of miles westward? He would try for a dozen.

He must take back proof of this place to convince them— David Iron, of course, with all his Yuchi regalia. And some of the Shawnee. That would prove the reality of his new Cymru, so he could get enough people to begin a real colony, wives and children and oxen, horses, all the animals that men lived by, pigs and sheep, of course, for their many gifts; and books, he thought, recalling the books Brian left behind. He hoped they still had the Psalms, because, like Wyn, that was his favorite.

Everyone must learn to read. He must demand that every-one speak Cymraeg, that the Shawnee adoptees must speak it and not their native language. The monks must make them-selves useful and start a school for the children, red and white, otherwise the red way would win out. Now they had only one large volume and the monks' little traveling library— Genesis, the Gospels, and Revelation, a couple of missals, a breviary, and a few men among them who could read Latin.

Wil's boys and Einion were already little red men. The children changed the quickest, he had observed. The men who had taken Shawnee brides had changed, too, become more and more red in the way they did things. They were all peppering their Cymraeg with Shawnee phrases and names. Rhys was singing in Shawnee. Madoc had no doubt that he would see less and less of the sash and more of the face paint.

How long, he wondered, would it be before they forgot who they were? He knew he must bring more of his people here if their language and ways were to survive.

Lost in these thoughts, he realized someone was standing behind him.

"Captain—?" Wil said politely.

"Uh, yes?" Madoc asked, looking up from his seated position, where he had been gazing at the embers.

Wil reminded him that he had not yet disclosed his plans. "I asked if you want me to travel in the lead again tomorrow."

"Uh, Wil, I want you to bring up the tail," Madoc said, glancing at the river, making the decision at that moment.

"Well, then," Wil said, embarrassed that his chief seemed preoccupied and inattentive, and wondering if his own performance as point today had displeased the captain, "it will be interesting to see what this country is like in its northern parts."

"Wil..." Madoc pulled at Wil's tunic, urging him to sit down.

"Yes, sir?"

"We are not going north."

Chapter 36

Flood tide and ebb
dwindling on the sand.
What the flood rides ashore
the ebb snatches from your hand.

—The Hag of Beare
Irish
c. A.D. 800

Wil sat back on his heels and gave Madoc a good long stare. "You mean go upriver instead of down?"

"Yes."

The Cumberlander stared off into the misty night toward the west bank, where the Chickasaw were said to roast their victims for three days before they died.

"We will stick to this shore," Madoc said.

Wil looked around as though implying something beyond in the darkness. "I feel eyes watching."

So, Madoc thought, I was right. But all he said was, "It will not matter if we move fast enough. According to what David Iron said, we can make it to the portage in a few hours." The journey upriver on the Yuchi actually was about thirty leagues—ninety-one miles.

Rhys, who had been silent, said, "Fox will be unforgiving."

"We will move so fast, we will be at the *Horn* before he knows we took a different direction."

"So it is the ship, is it?"

"I cannot leave her, not when she gives us a better chance."

"We would have a better chance if we go north to the Kantuck," Winnowed Rice said in sign, her own language, and a few words of Cymraeg.

527

Madoc regarded this spirited woman. In the absence of David Iron, she was his best guide through this country; her band's range was Muscle Shoals in the south, the Great River Road in the west, and the Cherokee hills to the east.

"I know your people would help us. But we do not want to remain wanderers, you see. We do not want charity. We must find open farming country where our wheat and oats will grow. We must bring our sheep here to make our livelihood. We must settle near water so that our ships can come and go." He tried to make it simple—he was explaining a foreign way of life to her, who had lived all her own as a hunter in the wilderness.

She watched her own red fingers entwined in Rhys's white ones. "I know there is much I do not understand," she said in handsign. "I only give counsel to my chief."

"Thank you, Winnowed Rice," he said, deep shadows etched on his chiseled face as the ashes of two logs settled, darkening the glow. "Your counsel is important. I need to be able to depend on your wisdom about the land and the people around us."

She thought he was making a mistake in crossing Fox but saw he had made his decision and further words would be useless.

"How long to Muscle Shoals?" Madoc asked, using handsign; he had learned only a few words of Shawnee. He wanted the red women to learn his language.

"Light current," she said uncertainly, "but paddling against it." They would in fact make about half the time of the Duck River trip, lucky to get ten miles of river under their coracles in an hour. At that it would take them at least nine hours of hard paddling barring no interference.

"We would make better time if the strongest rowers took along a passenger each," Rhys said.

"Make the holy men ride with women!" Madoc said, delighting in the possibility.

Beside him Wil chuckled cynically. Madoc grinned at him—they both wanted to see it.

"Even then we should raft the coracles together," Madoc said, thinking fast, already anticipating problems with the plan, so they could be solved before they doomed Madoc's Hundred. "The women will have to help, and there is cargo to think about." In his imagination he saw the string of sixty-odd coracles with precarious cargoes tied together.

"Two sunrises to Bear Creek, if lucky," Winnowed Rice said, after calculating as best she could.

"Not if we traveled at night."

"At night?" She could not believe she understood him. It was something no red man would contemplate.

"No reason not to, really. David Iron told me it is gentle, wide, and slow this side of the Shoals."

Winnowed Rice looked at him with a tilt to her head. It was not her place to question the chief's decisions. But she could not resist an attempt to enlighten him, since he was pointedly asking her opinions. "A river can throw more than a few rocks against a canoe."

"Spirits, eh?" He laughed in a downthroated way and shook his head. He had not thought any people could be as superstitious as the Celts—he could not resist feeling superior.

Winnowed Rice flashed an angry look at him but out of respect to Rhys's chief and friend limited her remarks: "All rivers are alive."

"Then they can be charmed like any living animal. Charmed, tamed, or killed. We will charm this river with a surprise— we will ride her in the dark."

They lashed the coracles together like a string of brown beads, woke everyone in ones and twos, and explained that they must hit the water before dawn.

"What about Gwen and David Iron?" Wyn asked.

Madoc gestured upriver. "They must pass us in any case."

It was something he had worried about, but only briefly. The plain truth was they faced another terrible gamble.

The sailors did not question their captain but sprang to obey his orders with renewed energy. Dag and his men slapped each other's shoulders and grinned privately—a return to the ship was their greatest desire. The civilians were excited and scared, but ready to do what the experts said.

Wyn insisted on knowing why he endangered everyone by breaking his promise to Fox. Madoc continued working with Rhys on the lines as he answered, "You and your brothers can do what you will, Domme, but I am going south."

The abbot swallowed further comment

"What about the dogs?" Madoc asked Winnowed Rice, who assured him they were trail trained. They would follow quietly, probably choosing to run the east bank rather than fight the current.

"Everyone," Madoc said, making handsign so they all could see. "You children, you must be quiet—understand Einion?" The boy would ride behind one of the monks with another child, one of the Shawnee, whose mam had one too many children to watch out for.

Einion nodded under mud paint. "Yes, father," he said in incongruous Cymraeg. Well, Madoc thought, he has not lost everything.

They launched their strung flotilla from the bank of the larger river at a protected beach. He tied the lead coracles to a snag at the water's edge and helped get the women and baggage aboard. The rowers scattered along the line. Madoc and Teleri boarded the lead canoe.

He started paddling to take up the slack in the tieline, then told Teleri to loosen it quickly from the snag.

He began the paddling chant.

The river grabbed at them, but only gently, as their strokes parted the waters, moved them beyond the surge of the Duck River's convergence and on up the Yuchi stream. He could feel the line stretched out behind him as its many parts heaved on the connections and the rowers synchronized their strokes.

The mist could not have been better planned to keep them hidden from any but the closest eyes. The head of the flotilla could not begin to see the tail, and those riding the end saw themselves pulled along the taut lines into a vague, pearly curtain that hid all but the next five or six coracles ahead. But it was not still dark. Behind the vapors dawn threw a glow onto the water past the underbrush of the bank. They settled into a comfortable rhythm, each man regulating his breathing for the pull on the oar.

Only after they were well on the river, moving against its gentle flow under the strong paddling of their best rowers strung out on the line with women, children and baggage between—only then did Madoc feel that they really might have a chance after all. He looked quickly back with each stroke: They were strung out behind him, so long a line they faded into the mist.

Behind them the line played out tautly between each coracle. Their low chant was just under the river's sound. So far there was no sign along the banks that anyone was watching.

By that time it was just past dawn. There was still no horizon, because the perpetual mists of the river cloaked all views. Behind the eastern pale lingered the sun's first light.

But it was a dark day that never enjoyed sunshine. It was a blessing, and the silvery water threw only a mild current against them. Madoc figured they were making better than

ten miles an hour on this broad river that had few kinks like
the Duck.

Even at noon, when by prearrangement they munched
from travel stores without slowing down their flotilla, everything was gray, as though the whole earth were smoldering in
clean silver smoke. The western bank was still hidden, but
the east bank at this point was a boggy lowland with few
beaches. Quicksand patched the shallows where long-legged
birds stalked creeping edibles in the reeds.

It seemed to him that once or twice he went to sleep while
paddling. He was used to going long watches without sleep, but
the continuous stroke, pull, stroke was a killing pace to keep up.
Midday they pulled over only briefly to give the rowers a chance
to stretch and reload off-balance cargo. They ate from stores and
were back on the water before the sun stood at noon.

Madoc felt his second wind, and by late afternoon, when
they had been on the water about eight hours, he saw the red
flag Gwen had tied to the snag. They could hear the faint
rumble of the shoals, though they could not yet see the black
rocks until they rounded the final bend. The general mist had
evaporated. The sky was a weepy azure in the west, but over
the shoals pink plumes piled up in a cloud column.

He was unable to catch the flannel as they skimmed by.
Teleri grabbed at it but held on too long and got a rope burn
for her trouble. "What do you think it means?" she asked
over her shoulder.

Madoc made a sound kin to the one David Iron made in
these same waters.

This time there was no fake hawk cry, just the slicing whine
of arrows and atlatl darts zipping through the air from his
sudden right. Madoc hauled on the paddle, calling back up
the line the cry that meant, "Do not stop now!"

Against such an attack he had ordered the Norsemen to be
armed—already he could hear William's hooting cry that
meant an arrow had been released from the crossbow.

Projectile weapons were almost useless to both defenders
and attackers. Their aim was to capsize or ram the foreigners'
fragile-looking boats, so they came in close in the sturdy
dugouts, with poles from many points to the right. Here they
made a mistake, because the Norsemen and sailors were not
loathe to leap into the river, swim under the offensive craft,
and spill them. There they finished the job with iron knives.

The sailors came exploding out of the river that turned

pink here and there around surfacing corpses. At least six men had gone overboard. Madoc could not see anything behind him, but they must slow down so the men could climb back onto the convoy—not an easy task with a single stationary coracle, and next to impossible in one that was moving. Finally, amid splashing and cries from those in the boats, five men called out one by one, signifying they were reboarded. One of the Shawnee women let out a long, low moan but broke it off.

So, he thought, one more down. How many hit in the attack? He called back, heard people sounding off.

Madoc was breathing long and slow, as deeply as he could pull. Water sloshed into the boat around his feet. There was a ringing in his ears. He heard Teleri speak very close and remembered she was right behind him. He could feel her comforting warmth. Glancing over his right shoulder and through strands of her wind-loosened hair, he saw the last of the bottom-up Chickasaw canoes slicing off down the current. He darted a glance to see if there were any more comers, but apparently that was a single hunting party separated from a main force, because there were no other boats on the broad river.

He was coming close to the bend eastward. The roar of the shoals was loud now, louder than the river sliding like a dream.

"Teleri—there!" he called back to her, almost forgetting to continue paddling as he looked upstream at a tongue of black rocks over which the last of many leagues of white water had plunged foaming. Even at its strongest the river could not beat him—throw me all you have, you river-spirit, he was thinking as he cut for the now-southern bank, where he suspected he had come upon the sudden mouth of Bear Creek.

Ahead—now due east—the south bank of the river began steadily to rise until far off in the wide, silvered distance near the black rocks the bank terraced into a raw pink cliff. The north bank was furred with green down to the water's edge, but Madoc ignored that side because David was emphatic about Bear Creek spilling into the Tennessee from the southern reach.

He watched for the stream of greener water that would be the beard of the Bear.

He slotted his craft and yelled back to Teleri, "We made it, by God, we made it!" She pressed closer to him as he pulled for the debris-littered shore, where the current beached them nicely, tottering like a top. Behind him the others came in, causing some pileup. Madoc tried to rise and found that he could not; something heavy he could not see held him back.

People were splashing around him, dragging in the coracles.

The ringing grew louder. The roaring of the water was a booming bell. The usual river-glare on the undersides of his eye sockets pulsated like a sound. It infuriated him when he looked down to see the slender cane shaft of a feathered arrow sticking somewhere about midsection. He tried to pull it out, but it would not budge. He continued to feel no pain but only fury that this thing had pierced his body. Someone at his ear admonished him to leave it alone.

"It is barbed, lord!"

"Put him here—"

They still seemed to be spinning down the Duck River with the incredibly blue sky roaring over the faces around him.

"Oh, God—"

"Get them apart!"

"I cannot."

He saw their lips moving, but their voices became silent. Even the river was still. Why were they acting so mindlessly, he wondered from inside his silent crystal shell. He reached down and broke off the feathered end of the arrow, as he had done for others on many a battlefield.

Suddenly he could hear again. There was Wyn's voice and Rhys's, then rough hands lifting him up, up, up, offering him, it seemed, to the dazzling sky. He had a vision of their convoy skimming smartly along on its string, a necklace of rough pearls, everyone pulling together. He was being lifted off the string, a bead sliding off the hot wire.

Again everything was quiet. The river hushed. He heard his own breathing, gravel rattling beneath his skull, the rough rustle of his leather clothing as someone—Evan, yes, is it you?—put something soft beneath his head.

"Yes, sir."

"What did I do, stop one for Teleri?"

"Yes, lord," Evan said, his face slick. He was soaking wet. He must have been one of those who capsized the Chickasaw.

"Teleri?"

"You have been wounded, master." It was Ari.

"Not so bad, eh?"

"It just nicked you."

It must be true, Madoc was thinking as he sat up.

Teleri had lost her hat. Madoc saw her beside him on her side as though she were merely sleeping, her freckled hand curled under her face, her clothing wet and tumbled around her. He saw the wink of the gold coin sewn into her apron hem. One of her common leather slippers had fallen off. He reached out and touched her small foot, still wet, pink, and slightly wrinkled from the bilge water they shipped.

She slumped forward. The back of her linen shift was pierced by the thin shaft, off which they lifted him. So strange that there was almost no blood. She had been sitting right behind him. The arrow had gone into his right side without much damage, slipping as a fast projectile sometimes will neatly between the intestines and the kidney. It was only a fragile splinter of cane, tipped with a knapped flint, sent with great power. It slammed through his soft parts and into Teleri's back on the left side directly into the heart, a perfect bull's-eye.

Strange, so strange that there was only a trickle of blood.

"Ohh," he started to say to someone leaning over him. It was Wyn looking very stern. Madoc held onto his cassock, fighting to stand. "She is dead, Wyn . . . Teleri . . ."

"We lost three, son." He crossed himself and laid his hand on Madoc's shoulder. "But she heard me give absolution—I am sure of that." His face beamed; such news would have comforted himself.

Madoc looked around, trying to focus. "Domme," he cried, "there is an arrow in your back."

Wyn twisted as best he could with the bulky backpack upon him and saw the shaft, but he couldn't reach it.

Madoc grabbed it and fell back, ripping away the torn pack and spilling its contents out into the light. Ari behind them and Evan leaned over to stare at the brilliant plaque of gold with a flint arrowhead embedded in the outline of the Orient. Wyn stared at it, his lips moving soundlessly because it seemed to him to be a divine sign that the arrow pierced the Holy Land instead of his own body.

The bedraggled company turned one by one to see the marvel of the arrow embedded in the golden map, while Wyn sank trembling beside their chief, who sat in the sand making a sound that was both laughter and crying.

He had missed the mouth of Bear Creek by a mile and landed them in a neat bight behind a pile of driftwood on the downriver tip of a long, slender island like many along that stretch of the Great Bend. Behind them was the phenomenal tower of mist pouring up off the black shoals that marched in wide stairsteps, up, up, and over the cascade for many leagues up the river.

On either side of the island lay the dark rocks that marked the end of the shoals. The pink cliffs held the river on the south, while the gently rising northern slope was littered with a continuation of the same stones in the river. These wandered down to the water, where their crevices were stuffed with long gray-blue and white fingers of the mussel shells that named the rapids, and off which generations of red people had survived.

The black rocks were a giant's path leading up the nearest shore, where a pyramidal structure surfaced with short grass rather than clay, but otherwise like the one at Mabila, and rose to a flat top crowned by a pavilion hung with colorful pennants and coils of blue smoke.

He found himself sitting, amazingly, fascinated by the blue puncture in his abdomen, palpating it to force blood to cleanse the wound, but feeling no pain, and he heard his own voice as though disembodied, "Evan, dig a fast grave . . . we cannot linger. . . ."

Evan glanced at the perimeter saying, "Here they will wash away in the first high water."

The island was gravel and sandy loam, but Madoc's eye found its heart where a circle of strong, tall honey locust looked as though they had been standing many seasons.

On the beach the monks were covering one of the sailors, a Shawnee woman, and Teleri with shrouds of buffalo hide.

Madoc's vision was shimmering with the colors of the sky; it all had the evanescent quality of a dream. Already the Shawnee were keening for the dead, and he would not let himself think the awful thought, that Teleri . . .

"No!" yelled a small voice from the crowd, and Einion threw himself onto his mother's body, clinging to the shroud.

Madoc plucked the child away from her, kicking and clawing, but without much fight in him. Madoc held him and patted his back, saying things only the boy could hear. "Son. I will take care of you." The boy sagged against him, his painted face on Madoc's shoulder, utterly given in to sobbing.

Winnowed Rice made a motion to relieve him of the child—Rhys held the sleeping baby on his back—but Madoc shook his head.

"Mama."

"We have to say good-bye to her now, son," Madoc said, and felt the withering truth twist inside him. But despite it, still holding the child, he told Ari to prepare one of the young pigeons for another attempt to contact the *Horn.*

Later he slipped a one-word note—wait—into the capsule on the bird's leg, blew his breath into her feathers with a traditional whisper of encouragement, and let her loose, hoping that she would spy the pennant atop the ship on the swamp lake only a few leagues from here from a bird's point of view.

Gwen had worked the young flock to the pennant, but this would be the bird's first long homing trip. Madoc did not have much hope for her success. She climbed and circled in what appeared to be confusion, then headed southwest.

He watched the gray bird grow smaller and finally diminish to a speck, then vanish into the sky. At least she was headed in the right direction, he thought, while the monks found the spade heads in the tool cargo and were fitting them with handles.

To add to their misery, small stinging flies suddenly descended from nowhere to buzz in the ear and put pulsating red welts on the skin.

Wyn approached John, who laid back with his eyes closed. The old man had taken a tumble, so Wyn started to back off, thinking their priest was resting from the ordeal, but John caught his cassock hem, drawing the abbot to his knees beside his elder.

"We must hold another funeral," Wyn said.

John did not open his eyes. "I am so weary, my son."

Wyn saw no visible wounds on the old man.

"Let Brian celebrate Mass in my place."

"But—" Wyn looked up to see Brian standing there, arms folded across the cassock he still wore. Behind him his wife knelt swatting insects from the babies in their cradleboards and began rubbing their exposed parts with the dark jelly she kept in a tied length of deer gut.

John roused himself, and with Wyn's help, sat up. "How can we gainsay the lord, who gave him a permanent tonsure?"

"Celtic priests traditionally were married, Domme," Brian said, scratching his neck where something was crawling.

Hayati was on her feet, smearing the mixture on her own arms. She offered a dollop to Brian, saying, "Take it for the cousins, husband."

"What cousins?"

"The little stinging ones, yes?" She expertly smeared the stain on his wrists and the backs of his hands, leaving enough with him to plaster his face.

Shyly she offered a glob to the old man, who drew back from it wrinkling his nose.

"The cousins hate it," she said.

Behind her Brian found that it did feel cooling on the itch. The smell was pleasant, aromatic like pine oil.

But Father John waved it aside. Hayati gestured for another woman to come, and gave her the excess. Behind them other red women were applying the salve, offering it to the white people, who did not fail to sniff it suspiciously.

Wyn saw how tired John looked. There was no blood, but he knew the old man was greatly weakened. No one knew how old he was, but he must be in his seventies, at least. He had never looked more feeble to Wyn, who had known him longer than anyone present.

He knows he does not have much time, Wyn thought with an aching loneliness for his friend and teacher. That is why he was encouraging this heretical young priest, the only ordained man among them after John.

But when he prevented the old priest from standing, John growled and leaned heavily on Wyn to gain his feet: "Do not look so grim, brother. I still have life left in me."

The soft heart of the island's little grove proved an easy dig with many hands helping. Away from the water the flies thinned out. Brian intoned the requiem Mass, and afterwards Rhys played. Everyone sang an old hymn, and even the Norsemen stayed close to the graveside, where everyone shoveled in the fill.

Then they walked back to the beach as a long, meandering string, swatting at the insects as they neared the water.

The river glowed with reflected colors, its broad and brilliant surface pointing like a road directly into the orange sun on the western horizon.

Madoc, with Einion asleep over his shoulder, walked with John and Wyn, muttering a droning prayer near the end of the scattered procession with the grave diggers bringing up the rear. Things had still not lost the glow of dream, which persisted in the arglwydd's vision as he walked slowly without speaking through the tall grass.

Suddenly from ahead someone screamed—a man, a woman—he could not tell. Everyone surged forward. Evan and several others dropped their shovels and drew swords as they ran past Madoc, who handed the sleeping child off to Wyn, then shoved through the final underbrush and onto the strand near the coracles, where they had been pulled ashore.

Those who had arrived earlier stood gaping as Madoc forced his way past their frozen shoulders to see what on the near shore had their attention.

The ridges above the river channel still were brushed with the golden sun of a lingering September day, and there was plenty of light left to see, walking over the debris of shells thrown by the river, by birds, and by human beings, a host of red men that appeared to be erupting from the earth itself as a long stream of red flesh stretched back over the ridge.

Fox had force-marched his war-party south on the trace as soon as his Chickasaw allies had sent runners with the news that Madoc turned south instead of north. Knowing that the whites could go no farther upriver than Muscle Shoals, he collected Muskogean allies along the way, at the same time sending out runners to other nations, asking for a big gathering there.

They kept coming, tens upon tens of them, staunch red men colored with fantastic war-paint, each an explosion of color in the feathers of a dozen flamboyant species, in rattling shells and dangling loops of pearls. They carried every imaginable kind of weapon; their faces were set behind their paint and tattoos. They made no sound except the crunching of their hundreds of moccasins on the crushed shells.

They filled the northern bank, flanking the hem of the grassy pyramid and blanketing the shore so that they spilled out onto the wet rocks, hundreds of red warriors in full battle dress. The intense colors flashed before his eyes, the strange pyramid beyond, the red people in their red, yellow, and green paint and feathers, the water glimmering by, the pillar of silver mist boiling up to the sky behind them.

Madoc's Hundred stared spellbound at the size of the red host that continued to pour from behind the ridge to line the riverbank across the few spans of swirling water. They were twenty deep and still coming, easily a thousand armed soldiers, none of whom spoke so much as a word. Now it could be seen that they were of many different nations but looked to be mostly Mabilan and Chickasaw, with Cherokee here and there.

The Cherokee stood out because of their nearly bald scalps with the stiff war-lock running from widow's peak to nape. They were also generally taller than the Muskogeans, who covered themselves with armor made of shells, while the Chickasaw were almost naked except for their braceletlike blue tattoos. On the ridge the wave of red warriors seemed to be ending. In less formal ranks there followed close on the heels of the warriors a lesser army of women and younger braves carrying supplies and hauling gihli-gasi. They staggered down the zigzag path until the slope was paved with red people.

Leading them all was Fox, face and chest painted dramatically red and black. He stepped nearer on the closest black rocks that provided a rough stair-bridge to the island. He stopped on the promontory, avoiding the flow that would have stained his immaculate war leggings and smeared his paint. Battle lance festooned with dancing ribbons, his weight on one booted foot, the war-chief looked down upon the white people.

In a voice that boomed out above the sound of the river and the ringing in Madoc's head, the Cherokee said, "You broke your pledge."

"We go to our ship a little south of this place, with which we keep our pledge to leave."

Winnowed Rice just behind him translated as Madoc and Fox spoke, but both men used sign.

The Muskogean chiefs screamed as one voice—no! when they heard this.

Fox regarded the Muskogean host, letting that be the answer to Madoc's request.

Madoc was chilled by the curl of Fox's lip; he was playing a game, which Madoc read as a challenge man-to-man. "This is between you and me, not our people."

"Are you out of your mind, man?" Wyn gasped behind him. "You can barely stand much less fight that creature."

But Madoc waved him aside, gesturing that he and Winnowed Rice should get away.

Fox observed the arrogant kanegmati chieftain swaying and

about to pass out before him. He saw that Madoc was wounded, which would be a good excuse not to fight him, but when one of his men, Evan it was, handed him a blue-metal sword from his own backpack, Madoc looked suddenly stronger as he took a firm grip on it and stepped forward.

Fox scanned his people and allies on the northern shore. In all the crowd he could not see Black Pearl, but as though she stood beside him, her words rang in his recall—"Let them go or I will walk into the forest."

He regarded Madoc, who, despite the swagger, did not look as though he would last a round in hand-to-hand combat. Fox was furious with him, forcing the issue in front of all these witnesses, which Fox must answer or lose face. He stepped closer to Madoc but did not draw his own long knife, a magnificent ceremonial flint with an edge much keener if not as durable as Madoc's iron.

"I do not want to fight you, white man," Fox said softly, but Madoc did not understand completely, and Winnowed Rice was slow to translate the Cherokee's words.

"Fight me now, before the sun sets," Madoc cried, taking a stance with the weapon.

Fox grimaced—this was too much of a challenge to parry, and he whispered so that only the crazed white man could hear: "I say I do not want to kill you."

Winnowed Rice heard and got it right this time, but Madoc was unable to believe her interpretation and threw further challenge at Fox by tossing his sword hand-to-hand and stepping out onto the rocks within a pace of the red chief.

Instinctively Fox drew his weapon, forced into it now with no way to turn back without terrible loss of face. He spat out his remark again—"I do not wish to kill you, Weather Eyes!"

Madoc was goaded by the name the red people called him. He leapt into frontal confrontation with both hands wielding the ancient sword. Now the dream began in earnest: Nothing else mattered, not the bone-killing ache of muscles too long without rest and too long at labor, or the dull ache of his wounds, or the fever he could feel prickling his forehead with deceitful coolness. Teleri's death, or even the larger goal of returning to claim the *Horn*—none of these considerations clouded the swift and sure knowledge in his hands around the heavy steel.

He took the first action, forcing Fox to quickstep back over the boulders and through a swift spit of water that threw up wings of spray against his ceremonial leggings.

A groan from many throats rumbled behind the two men. The wall of surprised but delighted red men pressed close to the water's edge, calling in unison Fox's name and title. This meant that they could have the pleasure of battle, all the gamble on wagers, without having to actually fight. Already the braves laid odds as they gave the kanegmati chieftain the once-over.

Likewise the white people leaned as a group in the direction of the fight as the red man found his footing, sidestepping up onto dry rocks as the white chieftain splashed through the watercourse and lunged again with his terrible weapon.

Fox saw that it was of the same hard metal as Black Pearl's little knife. A small streak of fear raised his hackles when he regarded the double-edged blade this close; it danced before his eyes to the left, then the right, barely missing Fox who took another gambling step backwards.

Fox had almost no hope of getting out of this without killing Weather Eyes except to try again with rhetoric. But the white man would not let them rest and pressed his attack further, catching Fox off guard at the left.

The blade clanged with sparks off the rock where Fox had been standing. Madoc called something that sounded like a battle curse and locked blades with Fox, who tried to speak to the snarling wild-eyed white man. "I promised the woman I would not kill you."

Madoc recognized the word for woman. He could detect that the opponent was feinting with him, not playing for keeps, but thought it was a trick to divert him. He threw weight against the red man's defense and backed away just out of reach, but kept his weapon poised for a lethal strike.

Fox eyed the sword's progress and repeated the word, tossing his own weapon into his other hand and whisking off the quick handsign for woman and promise.

They danced around each other, apparently evenly matched with Madoc's longer sword against Fox's generally longer reach and more formidable size.

Behind them the people on both sides of the river screamed for their man. Out of the corner of his eye, Madoc saw Evan lurking at Fox's right with a sword, and circled, jumping from slick stone to stone, calling, "Put it away, Evan!" praying that the others would follow.

Seeing Evan obey, Fox shifted his own blade from hand to hand in a graceful display of dexterity meant to stall a little longer. He was smug with the knowledge that his warriors would never dream of interfering with single combat. It was up to the war chief to do this work. If only he had something to use as an excuse, a sign to cease fighting, he could still keep his promise to Black Pearl and save face among the war leaders.

Madoc shook the sword tip at Fox. "What woman?"

Fox relaxed his blade in a slightly less menacing angle. "The woman with eyes like yours," he mimed in clear handsign.

Madoc blinked, right hand trembling with the heft of iron.

"The woman," Fox stammered, "the woman"—he gestured at his own eyes and then pointed to Madoc—"with your eyes."

Rhiannon, Madoc thought, her name upon his lips. He took another half step back, retiring the attack.

Fox subtly nodded, praying that he had a good excuse to stop the battle. He did some fancy footwork that took him around Madoc and through the stream to the most prominent boulder at the tip of the island. Then, away from the opponent, he raised his arms and called to his assembled warriors crowding the other shore where campfires flickered.

"It is almost sunset and no time to be fighting to the death!"

A roar erupted from the red horde, screaming for the white man's blood.

"Then kill him quickly!" the Muskogeans called, joined by some of his own men.

Sighing, Fox looked at the opponent and shrugged. "I tried to keep from killing you, Weather Eyes, I really tried."

Madoc recognized the temper of the enemy host. His own people were screaming for the red man's blood.

The two combatants' stillness hushed both sides, made one quivering throng of audience by promise of combat.

"Now I must kill you," Fox said in elegant one-handed sign, his knife poised in the other.

"You can try," Madoc said in his own language as he wiped sweat from his face with the crook of his arm. "But no matter what the result of our fight, let them go." He gestured at the Hundred and used the one-hand-sign for freedom—the profile of an ascending bird.

Winnowed Rice was close enough to witness this and translate for both nations to hear.

"Very well," Fox said, but doubt creased his forehead as he wondered, would Black Pearl see it his way?

Fox hoped that he could wound the white chief and thereby spare his life. A glance at the northern bank revealed the vast red human sea washing down the slope there. Lost among them somewhere was Black Pearl. He hoped she could appreciate his dilemma.

But to be sure, he turned and called so that everyone could hear his echoing voice above the water rumble, "Let every man and woman here witness that this kanegmati has given me a bargain. If he wins, they all go south the way they came. If I win, I take his life, but I will not kill women and children. We get their blue-metal weapons in any case. Let nobody here blame me for killing him who forced me into combat!"

Winnowed Rice translated as best she could for the Hundred.

"I cannot believe he agreed," Rhys said, near at hand but out of Madoc's view. "Why would he spare us?" he asked, but Winnowed Rice did not have an answer.

"But," Fox continued loudly, "understand I do not have to let any of them go. I am a man of honor, who does not break any vow." He hoped she heard. Would she understand that this man's challenge freed Fox of his promise to her? She must understand that if challenged Fox could not keep his honor and refuse.

He turned to see Madoc advancing.

They fought in earnest while the sun slipped into the river. It seemed to Madoc that his arms worked without his thought. He could not remember a time before this battle, as he watched it from somewhere deep within himself, when all he could hear was his own breath and heartbeat.

He was so weary. For the first time he feared he might not be able to hold out against the larger opponent, despite his superior weapon and skill with it. His side had begun to stitch. Missing the last thrust, he glanced down to see that his tunic was stained with fresh blood—the earlier wound was weeping.

His sight was dizzy. The fever ascended, leaving him alternately hot and cold. He had to spend more effort getting out of Fox's way than engaging him and was behind three or four offensive moves. The game was going to the opponent, as Madoc's strength ebbed.

Fox almost lazily brought his flint blade in so close Madoc was forced to stumble back to gain the reach to deflect the blow. Flint hit iron, sending sparks into the gathering dusk. Fox groaned when he saw his weapon broken in two; his hand rang with the impact. Madoc stared numbly at his sword. He lifted it and went for the kill, but he was put off by his weakness, confused by the colored sky, and distracted by Fox, who spun around and caught the other with his stony heel against the jaw. It would never have happened if Madoc had not been weakened. Fox picked up the great French sword, shocked at how heavy it was, dazzled by its color and its power in his hand. He almost forgot the opponent, who was down on his knees. Then he remembered and moved closer, thrilled that he had taken possession of the dream weapon and now would take the life of its owner to set the claim.

The Hundred moaned. Evan and several other men moved in closer, but Madoc warned them back. A dozen red warriors sprinted across the boulders but stopped when Fox cried out.

"We will keep our promise," Fox called to them, but it was meant to be his last remark to Madoc, who knew this was it when he saw Fox straining at the weight of the sword, understanding why the white man had used both hands to wield it.

In the hasty camp of Madoc's Hundred, the little gray pigeon fluttered back into the dovecote in a cloud of hysterical feathers beneath the staff with the pennant, which Evan had stabbed into the sand. Yngvild saw it. Rhys heard it but like everyone else was too absorbed in the combat, which Winnowed Rice was describing for him.

"He is down," she barely whispered, and made a small sound of regret. She clutched Rhys's hand.

A communal moan escaped the congregation. Down the line someone cried out as Fox brought the sword up to deliver the death blow.

Chapter 37

Blood rains from the cloudy web
On the broadloom of slaughter.
The web of man, gray as armor,
Is woven. The Valkyries cross it
with a crimson weft.
The warp is made of human entrails;
Human heads are the weights.
The heddle-rods are blood-wet spears.
The shafts are iron-bound.
And arrows are the shuttles.
With swords we weave
this web of battle

—Njal's Saga
Norse Oral Tradition
A.D. 980

Because of the swift shadow across his bent and bleeding enemy, Fox hesitated. His hunter's eyes flicked upward, where he saw Gwen's eagle floating in the air between the westering sun and the killing ground.

Sunset painted the bird's wing with fire. The talons blazed with points of light. Its eye seemed to be targeting him, giving Fox a chill up the back that it knew him as prey and might drop an attack against his bare shoulders as though he were a field mouse or cringing rabbit.

But the eagle did not stoop. It swept a lazy circle above Madoc and Fox, opening and closing its beak in fake shrieks, flexing those talons. Beyond the combatants red and white people gestured at the apparently purposeful bird. Christians who had expected to see their leader beheaded crossed themselves. A couple of them, though all knew it was Gwen's pet, fell to their knees, praising the Creator for its timely arrival.

Everywhere the sharp buzz of speculation whipped through the crowd like fire across a dry field. Circling the two men, the eagle could not fail to be interpreted as a potent sign by everyone there, red and white alike.

It would have been amazing had any bird behaved like this, but for it to be the most esteemed of all animals to the red men and not disregarded by the whites—this was a mighty sign right out of both their legends.

Then from the northern bank some red lookout with a downriver view around the headland below the shoals saw something that was even more astonishing. His cry alerted his nearer brothers, who were alarmed by the tone of his exclamation.

Madoc was still on one knee awaiting the blow, oblivious to everything but his expectation. His view was of the dark sand and eternity. He began a prayer he had been saving all his life and found the spot high up between his shoulder blades where he knew the warrior would place the blade. He willed the flesh there to relax so that there would be no resistance and it would be swift. He was floating. A rush of wind filled his ears, stifling the prayer he figured could not do any harm at this point: "Lord, bring me home..."

But he never said the words and did not finish the thought, because the blow that was supposed to cleave his spine and send him homeward never came.

He was aware of the sound of wind, or the voices of many people raised nearby. He opened his eyes and saw his long shadow on the trampled sand, and the opponent's stubby, cedar-colored toes still planted wide to deliver the blow.

Madoc felt a twinge of regret that he was still alive. His body screamed with pain in many places. The taste of blood salted his tongue. His heart ached with loss and despair; he longed to follow Teleri quickly. It would have been so good to sleep at last, to ease the grief of all these lives and this insane mission from his bent shoulders. He felt a hundred and one years old and with an ache recalled his father that last day on the sand. Owen must have felt like this, dusty with regret, tired to the marrow, grieved by loss, willing to let it all go but held back by some further duty.

He felt he might pass out, vomit, or lose his bowels and spoil what should be the dignity of a warrior's death.

But none of that happened. Nothing happened at all. Vision cleared as he leaned back on his knees. The river's continuous rough whisper filled every silence. The sky burned a fleshy purple overhead, while the eternal mists off the shoals bent by the prevailing westerly caught a flagrant orange glow from a sun just about to set on the horizon. The lay of the westward river made it look as though the sun would sizzle in its nether waters. A few high, stringy clouds moved swiftly enough eastward to see them change colors as they merged with the river vapor.

Madoc recognized Gwen's Arrow-Eye lounging against an updraft, so close now he and Fox could see individual pearly feathers on its chest. From a sudden angle the eagle looked like a ship banking against the wind. Arrow-Eye shrieked.

Fox heard Madoc's grunt of laughter, but he could not tear his gaze from the creature, who seemed to be looking at him, Fox, hunter of eagles. He was suddenly aware of his now-trembling arm muscles poised high over his head to deliver the blow two-handed in the ritual manner as though the kanegmati's weightier sword were the sacred obsidian of the harshest games.

Fox let his shoulders relax without taking his eye from the eagle, whose appearance must at last delay the work begun. He brought Durendal down slowly to one side, straining against its weight, his mouth working in the habitual formula his people recited upon seeing the sacred bird.

One woman among the Cherokee had not moved since the hand-to-hand started. When Fox lowered the sword without striking, she blinked, breaking her trance.

Then, majestically plowing against the current, the *Horn's* single square sail full of western wind bounded from behind the rocks, small at first, but enlarging against the magic light and under various labors, headed in this direction, its several long oars pumping in time with a deep, booming chant punctuated by the rhythmic banging of a drum. On deck Snorrison himself was blowing the curved war-horn, which completed the impression of a great bawling beast roaring up the channel.

The mightiest war-god could not have better placed the low glow behind the ship. A nimbus of molten gold light outlined the craft, turning it and its shadow menacingly black on the glaring water.

Praise and amazement rang from Madoc's Hundred, who began applauding and whistling encouragement, which the men on board could hear as they plowed closer to the island.

Cries of wonder and fear echoed from the red encampment.

Black Pearl had been prepared to turn and walk directly into the forest if Fox killed Madoc. At her feet a small bag lay packed for just that purpose, though she had only a vague plan of where to go. Perhaps north and east over the Warrior's Path. She had heard the Cherokee men speak of a mixed white and red tribe up near a great eastern salt water, presided over by a yellow-bearded chieftain. It sounded like Norsemen to her, especially after hearing the sagas.

She was too nearsighted to see Gwen's eagle, but she heard comments about her and fuzzily glimpsed the bird when it angled closer. Fleetingly she praised St. Brigit, who still seemed to be sending birds to help this poor colony. Black Pearl had not kept many artifacts of her old life, but she kept the prayer to St. Brigit, who seemed to be at home among these red tribesmen as she had been among the white ones back in the hills of Cambria.

Black Pearl would keep all the old stories, prayers, and songs from her former tribe and teach them in the coming years to her adopted people. She would recount Aesop's Fables, the Welsh stories of the Mabinogi, the bible stories of creation, the Flood, Moses, and the Gospels, telling them into the eight decades of her Cherokee life around a Cherokee fire to her Cherokee grandchildren, and the stories would trickle down through the years to change and meld with native stories, keeping traces that would mystify later Christians, who were eventually to settle in these river valleys.

The war-horn bellowed echoes off the wet stones.

Feeling as though she had been set loose in a dream, Black Pearl turned to see the ship approach. It was close enough now for her to recognize the bright colors and simple pattern of the dragon pennant, which she had copied in her weaving. And behind it came her many escorts, at least fifty coracles or Natchez canoes decorated with poles topped by bright feathers, each boat full of painted, chanting warriors waving their weapons.

People jostled against Black Pearl, suddenly yelling, pushing closer for a better view nearer the water.

No warrior was so amazed that he could not grab his nearest weapon—atlatls and blowguns rattled, arrows nocked, and a forest of spears sprang up. But none let fly. How could the gnat of a man's spear point pierce such a creature as this, bearing down on the red shore in a steady line that would take it by the island a narrow channel's width away? The red canoemen on shore were calculating the spot where it would hit the rocks.

Several red women screamed on the run for higher ground behind the north shore. But the wonder drew them up shorter than the ridge. About halfway there they turned, one with a suckling toddler, who let go of the teat to stare transfixed like everyone else.

The great canoe—for by now the Muskogean war-chiefs recognized this thing—did not appear hostile, just shockingly flamboyant. Word spread like lightning from the knowledgeable lowlanders to their highland neighbors, who had not seen this and its sister ship on the southern waters. Their primary wonder was how the great canoe got here overland.

Drums sounded from both sides of the river as flutes, harps, and tambours joined in a tuneless jubilation from Madoc's Hundred. Soon Cherokee bells, Mabilan log chimes, and Chickasaw gourd rattles swelled the tumult as shamans began hasty magic against the very big medicine down on the river.

Perhaps I have died after all, Madoc was thinking, because pain and misery seemed to have fled at the sight of his splendid ship as full of heart and spirit as any living creature. At the sound of Fair Beard's familiar yodel, he felt in his bones a wave of joy that would have knocked him to his knees had he not already been there.

"The *Horn*, the *Horn*, the dragon ship," he heard his people shouting, whispering, laughing behind him.

"Snorrison," Madoc said in wonder and disbelief.

Yngvild's voice rang with her husband's name as she ran with her babe tied up in her shawl. Incredibly in the noise and commotion, Fair Beard saw her and waved; she halted and held their wriggling son high for him to see.

Across the water red men called, "Uktena, Uktena—the Snake—River Serpent—Uktena—but how?" in several languages.

Madoc heard Fox whispering, "Uktena," as the Cherokee chief was now believing the Muskogean report about a snake canoe. All red nations told the legend. Every one of these warriors—Mabilan, Chickasaw, Cherokee, Yuchi, and several others—had grown up believing in the monsters who inhabited these waters in the ancient days before the world had set into its present shape. Several sachems among them had visited secret cliffs along this river where erosion exposed the Uktena's massive bones in the rock. Conventional belief held that the monsters survived only in vision, song, and in the rock paintings of a thousand local caverns and cliffsides. Women incised the figure of the Uktena as blessing work on their pottery. It was a venerable legend they never expected to see in the flesh, yet here appeared to be the incarnation of the old dragon in all its feathered glory with painted, hooting bowmen riding beneath its wing.

The Norse sailors had adorned themselves like the ship. A few, including Fair Beard himself and young Lev, full of the old fighting spirit he had heard about in old sagas, were stripped naked save for their paint, iron helmets, and battle-axes. Others clung to the rigging, yelling fierce cries their great-grandfathers had echoed off icebergs in the far northern fjords of eternal winter country.

"We will eat them—"

"Make them eat themselves—a piece at a time!"

"Kiss my thin-lipped blade—"

"We cannot be defeated!"

—this in a variegated mixture of Western Norse and Welsh and Irish not unlike David Iron's Yuchi war-cry rolling in echoes up the river valley.

The red dragon banner rippled like a tongue of flame on the mast. The sail itself snapped in the western wind; the rudderman yelled out to the captain about rocks dangerously close there! The very modifications that enabled this ship to brave the ocean made it vulnerable in channel navigation and shallows. The trick of weighting her so that the deeper bow-keel was raised out of the water further gave her the look of a charging beast. She bucked under the wind, a fair imitation of animal rage.

Despite his apparently triumphant cries, Fair Beard at the prow expected that at any moment the teeth of the river would chew his beauty. The water of the main channel did not rush as it must during the spring flood season, but it was thick with foam from tumbling over the shoals, making it impossible to see what lay below the surface. Silently he thanked the gods for steadying the wind, or they would be kindling by now. He saw the spot where he would take the ship and called this information back in the form of instructions in song to the sternman. It was an ancient technique that demanded unerring teamwork developed amid icebergs, slender fjords, and hostile weather, but it seemed to be working on this wide river quite as well.

Back and forth rang the battle cries mixed with instruction in a stew of song, chant, and yodel, as Fair Beard aimed the ship for the peaceful-looking little bay just below the island where Madoc and Fox seemed planted on the sand. It was the only apparent nook of safety for her and had a natural dock evidenced by the pile of washed-down debris caught there and the company's coracles upended on the shore.

An approach that would accommodate a coracle was one thing: the *Horn* was quite another. Beneath the war-paint and a snarl, Fair Beard bit his lip. He was worried, not at all sure they would bring her in without calamity.

The water was deeper there. Submerged rocks disturbed the flow on either side of the little harbor, but the surface where he aimed appeared placidly deep behind a snarl of uprooted trees and other high-water debris that was a reminder of what this river could do when angry. Reeds, cattails, and willows that denoted shallows grew farther up the island's long margin. They drew nearer. A moment came when it was time to roll in the sheet. Fair Beard poised, determined the moment, then shouted for the men in the rigging to reef the sail.

It was done; they were committed to the slot. One of three things was about to happen. They would either make it to berth, be yanked downriver in a wrenching turn that would probably throw them onto the headland rocks, or ram the first shallow bottom—it would lie either there, off the foot of the island where the stumps and snags had caught, or over there on the north shore where the red horde gaped. An eye as sharp as Snorrison's could always tell where moving water took its toll. With the dark turn of mind his philosophy encouraged, Snorrison imagined it would be a more splendid crash if they hit the rocks of the shore, which might send himself and his men immediately to the Halls of the Dead in grand style. He kept his hand on his ax handle so to be ready to enter Valhalla properly.

He ordered the several anchors to be deployed according to a rhyming song he bellowed. Each anchor had a name, so that in sequence they might stay a part of the ship and thereby maneuver her in tricky waters. Each man answered back a staccato response, a meaningless word like "Yo-aaa!"

that meant the order was obeyed. They had worked so long together, the *Horn*'s crew had the timing of a choir. Madoc felt privileged to witness the performance, which was rarely attended by anyone other than crew.

"Old One-Eye!" the captain sang, meaning their stone stern anchor shaped like a giant's bead, not meant to grapple the bottom but just to drag, thereby slowing down their rate of advance. The great vessel's stern suddenly seemed snagged. She bucked her head even higher out of the water, losing some forward momentum and veering obliquely against the current, alarmingly close to the mussel-covered rocks of the shore.

Madoc stared in wonder like the dazzled landlubbers—he could not believe that Snorrison was alive and the ship still sailed.

Fair Beard's voice rang with the call for the two oarsmen to hasten starboard and use the oar shafts like poles. Lev on one and David Iron on the other leaped to obey, assisted by four sailors to maneuver the still-green pine oars out of their deckblocks and into position at the starboard rail fore and aft, where they could push against any obstacle.

The *Horn* nosed away from the mussel beds. She bobbed, seemingly to sniff in the direction Fair Beard wanted her to go. When it was clear that the rocks would not get her, a cheer rose up from Madoc's Hundred.

Wonder and other emotions silenced the red host. This was beginning to look like loss of triumph for their side. Already the battle sacrifice was interrupted. A trio of Cherokee sachems moaned chants, trying to undo the damage, while warriors renewed handholds on their weapons. A war-cry is a war-cry, unmistakable in any language; several Cherokee subchiefs and their men pushed off in canoes toward the island.

Their movement from the north shore did not escape Fair Beard's notice as he prepared to signal the rudderman with his right hand raised above his head. When it dropped, the pilot translated the gesture into an obedient movement that swung the ship gently sideways and neatly into the little bay. Snorrison gave a final barking shout: "Odin's Nosehair!"

The last clawed anchor dropped with a splash. The ship kneeled toward Madoc, who had found his feet and was staggering into the shallows toward her. Fair Beard marked her a good way off the beach for fear of grounding. He was no less amazed than anyone else not to hear the grinding scream of her disembowelment. But here she was, peacefully nodding in place like a mallard.

Another cheer rose up from Madoc's Hundred as the arglwydd plunged into the water and with great affection threw his arms out to embrace the mossy prow like a child against his mother's apron. At a shout, he looked up to see the outlandishly painted Snorrison Fair Beard handing his bearded battle-ax to Lev behind him at the rail.

"Fair Beard—can nothing kill you?"

"T'would take more than Skraelings to do the job!"

"How in God's name did you find us?"

From onboard and unseen Gwen whistled. The eagle lazily turned, threw Madoc one last shriek, and aimed itself toward her outstretched and gloved arm.

"Your little gray pigeon, man," Fair Beard explained as he straddled the rail and found purchase among the new-tied sidelines. "We were already headed down the Yuchi when she came home. We turned her loosed with a reply, and she took off upriver, but we lost her, so we loosed the eagle after her, and all we had to do—"

Fair Beard leapt from the starboard rail, calling on the way down, "—was follow!" With a splash he hit the water, which was clear enough for him to see below the *Horn* less than a man's height to spare above a stone embankment. Still not quite believing their luck, he came up sputtering, his toes finding a ledge that led to sandy bottom.

Around him the water churned with wildly painted sailors and squealing women, singing monks and shrieking children, as Madoc's Hundred surged to greet their heroes. Many grinning Shawnee faces were among the whites. Lev and the other sailors let themselves be hugged, kissed, stroked, and petted, wondering in undisguised pleasure at the change in feminine ratio. The Shawnee were likewise glad to see a few more tangletongues of physique and face who pleased them.

David Iron scrambled down the sidelines, while the uproar increased with the Natchez canoes pulling in. He could see Fox edging toward his line and away from the Hundred, still holding Madoc's sword, and the Yuchi was determined to stop him.

Madoc felt himself fall against Fair Beard. "I knew you were alive, I knew you were alive," the arglwydd cried out. Up to their waists in water, they bear-hugged until the

Norsemen realized his commander had passed out and was bleeding from many wounds. Fair Beard dragged Madoc out of the water, shouting an order, observing his own crystal amulet hanging from Madoc's neck, and wondered what story lay behind its recovery; he last saw it when he was taken by the Alabamans.

Evan, Ari, and Gwen reached him before Snorrison pulled their unconscious lord up onto the sand.

As he stood, Yngvild stepped close to him with their son. He had a moment of joy looking at his fair woman, then holding her. But out of the corner of his eye, Snorrison saw that the fellow holding his weapon at the rail appreciated how the situation was changing with red movement on the north beach.

He called for his shield. Lev skipped it like a stone, but Fair Beard let it roll to one side as he yelled for the ax, stepping on the shield rim so that it flipped into his left hand.

Lev then let the ax go underhand so that the great blue blade was the center point of a circle described by the handle. Fair Beard, with his eyes on the spinning ax, took a shifting step to position himself under it, lifted his hand, and with deceptive simplicity caught it by the handle and brought it down and back before lifting it again, following the momentum of the weight without interrupting the spin.

When he had widened the orbit to his satisfaction, so that the ax began to hum its unique tune, he called to specific others, "Get the women aboard!" "Attack—there!" Then he called to his Natchez allies, bellowing in their language, throwing them into a wild, screaming display as they came around in their many smaller vessels and pointed their fury at the northern shore.

Evan had stabbed his own sword upright in the sand; Ari helped him shoulder Madoc. Staggering under the burden, Evan waded back into the water, misstepping and almost going under in the sudden deep. He found ropy purchase and began laboriously to climb the sidelines. Leaning over the rail, Wyn and two sailors relieved him of their fallen leader's body.

From the higher vantage point of the ship, Evan saw Fair Beard's blade advancing on the red men leaping from canoes. He dived into the water and came up near shore, where he gained his feet running, snatched up his weapon, and joined

Fair Beard, who faced the growing contingent with only a handful of men.

Behind the red chiefs a swarm of armed warriors clogged the river, some in canoes, many wading up to their armpits, holding high their weapons and all headed this way. Many had already encountered the Natchez, who had let go a flight of arrows.

Fair Beard took his stand, his men fanning out on either side. Glancing around, he saw that it was good ground, level, with low trampled grass patching the sand, no large vegetation other than a couple of willows, no boulders or gravel to impede the main play—almost an arena.

He kept the Kisser orbiting nicely as he began a slow yell that ended with famous battle poetry composed a hundred years before by Norway's King Harald: "I will persuade my enemy to kiss my thin-lipped ax!" He repeated the last phrase until the singing blade and screaming chant blended into a single continuous sound.

Someone called a halt, perhaps Fox, perhaps Madoc tried to yell it down, but by that time it was too late, because red men's arrows were loose and targeting, while bowmen aboard the *Horn* had already replied. William the Saxon's crossbow claimed a token, pinning a furious red warrior's thigh to the inside wall of his dugout adrift among cattails.

A horrible roar of more than a thousand combined warcries issued from the red advance. They drowned out the dozen or so white men howling as they moved behind Snorrison, practiced at staying two ax-circles from each other, advancing like some fierce, whistling, many-geared siege engine. Each battle-ax had its own distinctive whine, depending on the shape of the filigree cut into the blade; even these and the grumble of the river itself were drowned out by the red uproar.

But iron against antler, flint, and cane knives can even out the worse numbers. Brown bodies had begun to fall despite a rain of lances and blazing arrows toward the *Horn*. A few of these slew coracles, but most merely nicked impotently at the *Horn*'s impervious oaken strakes and fell into the river.

The blur of the Kisser had already taken down three red men and a fair-sized willow tree with the battle less than a minute old. Fair Beard's shield bristled with numerous shafts. He seemed to be sweeping arrows from the air before him, but none had gotten through it.

Behind the Norse axes came the two-sided Celtic swords, hardened with Wyn's metal-magic, slashing in wide figure eight sweeps, cleaving, each two-handed swing scoring a hit. Already members of the second wave were falling back under the blades. The iron mowed through red men without resistance, not even slowed. Fair Beard's eyes appeared sewn open, his mouth a fanged hole as he reaped his way through the red field.

The Natchez kept up their attack from the canoes, bringing down many coming from the other side. Some of the allies had already landed on the north shore—red noncombatants were fleeing back up the slope.

On the ship women, children, and clergy crept up behind the rails to watch. Two sailors were dousing flames from a pitch-pointed arrow that had fallen into rope. The several bowmen still aimed at the canoes, fewer now as latecomers stopped their river-crossing midstream when they saw the invasion force to a man falling without delivering a single blow. None stood against the advancing wall of white men, who reached the water's edge, hacking at canoemen before they could jump free.

Madoc on deck under Wyn's hands felt the ship shudder beneath him. Home again, he thought, about to sink back into blissful unconsciousness. He willed himself awake despite the tempting darkness and the abbot's protests. Beyond his vision he heard unmistakable battle clamor.

Someone was cutting the tunic off his body.

Madoc did not remember fighting or how he got here with a battle wound. He seemed suspended with nothing real to cling to except the briny boards under his face and the cries, beyond, of the dying. He willed himself to stay conscious, to turn over, and when he did, he saw Rhys, who reached out to stop him when he felt Madoc trying to move. "Be still—"

"Rhys," he cried, grabbing his arm, "I think this is it. After all the trouble, this is it." His strength failed him, and he fell back to the deck, vision blanked for a moment. "And I never got to hear your new song." He heard Rhys speak to someone else and opened his eyes as he said, "What was it about?"

"An impulsive sailor prone to sudden decisions," Rhys said, his hand against Madoc's shoulder to make him lie back down. "Caradoc says you will live to hear it sung."

Caradoc's startled face appeared above Madoc like a sunburned moon.

"You . . ." Madoc said, grabbing the mediciner's tunic, pulling him close. Memories flooded him, almost drowning out the war cries and faint screams out on the edge of awareness.

"Lie still, sir," Caradoc urged, wiping at Madoc's blood.

"You were the viper," Madoc said with unnatural clarity.

"Sir?" The man seemed truly distressed.

"The viper my brother said he put on board, the day we left."

Caradoc's wattles quivered when he swallowed the accusation.

"I am dying—you can tell me the truth." This close Madoc could see sweat bud in the folds of Caradoc's pink neck.

"Not I sir. Prince David hated me, and the feeling was entirely mutual. My happiest day was when he exiled me." His lip trembled, but he made himself stern. "It wounds me, lord, that you would distrust me after all my service." Behind him Winnowed Rice handed the physician a dripping cloth, which he used with great gentleness on the arglwydd's face and neck, speaking softly as he worked. "And you most certainly are not dying—you have lost some blood, but it is one of the luckiest wounds I have ever seen, right between this and that like grease through a goose." He knew that if the kidney or other organ had been punctured, there would be blood and agony especially when he palpated the neat puncture, which was closed by now. The other cuts given by Fox were all superficial.

"No bones broken, no parts missing."

"Why do I hurt so?"

"You took some blows, a cut or two on a muscle, and you hit your head, but you will live," Caradoc said earnestly.

"You hoarded food."

Caradoc blushed. "I guarded the food, sir, on the island, to prevent that Norse gang from taking it all." Actually he had hoarded in the form of nibbling during the entire sea journey.

"You hoarded, else how did you stay so plump?" Madoc asked, giving the mediciner's pink arm a tough pinch.

Caradoc shrank under the arglwydd's tweak. "Well . . ." he murmured, rubbing the bruise Madoc put on him.

"Admit you did."

"But I am loyal, sir, to you."

Madoc fell back, the memory of his brother's voice like a splinter. "Then, who?"

"There was no spy, no enemy at all. It was like him to hurt you any way he could. To make you distrust your crew. He hates you and feared you would contest the throne." As part of his battle camp, Caradoc had overhead Prince David say many things. "Here, sir, lie still."

But Madoc would not. He struggled to sit against Caradoc's protests and shook his head to clear it. "No, David meant someone, someone I did not know who came with us, some-one unseen, someone he put among us—"

Realization like the dart pierced him, the biting clarity of pain removing all doubt. "Rhiannon!"

"Not your lady-sister, sir—she loved you!"

"David was the father of her child," Madoc said, and he knew it was true. It had been worrying him since he saw the dark-haired baby, something he pondered just before falling asleep on many a night. How had he not seen the obvious?

This was no news to Caradoc, who figured the math of Rhiannon's pregnancy long before he saw the black-haired baby but kept it to himself. He nodded. Alone among the Hundred he had been part of David's camp. He had heard more than rumors that the prince had raped his sister, because David had bragged of it quite openly. "I suspect that is true, and it broke her heart."

"That is why she would not tell me—she did not want me to hate the baby as David's viper. I remember a look she gave to him the day we left—lord." He shook his head. "Why did I not believe her?" At least he knew, he consoled himself, a thousand miles from what was happening around him. "Am I really all right?"

"Thank the lord, sir," Caradoc said, a little too enthusiastically.

"No need to fear, physician, I believe you."

"Thank you, sir," he answered, sniffing a little and still rubbing the pinch mark his lord had given him.

"They are fighting—why are they fighting?" Madoc de-manded, reentering the here and now. He roused himself, pulled free of strong hands that tried to stop him. With some help he stood and focused on the beach. A wake of copper-colored bodies littered the slope behind Fair Beard, who had finally found his obstacle—the Kisser had beheaded the red warrior pinned by the Saxon's arrow and continued on until it slammed into the log canoe where the headless man still sat under a crimson cloak. Snorrison screamed in fury but could not free the blade.

"There is no need to be fighting," Madoc called. None could hear him in the din. They continued slashing around him; battle had turned into slaughter. He swung the war-horn hanging on its peg to his bleeding lips and blew the single note ordering the battle to cease. The sound and its ringing echo settled over the bloody sand; small children cringing in the hold below tearfully covered their ears against it. The sound pealed out over the water to bring the Natchez up short on their beachhead. It pierced Fair Beard's battle rage; he let go of the ax. Its weight dunked the canoe sideways, depositing the decapitated Cherokee into a river foaming pink against the bank.

The horn blast stopped David Iron, who had engaged Fox with Madoc's sword. The Yuchi was playing with the inexperienced though incredibly strong red man. David Iron stepped back, obedient to his commander's horn-blasted order.

Despite his unusual strength, Fox sagged with the heavy blade, the densest weapon he had ever hefted other than the boulder he had once used to bash a wolf's skull. He was aware Madoc had called the battle—everyone could hear him blasting away with that one commanding note that stilled the battle-axes, lances, arrows, knives, knuckles, teeth, fists, and fingernails. But the Cherokee chieftain still found within himself amazement at the heft of this weapon. He was thinking that with such metal blades the Principal People would have no enemy.

David Iron's sword tip was suddenly at his throat.

"Stay your hand, David Iron!" Madoc yelled. His son-in-law obeyed, but he did not remove the blade. Fox was cross-eyed looking up that long blue ribbon ending at David Iron's steady hand. With the left, he gestured at Durendal. Fox let go as though the sword had grown white hot.

David Iron precisely lowered his own blade and motioned for Fox to withdraw. With great dignity the Cherokee stepped back, his chest bared for what he expected.

The strike did not come. A cry of amazement went up from the northern shore.

He thought, Do these kanegmati do battle only to set the loser free? Around him on the blood-soaked sand was evidence that they did not.

Fox rubbed dust and sweat from his eyes and staggered a little, seeing that the whites had herded together ten and five of his warriors with hands bound as prisoners.

No other red men splashed ashore. Fair Beard stood panting, pink-tinted water lapping at his bare feet.

When the horn's last blast faded, a hush fell over the river canyon. After so many sounds it was strange to hear only water and wind, which amounted to silence after the roar.

"David Iron!" Madoc called at the rail, the strength of his voice surprising everyone who had seen him falter.

"I hear, my father."

"Tell Chief Fox that we will talk."

Chapter 38

*After a warm battle at Muscle Shoals
the whites ... said they would leave
the country and never return, and
after the exchange parted friendly ...
then descended the Tennessee down to
the Ohio, thence down to the Big
River then up to the Muddy River and
thence up that river for a great
distance ... but they are no more white
people; they now look like other red
people of the country.*

*—Cherokee Chief Occonostota in
1782, quoted by Tennessee
governor John Sevier*

Black Pearl looked up from the corn ear she was shelling.

Rhys's unmistakable voice fragmented on what was left of the western breeze. The corn was hard, the clam shell sharp and rough in her hand already blistered with the work, but the sweet song from across the water caused her to smile with recognition.

Rhys was singing a lullaby in Shawnee. Black Pearl had heard the language used for many kinds of music—love, battle, death, joking, conjuring, wood gathering, rain—but never before for such a gentle song. The words were simple, something a child might compose, but the music behind it held the shape and complexity of a Cymreig ode. Strange combination, she thought. As lovely as a dreamed kiss.

And he was playing Llais Mel. The old spruce wood from some gone northern forest boomed brightly under his fingers; he was getting good. The harp was happy.

561

Black Pearl sat with several other women amidst a pile of husks, the small mountain of the Muskogean temple pyramid a dark triangle topped with fireglow behind them. The Cherokee, taking Fox's example, called the mound a pimple. To belittle it was to hide their fear of the fifty-foot high earthwork, which the Cherokee for the most part pointedly ignored, except Fox who must climb its steep steps for official meetings with his new allies.

Sweating, exhausted, gritty with dust, sticky with sweat and the oily mixture against tiny stinging flies, Black Pearl nevertheless felt exultant. The triumph of her will was still with her hours after she had seen Fox spare Madoc.

This dirty but sociable task was nearly finished. The dozen baskets of shucked kernels they had filled since sunset shimmered in firelight from the nearby council lodge, as though the pent-up life inside each grain were trying to escape, leap to the earth, and start a new corn generation.

They had uses for the empty cobs and the husks, so there were more full baskets of those. While they worked, the Cherokee women speculated among themselves about the appearance of the great Uktena on the river across the narrow channel, where the silhouette of the legendary monster loomed against rippling water, reflecting a starry sky and a sliver of new moon. Fox had returned from negotiations that would let the whites depart downriver, escorted by the Natchez contingent, to western regions, never to return. Now Fox and his subchiefs were locked in their own meeting in the temporary willow-branch-and-hide lodge that served as the chieftain's bedlodge and the official seat of Cherokee council.

But the women had said about all that could be said of the Uktena and the white people who rode it and now could only repeat themselves amid the dusty pile of rustling husks, from which two of the women were tying small, tight bundles to be used later in cooking. They drifted onto other subjects as people will who bend together over boring labor.

Black Pearl's mind wandered; she wondered again who among Madoc's Hundred had been buried. She knew only that some bodies were shrouded. Black Pearl did not blame Fox for those deaths—she had seen Fair Beard's contingent attack. Fox had spared Madoc; that was their bargain, and he had kept it.

None of these women lost relatives in this afternoon's battle, but several had smeared soot and bear-grease on their foreheads to honor the dead, who had been wrapped and would be taken with honor back to various villages. The weapons of all the fallen would be displayed and their triumphs recounted at this evening's dance.

By then these women would have washed off all the soot but for a token spot on the forehead, and they would socialize. A couple were wives, but most were unmarried or widowed sisters who had been invited to attend specific warriors, their uncles, brothers, or fathers, for this campaign—a common practice in red warfare that required travel. Some had children, but none were along on this fast-moving warparty. The cornhuskers were looking forward to the dance, but they did not speak of it now; anticipation of it only sparked their talk about common things.

Someone wondered about the taste and yield of this rich amber variety of lowland tsalu given them by their new allies, the Muskogeans. The color was so deep it bordered on blood at the base of every third kernel. Immersed in the labor of ripping grains from the cob, Black Pearl could imagine each uttering a cry under the sharp edge of the shell. A little puff of dust broke free with each shucked leaf, easy to imagine the breath of Agawela—the corn-spirit herself—yielding up under a human hand the way dying animals breathed out their vitality into the hunter's mouth for the hunter wise enough to capture it.

Fawn-Face remarked the beauty of the kanegmati sachem's voice from across the river, though it seemed odd, because Cherokee men did not sing lullabies.

"He has a funny accent," an older woman said.

"Sexy," a young woman giggled, and several of the other women rippled husky laughter full of knowing that made the girl simper with self-consciousness, as though she had stepped into the women's lodge before her time.

For a while their circle was full of scraping and the small screams of corn kernels.

Across the river the song began again, again with old Honeyvoice alone improvising on the melody.

Black Pearl wondered if her baby had gone to sleep after the earlier burst of infant crying that had made her tad play some more. It could have been Yngvild's Bjorn, except that the cry had the peculiar note of the newborn in it. Little Bear would have nearly—how many, eight, nine moons by now? She had lost track, realizing that she had thought it in

Cherokee, not translated but directly. She was beginning to think in this language.

She shivered with a chill of quiet joy. This is what I want, she thought. I never thought I would get what I want, but this is it, and here I am, and it is mine. She made no sign of this for the others to see, but because she must make some action that confirmed what she was feeling, Black Pearl plunged her hands among the cool, silken kernels of tsalu, pulled up a handful that poured rattling like golden pearls through her fingers.

The older woman caught her eye and laughed a little at the new Shawnee woman for her strangeness; her eyes were glistening—was she from so poor a tribe that the sight of all this tsalu made her cry?

Listening to Rhys sing, Black Pearl was pleased to reflect that he would make a fine father. And Winnowed Rice would be a good mother to Rhiannon's little girl. Rhiannon, Black Pearl thought, as though Rhiannon were a woman she had known of long ago back in Britain, not herself, but a stranger in a song. The thought made her smile again.

The women drifted off the subject, discussing what kind of cornmeal these reddish kernels would make, pink or brown, oily or dry. The soft murmur of their voices faded as Black Pearl concentrated on Rhys's song. Until now she had heard only a repeated word here and there—cradle, child, rocking water—something like that, enough to tell it was a lullaby.

Smelling the western wind, Black Pearl tested the Shawnee premise that it was friendly. She faced it, drew air into her lungs, and breathed out a request for it to strengthen.

Sure enough, it picked up, stirring the smell of cedar incense from the ceremonial mound, so she heard the whole song several times before Rhys fell to idly strumming Llais Mel's strings. The baby must have fallen asleep.

The baby, my baby, my baby girl, Black Pearl mused. What had he named her?

The women tossed the last cobs onto the pile and began to stand with a groan or two on stiff legs. They tied down each basket with hides, while Fawn-Face put what grains had spilled into her skirt. Two women each grabbed up a basket and began hauling it to the storage lodge some distance away. Others began to gather up every scrap of husk and cob in separate baskets.

Though she longed to bathe quickly in the cool river, Black

Pearl stooped to help Fawn-Face, hoping to remain where she could best hear as much of Rhys's music for as long as possible without appearing to be really interested at all.

Fawn-Face counted each retrieved grain, which she said was good luck, while the harp poured out the unsung melody.

Then, as though he were composing extempore, Meredydd's son added a verse he had not sung before.

> "Cari, fair girl-child,
> ride the small boat on down
> gentle water rock the cradle,
> Mary's hand rock the girl-child
> Cari of the waters
> Child-boat ride the water."

Then he immediately sang it again, playfully rearranging the individual lines.

"Seven tens and two, seven tens and three," Fawn-Face was saying, keeping the beat. "He is good."

"—seven tens and four, seven tens and five, seven tens and six," Black Pearl said, plucking what seemed to be the last grain from the dust.

She and Fawn-Face both saw one more sparkling kernel near the fire. Both reached at the same time, hand over hand.

"Seven tens and seven," they said in laughing unison.

Seventy-seven was a very lucky number, they both were thinking as they hefted the basket between them and followed the other women. Black Pearl felt good, better than she had felt in many a night; Rhys had done an honorable job of naming.

His song faded behind them

> "Do not worry, mam, all is well
> with the small strong Cari-child."

In Black Pearl's native tongue, "cariad" meant love.

The moon climbed higher, not enough to illuminate, but enough to glow against the stars. The women ran down to the river, where the young warriors with torches were gathering mussels for the feast. Farther upriver there was a hidden nook along the bank, where the corn-huskers built a small fire and bathed like otters splashing in the water.

It was a mild night warmed by the crescent moon. Eternal mist off the river melted away as it lifted toward the star fields. Crickets and frogs trilled all around them. Back in camp hypnotic drums began building the beat for the dance. Black Pearl left the water first, walking toward Fox's distinctive white lodge in the center of camp. She knew he could have appropriated the high earthwork that hunkered over near a rise but eschewed the need. He did not care if the Muskogeans continued clattering their old bones up on that spooky place—his power was so great he did not need to seize useless artifacts. Instead his men had set up his lodge beneath the temple mound between it and the riverbank, a practical military position.

Black Pearl saw an entourage with the Yuchi headman Sun Caller at its center, obviously arriving under blazing torches from a long journey, solemnly coming this way. Every Yuchi, except Sun Caller himself, was burdened with baskets and hide-covered parcels in hand and strapped to their backs. Even a black-feathered sachem carried something wrapped in hide. The string of at least twenty-five Yuchi women amid a few men wound its burdened way into the Cherokee camp and toward Fox's lodge. Along the way the bedraggled Yuchi picked up hangers-on until half the braves on the north bank followed the smell of happenings in the air as the Yuchi approached. Only Sun Caller went inside; his bearers set down their burdens and stretched, speaking to nobody. Several brought up the rear with a team of stubby red dogs in harness pulling three gihli-gasi loaded with more objects. The dogs stretched and shivered when their masters unharnessed them and gave them water.

A quiet but curious crowd of Cherokee, Muskogeans, and Yuchis thronged around the headman's lodge where Fat Tongue stood guard. He was stationed at the open flap, staring stonily ahead like a tree or something inanimate.

Black Pearl stopped before him. He was trying to ignore her, as he had vowed, but she knew she could pull his eyes if she stared long enough. She did not have to do this. His approval of her was not necessary. He would make no move to prevent her from entering. All she had to do was go around him—his stubbornness was to ignore her as though she were invisible. She was thinking, this one will never accept me. He will hold out forever. She was just about to give up on him when she saw his eyeballs were quivering.

He was wounded in several places, on his shoulder streaked a blue welt. Dried blood caked his ear and one thigh. His war-paint was smeared with soot—one of the dead must have been of his clan. With a pang she remembered his son, whose name she did not know. She realized what Fat Tongue had lost. Without thinking, obeying an urge that swelled from her deepest heart, Black Pearl touched the mourning soot on the warrior's face.

It startled him; women did not touch warriors. He might strike her even if she did belong to the chief. But he did not. His lips parted as though he might break his self-imposed embargo on this woman's existence and speak, but instead he just watched her with that same look of surprise on his dour copper features as she smeared his mourning paint across the bridge of her own nose. She looked him right in the eye and had the boldness to touch his sooty forehead yet again, just lightly, then smear on her own face so there would be no chance for him to miss that she was saying she mourned with him.

He drew himself up with heavy dignity and stared directly back at her, then with a curt nod acknowledged not only her existence but her gesture.

A Cherokee woman would not smile, she was thinking, to keep herself from smiling. She felt immensely gladdened, though, and could not repress the pounding it made of her heartbeat.

As though movement caused him pain, Fat Tongue stiffly stood away from the door, his gaze once more pointed into emptiness, giving her entry to the lodge. It was a long, loaf-shaped affair with bent river-willow ribs and bleached deerskins for the covering. She slipped behind the buffalo hide that draped the doorway while the Yuchi chief ahead of her approached Fox, who had had advance notice of the arrival.

Fox was ensconced at the far end of the enclosure, in front of hanging cane mats, behind which was his sleeping space. He was sitting cross-legged on buffalo skins, his ceremonial pipe on its stand of horns before him. His counselors ranked behind him, all of them in ritual paint and feathers, along with the chiefs of allied nations, including Shell-of-Many-Colors of Mabila.

It could be interpreted as a sign of disrespect that the Yuchi had not stopped on the trail to clean up for this meeting. Sun Caller still wore soiled travel clothing and little decoration.

She looked anew at Fox in the firelight. He seemed almost not to be material, he was glowing so brightly. What had happened here to polish him so?

Before this interruption they had been discussing the ceremony they would stage upon return to the Cherokee's eastern homeland. She could not know that they had voted unanimously to bestow upon Fox the title of Most Beloved Man, thereby placing him above all chiefs of the entire nation, which at that time amounted to more than two hundred villages. It had never happened before that a war chief, elected for a single battle, was nominated for life to the highest civil office among the Principal People.

Without quite knowing what it was she witnessed, Black Pearl saw all this shining upon Fox as she observed him from the crowded shadows of the lodge. Out in the distance the combined voice of Cherokee, several Muskogean dialects, and Yuchi had joined the drums; warriors had begun the dance. The vibrations of their stamping feet trembled up from the ground like the heartbeat of earth herself.

Here inside the council lodge the air vibrated with formality. Black Pearl edged closer to stand behind one of the seven lodgepoles ranged down the center, where she could better hear and see the faces of the players.

After the host offered smoke to the four directions and muttered a secret formula, they smoked a long round as was their custom without conversation. Fox looked magnificent to Black Pearl, even more so than usual, despite bruises and slashes from his earlier combat. His new and exalted office had not been announced yet, but she could see that he was rubbed to this glow about some important matter just recently decided; something in the manner of his subchief bespoke it.

When she recognized the three simple eagle feathers in his quoit, she knew he was now eagle chieftain. She could not help thinking, my beloved, you too have what you most desired.

His greenstone pipe carved as Sun Woman with the bow in her belly, moved hand to hand around the circle in accordance with each man's status. Finally it came back to himself, who puffed on it enough to keep the coal alive, then launched into a short discourse about the longevity of the relationship of his own Ani Yunwiya nation with that of the Tsoyaha Yuchi.

He spoke at length on the mutual histories of the two nations, discreetly avoiding mention of the fact that they had been bitter enemies since either tribe could remember, or that his tribe outnumbered Sun Caller's a hundred to one. He used the formal names that each tribe called themselves, then he pointedly said to Sun Caller that from this day forward would be a new time—under a new sky, was the way the Most Beloved Man put it. He took a leisurely drag on the pipe's carved wood stem, which rose like a slender feather from the Sun Woman's head.

"An amazing thing happened while you were cleaning the game field," Fox continued, a long, thin stream of pale smoke issuing from his nostrils. It was traditional in such a meeting that the principal speaker not be interrupted until his discourse wound to its finish, so while he paused, none dared leap into his silences. During those moments the huge lodge simmered with the blue drone of flames in pine knots.

"This amazing thing is a sign of the new time—you may have seen it out on the river." At this Sun Caller shifted his eyes indirectly at Fox to say, yes, he had seen the Uktena in the last light of the sun when he approached the riverbed from the far northern ridge—had in fact taken a long view of the entire battle. Then the old man returned the stare.

"For too long the Head of Waters has been empty of people except for the honored Tsoyaha Yuchi on its border. Ancient battles made it so. But now I say that it will be called blood country no longer. All debts are canceled. All revenges are settled from this day forward. The Yuchi will have neighbors with whom to enjoy and to share the gifts of the Ancient One."

Fox took another deep puff. "Or, of course," he continued smoothly, "Sun Caller and any of his people may depart with the kanegmati, if they so choose."

Sun Caller sat immobile beside his host while the fire heightened the angles of his cheekbones, nose, and forehead. He seemed stuffed into his huge, painted, fur-lined robe, and the massive coil of blue kanegmati beads wound around his neck as he stared into the flames. He gave no indication he heard Fox, who now spoke of this new era of friendliness between his people and Sun Caller's, explaining how the Yuchi were a small nation and so would contain themselves east of some river and another and hunt no farther north than a certain ridge on the Warrior Path. She caught most of this with admiration for Fox, who continued in a voice of utmost friendliness as he outlined the total enclosure of the Yuchi nation.

Fox took the Yuchi silence for acceptance. His counselors nodded august approval behind him, their feathers bobbing, copper rattling on their long-stretched earlobes. The Muskogeans in the company, including Shell-of-Many-Colors, looked on with self-satisfied approval—the Cherokee had neatly tied up their perennial enemy. Only much later would they realize a protective buffer had been removed that would bring Cherokee much closer than ever before to the homeland of the various Muskogeans—Mabilan, Chickasaw, Choctaw, and later the nation that would be called Creek.

Finally Fox said, "That is all." This was a formal pronouncement that freed the highest-ranking counselors behind each chief to buzz quietly among themselves, shift position, and generally absorb what they had heard.

After a decent pause Sun Caller cleared his throat. Black Pearl thought she had never seen such mourning displayed in a human face. Every line was scored descending. He wore no mourning soot but seemed the grave personified. From her shadowed but clear view in the shadows, the Yuchi chief looked much older than when she had first seen him in conference with Madoc back in the spring.

"The Most Honored Man of the Principal People does this humble one great honor," Sun Caller said mildly.

There flashed on Fox's placid face recognition that Sun Caller had found out very quickly about Fox's election as Most Beloved of the Cherokee nation. Too quickly, his narrowed eyes seemed to say, and he cast a glance around at his own subordinates and allies, perhaps wondering which one leaked this information, and how, since it had only moments before been voted.

But he had misjudged the situation and realized it immediately: Sun Caller knew the Cherokee counselors would elect Fox their high miko. The canny old Yuchi did not need a spy to know how a hero of Fox's accomplishments would be honored, especially after men loyal to him met him on the trail to report events that happened this afternoon at the Shoals.

Now Black Pearl could see that Sun Caller was doing

something beneath his robe, manipulating something in his hands. Fleetingly she thought he might be drawing a weapon, a blade with which the defeated headman meant to strike Fox. In the time it takes to draw a breath, she saw that his gnarled fingers were toying with something too small to be discerned but surely not a weapon.

He did not look up as he spoke. "The Tsoyaha Yuchi are grateful for the generosity of the Cherokee." It was far too short a speech for the occasion, without formal oratory, just barely enough to be civil. While he employed the formal name for his own nation, Children of the Sun From Far Away, he had used the Muskogean name for the Ani Yunwiya, a common word that meant simply, cave-dwellers. He had backed the wrong aggressor. He had lost his only son, and now he had lost his people's vast exclusive hunting territory. Black Pearl, long familiar with such politics, felt sorry for him but was sure Fox would take only face and not the old man's life.

She suddenly smelled the delicious aroma of boiled corn bread and steamed clams from the cooking pots at the main fire.

Now, still except for four fingers pulling and pressing what appeared to be a lump of gray clay, the Yuchi waited to see what else his miscalculation might cost himself and his people.

Ignoring Sun Caller's slight response, Fox remarked in a pleasant tone, "Tell me, brother, about the gaming field."

"Clean."

Fox looked at the faces of his chiefs scowling at Sun Caller's brusque manner. But Fox, full of generosity in triumph, refused to take insult. "Tell us everything."

Sun Caller drew his hands from the folds of his robe and proceeded to pinch the clay in full view of the assembly. Black Pearl was surprised that he spoke unhesitating Cherokee, far better than her own, though with a strange accent. "As you know, Most Honored, my people bury their dead in stone graves inside the earth. We dig deeply for this purpose, the height of a full-grown man." The truth was the Cherokee considered the deep, stone-lined tombs of the Yuchi almost as excessive as the Muskogean bonepicker's mounds. Sun Caller knew this, in a subtle kind of one-upmanship. He leveled a lance at his tormentor. "It was to Yuchi grave depth that we lifted the ball field."

Fox thought this must be a Yuchi exaggeration but let i
pass.

Sun Caller seemed to have finished molding whatever i
was he held in his dry fingers, which had taken on the
whitish clay dust. It gave his hands a ghostly pallor. "I lef
people to dismantle the kanegmati lodges." He made a fina
pinch on the clay and looked directly at Fox for the first time
during the meeting. "However, they made serviceable reinforcements along the western face. These we will leave, since
they used only the river stone like the other rockwork."

Fox sighed heavily. "Come spring, I do not want to see one
spout of their vile pale grain breaking the sacred earth."

Sun Caller sagely nodded, again apparently interested only
in the object in his hands.

"So great is the disrespect the whites brought to the
gaming field that one could be justified taking a life for each
such sprout."

"One could. Come spring, I will walk the plateau with the
Most Beloved so that I may expose my throat to his knife
should he find one defiling sprout." Fertility was considered
as bad for sport as menstrual blood was for hunting and war.

Sun Caller's answer pleased Fox, who gave his highest
officials a broad grin, as though settling some private wager.

"The whites also enlarged the mystery gate and put a roof
on the maze," the Yuchi continued. "But my men are removing all traces of this construction." Sun Caller made a subtle
motion to one of his young warriors who stood holding
something near the lodge flap. The brave trotted forward and
placed at the Caller's feet a large parcel wrapped in a shaved
deer hide. "We have brought all the objects left by the white
people on the mountain," he said as he motioned for his party
to enter.

At least two dozen Yuchi warriors filed in, placed huge
heavy baskets full of objects before Fox, and departed. Two o
Sun Caller's burliest warriors hefted Wyn's anvil between
them. Murmurs of amazement and speculation buzzed around
him as Fox inspected the booty, most of which had n
discernible purpose to him or to anyone in the lodge excep
Black Pearl.

Before him lay only a small portion of the tools and
supplies Madoc's Hundred were forced to leave behind
adzes, axes, hatchets, saws, awls, wedges, plowshares, swords
knives, scissors, rings, hooks, clippers, forge implements

olts, pots, nails, buckets, brackets, spades, hoes, forks and
ammerheads, winches, chains, chain mail and armor—helmet,
auldron, greave, and gauntlet—in short a smith's store in
on and brass, for it was the heavy, undentable metal objects
ae whites had to abandon and red people held in highest
ascination.

Black Pearl glimpsed pieces of her loom and its instru-
aents amid bolts of woven cloth, surely another strange thing
o these people who did not yet weave on the broadloom.

Fox lightly touched the foreign things while his counselors
auttered warnings over his shoulder. His hand stopped over
wire loop strung with a dozen horseshoes, a common way to
rade iron back home. But Wyn would have had no reason to
aake shoes for horses here. These must have been part of the
ast of Owen's gifts to Madoc. She had not seen one horse
mong these people, and they made no reference to such an
nimal. She supposed they did not know of them, though she
ad not really thought about it until this moment, seeing Fox
aspect the incongruous horseshoes.

From the pile of rusting junk he pulled a breastplate. At
east this was an object familiar to him, which he recognized
s the one Madoc wore the day of their first negotiation.

Everyone quieted as Fox inspected the thing, obviously
ae form of a man's chest hammered into the strange metal,
ut harder than any metal he had ever known. How did they
o it? he wondered again. When he put it against his own
erson, there was a hushed silence as though his sachems
vere waiting for lightning to strike or something of equally
ad medicine to occur.

Black Pearl was struck by the almost innocent look on his
ace—How do I look? he seemed to be asking, and immedi-
tely all around him save the Yuchi assured him that he
ooked magnificent. Black Pearl recognized the same servile
bsequity she had grown up seeing in the men who served
er father, and with the same result—the monarch was
leased to be agreed with.

Fox accepted their flattery and handed the cuirass enam-
led with the red snake to one of his lieutenants.

Sun Caller nodded to the first brave, who had stayed in the
odge after the other bearers left. The man, who was one of
Caller's most honored sachems, bent in his dour black raven's
eathers to unfold the wrapping on the first parcel.

In the firelight was revealed a squarish brown object. Fox leaned forward to see better.

Sun Caller, bent by fatigue and loss of heart, said in a hollow voice, "This is the strangest thing of all."

Chapter 39

The Chronicles of Wales *report, that
Madoc, son to Owen Queneth, Prince of
Wales . . . prepared certain Ships, with
men and munition, and left his Country
to seek adventures by Sea; leaving
Ireland he sailed west til he came to
a Land unknown, Returning home and
relating what pleasant and fruitful
Countries he had seen without
Inhabitants, and for what barren
ground his brethren and kindred did
murther one another, he provided a
number of Ships, and got with him such
men and women as were desirous to live
in quietness, that arrived with him in
this new Land in the year 1170; Left
many of his people there and returned
for more. But where this place was no
Historie can show.*

> —Generall Historie of Virginia
> by Captain John Smith
> 1624

Fox touched the book, for Black Pearl saw that was what it
was, one of the monks' illuminated manuscripts. It was not
one of the miniature breviaries, but a full folio inside waxed
leather covers, one of the books unbeknownst to her that
Brian had left behind. Fox moved his hands around it,
exploring its edges. Such a perfectly square object was a
curiosity. Soon he found that the cover opened—the brass
latch had been ripped away.

He did not remove the book but opened its cover within

the box. The first page glared under the heading that identified it as the Gospel of St. John. The initial capital in the Latin script was richly colored; in the flickering firelight the blue spiderlike letters seemed to move on the parchment.

Delicately Fox lifted the edge of the page. The glow from the fire shown through the translucent material, which his fingers said was the inner skin of an animal, and gave a shimmering intensity to the colors.

Black Pearl was close enough to read the larger introductory verse: "Before all time was the word and the word was with God, and the word was God himself."

"What is it?" Fox asked Sun Caller.

"My sachem thinks it must be some kind of triumph-hide."

Fox gave the object the once-over, then without warning looked sideways directly into the shadows where Black Pearl thought herself to be hidden, his eye loaded with the question he would ask when they were alone: What is this thing your people brought so far only to leave behind?

Fox muttered to himself, leafing through the book for more colors. Strange triumph-hide, he was thinking, to have so few pictures. Flowers twisted into weird shapes did not denote a warrior's triumphs. He doubted the Yuchi interpretation but did not wish to argue out of respect for the venerable sachem.

He raised a questioning eyebrow at his own crystal gazer, who stepped forward. Fox gestured at the object. Clear Seeing Man took it, after gingerly closing the wrapping without touching it, handed it to an assistant, who departed immediately to perform cleansing rituals before the gazer conducted official examination.

"Thank you, Chief Sun Caller, for your scrupulous obedience to duty," Fox said as he tossed two cedar twigs onto the fire, then rubbed his hands as though washing them in the smoke to clean them of whatever pollution the object might have imparted.

"I believe by these actions you have cleansed your people of the taint the kanegmati brought to the gaming mountain. You must be hungry. Let the women feed you, go to the sweat lodge, and rest from your labors and your journey. Let your young men join us in the victory dance."

It was clearly dismissal. Sun Caller and his people did not linger. They filed out of the lodge along with everyone else who moved toward the cooking fire where good smells beckoned, leaving the trove of foreign objects where they lay.

Black Pearl had seen the Yuchi chief toss what he was holding into the fire. Now, alone in the lodge, she used a stick to tong the clay object from the coals. It sizzled on the packed clay, wisps of steam and smoke curling up from the blackened shape. She poked it but discovered little that might identify it or its purpose. It had none of the beauty of the women's pottery but was a crude lump of work and less than a child could do to have had so much attention. It looked like a stubby rope of clay with two knots on one end.

Her stomach growled.

With a quick moccasin Black Pearl toed the meaningless thing back into the fire and followed the others. It would be good to eat after this long day, she thought. She had grown fond of the taste of corn. For a moment she was alone under faint stars. Without thinking she lifted and sniffed her fingers, sore from labor but smooth and slightly oily from handling the golden kernels. The abundant oily corn smell was on her skin, delicious, the smell of yellow, the smell of edible gold.

In addition to the rumbling river she could hear the red people taking their celebration. Faintly she detected the pungency of burning pitch that must be coming from Madoc's Hundred across the water. Must be making repairs on the ship, she thought. One last glance; but she saw only blurs of several fires and torches, no shapes of white men or women, no sound, because any they might be making was drowned out by the Shoals' muted roar and the calling drums ahead.

Black Pearl hurried to the feast and did not look back.

The dance was informal and did not last all night as would later dances celebrating today's events. By midnight all fires but one were banked on the north side of the river. Nearly everyone but the lookouts in the camp of the red nations found their bedrolls. The one fire glowed from the firepit under the three-walled pavilion on top of the ceremonial pyramid. Two men sat close enough to the softening embers for their features to be seen by each other. Fox had left his camp below and trudged up the eastern steps of the mound. He could have appropriated it from his Muskogean hosts but did not need that show of force.

The Cherokee respected the antiquity of the pyramids, which they found when they came from the northeast to this country. They had good stories about them. But theirs was a different tradition. They felt they did not need the mounds or a few priests to climb up into the lower reaches of the overworld to commune with the Ancient One on behalf of the people.

Among Cherokee each man and woman was his or her own communicant with spirit, and Cherokee sachems were less priest and more agents. Cherokee communed with the same Ancient One Above as the Muskogeans, but the former were more action oriented, more involved with sign and portent, with cleansing and balance, and with a man's correct behavior in all circumstances than in decaying burial customs and sun ceremonies. Fox did not want to sleep on the earthwork with its grim funereal mementos of a decadent, and in his estimation less enlightened, religion.

So he left what he privately called the daguna, or pimple, to Shell-of-Many-Colors, but with victor's generosity deigned to visit the Muskogean miko on his own turf.

The pavilion's fourth wall, swags of woven cane, had been rolled up. Smoke from the sacred fire nudged the ceiling of cane fronds, then coiled sinuously out into the still night air. He and Shell were sharing an informal pipe near the fire while watching the silvery surface of the river from their perch.

The mist thickened, muffling the river's murmur. Far overhead the thin moon glowed like a rip in the sky, turning all below pearlescent, while most of the stars had been blotted out by vapor continuously boiling up from the shoals.

Across the river Madoc's Hundred still moved around the fires. Torchlight and lantern glow appeared here and there in the pearly darkness and on the silhouette of the Uktena.

All this passed below the watching eyes of the two men up on the pyramid. Old enemies, drawn together as allies, they found this an occasion to philosophize as they perused the silhouettes down on the island.

The Muskogean thought that the white devils were an aberration, a wild event without explanation. "A passing cloud," he said between puffs that enlivened the coal in his small personal red stone pipe.

But Fox had forebodings that more kanegmati might arrive from the east. "Why do you think the white chief broke his promise and tried to return the way he had come?"

Shell-of-Many-Colors shrugged; his bones squeaked, an oddly appropriate sound in the gloom. His mother's people were from this chiefdom. Around him lay the meticulously picked, age-browned bones of many ancestors stacked in neat piles according to their parts—legs there, forearms over here, and the pyramids of skulls between trays of finger and toe knuckles. Ribs in bundles bailed with ropes of strung vertebrae were cribbed between tall carved poles hung with festoons of hundreds of scalp tassels, just the coin-sized crown, each stretched over reed hoops, painted and adorned with seed pearls.

It was a very sacred place. His own remains would someday repose here. For Shell-of-Many-Colors this was a comfort. Ropes of freshwater pearls—pink, white, gray, and blue among the more common yellow—hung in loops as thick as vines around the three inner walls. Baskets of more pearls and human teeth, the similarities of which had been anciently discerned, crowded the hard clay floor back near the bone shelves—testament to generations of shellfish subsistence.

Feather bundles dangled from the beamed roof, intermixed with strings of carved and painted shells that rattled grittily against the slow movements of a bald, withered bonepicker-priest, as brown an ivory piece as the skulls stacked in three pyramids, who moved in the shadows performing intricate rituals behind Shell-of-Many-Colors and his guest.

Fox repressed a shudder lest he look unmanly when he caught a glimpse of the bonepicker's long picking nail on a gnarled forefinger as he threw dust of cedar onto coals in a stone brazier. The fragrant smoke wafted in lazy blue ropes on the damp air. The Muskogean took another puff and handed the pipe to Fox, who continued: "I will tell you what I think. He wants to go back and bring more of his kind here." Fox let that sink in as he drew on the pipe. "If many of them come here armed with the blue metal..." he said, offering the smoke to Shell and remembering the heft of that blade he held this afternoon, "...well, the great gambler Untsaiyi might take their side."

They passed the pipe back and forth as they talked, with the droning chant of the bonepicker a rough whisper behind them.

"Not in our lifetimes, my worthy opponent," the Muskogean chief assured Fox. "And if they are unwise enough to return, they will have you and me to fight."

"But look what it takes to keep us on the same side of the fire," Fox replied. "When was the last time a Cherokee sat down with one of your chiefs like this?" He used the informal

Muskogean word for his own nation. "We are bears and panthers, honored enemy, bears and panthers."

"Bears and panthers both hate snakes," Shell replied. His nephew died because of those blue-eyed snakes, and his choice would have been blood revenge except for his alliance with Fox, to whom he must defer. He did not mention it, because there was loss of face in the fact that Aligapas died because of a woman.

"But," Fox replied, "will we be able to battle the snake together again?" He shook his head, morosely answering his own question. "Perhaps we should kill them every one and bury their parts on a hundred ridges."

Shell shrugged again and tapped out the dead bowl. "You are wiser and more powerful than I," he said as he wrapped the pipe in its beaded bag.

Fox nodded and Shell continued. "I will personally defy even the Uktena if you decide to chop them to pieces in the morning," Shell said, straightening his feather robe. The corrugated frown deepened on his high forehead. "When we must kill serpents, that is the way we do it." Because he was the highest ranking miko of his people in attendance at the temple, he not only occupied the high house but wore ceremonial regalia.

"No," Fox said, glancing down at the dark, long-necked silhouette outlined against the river water. Not for one moment did he believe the ship was the legendary Uktena, but it was serious matter to kill any snake even with cleansing rituals. His more gullible warriors would hesitate to attack such a power object after the display of force from it this afternoon, no matter how greatly their numbers outweighed the enemy's.

And there was Black Pearl to consider. Out on the killing ground he had hesitated when the moment came to take the kanegmati chief's life. He knew it was Black Pearl's vow that stopped him. Sun Woman would have abandoned him and the old-bone would return to the void she left in his spirit. His personal power would dwindle, his wrists and elbows would stiffen and grow knotty while his manhood would go lame, and he would quickly grow old before his time.

"But if that white chief breaks his vow again..." Fox purposefully left the thought dangling.

"One can hope," Shell remarked dryly, his artificially flat and wide forehead catching flickering shadows from the fire

All canoes had the necessary shape of serpents (except the kanegmatis' round ones, which he considered serpent's eggs for the comfort of his categories). He knew that another large canoe similar to this Uktena had been burned in the saltwater bay of his homeland. His men had reported its skeleton sticking up out of the water at Two Rivers Island, so he personally had little scruple against destroying this one. People who live in swamps have plenty of rituals for killing snakes.

As though anticipating his thoughts, Fox suggested an alternative. "Send your young men out on the long hunts. It will be an early cold. This little battle of no consequence is over."

The Muskogean observed that even as Fox spoke, he wore the famous triumph robe. How long, the Muskogean wondered, before today's events were painted there? But to be polite, Shell-of-Many-Colors agreed to begin the fall hunt. They had given much corn to these new allies, enough to deplete winter stores. It would not hurt to begin laying in for winter.

For a while they spoke of other things: the possibility of a hard winter, game that season, portents and signs, deaths in their clans, mutual matters between their territories, such as the birth of a two-headed dog, and the like. Fox indicated that Shell should take his pick of the booty the whites left behind, except for the strange triumph-hide in the square box. That the Cherokee wanted to keep for further study.

As guest under the pavilion, Fox had the prerogative of departure. He stood and after politely quoting a leave-taking formula in the miko's own language, exited the sacred pavilion by a path marked in brighter clay that led him out the west side of the pavilion and back around to the eastern steps.

The fire behind Fox was extinguished only once a year in solemn ceremony, but in the hours from midnight to dawn each night, it was kept as glowing embers, to allow the sacred flame to rest along with everything else on earth. It was the old bonepicker's task to keep it just below flames without letting it go out, for which offense his throat would be cut. Fox was in sudden darkness beneath a sullen sky, where most of the starlight was already veiled and only a thin moon promised but did not deliver illumination.

He hurried down the embedded stone steps with a foreboding chill. Many of his people's stories concerned ghosts who resided in places like this. The Cherokee buried their dead in the earth; the Muskogean tradition of disinterring bones, scraping off flesh, and depositing them in open charnel houses like the one behind him—these habits disgusted and frightened the warrior beyond physical concern. All those bones back there represented ancestors whose spirits resided inside the earth of the mound, which had been piled basketful by basketful on this spot for centuries.

He hurried to leave this place. His nightwise eyes found the steps that led downward to the riverbank, where he went to his own bedroll in the council lodge in the center of the circular throng. Warriors from ten tribes and their women slept around him, a vast host, a red blanket spread out beneath the night.

Wolves howled their relays from the slopes.

Any trace of the west wind had died. Faintly on the mist Fox could smell early winter coming on stealthily like a thief. Despite the mild evening under faint starglow up where the dog ran, he drew more tightly around his shoulders the bear robe with his illustrious battle record painted upon it.

The several persons of his household slept inside. Black Pearl snored gently, like a little bird, beneath their blanket. On the other side of the banked coals of a small firepit, Fox's grandfather, the oldest known grandfather of any tribe, ten tens and three winters old, nodded against his power pole.

All was well in the camp.

All was well with the Overhill People, the Ani Yunwiya and their people throughout the blue mountain land called Head of Waters. They were all-powerful. Truly the Principal People. Not even the Leni Lenape or the Iroquois could contend for these regions now. Fox had accomplished, like Sun Woman in the story, what he set out to do and had won many prizes in the process. He had grown strong and likewise his children and his people because he had lived the Way. Now he could have painted upon the robe his victory over the kanegmati, who would depart in the dawn on his orders, and who had given him victory over the Yuchi and neutralizing alliance with the Muskogeans.

He would get credit for chasing the Uktena from these waters. With the Yuchi contained and the Shawnee gone, the

Cherokee were supreme in these parts from now on. And among the Cherokee he would be Most Beloved Man. When they returned to the heartland, the council would have to create the new title for him, because no war chief had ever held a supreme chiefdom over that nation's many chiefdoms.

He was only sorry that he had not been able to talk the white chief out of the secret of the blue metal. He had offered to adopt the frail white tribe, but Madoc had refused, swearing for the second time to abide by a promise to take the river downstream to some other territory and never come back this way again. This time the Chickasaw would follow them along the western bank of the river to make sure they did as promised.

There was a place on the hide, here—his hand stroked the bearskin where Black Pearl would sketch with her paints the last confrontation between himself and the hairy kanegmati chief. The lightning of Fox's power would flash in small neat zigzag lines. Black Pearl would know just how to outline his lightning strokes of power with her amazing blue beads. His hunter's eye imagined the little stick figures and geometrical power symbols she would paint with her strong, steady hand marked by the calluses from her harp. He never doubted she was his, but still, a man with a young, beautiful wife should take no chances. He looked around to insure his privacy, then breathed his life's breath onto his fingers and touched them to Black Pearl's throat, where he felt her unsleeping heart's drum. For three nights now he had recited the secret formula to keep her faithful. Tonight was the final night. So softly that his voice was below a whisper, Fox chanted the formula for the fourth magic time:

"Listen to me, Ancient Red. This woman's soul has come to rest at the edge of your body. You are never to let go your hold upon it. Never let her think of another man. Never let her think of another place except beside me." He hummed a monotone of repeated words that meant, "This is to be so many times over," then added, "I am an honorable man. I stand in the sunrise. Here where I stand her soul has attached itself to mine. There is no loneliness where my body is." He hummed the monotone again, which was the equivalent of repeating the formula seven times.

Withdrawing his touch from her, he stared at his robe, imagining the Uktena she would paint fleeing from the power of Fox. But not even that pleasant fantasy cooled his heart;

still he could not sleep, so he stood from his thinking spot beside the fire and stepped into the night, leaving his exquisite Black Pearl deep in the country of sleep: O what a blessing she was, this unbeaten gold nugget given to him from Ancient Red, a gift and reward for his later years. Looking back at her, he loved her far more than a warrior should. He knew it. Yet he felt it would be spurning the Ancient One's generosity not to love her.

Her eyes moved beneath almost-blue lids.

He knew she had come from them. The kanegmati. Therefore they must be human, just as were the Cherokee and Muskogeans. Black Pearl proved it. He smiled. The sky-eyed serpents. That is what his Black Pearl was, the best of them. You are my own, my beloved, my treasure, my rare black pearl, my reward for being a scrupulous man of power.

The voice of the river called to him. The path was dusty beneath his moth-quiet heels as hard as chert, so that he moved without waking the watchman. The negligent buck would regret that nap tomorrow, but tonight Fox was glad to be the only conscious soul in his camp. He was its heart and brain, diligent when all other eyes closed in sleep.

The bursting cattails along the river were small warriors in eagle-feather bonnets. Their topknots loosened and escaped lazily into the mist as Fox moved among them, looking beyond the dark horizon upward toward the light in the eastern sky. He muttered the ritual words, "Greetings, Brother Moon. In thirty days and nights, you and I will meet like this again."

The crescent throbbed in the steamy river vapor high above the old woman mountain. Old One-Teat, the warriors called Her, but never within her hearing. She was the Earth, Daughter-of-Sun, the last embracer.

Tonight he would have called her Mother, but Moon would hear and be jealous, so he shut up and contented himself with listening. Moon was still jealous of Earth, his daughter through trickery with his sister the Sun. Sun was so furious with her cunning brother, she chased him from this side of the sky, where she gave birth to Earth, who continues to get most of Sun's warmth and love. Moon wished he had creatures to call him father, but he was scarred ugly, lifelessly cold, and far away, too far away even to know that Earth was his child.

Around Fox night creatures spun incredible tales if one

could only understand their language. He wondered what tales the kanegmati would have told if only he understood them.

Perhaps someday, he mused, my Black Pearl will trust me strongly enough to confess her secrets to me, and we can talk of many things. Perhaps she would explain why they made triumph-hides without pictures. She can satisfy my curiosity about the eastern place where the kanegmati nation lodged.

Dazzled by the possibility of learning more about the place the Sun's home, his obsidian eyes stared into the soft night. Tree frogs reached some kind of agreement that silenced them for a lull—their ringing echo subsided in his ears, and the night was suddenly still except for the voice of the river, more like a color or smell than sound, so consistent was its one note. Beyond the willow and poplar trees at its murmuring edge, out past its knurling surface, he could just make out the faint kanegmati voices across the river in some strange kanegmati song.

As familiar as these strangers were to him by now, he had never completely gotten used to them. Their wonderful metal was something to be valued. Likewise the blue beads. And the mystery of their great serpent-canoe would long live in story and song among the people of this region.

But the whites themselves, other than she among them who chose to become red—they were surely not really normal beings like himself. Perhaps once they had been red humans, but now they had grown hairy and pale because of their bad practices without honor. They forgot the Way, and now they were forgotten.

They must be degenerate. He hated the idea of their existence, and he was sorry again he had let their Uktena-canoe intimidate him. What if his intuition was right, and there were more of them on the way to this country? he wondered with a sharp, chill gut-grab, as though a corner of the world had dropped a little as it inevitably must when age frays the ropes that holds up its four corners. He shivered; it was an ancient nightmare that haunted many a Cherokee night.

He tried to hear some good omen in the sounds of the strangers across the river. Earlier one strong-voiced man sang childish Shawnee, but now many of them were making music together in their foreign voices. It sounded too joyous to please Fox.

They were preparing for departure, eating, packing belongings, repairing weapons and binding their wounds, getting their big canoe into good repair, deciding what was more important to keep and what must be left behind, all while they sang together in a more regular music than Fox was used to, making harmonies like paints swirled in water.

The mist thickened.

You have shown too much kindness, he thought to himself. Your enemies will call you a weak woman who was afraid of the great Uktena. He brooded on that. Then he thought about Black Pearl and how she bargained with him for the life of the hairy chieftain but had chosen him, Fox, Most Beloved Man of the Overhill Ani Yunwiya for her prize. She would become his war-woman, though she did not know it yet. He would teach her, lovingly, and between them they would guide the Cherokee to become the greatest nation in the Land of Head of Waters, so that the name of Fox would be remembered down through the children that would spring from this woman's loins, to their children's children's children.

Ah, yes, he thought, finally satisfied. It would all come about because he had won her, his gift from Grandmother Sun, Old Ancient Red One. What more sign did he need than this? His moment of doubt was over. He shook off the chill of foreboding. These white strangers are so puny, he decided, it would be beneath the dignity of a warrior to kill them. The wilderness will accomplish that, or—Ha!—the Leni Lenape.

He amused himself with the thought that perhaps the Grandmothers, which the Cherokee considered the Leni Lenape to be to their own nation, would chop up the kanegmati for him. He would be rid of them without the bad luck of snake killing, and also keep his promise to Black Pearl. His people would never have to worry about white interlopers again. They would settle like silt on the bottom of a lake, into the mud of myth and legend.

"They came. They go. So what?" he asked nobody but himself, finding comfort in his own voice. Shell was right; the kanegmati were no more than a cloud passing. The Ani Yunwiya nation would hold this river and these hills and pray with arms outstretched against these skies forever, and for the rest of his life he would hold in his arms the love of the rare Black Pearl.

He stared too long, leaving an afterimage he could not blink away as he made his way back to her blanket. In his eyes and not far across the dark water winked the campfires of the enemy.

BIBLIOGRAPHY

(The starred [*] items are sources of direct quotes used in the chapter epigrams or within the narrative.)

* Armstrong, Zella. *Who Discovered America: The Amazing Story of Madoc*. Chattanooga, Tennessee: The Lookout Publishing Co. 1950.

  Catlin, George. *North American Indians*. Edinburgh: John Craft, 2 vols., 1844.

  D'Arcy, Mary Ryan. *The Saints of Ireland*. St. Paul, Minnesota: Irish American Cultural Institute, 1985.

  Davidson, Donald. *The Tennessee*, Vol 1. New York: Rinehart & Company, Inc., 1946.

  Deacon, Richard. *Madoc and the Discovery of America*. Frederich Muller, 1966.

  Faulkner, Charles H. *The Old Stone Fort, Exploring an Archaeological Mystery*, The University of Tennessee Press: Knoxville, 1968.

* Ford, Patrick K., ed. and trans. *The Mabinogi and Other Medieval Welsh Tales*. Los Angeles: University of California Press, 1977.

  Gatschet, Albert S. *Migration Legends of the Creek Indians*. Philadelphia: Reprinted from the original 1881 edition by Kraus Reprint Co., 1969.

* Gerald of Wales. *The Journey Through Wales/The Description of Wales*, 1178. Translation: Harmondsworth, Middlesex, England: Penguin Books Ltd., 1978.

  Hadingham, Evan. *Early Man and the Cosmos*. Norman, Okla.: University of Oklahoma Press, 1984.

* Howard, James H. *Shawnee!* Ohio University Press, 1981.

  Hudson, Charles. *The Southeast Indians*. Knoxville: University of Tennessee Press, 1976.

* Jones, Gwyn. *A History of the Vikings*. Oxford: Oxford University Press, 1985.

Knight, Bernard. *Madoc, Prince of America*. (fiction). London: Robert Hale, Lmtd., (Plymouth: St. Martin's Press), 1977.

Lewis, Thomas M. N. and Kneberg, Madaline. *Tribes That Slumber*. The University of Tennessee Press: Knoxville, 1982.

* Magnusson, Magnus & Hermann Palsson, trans. *The Vinland Sagas: The Norse Discovery of America*. Harmondsworth, Middlesex, England: Penguin Books Ltd., 1985.

* Montague, John, ed. and trans. *The Book of Irish Verse*. Collier Books, New York: MacMillan Publishing Company, 1974.

* Mooney, James. *Myths of the Cherokee*. Washington: United States Government Printing Office, 1902.

* Oxford University Press. *Oxford Book of Welsh verse*. Oxford, 1977.

Roderick, A.J., ed. *Wales Through the Ages*. Vol. 1 Llandybie, Carmarthenshire, Christopher Davis Ltd., 1971.

Schele, Linda and Miller, Mary Ellen. *The Blood of Kings, Dynasty and Ritual in Maya Art*. New York: George Braziller, Inc. 1986.

* Sayers, Dorothy L., trans. *The Song of Roland*. Harmondsworth, Middlesex, England: Penguin Books Ltd., 1957.

* Smith, Capt. John. *The generall historie of Virginia and the Summer Isles . . . from 1584 to the present 1624*. I.D. and I.H. for Michael Sparkles, 1624 reprinted by University Microfilms, March of America Facsimile Series, No. 18, 1966.

Southey, Robert. *Madoc, An Epic Poem*. London: Longman, Hurst, 1805.

* Sturluson, Snorri. *King Harald's Saga* from "*Heimskringla*." Translated by Magnus Magnusson and Hermann Palsson, New York: Dorset Press, 1966.

Tedlock, Dennis, translator. *Popol Vuh*, The Mayan Book of the Dawn of Life. New York: Simon & Schuster, Inc., 1985.

* Velie, Alan R., ed. *American Indian Literature, An Anthology*. Norman, University of Oklahoma, 1979.

Afterword

There are many Welsh, Irish, Norse, English, and Dutch references to pre-Columbian voyages to North America—I used some of these as chapter epigrams to show how Celtic navigators might have known about the western isles. But the trail thins out on this side of the Atlantic. The red nations achieved a rich oral culture, but they used only pictographs, and not writing, so what we know of their early history and legend is what has survived in rock paintings, pottery, and fragments of oral tradition translated long after European contact.

The earliest historical Europeans to these shores were aware of predecessors. At least one Irishman crewed Columbus's famous voyage, and there is evidence the admiral sailed to Galway as early as 1479, where he would have heard of St. Brendan and Madoc. Explorers, soldiers, artists, missionaries, farmers, and white captives have added to the anecdotal material.

Tennessee governor John Sevier said in 1810 that the Cherokee "Chief Occonostota informed me an old woman in his Nation, named Peg, had some part of an old book given her by an Indian living high up the Missouri, and thought he was one of the Welsh tribe. Unfortunately before I had an opportunity of seeing the book, the old woman's house and its contents were consumed by fire."

Throughout the past two centuries stories have circulated about European coins dug up in Georgia, paleface mummies in Alabama caves,* and red-haired, blue-eyed Indians surviving in the vast American west. Several published Indian captivities end with the red captors adopting a conde⌐

---

*As told in Louis L'Amour's *Jubal Sackett*.

white man after hearing him pray in Welsh, which was understood as their own language.

My primary sources for the American material are Shawnee, Creek, and Cherokee legends of early Alabama, Kentucky, and Tennessee, and later Mandan reports from the Upper Missouri. Prayers and other religious practices imagined here are based on Spanish, French, and English first-contact journals, James Mooney's Cherokee interviews, and archaeological evidence from hundreds of pre-Columbian pyramid sites on the rivers of the American South.

Captain John Smith and other British writers believed Madoc made more than one journey to western lands. I am presently working on *Madoc's Hundred*, the next book in the series in which Madoc settles his colony in Kentucky and returns to Britain for reinforcements.

There is some evidence that over the centuries the colonists made their way, as Cherokee legend says, along the Tennessee to the Ohio, the Mississippi, and finally the Missouri River, where the artist George Catlin was sure he found their descendants in the 1830s. He based his argument on the Mandans' light skin and eyes, round canoes, migration route, unique glass-making art, and similarities between their language and Welsh.

We are fortunate that place names tend to remain the same over the generations. Many Southern states, rivers, and towns retain native languages. For clarity I've used modern spellings. Tribal names can be confusing, because people usually don't call themselves what others name them—the Welsh and Cherokee are cases in point. The Yuchi is one of the few self-named tribes. Except when specifically explained, I used the most familiar terms despite the temptation to recall more of the wonderful old names of people and things that figure in this story.

The portage between the Tombigbee and Tennessee rivers in the story anticipates the Tennessee-Tombigbee Waterway. Conceived right after the Civil War and completed in 1985, the immense U.S. Army Corps of Engineers project and the Tennessee Valley Authority have erased features of the old rivers, including Muscle Shoals. They are described in this story from eighteenth-century eyewitness reports rather than from the way they look today—a string of lakes, locks, and ms with which we like to think we've conquered the nt spirit of the wild old streams. However, still standing below Wilson Dam at Muscle Shoals are the pyramid mound, island, and a few broken fragments of the original thirty-five miles of black rocks where Cherokee legend says they defeated the Welshmen.

Wendel Norton helped me see Madoc's world view by drawing the map imagined to be based on Madoc's charts and Brother Wyn's golden map.

Many thanks to Kim Miranda, Leni Sorensen, and Judy Lalah Simcoe for help with the manuscript and research, to Alexei Kondratiev of the Irish Book Loft in Manhattan for historical and linguistic consultation, and to Michael de Buys for nautical and technical expertise. Gratitude to the staffs of the New York Public Library; Toltec Mounds State Park in Arkansas; Desoto State Park of Alabama; the Indian Mound and Museum of Florence, Alabama; and the Old Stone Fort State Park of Tennessee, the site of the mountain gaming field in this book.

Grateful thanks also to Eileen Campbell Gordon of Rivendell Bookshop Ltd. of New York, Lydia Galton, Greg Tobin, and editor Barbara Alpert.

Special thanks to L.L., who speaks through the chiefs in the last chapter of this story: The whites came. They went. So what?

Pat Winter
Manhattan
July 1989

Excerpt from

MADOC'S HUNDRED

Book II in the Madoc Saga

High on the mast as lookout, Madoc's gut clutched when he shifted his attention to the river, thicker it seemed and darker with floating objects, tree boughs, tangles of roots and river grass, a small dead animal. He glanced toward the rudder where Fair Beard and Huw shared the labor of keeping it steady so that the Horn aimed toward the Shawnee but without the wind, the current was quickly gaining against them despite their heroic effort.

Still the wind stalled; the sheet flapped, bellying under its own weight in the teasing gusty puffs.

He heard someone yell forward. The current had snatched an oar. It angled parallel for a moment then was caught in its socket by the stream and snapped like a twig and whirled away while the two men it had thrown struggled to get to their feet amid the legs of others at the paddles and of the line crew working on the rigging.

Madoc thought he saw a flash of blood, but was too far away to be sure.

"There is a bay back there," he called, giving its distance in leagues, about three English miles.

Fair Beard was standing with straining arms braced against the tiller while Huw pulled against it from the opposite side; it was vibrating up into both men's bones, rattling the

Norseman's teeth as he strained to hold it in a position that gave some resistance to the current and kept their stern in line with their prow. But it was finally too much even for the two strong men on the rudder who were nearly thrown overboard when the thing surrendered to the press of the river and slammed in a halfturn in its pintle against the ship's waterline, flapping like a leaf and completely useless.

Dreamlike, Madoc felt them haul around so that for a sickening moment they were about to go broadside downstream, with the odd vision of the muddy Ohio to port and the clearer Shawnee to starboard, the oars tangled, the rigging loose, the sail tilted with the linemen and passengers thrown into confusion and slipping on the washed deck.

The ship's sleek, unresisting shape prevented them from broadsiding but they were careening fully out of control downstream and backwards, any chance of making the mouth of the Shawnee lost, their sail hanging without wind like a broken wing, the rigging slipped under the hands of the linemen.

Helpless to do anything except witness, Madoc was sickened to see someone overboard out on the water close to the ship but moving swiftly away as the stream toyed differently with different pieces of flotsam.

The various coils of the river's flow collided midstream to yield a frothing brew that sucked at the ship fore and aft and side to side so that she jerked along, a heavily-laden cork in the unremitting grip of the stream.

The man in the brink waved a long pink arm and shouted something the moving water drowned out while Wyn and a sailor at the closest rail tried to send him a line, too late. Madoc saw that it was young Brother Andrew in the fraction of a second before the undertow took him down and out of sight.

The sky perceptively darkened as clouds squeezed off the ball of orange sun just touching the western horizon, forging narrow rays and beams to lance the purple thunderheads.

They must have hit a deeper channel which their passage upstream had avoided, because the river flattened out, her current no less, but the surface was more glassy; this had the effect of spinning the ship in a long, almost lazy circle of itself while on deck something had happened among the oarsmen. He could not see from this angle but it looked as though one of the monks was face down with Mary bending over him, looking back and calling for help.

Caradoc, who had been pulling in another oar with one of the seamen, held on to tangled line and other people and made his way to the woman to help her turn the fallen monk over.

It was Father John.

The useless tiller abandoned, Fair Beard was making his way forward to help get the sail up because now the wind had sprung suddenly alive again from the southwest and if they could just catch it they could at least get to the nearest shore, the gravel beach down at the bend for that was what appeared to be their best chance coming up very fast behind them.

But they must escape being thrown onto one of the long sandy islands, so the only hope was to use the sail to guide them, a tricky task under any circumstances and too positively close for a captain's comfort under those prevailing, oarless, rudderless and now approaching darkness.

Through cupped hands Madoc called to the pilot their distance to the first low island, which he could now see by twisting around to peer over his shoulder. Fair Beard called back an affirmative without looking upward as he grabbed a halyard to help the men get the sail up from the canted position into which it had slipped. Growing fat under the wind, the heavy patchwork leather sail groaned up below Madoc's position, cutting off his view of the deck where Wyn left the rail and hurried across the deck to drop to his knees beside John.

The renewed wind in the sail slowed their breakneck run sideways and backwards, and as the crew hauled on the sheets and oars the ship came around to point toward the beach ahead well away from the pull of the first island. But here they must do the delicate thing and come not so close to the second yet be ready to swing to what was now portside since they were running backwards, and make for the harbor, praying for a channel between the bottom of the second island and the cup of land below it.

There was still a strong current close to shore, a current that would be against them suddenly pouring as it did from the north around the island and scooting with cutting speed.

Thirty feet up, Madoc swayed with one hand on the king-knot in his harness as the wind action brought them briefly but directly across the current, Fair Beard hanging onto the sheet now to keep them in line with the landing, controlling her totally with the sail.

It looked like the ship could overcome all obstacles under the effort of her crew and passengers with the help of the wind despite the current which pressed them as they made for the sheltered bay the water action had carved over the eons.

The water was stirred and the light was not good but it seemed that they were not in shallows—no indication that the island had laid a treacherous sand trap for them.

At that moment they felt and heard a terrible low crunching sound belowdeck.

MADOC'S HUNDRED

To be published
Soon by Bantam Books